The
WELL
of Tears

Also by Cecilia Dart-Thornton

THE BITTERBYNDE TRILOGY

Book 1: The Ill-Made Mute
Book 2: The Lady of the Sorrows
Book 3: The Battle of Evernight

THE CROWTHISTLE CHRONICLES

Book 1: The Iron Tree (2005)
Book 2: The Well of Tears (2006)
Book 3: Weatherwitch (2006)

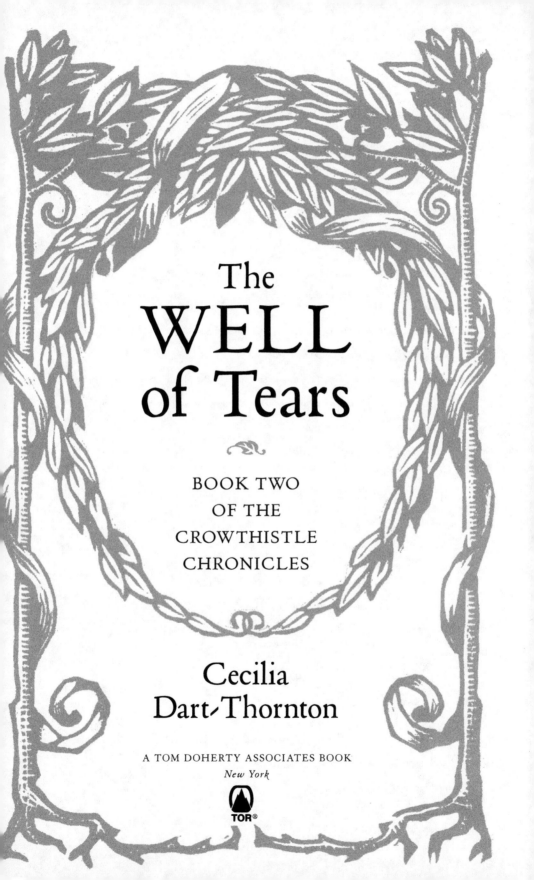

The
WELL
of Tears

BOOK TWO
OF THE
CROWTHISTLE
CHRONICLES

Cecilia
Dart-Thornton

A TOM DOHERTY ASSOCIATES BOOK
New York

TOR®

THE WELL OF TEARS: BOOK TWO OF THE CROWTHISTLE CHRONICLES

Copyright © 2005 by Cecilia Dart-Thornton

Originally published in 2005 by Tor Australia, an imprint of Pan Macmillan Australia Pty Limited.

This book is printed on acid-free paper.

Map and Crowthistle logo by Elizabeth Alger

Edited by Claire Eddy

A Tor Book
Published by Tom Doherty Associates, LLC
175 Fifth Avenue
New York, NY 10010

www.tor.com

Tor® is a registered trademark of Tom Doherty Associates, LLC.

Library of Congress Cataloging-in-Publication Data

Dart-Thornton, Cecilia.
    The well of tears / Cecilia Dart-Thornton.—1st ed.
      p. cm.
    "A Tom Doherty Associates book."
    ISBN 0-765-31206-9 (acid-free paper)
    EAN 978-0-765-31206-8
    1. Orphans—Fiction. I. Title.
    PR9619.3.D253W45 2006
    823'.92—dc22

                                        2005016723

First Edition: February 2006

Printed in the United States of America

0 9 8 7 6 5 4 3 2 1

*Dedicated to Marisa,
for being courageous, wise, caring, funny, talented,
and all things marvelous.*

*Cecilia
Dart-Thornton*

CONTENTS

GLOSSARY

Álainna Machnamh:	(AWE-lanna Mac-NAV)
a stór:	darling (a STOR)
Ádh:	luck, fortune (AWE) Lord Ádh is one of the Four Fates
Aonarán:	loner, recluse (AY-an-ar-AWN)
áthair:	father (AH-hir)
brí:	the power possessed by weathermasters enabling them to predict and control the dynamics of pressure systems and temperature inversions, wind currents and other meteorological phenomena
cailín:	girl
Cailleach Bheur:	The Winter Hag (cal-yach VARE or cail-yach VYURE)
carlin:	wise woman
Cinniúint:	destiny, fate, chance (kin-YOO-int) Lady Cinniúint is one of the Four Fates
cruinniú:	a flotilla of pontoons used as a central meeting place, from the Irish word for "gathering, meeting, collection" (crin-YOO)
Cuiva:	(KWEE-va); in the Irish language this name is spelled "Caoimhe"
Earnán:	(AIR-nawn)
eldritch:	supernatural
Eoin:	(OWE-in)
Eolacha:	(o-la-ha)
Fionnbar:	(FIN-bar or FYUN-bar)
Fionnuala:	(fin-NOO-la)
gariníon:	granddaughter (gar-in-EE-an)
garmhac:	grandson (gar-VOC)
Gearóid:	(gar-ODE)

gramarye: magic

gramercie: expression of thanks

Ice Seven: a crystal that will not melt, created by the weather-masters

Lannóir: Goldenblade or Fallowblade, the golden sword, the only one of its kind, slayer of goblins and heirloom of the House of Stormbringer (lann-OR)

Liadán: (LEE-dawn)

Luchóg: (La-HOGE)

Maolmórdha Ó Maoldúin: (mwale-MORGA oh mwale-DOON)

máthair: mother (MAW-hir)

Mí-ádh: bad luck, misfortune (mee-AWE) Lady Mí-ádh is one of the Four Fates

Míchinniúint: doom, ill-fate (mee-kin-YOO-int) Lord Míchinniúint is one of the Four Fates

muirnín: darling (mwirr-NEEN)

Odhrán: (o-RAWN)

Páid: (PAWD)

Ragnkull Island: (RAGG-en-kull)

Ruairc MacGabhann: (RORK mac-GAVAN)

Saibh: (say-EVE)

seanathair: grandfather (shan-AH-hir)

seanmháthair: grandmother (shan-WAW-hit; "waw" as "au" in "Maud")

seelie: benevolent to humankind

Stryksjø: (STRIKE-syo)

To *sain*:   to call for protection from unseelie forces

Uabhar: (OO-a-var)

Uile: the All, or universe (ILL-e, "e" as in "best")

unseelie: malevolent to humankind

To *wassail*:   to greet someone

CROWTHISTLE

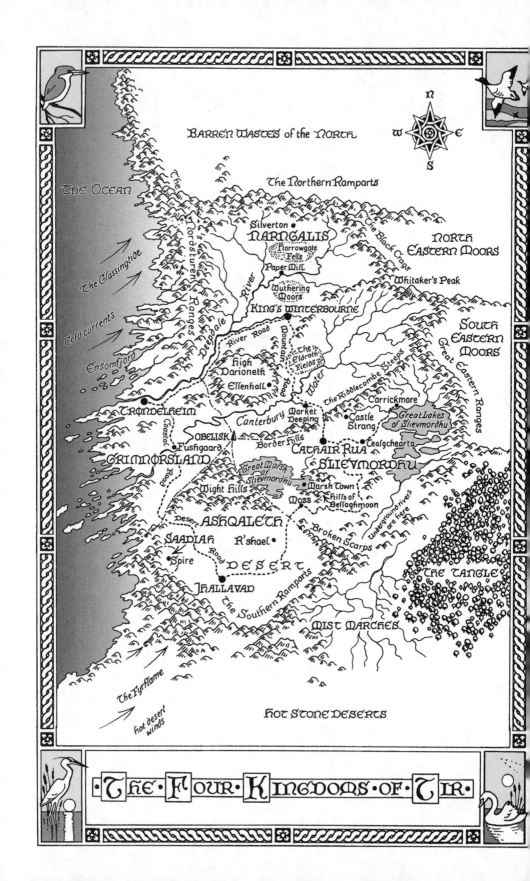

BARREN WASTES of the NORTH

The Northern Ramparts

N
W   E
S

THE OCEAN

The Glassingtide

Cold currents

Ensomfjord

The Nordsturien Ranges

The Black Crags

Silverton
NARNGALIS
Harrowgate
Fells
Paper Mill

NORTH
EASTERN MOORS

Whitaker's Peak

Wuthering
Moors

Deepdale River

River Road

KING'S WINTERBOURNE

SOUTH
EASTERN
MOORS

High
Darioneth

Mountain Road

The Eldroth
Fields

Ellenhall

The Mountain Water

The Riddlecombe Steeps

TRONDELHEIM

Canterbury

Market
Deeping

Carrickmore

Castle
Strang

Great Lakes
of Slievmordhu

Great Eastern Ranges

OBELISK
Fushgaard

Border Hills

CATHAIR RUA

Tealgchearta

GRIMNORSLAND

Coastal Road

Great Marsh
of
Slievmordhu

SLIEVMORDHU

Wight Hills

Marsh Town

Moss

Hills of
Bellaghmoon

Underground rivers
are here

ASHQALETH

Broken Scarps

THE TANGLE

SAADIAH

Desert Road

R'shael

Spire

DESERT

JHALLAVAD

The Southern Ramparts

MIST MARCHES

The Fyrflame

hot desert
winds

HOT STONE DESERTS

·THE·FOUR·KINGDOMS·OF·TIR·

Preface

The Well of Tears is the second book in the CROWTHISTLE CHRONICLES.

Book 1: *The Iron Tree,* told of Jarred, a young man who lived in a village in the desert kingdom of Ashqalêth, and possessed an amulet that apparently made him invulnerable. He and his comrades decided to travel to seek their fortunes in distant realms. On the way, they visited a town built amongst the intricate waterways of the Great Marsh of Slievmordhu, where Jarred fell in love with a marsh-daughter named Lilith.

Slievmordhu is a kingdom situated in the southwest of Tir, a continent throughout which grows a disliked but beautiful common weed called "crowthistle." Eldritch wights dwell in the marsh but seldom harm the marshfolk, who understand them and their ways. An urisk, a seelie wight like a dwarfish man with the legs of a goat, often loitered near Lilith's cottage, where she lived with her mother, Liadán; her step-father, Earnán; Earnán's son, Eoin; and Earnán's mother, Eolacha, a wise carlin. Nearby lived Old Man Connick, a demented and elderly man who was the father of Liadan. Unknown to her family, Lilith's mother kept imagining she could hear footsteps invisibly following her, and privately sensed that she was falling prey to a mysterious madness.

When Jarred and Lilith fell in love, Lilith's step-brother, Eoin, became jealous. Jarred and his comrades departed from the marsh and continued on their travels, but Jarred could not stop thinking about Lilith. Back at the marsh, Lilith's mother tried to flee from her growing madness, but instead was accidentally drowned. Jarred made excuses to his friends and returned to the marsh to settle. His arrival helped Lilith endure her grief over the apparently inexplicable death of her mother.

Jarred learned the ways of the marsh-dwellers and began to court Lilith. Around his neck he still wore the protective amulet. Rivalry grew between him and Eoin, who was resentful of Lilith's affection for Jarred, and who guessed the power of the amulet.

During celebrations of the traditional Festival of Rushbearing, Lilith became lost and injured. The urisk, usually surly but in this case benevolent, helped Jarred find her. Upon her rescue the two lovers plighted their troth. Jarred gave his bride-to-be a ring, and his amulet.

Their happiness, however, was short-lived. After Old Man Connick died, completely insane, the carlin Eolacha and young Lilith realized that there was some kind of curse on Lilith's bloodline. Lilith declared she must never marry and beget another doomed generation. Jarred swore he would find the cause of the curse, and break it.

Lilith and other members of her household traveled to the Autumn Fair at the capital city of Slievmordhu, Cathair Rua. There they saw druids of the Sanctorum, who are the official "intermediaries" between the people of Tir and the "Four Fates." In the city, Jarred sought to learn the history of Old Man Connick. He visited apothecaries and made inquiries, but to no avail. Eventually a yellow-haired street-urchin called Fionnbar Aonarán led Jarred to the hovel of half-senile Ruairc MacGabhann. The old man related the decades-old history of the brave youth Tierney A'Connacht, who, wielding the golden sword Fallowblade, rescued beautiful Álainna Machnamh from Janus Jaravhor, the long-dead Sorcerer of the (now sealed and abandoned) Dome of Strang in Orielthir.

Jaravhor, powerful and malign, then cursed the heirs of Tierney A'Connacht and Álainna Machnamh with madness and death. Old Man Connick, his daughter, Liadan, and her daughter, Lilith, were all descended from the cursed couple. This tale of the past explained the nature of the malediction, but not how to break it. Jarred returned to his friends and sweetheart and told them what he had learned. The news cast a pall of gloom upon them all.

On a subsequent visit to the city Fionnbar made a second appearance, and guided Jarred back to Ruairc's hovel. On the way he led Jarred near a strange indestructible tree that grew in the city. Enclosed inaccessibly within the Iron Tree's fretwork of thorny boughs was an extraordinary, sparkling jewel. Jarred was tricked into retrieving the jewel—a feat no man had been able to achieve before—thus inadvertently proving he was the grandson of the sorcerer. It was further revealed that Jarred's amulet had no power. The talisman was a decoy employed by Jarred's father, to disguise the fact that Jarred himself was immune to harm because the sorcerer had left an enchantment of invulnerability on all descendants of his own bloodline. Despising his malicious grandfather, Jarred flung the jewel back into the Iron Tree and vowed to have nothing more to do with the Sorcerer of Strang.

Joyfully, Jarred and Lilith returned to the marsh. They believed that they could now safely marry: the benison on Jarred's blood would surely cancel the curse on Lilith's. Eoin was not so happy, despite the fact that recently he had happened to do a good turn for some eldritch wights who, as a reward, granted him good fortune. But Eoin's jealousy festered. He became wealthy, and built himself a floating house, while Jarred remained in poverty.

A year after her marriage to Jarred, Lilith gave birth to a daughter. They named her "Jewel." Despite his earlier misgivings, Eoin discovered he adored the child.

Lilith and Jarred enjoyed twelve years of happiness together. They were convinced the curse had been broken. Unwilling to compromise their daughter's happiness, they concealed from her the curse and its history. Furthermore, Jewel had no inkling of her own innate invulnerability. However, Eolacha, the old carlin, eventually died and, as if her grief were a trigger, Lilith began to fall prey to the ancestral paranoia. She heard the first, distant footsteps of madness.

Desperate to save his wife from a gruesome fate, Jarred traveled to Cathair Rua in search of a druid called Adiuvo Constanto Clementer, who was reputed to be a healer of lunatics. In order to pay the healer, Jarred once again retrieved the jewel from the Iron Tree, but a passer-by spied him doing the deed. Soon, word of the jewel-taker came to the ears of King Maolmórdha and his profoundly flawed family, including the conniving eldest son, Crown Prince Uabhar. The executant of this deed would necessarily be of the sorcerer's blood, and they suspected that only a descendant of the sorcerer would have the power to open the sealed Dome, revealing the reputed treasures hidden within. Uabhar convinced his weak father that it was in the Crown's interests to capture this "jewel-thief" and make him unlock the Dome of Castle Strang.

Ruairc MacGabhann's niece, the drudge Fionnuala Aonarán (half-sister to Fionnbar), came in haste to Jarred, whom she loved. She informed him that the king's men were hunting a man of his description, and also seeking any offspring he may have. Jarred wished to have nothing to do with the mysterious Dome. Besides, he knew Maolmórdha was untrustworthy and in all likelihood would harm him. Fervently he hoped that the king was not aware he had a daughter. Fionnuala and Fionnbar helped Jarred to escape, but only after they had forced him to promise he would later leave his family and go with them to unlock the secrets of the Dome.

Eoin, also visiting the city, witnessed a strange funeral, conducted by eldritch wights. When he looked into the coffin he saw a corpse with his own face and understood, to his horror, that he had witnessed an omen of his own impending death.

With Maolmórdha's cavalry hot on his heels, Jarred hurried back to the marsh. On the road he encountered Eoin, who eventually admitted that his jealousy had led him to betray Jarred to the king. When Eoin realized that in betraying his rival he would also be bringing danger to Lilith's daughter, Jewel, he became utterly distraught, and filled with self-loathing.

At the marsh Jarred angrily bade Eoin help him, and told Lilith and young Jewel to make ready to journey in secret to the safe haven of Narngalis. But before they had a chance to leave the marsh the madness came upon Lilith again, triggered by the fear of pursuit. Running in terror, Lilith tumbled over a cliff and was mortally injured. Jarred, trying to retrieve her broken body, slipped and fell a short distance. By ill-chance his heart was pierced by a branch of mistletoe sprouting from a tree leaning out from the cliff part-way down. Mistletoe was the only thing in the world (besides old age) from which the sorcerer's enchantment could not protect him.

Jewel's parents were now both dead, and Eoin, racked by the agony of remorse, was determined to save the child on his own. They set out together in their boat—just in time; the king's cavalry arrived at the marsh soon after they had left. Toward the close of the book the following words are written:

> On the lightless staithe of the Mosswell cottage, Cuiva and Odhrán Rushford stood together, the moon-pale and the sun-browned. Their faces were folded in on themselves, creased and wet with crying, and they leaned upon each other's shoulders.
>
> They could hear the king's men crashing and splashing through the marsh. Frogs twanged. Stars had fallen into the water, or perhaps they were dying blossoms.
>
> "So," said Odhrán, "in the end the sorcerer wreaked his full measure of vengeance."
>
> They stared out in the direction Eoin and Jewel had taken, and after a while Cuiva said, "I wonder what will become of them."
>
> Toward morning, Jewel and Eoin reached a northwestern edge of the marsh. They came ashore and set the canoe adrift. Shouldering their bundles, they disappeared into the gray woods, like trows hastening to depart the haunts of mortal men before sunrise.

Jarred and Lilith had perished, but their child lived on. In later days it was said that the wraiths of the doomed lovers could be seen walking joyfully, hand-in-hand, through the marsh twilight.

The
WELL
of Tears

Prophecy

For five nights and five days Jewel and Eoin fled on foot across sparsely wooded countryside, northward from the Great Marsh of Slievmordhu. Often they looked back, scanning the uninhabited landscape to see if anything was coming after them.

They could not discern any obvious signs of pursuit, but they made haste, nevertheless.

By day, sunlight silvered the ferns carpeting the bracken-woods, where tree-boles leaned against their own shadows. By night, the far-off constellations were gauzy scarves of white mist sewn with nearer stars as brilliant and hard as splinters of glass. The dark hours were also the wighting hours, their wind-murmuring quietude randomly punctuated by dim sounds of sobbing, thin, weird pipe-melodies, unintelligible singing, or bursts of rude, uncontrollable laughter.

The rations the wayfarers carried in their packs were scant, and dwindling fast. Their departure from the marsh had been precipitous; in their haste to escape before King Maolmórdha's troopers arrived, there had been no time to throw anything more by way of provisions into the canoe than a few lotus-corm loaves, some packets of dried fish, and a couple of leathern flasks.

"I'll catch a tasty treat for your supper this evening, little one," Eoin said to Jewel, in an effort to coax her out of her gloom, but she answered not a word. The girl spoke rarely, and her eyes, her blue eyes like two amethysts in caskets lidded with lapis lazuli, gazed out with a dreary and haunted look.

It was agonizing to dwell on the recent past, yet somehow she could not prevent herself from doing so. She had lost nearly everything she loved, everything that was familiar to her: family, home, pets, and possessions. Seeking for some comfort, Jewel glanced over at Eoin, her step-uncle and protector, for whom she felt an earnest fondness, knowing nothing of his role in her downfall.

As they plodded onward, the marshman was himself buried deep in thought, endlessly rebuking himself for the part he had played in Jewel's suffering. Had Eoin never revealed Jarred's identity to King Maolmórdha's minions, the king would not have learned that Jewel's father was descended from the notorious Sorcerer of Strang. Then the royal cavalry would not have come thundering along the road to the Great Marsh of Slievmordhu. Their pursuit would not have triggered Lilith's madness, and she would not have run to the cliff-top in a blind panic. Jarred would not have died trying to save his wife, and twelve-year-old Jewel would not have been forced to flee from her home.

Eoin blamed himself for all these tragedies. None of this would have happened if he, displaying a pettiness unworthy of a truly upright man, had not informed against his rival. Driven by his own vain jealousy, he had brought this fate of loss and exile upon the child he doted on, daughter of the woman he adored—and now he must do what he could to make reparation, although he ached, as if the fibers of his sinews had been shredded.

The marshman unhitched the slingshot from his belt and couched a stone in the strap. He was ready when, with the whirring of a hundred rapid spinning wheels, a brace of grouse flew up from the ferns beneath their feet. After whirling the weapon around his head, he let fly. He was lucky; a plump bird fell, wounded. Eoin wrung the bird's neck, plucked it, and roasted it over a campfire on the banks of a narrow stream. Succulent juices ran from the meat, but as enticing as the meal appeared, it tasted no better than sand in the melancholy mouths of the diners.

As if to punish himself, Eoin brought to mind the uncanny funeral he had lately witnessed in the city of Cathair Rua: a mock, staged affair, conducted by eldritch wights, the coffin containing a corpse whose face was the exact image of his own. Eoin had comprehended at once that he had viewed a prophecy of his own death; within a twelve-month he would perish. Somehow, as he brooded by the campfire, the prospect lent him some relief. If only he could bring Jewel to some safe haven before his final hour, he would be quite glad to lie down, relinquish his gut-wrenching remorse, and find peace.

After the joyless meal was over, Eoin went down to the stream to refill the water flasks.

As he knelt by the water, the flesh clenched on the nape of his neck and un-accountable fear shivered through him. A harsh voice had called from the brakes of fern, a voice like a cry from the long, hoarse throat of some wild bird.

Raising his head apprehensively, he saw a strange entity watching him from the other side of the stream. It was a stunted, man-like thing, strongly built and doughty. Its umber tunic and leggings were so ragged they appeared to be fash-ioned from withered bracken, and its frizzled hair was as russet as the sap-starved leaves of Autumn. Its eyes were bulbous, outlandishly huge, and they rolled beneath its shaggy red brows like the eyes of a wrathful bull.

"How dare ye come here slaughterin', ye miscreant?" it growled. "The wild creatures in this place are under my guardianship. If nuts and blackberries sus-tain me, that am their custodian, should they not be good enough for you? Step over to this bank, and I'll show you the victuals I gather."

Eoin guessed this was the Brown Man of the Muirs, a wight he vaguely re-called from old tales. As far as he could remember, the wight forbade hunting in its own domain. Horror engulfed Eoin, that he had offended an eldritch being, and for a moment he was daunted. Then it came to him that he was acting like a coward and, despising himself, he sprang up and set his foot on a tussock, preparing to jump across the stream. As he did so, he heard Jewel's young voice from somewhere behind him, crying out pitifully, "Uncle Eoin, where are you?"

He wheeled about. The little girl was running toward him, her hair and gown streaming behind her on the wind.

"Go back! Go back!" Eoin warned, but when he turned back again the Brown Man had disappeared. "Did you see it?" Eoin asked, as Jewel rushed up beside him.

"See what?" demanded Jewel. She tossed back the dark tangle of her tresses and folded her arms across her chest.

"That was the Brown Man of the Muirs, if I'm not mistaken," said Eoin, craning his neck to peer in amongst the crochet of fronds on the opposite bank. "He bade me cross the stream and join him, saying he would show me how to find nuts and berries. Come, let us ford the brook and seek him."

"Are you mad?" shouted Jewel disbelievingly. "If 'twas indeed the Brown Man, then 'twas only the running water that saved you! If you had crossed over, the wight would have torn you apart and not even your druid-sained amulet would have protected you!"

Bewildered, the marshman shook his head.

"Come away," said the little girl, her mournfulness now replaced by anger, "and hunt no more. Do you wish that I should lose you, too?"

Then, as suddenly as her mood had changed, it changed again. The light in her eyes dulled and her hands dropped listlessly by her sides.

Strung up on a gallows of jealousy, betrayal, and premonition, Eoin felt guilt tighten like a noose around his gullet. The child's evident wretchedness pained him excruciatingly. It was *he* who was to blame for her bereavement and exile, no one else.

"No," he mumbled. "Let us go on."

Once, as evening deepened to night and they passed through a young oak wood, they spied a twinkling of lights through the trees and caught the babble of voices. Not wishing to be discovered by bandits, they crept forward silently. There in a clearing they beheld a scene of feasting and revelry set out on the greensward under the stars: a long table, garlanded with moon-roses, laden with dishes piled high with delectable fare. As the two mortals cautiously approached, musicians struck up a merry jig and the guests began footing it around the table.

Marvelous to look upon were these dancers and musicians, some as fair as flowers, elegant, silk-haired, clad in rainbows of finery. Others were foul nightmares, squat as toadstools, crooked and lopsided as trees rooted on a windswept sea-cliff, bloated as leeches, quick as rats, long-legged, gangling, and knock-kneed as newborn foals, grinning like pumpkin lanterns, hopping like frogs, graceful as cats, scowling like belligerent gargoyles.

Knowing full well that they looked upon a gathering of no mortal creatures, Jewel and Eoin scarcely dared breathe, lest they betray their presence. Eldritch wights could not bear to be spied upon, and might exact some terrible revenge for such a crime.

Slowly the intruders backed away, but an incautious step snapped a twig. In that instant the twinkling lights went out as if the eyeballs of the mortals had been gouged from their sockets. Simultaneously the strains of music were cut off in mid-bar, and the babble of voices stopped in mid-word. All was silence and darkness.

Fortunately, the stars let down enough filaments of light through the oak leaves for the wayfarers to relocate their forest trail. Soon they were on their way once more, putting as much distance as possible between themselves and that spooky place before weariness overcame them and they made camp for the night.

Eleven days after the wayfarers had fled the Great Marsh of Slievmordhu, they found themselves in open country that climbed to meet the rounded shoulders of the Border Hills. Eoin had cut a staff of blackthorn-wood for himself, and a shorter length for Jewel. Using these for support, they plodded up a gentle slope of turf that had been cropped short by deer and wild goats, a smooth greensward strewn with low boulders and occasional clumps of the weed crowthistle.

Glancing ahead, Jewel fancied they were ascending a stairway to the sky. Out of the northwest, low, livid rainclouds were moving swiftly eastward, heavy with rain. Where sunlight struck them, they boiled out into puffs of luminous dazzle, pristine pillows of steam. Farther east, they broke up into islands in a blue sea that faded from cobalt at the zenith, merging to a haze of softest gray at the horizon.

A drawn-out sighing greeted them as they reached the top of a ridge, the sound of cool breezes breathing through a copse of beeches that crowded close together. Magpie-larks swooped, uttering their rusty-gate-hinge calls. As the wayfarers walked over the spine of the ridge and down into the copse, the trees loomed taller, towering overhead. Their wide-reaching boughs nodded gently, whispering; their shade was cool and dappled, the ground patterned with tender green blades and butter-curls of leaves, gold and brown. A path of sorts went winding between the boles. Here they rested for a while, seated with their backs against corrugated bark.

"When we come down out of these hills," said Eoin presently, "we shall leave Slievmordhu behind us. These are the borderlands. Narngalis lies ahead."

Solemnly, Jewel nodded.

Throughout their journey together, Eoin had never seen her smile. This was not to be wondered at. There was no reason for either of them to be mirthful. Wretchedness and weariness weighed upon him. He wondered how much Jewel knew, or guessed, about the part he had played in the ruination of her family, of her life. As ever, his thoughts flickered miserably back over the recent series of events, precipitated by a single, spiteful act born of his vindictiveness. Privately—so as not to cause further distress to Jewel—he pined grievously for Lilith. He was consumed by an unassuageable longing to return to that pivotal moment in time when he had stepped into the palace, so that he might erase his errors and change everything.

Having swallowed a mouthful of water, he and Jewel got up and continued on their way.

The colors of the wayfarers' raiment blended with those of the landscape. This was because they were covered in much of it. The marshman, gangling and long-jawed, was clad in the same gear he had been wearing throughout his helter-skelter ride from Cathair Rua. His soft leather leggings were travel-stained; his fine linen shirtsleeves had been rent, in places, by the protruding spurs of low vegetation through which he had pushed in haste. The gray stocking-cap he had purchased from the landlord of the "Ace and Cup" in Cathair Rua had fallen off long ago. The reddish knee-length tunic, now dirty brown, was coming unstitched at the seams. Its cheap woolen fabric was thin, and provided little warmth. When he woke from his brief slumbers, he was always shivering. His boots, however, were stout, and well endured the trials of swift passage across rough terrain.

The smudges on the face of the twelve-year-old girl walking at his side could not obscure her beauty. Her hair was as black and shiny as a handful of acacia seeds, and the dark locks clung together in a singular fashion, so that the tapered ends spiked forth like the new-budding tips of a fir tree. Narrow was her waist, no wider than the thigh of a grown man. Her skin was peaches-by-firelight; her mouth was the softly curved petal of a pink rose. She wore a linen kirtle beneath a woolen gown, and over her shoulders a traveling-cloak, lined with fur, clasped with a brooch of bronze. The matching traveling-hood hung behind her shoulders. Like her step-uncle, she had lost her other headgear; her scarf was dangling from a twig somewhere, having been swept from her scalp during that first frantic scramble away from the northern shores of the marsh. Her boots, like Eoin's, were well made. In happier days he had purchased them for her, as a present, from the most reputable cobbler in Cathair Rua.

Trudging beside Jewel along the verdant vales and wooded slopes of the Border Hills, Eoin was glad of his gift to the child. It was his fault she had been hounded from her home in search of an uncertain future, his fault, indirectly, that she was orphaned. The irony was that of all things that lived in Tir, he cared most for her.

The two wayfarers met no human being in these high places, only the mortal creatures of the wilderness, such as birds, insects, reptiles, beasts of hoof and horn. Sometimes in the gloaming they spied more wights—whether seelie or unseelie they could not tell, but they kept their distance. If human beings had ever dwelled in the Border Hills, they were long gone.

These were lonely lands.

As they journeyed, Eoin never let down his guard. The fear of pursuit remained strong in him still, accompanied by the awareness of clandestine eldritch activity all around. Furthermore, he was heavily burdened with a sense of responsibility for his step-niece, a desire to protect her from all harm, both because he loved her and because while defending her he could deceive himself that he was relieving his guilt.

He was unable to bring himself to talk to his young companion about the terrible events that had befallen her, never tried to break her long silences. Above all, he could not bear to incur the child's hostility by revealing the role he had played in her family's tragic fate. Of course, she had been audience to her father's harsh words to Eoin shortly before Jarred's death, and she must have perceived there was more ill-feeling between them than usual, but she never confronted Eoin with demands to be told exactly what had happened. Perhaps she believed it was all too appalling to contemplate and was best left unvoiced. Perhaps her overwhelming grief clouded her reason. For Eoin's part, his remorse and self-reproach prevented him from broaching the subject with her.

At nights he did not sleep, preferring to keep vigil. During the days he and Jewel would halt at noon, when he would fall into a dreamless slumber for a few hours. Relentlessly his body stayed taut as a spring, his muscles involuntarily twitching at random intervals, ever ready to react to the first hint of peril; and his sharp eyes flicked back and forth, noting the shape of every boulder, the motion of every bough and pool of shade. He watched, also, for suggestions of disturbance amongst the wild fauna of the hills, which might provide clues to impending danger.

Crickets whirred rhythmically in the seeding grasses of Autumn, counterpointed by the dark, oceanic soughing of the wind through drifts of living leaves. The wayfarers were passing through another scattered beech wood when two events occurred simultaneously. Although they scarcely engendered any sound, alarm screamed through the skull of Jewel's guardian.

Not far off to the right, a flock of wood-pigeons fountained into the air, their wings flapping like a multitude of white hands waving farewell. And a vertical litheness detached itself from a tree-bole before gliding into a thicket.

Instantly, Eoin spun around. Jewel had been dawdling behind him. Now he discovered that she had dropped back several paces and was leaning over, intent on examining some weed or wildflower sprouting from the crevice of a mossy boulder.

"Hide!" Eoin hissed through his teeth, signaling urgently to reinforce his words. Surprise flared momentarily across the girl's features; then she obeyed, dropping out of sight amid the lush foliage of a bank of foxgloves.

Where Eoin had stood, he stood no longer. He, too, had thrown himself to the ground, and now lay rigid. Between thin wands of tussock-grass he could see the figures of men who might well have been mistaken for part of the countryside, had they not been on the move. His first thought was that the king's soldiery had discovered Jewel's existence, had somehow tracked her down, and were quartering the hills in their search for her. Almost at once he realized the folly of such an assumption—the men he was watching were making their way on foot, not on horseback. Neither were they clad in the uniforms of the Royal Guard, but in motley garb, dun-hued, their visages largely obscured by leather helms. As well, they advanced with an easy stealth that could only be learned from practice in the wilderness, never by routine drill in the training-yards of a military barracks.

These men were bandits—or, worse, the warped mountain-swarmsmen known as Marauders.

Most likely Marauders, Eoin concluded to himself, *using the shelter of the Border Hills to conceal their passage toward Grïmnørsland and the coast.* The men, spread across a wide front, were stepping noiselessly between the trees. Soon, one of their number appeared from behind a scabrous beech growing quite close to Eoin, and the marshman held his breath. *Lie tranquil, Jewel.* His lips formed the words without uttering them—yet he knew with certainty that the child would lie immobile, unflinching. She was not one to startle easily, and he had great store of respect for her common sense.

The walker went past without spying the refugees in their makeshift coverts.

The farther-off Marauders were no more than a shaking of leaves, a mellow crunch of dry seed-pods underfoot, an erect form ducking beneath a bough. Those passing closer to Eoin's hiding-place resolved themselves into unsavory-looking fellows whose belts and baldrics sported a vast array of portable weaponry. Some carried bundles on their shoulders. They did not speak to one another, but now and then one would cup his hands around his jowls and make a call like an owl, a signal to his accomplices.

Foolish, thought Eoin. *Owls are nocturnal. . . .*

Eoin counted eighteen mountain-brigands. The wind began to rise as the last of them disappeared into the woods to the west and blended into the scenery. When the sounds of their excursion had died away, Eoin dared to draw a deep breath and raise his head.

As if struck in the face, he reeled.

He had been mistaken. Buffeted by a swirling tide of golden leaves, a nineteenth swarmsman was following in the wake of the rest. His footfalls as muted as a deer's, the Marauder happened to be making straight for the weedy bank where the child lay concealed. At any moment, he must surely stumble over her.

Jewel, curled up in her bower of late-blooming foxgloves like some elfin princess in a castle of purple turrets, heard someone approaching. Judging by the tempo and style of the pace, she guessed it was not Eoin. Notions of incorporeal footsteps flitted through her consciousness, and in that moment she believed her mother's madness had descended upon her.

Then the stately flower-towers, dripping with clusters of hyacinthine bells, shuddered. They swished aside, and a thick-set, bearded fellow stood looking down at Jewel. She kept her wits and did not cry out, even when a yellowish grin split the beard and he bent to seize her.

Something came flying out of the sky, landed on his shoulders, and knocked the man over. Jewel rolled aside with well-timed presence of mind—he came crashing down on his face, into her nest, with Eoin riding atop him. The marsh-man grabbed the brigand in a stranglehold, so that he had no breath to summon his comrades—but the bearded fellow was no weakling. After a manic struggle he managed to throw off his attacker and twist around to confront him. Eoin jumped to his feet, fists at the ready. The rustling of windblown leaf-showers drowned out the noise of combat, and the swarmsman gasped for air, too short of breath to cry out to his distant comrades, who by then had passed out of earshot. He lumbered upright and lunged forward. The two men locked together in deadly combat while Jewel frantically cast about for a stick or stone with which she might assail their enemy. It was obvious Eoin was no match for this thick-thewed ruffian.

Laying hands on her blackthorn stick, the child thwacked the Marauder mightily across his back. Emitting a grunt of astonishment, he turned his head to see what harassed him, and at the fulcrum of his distraction, Eoin gave a sudden, hard shove. Off balance, the brigand stepped backward. His boot-heel slipped on a small rock overgrown with grasses and he toppled for a second time, dragging his opponent with him. Yet when he hit the ground his arms loosened and fell by his sides, flaccid as rope. He ceased to move. A scarlet worm crawled from the hollow of his left temple, where his lopsided skull had made contact with the mossy boulder whose crevices harbored wild orchids.

Staggering, gasping, Eoin stood up. The staff dropped from Jewel's fingers. She glanced from her step-uncle to the prone man, and back again. Her vivid eyes seemed huge and luminous in her pearl of a face. Underneath, they were smeared with bruised arcs, like the juice of nightshade berries. A tremor ran through her lower lip.

Eoin grasped her by the hand. "We must depart with all haste," he rasped, his voice cracking with exertion, "before they discover this man is missing, and come seeking him."

He grabbed their packs and away they sped, to the north as ever; far from the Marauders' westward path, far from King Maolmórdha's soldiers, far from the scene of Eoin's treachery, though he was never able to outrun his guilt.

A strewing of birds shivered across the sky, flashing from dark to light with every beat of their wings. Leaves, detached from their stems by the cool touch of the season, spooned down cascades of air, like tiny boats.

The wayfarers went on at a cracking pace, without their usual brief halts for respite. Jewel had made no complaint, but it was obvious to Eoin that she was exhausted. When the deepening twilight began to pool in the valleys, they finally made camp in a grove of lime trees on the eastern slope of a hill. Radiance poured, green and gold, through the foliage. Amongst the million upon zillion floating points of light and color that were the leaves, the intertwining trunks and branches could be glimpsed, standing out starkly, as if drawn with charcoal strokes.

The marshman left the tinderbox in the leather pack and did not light a fire, in case Marauders lingered in the vicinity. A column of smoke, no matter how ethereal, would surely attract their attention. Neither he nor Jewel had much appetite for the fragmented remnants of dry foodstuffs that remained.

"This night I shall catch a coney or two," said Eoin without enthusiasm, breaking a long silence between them. "We are far from the haunts of the Brown Man."

The child nodded.

"Do you think he died, that fellow with the knives?" she said, after a while.

"He did not," answered Eoin. "He was breathing. I saw his chest rise and fall. The senses were knocked out of him, and with luck he'll remember naught of what happened, but he lived, and maybe lives still."

"I am glad."

"You should not be. He saw you—"

"Why does that matter?" she asked.

He pondered, then shook his head. "I am all a-muddle," he said wearily, rubbing his eyes. "It matters not, after all. The people of the marsh would never betray you. They will swear Jarred had no child."

Listlessly, Jewel picked at the ripening seeds of panicum grass growing within her reach. "I do not understand," she said.

"What is it you do not understand?"

"My father—"the girl paused, drew a long breath, and continued—"my father explained to me why I had to leave the marsh. But it all happened so quickly and there was no time to ask questions. And then he was gone—" Again, she broke off. Her knuckles bleached as she clenched her small hands. "I do not properly understand why the marsh-folk must not tell Outsiders that my father had a daughter. And why would King Maolmórdha send his soldiers to capture me, if he found out I exist? And if these soldiers took me, what would happen to me?"

She reached beneath the front of her gown and extracted two pendants. One, like a creamy coin, hung around her neck on a fine silver chain; the other, an extraordinary jewel, depended from links of white-gold. Reflected rays shot from the jewel. Fire-of-snow, it twinkled, fascinating, brilliant.

"Is it something to do with this?" asked the child, holding up the precious stone. "Where did it come from? How did my father obtain such a marvel? To whom does it belong?"

"That pretty rock belongs to you and no other. Your father managed to take it out of the boughs of the Iron Thorn that grows in Cathair Rua. It belonged to him by right of birth. His father's father was Janus Jaravhor, the Sorcerer of Strang, who cast the bauble into the tree, where it could only be retrieved by one of his descendants."

Jewel fingered the other pendant strung about her neck. It was an amulet, an unpretentious disc of bone engraved with two interlocking runes. "My father gave me this amulet. He used to tell me it would keep its wearer from hurt. But I know that after all, 'tis not the amulet that protects me. 'Tis the blood of that sorcerer, flowing in my veins."

"What?"

"In faith. My father revealed the truth to me the last time I saw him, before he went searching for my mother. Naught in the entire world could harm me, or him." The child's face darkened. "Save only for one thing, as has now been discovered."

She was referring to the fact that just before Jewel and Eoin had fled from the marsh, Cuiva, the White Carlin, had told them how she had discovered Lilith lying dead on a narrow ledge that jutted below the edge of the precipice. Jarred, having tried to reach his wife, was lethally impaled upon an upthrusting, jagged branch of mistletoe an arm's length away, his fingertips lightly brushing Lilith's face.

Slowly, Eoin assimilated Jewel's astounding revelation about the disc of bone. *So,* he thought, *that is why Jarred remained unscathed after our scrimmage. That is why he never took harm from the marsh-wights. I believed it was all due to the amulet. Ardently I wanted to possess that talisman, until he bestowed it on the child. And as it turns out, the power was never in it after all!*

It was curious, the way Jarred had met his fate, curious, terrible, and unbearably sad. A branch of mistletoe, sharp as a spear, must have been the only material in the world capable of causing harm to a near-invulnerable descendant of Janus Jaravhor. Since then the child, as far as anyone knew, was the sole heir of the malign Sorcerer of Strang. Anew, remorse struck through Eoin like a bolt of pure ice.

Jewel is armored by her ancestry, the marshman ruminated to himself, *and on hearing that news I am now blithe! Yet she must beware . . .*

"Aye," he said softly, "and because of that same heritage of the blood, you alone possess the ability to unseal the Dome of Strang, and reveal all its hidden treasures. That is why King Maolmórdha would seize you, if he knew of you. You must not tell anyone who you are."

But Jewel was scarcely heeding his words. Deliberately, she was staring at the amulet of bone. She pulled the silver chain over her head and threw it away. "I do not want that thing!" she cried. "It is a counterfeit. My father lied when he gave it to me. I wish he had not lied."

"Peace, little one," soothed Eoin. "If he told you an untruth, it was for your benefit. That cannot be doubted. Be certain, moreover, that in all other ways he was honest with you. Jarred was a good man."

Having uttered these words, he suddenly averted his face. Violently, his shoulders began to shake. As he sobbed achingly beneath the lime trees, Jewel fetched the amulet from where it had fallen. She crept close to her step-uncle and dropped it in his lap.

"Here," she said softly. "You wear it. Perchance it contains some effectiveness, despite all."

"Nay," he replied in muffled tones, "I own an amulet, a good druid-sained one from the Sanctorum." He groped for the talisman he usually wore beneath his tunic, but it was no longer there. His fingertips traced across the nape of his neck, detecting a long weal, and it came to him that during the skirmish with the Marauder he had felt the chain bite into his flesh. It had snapped apart as his enemy ripped it off in an effort to garrote him.

"Well," he said, "it seems I do not have an amulet, after all."

Jewel looped the silver chain over his head and carefully cleared his bedraggled locks from his collar. "Now you will be safe from unseelie wights."

The child's kindness came near to undoing the man. "Gramercie," he whispered.

"Do not catch coneys this night, Uncle. Let us rest." She drew a corner of her traveling-cloak over both of them and, placing her head upon his shoulder, closed her eyes. Her lashes were fringes of sable silk against her creamy skin. Eoin dared not glance her way—she resembled Lilith so closely that if he looked upon her for more than an instant his heart began to decay like moldering stone, and his anguished spirit screamed its fury at the horror of his loss. Instead, he stared down at the amulet of bone. Another irony—thirteen years ago he would have given almost anything to possess this object. He surmised, now, it was a purely decorative trinket with no life-warding properties, no efficacy at all against malignant wights, but he did not care.

I am as good as dead already, he thought to himself, remembering the portent he had seen, the prediction of his own imminent death within the twelve-month.

He had been walking through the streets of Cathair Rua in the evening, leading his horse.

The street running alongside the Sanctorum was deserted save for a man in rags, picking about in a gutter. Spying a traveler with a horse, this beggar made ready to ask for money. As he approached Eoin, the deep, solemn pealing of a bell boomed out from a lofty belfry within the Sanctorum.

Forgetting his purpose, the beggar quickly looked up and made a sign to ward off evil. He grabbed Eoin's arm. "By the bones of Ádh," he said fearfully, "'tis the passing-bell! I have never heard it ring at such a late hour! It's the bell they ring when someone dies. But there is no light in the belfry!" shrieked the beggar, gibbering with fear as he rounded a corner and disappeared from view.

The brass tongue in the bell's mouth made its voice say *doom, doom, doom.* Eoin counted the strokes. They ceased at thirty-seven. As the terminal vibrations thrummed away out over the city, Eoin realized the bell had numbered the years of his life. . . .

When Eoin drew near a side-gate it sprang open and a strange child-size funeral procession emerged. On their shoulders they bore a small coffin, the lid of which was askew. "Ach, I've seen such wights aforetimes," the reappeared beggar spluttered startlingly in Eoin's ear. "Fear not. They're seelie enough if no man meddles with them."

"But this is impossible," muttered Eoin. "Wights are immortal. They do not truly die—yet this looks to be a funeral!"

The inquisitive beggar tapped the side of his nose knowledgeably. "It'll be one of their mockeries."

"Why do they do it?"

"'Tis a death portent."

Nausea billowed through Eoin's belly.

"I want to see what lies in that coffin," he said impulsively. "Hold my horse for me and the job'll earn you sixpence."

"Give me the halter," mumbled the beggar. "But I warn you—those of their kind take offense if mortal folk try to speak to them. They might hurt you if you do."

Without reply Eoin threw him the rope halter and strode after the procession. As he came up with it he peered into the coffin. A shock bolted through him.

The figure lying there wore his own face.

The enormity of the portent sank in.

Heedless of the beggar's warning, he spoke to the coffin bearers in sick and quavering tones, saying, "When shall I die?"

They answered him not.

He overtook the leader, but when he reached forth his hand to touch him the entire procession immediately disappeared and a violent wind came barreling down the street.

The beggar dropped the halter and made off without his sixpence.

Under the lime trees, lying protectively beside Jewel in the wilderness, Eoin thought, *I can only hope I will live long enough to see her safe to shelter.*

"Where are we going?" Jewel asked next morning. After making a rudimentary breakfast they had refilled their water flasks at a freshet that tumbled from a crevice in the hillside, beneath the knotted roots of an overhanging linden tree. Now they set off downhill again, their boots rustling through sparse layers of leaves that lay like fragile seashells cast in copper, bronze, and red-gold.

The child had not asked that question before. In the last day or three she had begun to speak more frequently, but she never referred to the loss of her parents. Eoin understood she was still too stunned by the enormity of the disaster, too numbed to fully comprehend either the past or the possible future.

"Far from Slievmordhu," he replied, "to King's Winterbourne, the chiefest city of Narngalis. Warwick Wyverstone, sovereign of the north-kingdom, is a wise and just ruler, by all accounts. As you know, the foremost amongst his noble warriors, the famous Companions of the Cup, are as chivalrous and honorable as they are valorous. There is little or no love between Warwick Wyverstone of Narngalis and our King Maolmórdha Ó Maoldúin. We will keep your identity secret, but even if it were discovered, 'tis unlikely Narngalis would hand you over to Slievmordhu. King's Winterbourne is a most prosperous city. We shall find a place to stay, and I shall seek employment."

"I want to go back to the marsh," said Jewel. "Perhaps in a twelve-month or two it will be safe, and we can go then."

Eoin grunted noncommittally. He knew that as long as King Maolmórdha required a descendant of Jaravhor to unlock the Dome she could never return, yet he could not bring himself to shatter her hopes.

Farther away, through the spindly stems of larches, motes of snow seemed to be drifting. It was a flock of sulphur-crested cockatoos, so frostily pure-white they seemed unreal, as though shavings of highly polished platinum had been cast in handfuls on the wind. Above the heads of the wayfarers the woodland canopy hovered, shimmering in the breeze like an explosion of butterflies, jade and saffron.

"I have been thinking," said Jewel, marching along. "Is it possible the sparkly *stone* is the key to this precious Dome of Strang, rather than the sorcerer's only blood-relative?"

Eoin shrugged.

"If it is," she went on, "I would gladly give it to King Maolmórdha in exchange for the freedom to go home."

"Little one," said Eoin earnestly, "you are young and not yet learned in the ways of the world. Hearken. Maolmórdha is a weak man, despite that he rules over one of the Four Kingdoms of Tir. He dances to the tweakings of his druids, like a puppet on cords. The druids jealously guard their authority, their status and power. Do you think they would blithely allow a scion of Jaravhor to dwell freely in Slievmordhu? Janus Jaravhor was a mighty sorcerer, the most potent of his time, if the stories are true. When he died, the druids rejoiced. When no successor appeared, they were relieved. You are a child, but if they knew of your existence, I've no doubt they would wish to confine you—"

"But they cannot harm me!" argued Jewel. "I am close to invulnerable. My father told me so!"

"Let me finish! Although you are impervious to hurt, they might imprison you for life, in some forgotten dungeon. They would yearn to be rid of you before you reach maturity and come into your full strength, whatever that may be. Key or no key, 'tis you they would want."

"What *full strength*?" cried Jewel angrily. "My father wielded no gramarye! He was immune to injury, that is all. As I am, too, so it seems. But I have no special powers." She leveled her forefinger at a tall larch. "Fall!" she shouted. The tree stood unaffected, a bottle-green cone pointing up against the sky. Jewel stabbed her finger at a boulder, lichen-mottled, peeping from a filigree of wild sage. "Split!" she commanded. "Fly apart!" The rock remained unmoved, as it had for seven hundred and thirty-five years. "There, you see?" she declared, pouting. "I'd be no threat at all to the druids. They might as well leave me alone."

"Ah, but they would not. Their suspicious minds could never be certain of your innocuousness. And they are ruthless."

"Then I say, *cursed be the druids,*" Jewel said with vehemence. "Here, Uncle," she added impulsively, "you take the stone." Having drawn the necklace over her head, she held it out to him. In her palm it glistened, as though she had torn a piece of radiance out of the sun. "I do not want it anymore."

Eoin pushed her hand away. "What are you saying?" he muttered incredulously. "It was your father's gift."

"Aye, but 'tis of no use to me. You, on the other hand—you have forsaken your house, your friends, your living, all just to go traipsing across the countryside looking after me. I owe you something in return."

"My breath and blood!" exclaimed Eoin, his features collapsing in mortification. "Oh, by my troth! Never say that, Jewel. Never say it. 'Tis I who am indebted to you. But do not ask me why, for I cannot endure to tell you."

Slowly she retracted her hand, yet she did not replace the chain about her neck.

"Anyway," said Eoin hastily, evading her inquisitive stare and hoping to put her mind at ease, "I own riches enough."

"All your coin and possessions remain back at the marsh."

"You are mistaken. I carry my good fortune with me."

"I cannot believe it."

"In sooth! Several years ago I did a good turn for some wights, and they re-warded me with luck in all my enterprises."

She was entranced. "Is it so? How did it come to pass?"

They forded a pebbly brook and started uphill again. As they plodded through the wiry grasses, Eoin told the tale of that night in the marsh when he had crossed an island, through groves of trees whose starlit boles were slender, silver dancers, shadow-haired. When he walked out upon a grassy, open space, a sense of strangeness had overtaken him.

An alarming racket had arisen on all sides. He knew he was amongst el-dritch wights, although he could not see them, and he was afraid. Some were laughing; others were weeping. One of the wailing voices suddenly said, "A bairn is born and there's nowt to put on it!"

At this, Eoin jumped backward and sideways, for the voice had seemed to come from almost under his feet.

"A bairn is born and there's nowt to put on it!" squeaked the woeful voice a second time.

In the name of all good sense, what am I doing here? Eoin thought, in growing apprehension, *out here alone with no one nigh for miles to hear my screams should any ill befall me. . . .*

"A bairn is born and there's nowt to put on it!" shrilled the melancholy voice again, but Eoin saw nothing except the gem-encrusted night sky, the dark grasses bending in the breeze, and the glint of starlight on black water. Swiftly unfastening two bronze shoulder-brooches, he doffed his cloak and cast it to the ground.

"Take this!" he croaked, his mouth dry with terror.

Instantly, the cloak was seized by an invisible hand. The howlings died away, but the sounds of mirth and celebration intensified. Hoping his action would content the wights, Eoin took his chance and fled.

"My action did indeed content them," he said, concluding his tale to Jewel. "From that night forward, I had great luck in gambling and trade."

"Why, that explains many things! How wonderful!" With that, the child slipped the chain of the white gem around her neck once again, and concealed it beneath her gown. "But—oh!" Abruptly, she halted.

Eoin stopped beside her.

"Won't your good luck cease now you've told of it?" Jewel said, frowning up at him, "That is the way with wights. It is astonishing you are not aware of it! Their gifts only remain as long as their source is not disclosed!" Her voice sank to a whisper and she darted furtive glances over her shoulders.

The marshman, however, knew exactly what he had done. Deliberately, per-haps as a kind of self-punishment, he had made known the origin of his luck and thereby surrendered it forever. In their mysterious way the wights would know what he had done, and instantly withdraw their endowment. Time past, the knowledge would have troubled him, but now it made him perversely glad. In his own view, he deserved to pay for his transgressions.

"Aye," he affirmed, giving a wry smile. He patted the child on the shoulder. "It never did me any good, being prosperous. I care naught if the eldritch gift is taken away."

"But you should *not* have told me your secret!" she protested, with irritation. "I hope no wights of eldritch overheard." Disconsolately she kicked out at a clump of red-capped toadstools sprouting near her toes. Her companion fancied he heard a burst of chatter, as of shrill voices, but he could not be sure. Perhaps it had been the twittering of small birds. . . .

"Somehow, they will know," he said. "They always do."

Distraught, the child began to rail at him, but he soothed her, saying, "Hush, little one. Give a man leave to choose his own direction. Now, we must continue on our way if we are to reach shelter before our supplies run out."

Sulkily, she complied.

As they went on together he began to sing to her, to calm her. It was a song he had first invented when she was an infant, and he used to rock her in his arms:

> "I'll make you a bonnet of a bluebell, silver shells for your shoon,
>   And me and baby will go dancing all by the light of the moon.
> I'll make you a carriage of a pumpkin, white mice for the team,
>   And me and baby will go driving down by Watermill Stream.
> I'll make you a song of pretty rose-buds, white and pink and gold,
>   And me and baby will be singing until the day is old.
> I'll make you a necklace of bright raindrops falling one by one,
>   And me and baby will be laughing until the day is done.
> I'll make you a cradle of a walnut, lined with down so light,
>   And little baby will lie sleeping, peaceful through the night."

Late in the afternoon a rain-shower blew away into the east and the sun, slipping through a gap in the clouds, flooded the western hillsides with amber radiance. Eoin and Jewel emerged from a straggling copse of linden trees. They had reached the other side of the Border Hills. At their feet, the ground sloped gently down. The trees opened out and they looked out over a vast windswept land striated with overlapping belts of trees, dark green, tinged with a dusting of topaz at the leaf-tips. Great draughts of fresh air swept up the rise, so intoxicating they took the breath away.

This was Canterbury Grasswood, an undulating region reaching from the Border Hills to Canterbury Water, the great river whose sources sprang amongst the mountain ranges of the east. Its rounded shoulders were lavishly clothed in grassland, scattered with open woodland. In places, the trees clustered closely together, forming dense patches of forest. Copper-beech proliferated here, and horse-chestnut, maple, elm, and elder. The northern horizon was veiled by a low band of mist rising from the distant river. Above the mist reared a line of peaks, the southernmost of the mountain ring that encircled and buttressed the distant High Plateau.

The wayfarers descended the final incline. It was a lonely spot, far from human habitation or the routes of Marauders, so Eoin decided to risk lighting a short-lived cook-fire. That evening he snared a rabbit, which they roasted for supper over the orange flames.

Seven days after leaving the Border Hills they were trudging, bound by their customary silence, along a footpath sunk between high banks of thyme, and overhung by elder trees gaudy with scarlet berries. The sky was overcast, and the wind had swung around, bringing a bitter chill down from the north. Instinctively, Jewel tugged her hood over her ears and pulled her fur-lined cloak more closely around her slight form.

"How do you know the way to King's Winterbourne?" she asked. "Have you been there?"

"I have not. Nonetheless, I know enough about Tir to be sure that if we head north we shall eventually arrive at the Canterbury Water, and if we veer somewhat east as we travel we shall find the bridge where the Mountain Road crosses the river. That bridge cannot be crossed without paying a toll to the watchmen of Narngalis."

"What if the watchmen suspect us?"

"We'll confront that predicament when we come to it."

"Can we not cross the river elsewhere, and avoid predicaments?"

"I know of no other way across the Canterbury Water, unless one journeys far upstream, or finds a ferryman, or goes far downstream to the bridges over the border in Grïmnørsland."

The sunken path dipped and ran rapidly downhill. At the bottom of a flowery dell a little wooden bridge spanned a stream. It was a rotting, rickety construction built on piles of moldering stone, the patched-up remnants of a more robust structure that had once spanned the watercourse. When they had reached the opposite bank the trail led them into a stand of maples and copper-beeches. Here Autumn flamed in its glory, splashing color far and near in vibrant shades of red, yellow, and orange.

"By all that's uncanny—what's that ahead?" Eoin said sharply. He thrust out his arm to bar the progress of Jewel, who was following behind him. They both halted, peering into the dappled shade that hung across the trail like a richly embroidered curtain. Something moved between the trees, then gathered shape to itself from contrast and dimness, from hue and saturated luminosity.

"It looks like a coach-horse," muttered Eoin.

"Which signifies it probably isn't one," Jewel hissed back.

A loud whinny emanated from the vicinity of the creature. It switched its ivory cascade of a tail back and forth, then trotted off up the path. As its palely glimmering form disappeared around a bend it nickered, rudely and brazenly.

Without thinking, Eoin clutched the amulet at his throat. "Sain us," he said. "Methinks 'tis a waterhorse! Who knows what kind it might be—a cabyll-ushtey, a shoopiltee, or a kelpie; an aughiski, maybe."

"Aye, but we are far from the marsh, and farther from the sea," said Jewel reasonably. "In which case 'tis unlikely to be any of those types."

"We crossed over a stream back there," Eoin reminded her. " 'Tis some sort of horse-wight, there's no denying, but whether 'tis seelie or not I cannot tell."

"We must go forward unafraid," Jewel decided. "Wights get power over mortals if we show fear. Besides, if it *is* a malevolent waterhorse, 'tis easy to avoid their clutches. All we must do is refuse to get on its back if it invites us."

"And be able to run very fast when it waxes wrathful at our refusal," Eoin murmured under his breath.

"Your blackthorn staff will help to ward it off," said Jewel optimistically. "What's more, you have knives of cold iron, and I picked a bunch of bright red elderberries this morning. We have your amulet of bone, and my gemstone for added protection. We can turn our clothes inside out, and we can whistle. If all else fails we can turn back and make for that stream. Once we cross running water we'll be safe for certain!"

"Very well." Eoin began to shrug off his pack.

"Oh," said Jewel, "but I shall be safe anyway. I forgot. Sometimes I overlook my own invulnerability."

"We shall both be safe," said Eoin, endeavoring to sound sincere.

They removed their outer garments, turned them seam-side-out, and put them on again. Whistling, they began to walk on, so filled with apprehension that they were unaware they were whistling two different tunes, that wove together in eerie discord.

Every time they rounded a twist in the narrow woodland path they would see the horse-thing again, poised as if waiting for them, whereupon it would flounce off as before, uttering clamorous and prolonged horse-noises. After they had gone on in this fashion for more than a hundred paces, the woods thinned, and when they came out into the open, the wight had vanished.

"I wonder what happened to the calf with the kerchief at its neck," said Jewel.

"Did you see that, too?" Eoin exclaimed. "I thought my eyes were playing tricks. First a coach-horse, next a calf with a horse's tail." Suddenly he turned around and slapped his thigh in a revelatory manner. "I wist I know what that wight was!" he said. "'Twas a brag!"

"Are brags seelie?" Jewel wanted to know as they recommenced their journey at a somewhat swifter pace.

"Indeed," her step-uncle advised, "yet 'tis mischievous they are, as well. They are shape-shifters whose usual form is a horse, but not a horse associated with water. Like their cousins the phoukas, they are practical jokers who sport with humans for their own wayward delight."

"What is their custom?"

"Oh, the usual thing. They entice folk onto their backs and give them wild rides to bruise their seats and bemuse their wits, before flinging them into some duck pond or muddy puddle and galloping off, guffawing with laughter. Unlike the true waterhorses, they do not devour their victims. Brags can take certain other shapes, too. They may appear as a bushy-tailed calf with a white handkerchief tied around its neck, or as a naked, headless man. Once it appeared as four men holding up a white sheet . . ."

"Yes?" prompted Jewel.

". . . but that was when myself and three other fellows were trying to make fools of some of the marsh Watchmen," Eoin confessed.

"Did the trick work?"

"Not exactly."

Jewel smiled. At this rare sight, Eoin felt his heart must break.

"Do you know anything else about brags?" she inquired.

"A traveler's gest tells of a man who had a tailor make a set of garments for him, all in white. The first time he wore them, he met a brag, and ever since then whenever he wore the white clothes some ill-chance happened upon him."

"Then he was a fool to keep putting them on," remarked Jewel.

"That is the way of most folk," said Eoin, "ever hopeful that their luck will change. Moreover, he must have been a fearless man. It is told that he met the same brag a second time. All dressed in his white, he was returning from the naming ceremony of a nobleman's child. When he saw the brag in its horse-shape, he was undaunted. Probably longing for revenge, he leaped on the wight's back. They jogged on all right for a while, and he thought he'd get a good ride home, but when they came to the crossroads by the village green, the brag began to leap and arch its back so mightily that the fellow had all he could do to cling on. You may guess the outcome."

"It bucked him off into the middle of the duck pond and frolicked away, laughing like any mortal man?"

"Even so!"

Jewel smiled again, but it was a wan smile, and the dark smudges arcing beneath her eyes made her appear, to her step-uncle, like some waif.

By sunset, the wayfarers had not yet found a suitable place to make camp. They plodded on through the accumulating twilight, before settling at last at the margin of a thicket of elms, in the lee of a low embankment. There had been no sign of Marauders for many a mile, so it seemed safe to risk lighting a fire. Kindling was easily found. They had a good blaze crackling away when Eoin announced, "I'm off to catch something for supper." After a nod of acknowledgment from Jewel, who was busy reversing her cloak and hood to seam-side-in, he took the coils of snare-wire and fishing-line and slipped away into the dusk.

The wind had dropped. The evening was so still that the fulvous elm-leaves hung static. Hardly a one floated down to become part of the sumptuous mosaic on the woodland floor. Eoin backtracked until he reached a shallow ravine, whose steep walls he and the child had negotiated shortly before sunset. Roughly fifteen feet deep, it had been gouged from the sandy soil of the hillside by a bubbling beck that flowed along its nadir. To the marshman's eye, this had looked like a trout-stream. As he approached, the tinsel gurglings of moving water intensified. He had just let himself down the fern-decorated cliff-face when an awareness grew in him that the water's merry song was mingled with another sound. It was a soft, protracted cry, and the voice that made it was clear and melodious beyond human ability. Through the gloaming he discerned the silhouette of a woman. He stepped closer. When he saw her face, he felt a sky-bolt smite him. She was beautiful, but pallid as a marble tomb. A smoke of charcoal-hued hair tumbled down over her shoulders, and her eyes were two melts of the most vivid, concentrated blue he had ever seen in his life.

Lilith.

She made as if to speak to him, but gave voice merely to her weird wailing. Then, beckoning him to accompany her, she turned away. Eagerly he followed, until without warning, he was following nothing. Only moonlight stood in sky-high columns at the ends of the ravine, pleached with the first tendrils of a slowly elevating mist.

Tormented, he hurried back to the place where he had originally spied this vision, but there was no clue to her whereabouts. Forgetting the object of his excursion, he began to run wildly up and down the shores of the stream, calling the name that pounded through his head.

"Lilith!"

Much later, spent and gray-faced, he made his way back to the campsite empty-handed.

"What's amiss?" Jewel asked at once.

Having just witnessed a vision of the love of his life, whose death he had brought about, Eoin was shaken to the foundations of his being, shocked and utterly unmanned. "Naught," was all he would say, and he lay down as if to sleep, without taking so much as a bite of their meager fare.

The lightless hours crept onward, and far off in the elm-wood a masked owl gave a drawn-out, rasping screech. Jewel roused from a shallow doze to discover she was alone in the moonlight, beside the ruddy embers of the fire. Eoin's pack lay nearby. It was thoroughly uncharacteristic of him to abandon her in the night, so she sat up, alarmed, looking about. He was not to be found.

Immediately she concluded he had gone back to seek whatever it was that had been troubling him since his unsuccessful fishing trip. After quickly stamping out the glowing coals as a precaution against wildfires, she picked up her dilapidated skirts and hastened in the direction she supposed he had taken. Along the leafy trail she ran, leaping over gnarled roots that sprawled athwart her path, dodging a sleepy hedgehog, paying scant heed to the occasional eldritch squawks erupting from deep in the undergrowth.

Near the ravine, she found him. By now a dense mist had built up in the cleft and was spilling out in diaphanous waves across the ground. Half-hidden by serpentine vapors, Eoin was roaming eccentrically about. He seemed to be remonstrating with a being Jewel could not see, pleading with it to return.

Screaming, Jewel sprang toward him and gripped him by the arm. "Come away! Come away!" she shrieked, " 'Tis some spell on you. Come away!"

He regarded her with a clouded gaze. His drooping eyes seemed to be swimming with dreams and she thought he stared straight through her.

Into his wrist she sank her teeth.

"Ouch!" His lids flew open.

Dragging at his elbow she shouted, "Come away, lackbrain!" Harsh words were the only other strategy that occurred to her, on the spot, to capture his attention.

Eoin, shocked from his enchanted stupor, looked down. Through the mist he perceived that he and Jewel were standing on the very brink of the ravine. One false step and they would both hurtle down the cliff. Fifteen feet was not far, yet it was far enough to break one's neck. Smothering a yell he caught the child by the hand, and they fled.

At their backs, the mist reached out frayed strands. Muffled by humidity, the song of the water sounded like wailing, sweet and low, and two powder-blue moths fluttered out of the moonlight.

Later, back at the fire, Jewel demanded, "Who did you think you were talking to?"

"Nobody."

"That is not true!"

Eoin seemed to have found Lilith only to lose her again, and in the process he had endangered the life of Jewel's sole protector. Tortured by his distress, he responded with unwonted harshness, snapping, "Leave me alone."

The child was stung by his gruff retort. She withdrew into her protective shell of silence, feeling that she ought to have guessed he would eventually lash out. The world had recently proved itself a cruel place—how could she expect unfailing kindness from any quarter, even from her beloved uncle?

Other eldritch wights manifested themselves along the way, but after that night none of them greatly troubled the wary wayfarers. Over the next seven days Eoin and Jewel forded many lively tributaries running down from the hills. At length, hungry and weary, they entered the valley bordering the Canterbury Water. These river-drained slopes were broad and shallow. Indeed, they descended toward the watercourse so subtly that the incline was scarcely noticeable. Darkly gleaming forests of evergreen lilly-pillys and silkwoods clothed the valley sides.

Eoin steered by the sun. This was not effortless, now that he and Jewel had penetrated the close-ranked timber. Little trails made by wild things meandered haphazardly, before fading into the creeping herbage. The wayfarers were continually forced to leave these paths when they twisted in the wrong direction, to push their way through a tangle of woody lianas and webs of blossom-starred clematis. Fallen branches and drifts of rotting leaves littered the forest floor.

"We ought to turn east right now, and make for the road," said Jewel. She twitched the hem of her skirt aside, tearing it from the opportunistic grip of a briar. "We must find the road in any case, since it leads to the bridge—we might as well be striding along in the open spaces, instead of struggling through this wretched gallimaufry. In sooth, we'd be going more swiftly than at present."

"We cannot risk it," replied Eoin. "Crossing the bridge will be perilous enough. I do not want to be on the road for longer than necessary."

"What is so dangerous about the road?"

"We cannot be sure King Maolmórdha's soldiers did not worm the secret of your existence from the folk of the marsh."

"Ha!" snorted Jewel, "No amount of gold would make our people betray their own kind to out-marshers."

"Not gold," said Eoin somberly. "Maolmórdha and his druids would have other means of extracting information from those who are reluctant to divulge it."

"Oh," said Jewel. After a moment's thought, she added, "I feel ill."

"Do not," Eoin instructed briskly. "We have no time for illness on our journey. You understand, little one, that if Maolmórdha has heard of you, the roads will be patrolled by his men."

"Not here in Narngalis!"

"Even in Narngalis, they may well be able to find some pretext to ride the highways. A species of arm's length cordiality officially exists between Cathair Rua and King's Winterbourne, in spite of the fact that the two kings have no love for one another."

"Does this signify we shall be traveling off-road all the way to King's Winterbourne?"

"Perhaps."

"Pish! A plague on't!" muttered Jewel, wrenching a fold of her skirt off a dead bough and ripping the fabric in the process.

Had he been in a better frame of mind, Eoin might have secretly smiled at his protégée's outburst. She looked so small, so fragile; yet by nature she was tempestuous and valiant. Instead of wilting like a fallen leaf in the face of adversity, here she was uttering curses, railing at her lot, like some hardy, blustering soldier in the guise of a girl-child. Like anyone she had her faults—indeed, she could be selfish and even somewhat conceited—but Eoin, the indulgent uncle, deemed that any flaw was not her fault; it was due to her being an only child, much spoiled and fussed-over. Her imperfections had always been outweighed, in his view, by her disarming qualities of generosity, kindness, courage, and perseverance, and by her exuberant zeal for knowledge.

Clouds blew across the sun's tawny countenance. That night, it rained.

The rain kept up, on and off. Their supplies of food had long since run out, and they were living on the wild fruits of Autumn gathered along the way: hazelnuts and blackberries plucked by the handful, dandelions and astringent rose-hips, mushrooms and watercress, the roots of pignut, silverweed and wild parsnip, and the seeds of the common weed Fat Hen. Eoin became gaunt and haggard, but Jewel appeared to experience no ill-effects from this meager diet.

By the morning of the thirty-second day since they had departed from the marsh, they reached the banks of the Canterbury Water, which were lined with a spangle of willows and river peppermints. The sight of willow trees and large expanses of water was familiar to them both; their spirits rose as they picked their way upstream. The sun was a silver disc behind thin sheets of altostratus cloud. It hung directly overhead by the time they glimpsed, at last, through the vertical slats of the lilly-pilly boles, the gray sash of the road, its rain-puddled surface shining. To the left, they could see the massive stone bridge with its twenty-one arches, soaring across the water. A small building squatted at the bridge's far terminus: the toll-house.

Traffic was passing to and fro along the road to the bridge. On the north bank, three travelers on foot had come to a halt at the toll-house. A coach-and-four was bowling across the bridge, moving south. From the other direction an ox-cart and a donkey-cart, widely spaced apart, were rattling up the road.

"Have we money for the toll?" questioned Jewel.

"I carry coin," said Eoin absently. Frowning in concentration, he was peering between heavy draperies of dark, glossy leaves and ripening lilly-pilly berries.

"If the toll-house sentries have been warned to watch for a girl-child who speaks with the lilt of Slievmordhu, then we are indeed in danger," he mumbled, speaking chiefly to himself.

"But the sentries are Narngalishmen. Why would they heed King Maolmórdha's edicts?"

"Some fabrication might have been spun, possibly some falsehood about thievery or other crimes. And as I said, *officially*, goodwill and cooperation are firm between the two kingdoms."

"In that case we ought to cross the bridge in the company of some Narngalishers returning home," said Jewel. "The sentries will hear them speak, and believe we are of their party."

"A profitable notion," said Eoin, nodding thoughtfully. "However, we can hardly jump out of the bushes at the next group of travelers and begin walking alongside them. If strangers appear unexpectedly from the wilderness, folk naturally demand explanations."

"We must double back," said Jewel, "traveling south and staying parallel with the road but hidden from its traffic. At dusk, these comings and goings must surely cease. Most folk mislike being abroad after dark, and will have found themselves shelter at some wayside inn. When the road is empty, we ought to make camp on the very verge, just the other side of the ditch. Come morning, we must listen to the language of passers-by when they hail us. If any prove to be Narngalishers, we should join them."

Her step-uncle scratched his head. "I can think of no better way," he admitted eventually. "Very well, little one—let us put your plan into action."

As they set off again it came to Eoin that during this exchange Jewel had somehow become the authoritative member of the expedition. The insight reinforced his fond opinion of his niece as a competent, self-assured damsel who would never meekly stand back and allow ill-fortune to get the better of her. He allowed himself to dare hope that she might ultimately prevail over their current trials, even though he was irrevocably doomed.

Slowly, majestically, the treetops bowed and swayed, their foliage glinting in the morning sun as if the underside of each leaf were lined with thinly beaten metal. Near at hand, small wrens chirruped peevishly, bossily, in low bushes of tea-tree. Above the forest roof, a flamingo sunrise painted the eastern skies. Elongated tree-shadows lay across the trampled dirt of the road.

By the roadside the wayfarers were kicking loose soil over the remnants of their diminutive fire when a faint snatch of sound drifted to their ears.

"Voices . . ." said Eoin. Hurriedly, he hoisted the leather pack onto his shoulders. With their provisions gone, he had crammed Jewel's small bundle inside it, and now carried both.

The hint of conversation ceased, but it was not long before there came into view a straggling group of pedestrians carrying bundles and a basket. Three were adults; two were half-grown children. Eoin and Jewel turned away and feigned ignorance of their approach, busying themselves with adjusting the pack-straps. In low tones the marshman said, "It looks to be a family—husband and wife, children, and the grandfather."

"Good morrow, strangers!" a man's voice called. The wayfarers exchanged a quick nod of relief. By his pronunciation, the man was a native of Narngalis.

"Ah! Good morrow, sir!" returned Eoin, trying to appear surprised.

"We are of mortalkind," said the husband, employing traditional etiquette.

"We also are of mortalkind," Eoin responded, according to the time-honored formula. Wights of eldritch could not tell outright lies, so this was as good a way as any of finding out who one was dealing with, when one met a stranger on the road or in untame regions. The converse side of the coin was that humankind *could* lie, and swindlers would not hesitate to do so, with eloquent flair.

With Jewel in tow, Eoin jumped the ditch and walked toward the group. "My niece and I were about to set off again after a cold night spent sleeping amidst the weeds of the wayside. How far is it to the bridge?"

"Not far. Noon should see us all there," said the man.

It was obvious these people were not affluent. They were not aided in their labor by any beast of burden, and their simple, homespun garments were copiously patched. Yet as Eoin glanced from parents to children he noted they were clean and red-cheeked, their hair combed, their eyes bright.

"I am Daithi, son of Donncha," said Eoin, "and this is my sister's daughter, Aisling. May we keep you company for a while?"

"Gladly," replied the man. "I am Leofric of Fiddler's Hamlet." He introduced his smiling wife and children. "We are on our way home," he continued, "after calling on my wife's sister in Cathair Rua."

"She has a newborn infant," volunteered his wife.

The two children stared at Jewel, whispering to each other.

"What coincidence," said Eoin, thinking quickly. "We are on our way to visit cousins in King's Winterbourne." He turned to the fifth member of the Fiddler's Hamlet expedition. "But we have not yet been introduced to you, sir—" The marshman's words were chopped off as if his throat had been squeezed. His eyes bulged like a frog's as he stared at the ragged, filthy old man.

Leofric of Fiddler's Hamlet said, somewhat sourly, "In sooth, this graybeard is a stranger to us. He fell in with us three leagues back and continues to follow."

It was the beggar from the streets of Cathair Rua.

Eoin had no difficulty in recognizing him—that decrepit face was imprinted on his consciousness. . . .

"Good morrow, sir," he said. Acid was churning in the pit of his stomach. Would the man recognize him? He had encountered the fellow little more than a month ago, yet to him it seemed a lifetime. . . .

"Cat Soup," the beggar was saying.

The marshman flinched, startled from his ghastly reminiscences.

"Cat Soup," the beggar repeated. " 'Tis what they call me, in the city."

Jewel said demurely, "May the Fates smile upon you, Master Cat Soup."

The beggar stretched his thin slash of a mouth, uncovering eight brown teeth distributed between gummy gaps. Eoin stepped back, blasted by the stench of the old man's breath. Alert to her step-uncle's discomfiture, Jewel diverted attention by asking the others, "Good folk of Fiddler's Hamlet, prithee, have you any victuals for sale? We carry small coin. We can pay."

At the mention of coin, the beggar seemed to prick up his ears.

"No need for payment," said Leofric's wife affably. "We have food to spare." She began to rummage through her covered basket.

Meanwhile, Eoin rummaged through his memories. What had altered about his appearance since his first meeting with the beggar? He was wearing exactly the same garments—the dark-red tunic purchased from the innkeeper at the Ace and Cup, the same buckskin leggings. Every item of his clothing, however, was stained, wrinkled, sagging, torn. His face, too, must have changed—a month's worth of beard covered his jaw, and dirt ingrained the furrows of his skin. Hanks of unkempt hair fell across his forehead and into his eyes, which felt sore and bloodshot. Surely he must be unrecognizable.

From her basket, the goodwife extricated a strange, green fruit slightly larger than a man's fist, lumpy and knobbled.

"By all that's wonderful!" exclaimed Jewel wonderingly. "I've never seen such a grotesquerie. What is it?"

"A custard apple," said the woman, bringing out a small table knife.

"It looks like a goblin's head."

"How would you know, little one?" asked Eoin, regaining enough composure to attempt joviality. "You've never seen a goblin!"

"I can imagine," said Jewel.

Eoin fossicked in his money-pouch for some coppers to present to the woman. Having waved away his offering, she sliced some chunks off the fruit and handed them to Eoin and Jewel. After the first nibble they commenced to devour the creamy flesh with gusto.

Cat Soup was by their side, his dripping nose somehow inches from the fruit. The goodwife cut up a second custard apple and gave him a piece, to the evident disgust of her husband.

"Come," he said brusquely, "let us walk on, if we are to reach the bridge by noon."

The party of seven moved off.

The road was wide and curved gently between the walls of trees. As the sun lifted, the clouds began to disperse. The few sky-sheened puddles on the road's surface shrank and disappeared. On Eoin's brow, perspiration stood out like granules of quartz. *Any moment now the old fool will recognize me and say something,* he thought, *yet we cannot simply part company with these folk. To walk away into the forest must invite speculation of the most detrimental kind.*

What if the beggar suddenly blurted, "Have I not seen you in the streets of Cathair Rua? I remember that day, for it was the same day an eldritch funeral mockery came out of the sanctorum, and the jewel was taken from the Iron Tree, and the city was all a-buzz with the news that the king was searching for the thief!" What if the old man went on to demand, "What is your business on the road to Narngalis? Do you know the man they are seeking? Are you he?" And the suspicions of everyone would be aroused. Eoin forced himself to march, rather than breaking into a run, dragging the child with him. He kept steadily on, though needing every particle of effort to maintain his mask of nonchalance. By his side, Jewel glanced frequently up at him, aware his thoughts were troubled, but unsure of the reason.

The sweetness of wild clematis perfumed the air. Contralto magpies warbled in the lilly-pilly forests. Apparently cheered by this, or by his gobbet of fruit, the beggar began to wax voluble.

"I've been on this road aforetimes," he said knowledgeably.

"No doubt," said Leofric of Fiddler's Hamlet, "as have we."

"Ah, but have *you,* sir?" the old man said, leering up at Eoin from his stooping posture.

"Nay." The marshman shook his tangled locks further over his features.

"Be warned then," said Cat Soup, "for if you think the road so far has been perilous, 'tis naught by comparison with the other side of the river."

"The road north of the bridge is safe enough during daylight hours," said the goodwife.

"Maybe, maybe not," the beggar chuckled, "for you see, sir," he said to Eoin, "before it reaches the village of Saxlingham Netherby, it passes right through a certain field they call Black Goat, which has a dreadful reputation, dreadful indeed. Murderous wights haunt it, they do. 'Tis a brave man who'd set foot there between sunrise and sunset, and a fool who'd try it any other time. I have heard—"

"Prithee, Master Soup, do not repeat any tales of horror you have heard," said the goodwife. "My husband and I would prefer it if our children were to sleep soundly this night, their dreams untroubled by lurid fancies."

Cat Soup's eye alighted on her basket of provisions and his mouth slammed shut like a trapdoor. His silence was annulled by the soft chatter and giggles of the two children from Fiddler's Hamlet.

Only a trickle of southbound traffic went past in the other direction, and no northbound equipage overtook the party. Well before noon, they reached the Canterbury Water.

"How much is the toll?" Eoin asked Leofric as the bridge again loomed in sight, arches and stanchions formed from huge blocks of granite, solid as a castle.

"Tuppence. 'Tis free for children to cross."

The marshman dug two pennies from his money-pouch and clutched them in his fist.

As they walked across the broad span of the bridge, the members of the party were able to look out over the stone parapets at the lustrous black-gray waters careering toward them from the right, rushing away on the left. Mustard-yellow willow leaves and the pellucid domes of bubbles swirled on the river's surface. Where the bridge poured itself onto the opposite shore, two strong gates reached across the road, meeting in the middle. To one side stood a slate-roofed edifice constructed of the same hoary granite as the bridge. It was small in diameter, but quite tall.

"That is the toll-house," Eoin murmured in Jewel's ear. "Fall back beside me, and say no word."

At the distance of a bowshot from the toll-house there arose an artificial hill, perfectly cone-shaped. On its flat top crouched a structure resembling a haystack, which was, in fact, a huge pile of kindling and dry logs, thatched to keep out the rain. In times of danger, this beacon fire could be lit by a flaming arrow sent from the toll-house. It would be seen by fortified settlements within eye-view of the beacon, on hilltops farther away. On the pinnacle of the toll-house perched a watch-turret whose narrow windows faced every direction, and atop the turret, under its own tiny roof, hung a bell.

A helmeted sentry dressed in the colors of Narngalis came out of this robust edifice. He stood facing them, with his back to the gates, similarly barring their path. His tabard was the color of black raspberries, bordered with orpine and emblazoned with the sigil of the sword.

"Travelers, hail," he recited in a voice like river-gravel. "The toll is tuppence a head, be that head sixteen Winters' age or more."

"Hail, sir. Well met," Leofric greeted the official in his congenial manner.

Eoin and Jewel hung back to the rear of the party, but try as they might, they could not get behind Cat Soup, who always managed to slip adroitly into last position. Goodman Leofric was in the lead, and as he fumbled with the knot in the drawstring of his belt-purse, the drubbing rhythm of fast-approaching horses came up the road from the south.

Cold claws of dread laid hold of Eoin, and the galloping hoofbeats throbbed in the blood through his temples. In a foment of panic, he could only shuffle from one foot to the other, trying desperately to maintain his charade of indifference, itching to throw his coins at the feet of the sentry, grab Jewel, and make a dash for the hedges bordering the road on the northern shore. Jewel showed no signs, but he understood her well enough to be certain she, too, had picked up the rumor of swift riders, and knew what it might mean.

"For myself and my wife." Leofric's four copper coins dropped *clink!* into the upturned hand of the sentry, who stared past the Narngalishman, shading his eyes with his other hand.

"Riders from Rua, eh?" he said. "King's men, by the look."

The marshman stepped forward and dropped his pennies into the still-open palm. The bridge guard stood aside, pushed one of the gates ajar, and motioned for him to pass, along with Jewel and the family from Fiddler's Hamlet. Simultaneously, he called out to his fellows in the toll-house—

"Sigeweard! Hunfrith! Look lively and show yourselves. Here's riders from Cathair Rua, and they look to be in a mighty hurry."

A clatter as of spilled ironmongery emanated from the unglazed windows of the toll-house and somebody let fly a curse. By this time, the entire party had stepped off the bridge, but the gritty voice of the sentry shouted, "Hey, you there! Stop!" and everyone came to a halt.

Eoin felt the muscles in his scalp slide on his head-bones, of their own accord.

They all turned around, to see two other sentries emerging from the toll-house, while the first strode toward Cat Soup, beckoning and snapping his fingers, saying, "You, sir, may not pass. You have not paid the toll."

A surge of relief made Eoin weak at the knees, yet it was mingled with mounting horror at the riders' relentless approach. The old man began to protest. Paying no heed to his objections, the sentry indicated with a wave that the rest of the party might proceed unhindered. As they set off, they heard Cat Soup insisting, "I have no money, but I have special powers and can tell you things that will be greatly to your benefit!"

The bridge guard rolled his eyes. Wearing a look of boredom, he continued to conduct the beggar back through the gates. It took great effort on Eoin's part to resist taking Jewel by the hand and making a dash for freedom. Each step seemed unbearably slow, as if they all waded through knee-deep mud. His ears twitched, for he kept expecting to hear someone call out from behind, bidding him halt immediately.

On the northern side of the Canterbury Water, the road was paved with flag-stones and cobbles.

"Now that we're across," said the goodwife to her husband, "I should like to rest over there beneath the trees. The children are hungry, and 'tis high time we had a bite to eat."

Aware that the family's provender was scarcely ample, and desperate to get away from the converging riders, Eoin spoke rapidly. "Alas, we cannot tarry with you, for we must make haste. We are grateful for your kindness and hope we may meet again." He bowed, and when he looked up he saw by their facial expressions that he had eased them of a burden—yet also they were concerned for the welfare of their companions.

"Take this, child." The goodwife thrust a wedge of hard cheese into Jewel's hand. The marsh-child thanked her with a polite curtsey and thus they took their leave.

From the bridge, the road barreled on, straight as a javelin. The land to either side had been tamed into hedge-bordered fields and meadows, interrupted by copses and spinneys and laced with slender brooks. Eoin and Jewel strode along as fast as they could without actually breaking into a run. "With all speed we must reach that bend up ahead," the marshman muttered fervently. "Even a slight curve will suffice to put us out of view of the bridge."

Neither of them dared to look back, but Eoin felt as if his ears had somehow lengthened, stretching behind him like the ears of a hare, straining to pick up sounds of hoofbeats. It could not be long until the horsemen caught up with them. Just before they reached the bend they risked a glance back toward the bridge. One of the gates, left ajar, had swung wider on its well-oiled hinges, revealing a clear view. Outside the toll-house, four riders had drawn rein. They wore the uniform of the King's Guard, emblazoned with Slievmordhu's sigil of the Burning Brand. Still on horseback, and in the company of the toll-house guards, they were grouped around the beggar. Indeed, Cat Soup appeared to be the focus of attention. One of the riders was leaning down, speaking to him. Then the beggar spoke, and the riders were obviously heedful.

"He is betraying me," said Eoin, suddenly. "He recognizes me from a chance encounter in Cathair Rua, and he is telling the king's cavalrymen." Jewel gasped. Fear shadowed her eyes of glacial blue. "Hasten!" cried her step-uncle. "Once around this bend, we'll be hidden from their line of sight and we can leave the road once more."

Even as they fled around the curve in the road they heard it start up again— the clop and clatter of iron crescents on flagstones. After jumping the ditch on the left, they ran alongside a berry-ornamented hawthorn hedge until they found a stile. This they vaulted swiftly in their terror, and were thus able to keep sprinting on the other side of the hedge, along the margins of a field, concealed from view of the road.

From behind them the sharp drumming of a fast-moving cavalcade grew louder. In front loomed a belt of old pines, probably planted long ago as a windbreak. The two terrified wayfarers plunged into the verdurous twilight beneath their boughs, with the clap of iron on stone racketing through their heads. The marshman threw himself to the ground, pulling Jewel after him. The cacophony crescendoed to its peak, as if the horsemen rode across their very spines, but no iron-shod hoof planted itself in the sumptuous carpet of pine-needles, no harsh voice shouted a command, and as the hammering of hooves faded up the road the wayfarers opened their eyes and sat up.

They listened.

In the branches above, a blackbird sang a poignantly beautiful melody. The wind crooned through the dark green needles. There was a muffled thud as a pine-cone hit the ground.

Nothing else.

"They will return," said Eoin, his eyes flicking nervously from side to side as he scanned their surroundings for hints of any further peril. "I daresay they will eventually guess our strategy and come hunting. Let's go! We must hasten from this spot, but we must not return to the road. Not in daylight. We'll wait until dusk."

As they picked themselves up and resumed their journey, Jewel said, "But Uncle, this is likely to be the very region the old man warned us about—the field called Black Goat, with its reputation as a haunt of unseelie wights. It will be too perilous here. Let us go back to the road at once."

"You are invulnerable, little one," her step-uncle reminded her.

"Except against mistletoe," she amended.

Paying no heed to the interruption, he repeated, "You are invulnerable, and I can take care of myself. The need for speed and secrecy is paramount. We shall take our chances off-road during daylight hours and return to the road at nightfall. And we shall stay wary at all times."

He was determined, and in the end she gave way to his decision.

The fields across which they were passing looked innocent enough, though rather wild and neglected, knee-deep in a profusion of weeds and wildflowers. Amaranth-pink blooms climbed the tall stems of common fumitory, the delicate albino racemes of shepherd's purse trembled, brushed by the corner of Jewel's cloak, and the sepals of charlock, bright yellow, glowed like warm butter. There was prickly crowthistle, too, grown lanky from the fierce need to reach for sunlight from amongst the shadows of its neighbors. Its blossoms perched on their stalks like colonies of purple birds.

Screened from the road by hedges and windbreak plantations, the wayfarers plowed on, stopping now and then, when Jewel's exhaustion overwhelmed her. Eoin was anxious to keep moving. He strapped his pack to his chest and bade his niece climb on his back, so that he might carry her. She went to sleep on his shoulders and almost slipped off.

Whether it was the fragrance of the wildflowers or the fact he had not had a good night's sleep for more than a month, or whether due to the aftermath of the terror engendered by the king's horsemen, or some other reason, Eoin, too, began to be affected by somnolence. With his lids sagging, he plodded stubbornly on, partially supporting himself on his blackthorn staff. His right arm, supporting Jewel's weight, was locked painfully into position; his knees creaked; his head throbbed. His sole notion was to keep moving north while staying out of sight of the road. It did not occur to him that after the single burst of speed and noise from the horsemen passing by, there had been no sign of them again. The king's riders had not doubled back to search for him and Jewel.

This was because, unknown to Eoin, the riders were not pursuing these two refugees at all. They were merely delivering a letter from Primoris Asper Virosus, the Druid Imperius of Slievmordhu, to the Druid Imperius of Narngalis. The letter had nothing to do with any descendants of the Sorcerer of Strang. At the toll-house Cat Soup, whose half-demented brain had not recognized Eoin, had been spinning the king's men a tale of his "unusual powers," of how he "knew" what was in the letter they carried, and they had better beware, for it was not to the letter bearers' advantage. Because of everyday association with the Sanctorum of Slievmordhu, the soldiery of Cathair Rua were highly superstitious. Unlike the Narngalish toll-house guards, they were inclined to believe the old man, even though they feigned skepticism. Before they rode away they tossed him a couple of coins, with which he paid the toll, and crossed over the Canterbury Water.

Eoin, however, was unaware of this and in his miasma of weariness, or enchantment, he was also unaware how far he had strayed from the road.

A gray gloaming crept over the fields. On her uncle's shoulder, Jewel stirred. "Should we not be returning to the road now?" she murmured sleepily. " 'Tis getting dark."

"Aye." Eoin veered to the right, then stumbled.

"Put me down," said Jewel. He let her slide from his back, and flexed his stiffened arms, passing his staff from hand to hand.

"Come on," he said grimly, looking about as if he, too, had just awoken. "We must head due east. Somehow I've blundered too far from the road. 'Tis nowhere in sight."

He reinstated the pack on his back and again, they set off.

A wall of cloud, iron-gray, stretched across the western sky. As the twilight thickened, translucent steams arose stealthily, and the weeds through which the wayfarers were wading looked taller than they had appeared by daylight. Their leaves now seemed blackish instead of green, and amongst them nightshade proliferated, heavy with orbs of poisonous fruit. Hidden beneath the rank growth were rocks and odd-shaped things, ready to turn one's ankle if stepped on. And instead of birdsong, a weird, acute melody was spurling across the fields, thin as a razor's edge.

In the distance, a cluster of red-gold lights flared. "Look yonder," said Eoin. "Bonfires on some hilltop. Perhaps folk are making merry there." Gold-tinged smokes haloed the remote blazes. If the fires had an uncanny look, the travelers were too weary to note it.

The mists that had been conspiratorially exuding from the ground floated ingenuously across their line of sight. They dimmed the lights and ultimately obscured them completely. Without reference to the descending sun, the marsh-man felt even more disoriented. He wondered if he had stepped on a Stray Sod—an eldritch piece of turf with the power to disorient any mortal creature that set foot on it—and muttered an age-old protective rhyme under his breath: "Hypericum, salt and bread, iron cold and berries red . . ."

The humid haze commenced to slowly circulate, and Eoin was vigorously re-minded of his encounter with the blue-eyed woman-seeming wight. That had all been glamour, nothing but an illusion created at the whims of supernatural be-ings for the purpose of luring mortal men to their deaths. *I'll not fall for that trick twice,* he decided, yet an inexpressible horror pressed on him. It struck him that for some while he had heard scant sound of Jewel beside him, swishing through the weeds. "Stay close," he said, turning toward her, but she was no longer there.

"Jewel?" he called, squinting through the murk and mist. "Jewel!"

No voice answered. He panicked, and started to run.

Alone in the dark, Jewel was beating through the tares, calling out the name of her step-uncle. She could not understand how the two of them had become sep-arated. Clammy tentacles of apprehension crawled across her flesh. Spying a rowan tree that stood alone, laden with its Autumn jewelry of scarlet beads, she hurried to shelter beneath its branches.

I shall wait for him, she thought. *It is safe here, beneath the rowan.*

She was too tired to walk any farther. The wighting hours were upon the land and she knew there might be trows about, or worse. Trows were apt to abduct folk. They did not harm them, but they kept them, trowbound. If that should happen, her invulnerability would avail her naught. At all events, trows and other minor unseelie creatures were unable to approach rowan wood.

"Uncle!" she called into the night.

The thin music was joined by distant voices, singing.

The fog had become so dense that Eoin could not see where he was going, and he was forced to lurch to a halt.

As the vapors thickened, the singing sprang up around him, louder than be-fore. He knew then that he was surrounded by wights, who at best would hin-der and mislead him. He turned back, heading in the direction from which he thought he had come, but a hedge barred his way. Its ends, if ends it possessed, were lost in the mists. Eoin was certain the hedge had not been there earlier, and this reinforced his suspicion that he had inadvertently stepped on a Stray Sod.

The hedge was of cypress, not prickly hawthorn, so he left his staff propped against it, pushed his way in amongst the springy foliage, and began to climb. As he ascended, however, the hedge-top never came any closer. It was as if the cypresses were growing taller, the higher he went. Eventually he surrendered and jumped down, before retrieving his staff. Striking out to the left, he made his way along the line of the hedge, bewildered and alarmed by the loud chorus of eldritch song issuing from all sides.

Foremost in his mind was the desire to locate Jewel. His heart was thundering like a rampage of mad horses, and every breath puffed in short, shallow gasps. He must find Jewel, protect her. Guilt was ripping his spirit apart. She was lost alone in the wilderness, and it was his fault. He had catapulted her into this predicament, and now he had failed her.

The aqueous gases clung to him stickily, chillingly. Damp, intangible wool pressed on his eyes. He began to stumble, and every time he did so, jeering laughter broke out. After a while he could endure the invisible mockery no longer. He sat down and took off his pack, then brought out his tinderbox.

A spark jumped from his flint and steel onto the curls of dry bark in the box. A flame flowered. Light blossomed.

A pile of jagged stone ruins leaned suddenly out of the nearby darkness. The radiance of the tiny tinder-fire flowed over it like rose-water, describing savage perforations and rude projections. The openings gaped to reveal the interior of this relic, which was filled with wildly gamboling figures, ludicrous mockeries of human shapes. Many possessed long-snouted heads, splayed hands, skinny limbs, and monstrous feet. Others were perverted to the degree of indescribability.

Eoin picked up his staff and sprang to his feet, but as he was about to escape, he was intercepted. Right in front of him capered an incorporation of the macabre; it looked like a black buck-goat, with horns a yard long, flaming eyes, and a long, twirling tail. Around the marshman it bounded, attempting to grasp him. Choked with terror, Eoin comprehended that instead of hooves, its forelegs terminated in hairy paws.

The numinous music and singing squealed from every point of the compass. It streamed into the ears of the mortal, flowing down his canals to his cerebellum, and down nerve fibers to his toes. Absurdly, his feet danced, compelled to move in rhythm with the eldritch minstrelsy. These wights, with their musical tricks, were making him look like some awkward, jiggling clown! His terror changed to fury. He was being forced to perform like a string-puppet, and this monstrous goat-thing appeared to be trying to lead him in the dance. But if it gripped him, what then? Would he be made to dance endlessly in some eldritch place, forever lost to mortalkind? In the past, he had survived many an encounter with wights, some tricksy, some malevolent. And he might do so again! With a surge of anger, forgetting he no longer wore an effective amulet, he brought up his fist with the cudgel of blackthorn and lashed out at the bizarre actuality leaping before him.

The weapon was torn from his grasp.

The guttering lambency from his tinderbox extinguished itself.

Something tripped Eoin and he fell flat on his back. A heavy blow sent him rolling down a slope. He felt himself crash into a thorny hedge at the foot of the incline; then two prongs of burning agony lifted him and he was thrown over the hedge on the horns of the goat-simulacrum. After that it was as though an unnaturally violent wind manifested, tossing and spinning him as if he were no more than a speck of dust, dashing him against rocks and briars, stripping the clothing from his back and the flesh from his ribs.

There was no lull, until at last he lay broken and insensible at the foot of a great rock. After a long while, consciousness returned briefly to him. He looked up at the sky, which was now visible, since the mists and cloud had cleared. He was alone. The stars shone kindly down on him, and all pain receded.

Thus it comes to pass, he understood, *that the forecast of the eldritch pallbearers is validated. I am departing from this world.*

The idea made him forlorn.

I am leaving Jewel. I am abandoning her to an uncertain fate, she whom I love more than anyone alive. It is I who am the cause of all her past sorrows, and probably her future suffering as well. What tribulations will tomorrow bring for my lost little one? My heart bleeds for her. Oh, if only I had not acted out of spite, if only I had never . . .

The dying man sensed a drawing back, a departure. Oddly enough, no more was he afflicted with wretchedness; instead he became flooded with a sublime peacefulness. He believed himself to be floating, as if his point of view had flown from his body and he gazed from a distance at his own person lying bloodied on the ground. Detachedly he thought, *I have suffered for my mistakes, but suffering is now at an end. May the child find protection, for I can be her guardian no longer.*

Suddenly his physical eyes opened wide, as if he were staring at some wonderful, unexpected sight, or someone he had fervently longed to behold, and a look of joy illuminated his features.

"Is it thee, at last?" In tranquillity, his lids closed. That final whisper condensed into a puff of steam and wafted away.

The night went on and on.

Far away beneath the rowan tree, worn out from calling vainly for her step-uncle, Jewel was fast asleep.

Deliverance

A half-moon rode the dawn sky.

Its mountains looked as if sketched and blocked in with raw chalk, while its meres had captured the same ineffable gray-blue as the skies. Thus, it appeared translucent, a glass bowl, haphazardly frosted.

Jewel woke, alone beneath the rowan tree.

She cried out a name, and then she called a second time, but the only reply was the wind breathing through the rowan-leaves, the distant *chint! chint!* of bellbirds, and a scattered flurry of airborne dandelion seeds, pirouetting like miniature ballerinas.

The mists had dissipated. The clouds had shredded and rolled away to reveal a clear, bright day. Beneath a sky of pale azure, trees let fall leaves tinged with the poppy-hues of Autumn. Weed-studded grasses dipped and waved under the combing of the breeze. All morning, Jewel called and searched, to no avail. Kneeling beside a trickle of a brook, she drank, then rose and searched the forsaken fields again.

Her efforts were useless. Eoin had vanished.

After noon, she wandered through a gap in a cypress hedge, where one of the trees had died, withering to a blackened stump. On the other side stood a convocation of partially collapsed walls jumbled with piled rubble—perhaps the remnants of some ancient Oratorium or watchtower. The stones were dark with age and slime. Velvety mosses probed at their seams. Bindweed roped them.

Not far away was a circle of turf that, in places, had been trampled. Beyond stood a clump of buddleia shrubs, from whose tiny cone-shaped flower-clusters the last magenta florets were dropping. Under the buddleias, half-hidden by tussocks of gold-sprinkled ragwort and groundsel, lay Eoin's pack. As she rushed toward it, Jewel stumbled over his blackthorn staff. She sprawled head-long in the weeds, crawled to the bundle, and threw her arms around it.

There she sat.

A swift, solitary breeze rustled the groundsel's dagged foliage. Small furry bumblebees droned in and out of the overhanging buddleias, whose purple-red petals rained down sporadically, like fragments of torn tissue. Sparrows perched on top of the ruins, quarreled, and flew off. In the tranquil morning, only the wind and wild things moved.

Jewel called out again. Her voice in her own ears sounded small and weak, but the corrupted walls seemed to lean forward and listen. All of a sudden the child took a strong and unaccountable dislike to this place. After scrambling to her feet, lugging the pack and the staff, she moved off with as much pace as she could muster. She left behind the decomposing edifice, the grinning cypress hedge with its rotten tooth. By the gaudily ornamented rowan she passed, and beyond. She must keep the falling sun to her left. She must keep moving north-ward.

For she knew there was no chance, now, that she would find Eoin alive. There was no doubt in her mind that he was gone, and that wights of unseelie had proved his undoing. Following so closely on the deaths of her parents, this loss seemed too much to endure. Almost everyone and everything Jewel had ever loved had been stolen from her: her mother and father, Eolacha and Earnán, her friends and pet, the marsh itself, and now her beloved uncle. All that remained of her past life were memories, a white jewel, and a small bundle of objects. Her body ached, as if her viscera had been scooped out and her hide had become a hollow, clenching thing, curling like a dead leaf around the emptiness of its own misery. Pain was unfamiliar to her—this was no flesh-and-blood hurt, however, but the agony of the inner spirit.

As she walked on, Jewel's thoughts tumbled in tumult. These catastrophes had sprung largely from a single source—the inescapable fact that a sorcerer's blood coursed through her veins. For this reason she had been exiled. Combined with her anguish, she felt a terrible rage against Jaravhor of Strang and all his works. Picturing the famous fortress in Orielthir, of which so many tales were told, she imagined it broken open, and ardently wished that all its secrets could be laid bare for her to plunder at whim.

For there was, after all, something else left to her among the ruins of her life—her rightful legacy, the Dome of Strang.

She did not weep. She had crossed the desolate boundary beyond tears, the border that is only reached in the direst of extremes. As a child who is hurt restrains his crying until he has reached the haven of his mother's arms, as an injured beast does not permit itself to die until it has dragged itself to refuge, she did not weep. Her cornflower eyes remained arid, and blank as a snow-bound Winter sky.

Onward she went.

The desire for food induced a dull ache beneath Jewel's ribs. In the late afternoon she rested in a fair meadow of fescue and daisies, where sheep grazed, although there was no shepherd in sight. After sorting through the leather pack, she ate the last of the goodwife's cheese and some leftover chestnuts Eoin had roasted. Then she extracted the pack's contents and laid them out on the grass around her knees. The tinderbox, she noted, was missing. There would be no way of making fire. Everything else appeared to be present—the bronze snare-wire, the fishing-line, rope, fish-hooks, soap, a small whetstone, a wooden plate, and a diminutive saucepan. Even on such short notice, her father had planned well. Jewel herself had packed a comb, the book of stories Eolacha had given her, and the clockwork serinette that had been a present from Eoin. Her father's white gem hung at her throat. What did she carry that had been gifted by her mother? Nothing. The notion distressed her intensely, and she sought wildly for some reassuring answer. Finally, looking down at herself, she concluded, *I have myself. She nurtured me. Life is her gift, and this will always be mine.*

In spite of this self-reassurance she had been so deeply hurt by all the losses she had suffered that she felt as if she were trapped at the bottom of a plunging pit of despair, whose walls were unscaleable, and into which no light could enter from above. A dimness had drawn across her vision, so that she viewed the world as through a curtain of gray glass. Each heartbeat was a hammer blow knocking painfully against raw flesh. Everything had been taken from her, and there seemed to be little reason to keep going. Indeed, when she walked forward she felt as if some invisible hand against her forehead were pushing her back. Nothing appeared real; it was as if she moved within some ghastly dream. Panic ensued as an inconsolable feeling of loss and loneliness rushed upon her, and when the terror subsided, she wept.

Yet the day's peaceful breezes lapped her like a lullaby. Sheep bleated lazily, shoulder deep in cream-and-green grass. Small birds squeaked, darting in and out of crevices in the dry stone walls enclosing the meadow. The sweetness of the afternoon soothed her wounded spirits and temporarily allayed the agonies of bereavement. She dried her eyes. Deliberately she forced herself to push away sorrowful reflections. With renewed courage she re-packed her bundle, then gazed at the meadows rolling away to the mountains in the north. A bird hovered high above—a kite, judging by the shape of its tail. What a view its keen eyes must command, at such an altitude! The pleats of the land must look like a gigantic swathe of parti-colored velvet, embroidered with stone walls and hedges, stitched with trees, beribboned with watercourses, threaded with roads, and appliquéd with the farming settlements of Narngalis. Here and there a piece of mirror would wink, a lake or pool flashing in the sun. Tatters of light and darkness would chase one another across the meads as clouds raced across the sky. Mile after mile, league upon league, Narngalis unraveled. Somewhere far off—so far it would not bear contemplation—resided the solid, wealthy city of King's Winterbourne: shelter, safety—perhaps—for a wanderer.

How could a child, alone, make such a long journey? Would she be forced to seek out some of the remote villages and beg for food? And if she did so, would they guess her identity and turn her over to their watchmen?

The kite folded its wings and dived. Altering her position so that she might follow its trajectory, Jewel felt the precious stone shift on its chain. She touched a fingertip to the lump beneath her clothing. There lay the ice-like crystal, warm against her skin—her father's parting gift. *I am of sorcerous blood,* she thought, watching the raptor rise with a struggling shrew clutched in its talons. *I am invulnerable. But what does that signify?*

By comparison with the hurts of other folk, any scratch or bruise on her flesh had always healed with astonishing speed. *What, then, can harm me?* she thought. *I know what slew my father—Cuiva said he fell upon a sharp stick of mistletoe that pierced him to his poor heart. Mistletoe can hurt me, but what else? Surely not hunger and thirst?*

She drew a deep breath. As she expelled it, she reasoned, *If lack of food cannot hurt me, why am I hungry? Is it because I expect to feel this way?*

Softly she chanted, "I require no food to survive. Without food, I will live. I can draw nourishment from—from nothing! From the air!" And promptly, her hunger was annulled. Through her, in its place, there welled a consciousness of strength and durability. Too astounded by this phenomenon to feel ecstatic, she merely stood up, hoisted the pack, and resumed her journey.

No thirst either. Nor weariness of the body, she reflected as she wandered on, *but weariness of the mind? Fear? Loneliness? Grief? I am not immune to them. . . .*

When she came upon an ancient elm, hollow and dripping with wild honey, Jewel took some of the bees' store, simply for the pleasure of it, and in the knowledge that the insects habitually manufactured an over-abundance of their larval fare. With the innate wisdom of bees, somehow understanding she meant no harm, the creatures did not sting her. The viscid fluid lent her comfort and true vigor. Later, spying a gnarled and ancient fig tree, she plucked the fat teardrops of fruit, dark crimson. Again she consumed them for pleasure, and because it seemed fitting to do so. *I can live on air, but I cannot thrive on it.*

Three days later, as the afternoon waned, Jewel climbed a steep, grassy slope and came over the top of a ridge. She was greeted with a sweeping vista of undulating lawns patched with sunlight and cloud-shadows, dotted here and there with ancient aspens and hoary poplars. It fell gradually toward a sheet of metallic gray—a small lake nestled in a pocket of the land. The surface was dimpled with patterns, like a spillage of molten pewter. Near the shore, clumps of knot-headed reeds stood up out of the water. Fallen logs jutted like blackened ship-wrecks.

The mountains appeared to be very close now. Their uttermost tops were dolloped with a cream of snow, while their flanks, sweeping graciously to the lowlands, were stippled with slate-blue shadows. They appeared to be steaming, as if gargantuan cauldrons boiled inside. Gray-white smokes billowed thickly from behind their peaks, curled themselves up like foaming surf, and coasted away in long, roiling cylinders. The entire sky seemed to be pouring away to the east. The sun kept breaking through for an instant, only to be swiftly obscured.

The remnants of an old dam-wall meandered along the edge of the mere, leading to the other side of the vale. Jewel climbed a stone stair and walked along the weather-bitten road that ran along the wall's top. The way was farther than she had imagined; dusk had drawn in by the time she reached the end and began to climb a gentle incline through a sprinkling of stunted trees. A moody wind was brewing in the west, and it bore in its dull fingers a vast curtain of cloud, which it dragged across the sky. Ragged rents tore open and closed in the curtain, through which the waxing moon peered fitfully before being swallowed up again.

North of the vale, the child found herself in open country studded by low vegetation. The sky was pressing down on these exposed hills, weighty with imminent rain. Wanting to find shelter, but unwilling to turn back, Jewel trudged forward, wrapping her cloak more closely about herself. She could kindle no light, and in the deepening gloom she could barely see her way ahead.

Her courage began to ebb. Had she not been burdened by sorrow, she would have cursed silently, asking herself why she should find herself in such miserable straits, since she had done nothing to deserve it. In the next instant, the morose thoughts cluttering her head were abruptly scissored.

Something had laughed.

A clenched fist banged and thumped inside Jewel's ribs. *By all that's strange,* she said to herself, *I am not alone.* She reached for the amulet hanging at her throat, but found only the icy gem.

The laugh sounded eldritch. All manner of wights were wont to laugh, yet this laugh was unfamiliar to the ears of the marsh-daughter.

'Tis merely the wind grating two boughs together, she said to herself. The moon appeared again, and heartened by its wan radiance she pushed on, looking for shelter—some hollow cliff, some leafy nook or scoop in a hillside. A gust came howling out of the atmosphere, tearing at her cloak and hair and hood, stirring up swathes of debris to swirl angrily about her. As before, the wind dragged the clouds over the moon. On the back of the wind, the rain came blowing aslant, a silvery barrier so solid it was blinding. Its noise filled her ears.

Soaking wet, violently buffeted, the child was eager to find refuge. When a gap appeared in the fence of water, she fancied she could distinguish, on the hillside ahead, a solitary tree, its boughs flailing in the squall. Wind and water slapped across her face and she lost sight of the tree, but fighting the wind, she directed her steps toward it.

When she reached the place, however, the tree was not there. Assuming she had miscalculated she peered into the storm and saw it standing farther ahead, still thrashing about in the gale. She went on pursuing the tree, but every time she thought she must certainly have reached it she discovered she had been mistaken; her judgement of distance flawed, perhaps, by the deceptions of darkness and the elemental forces lashing the hills.

Jewel had been walking after the tree for almost a mile when over the top of the storm's wail there grated a repetition of that same queer sound that might have been a laugh, or two branches rubbing together. *'Tis branches,* she perversely told herself, and she kept on following. The wind battered, the rain drenched, and a fierce chill was endeavoring to embed itself in her unassailable bones, but she was determined to reach that tree, and finally she did.

After putting her hand on the rough bark of its trunk to assure herself she had truly attained her goal, she dropped slowly to the ground in exhaustion. The trunk sheltered her from the worst of the wind's cruelty, although the twigs and branches were so water-laden that they did nothing to keep out the rain. Still, she snuggled into her cloak, glad enough merely to be resting.

She began to drowse.

A moment later, through her stupor, a voice creaked.

"I don't know about you," said the tree, "but I'm getting soaked through. I'm off home to a nice warm fire."

And it departed.

Jewel jumped up and looked around. Crooning silkily, the wind commenced to ease. The rain's song abated from furious drumming to a dulcet lilt. For a few moments the moon, or her ghost, appeared. Row upon row, beaded necklaces of water-drops hung from acres of clouds. Raindrops pelted into Jewel's eyes. The nearest trees were a glaucous smudge about half a league away, along the out-skirts of a neighboring hill.

She cupped her hands around her mouth.

"A plague on you, tricksy wight!" she screamed into the somber, saturated landscape, which appeared empty of anything but grass and stones and distant blurs.

Indignation heated her blood. She started down the incline toward the line of trees, hoping they were real.

As it turned out, the trees were chestnuts, not shape-shifting wights. Down amongst their honest roots the child slept the night away. If not for her great-grandfather's legacy, she must surely have perished of cold.

Come morning, the storm had fled.

The sky had been wiped away, and in its place an all-encompassing wad of teased wool battened over the land from horizon to horizon. The sun had vanished, and in the mists of morning so had any landmarks. Jewel continued on her way, but down in the valleys it was easy to lose one's sense of direction. Whenever she emerged on the ridge-tops and stared searchingly through the haze, she imagined the mountains were marching across her path. Moreover, the land was rising as she traveled. Had she strayed too far west? In her studies, she had never paid much attention to maps of Tir. North was where Eoin had said they must go, so she kept to that heading, as well as she was able.

Yet, eventually there could be no doubt—she was moving ever higher into the foothills of the mountain ring in western Narngalis. She was assailed by vivid fancies about the wicked gwyllion and other unseelie mountain wights, and rec-ollected old tales of goblin hordes surging down from the heights, augmented by grotesque kobolds, and the weird horse-beasts called *trollhästen*. Despite these notions, which imbued her with terror, she doggedly persisted on her way north, now bearing east. Sheer rock faces echoed the *crack* of loose stones, when her feet dislodged them. Tall crags reared against a featureless sky. No food was to be found, but there was plenty of water, and crisp, invigorating air.

With only elusive birds for company, however, and loud cascades tumbling rapidly down cliffs, and mocking echoes, and elusive hints of unwholesome presences, the mountains seemed vacant, aloof, and utterly desolate. Higher she climbed, seeking a way through, and found herself among steep alpine fields spangled with silver-leafed snow daisies. It was as if a welter of molten silver flowed around the boulders that strewed the ground, tossing up sprays of glitter-ing, flower-shaped sparks. Little pools of water, cupped in the hollows, danced and sparkled as if alive. Always when she looked up, there they were—the heads of the mountains; untouchable, ancient, dreaming in their purple haze, dozing behemoths of soil and rock, of fire and water, of hollows, and deep, secret places; white-haired, cloud-tressed giants clothed in viridian velvet.

Jewel had been following a thin track that meandered uphill through a stand of eucalypts when a soft air current came ruffling, and the clouds cleared, and the sun shone. The breeze rippled through the trees, tipping each leaf so that handful by handful they spilled their burdens. It was like a second rain-shower, sparser and slower than the first; drops fell without haste, glittering as they caught the light, each vertical trajectory on exactly the same angle, like harp-strings threaded with crystals. Amid the slow fall of scintillants, gold flies glided, cupping sunrays in their wings.

Following the track around an outcrop, the child entered a grassy dingle. On every side, the wet flanks of the granite walls glistened, capturing the light. After the darkness of the previous days, the dingle seemed a vase of luminescence. A pool nestled in this hollow, but it was unlike any other pool Jewel had ever seen. Its shores were rocky and barren of greenery, and neither reed nor rush sprouted at its margins. The surface was alive with thousands of wisps of steam, dancing like white flames ignited on a spillage of perse liqueur.

Fascinated, she ran to kneel at the brink. A sigh of tepid air enveloped her. She dipped her fingertips in the water and warmth enfolded them, spreading luxuriously through her hand. Such pleasure was tempting. It would be agreeable to immerse in this temperate bath, but far too hazardous in such wight-ridden countryside.

And kneeling there, she was getting no closer to King's Winterbourne.

King's Winterbourne—the chief city of Narngalis, the mightiest center of population, commerce, and culture in the north. Uncle Eoin had spoken of starting a new life there. The place hovered in her imagination like some castle in the air, or crock of gold at the end of a rainbow. If she ever reached it, what would she discover? Nothing could ever replace all she had lost. Would there ever again be happiness for the bereft daughter of Lilith and Jarred?

She did not linger long. Soon she was wending her way uphill once more, gasping with the effort of conquering the steep trail.

After another hour's climbing, she arrived at a slim defile. Looking ahead, she perceived that the trail ended at a wall of corrugations and jagged projections. It simply ran straight up to the foot of the wall and ceased, as if the buttresses of the mountain had fallen across it and chopped it in twain. Studded liberally with overhangs, the precipice was too difficult and too high to climb.

Two thoughts occurred to her at once: first, that this might be some enchanted path leading to a spellbound door in the mountainside and therefore dangerous; second, even if the path were not enchanted, it plainly came to a dead end and there was no profit in pursuing it.

Wondering for the first time what agency had actually created the abruptly terminated path, Jewel turned back. She was starting downhill when she began to hear the sounds, echoes of a rattling clatter overlaid with a modulated murmur of voices. Whatever was causing the hubbub was coming nearer. She started to run, but slipped on the wet ground and fell, twisting her knee. It did not hurt, but the unexpectedness of the accident and the awkwardness of her fall discomfited her. As she dragged herself upright she was aware of how the noises had gained on her; they seemed to be emanating from the very cliff at her side. Loud laughter erupted, seemingly just beneath her ear, and without thinking she threw herself into the closest rocky niche, amid an overflow of saprophytic creepers, and attempted to press herself and her pack into the unyielding fabric of the mountainside. As an afterthought she quickly unfastened the chain about her neck and stowed the white jewel in a hidden pocket of her clothes for safekeeping.

The laughter and voices burst forth. There was a *swish* and a rustle, a chiming of metal, and a din like pebbles being shaken in a jar, or horn striking stone. The ruckus originated higher up; impossibly, from the direction of the dead end.

Human-seeming figures were filing down the narrow trail, leading horses on reins. The first three, conversing merrily, were not looking in Jewel's direction, and clearly did not notice her as they passed by. She squeezed herself more tightly into the narrow gap, desiring fervently that she should escape attention, and that they would proceed on their way without discovering her.

The fourth, however, turned his head. His gaze alighted on her, and he drew to a halt. Behind him, others of the company stopped also, because he was blocking their path; and those in the fore looked back to see what had occurred.

He who was staring at Jewel had the form of a youth aged about eighteen Winters. Like the youths and damsels accompanying him, he was dressed in richly dyed raiment, of excellent fabric and elegantly tailored. At the shoulders and in other places, their clothes were embroidered with bands of swirling patterns. Their belts and baldrics were fastened with ornate buckles, fashioned from some lustrous, bluish-white metal. With their gleaming rings and bracelets, their garments of costly fabric and their long, well-dressed hair, they looked to be heirs of wealth.

If they were indeed human.

Surely it was impossible that they could be members of her own race, out here, so far from the towns and villages of humankind? They were certainly too normal in appearance to be Marauders, yet they could not be traveling peddlers, for they had no wagons and were not following a main road—this was merely an aimless trail among the mountains. Could they be woodcutters, or charcoal burners, or other such craftspersons who dwelled in the wilderness? Jewel thought not. These folk had the appearance of nobles rather than poor artisans. They must, after all, be eldritch wights of some unknown species: heroic trooping types, or else tiny, self-important siofra, hugely magnified and disguised by the illusions of glamour. It was best to avoid wights, even when they were not known to be unseelie: their habits and moods were infamously unpredictable. Jewel neither moved nor spoke. Irrationally, it flashed into her thoughts: *If I close my eyes, perhaps they won't be able to see me. . . .*

"Well," said the youth who had first spied Jewel, "what have we here on this fine Ninember morning? A little trow-daughter—but too pretty! What are you doing here, wightlet? Are you landbound? Did the sunrise surprise you before you reached Trowland, forcing you now to wander aboveground until sunset?" Without waiting for a reply, he went on, "Sponge away the glamour and let us see you as you really are!" He turned to his companions, saying, "Does anyone carry a four-leafed clover, or any other charm that gives True Sight? I would fain behold this eldritch thing in its native shape."

Jewel had no words to utter. The youth's words indicated that he was human, yet wights could use language to prevaricate and mislead with a skill stemming from centuries of practice. She could only keep hoping, against reason, that these unwelcome visitors would all go away. She tried to blend in with the creepers, to give the impression of insignificance. This did not avail her, because it appeared the youth, human or not, was in pursuit of diversion, delighted to stumble across potential entertainment. His companions crowded around him, craning to see what he had found. Someone had handed him a small stone with a hole in the middle. He held it up to his eye.

"By rain and thunder, there's no glamour!" Jewel's harasser cried in astonishment. He passed the stone across to one of his fellows, to verify his verdict. "What are you?" he said, half-teasingly, to Jewel. "One of the baobhansith, with your temptress's eyes? By fire and flood, if you are, 'tis a novel manner to seduce men—blackened with dirt, dressed in rags, your hair as rumpled as an overused besom. And so young!" He frowned. "You are human, are you not?"

Tight-lipped, she made no answering sign. This might be some trick.

"Out with it—speak!" he insisted. "Who are you? Why do you come prying around the inner places of the mountains? Where are the rest of your kin? How many of them are there?"

His accusing tone frightened her. Dumbstruck, she merely gaped.

"Ryence, leave her be!" some of the damsels protested ineffectually. "You are entirely alarming!"

Ryence stepped toward Jewel. She felt cornered. In sudden terror she darted out and tried to knock him aside, but he was too quick. A manacle of steel closed around her forearm. He had her in his grip. Struggling, she kicked him in the shins, but he merely laughed.

Then another youth came forward. "Let her go, Darglistel," he said. "She's only a child."

Ryence, or Darglistel, dropped Jewel's arm. The young men and girls with their horses surrounded her; there was nowhere to run. She froze.

The second youth released the reins of his steed. Then he deliberately hunkered down to crouch on his heels, so that he had to tilt his chin and look up at Jewel from grave eyes of jade. He said, "My name is Arran. I suspect you fear that we are not as we seem, but I assure you that I am human and so are my companions. We will not harm you. That is my promise. Would you like something to eat?" He unwrapped a small parcel and held out a cake. It was made of some crumbly substance, like lotus-corm meal, with dried berries baked through. *It looks delicious,* thought Jewel, her mouth watering. She was relieved at the revelation that her inquisitors were not eldritch, although human beings might equally mistreat her or betray her to her enemies. She had no desire to fraternize with anyone at all, and therefore shook her head. *Go away.*

"Are you lost?" asked the youth with the cake.

No reply.

"If you are, we can offer you food and shelter, and help you find your kindred."

Silence.

"Will you at least accompany us on our picnic?"

A demurring shake of the dark head.

"Very well." With a nod, Arran stood up and withdrew. To his companions, he said, "Let us move on." They made no protest, obeying him as if he were their leader. *"Giddap!"* they murmured to their mounts, and soon they were filing past again, wide-eyed and inquisitive, studying this surprising apparition in the creepers.

The child's mind conjured the terrible loneliness and fear haunting the mountains. She no longer had a home, or the protection of strong, loving parents—she did not even know, exactly, *where* she was. There was no comfort for her between these soaring walls of stone, no warmth upon the hard cold ground, no murmur of affection from the heartless wind. In the eyes of the youth called Arran she had divined concern and kindness. Suspicion warred with desperation. Her heart fluttered like a pinned butterfly.

"Wait," she cried, then added uncertainly, "Are you truly human?"

The richly clad company laughed, and averred yes, they were.

"Then I will come with you. But only for a while."

"It talks!" commented Ryence, but it was plain his banter was not ill-meant. Jewel joined the procession in its march. Once past the narrow section of the trail, they mounted their horses. "Ride up here with me!" one of the girls called, reaching her hand to Jewel. Vehemently, the child shook her head a second time. She trusted no one. They might ride, but she would walk. Ever on the alert, she would follow these folk with caution. For a while it would be refreshing to dine in company. For a *while*—that was all. When their picnic was over, she would take her leave.

Jewel counted fifteen young folk, all of whom made the newcomer welcome. As they proceeded along the mountain trail they slowed their steeds to keep pace with her. They leaned from their saddles and gave her tidbits of food. Amongst themselves they joked blithely and kept up multiple conversations. At the same time, however, the child noted the way many of them were looking into the sky, as if scanning for something, and some positioned their hands near the decorated hilts of their daggers. Most peculiarly, a rogue wind sprang up. As well as she could discern, there in the shelter of the mountain, it veered rapidly from the north through west and south, then from the east and back to its starting place, performing a complete revolution. It was the strangest wind she had ever experienced, but the riders, instead of sharing her bemusement, sat upright and appeared to be sniffing the air, like hounds on a hunt.

Jewel did not ask why. Deeply suspicious, she spoke very little to these strangers. Her father had said, at their parting, *"Tell no one of your invulnerability."* She would tell them nothing at all about her background. As she walked, she invented lies in her head, in case she should be questioned.

Their route took the cavalcade back down to the bright dingle with its thermal waters. After throwing off their outer garments, the party swam and sported in the balmy pool as if it were harmless, and free of drowners. Jewel supposed it must be; there were no sudden vanishings. Notwithstanding, she seated herself somewhat apart from the rest and watched, eating some more of their fare and listening to their songs. It was impossible, however, not to relax a little, surrounded by this convivial consortium, and by scrutinizing them carefully she even began to trust them to some degree.

The dingle became steeped in late afternoon shadows. At the conclusion of their sojourn the party was packing up to depart when two of the older girls came over to Jewel and sat down beside her. One was tall and graceful; the other was of medium height, with hazel eyes, a pointy nose, and frizzy hair.

"I am Elfgifu Miller," said the latter, "and this is my friend Ettare Sibilaurë. You seem to have strayed, or been abandoned. Will you return with us to our home?"

All around, the young riders were tightening the saddle-girths and ensuring the panniers were secure. In easy camaraderie they called to one another, still as blithe as ever. Some of the youths were indulging in horseplay at the water's edge, and a couple of the damsels had collapsed in hilarity at their antics. Others were flicking spangled droplets from their nut-brown hair.

A pang of homesickness and loss swept through the marsh-daughter. How could she leave this mirthful company and go on again in solitude, braving the unknown dangers of the wild? What if Maolmórdha had discovered her identity and issued a reward for her capture, or posted spies throughout the kingdoms to watch for her? She had no idea how far it was to King's Winterbourne, and the cold season was drawing in. Already it was Ninember. Despite her invulnerablility, she might be captured by trows, or lost forever, wandering alone and in misery. Still, she must try to fulfill Eoin's goal. . . .

She drew breath to say *no* to Elfgifu's invitation. It was then that she perceived the expression of motherly concern on the faces of the older girls. A hardness inside her crumbled and gave way. It was a struggle to save it from deliquescing to tears.

"Even so," she said at last, "I am lost. I will go with you."

"What is your name?"

She told them.

Instantly she regretted her carelessness. In her fraught state of mind, distracted by woe and anxiety, she had imprudently blurted the truth before she could stop herself. It was now too late to repair the mistake.

All was rejoicing when Elfgifu's friend Ettare imparted the news to her comrades. Ryence, called Darglistel, lifted Jewel as if she weighed no more than a daisy-petal, and set her on his horse behind him, saying, "Hold fast, wightlet!" This sudden close contact with a stranger disconcerted and affronted Jewel, but there was no opportunity to complain, nor did she deem it wise. She closed her mouth tightly and gripped the steed with her knees, for there was no side-saddle riding for the ladies amongst this mettlesome group. Then the company ascended the mountain trail at a fast trot, until they came near the place where she had first encountered them.

Having dismounted, they led their horses along the narrow section and through the slim defile, but Jewel hung back, wary of the dangers of enchanted paths.

"What's amiss?" her companions asked.

"This path leads nowhere!"

"Come with us and see," they said, smiling, and they took her right up to the dead end. Now Jewel was able to perceive that this was no blind alley after all, but an optical illusion. She was greatly taken aback and, after her initial incredulity had dissipated, she wondered, not without alarm, how many other seemingly undistinguished places she had passed on her travels, unaware they concealed some secret.

The trail did not finish; instead, it circumnavigated a massive granite boulder and, passing behind it, entered a tall, narrow opening in the mountainside. This opening, shielded by one monolith among many so similar, was invisible to anyone standing at the lower end of the defile. Nevertheless, some members of the company were observing to each other, "The path is becoming much too obvious. 'Tis time we camouflaged it again." A minor argument broke out. "It was *your* turn to strew leaves . . ."

The opening gave on to a rocky passage driven right into the flanks of the mountains. Fine strings of water trickled along the sloping floor, and the sides leaned in like the walls of a tent. Soon the floor became a stairway, its treads wide but steep, winding up through the living rock. Cheerfully, the company led their horses up the steps, making a clatter that echoed like a spilling of rattles in that confined space. Jewel followed, not without trepidation. She had never before seen anything like this underground ascent, dank and rough-hewn, whistling with cool air. Here and there, light entered through thin overhead shafts.

"We have entered through what we call the Southeast Door," said Elfgifu, climbing at her side near the rear of the procession. "It is a secret way, known only to our folk, but because you have been lost, you would not know how to find it again. Therefore we can trust you with the secret."

For the first time, Jewel comprehended they were almost as suspicious of her as she was of them. The notion was mollifying.

At length the lofty stairs came to an end. Ahead of Jewel, the company made its exit, and then it was her turn. Orchid-pink light streamed in from outside, and the rocky walls opened onto a vista so spectacular that the child stood stockstill, trying to assimilate what she saw.

She found herself on a wide ledge above an immense wooded plateau, many miles in diameter, encircled by saw-toothed mountain peaks. Over the western ranges the sun was setting, casting peach-colored luminescence across orchards and fields. The fading light caught the glimmer of a lake, and smoke was rising from the chimney of a distant cottage.

The ledge was not much higher than the tops of the nearest trees. When she glanced to the right, Jewel saw a much loftier platform jutting from an escarpment about half a mile away, like a gigantic shelf, overlooked by a cloudmantled crag. It was greater in all dimensions, so wide that large buildings had been erected all over it. A fence of stone ran along the platform's outer edge.

"Behold!" cried Elfgifu, her extravagant flourish indicating the entire tableland. "High Darioneth!" Awed, Jewel merely gaped, absorbing the dramatic loveliness of the scene.

"And," Ettare added, nudging the child's shoulder and pointing to the cluster of buildings on the cliff-top, "Rowan Green, the Seat of the Weathermasters, where stands Ellenhall."

Weathermasters!

Jewel wondered how she could have become so slow-witted. Of course! These folk were children of the weathermasters, that mighty kindred who made their home in the mountain ring of Narngalis. She had seen men of their number before, at market-fairs in Cathair Rua, striding along the aisles between the booths, grave and self-possessed in their storm-gray cloaks, their belts buckled with sun-forged platinum, a trio of three curious hieroglyphs blazoned on their shoulders.

Weathermasters were well respected by all of humankind, for, of all mortals, only they were born with puissance of the blood called the *brí*—a talent very different from the power of eldritch wights. Their far-reaching faculties could sense and predict the dynamics of pressure systems and temperature inversions, of wind currents, of the interfaces between air masses of different temperatures or densities, and most other meteorological phenomena. A strong people were they, and prosperous. Their weather-modifying abilities were in great demand throughout the Four Kingdoms of Tir.

Once, Jewel had heard her beloved Eolacha say, *"In days of yore I was well acquainted with several of the weathermasters, but no longer."* She had been speaking of her youth, when she was wont to make excursions from the marsh.

If Eolacha had invested faith in them, it was likely they could be trusted. Eolacha Kingfisher Arrowgrass, Eoin's grandmother, was a carlin, a wise-woman who had been chosen to receive a Staff of gramarye from the eldritch hag of Winter, the Cailleach Bheur. The old woman, now deceased, had been compassionate and erudite, the embodiment of sound judgment. Jewel had admired and loved her profoundly.

Down a winding path she made her way with the children of the weathermasters, until they reached the plateau floor. At the foot of the incline they remounted, and once again Ryence took her upon his horse. Away they cantered, along a cart-track through groves of trees burgeoning with walnuts and chestnuts. Along the way they were hailed by a farmer driving a cart, and later by three fellows in light mail, who Jewel supposed were watchmen. After passing through the orchards and alongside a meadow the road climbed steeply up the side of the great platform jutting from the mountainside. More than three hundred feet above the floor of the plateau the road leveled out. It passed though an open gate and into the precincts of Rowan Green.

The final caress of the dying sun gilded the walls of nine imposing half-timbered houses. Most of the lower stories were built of granite, while a great many of the upper stories, which often projected out over the ground floors, were constructed of dark oaken frames filled in with brick and whitewashed plaster. Clusters of chimneystacks protruded from among the slate tiles of the steeply gabled roofs, each column fluted, twisted, and decorated with checkerboard or herringbone patterns of variously colored bricks. Solid blocks of granite surrounded the heavy oak doors, ornamented with their ironmongery of hinges and studs. Stone mullions encased diamond-paned leaded-glass windows, whose flattened arches were capped by simple squared-off moldings. Some of the manors boasted impressive oriels; jutting, multi-sided windows cantilevered out from the upper floor, and supported on a corbel from beneath.

These stately homes were arranged around the outer perimeter of the shelf, centering on a spacious village green carpeted with short turf, wherein a snow-drift of geese and ducks congregated at a pond. Between the houses majestic rowantrees, far taller than the rowans of the lowlands, put forth their boughs. White birds orbited overhead, and fled down like sudden gusts of leaves to alight in the loft built above the stables, set apart from the dwellings. The air was mellifluous with their cooing. From high on the mighty crag overlooking Rowan Green a waterfall draped its silken threads down the precipices. Glittering, it bypassed the horizontal apron on which the houses stood, hurtling straight down to the flat lands at the foot of the cliff, where it flowed, burbling, away amongst the orchards.

In the middle of the green, abutting an octagonal tower, stood a long building constructed of the same materials as the houses. A slender belfry-turret topped the gable. A larger, longer edifice was set at right angles to the first, and somewhat apart. At one end, veils of smoke plumed from three chimneys. Primrose lamplight was exuding from the windows, and much activity was evident within. On catching sight of the incoming cavalcade, a group of small children shouted greetings and scampered to surround the riders.

"Who's that with Ryence?" they demanded, skipping alongside the horses. "What's her name?"

"Be patient," said Arran, holding up his palm. "All will be told over supper."

"I won't tell you anything over supper," Ryence informed the children. "My business will be dining."

Savory fragrances floated from the vicinity of the long hall. After the riders had dismounted, Ettare said in Jewel's ear, "Come with us." Still flinging badinage at one another, the erstwhile picknickers split into groups, each group leading their horses to the salubrious community stables, where they unsaddled them before heading to their dwellings. Elfgifu, Ettare, and Ettare's three sisters took Jewel to the house at the farthest end of the Green.

"Will you bide here in the Sibilaurë house tonight?" Ettare asked the child. "Elfgifu will be staying with us until the morrow."

"Aye," said Jewel, glad of the invitation from the amiable Ettare and her sisters.

The interior of the Sibilaurë family's house humbled her with its size and astonished her with its grandeur. To the marsh-daughter, accustomed to small wooden cottages hoisted on stilts and thatched with reeds, this grand abode of many rooms seemed like a palace. The walls were lined with paneling made from dark, fine-grained wood. A sweeping staircase led up to a second story. The wide, low-ceilinged chambers were disposed with intricately carved furniture fashioned from the same dark wood, glowing warmly with the layers of beeswax that had been applied over the years. The windows, instead of being unglazed, were filled in with the kind of diamond-paned lattices Jewel had seen in Cathair Rua, and draped with sumptuous folds of curtains. There were carpets on the floor, rather than rushes. Lamps seemed to be everywhere, and candles of pure beeswax also, in contrast to the tallow-dipped rushlights common in the marsh. Their long stems were upheld by candelabra made of a silver-white metal, not baked ceramic.

In wonder and delight, Jewel gazed at her surroundings. She was introduced to Ettare's family—a confusion of names and faces. In a tiled room, water came pouring from a spigot, steaming hot. She washed her face and tried ineffectually to drag her comb through her tangled hair, before being escorted to the long building on the Green.

"This is the Common Hall," said Elfgifu, her guide, "also named 'Long Gables.' 'Tis where we have banqueting and dancing. The other large building, that one in the middle with the tower and belfry, that is our Moot Hall, where our Council meets. We call it 'Ellenhall under Wychwood Storth.' Tonight all the families of Rowan Green, and some from the plateau below, are feasting together in honor of the birthday of the Maelstronnar. My friends and I managed to evade the preparations by escaping on our jaunt to the Hot Pool. Our excuse was that we needed fresh air, after being cooped indoors during the rainy days."

Venturing a comment, Jewel said, "But you are weathermasters. You might have commanded the rain to cease, if it inconvenienced you."

"I am like you—not a scion of a weathermaster family," replied Elfgifu, "unlike most of my friends. But, even if I were, I would not stop the rain of Tir's-law from falling merely for the sake of convenience, and neither would they."

Instantly, Jewel understood. She recalled the philosophies of her carlin great-grandmother, who had always taught that the upsetting of natural balances and the bending of the world's laws was not to be undertaken lightly. *"It is the responsibility of the powerful to maintain the equilibrium,"* Eolacha used to say, when Jewel asked her why she did not wield her eldritch-bestowed abilities more extravagantly and indiscriminately. As a small child, Jewel had considered this a tiresome ethic. Where was the joy in possessing power, if one could not use it as one pleased? These days, with her freedom threatened by a monarch whose political powers were unbridled in his own realm, she had revised that opinion. She was convinced, however, that if she ever had the good fortune to become powerful, she would wield her influence with far greater justice and mercy than a spineless king such as Maolmórdha.

Nonetheless, she could not help thinking that to own the talent to make the wind blow and not be permitted to raise gales at whim must be as vexatious as being heir to a fortress full of secrets, with no opportunity to reach and breach it, as irksome as loathing one's ancestor for causing catastrophe in one's life and being incapable of wreaking some form of belated revenge. It was conceivably almost as devastating as having one's loved ones stolen away and being unable to grasp any security in this fickle world. . . . At this point Jewel realized she was allowing her sensibilities to escalate out of proportion. Stubbornly, she thrust aside her grief before it welled afresh and overpowered her.

An elongated table ran down the center of Long Gables. The spacious interior was packed with well-dressed people, firelight, lamplight, and shaggy-haired dogs the color of bleached yarn. To find oneself amongst such a large crowd of strangers was quite daunting. Jewel gathered her courage and tried to make sense of all that was happening. After telling the tale of her discovery, her newfound friends fended off undue attention and, as soon as the concourse turned its attention to social matters, the stranger was apparently overlooked. She was given a seat on a wooden settle, between Elfgifu and Ettare, where, overwhelmed by a sense of awe, she gaped at her magnificent surroundings while endeavoring to shrink into obscurity. From there, as the evening progressed and a lavish supper was merrily consumed, she was able to observe and learn much.

At the head of the table sat Avalloc Maelstronnar, the Storm Lord of Ellenhall. He, whose family name meant *Stormbringer* was the leader and most powerful of all weathermasters. The jade eyes of the Storm Lord were hooded by deep lids; his nose was hooked like the beak of an eagle. Straight-backed and snow-haired in his ash-colored robes, he seemed as sturdy and enduring as an antique oak tree. Jewel had no way of knowing it, but the Storm Lord had inherited the striking looks of his grandsires. His immediate family was seated near him, along with his closest comrades amongst the weathermages and councillors of Ellenhall. They were surrounded by the various branches of the Maelstronnar family and the stewards of his household also.

The benches up and down the table were occupied by descendants of other lineages, young and old; *brí*-child, prentice, journeyman, and weathermage.

"The chiefest among the weathermaster familes," Ettare instructed the guest, "are those of Maelstronnar, Darglistel, Sibilaurë, Longiníme, Ymberbaillé, Dommalleo, Cilsundror, Heaharním, and Nithulambar, but each family has its branches, and those branches bear sundry other names."

Jewel promptly forgot these foreign-sounding cognomens. She reckoned there must be more than a hundred folk occupying the hall, every one of goodly bearing and appearance. Some were dressed in richly patterned raiment of various colors, like those she had first met. The elder weathermasters, however, no matter were they man or woman, were invested with splendid raiment in many shades of gray; storm-cloud, ash, iron, and slate. These were the weathermages. Their garments of voluptuous velvet and copiously embroidered satin were emblazoned with the emblem of their calling: the runes for Water, Fire, and Air: ¥, Ψ, and §.

One of their number rose to his feet and, as a hush fell, he began to sing:

"A wondrous sword was Fallowblade, the finest weapon ever seen,
Forged in the far-famed Inglefire, wrought by the hand of Alfardēne,
Famed master-smith and weathermage. Of gold and platinum 'twas
   made:
Iridium for reinforcement, gold to coat the shining blade,
Delved from the streams of Windlestone, bright gold for slaying
   wicked wights,
Fell goblins, bane of mortalkind, that roamed and ruled the
   mountain heights
Upon a dark time long ago.

"To forge the mighty Fallowblade upon the peak of bitter snows
The Storm Lord labored long and hard. The heights rang with his
   hammer blows,
Hot sparks flew up like meteors. A lord of fire was Alfardēne;
With power terrible he filled the sword. And all along the keen
And dreadful blade he wrote the words in flowing script for all to
   find:
Mé maraigh bo diabhlaíocht—'I am the Bane of Goblinkind.'
Upon a dark time long ago.

"When weatherlords to battle fared, the glinting of the yellow blade
Was spied from far off. Wild and strange the melody, the blood-song
   played
By winds against the leading edge. The wielder of the golden sword
Smote wightish heads, hewed pathways of destruction through the
   goblin horde.
Their smoking blood flowed on the ground. Unseelie wights were
   vanquished. Then,
'To victory!' sang Fallowblade. 'Sweet victory for mortal men!'
Upon a dark time long ago."

The audience applauded heartily. Food and drink were plentiful. Conversations were lively and manifold; songs were chorused with enthusiasm. *Have these people an endless appetite for roistering?* thought Jewel, yawning. *I am not weary,* she told herself. *I do not expect to be weary.*

Then she fell asleep, her head cradled on her arms, which rested on the table.

When she opened her eyes in the morning, Jewel was lying in a soft, canopied bed. She was sharing it with Elfgifu, who was still asleep, her face framed by the frilly nightcap of white lawn covering her fountain of flyaway hair. Elfgifu was clad in a matching night-dress. Jewel was wearing a clean linen shift, which her hosts had lent her to replace her travel-stained rags. She grimaced, noticing that her grimy clothes were piled in a corner on the floor beside a heap of laundered ones, and left the bed. After checking that her father's white gem was still hidden in her pocket, she tiptoed to the window.

Out across the stable roofs she looked, and through the foliage of a rowan-tree, and past the parapet bordering the cliff edge. To the left, the fertile plateau of High Darioneth stretched away toward the far side of the mountain ring. To the right, towering steeps soared up like a colossal palisade. The lofty waterfall was making music. Dark double bows of bird-shapes were circling in a sky that seemed impossibly huge; pale blue and depthless. When they flew closer, Jewel could see that they were pigeons, glistening white as blowing blossoms against the shadowed trees and roofs. Behind the cloud-wrapped peak of Wychwood Storth, the sun was rising. Attenuated shadows, stains of etiolated blue, lay peacefully across fields and orchards hazed by morning mist.

"You can almost see the mill from that window," remarked Elfgifu, sitting up in bed.

Jewel jumped.

"Oh, forgive me. Did I startle you?" said Elfgifu, climbing from the bed and joining Jewel at the window. "Look there," she said, extending a finger. "If we were birds, and could fly over that last hazel thicket this side of the lake, we would be able to see the mill. That is where I live. My father is the miller. Yes, I know it is a foolish thing to be called 'Miller' and to *be* millers. But that is the way of it. My grandfather was a cobbler, but his forefathers were mostly millers, and the name has remained with the family."

How she chatters on, thought Jewel ungratefully. *Just like a freckled duck at nesting-time.*

"You must come and stay at the mill with us, you poor little lost one," Elfgifu said.

At once, Jewel felt ashamed of her ungracious opinion.

"Only until your people come looking for you," the miller's daughter added, in reassuring tones.

"I could not impose—" Jewel began, dredging polite demurs from the uttermost corners of her memory.

" 'Twould be no imposition at all!" cried Elfgifu. "Besides, we cannot let you go wandering about in this season. In a few weeks it will be Midwinter's Eve, which falls on a Moon's Day this year. I always think it strange that Midwinter's occurs in the first month of Winter, don't you? By rights it should be in the middle of the second month. Anyway, it always gets colder after Midwinter's—"

"Gramercie," Jewel said forthrightly, interrupting the flow of words. "I will bide with you, Elfgifu. For a while. You are generous, to offer such hospitality to a stranger."

"A stranger, but a child," said Elfgifu. "Children need food and shelter. And we know you have not told us untruths."

"What is your meaning?"

"We know you are indeed alone. The weathermasters among my friends could detect no sign of other folk within miles of the place where you were found."

"How could they be certain?"

"Did you not feel the curious wind that arose and swung precociously around through the four quarters of the compass? Arran Stormbringer summoned that current, and made it wheel about so that it would carry to the heightened senses of his kindred any whiff of intruders. Furthermore, they searched the skies for hovering flocks of birds which might have flown up, disturbed by human presences."

"I did feel that wind." Drawing a deep breath, Jewel said, "But someone *was* with me, until he disappeared. I do not know what happened to him. And then I was lost."

"Oh!" exclaimed Elfgifu. "Who was with you?"

"My uncle."

"Where did you last see him?"

"It was in a field, south of here, which I think is called 'Black Goat.' "

A look of concern crossed the features of the miller's daughter, but she only said, "Hmm. And when was that?"

"I'm not certain. Maybe five days ago, or seven. After he disappeared, I was confused."

Elfgifu put out her hand as if to comfort Jewel, but the child subtly evaded her touch.

"The Maelstronnar has asked to see you this morning," the miller's daughter said quietly, drawing back her hand.

"No! I mean, why would that be?" Surprise and nervousness accelerated Jewel's pulse.

"I daresay he wants to learn how we might help you. Indeed, he might send riders to find out what happened to your uncle, if you ask."

Brightening, Jewel clasped her hands tightly together. "Then I *will* ask."

"But that is enough talk!" Elfgifu cried. "See, we have lent you some clean garments to wear. Let us get dressed and go downstairs to breakfast, and afterward you will have an audience with the Storm Lord. Then without further ado we'll descend to the plateau, and you shall come with me to my father's mill!"

The interview with Avalloc Maelstronnar-Stormbringer took place in a small, paneled chamber within Ellenhall. Between respect, dread, and wonder Jewel stood before the great weathermaster in her borrowed apparel, intensely aware of his comprehensive authority, glad that Elfgifu and Ettare had accompanied her.

The Storm Lord regarded the child attentively from his sage's orbits, saying, "Greetings, Jewel of Slievmordhu. You are welcome at High Darioneth."

Jewel curtseyed and mumbled her thanks. She was not surprised he had identified her country of birth. Her accent must have betrayed her.

Then she balked. Once more it came to her that she ought to have proffered some name other than "Jewel." Her own honesty had put her at risk. If King Maolmórdha ever discovered Jarred had a daughter, he would also discover her name. In due course the connection would be made—Jewel of the marsh was one and the same as Jewel found roaming in the mountain ring. Inwardly, she railed at herself for her naïveté. Now, however, it was too late. For better or worse, her name had been spoken, and that could not be undone. What might come of it she could not tell.

"How came you to be wandering alone near our mountain fastness, hmm?" asked the Storm Lord. His voice was calm and deep.

"Sir, I was traveling with my uncle. We were on our way to King's Winterbourne, there to seek employment. He vanished in a field called Black Goat, and I lost my way."

"I see. How came you into that notorious field? Why did you leave the highway?"

His probing questions were discomfiting. If Jewel admitted that she and Eoin were trying to evade the men of King Maolmórdha, the Storm Lord would wish to know why they were being sought.

Fidgeting with her sleeve-cuffs, the child cast about for some feasible reply. "Well, sir, we were trying to avoid highway robbers. And my uncle was drunk, and mistakenly chose the wrong path."

The alibi sounded absurdly feeble, and she knew it.

Somberly the Storm Lord studied her, and as she boldly returned his penetrating gaze it came to her that his eyes were of the same leaf-green as those of Arran, his eldest son. Plunging recklessly ahead, she said bluntly, "I beg you, sir, to send men in search of my uncle."

Avalloc Stormbringer's dove-white eyebrows twitched. "Are you aware, Jewel of Slievmordhu, of the expense of sending my riders out to scour the countryside?"

"No, sir. But I should like to find out what happened to my uncle."

"Bravely said." The weathermage smiled, and went on, "I will do as you request—not least because I wish to uncover recent tidings of that place and its inhabitants. Ellenhall should always be well informed. If any mortal men in Tir can discover what has become of him, it is my kindred."

"Sain thee, gentle sir!" Jewel cried, heedless of good form.

"I wist there is more to your tale than you have revealed, dear child," said the Storm Lord perceptively, and at these words the ice-water of impending doom doused Jewel's enthusiasm. Her hand flew to the pocket where the white gem was now stowed; she found it reassuring to feel the stone's shape through the fabric. "But I judge there is no wickedness in your young heart," Avalloc continued. "Therefore keep your secrets from me, or reveal them when you see fit. Meanwhile, be welcome here and remain as long as you wish."

Having braced herself for disapproval or further interrogation, Jewel was disarmed. The kindly look she glimpsed in her host's eyes moved her more than she expected, and she found herself on the verge of weeping. Even as she strove against tears, she knew it was longing for her own parents that made her yearn to remain in High Darioneth, safe with the weathermasters and their people.

Courteously she took her leave.

Away down the steep cliff-path rode Jewel and Elfgifu, on the back of Elfgifu's pony. Their journey took them past the meadow and along leafy lanes hedged by brambles abundant with ripe berries. Through the flourishing nut-orchards and apple-orchards, over picturesque bridges that spanned clear streams of fast-flowing ice-melt, past fallow fields they went, and fields planted with Winter vegetables, until at last they came to the High Darioneth Mill.

It was a large, multi-storied building with living quarters attached, surrounded by outbuildings including a byre, stables, and a kiln. Stolidly, as if it brooked no argument, it stood below the weir, which had been constructed on the millstream to supply it with water all year round. Water surged down the head race and through the wooden gates that controlled the flow, to pass through the wheel pit, before being discharged, by way of the tail race, back into the stream below the mill buildings. With no sound other than the loud gushing and gurgling of liquid, the monstrous water-wheel turned slowly and ponderously on its well-oiled axle-tree.

Because no wheat, barley, oats, or rye would grow at these high altitudes, this was a nut-mill. Its well-ventilated upper stories were used to store nuts, which had to be hoisted up in bags, by rope-and-pulley. The storerooms, or "squirrel-ries," as Elfgifu called them, contained several compartments for different types and grades of nuts. Besides the massive grindstones for making nut-meal, the mill boasted water-powered shell-cracking rollers.

"The nut-shells are never wasted," chattered Elfgifu as they entered the mill precincts amidst a din of hooves on flagstones. "Hazelnut shells can be used as mulch, or blended with powdered black and brown coal to make cinder blocks. Finely ground walnut-shell flour is used for polishing metal, and the scholars use walnut shells to manufacture ink. Pecan shells make good fuel, and they are used by leather-tanners to concoct their foul-smelling compounds, and some-times we mix them with charcoal in hand-soap to make a really good scrubbing-agent. My sisters fashion nut-shells into beads and buttons."

The interior of Elfgifu's house was not as grand as the dwellings of Rowan Green, but it was comfortable, and much finer than any marsh-cottage. The Miller family was extensive. Elfgifu had an older brother and six younger sib-lings, three girls and three boys. Her father, Osweald, was a tireless worker, al-ways intent on business. A bald-crowned, bearded, nuggety man, he was also energetic, single-minded, and somewhat intolerant. He cared deeply for his chil-dren, but driven by the desire to operate the mill at optimum efficiency and to goad the mill-hands to do the same, he spared scant time for them. Hardly con-cerned, they ran wild. Mildthrythe, his wife, was carefree, easy-going, and prone to laughter, happy to include another child in her household despite the fact that she would soon give birth to her ninth. Jewel settled in among this harum-scarum brood, willingly learning to help with the myriad duties of hearth and mill.

In private, Jewel continued to mourn for her family. Every night she sobbed silently into her pillow, and concocted fanciful tales in which she met her par-ents once more, and her uncle as well, and all were reunited in happiness. Such imaginings were like twisting a knife in a wound, yet perversely she continued to dwell on them, as if she felt she was in some way responsible for their deaths and ought to pay with sorrow. She also suffered desperately from homesickness, craving the sights and sounds of the wetlands.

Secretly she vowed she would never again allow herself to be so vulnerable, such easy prey to catastrophe. The conclusions she drew from bitter experience were that it was preferable not to *love* people, because then one could not be hurt when they were stolen away. It was desirable also to acquire influence in the form of property or immense knowledge, so that one had more chance of defending the defenseless and innocent, more chance of determining the outcome of events in an unpredictable and uncaring world. She resolved to face life's future battles well armed with buckler and weapon, if she could; for her shield, the eschewing of love; for her sword, the accumulation of great wealth or marvelous lore with which to direct her own destiny and the fortunes of the meek. At such times her thoughts would inevitably drift to the far-off Dome of Strang, and its hidden arcana.

The riders sent forth by the Maelstronnar returned with the tidings that they had searched Black Goat and found the remains of a man, badly battered. It was obvious the corpse had been lying there for many days, so they had taken it to the cemetery at nearby Saxlingham Netherby, and buried it with honor and due ceremony. There was not much on the victim to identify him, but from around his neck they took a silver chain strung with an amulet, a disc of bone engraved with two interlocking runes. This was shown to Jewel, and she knew then, for certain, that Eoin had perished. When she perceived the sympathy in the eyes of Elfgifu's mother she could contain her sorrow no longer, and wept in the woman's arms until she was drained of tears, all passion numbed.

The Uncanny

Over the next few weeks Jewel slowly approached the knowledge that she had no de-sire to leave High Darioneth in the near future, although she was not willing to refute her original intention that she would one day continue onward to King's Winterbourne. *Next Summer,* she said to herself. Her grief at the loss of her parents and uncle was ever-present, and severe. Being part of a family again could not cancel that grief, but the sense of liveliness and companionship assuaged the pain, making it easier to endure.

She had unpacked the bundle she and Eoin had brought from the marsh. Discarding her disreputable traveling-outfit, she put on a linen kirtle and an over-gown of woven wool, cinching them at the waist with her old leather belt. The style of these clothes differed from the prevailing mode in Narngalis, but she cared little. Elfgifu's mother gave her a pair of wooden clogs and a fur-lined cloak.

"Wear these pattens over your shoes, if you go outside after rain. The mill-yards get very muddy. And you will need this cloak. Mountain nights can be bit-terly cold."

In a grove of liquidambar trees on the far side of the mill orchard, Jewel built a cairn of river-stones. She placed leaves and berries on it, making it a memorial to loved ones lost.

After Harvest the season deepened from Autumn to Winter. Ninember passed, Tenember took its place, and Midwinter's Eve arrived, engendering boisterous festivities at Rowan Green and on the plateau. Soon afterward the old year gave way to the new, ushering in the month of Jenever with yet more rejoicing. Wistfully, Jewel reflected on the way her own people in the marsh had celebrated these occasions, far away in the south.

When people asked her the name of her home village, she always replied, "Cathair Rua," in the hope that the population of that metropolis was large and anonymous enough to hide her true origins.

"Is Slievmordhu very different from Narngalis?" the miller's children would sometimes ask.

"Yes, it is different," she would reply circumspectly, having quickly learned how to divert the course of conversations that threatened to reveal too much, "but one thing is the same. In this kingdom the hardy weed crowthistle grows, as it grows throughout Slievmordhu. People dislike it as much here as they do in my homeland, because it prickles bare feet, and stock cannot eat it."

"Yet it has a lovely flower," Elfgifu would murmur.

"And mistletoe grows in Slievmordhu," Jewel once added, with an air of being scarcely interested.

"What is mistletoe?" the other wanted to know.

"Oh, 'tis a parasitic shrub that grows on other plants."

Elfgifu shook her head. "We do not have any mistletoe at High Darioneth."

Jewel shot a quick look of delighted surprise at her friend, then glanced away as quickly, to hide her reaction. This discovery lifted a weight from her spirits, a burden she had not been aware she carried.

Slievmordhu. Often, Jewel wondered if she would ever see her native land again. High Darioneth seemed such a safe haven, and the longer she remained there the less willing she became to face the dangers of the world outside. Sometimes, especially at nights, it would come to her that she was poising frozen, tense, staring in the direction of the East Gate and listening for the distant sounds of an incoming cavalcade of soldiers.

As time progressed and she became more and more comfortably entrenched in the life of High Darioneth, her trepidation decreased—although that edge of fear was never completely blunted.

Her curiosity about her new environment was avid. Keenly she studied it. The high country in which she dwelled comprised shallow valleys and flats cradled amongst mountain peaks that the inhabitants called "storths." In addition to Wychwood Storth there were crags with names such as Weatheroak Storth, Windrush Storth, Woodgate Storth, Wolf's Castle Storth, Wellwood Storth, and Oakdale Storth. Hanging pools and lakes, blanketed with steam, lay cupped here and there in the upper hollows of the ranges. Waterfalls splashed down the faces of the storths, and small fast streams, such as Stony Creek, which powered the mill, flowed across the plateau. On the western side they joined to become one large, turbulent waterway, the aptly titled Snowy River. The river drove down through a deeply cloven, steep, unnavigable canyon straight through the mountain ring toward Grïmnørsland and the sea.

Only one main road led out of High Darioneth, and that was in the east. When anyone approached the outer gate from the lowlands, an eldritch frightener, which had haunted those heights for centuries, habitually set up a clamor like a baying of hounds, a rattling of chains, and a slamming of doors. This racket conveniently warned the watchmen, who would swiftly double their vigilance at the inner and outer gates of the East Road. There also existed four secret, subterranean ways out of the circle of storths. Their exits were skilfully hidden. The whole place was well protected from invaders, not least by the widespread fame of the power of the weathermasters.

Up on Rowan Green, each sprawling house sheltered several branches of the same family. The dwellings were supplied with heating and hot water from thermal springs deep inside Wychwood Storth. North of the village green, by the parapet overlooking Wychwood Waterfall, there spread a circular apron paved with flagstones and edged with small-leaved creeping mint, from which the four great sky-balloons could be launched to carry the weathermasters swiftly to wherever their skills were needed. From time to time, the plateau-dwellers would feel breezes from an unexpected quarter blowing on their faces, and look up to see one of the great, pearlescent teardrops floating across the sky. Jewel's inquisitiveness extended to the weatherlords and their astonishing skills. There was little chance, however, to discover much about the wielding of the *brí,* for the chief secrets of weathermastery were shared only among the practitioners and their students.

On the plateau below, dotted amongst the farmsteads and orchards, dwelled the many tradesfolk necessary to the community of High Darioneth: the cobbler and the carpenter, the cooper and the wainwright, the bowyer and the thatcher, and others possessing specialized skills. The blacksmith was also the farrier. Over the forge-fires of his smithy he worked in bronze, iron, and brass, shaping the metals with hot and cold forging, annealing, grinding, and casting. But the relatively low temperatures produced by his charcoal-fueled conflagrations would not make malleable the platinum so well loved by the folk of High Darioneth. For that, there was the Foundry.

The Foundry was situated inside Wychwood Storth, high in a huge, airy cavern accessible through a doorway set into the cliff behind Rowan Green. The tremendous heat required for melting platinum was provided by upwelling lava in natural pipes and shafts that thrust through the fabric of the mountain, jetting liquefied rock from unimaginable depths at temperatures of thousands of degrees. For cooling, the foundrymen used waterfalls of snow-melt from the high crags. Steam and flickering heat hazes rose from the chimneys of the Foundry as the men mixed platinum with iridium to produce a metal of a silver-white color, or with osmium for bluish white. Alloys of nickel they made also, and for hardening they used rhodium, or metallic elements found in platinum ores, such as palladium, ruthenium, and osmium.

Many other industries prospered on the plateau. Farms produced mushrooms, chestnuts, hazelnuts, walnuts, pecans, berries of sundry kinds, apples, asparagus, peppermint, and lavender. There were vineyards and dairies. Hunters bagged deer in the mountain forests; fishers caught salmon and trout in the lake and streams. Prospectors panned alluvial gold from river-gravel, occasionally building complicated water races to aid their efforts. Walnut and chestnut trees provided ample timber for the carpenters and joiners. Other artisans created paintings, sculptures, poetry, and patchwork. Those with a musical bent practiced singing, dancing, or playing the bagpipes.

The human inhabitants had dwelled on the flatlands of High Darioneth for centuries, but they had cleared only a small portion for farming. This was partly because there were relatively few of them on this vast plateau, but chiefly because they had enough respect for the supernatural creatures of the wilderness to leave large tracts of natural forest well alone. Acres of ancient timber covered most of the plain, particularly toward the misty foothills of the mountains. These mysterious forests had been untouched by humankind since the dawn of time. Even within the farmed areas of pasture, meadow, and orchard, many pockets of wildwoods remained intact because some eldritch guardian haunted them. The greater part of the plateau was covered with trees, and no one really knew what was hidden amongst them. It was understood that there were many secret brooks, bogs, ponds and hidden waterfalls, secluded glades, undiscovered dells and hollows, caverns and lairs where unimaginable beings lurked; some kind to mortals, others not so well-disposed.

Fewer than seven hundred people lived in the close-knit community of High Darioneth. Of them all, the weathermaster families were most prominent. Jewel soon learned their names, and the meanings of those names: "Darglistel" was the ancient weathermaster word for *Blackfrost,* Sibilaurë signified "Whistles-For-The-Wind," and Longiníme meant "Longcloud." The translation of Ymberbaillé was "Rainbearer"; of Dommalleo, "Thunderhammer"; of Cilsundror, "Skycleaver"; and of Heaharním, "Highcloud." Nithulambar was rendered as "Walks-In-Mist."

Avalloc Maelstronnar was a widower. Arran was his eldest son; his other children were two daughters named Galiene and Lysanor, and an infant son, Dristan. The Storm Lord's sister, Astolat, was married to Branor Darglistel-Blackfrost, a man burdened with poor health. They had four sons—the eldest of whom was Ryence—and one young daughter.

The carlin at High Darioneth was a woman named Luned Longiníme-Longcloud, a steely and business-like body, not friendly, as Eolacha had been. She walked with a skewed gait. All the toes were missing from her left foot. When first she set eyes on Jewel, she said, "What is that about the child's neck?" and took hold of Jewel's amulet, which had been retrieved from the body of Eoin. This action pulled Jewel close to the carlin, whose flinty eyes studied the disc of bone, while her sour breath caused Jewel's nose to wrinkle. "This thing is useless," snapped Luned Longiníme. "It has no power. Somebody give the child a proper talisman, for goodness' sake."

Unseelie wights were seldom glimpsed within the ring of storths. Brownies, on the other hand, were everywhere. It seemed the place was teeming with them; almost every household had one.

These seelie, domestic wights were generally nocturnal. Helpful and strong, they were hard workers in homes and farms, and could perform the labors of ten men. Like all wights, brownies had their system of moral precepts; they hated being spied upon, and despised laziness in servants. They could turn mischievous or even unseelie if mistreated, and if anyone gave them presents, they would depart forever.

The brownie of High Darioneth Mill discharged his self-imposed duties with exceptional zeal. He was particularly fond of one member of the household—in this case, Mildthrythe, Elfgifu's mother. Mildthrythe had grown up at the mill, an only child. Her father was the miller, and in due time her husband, Osweald, became master of the mill. The brownie's loyalty to Mildthrythe never swerved. When she spoke of him she affectionately called him "Robin," although everyone else called him "the brownie," and outside his own home he was often feared. Visitors to the mill avoided traveling along the path that went by the "Auld Pool," above the weir on the millstream. Although that path was the most direct, it had an ill-name; it was said the mill's brownie liked to linger there.

Mildthrythe's friendship with the brownie was so close that she kept no secret from him. When she fell in love with Osweald, the brownie helped smooth the path of the courtship and administered to the particulars of her wedding ceremony. Each time she gave birth to a child, he was solicitous in the extreme. Every night he was busy cleaning out the fireplaces, bringing in new kindling, putting water on the fire to boil, sweeping, washing, hanging out the clean linen to dry, and generally setting things to right in the house—all with barely a whisper of sound. Come morning he would severely pinch the cook and the nurserymaid if they overslept.

A few weeks later, in late Jenever, it happened that heavy rains fell for several days, and the rivers of High Darioneth were roaring in full spate. So much water was pouring down from the mill-weir that the excess flow had to be diverted from the head race through the spillway. At the height of the flooding, the pains of motherhood came upon Mildthrythe and she knew it was nearing time for her ninth babe to be born. Osweald ordered the stable-boy, "Ride at once to fetch the midwife. Make haste!"

"Yes, sir," said the stable-boy, and he went to the tack-room to put on boots and greatcoat.

The rain pelted on the roof, ranting and racketing. From the window, the boy peered out at its sheer, drenching curtains. The watercourses were all running at full capacity, and word was going around that farther down, the water had inundated the bridge over the swollen millstream. That bridge lay between the mill and the house of the midwife. He knew he would have to go by the Auld Pool, and the thought filled him with dread. So he loitered, fussing with boots and saddle, delaying the moment of departure.

Elfgifu came running into the tack-room, with Jewel following a few paces behind.

"Cynric! Are you not ready yet? You must go straightaway!" cried Elfgifu, thumping him urgently on the shoulder. "Mother says this child is eager to be born. Her time is at hand! Go now!"

"I am dressing as fast as possible," protested the stable-boy, but even as he uttered the words, a hulking figure came rushing into the room. After flinging the greatcoat over its shoulders, it dashed into the stables next door, mounted the fastest horse, and galloped out into the rain.

"May all that's charitable protect me," said the stable-boy, ashen-faced. He propped himself against the wall. "The brownie has gone for the midwife, and my life is not worth tuppence."

He fled to the servants' quarters.

A remarkably short while later, the shape of a horse with two riders loomed out of the rain's silvery draperies. The midwife, in a state of shock, was deposited at the steps of the side door of the mill, whereupon she was hustled indoors and shepherded directly to Mildthrythe's bedchamber.

Soon afterward the babe was born. Eager to view the new arrival, the entire family, including Jewel, congregated in Mildthrythe's chamber. The cries of the newborn presently mingled with roars of pain from the vicinity of the servants' quarters.

"Herebeorht, go and find out what's amiss!" said the miller to his eldest son. The youth returned, laughing. "Poor old Dobbin is back in the stables, in a sorry plight. He looks as though he has been pixie-ridden! And the brownie has been in the servants' quarters, dispensing a sound thrashing to our Cynric, with his own horsewhip!"

"Mercy me!" said the midwife, handing the swaddled infant to Mildthrythe and plumping herself down on a stool. She fanned her face with a folded swatch of linen, saying, "I was on my way here with your manservant—as I thought— riding like thunder, when I discovered what a dreadful road he was taking. I screamed, 'Do not ride by the Auld Pool! We might meet the mill's brownie!' And he replied:

> "'Have no *fear,* Goodwife Stanford.
> Hold tight; keep your seat.
> You've met *all* the mill-brownies
> You're likely to meet!'

"With that, he plunged the horse into the water and bore me safely to the other shore. Mercy me! I've never been so flummoxed in all my born days."

The nurserymaid handed the midwife a cup of blackberry wine, which she gulped gratefully.

"I'll not be going back by the same road," she declared, "nor with the same rider!"

"Have no fear of that," answered Mildthrythe, still smiling fondly on her youngest child. "Osweald will see to it. Ah! What a bonny boy this is. I have you to thank for his safe delivery into this world, and Robin to thank for your safe delivery to our doorstep!"

The midwife shuddered, and held out her cup to be refilled.

The other kinds of wights sporadically glimpsed around High Darioneth were chiefly trows and siofra. The latter, who looked like tiny men and women dressed in leaves, mouse skins, and insect carapaces, were relatively harmless. They could play tricks with their glamour, but usually it was nothing worse than creating the illusion that their clothes were tailored from gorgeous fabrics, or making the indigestible fare sold at their charming, miniature markets appear deliciously inviting to the unwary mortal purchaser.

In the days when Elfgifu's grandfather worked the mill, he had used his picks to help the siofra scoop out numerous circular basins in the rocky sides of the millstream. On many a moonlit evening the queen of the siofra and her entourage could be seen, like finches and sparrows, flicking and laving in these little pools.

Trows were much larger than the siofra, and less inclined to disguise themselves. Most trow behavior did not threaten humankind. The long-nosed, gray wights were wont to enter houses at night and wash their babies in the clean water set out for them on the hearth. Sometimes they could be seen performing their quaint dances beneath the light of the full moon. But trows, by nature, were thieves. They loved silver, which they stole whenever possible, absconding with it to Trow-land under the ground. They pilfered the fruits of garden and orchard. Sometimes they made off with animals. Other times they stole human beings.

When Spring came strewing buds across the high plateau, Herebeorht, the eldest son of Mildthrythe and Osweald, married his sweetheart and brought her to live at the mill. Her name was Blostma, meaning *flowers,* and she was as pretty as her name. The trows had long been watching Blostma, and had ofttimes tried to entice her away to Trow-land.

Early Winter had brought heavy rains, but come Spring, not a drop had fallen for weeks. The weather remained very cold, so that the snow on the heights of the storths failed to melt. The mountain streams slimmed to a travesty of their normal flow, and by Mai Day the waters of Deeping Lake had retreated.

By this time Jewel had become firm friends with Hilde, Elfgifu's young sister.

"Come down to the lake, Jewel," said Hilde after the equinoctial festivities were over. "You should see it—the water has gone down so far that the old mill has risen up out of the depths!"

So Jewel accompanied her to the lake, but she could not resist the temptation to say exasperatedly, "The weathermasters ought to exert more control over the climate here. One moment we're inundated so enormously that even the bridges are flooded—next instant the streams are drying up."

Hilde only shrugged.

Draped with waterweed and bedecked with slime, stone ruins protruded from the diminished lake. On seeing these once-sunken remains Jewel was intrigued. She thought they looked eerie, like the ancient skeleton of some drowned city. Gaps in the walls where stones had fallen out, or where windows once had been, now predictably resembled staring, misshapen eyes.

"Why is the Old Mill underwater?" she demanded curiously.

"It became too severely haunted, in the end," said Hilde. "But that was a long time ago. The folk of olden times drowned it, and there was no more trouble after that. Only, when the lake ebbs, which is once every ten years or so, the ruins come up, and at nights, passers-by can see strange lights moving therein, and hear voices."

Jewel wanted to borrow a boat so that they could row over and inspect the ruins, but Hilde said, "No, it is too dangerous. Besides, it is forbidden."

And Jewel had no choice but to be content.

Six weeks after his marriage, Herebeorht Miller took his nets and went to the lake to catch some fish. The waters were down at their lowest mark, and the skeleton of the Old Mill was clearly visible, thrusting up from the water, suspended over its own solemn reflection.

Herebeorht had not been fishing for long when he heard loud noises coming from the ruins. It sounded as though carpenters were at work inside; he was sure he could hear the rhythmic grating of a saw, the percussion of a hammer, the thud of a mallet driving a chisel.

Carefully and quietly he began to gather in his nets. He had drawn them all in and was rolling them up when a hollow voice from the Old Mill said, "Ho, what're ye doing?"

Herebeorht dropped his nets and stood, petrified. Then a second voice, with an equally strange accent, answered, "I'm making a wife to Herebeorht Miller."

Instantly the young man understood that the first voice was not addressing him after all, but the words of the second voice astounded and horrified him. Leaving his nets where they lay, he raced back to the mill and called the family together. They all came, except his father, who was busy with a chisel, "dressing" a pair of mill-stones.

Wrapping his arms about his bride, Herebeorht said breathlessly, "I heard voices in the Old Mill. 'Tis certain the trows will come for Blostma this very night. What shall we do?"

Blostma, despite her amazement, reassured him, "My love, do not be afraid on my account! Any sounds you heard in the Old Mill were, in likelihood, only the wind!"

Emphatically he shook his head.

"Well then," said his new wife. "Perhaps the voices were those of mischievous siofra, up to their tricks."

"No," he said, clasping her more firmly. "They were trows."

"But surely there is no need to fear," said his mother. "Robin is here. He will not let trows come in."

"Of that we cannot be certain!" cried Herebeorht. "The brownie might choose to guard only you, Mother, and those who are of your blood. Or he might have no power over trows."

"Send Cynric for the carlin," suggested Hilde.

"Luned is not at Rowan Green today," said Mildthrythe. "She is sixty miles away. Cook says she has been called to a cottage in the northwest."

"Then Blostma is in dire peril!" insisted Herebeorht, in anguish.

"There are druid-sained charms aplenty nailed over every door and window," Blostma pointed out.

"They will avail you naught," Jewel advised. "When the trows come for humankind, no charm of stone or wood or iron can stop them. This I know, because my great-grandmother was a carlin and I learned much from her."

"The child speaks truth," said the nurserymaid. "I have heard the same."

"What shall we do?" repeated Herebeorht.

"Will you let me help?" asked Jewel, stepping forward. "I know how to prevent trow-thefts."

Herebeorht eyed the child askance, but he nodded. "Say on."

"This is what must be done," said Jewel. "Tonight you must seal up this house, making it secure against all comers. Bid the entire household remain indoors until sunrise. Tell them they must not be lured outside under any circumstances, and furthermore they must speak no word during the dark hours. Herebeorht, you must prevent Blostma from leaving the premises."

"But I shall not try to leave!" Blostma said indignantly. "Why should I step beyond the door tonight?"

"Wait and see," cautioned Jewel. "With respect, Mistress Blostma, you will discover the power of a trow-spell. Be forewarned, all—you will be sorely tempted to cross the threshold and venture forth. Many of you will also yearn to cry out, and methinks it is too much to ask that the object of the spell resist this urge, but at all costs no one else must succumb to the bait. Be prepared!"

That evening, they locked every gate and door of the mill.

"Nobody must set foot outside these walls this night," Herebeorht told the servants grimly. "Neither door nor gate nor window must be opened, no matter what chances, or seems to chance, outdoors."

The servants promised to adhere faithfully to his orders.

After sunset, only the youngest children went to bed. Everyone else was too nervous and apprehensive to even consider rest.

Family and servants waited together in the huge kitchen.

In the fireplaces, flames flickered. Shadows wavered. Out in the darkness, water chuckled. Mist would be rising from the millstream and the weir, to steal like heavy smoke across the ground.

At midnight there came a soft knock at the kitchen door, *rap-rap-rap.*

Blostma began to rise from her chair, but without a word her husband gently clasped her in a firm embrace. Her eyes widened in fear or astonishment, yet she uttered no word.

Not one of the mill-dwellers made any sound.

In the frangible silence they could all clearly hear the crunching of footsteps departing from the door, and immediately the new milch-cow in the byre began to low and bellow, ramping as if trying to break down the walls. The miller stared hard at the goose-herd, who bowed obsequiously. Neither of them spoke.

It was Blostma who breached the uncanny hush. Suddenly she was squirming and writhing in her husband's arms, begging him to let her go. Unmoved, he held her more tightly. Out in the hen-coop the chickens began to squawk and the rooster to crow, as if a fox were rampaging amongst them. A prolonged buzzing arose, so penetrating it was like the droning of all the bees swarming from their hives. Next came the roar of a mighty updraught and the horses in the stables started a tumult, neighing and snorting, striking out with their hooves, as if the stables were afire and the animals were trying to escape the flames. The miller's features contorted in desperation, and he made as if to rush to the door, but one glare from his eldest son was enough to quell him.

Blostma was struggling to wrench herself from the grasp of her husband. She, alone of the company, was unsilent. She entreated, cried, wept, and smote him with her pretty white hands, but he would neither move nor speak nor quit her. Meanwhile, outside in the stables and the byre the uproar worsened. Hour after hour it dragged on, until, with the coming of morning, it faded at last.

In the hen-house, the rooster crowed, welcoming the first rays of the sun.

Those who had eventually fallen asleep in their chairs jolted awake. Simultaneously, everyone began to speak, and the doors were unbarred, and the miller hastened outside to survey the damage to his premises. Herebeorht remained seated. On his lap, worn out but secure, Blostma sat, resting her head on his shoulder, peaceful now.

From the yard came Osweald's shout. He rushed in at the door, followed by the stable-boy and the goose-herd, who between them were carrying what appeared to be a log of wood.

"All is well. 'Twas all glamour; neither beast nor fowl nor shed has been harmed—but look you here!" the miller cried triumphantly. "I found this piece of moss-oak leaning against the garden wall."

The wood had been cut to Blostma's exact height, and crudely carved into the shape of a woman resembling her.

"A trow-stock!" exclaimed Herebeorht, and he bade the servants fling the effigy on the kitchen fire, where it burned merrily until it fell to ash.

After the trow episode, Jewel was exalted to high regard in the eyes of the Miller family and their neighbors. Herebeorht and Blostma, in particular, doted on her. Despite the fact that Jewel still privately mourned for her family and home, life was relatively pleasant. All Summer long the marsh-daughter sported with the other children in the fields and orchards, or attended lessons with them in the little schoolhouse called "Fortune-in-the Fields," or helped with the less arduous domestic chores. Hilde, whose year of birth was the same as Jewel's, was her usual companion in adventure.

The Millers had accepted the orphan as a member of their family. For her part, she had adapted well to her new life, easily making friends and learning unfamiliar skills, fitting in with the daily routine. Her contentment increased as time passed, and happy memories overlaid the sorrowful ones. Moreover, she was so busy with chores and lessons and games that she could spare little time for sad reflections.

When she did ponder on times past, she would sometimes compare her pleasant life amongst the people of High Darioneth to the way things might have been. She loved the Millers and was entirely grateful to them for their kindness. If not for them, and the children of the weathermasters, she might have roamed long alone through the wilderness. She might have been enslaved by trows, or captured by the King of Slievmordhu, or even abducted by Marauders. The inhabitants of High Darioneth could never take the place of the family and friends she had lost, but they had become very dear to her.

Autumn was the busiest season at High Darioneth, for that was when the nuts in the vast orchards were ready to be harvested. At this time the mill-hands and the brownie were constantly occupied: hoisting sacks of nuts to the upper levels, grading the varieties, ordering the storehouse, feeding the nuts through the huge rollers, separating the kernels to be ground into nut-meal, and roasting or drying some in the kiln before grinding, sifting and bagging the nut-flour and dressing the mill-stones, as well as maintaining the cogs and gears, the line-shafts and axle-trees, and all the other parts that made up the mechanisms of the mill.

Not long after the annual celebration of the High Darioneth Horn Dance—at which men traditionally pranced about wearing on their heads the antlers of deer—Elfgifu's father received word that the mill at Coppenhall Moss had gone out of business and its machinery was going to be sold. The High Darioneth

Mill was in need of a new crankshaft for the crown-wheel, the old cast-iron pivot being fractured, and close to redundancy. Hoping to be able to obtain one at a bargain price, Osweald, rather reluctantly, left his foreman, Grimbeald, in charge of the Autumn milling and set off for Coppenhall Moss, almost a hundred miles away by road.

The mill's brownie had a jocular disposition, and was prone to entertain himself by making small mischief to the inconvenience of his fellow servitors. Notably, when he had a spare moment he liked to fling handfuls of broken nut-shells at them from unexpected quarters, which did little to endear him to them, despite the fact that his nocturnal labors lightened their work-load considerably. For all his gleeful nature, he was not especially quick-witted. He was artless and credulous enough for the servants to be able to take reprisals by making him the dupe of their pranks.

"How the brownie is clever enough to speak always in rhyme is anybody's guess," Hilde confided to Jewel.

"He's a wight," replied Jewel, drawing on Eolacha's teachings. "It is in the nature of some of them to speak in rhyme. They are unable to do otherwise."

Of all the servants, it was the boy Cynric who most disliked the brownie. Cynric had never forgiven the wight for the thrashing he had received at Robin's hands, and the humiliation that ensued. His resentment had simmered all through the Summer, and come harvest, he had formulated a plan for revenge. Assuming an air of transparency, he suggested to Grimbeald and the other mill-hands that they should enter into a contract with the brownie, whereby the wight must agree to do all his work and theirs as well, right throughout nut-picking-time.

"With His Lordship away," said Cynric, "there'll be no one snooping around. None of the household will be any the wiser!"

"I'd be more than partial to taking my ease," said the foreman, rubbing his lower back to iron out the aches, "but even Brownie-Dullwits would never bind himself to such a one-sided contract!"

"Inform him," said Cynric, "that if he does, you will give him the ragged coat and the worn-out traveling-cowl hanging behind the stable door. The old fool has always nurtured a liking for those cast-offs."

Grimbeald snorted. "You'd have us drive him away, would you? Nobody in their right senses would do that. All the tales tell that if brownies get presents, they depart!"

"Only if they get *new* clothes, not old, worn-out clouts," said Cynric persuasively.

Mulling over all the old stories he had heard, the foreman concluded Cynric was probably right. Still, he did not put the proposition to the brownie straightaway. Two days later five carts rolled into the mill precincts, piled high with sacks of walnuts and hazelnuts. After one look at them, Grimbeald felt his back twinge and made up his mind.

The brownie happily agreed to the proposal. The mill-hands were careful that no hint of the subsequent proceedings should reach the ears of their employer's family, or any servants with loose tongues. Throughout harvest-time they reclined at their ease in the hayshed behind the byre, while the wight worked on, day and night, performing such tasks of strength and perseverance as no mortal man could possibly endure for more than a week at most.

None of the mill-hands disliked the brownie with the same intensity as the stable-boy, and on the whole they were not a hard-hearted lot. Some of them began to feel sorry for Robin, and they began to talk amongst themselves. Gratitude and pity moved them. "Poor old fellow," they murmured, "working himself to the bone for a threadbare coat and cowl, the old simpleton. Let's give the garments to him now, and let him have joy of them during his final days of hard labor."

Just before the miller was due back, Grimbeald and some others went into the grinding-room one evening. They left the coat and cowl for the brownie on a pile of pecan-kernels, then hid behind a partition to enjoy his delighted response. When the wight came in to start work, he saw the gifts laid out for him, and a huge smile spread across his ludicrous features. Snatching up the coat and cowl, he frisked about in glee, crowing, then put them on. However, instead of getting down to his work, to the astonishment of the eavesdropping men he said loudly:

"Robin knows you're hiding all, spying there behind the wall!
Foolish clowns, to pay the fee before the work is wrought for ye!"

Triumphant at the notion of outwitting his fellow-workers he added in sneering tones:

"Since you're such clods I'll now decline to haul another sack of thine.
Robin has got a cowl and coat, and never more will work a jot!"

In the greatest consternation the men started from their hiding place, begging him to stay, but the wight had already disappeared.

He was never seen again at High Darioneth Mill.

The miller returned from Coppenhall Moss with the new crankshaft loaded on his ox-cart. When he was informed of what had eventuated during his absence, there commenced an uproarious hullabaloo. Cynric the stable-boy protested his ignorance of the fact that brownies will depart whether the gifts they are given are old or new. His assertions did not hold water with the miller, who instantly discharged the lad from his employ. Only Grimbeald's years of loyalty saved the foreman from the same fate. Mildthrythe was distraught at the loss of the wight, her life-long supporter, and for several weeks the atmosphere at the mill was one of misery and recrimination.

The labors of the miller and his hands were manifold after the brownie's departure, but otherwise all seemed to go well at the mill as the seasons turned again, and the snow-line crept down the ring of storths.

Osweald Miller was puzzled when, as Winter again yielded to Spring in the year 3467, queer incidents started happening around the mill. The strangest of these was the unsettling of the storerooms on the upper levels. No matter how carefully the laborers sorted the nuts and left them overnight ready for the cracking-rollers, when morning came they were scattered about and jumbled in utter disorder. This happened quite regularly, despite the door being locked. Although he searched methodically, the miller could find no evidence of breaking in, and he was at a loss to explain or prevent this occurrence.

At length, determined to discover the prankster, the miller couched himself one night underneath an old oilcloth, and kept vigil. The storeroom was dim and quiet. Only weak, watery starshine trickled through the windows.

He estimated it must have been around midnight when the whole length and breadth of the room was lit up by an extraordinary radiance, as though liquid moonbeams were flowing in. Thousands of miniature folk came sliding through the keyhole of the locked door. The miller knew at once that these were siofra, and the diminutive wights had apparently shrunk themselves even more, in order to squeeze through the keyhole. Without further ado the tiny wights began to gambol amongst the heaps of sorted and graded nuts, which soon became mixed up in thorough disarray. Hazelnuts tumbled in with the walnuts, pecans rolled with the chestnuts, large nuts mingled with the small, and low-quality blended with the best. The miller could scarcely contain his wrath. He was heedful, however, that the siofra, although diminutive and fetching, could be angered—like any other wight. If enraged sufficiently, they might take revenge. So he gritted his teeth, sat motionless, and stared without interfering.

At length, his supernatural visitors started to busy themselves in a way still less to his taste. Each wight commenced to pick up a nut and dart through the keyhole, which happened to be a somewhat larger aperture than most of its kind. So many of the little creatures were rushing in and out of the orifice that it resembled the opening of a bee-hive on a sunny day in Juyn. Watching the produce disappear in this fashion, the miller struggled harder to leash his ire. His entire frame was shaking with the effort and the cords on his neck were bulging like pipes.

One of the siofra was handing a hazelnut to another when it said in the tiniest voice the miller had ever heard, "I weat, you weat." At the smugness in the tone, and the air of propriety over the ill-gotten spoils, the miller could restrain himself no longer. He burst from his hiding place, bellowing, "Pestilence and boils upon you! Let me get amongst you!"

Like a swarm of disturbed insects the siofra flew up, or else some numinous wind swept them up like Autumn leaves. Squeaking with fright, they swirled about the head of the miller. He blinked. When he looked again, they had disappeared.

The miller had a bolt and padlock fitted, instead of a keyhole, and the siofra never disturbed his storerooms again.

But the tiny folk seemed more plentiful, or more active, that season than ever before. Or perhaps it was the lack of a brownie at the mill that made them bolder.

On certain moonlit nights the queen of the siofra and her retinue continued to be glimpsed bathing and sporting like small birds in the circular pools beside the millstream. Emboldened by this sign of the queen's ongoing favor, and by his success in driving the nut-thieves from his storerooms, the miller took a jaundiced view when one of the mill-hands came to him, grasping his cap in his fist, saying, "Sir, the kiln-house is being used at nights, when all proper mortals are in bed. Some of us have seen smoke rising from the chimney, sir, and heard little mousy-voices in there, after all has been locked up. In the mornings, the kiln is warm and there are signs that roasting has been going on."

For a few days the miller simmered resentfully, mulling over these revelations. He took to prowling around outside the kiln-house at nights, and sure enough, what the hand had told him was true.

It irked him intolerably.

By all the signs the culprits could only be the siofra again, using the eye of the kiln as their kitchen to boil their pottage and cook the nut kernels the miller had laid up for roasting. The siofra contributed nothing to the success of his mill, unlike the brownie, who had performed astounding labors, requiring nothing more than a bowl of cream and a quarter loaf of nut-bread to be set out for him on the hearthstone each night.

The siofra were tiny wights; a single hazelnut was as much as one alone could consume. But their population—which appeared to fluctuate dramatically, according to the incomprehensible ways of eldritch wights—could be enormous. That they should be dining extravagantly at his expense stirred Osweald Miller to extreme wrath. Every day he labored strenuously to feed his family, and these lazy imps wantonly thieved the produce! Since he had been so successful in driving them off the first time, he confidently decided to take matters into his own hands once more. On this occasion, the flames of his rage had been fanned to such intense heat that he wanted to do more than merely frighten the siofra away; he wished to take revenge for their impudence.

One night, while the siofra were preparing their supper inside the kiln-house, chattering and squeaking in their miniscule voices, the miller quietly climbed onto the roof. In his pockets he carried a sizeable sod he had cut from the bank of the millstream. Steeling his nerves and drawing a deep breath, he threw the sod down the chimney and instantly fled. As he half-clambered, half-slid down the ladder he could hear the tumult going on inside the kiln-house. The falling mass had dashed soot, fire, and boiling pottage among the wights. Before he could reach the mill the trembling fugitive heard the cry "Brunt and scalded! Brunt and scalded! The sell of the mill has done it!" And the queen set out after him like an angry wasp; just as he reached the door she touched him and he doubled up, bowbent and crippled.

And crippled the miller remained.

"Osweald, I cannot undo what has been laid upon you by the queen of the siofra," said dour-faced Luned Longiníme, standing beside the wicker chair where the miller slouched, wrapped in a shawl. "Nor can I tell if this affliction will ever be lifted, or whether you will have to bear it until your dying day."

With these reassuring words, she put on her cloak and departed.

It was up to Herebeorht to run the business now, aided by Grimbeald. Osweald was able to walk, albeit slowly and painfully, but he could neither ride a horse nor drive a cart nor lug heavy sacks. Parted from the hub of entrepreneurial activity, he became a morose figure, finding joy only in the company of his family.

The younger children especially were glad to have their father with them more often. Osweald was a master storyteller. His store of traditional tales about the exploits of weathermasters, and the goblin wars of ancient times, was apparently inexhaustible.

"Father, tell us about the olden days," the children would say, gathering at his knee as he sat beside the fire of an evening. Jewel loved these tales, too, and was always to be found in the thick of the audience.

Centuries ago, when the power of the weathermasters had been at its height, one had lived who had been the strongest among them, the greatest warrior-weathermaster of all. Avolundar Stormbringer was a forefather of Avalloc. It was he, leading the weathermasters, who had inspired armies to free the Known Lands of Tir from the scourge of the goblins, with their wicked kobold slaves and their daemon horses, the *trollhästen*. Many were the accounts of valor that arose in those times.

"Are there any goblins around here?" one of the youngest children asked her father.

"No goblins are hereabouts. None are to be found in the Four Kingdoms anymore. They are all long gone."

"I heard someone sing a song about them."

"Those were dark times, now passed out of living memory. More than a century ago goblins made their mark indelibly on history. The memory of those times remains to haunt us in tales, in songs, on headstones. The goblin wars were long and terrible, but in the end mortalkind defeated the wicked wights utterly. Not even a remnant of their once-mighty nation exists. Do not fret—we are safe from goblinkind. But we have enough eldritch creatures of other kinds to trouble us!"

There were stories, too, about sea-wights: the merfolk and seal-kindred, the wave-maidens and the benvarreys. There were tales about the wights that dwelled underground, in old mines, and those that dwelled in abandoned buildings, or submerged in fresh water. There were anecdotes concerning trooping wights and solitaries, shape-shifters and shape-keepers, seelie and unseelie.

"Tell us the strange tale of the Dome of Strang in Orielthir," Jewel would sometimes murmur.

"Well," the miller would begin, "it is said that great treasure is hidden there, and uncanny objects that possess supernatural powers. There are precious metals and jewels, and pairs of seven-league boots, and a magickal cauldron that produces limitless food, and a harp that plays all by itself."

Jewel always paid close attention to these stories. It both thrilled and disquieted her to recall that, unknown to any of the other listeners, this extraordinary fortress was inextricably linked with her own history. She wondered how much of the lore was truth, and how much was fiction prompted by the mystery and unassailability of the place.

"There is a bottomless purse that is always filled with gold coins no matter how often you empty it," Osweald was fond of repeating, "and a bag of seeds that, when scattered on the ground, instantly spring up as armed warriors. And there are amazing creatures, such as the goose that lays golden eggs. Have I told you the story of that wonderful fowl?"

"Tell us again!"

Osweald willingly obliged. He told these tales and more, with the vivacity and expression of the true storyteller, and during these sessions he could almost ignore the pain of his swollen joints.

Aeronautics

Whenever Summer cast her glowing mantle across the high country, Jewel's thoughts would turn to the marsh, and she would be beset by longing for her home and her people. The initial sorrow that had harrowed her at the time of her bereavements continued to become more bearable as the seasons revolved. Never was it completely erased, never would it be, but the agony gradually gave way to a sad nostalgia, at times a bitter yearning, and sometimes she dreamed she was falling from a great height. Her fear of being pursued also diminished over time. The mountain ring was a safe stronghold; geographically isolated from other centers of population, far from the royal palace in Cathair Rua, its charter wisely and justly administered by the Storm Lord and the councillors of Ellenhall. Jewel felt certain that even if her identity were somehow discovered and the king's soldiers tracked her down, the weathermasters and plateau-dwellers would guard her. Her friends would surely refuse to allow her to be taken away against her will. She grew up with the miller's family, and by the age of sixteen, she finally admitted there was no good reason why she should ever go to King's Winterbourne. She had made High Darioneth her home.

At that age, Jewel came into the full inheritance of her parents' beauty. Her eyes, fringed by two fans of luxuriant lashes, were two blue tulips sparkling in the dew of morning. She was lithe and slender, with a waist like a serpent. Her quick smile and the flash of her eyes were a virtual spell, although she was only half-aware of her power to charm. Except as part of her wide circle of friends, she had scant interest in the youths of the plateau or Rowan Green, preferring to ride or climb or trek on endless adventures and explorations, both within the ring of storths and without. Her inquisitiveness seemed insatiable. She wanted to discover everything about her surroundings, and sometimes this led her into danger. Somehow, she always managed to escape unscathed, even when her companions were less fortunate. Notwithstanding, her invulnerability was never noted. Who would think to look for such an obscure and bizarre quality in one who seemed to be conventionally human in every way?

Whenever anyone asked about her past, Jewel repeated the story that she and her uncle had been on their way to King's Winterbourne to seek employment when they met with disaster.

"What about the other members of your family?" people would ask.

"My parents died in an accident in Cathair Rua. I have no sisters or brothers."

Perceiving the sad look in Jewel's azure eyes, the questioners would take pity on her, and leave off their enquiries. Uncomfortable about practicing deception, Jewel made a habit of discouraging information-seekers. Deep down she yearned to share her history with someone, but dared not.

When Elfgifu climbed the steep road to visit the weathermasters at Rowan Green, Jewel was always invited to accompany her. The marsh-daughter enjoyed popularity at the Seat. The weathermasters' earlier pity for the plight of the lost orphan had turned to affection and even admiration. Jewel was quick-witted and seemed fearless. There was no physical challenge she would not tackle.

For her part, Jewel came to love and trust some who dwelled amongst them—in particular, Avalloc Maelstronnar-Stormbringer. Her confidence in him eventually grew so great, and her desire to confide her true history so pressing, that soon after her sixteenth birthday Jewel arrived at a pivotal decision and requested a private audience with the Storm Lord.

It was in the dining hall of his house that she met with him; a wide, low-ceilinged chamber paneled with walnut and comfortably furnished. Jewel's eyes were drawn to the great sword in its scabbard hanging on the wall above the fireplace. She knew the weapon by reputation, of course; its history was common knowledge. Here was Fallowblade, the golden sword, slayer of goblins, and heirloom of the House of Stormbringer. In High Darioneth many stories were told concerning this marvelous weapon, including a haunting tale from long ago, about a young man named Tierney A'Connacht who had wielded it to effect the rescue of his true-love from the clutches of the Sorcerer of Strang himself. Indeed, the hero A'Connacht had employed this very weapon to cut off one of the villain's hands! Jewel regarded Fallowblade with admiration. In an odd way, it was connected with her; it had tasted the blood of her infamous ancestor.

Turning her attention to the Storm Lord, the damsel hesitantly informed him she had a secret, and asked if he would guard it.

"That I will, dear child, as long as the guarding does not endanger High Darioneth," he replied.

"I think it will not," she replied, eager to share the burden with this wise and worthy leader.

"Before you begin, know that I might divulge your information to the other councillors of Ellenhall if the need arises. I keep no secrets from them, nor they from me. We are a tightly knit fellowship, bound together by the strongest ethics, and you can be certain we would never betray any confidences beyond our circle, not even to our close kindred."

"I would be honored if the esteemed councillors were to be made privy to my tale," Jewel replied without hesitation, curtseying formally. She related her story: how her father had been the scion of the deceased Sorcerer of Strang, and thus invulnerable to all harm except that which was caused by a rare plant and, as far as anyone knew, the ultimately lethal effects of old age; how the gift of immunity had been passed on to his daughter; how the sorcerer's descendants were the only ones able to open the Dome of Strang, and how King Maolmórdha had hunted her father in order to persuade him to unseal that very fortress. She explained that the Great Marsh of Slievmordhu had been her real birthplace and home. Before fleeing from the wetlands her father and mother had been killed, while she, Jewel, had escaped with her uncle. Should Maolmórdha discover her existence, he would send soldiers to look for her. Jewel could only assume the marshfolk had not been forced to betray her. To prove her story she produced a small drawstring bag from her pocket and opened it, displaying the white jewel from the Iron Tree. It sparkled in the palm of her hand, like a polished shard of starshine.

The miller's family knew of the jewel, of course. No material thing could be concealed from that large, boisterous lot, who treated all possessions with candor. They knew of it, and merely thought of it as Jewel's jewel. They assumed it was made of glass. She usually kept it in a small wooden box Herebeorht had made for her, alongside other objects in her collection: the desiccated corpse of a purple butterfly, a green feather, a handful of shiny red seeds, a tawny stone.

"Indeed," said Avalloc, nodding thoughtfully as he gazed into the dynamic brilliance of the stone, "I cannot help but recognize it at once. That is a renowned mineral. The news of its removal from the Tree caused a sensation in Slievmordhu, and was borne to the corners of the Four Kingdoms. Yet there is no need, Jewel, to provide evidence that you do not lie. I perceive you are being honest with me."

"I entrust the truth to you, sir," Jewel concluded humbly, as she tucked away the glittering nub of light, "because I hold you in the highest esteem. My great-grandmother, Eolacha the carlin, once walked among the weathermasters. She was a friend to them in her youth, and they thought well of her."

"Eolacha of the marsh," Avalloc Stormbringer said musingly. "That name is well known to me. She was a wise and great carlin, I have heard. I am sorry to learn she lives in Tir no longer. Marsh-daughter, your tale is extraordinary. You have endured much."

He looked at her gravely from his hooded eyes, and she bowed her head in acknowledgment. "What other legacies have you received from Janus Jaravhor, hmm?" he asked.

"I do not understand you, sir."

"Jaravhor was a man of skill. Is it possible he passed other talents to his heirs?"

"Not that I am aware of," Jewel answered truthfully. "In every other way I am like the rest of humankind. I cannot sprout wings and fly, or destroy objects with a glance, or become invisible, or anything of the sort, if that is what you mean."

"That is indeed what I mean. To me it makes sense that there was only one inheritable virtue. It is no petty feat for a mortal man to conjure a charm of the blood, one that can actually run in the family. No one else has ever achieved such an extraordinary result. I daresay Jaravhor must have striven life-long to succeed. With an enterprise of such magnitude there would have been no leisure for developing any other bequeathable spells."

"I am disappointed I possess no other powers," said Jewel. "If I had any, they would be at your service, my lord, and at the service of High Darioneth." She bowed once more.

The Storm Lord nodded. "I see." Presently he went on, "Many tidings are relayed to us here at Ellenhall, and many more come to us during our excursions—but amongst them I have never heard that Maolmórdha pursues a marshchild. Nonetheless, would it not put your mind at rest to find out, once and for all, whether Maolmórdha knows of you and seeks you?"

"It would indeed, sir!"

"Well, then, I will send one of my most discreet messengers to Cathair Rua. If anything is hidden, Rivalen Hagelspildar will be the one to uncover it."

"I thank you, sir! Prithee, is there any way I can send a message to my step-grandfather in the Great Marsh of Slievmordhu?"

"You might write a letter," he answered. "Next time one of our people travels that way, he or she shall deliver it. But it may be long ere that happens."

Jewel thanked the Storm Lord for his kindness, and took her leave. Her mind felt unburdened. She wrote to Earnán, her step-grandfather, desperately hoping that he still lived. After giving the missive into Stormbringer's keeping, she waited impatiently for the opportunity of its delivery.

There was only one matter she had neglected to mention in her interview with the mage—the fact that mistletoe was her bane. That was not of immediate consequence, Jewel decided, and indeed perhaps it was best that no one at all should know about the mistletoe, lest the information eventually find its way to the ears of any who might wish her ill.

A few days later, she was swayed by second thoughts. If anyone could be trusted to keep the matter confidential it was Avalloc Stormbringer. She could conjecture no reason why he should not be told. Next time she saw the Storm Lord she begged leave to take him aside, whereupon she imparted the information to him.

On hearing her words Avalloc raised his bushy eyebrows. "Mistletoe, hmm? How many other secrets are you keeping from us, Jewel?" he asked mildly.

"None at all, sir, I vow."

"Then be of good cheer, child, for now you have wisely shared your confidences and the truth is in safe hands."

Thus relieved and light of heart, the damsel directed her contemplations toward other topics of interest.

One of these topics was the wonders that were possibly locked within the Dome of Strang. The unknown had always intrigued Jewel; besides, the acquisition of sorcerous secrets could well provide her with life-long security in the form of prestige, knowledge, or wealth. Any of those three elements could help defend folk against life's tragedies. If Jewel had been privy to wizardly lore years ago, for example, then when King Maolmórdha's armed forces came looking for Jarred, she might perhaps have conjured illusory barriers to confound her father's pursuers, or cast a spell to make them forget their orders. Alternatively, if she had been rich with Strang's reputed treasures she might have bribed the soldiers, or purchased an impregnable fortress as a haven for her parents, protected by well-paid guards. If she had been famous as a sorceress and held in high regard, she would have been able to call on the aid of the mighty. Were she wizardly, wealthy, and wise, she would also be in a position to aid the powerless: blameless commoners like herself and her father, who were persecuted by those in authority.

Furthermore, the Dome and all its contents were hers by right of legitimate inheritance. The sorcerer's "gift" had indirectly been the cause of her original misery; by rights his legacy ought to redress that wrong.

Another subject of fascination for Jewel was the power of the weathermasters. When her visits to Rowan Green became regular, she was entranced by glimpses of their weather-handling skills.

"Show me how it's done," she would beg her weathermaster friends. "Tell me the words; show me the gestures!"

"According to our law, it is forbidden to reveal our secrets to any who are not studying for weathermagehood."

So she would ask the younger ones, when their elders were not listening. Most of her friends told her, "What's the profit in it? Only those with the *brí* in their veins can wield weather. You might say the words and make the gestures until you are hoarse and arthritic, but you wouldn't swing a puff of wind or summon a single drop of rain. The *brí* is sometimes called the seventh sense, and one is either born with it or devoid of it."

"If your secrets are useless to such as I," said Jewel, "why are they forbidden?"

Arran Stormbringer explained, "There are those who are born with the *brí* who might use it to work wickedness. Therefore, the lessons are taught piecemeal as *brí*-children grow up. Prentices must pass tests of ethics as well as skill, before progressing to each higher level. They become journeymen; then at the age of twenty-one they are ready to pass the ultimate test and become full-fledged weathermages. Only then is the final secret of weather-wielding given to them. If they are not suitable, then even if the *brí* is strong in them, they will not be given the final training. We call untrained *brí*-heirs 'gift-sundered.' Some name them 'the wasten,' but that is an unkind term."

"'Tis cruel to deny them their birthright," said Jewel primly.

"Wrongful use of the *brí* could upset weather systems, even destroy the world."

"Oh, but *I* would not tell anyone else the secrets," she coaxed earnestly. "Trust me!"

The son of the Storm Lord would not be moved by her pleadings.

Conversely, Ryence Darglistel-BlackFrost was always happy to oblige. He was twenty years old now, a swaggerer who enjoyed showing off his skills. "Come with me, wightlet," he would say to Jewel, elaborately glancing over his shoulders as if to check for eavesdroppers. "I'll teach you to summon the wind."

She needed no coaxing. Every time she tried to wield weather, she failed; nonetheless, she lived in constant hope that she might succeed, one day, if she practiced long and hard enough. Ryence did nothing to discourage this conviction. Together, they would stand atop a bluff that stood out into a chasm high on Wychwood Storth, overlooking the plateau. Raising his hands and sketching a subtle character on the air, Ryence would utter words unfathomably strange to the ears of the damsel, the commands of weatherworking gramarye. They sounded like words she recognized, but he said them in such a way, with such inflections and nuances, that they seemed no longer to be words but volant vectors, the sequels to atmospheric phenomena.

"Bɬāw̌, §ɛ£iř, ¥ɇ W̌ę§ṯ W̌ɏɳd̂ê, ť w̌ā h̃ũ̃ńd̂řêd̃ šĩ>Ꞁṭịg̃ ²F̃ðf̌ĉê," commanded the young weathermaster.

And an artful zephyr would come silking out of the west, picking up the sable tresses of Jewel's hair and causing them to dance gently about her face, before passing away like a sigh.

"Blaw, Sefir, ye west wynde," said Jewel, imitating his gestures, "two hundred and sixty, force two."

No breeze arose.

The more these failures angered Jewel, the more Ryence would laugh at her. Stubbornly, she mastered her indignation and said, "While I am learning to govern the wind, Prince Braggart, you might as well teach me the rest of your weathermaster lore."

"Unlike weathermastery, knowledge of the lore is not forbidden to ordinary folk," said the young man. "Therefore, 'twill not be so amusing."

"I," said Jewel with dignity, "am not ordinary. Teach me."

This she learned: that weathermages could govern three of the four elements. Air they could command, and Fire and Water, but not Tir, the rock and soil of the land. Over quakes, avalanches, and crystals they had no mastery. However, their ability to wield Air, Fire, and Water more than compensated for their lack of influence on Tir. Air pressure, fronts, winds, tornadoes, and hurricanes could be guided and altered at their will. Lightning, fireballs, fire itself, thermal springs, ambient temperatures, rays of the sun, and even volcanoes were subject to the influence of the *brí*.

Of all the elements, the most important was Water.

"Water," instructed Ryence, "makes Life possible. Life can exist anywhere there is Water, even in the absence of Air or the warmth of the sun's Fire. The bodies of mortal beings are made mostly of Water. Even trees are half composed of the stuff."

Rain, fog, mist, steam, rivers, waterfalls, ice, snow, frost, rime, dew, sleet, lakes, clouds, hail, humidity, tides, and the great flood-waves of the oceans could all be chastened by the weathermages. Waterweaving was the third and last of the skills taught to the students, after they became journeymen. Airmastery was the first, and Fireworking was learned in the middle years of their studenthood. It was within the compass of weathermasters to swiftly direct local elements, such as small puffs of wind, and tiny fires, but to regulate more extensive forces such as regional weather systems took time and patience and not a little skill and strength.

Ryence Darglistel liked Jewel; she was well aware of that by now. For her part, she would sometimes allow him to kiss her in return for information. He annoyed her, teased her. In return she deliberately tried to vex him. She half liked him, half hated him; he aroused her to fervors of varying sorts, and he was never dull. He was like a spark, bright, exciting, hurtful, quick to disappear, causing damage, yet kindling flame. When she paid attention to his face and form Jewel knew he was good to look at, strong and well made, comely of feature, his hair the color of hazelnuts, his eyes bright with mischief and mockery. Nonetheless, in the certainty that his attraction to her was due more to his liking of her looks than a desire for companionable conversation, she thought of him sometimes as a plaything, sometimes as a tormentor, rarely as a friend.

"Byrn, ye beorht brond!" Jewel would cry, bouncing the knuckles of her right hand off the upturned palm of her left, while wiggling her fingers.

"βȳřň, ¥ē βéøřħŧ βřöŋđ, ān ŧħêřмє!" the deeper voice of the journeyman weathermaster would ring out, and after a dextrous flourish his left hand was holding a tiny flame that danced between his fingers and never blackened or scorched them. Nettled, Jewel comforted herself with the secret knowledge that although she could not hold fire within her hand, she could hold her hand within fire.

Notwithstanding, she could not resist blowing out Ryence's flame.

After four weeks away, the Storm Lord's messenger Rivalen Hagelspildar returned from his journeys in the lands beyond the storths. He brought tidings that there was no hunt for Jewel. No watch was kept for her. Four years earlier, King Maolmórdha's cavalrymen of the Royal Horse Guards had witnessed with their own eyes that Jarred was dead, and the marsh people had vowed that he had no child. The search for a scion of the sorcerer had been abandoned long ago.

The last fetters of anxiety loosened themselves from Jewel. Finally, she felt she was at liberty. With freedom came thoughts of returning to the friends and family she had left behind in the marsh—Earnán, her grandfather; Cuiva and Odhrán Rushford and their children, Oisín, Ciara, and Ochlán; Neasán Willowfoil, the Tolpuddles, and even the Alderfens.

A prentice on a southbound journey had borne Jewel's letter with him. He returned, saying he'd given it into the hands of a Marsh Watchman. Jewel's hopes soared. As weeks passed, however, her excitement faded. No answering letter appeared.

She told herself it was difficult to find honest travelers who would deliver letters. She told herself that in all likelihood a letter had been sent from the marsh, but the bearer had been waylaid by Marauders or unseelie wights. Excuse after excuse vaporized. Eventually there remained no other explanation; tragedy had overtaken her people in the marsh. Her grandfather must be dead.

Then a letter arrived, carried into High Darioneth along East Road, in the dusty packs of a band of traveling hawkers. When Jewel unfolded the papyrus and saw it had been written by Earnán she flew into a mad dance, then eagerly sat down to decipher his old-fashioned spelling.

> *Beloved* Gariníon [he wrote], *my Heart is breaking. It hath been a hard Task to put Pen to Paper synce your News arryved. I am sorely grieved to hear of my Son's fate. May he rest in Peace. He was a fyne Lad. One of the fynest. I can wryte no more on thys Subject for now, lest my tears smudge thys Letter.*
>
> *We are all hale and we myffe you. After you departed we had to selle your Pony but we founde hym a goode Home. We have a new Upyall, fatter than the last, which lyved to a good age, Tralee is old but in found Health, and Eoin's Retryver Sally is dwellynge comfortably wyth the Tolpuddles in Eoin's old House which is styll flotynge, wyth the Weathercock atop. The Green Laydye haunts the Caufewaye stylle, but she is a seelye Wyte lyke all Gruagachs, and the Tolpuddles have growne ufed to her. Keelyn Styllwater is now marryed and so alfo her Brother. Floods have shyfted the high ground behynde the houfe and now our apple tree grows from the opposyte bank. There are no more Felle-cats in the Marsh. We thynke the Tiddy Mun hath dryven them out.*
>
> *The Weathermafters are worthy Folk and you wryte that you are well treated. But do not return to the Marshe. It would be too perylous. Here, we never speak of Matters furroundynge the Purfuite of your Father by a Certaine Authorytye. Your Return may well styrre up all that old Trouble. There is Nobody here who wysheth you Harme, but Harme might come in unlooked-for Ways. By Myftake or Ignorance. We yearn to see you again, but it is better that you remain in Safetye. My Bones are gettynge old and there is always Worke to be done. One Day, perhaps, Cyrcumftances myte allow me to vysyt you. But it is a long Way. For now I am glad you are safe and well. An old Man's Heart is lyter, for redynge your Sentiments.*

After perusing his letter several times, dwelling on every word, Jewel was forced to acknowledge the logic in her grandfather's reasoning. She showed the papyrus to the Storm Lord and he agreed.

"That does not signify you will never see your family and friends again," he added, gently. "Time brings changes. The future is never clear, no matter what the druids may claim."

The discontent of the marsh-daughter was scarcely quelled by the good news from the marsh. When she had received the tidings that she was not looked for by King Maolmórdha, restless longings recommenced to seethe and ferment in her brain, as though floodgates had been shattered. The desire to uncover the secrets of Strang's enigmatic Dome returned with redoubled force. Now, if she wished, she might journey to the mysterious region of Orielthir without fear of recognition and pursuit!

Yet the stories about the Dome told that it had remained heavily guarded for years. Old King Maolmórdha, taking no chances that a rival might try to crack the seal and steal the contents from under his nose, had set a permanent watch on the building. Jewel dreamed of leaving High Darioneth and journeying to Orielthir, but the prospect of being captured by Maolmórdha's guards was not one she relished; thus she was forced to dwell in tolerance of her unrequited desires, a situation she found vexing in the extreme.

The year that she turned sixteen was notable to Jewel's mind chiefly because of the new and fearless future that had broadened before her, and for two occurrences—one joyous, the other strange.

On an evening, hoop-backed Osweald Miller was making his way slowly along the willow-festooned banks of the millstream when he heard a thin weeping and wailing that seemed to come out of the ground. To his ears, it sounded like the cry of a sorrowing child. His heart was moved to pity, but when he looked around he could see nobody. Limping on with his head bowed down in its customary position, he came across the two broken halves of a child's shovel lying in the grass. It was a tool such as his own children were wont to use, digging in the vegetable patch or delving little water-channels from the mill-race, on which to float their toy boats. Painfully he leaned and picked up the two halves, turning them over in his hands. *I reckon I could mend this,* he thought, and he took the pieces back to the mill workshop.

There he sawed the splintered ends to form two neat parts of a joint, then bolted them together and wrapped them with a good length of thick twine soaked in strong glue. It hurt his aching body to perform these tasks, but the memory of the child's voice crying for its toy sustained him in his labors. Next morning he went out along the banks of the stream, and left the mended shovel where he had found it. The lamenting was still going on, but it had decreased to desultory sobs, interspersed with sniffing.

As he was about to hobble away, the miller noticed he was standing near a green hillock his children called "The Pixy Mound." *Well,* he said to himself with a wry grin, *perhaps I have been of help to some wight.* As he departed he called out, "There's your shovel—no need to cry anymore."

Instantly, the sobbing ceased.

On the following day, his curiosity aroused, the crippled miller returned to the hillock. The mended shovel was gone, and in its place was a new-baked cake, golden-brown, still warm and steaming. Osweald buckled his distorted joints enough to lean over and pick it up. He wrapped the cake in his kerchief and took it home.

"Go to the carlin at Rowan Green," he instructed his eldest daughter, "and ask her what I should do with this delicacy. I believe it is a wight-gift, but it is said to be unwise to eat their food."

Elfgifu dutifully rode to the Seat, and when she came back she said, "Father, Carlin Longiníme advised that since this is a gift in return for an act of kindness, it will not harm you and might, in fact, bestow some benefit. She warned that no one else should touch so much as a crumb."

Her father unwrapped the cake and scrutinized it. "It looks tasty," he said, and took a bite.

An expression of bliss transformed his face, and as he swallowed, the transformation appeared to spread from his face throughout his entire body. He straightened and stood up tall, threw back his head, and flung out his arms. "Ha!" he shouted. "I am cured!" With that he bolted down the rest of the cake for good measure and, with his mouth still full, grabbed his astonished wife by the waist and lifted her high in the air. "I'm more hale than ever I was!" he shouted. "Herebeorht, fetch the keys to the cellar. Tonight we'll all celebrate!"

The strange event of Jewel's year happened several weeks after the joyous occasion of the miller's recovery.

Autumn had rolled around again, the fifth Autumn she had seen at High Darioneth. The season was particularly bountiful. The boughs of the orchard trees bent to the ground with the weight of their fruit, and the colors of the turning leaves shimmered in the clear light of high altitudes, ruffled by fresh breezes.

Sevember had passed, and the occasion of the annual High Darioneth Horn Dance with its antler-headed entertainers had come and gone, as always with much merriment. It was now Lantern Eve, the last day of Otember, and nearing the hour at which the eldritch Winter Hag would begin walking the wild places of Tir, smiting the land to suspend propagation and invoke bitter weather. In the fire-bright kitchens of the mill the last of the cooking was taking place, in preparation for the evening's festivities. Clad in aprons and daubs of honey, with their sleeves rolled up to their elbows, Jewel, Elfgifu, and Hilde were helping the cook to bake nut-bread. On such occasions, the Miller sisters were wont to sing lustily, "to make the task lighter," as Elfgifu put it. A tuneless old nursery chant was well under way:

> "Nut-bread, nut-bread, we're a-baking nut-bread.
> 'How does one make *that* bread?' the milk-maid said.
> Four eggs, crack them up, fresh honey half a cup,
> Mix the eggs and honey till they're syrupy and runny.
> Two cups of grinded nuts, another half for Greedy-Guts,
> Mix the eggs and nut-flour; use a bit of elbow power,
> Quarter cup of melted butter, blend it in to make the batter.
> Soda next, half a teaspoon, pinch of salt, just to season.
> Bake it till it's golden-brown. Nicest bread in Hatfield Town."

"Why Hatfield Town?" Hilde asked, sloppily stirring a mixture in a bowl she held in the crook of her elbow.

"Because it fits with the rhythm," replied her elder sister.

"Watch that batter, Mistress Hilde!" scolded the cook. " 'Tis spattering every-where on the floor."

"I've eaten nicer bread than dry old nut-bread," said Hilde, still beating vig-orously with her wooden spoon. "I prefer the wheaten loaves they make in King's Winterbourne, and most of the lowland villages. They're so soft and *spongy*."

"What a pity for you," said Elfgifu airily. "You won't get too many of those hereabouts, not unless you marry a son of the weathermasters and go to live at Rowan Green."

Hilde glanced slyly at Jewel, who was measuring out walnut meal with small attempt at accuracy, her attention apparently wandering from her task. "When Jewel is living up there she'll invite us to visit every day, won't you, Jewel?"

"What?" said Jewel. Oblivious of their chattering, she had been staring out the window. Above the dulcet gurglings of the millstream, faint wight-sounds of lamentation and eldritch revelry floated in from the surrounding orchards. Close by, a barn-owl hooted. The first star had not yet appeared in the darkening skies, but behind the distant storths the moon was already rising, hanging low on the horizon like a faded image of the sun, full, copper-mellow, and luminescent.

Something had gone by, out past the water-pump and through the kitchen garden toward the duck pond. Initially, Jewel had assumed it was one of the children, but on second thought she was not so sure.

"When you're living at the Seat you'll ask us to visit you every day, won't you?" repeated Hilde.

"Yes," said Jewel absently. She turned away from the window, holding an overflowing cup of nut-meal in her hand. "What? What are you talking about?"

Hilde and Elfgifu chuckled.

"Now then, misses, stop your mischief and take heed of your work," reprimanded the long-suffering cook. "You are supposed to be helping me, not scattering food all over my kitchen. Mistress Jewel, you are dispersing nut-flour like a farmer sowing seed."

Energetically, Hilde roared, "Nut-bread, nut-bread, we're a-baking nut-bread. 'How does one make *that* bread?' the milk-maid said."

Jewel forgot the apparition in the kitchen garden, dismissing it as a fancy.

Then, three days after Lantern Eve she took a basket and went mushrooming on her own, partly to absent herself from the general hurly-burly of the mill and find some solitude, partly to thwart Ryence Darglistel, who had told her he would be riding down past the mill that day and might call in. Jewel loved company, but she also enjoyed teasing Ryence with unpredictable behavior, trying to throw him off balance, as he so often did to her. Besides, only when she was alone could she ponder her past, examine her memories, review the recollections that were fading day by day. She did not want her history to become lost to her. The marsh had been a happy home, and she thought of it wistfully, wishing there was someone with whom she might share her reminiscences.

Carrying the basket on her arm, she roamed the paths of the plateau until she had wandered far from the cultivated regions, down by a wild stream that ran through a patch of beech-wood. Here she had found mushrooms before, and here she found them again, popping up their creamy buttons between the roots of the trees. Her basket was half-full when she straightened, to ease her back. Not far away a small, man-like creature was sitting on a fallen tree-trunk, with its knees drawn up to its chest.

It was watching her.

She almost dropped the basket. Recovering her composure, she returned the creature's inspection, peering at it sidelong, lest she offend it by making eye contact. From the waist up it appeared like an ugly little man with pointed, tufty ears, a turned-up nose, and eyes that slanted up to the outer corners in the usual manner of wights. Its head was covered with a thicket of curly brown hair, from which protruded two stubby horns. It wore a threadbare jacket, frayed at the cuffs, and a tattered waistcoat of indeterminate color. Ragged breeches covered its shaggy goats' legs.

That this was an urisk Jewel knew from stories her mother had told her. She could not remember ever having seen one of these seelie wights. The one that had been attached to her mother's household had disappeared when Jewel was three years old.

Should she move? Should she speak? If she did, would it vanish? Her curiosity overcame her, and she said courteously, "Good morrow, sir."

It made no reply, but directed its gaze away from her. Encouraged by the fact that it remained, she inquired, "Can I help you?"

The look of scorn it turned upon her caused her to wilt. Deliberately, the wight rose from its perch. Jewel guessed that it was about to fade away amongst the trees, and at that moment it occurred to her that an urisk, being a water-haunting creature, might know something about the marsh.

"Wait!" she cried. "Are you familiar with the Great Marsh of Slievmordhu?"

It was too late. The wight had already become one with the beech-wood.

Crestfallen, Jewel returned to the mill.

She asked Elfgifu, "Are there many urisks around here?"

"None, to my knowledge," said the miller's daughter. "It's brownies this place is jumping with. Brownies, trows, and the siofra. Myself, I should like to see a swan-maiden; I have heard they are quite remarkable."

Visions of the urisk hovered in the background of Jewel's private musings. She caught herself watching for subtle movements in the kitchen garden, or in the lane-side hedges during her rambles. This way, she often saw wild creatures such as mice, echidnas, globe-bodied spiders, and small birds. More rarely, she snatched glimpses of tiny, human-like folk scurrying out of view.

News of the greater world never failed to reach High Darioneth swiftly, borne in miniature scrolls tied to the legs of carrier pigeons or brought by travelers, or carried by weathermasters in sky-balloons. From Slievmordhu on the seventeenth of Tenember, three days before Midwinter's Eve, came word that King Maolmórdha Ó Maoldúin was dead. Prince Uabhar, being of age, was to be duly crowned in the new year, and members of the upper echelons of the weathermasters were invited to attend the coronation, as they had attended the royal wedding the previous Spring. The Crown Prince had lost a father in the same year he had taken a wife.

This change of government in the southern kingdom failed to impress the inhabitants of High Darioneth. Amongst those few who had personally encountered the royal family of Slievmordhu, it was privately held that the son Uabhar was as false as the father had been weak. They rejoiced, as ever, that they were citizens of Narngalis and not subject to the arbitrary rule of the dynasty Ó Maoldúin.

The machinery of politics did not interest Jewel, unless it affected her daily life. She might have taken small note of the royal succession, if not that the demise of the old king reminded her yet again of the reason he would have sought her, had he known she existed.

She alone could unlock the Dome of Strang.

What lay inside that Dome of such importance?

Even more than the notion of enormous might or wealth, the idea of penetrating a mystery attracted her. The thought of closed doors made her itch to fling them wide. The contemplation of hidden secrets made her yearn to discover them. In addition to her desire to obtain the trappings of security, her inquisitiveness was that of an alchemist or philosopher, ever driven to delve deeper into the arcane.

Such was her frustration that all objects of a certain shape seemed a reminder: an enticement and a challenge. In the kitchen she became such a nuisance that the cook banned her from that domain. Without being aware of it, she had slipped into a habit of up-ending mushrooms, stoving in hard-boiled eggs, skewering freshly unmolded puddings with a carving knife. Never would she allow a bowl to be left upside-down, and she even turned hats inside out, when nobody was looking.

Winter stole in silently in white slippers. She had exiled her sister, velvet-clad Autumn of the red hair, and instead broadcast a cloak of frosted satin encrusted with ice-diamonds. Tenember, last month of the old year, was a time of great significance in all Four Kingdoms of Tir, for its twentieth day was Midwinter's Eve. By that date, Grianan the Winter Sun had diminished, becoming no more than a sullen, tarnished coin in the southern skies, and the strength of the eldritch hag, the Cailleach Bheur, was at its most potent. This was the season for the choosing of new carlins.

All across the kingdoms of Tir festivals were held in celebration of Midwinter's Eve. At High Darioneth the bells atop Ellenhall carillonned in the morning. Games and contests were held down on the plateau's Greatlawn Common in the afternoon: archery competitions, prize-fighting, races, hurdling, and football. A ram lamb was roasted on a spit. Then, as the day faded, the plateau-dwellers came up the cliff road to join the weathermasters. Bonfires were lit on Rowan Green. There was music and song, wine and conviviality.

In the Great Hall of Long Gables, warmed by log-fueled infernos in gigantic fireplaces and lit by pendant chandeliers on hoops of marigold brass, the traditional wassailing bowl was passed around. It was filled with "lamb's wool," a mixture of hot ale, nutmeg, and honey, in which floated roasted crab-apples and fragments of toast. The great bowl itself, an ancient heirloom, was carved from ash-wood, and cheerfully decorated with colored ribbons.

"Here we come a-wassailing amongst the leaves so green; here we come a-wassailing, so fair to be seen," inventively sang the happy band of wassailers who were taking the bowl around so that all might share.

The weathermasters, old and young, were attired in festive raiment. The men went bare-headed, their hair flowing to the middle of their backs. Their hose were of dark wool, their shoes of soft leather. Over their tunics, which reached to mid-thigh, they wore surcoats of velvet, lined with damask. The surcoats were pleated at the back, gathered in by waist-belts of linked platinum platelets engraved, inlaid, and chased with intricate patterns. The sleeves of several of the elders were long, and trailed to the floor. The women adorned their heads with couvre-chefs of soft silk, held in place with chaplets of delicate filigree. They were simply but elegantly coiffed, some with two long plaits reaching to below their knees, and braided with colored ribbons. Their bell-sleeved over-gowns of stout brocade were ornately stitched with motifs of their families' coat-of-arms, while the tight-sleeved kirtles showing beneath were of plain, rich satin. When not wearing the traditional gray, weathermasters favored warm tints such as ambers, honeys, crimsons, golds, and browns, contrasted with black. At their necks and wrists, these colors were accented by splashes of ivory, glimpses of bleached cambric shirts and chemises.

The men and youths of the plateau were garbed in long-sleeved cote-hardies of woolen cloth, some with dagged hems, all displaying bands of embroidery at the cuffs and collars. Their leather belts were lush with embossing, and their headgear consisted of a capuchon with liripipe, thrown back in the warmth of the Hall. After the prevailing fashion, the plateau-dwelling women wore their gowns open at the front to reveal the kirtle beneath. These were their best clothes, saved for special occasions. Along the edges of their garments they had worked complicated designs of birds and leaves in colored thread. Elderly women covered their heads with wimples and peplums, the married women preferred the couvre-chef with a simple band, and the damsels entwined their hair with ribbons or let it flow freely down their backs, held clear of their brows by fine chain-fillets.

The revelers stood and sat around the perimeter of the Hall to watch the mumming play. This time-honored branch of theater began with the entrance of a group of men who stood silently in a crescent-formation. The mummers always concealed their identities with elaborate masks, and their garments were thickly sewn with strips of cloth, so that that they resembled furry bears, or scarecrows. To aid in the concealment of their faces they wore splendidly decorated hats.

Led by a man dressed in jester's costume, called the "letter-in," the mummers took turns to step forward and deliver a short speech. After that, the rest of their display took place in silent mime.

The pivotal part of the ceremony ensued: the Hero-Combat. The "hero," whose name this year was "Old King Waldemar," commenced to do silent battle against a number of enemies attacking him in succession. These assailants bore names such as "The Bold Slasher," "The Black Prince of Paradine," and "The Turkey Snipe." After some lively combat, one of the contenders, not necessarily the miscreant, was inevitably "slain," to the consternation of some of the younger children in the audience.

Fortunately, a "druid" never failed to turn up at the right moment. He would proceed to eulogize his own skills in the most improbable terms, and tell implausible tales of his foreign peregrinations, until the audience was bent double, in fits of laughter. The "druid" would then marvelously revive the "dead" man.

When these enactments had concluded, the "druid" waltzed off to change his costume.

"Why are there no druids here at High Darioneth?" asked Jewel, suddenly struck by the dearth.

The miller and his wife exchanged glances.

Mildthrythe cleared her throat. "Not that the Maelstronnar lacks respect for that worthy brotherhood," she murmured, somewhat awkwardly. "On the contrary! However, he deems their presence here unnecessary. We send yearly tithes to the sanctorum at King's Winterbourne; in return the druids intercede with the Fates on our behalf."

"My great-grandmother used to say the druids were nothing but drones," said Jewel clearly.

Mildthrythe coughed. Her mouth pursed as if she were trying to suppress a smile, and a look of amusement flitted briefly across her husband's features. "Indeed? Well, ehrm"—delicately she cleared her throat—"such opinions must not be spoken aloud."

Jewel nodded, returning their smiles.

The wassailing bowl went around again, and as the garnet glow of sunset streamed through the windows, it was time for the longsword dancing. During the performance darkness drew in quickly. Afterward, bagpipers struck up tunes and feasting resumed.

The dancing commenced. Partners lined up for an eightsome reel, and the center of Long Gables exploded into a whirl of movement, a swirl of skirts, an eruption of leaping and galloping. As she skipped through a "strip-the-willow" with Ryence Darglistel, Jewel looked across to the far wall, along which a row of people without partners was seated. She felt a pang of pity for them. On the other side of the room the Maelstronnar's son Arran Stormbringer stood, framed by an architrave. Jewel had the impression he had been watching her, and when their eyes met she thought he smiled, but she was whisked away in the dance, and could not be certain.

After performing the "Dashing White Sergeant" and "Sir Roger of Coverley," the musicians paused to retune their instruments and the Master of Ceremonies announced a "Gentlemen's Choice." All the men were entitled to choose their own partners, and the lady they chose was not permitted to refuse. In order to prevent a stampede, the men had to form a queue in front of the Master of Ceremonies. This in itself caused a furore of jostling and pushing, to the hilarity of the onlookers, particularly Jewel, who doubled over in a fit of laughter.

Near the front of the queue was Arran Stormbringer. When his turn came, he began to stride across the Hall.

"Many damsels will hope," murmured Elfgifu at Jewel's elbow. "I conjecture 'twill be Ettie he seeks."

At these words, Jewel felt an unexpected twinge of vexation.

Yet it was not toward Ettare Sibilaurë that the Storm Lord's son was heading. He was moving toward the group with whom Jewel was keeping company.

"By all that's wonderful!" exclaimed Elfgifu. "He comes this way!" Her face was crimson and her hands fluttered ineffectually at the strands of hair rebeling from beneath her velvet cap. Impatient with her friend's primping, Jewel stood on tiptoe and craned her neck to peer past the shoulders of those surrounding her. She was wondering how Ryence had tolerated the ignominy of not being first in the queue, and felt unable to resist the delicious notion of taunting him. Ryence's mother, Astolat, was standing right beside her. She calculated she ought to move a little apart from that well-respected lady before she indulged in teasing her son, despite the fact that Ryence never paid much attention to either of his parents.

The young Stormbringer halted before the group of women and damsels, directly in front of Jewel. To her own surprise and confusion she felt her heartbeat racing, and the blood rising in her face. Arran, however, made a courteous bow to Astolat Darglistel and offered her his hand. The lady took it, with a smile and a curtsey, and they made their way to the center of the floor to await the other couples.

Quickly recovering her poise, Jewel glanced about to see if anyone had noticed her brief lapse of composure. Everyone, even the damsels who had hoped to partner him, was smiling in approval of Arran's decision to dance with his aunt instead of one of them. Next moment, Jewel's hand was taken by Bliant Ymberbaillé-Rainbearer, the son of Baldulf, and she was led into the fray.

As Jewel passed amongst the growing assembly of couples, young Darglistel was suddenly at her ear, whispering provokingly, "I avoided being first in line because you would expect me to choose you." Angrily she spun on her heel to deliver some caustic retort, but he had already disappeared into the crowd with his dance partner.

Bliant was slight of build and dark of hair, with a long face and a wide mouth. He was one of those people whose every thought and feeling was displayed on their countenance, whose expressions flit and change like cloud-shadows on a windy day. His motives were laid bare for all to scrutinize, and, like an eldritch wight, he was incapable of lying. All who knew him honored him as a true stalwart and a worthy young man. He was a capable dancer, although no expert. Jewel might have enjoyed his company, had her thoughts not been focused elsewhere.

Between dances, Ettare asked, "Jewel, why were you frowning at everyone so, after Arran took Ryence's mother to partner?"

"I imagined some people might be dissatisfied with his choice."

"Fiddlesticks! As far as I am concerned, I'll not deny I had half hoped, but he made the lady Astolat very happy. As all are aware, her husband, Branor, is quite ill, and unable to attend occasions like these. Arran has not offended anyone—certainly not Ryence, who is an unsolicitous son, and not even the many other damsels vying for his attentions. Besides, I have danced with him many times this night, and doubtless shall do so again!"

She was not mistaken. Later, she and the young Stormbringer embarked on an escapade of ridiculous capers, to the delight of a group of children. Gales of laughter blew across the Hall. Hovering at the edge of her circle of friends, Jewel was watching their antics when a youth stepped close and drew her aside. Not surprisingly, it was Ryence Darglistel. He offered a cup of wine that sparkled like carbuncles in the firelight.

"I refuse to speak with you," she said childishly, turning her shoulder to him.

"I will teach you to call the rain," he coaxed.

"I've done with all that."

"When I am made a mage, I will take you in a sky-balloon."

The temptation was too great, even though she knew his promises were generally hollow.

"Good!" She snatched the wine cup from his hand.

"Put on your cloak. Come outside to see the bonfires."

Effecting a shrug to display her indifference, she complied.

They walked under the stars. Vaporous ghosts hovered before their mouths as their breath condensed on the air. Rowan Green was illuminated by the bonfires, whose flames roared like the wind.

"Why have you been asking questions about the Dome of Strang?" Darglistel asked, causing Jewel to realize she had not been as discreet with her inquiries as she thought.

"None of your business," she retorted, whereupon he, simulating outrage at her insolence, grasped her in a firm embrace. She threw herself off balance and they toppled together, rolling in the dew-damp grass, laughing. Naively, she was viewing their high jinks as a child's game. Then all at once the laughter was gone and she became aware he lay across her, his weight pressing her against the ground. He was trembling between her arms; quivering, but not from the cold. The unexpected awareness of her effect on him rushed through her in a pulse of excitement. Yet it was also, suddenly, alarming.

Pulling away from him, she stood up, brushing grass-blades from her skirts.

"Now you've had your kiss, you must pay for it," she dared to say, undaunted though uncertain. Still lying on the sward, he leaned on his elbow, his head cocked slightly to one side, waiting, play-acting as if indifferent. "Tell me all you know about the Dome of Strang."

"That's easily done," he said. "I know naught."

With an exclamation of disbelief and disgust she stamped her foot. He sprang to his feet, but she was already off, running. With him in close pursuit, leaping over tussocks, she was breathless with laughter and exertion, torn between exhilaration and fear that he might catch her.

She doubled back toward the crowd gathered about the bonfire, and he was forced to abandon his pursuit.

For two weeks the weather remained comparatively mild, after which there came a sudden cold snap. Light powderings of snow dusted the ground, and the air cracked like crystal. Indeed, the landscape was so still and quiet that it might well have been entombed in glass. Pools and puddles were frozen solid. Glazes of translucent ice rimmed the duck pond and the mill-pond. The way bright sunbeams refracted dazzlingly through icicles and beads of frost reminded Jewel of the gem from the Iron Tree. She removed it from its storage box to admire it. Its beauty was such that she decided to wear it on its chain about her neck, concealed beneath layers of cold-weather clothing.

The dream of falling returned to trouble Jewel, and after one particularly restless night she woke early, on the cusp of dawn. Welcoming first light as her rescuer from nightmare, the marsh-daughter slipped from her couch without rousing the household. Jittery, unwilling to return to sleep lest she be plagued by monstrous visions, she dressed warmly and stole outdoors.

Gray-green, silver, and white was the world, striped with soft shadows the color of wood-smoke. The ground was alabaster. Frost lay in luxurious swathes across the mill-yard and the surrounding fields. Each sugar-coated blade of grass was fringed with spiky crystals. Each fallen leaf was edged with glassy beads, its veins picked out in lines of silver, its surface a constellation. On the roofs of the outbuildings, where the first rays struck, the frost was already start-ing to melt. The ends of the eaves glimmered with swift trickles that sang a merry, chortling melody. In the yards, the tops of the stone walls and wooden fences were lavishly slathered with a layer of fragile diamantes.

Out into the road went Jewel, over the stile in the hawthorn hedge and across the field toward the stand of leafless liquidambars on the borders of the orchard. Underfoot, the frozen grass rustled like crisp silk with every step. Small herbs amongst the grasses stuck out as stiff as crystallized angelica, each with its ice-powder sprinkling, each meticulously outlined in polar fur.

From down in the hedge to her left came the burble of tiny voices. Slowing her pace, she crept quietly up to the source. There, beneath an arched gap at the roots of the hawthorns, two dozen small figures were skating and sliding on a frozen puddle. Jewel was careful to emit no sound, although she could not stifle a smile. The siofra were cloaked in ragged furs, perhaps the hides of rats and voles. These were pinned at the shoulders with cockroach brooches. It appeared their other clothes were chiefly made of moss and shrew-skins. Their strange as-sortment of hats was adorned with wrens' feathers, and for scarves they twisted wisps of dirty sheep's wool about their necks. The mortal watcher could not guess how they had constructed the skates bound to their little snakeskin boots. Perhaps they had found and honed some blades of bronze, since they could not endure the touch of iron.

Beside the frozen puddle, now etched with a tracery of whorls, a siofran pic-nic was set out in various vessels. It looked indigestible, to say the least. Lush piles of insect eggs and dead flies were heaped in nut-shell bowls. Dried seed-pods were filled with larvae, withered berries, and objects that appeared to be the unctuous dewlaps of snails. To Jewel, the only palatable items were con-tained in the brimming acorn cups: clear dew, and droplets of honey.

Wisely, she did not study this curious gathering for long. Danger was always present; if they caught her spying they would be angry. Noiselessly she drew back from the eldritch hedge-party, and continued on her way.

High above the plateau hung the storths, tall snowy peaks in the sky, cloud-wreathed. As the sun ascended, its clear light stretched across the field. Ice glit-tered on rain-pools. Deep among the liquidambars one pool glimmered differently.

It was dappled silver, giving off iridescent greens and blues.

Approaching this strange puddle, filled with awe and astonishment, Jewel ex-perienced the abrupt awareness that she was being watched. She looked up, and

THE WELL OF TEARS { 121 }

jumped backward. Beneath the trees, a melange of gray dew and cobwebs had caught her eye.

"Oh!" she exclaimed, adding unnecessarily, "You startled me!"

The urisk made no reply. It was standing amongst the trees with its arms folded across its chest, watching her, as one of its kind had done before.

She did not know how to tell one urisk apart from another. They all possessed similar features: the pointed ears, the snub nose, the slanted eyes with vertical slits of pupils. They were all short in stature, with hairy goats' legs, and they all seemed more closely related to the mysteries of wood and water than to the mankind they resembled from the waist up.

There was no way of knowing if this was indeed the same urisk she had erstwhile met, but suddenly great hope sprang in her, and she said eagerly, "Prithee, do not go away too soon. Have you ever been to the Great Marsh of Slievmordhu?"

"Once I dwelled there," said the wight in a voice like the sound of low flutes.

Jewel fancied she heard a tinge of contempt in its tone, but she took a step toward it and said, clasping her hands together, "Were you ever acquainted with the families of Heronswood or Mosswell?"

The wight was silent for a time, while its interrogator watched it pleadingly. At length it said, "The house of your mother was not unknown to me."

The girl gave a cry of delight. She felt tears start beneath her lids. "You knew my parents. . . ." Her throat clenched on her words and she could no longer speak.

This must surely be the urisk of the marsh. Her mother and father had often told the story of how the wight had helped them, leading Jarred to the place where Lilith lay alone and defenseless with an injured ankle. Grandfather Earnán used to say, *"The wight was surly and shiftless, but at the crunch it proved worthy."*

"This garment," said the creature, offhandedly indicating the shimmering rain-pool, "is yours."

And it was then that Jewel realized the glimmer of iridescent greens and blues in the frosty grass was no pool of fractured ice, but a cool slither of shimmering scales, like the mail of opalescent fishes. Amazed, she bent down and gathered it into her hands, marveling at the smoothness of the texture, the pearly loveliness.

"The fishmail shirt!" she exclaimed in a low voice. "I remember this extraordinary thing. How could I not, even though I was so young? It used to hang on the cottage wall. My mother said she gave it to you, and you took it away when I was but three Winters old. Why are you presenting it to me?"

"I have no use for such a frippery."

"How do you know who I am?" Jewel asked.

The wight merely gave a snort of derision. Of course, Jewel reminded herself, wights were able to find out many of the secrets of humankind. They could often pass unnoticed amongst mortal beings, and they had their own methods of seeing and hearing things.

Due to its past connection with her family, to Jewel the urisk seemed like a link to the old times. Fervently, she wished she might form some kind of bond with it. The creature radiated the impression that it was constantly on the point of departing, and even as she watched it she was swept by an ineffable sense of loss, as if it had already gone.

"Prithee, stay with me, sir," she begged, as politely as she could. "Won't you tell me some stories of the marsh? Won't you come to live at the mill?"

Sourly, it gave reply. "I am no nursemaid, to tell stories to children. And are there no brownies hereabouts who will do your work for you?"

It was moving away, leaving again.

"Sir, I am sorry if I have caused offense!" cried Jewel in alarm. She cast about for some way of drawing it back, of entwining it with her so that this final, tenuous nexus with her childhood should not be destroyed. What might lure the wight—something beautiful and precious, perhaps? Something she did not value half as much as she valued the chance to converse with one who had known her parents and the marsh?

"Wait! I have a gift for you!" Carefully replacing the fishmail shirt on the ground, the damsel fumbled behind her neck, under her hood and scarf. Having unfastened the chain, she drew forth the sparkling gem her father had given her. "This!" she said, holding it up so that it trapped the sun's rays, breaking and scattering them as if a light-smith or a pixy jeweler worked with his hammers within.

The eyes of the urisk, black chips of jet, stared coldly from the curdled shadows of the grove.

"Prithee, take it," said Jewel, hanging the chain on a jutting twig and letting the jewel swing there. She backed away. "I will not come near you, if you wish it so. But prithee, do not depart."

Without looking at the incredible bijou on its delicate links, the urisk grasped it with one hand. Then the wight was gone.

It left behind both desolation and relief.

Seizing the fishmail shirt, the girl ran away. For some reason she could not explain, she was weeping.

In the light of the rising sun the white ground winked and sparkled. Frost lay thickest in the long, blue shadows of the trees and hedges. As Jewel neared the arched gap in the hawthorn hedge, her sobs alerted the eldritch beings who disported themselves beneath. Out from amongst the roots they came skip-ping, and this time they seemed to be dressed in splendid arctic pelts and gar-ments of richest velvet, stitched with gems. The diminutive fellows and dames beckoned to Jewel, turning up their teensy faces to her, bright as field-daisies. She understood they were inviting her to their festivities. Dashing away her tears with the heel of her hand, she followed them to the frozen puddle under the hedge and crouched there. The feast of the wights now looked delicious and enticing beyond measure. Ripe fruits, no bigger than dew-drops, glistened on golden dishes. White bread and creamy yellow cheeses were displayed be-side goblets filled with wine. Had she not seen these victuals in their native state, before the siofra had put their glamour on the feast, Jewel might almost have been gulled.

So as not to offend them, she extended her index finger and thumb, and made to take up one of the little goblets, which she knew was really filled with water or honey. The wights waved their arms and gabbled at her in their high, shrill voices. Guessing they wanted her to donate something in return for their so-called hospitality, she withdrew her hand. Shaking her head, she shrugged.

"I carry no food," she said. "Forgive me."

They jabbered some more, then, suddenly ignoring her, began busily to pack away the picnic things at a rapid rate. Jewel stood up. It came to her that the siofra had only invited her so that she might provide them with food such as mankind thrived on. She had none to share; therefore she was no longer of in-terest. They were removing themselves, now that a human being had stumbled upon their merrymaking and proved useless. Already most of them had disap-peared into the workings of the hedge. Only two remained, pulling off their skates before scurrying after their comrades.

Uttering a "Hmph!" of disparagement, the girl walked off and left the harmless hedge-lurkers to their own devices.

When she reached home, Jewel moodily folded the shirt of scales and stowed it in the small wooden box Herebeorht had made for her. It was difficult to thrust the morning's encounter with the urisk from her mind, but the busy round of daily activities eventually dispelled her gloom. She was grateful for the tumultuous life at the mill.

That evening as she retired wearily to her couch, recollections of the strange meeting returned with force. For, there on her pillow lay the white jewel, chain and all. Why the urisk had returned it, and how the creature had slipped in and out of the mill unseen, she could not fathom. It was impossible for wights to en-ter the households of humankind without invitation. Perhaps there had been such an invitation decades ago, issued by some previous mill-holder. Or perhaps the creature had thrown the jewel in through the open window. It was a puzzle.

The utter alienness of eldritch immortals was incomprehensible. As Grandfather Earnán would have said, *"Unaccountable are the ways of wights."*

She went to sleep clutching the jewel.

That was not the last she saw of the goat-legged wight. Sometimes, when roaming the orchards of the plateau or the timbered slopes of the storths, she would catch a glimpse of it loitering by an untame stream, or a lonely forest pool; but if she tried to approach, it would simply dissolve into its surroundings, like a wild deer, or a trick of the light. And if she called out, it would no longer be there. Nobody else at High Darioneth ever witnessed the wight, or if they did, they never mentioned the sighting.

Jewel cherished the letter from Earnán, frequently taking it from the wooden box to re-read. In her mind, Earnán was the most dependable, enduring pillar of the familiar past, and she longed to hear his voice, to see his weathered face, to talk for hours with him about her parents, and Eoin, and Eolacha. To be with him again would be to relive the childhood memories that must come flooding back, triggered by the fish-and-vinegar smell of his clothes.

Yet he had stipulated that she must not return to the marsh.

Thwarted, the marsh-daughter brooded. As a dog worries at a bone, she dwelled on the notion of a reunion with her step-grandfather, until at length she formulated a plan. In his letter, Earnán had written: *"My Bones are gettynge old and there is always Work to be done."* Doubtless, he still made the regular seasonal voyage up the Rushy Water to the Fairfield of Cathair Rua. It might be possible to meet with him there, if not at the Winter Fair, then in Spring.

Allusion to the fair evoked memories of childhood trips to market with her parents. In those days she had made the journey several times, for there had been no need to hide herself from public gaze. King Maolmórdha had had no idea that Janus Jaravhor had sired any living heirs. How sweet and secure life had been, back then! On this occasion it would be very different; she must go in secrecy.

Shortly after the commencement of the new year, to Avalloc Stormbringer she took herself, meeting with him this time in the Tower of the Winds, which abutted the Moot Hall on Rowan Green. The building was several stories high, and octagonal in shape, with the names and personifications of the eight winds displayed as sculpted friezes on each wall. A water-clock on a pedestal graced the center of the ground floor, and a few chairs stood beneath the windows. Here Jewel informed the Storm Lord of her decision to make a journey to the royal city of Slievmordhu.

"How do you propose to travel, hmm?" he quizzed, directing a quick but intense look in her direction.

"I shall walk," she said, with as much dignity as she could muster, feeling somewhat foolish all of a sudden.

He did not smile. "It is a long way, my dear child, and not without peril."

"That I know, sir," said she. "Nonetheless"—and her dignity gave way to an expression of such naive vulnerability that the sternest heart must have been moved—"nonetheless, I must see my dear grandfather again."

The Storm Lord deliberated, then gave a quick nod. He rose from his seat and walked to one of the windows. With his back toward Jewel, he gazed out over Rowan Green. She kept silent until he should speak.

"As Master of the Seat and guardian of all who dwell in High Darioneth," he said, "I cannot sanction such a venture."

The girl sprang to her feet with a cry of protest, but he held up his palm in an admonitory gesture. "Do not try my patience, Jewel," he warned. "I have given you my counsel. It is for you to decide how to conduct yourself. I shall not hinder you, but neither shall I indulge in argument. Now pray depart, for I have much business to attend to."

Subdued, Jewel bowed and quietly took her leave. In her heart she stubbornly determined to make the journey whether or not Avalloc gave his approval, and she began to formulate plans.

On the following day he unexpectedly summoned her to his presence again.

"Jewel, I have given further thought to the matter of your proposed expedition to Cathair Rua," he said. "You seem determined to go, and perhaps it is best that you do; otherwise you will be forever restless and dissatisfied. To journey alone and on foot would be foolhardy to the point of absurdity, however, so I suggest that you travel by air. You may make the voyage in one of our sky-balloons."

Jewel gasped at the enormity of this offer. She was dumbfounded—never had she expected such a response.

"Let me elaborate," the Storm Lord went on calmly. "You must be patient, and wait until the next message comes from Cathair Rua with a request for the services of a weathermaster. Then you may accompany whomsoever we send on the mission."

"Gramercie! Gramercie, sir!" cried the marsh-daughter, much astonished and grateful. Then a thought struck her. "But I must go in this month of Jenever, while the Winter Fair is being held, or I shall be forced to wait until Spring. How long will it be until such a request arrives?" she asked, endeavoring to keep the disappointment from her tone.

"Soon," he said. "Soon. Be patient!"

She went to him, and looked up into his face pleadingly. "How can you know it will be soon?"

"I sense weather systems from great distances. I can tell you, my dear Jewel, there are violent windstorms approaching Slievmordhu even as we speak."

At his words, Jewel felt she had been jolted roughly from one dimension into another. She had never guessed the extent and magnitude of a weathermage's empathy with climatic phenomena. What must it be like, to sense the approach of storms—like a dark premonition, perhaps? An inner vision of long walls of cloud rolling across the firmament, their boiling interiors intermittently lit by flashes of lightning? Or like a gentle, thrilling touch that makes the skin turn to gooseflesh? What must it be like, to know the rain as intimately as one's own tears, the wind as certainly as breath, the frost and snow as exquisitely as pain?

As her imagination soared, she was awe-struck. Reading her amazement, the Storm Lord smiled. "Good gracious, child, 'tis no hardship to bear," he said, turning away from the window. "On the contrary, to be deprived of the weathersense would be worse than being blindfolded, or made deaf. Besides, not all among weathermasters can reach as far as I."

"I cannot fathom it, sir, this gift you have," said Jewel.

"But will you do as I bid?" His tone was stern, now.

"Even so." She hung her head. "I will wait."

Placing his finger beneath her chin, he tilted up her head so that she must look into his jade-green eyes, profound behind their hooded lids. "That is well," he said gently. "Be blithe, for the nonce." There was merriment behind his wry smile, and she could not help but match it with a grin.

"It will be necessary, for your own security and for my peace of mind, for me to advise your eventual flight-commander and crew of the truth behind your escape from the south. I must inform them you are the invulnerable scion of Strang. Be assured, all our flight-commanders and crew-folk are trustworthy and will not betray you. Is this acceptable to you?"

"Of course!"

"Now off you go," Avalloc added, drawing away, "for I have tasks to accomplish. And you must tell the Millers what is afoot. Word will be sent to you at the appropriate time. Be prepared!"

Homing pigeons, white as day-old lambs, flew in and out of their lofts on Rowan Green, and circled the skies over High Darioneth. Sometimes carts or coaches or other vehicles would depart along the East Road, heading for distant lands, carrying wicker cages of birds.

It was a brisk afternoon in Jenever when a lad from Rowan Green arrived at the mill to announce that the sky-balloon *Windweapon* would be leaving from the launching place early the very next morning and the Maelstronnar's wishes were that Jewel of the mill should be aboard. A frenzy of activity followed this news. Somehow, amidst the running up and down stairs, the packing, unpacking, and repacking, and the loud offerings of conflicting advice, Jewel made ready for the excursion.

While continuing to conceal the fact that she was the heir of the Sorcerer of Strang, she had informed the Millers that she was going to visit her ageing grandfather in Cathair Rua. The fewer who knew the truth of her identity, the better—not that she did not trust the Millers, but she knew that an innocent slip of the tongue might cost her her freedom.

"My grandfather Earnán is my only living relative," she had told the family, which was true, as far as she knew, for she had no idea whether Jarred's father, Jovan, was still alive, "and I yearn to see him again. The Storm Lord said I may ride in a sky-balloon, but only if there is room, and only if an aerostat is making the voyage anyway, regardless of my request."

Her friends enviously jested that they ought to invent long lost relatives so that they, too, might ride in a sky-balloon. "You have charmed even the Storm Lord, Jewel," they bantered. "You have put some Slievmordhuan spell on him! It is rare that he gives permission for mere passengers to be transported, rarer still for him to allow anyone who is not a weathermaster to flit through the clouds in one of those aircraft."

Many among Jewel's circle began badgering her with demands, entreating her to use any influence she might have with the Maelstronnar to cajole him into letting them, too, travel in sky-balloons. At first, she responded politely, explaining that she held no sway over Avalloc and she was just as surprised as they that he had allowed her this jaunt, but the more she declined the more they pestered her, and the more exasperated she became, until she began snapping at anyone who asked. Hilde Miller, the last person to put the request to her, received the full brunt of Jewel's accumulated vexation.

"Hardly anyone from the plateau has ever been in a sky-balloon," Hilde said enviously. "Try to inveigle a place for me on some flight, won't you, Jewel? To anywhere—I don't care."

"Inveigle it yourself," Jewel cried impatiently, throwing up her hands. "I tell you, I exercise no authority over the Storm Lord!" As soon as she had uttered the words she rued her hotheadedness and wished she could better rein her temper.

Hilde glared. "A fine friend you are," she said, and refused to converse further with the marsh-daughter, even after she had apologized.

At dawn, Jewel rode up the cliff road to Rowan Green in a wain driven by Herebeorht Miller, accompanied by Elfgifu, Blostma, and the unspeaking Hilde. Already, the niveous dome of the inflating envelope could be seen rising tremulously over the steep slate roofs of the Seat houses, glimmering palely against the darkness like a simulacrum of the moon.

On arrival at the launching place, Jewel and her companions were greeted by the sight of a crowd thronging about the wicker gondola suspended beneath the balloon. Light luggage was being loaded on board. Galiene, the eldest daughter of the Storm Lord, hailed Jewel.

"Are you wearing your warmest clothes? 'Tis bitter chill up there," Galiene said, indicating the lightening sky. Around the rim of High Darioneth the mountaintops had disappeared into a layer of vapor. Giant cloud formations billowed and surged overhead, mist-edged for the most part, their borders hard-stenciled with silver-gilt when they churned across the face of the Winter sun.

Jewel, clad in wool and furs, assured her friend she had brought adequate costume. Staring in astonishment at the assembly gathered on the paved apron edged with small-leaved creeping mint, she said, "How many people will be going on this journey?"

"Six of us," said Galiene. "Customarily, only four are dispatched on weather missions, but since you are to take passage, I am to accompany you."

Jewel whooped with joy, and the two girls embraced. Herebeorht stood by with cap in hand, looking sheepishly pleased, while Blostma leaned on his arm and Hilde pouted.

"But why so many onlookers?" Jewel asked Galiene, as Bliant Ymberbaillé courteously took her pack from her and placed it in the basket.

"Since he became a weathermage, this is the first time he has commanded a mission flight. Many are here to wish him well."

"Wish who well?"

"My brother Arran, of course!" It was Galiene's turn to express astonishment. "Having come of age and succeeded in all trials, he is named weathermage."

"Tut!" interjected Elfgifu. "Jewel, has the eternal squeaking of the mill machinery made you deaf to the tidings buzzing throughout High Darioneth?"

"Now that you mention it, I do recall," said Jewel, with as much conviction as she could muster.

"Come!" Galiene grasped her by the arm and guided her around Bliant Ymberbaillé, who stood gazing at *Windweapon*. The young man, his honest face beaming in excitement, exchanged affable nods with the girls as they went by.

Galiene said, "Jewel, you must be introduced to the purser who will be traveling with us. You already know our two crewmen, journeymen Gauvain Cilsundror-SkyCleaver and Engres Aventaur-FluteWind. Looking after sky-balloons is part of the training of prentices and journeymen, as I know only too well!"

Almost fully buoyant, the aerostat was anchored to the ground by four thick cables. Tiny bells, attached along the rim of the basket, tinkled with every subtle vibration that passed through the framework. Their function was to guard against unseelie wights. The enormous satiny envelope shivered and swayed high above, its multiple gores rippling as the interior temperature increased. The source of the heat was a huge sun-crystal, mounted in a cradle directly beneath the balloon's mouth. Cut like an eight-sided pyramid, its triangular facets gleamed and winked like water in moonlight, but in its heart dazzling white-gold rays bristled like a miniature star, and none could look directly into those depths without being blinded, for some quality of the sun was trapped therein.

Before dawn, the aircraft had been brought out of its shed. The gondola had been laid on its side, the envelope spread out on the ground. Once set in place, the crystal was uncovered. Over several weeks of prolonged exposure to sunlight, the mineral had absorbed and stored an extraordinary amount of energy. The flight-commander, in this case Arran Maelstronnar-Stormbringer, caused the heat to be gradually released, flowing out from the crystal's peak. Meanwhile, balloon-stewards held open the sprung steel band at the lower edge of the fireproof skirt clipped to the mouth of the balloon, so that all heat was directed inside the silken envelope.

As the air warmed, *Windweapon* began to inflate. Greater it grew, like a swelling bud, until at last it lifted from the ground, still anchored. Then, with a jingling of bells, the gondola was set upright and the flight-commander climbed inside. The crystal rayed forth more energy and the envelope dilated like a bubble. Slung beneath, the basket strained at its moorings. The spectators were charged with excitement and expectation.

Ryence Darglistel was not amongst the audience, but it was not long before Jewel noticed him striding across Rowan Green, toward the launching place. As he passed the floral window-box of one of the houses he performed an agile leap. With one swoop of his hand he plucked a Winter rose. This he offered to Jewel, when he found her.

"Hmph, I saw you steal that flower," she sniffed, but she accepted it anyway.

"All aboard!" yelled the journeyman Gauvain Cilsundror, as the eastern sky glimmered like a reflection of fire on water, and the sun began to climb the back of Wychwood Storth. Jewel said her last farewells to her friends; then unexpectedly, Ryence scooped her up and lifted her into the gondola. Arran Maelstronnar gave a signal and the moorings were cast off.

The gondola skated a few feet sideways, before *Windweapon* rose straight up.

Jewel watched the land drop away. There was little sensation of lift. It was almost as if the gondola remained static in space, while the perspective of its environment drastically altered. The waving crowd below dwindled to a scatter of tiny upturned faces, like clover in a field. To the left, waterfalls splashed down Wychwood Storth from eyries so lofty they were still high above the balloon.

The damsel's fingers traced the rough texture of the willow basketwork, the swell and dip of the woven canes. The wight-repellent bells were silent, only chiming when the passengers moved about in the cramped gondola. Arran was standing with feet braced apart, hatless even in the frigid upper airs, his hair streaming down his back. He was murmuring soft words that unleashed potency with every syllable. His hands moved in a swift, intricate design as he commanded a rising wind to blow at a certain altitude, in a certain direction. As he scanned the horizon the line of his body was taut, as if his spine were a metal rod, receptive to every nuance of atmosphere. In common with his sister and the crewmen he was wearing garments of weathermaster gray, embellished with the triangular three-runes insignia at the shoulder. Glancing at his profile against the sweeping vista of clouds, the marshgirl was unexpectedly struck by his beauty. It had never before dawned on her how exceedingly handsome was the son of the Maelstronnar. Tall and lithe was he, with dark brown hair that rained across his shoulders and down his back. His eyes were as green as leaves.

In the next instant she forgot her discovery, overtaken by the sheer delight of floating through the welkin.

"How high do we fly?" she said breathlessly to Engres Aventaur, one of the journeyman weathermasters.

"About five hundred feet above Rowan Green, I estimate," was the reply.

Jewel leaned out over the side of the wicker car. *Windweapon* was lifting farther above the clusters of weathermaster houses, the rowans, the pond in the middle of the green, and Wychwood Waterfall; indeed, they had already been left behind. She could barely make out the house of Maelstronnar with its characteristic cupola on the roof. Cloud-shadows raced across the ground. The plateau was spread out like a tablecloth, knotted with orchards like knubbled yarn, and dusted with snow. Buildings scattered thereon resembled odd-shaped salt-cellars and spice pots. Winding roads, lanes, and streams lay as haphazardly as discarded scraps of braid.

The walls of the storths loomed lofty and sheer to either hand, as the sky-balloon glided toward the sharp alpine valley between Wychwood Storth and Wolf's Castle Storth. In the lucent mountain air, every detail stood forth with remarkable clarity: glistening mantles of snow, scree on the lower slopes, and jagged outcrops of rock gorgeously embellished with a patina of hardy lichens, pale aquamarine, green, and tea-rose pink. A spear of sunlight stabbed through a hole in the clouds, and snow-dazzle leaped out to gouge the eye-pits of watchers. It struck glints off the valley stream, and the thin cataracts trailing like metal shavings from the mountainsides.

Windweapon's shadow slid across the terrain below, its outline continually changing as it passed, like some eldritch shape-shifting wight. Arran spoke, moving his strong and graceful hands, and the sun-crystal's eerie fires died down to a smolder. The sky-balloon leveled out at a constant altitude, while the summoned wind strengthened, picking up speed.

Soon the mountain ring was barreling past at an exhilarating rate. Jewel clutched the edge of the gondola and could have shouted aloud for delight, had she not been mindful of propriety in such illustrious company.

"How swiftly we move!" she exclaimed to Galiene.

"There is ever need for haste when a request for our services arrives," replied her friend, drawing her fur-lined cloak closer about her person. "The world's weather changes rapidly, and consequences might be grave if weathermasters are tardy."

A mountain lake winked like a star. Its depths were saturated with cloud-images.

"Up here, one could be uncommonly joyous," said Jewel, "if the future were not disturbing. I am concerned lest the balloon's approach to Cathair Rua be noted by the watchmen on the parapets. As soon as we touch land, folk must come running to behold such a spectacle, and then they shall see me, and ask who I am. If they pry too deep they might learn something of my heritage. This enterprise *must* not attract attention."

Galiene patted her arm reassuringly. "Do you truly think my father has not foreseen and forestalled that possibility? It has been arranged that my brother will set us down at the city's outskirts, in some hidden place. Then he and the crew will take off again, proceeding to the palace grounds in the customary manner, while you and I go on foot. I am not well recognized in Rua. In all honesty, it is not one of my favored destinations. King's Winterbourne is far more to my taste. You and I shall walk to the Fair Field as two ladies on a jaunt to view the wares of the stall-holders."

Her eyes sparkling, Jewel said, " 'Twill be a treat!"

"Mind you, I was put to much inconvenience, in my efforts to dissuade my brother from escorting us," continued the weatherlord's daughter. "With my father, Arran has visited the city often, and his identity is widely known. Anyone accompanying him would certainly become a topic of popular discussion. I had to remind him that I have my weathermastery to arm and shield me, while I understand that you, Jewel, are not without wards of your own."

Jewel smiled, but made no other reply to the damsel's comment. They leaned their elbows on the padded edge of the basket and resumed watching the lands of Tir stream by, far below.

"If truth be known," Galiene continued confidentially, "you are traveling by air only because my brother put in a good word for you. When my father mentioned you wished to journey south, Arran asked him to let you make the trip by sky-balloon."

"Oh!" The marsh-daughter glanced in surprise toward the young man in question, but he was preoccupied with adjusting the vent-lines.

"Be not mistaken," her companion added. "I am glad you are with us. It never crossed my mind to ask my father to grant such a petition, and even if I had thought of it, I would not have done so, because I would never have believed he would consent. But here you are! One cannot always predict how my father will choose to act."

The damsels fell silent, both gazing at the clouds.

Later that morning they crossed the gleaming curves of the Canterbury Water. Jewel could see the stone bridge with its toll-house. The sight brought back memories of crossing the river with her uncle, and a pang of loss went through her.

"Well," said the young Maelstronnar, at Jewel's side, "how do you like flying?"

"Very much." Unaccountably, she felt awkward that he should be standing so close. This was the same Arran she had known for four years, but in his presence an unfamiliar shyness had come over her. Impatient with her own wayward sensibilities, she said loudly, without taking her eyes from the view of land and sky, "Yet I would prefer to fly as a bird does."

"Why?"

"There would be greater freedom. One would not require a sky-balloon, with all its paraphernalia."

"Weathermasters do not *require* sky-balloons."

"In sooth?" Disbelieving, she swung to face him. From such close quarters, the sight of the cleanly contoured structure of his face and the acute, almost savage vitality in his demeanor had the effect of a blow. A single pain knocked hard in her chest. She excused it as merely a symptom of altitude sickness.

"It is possible for tornadoes to provide transportation," Arran said, resting his hand on the edge of the gondola, next to her own.

"How is that possible?" she demanded. "From all the stories I have ever heard, such terrible winds can only destroy."

"Aye, they can slay and destroy if uncontrolled. With the right master, they can serve. Doubtless you have heard other stories—tales of fish, or frogs, or other small creatures raining inexplicably from the skies, over villages or farmland."

"That I have!"

"Those strange showers were engendered by natural tornadoes," said Arran, "unfettered by the bonds of the *brí*. However, the violence of the spinning winds can be concentrated into narrow paths, and—with proficiency and knowledge—directed. They are able to lift up a man and put him down again, miles away, completely unharmed."

"Unharmed but richly entertained!" said Jewel gleefully. "Such a voyage through the air sounds wonderfully stirring. Would that I might travel by tornado!"

" 'Tis stirring, but not without peril," said Arran.

"Peril means nothing to me," replied Jewel.

Arran glanced sharply at her. "Of course. The fact had slipped my mind. My father told us all about you."

For a while they stood without speaking. Avalloc's son was somewhat of a mystery to Jewel, and she wondered, fleetingly, what he thought of the revelation about her sorcerous ancestry. Soon the excitement of being borne aloft swept other thoughts from her mind. The snow-sprinkled landscape flowed past beneath their feet, while all around gray-white ash towers of cloud exploded in slow motion. At their backs, Jewel could hear Galiene chatting to the purser, a hollow-cheeked, middle-aged man with a grizzled beard. The basket rocked slightly as someone shifted position.

Birds darted and soared, in pairs or alone, or in great flocks. The heart of any watcher must have been moved, to behold these flocks; their innocence, their grace and beauty, the miracle of synchronized flight, the matchless aerobatics and extraordinary feats of navigation. Motes of thistledown swam past, pirouetting like toy spinning-tops. Jewel tried to pretend they were dancers, finger-high.

"I wonder whether wights can fly," she mused aloud. "I have never heard tell of any that possess wings."

Having caught this comment, Galiene and the purser joined their conversation. The Maelstronnar's daughter said, "Neither have I, but they *can* fly!"

"If eldritch wights take to the air," elucidated the purser, "they are obliged to use transport, just as we ourselves must do. They employ gramarye to transform twigs, or bundles of grass, or sticks of wood, or even broom-handles. After seating themselves on these strange aircraft they command them to rise into the air, by means of some word or phrase of power."

"Arran has seen them," said Galiene.

"Tell more, prithee!" begged Jewel, overcome by curiosity.

"One eventide, about five Winters ago," said Arran obligingly, "as my father and I flew home in *Northmoth,* returning from a mission in Narngalis, we came low over the Forest of Huntshawe Cross. It is a region of mighty timbers, one of the most ancient forests in Tir, dense and dark, the lair of many bizarre beings. Just after the sun dipped below the western ranges we heard a whirring and a fluttering in the tree-crowns below, as if a bevy of large, winged insects had stirred and was pushing its way through the foliage. We peered over the side of the gondola. There, riding upward out of the forest canopy like"—he cast about for similes—"like a flock of ragged flowers, or bird-skeletons threaded on sticks, was a group of perhaps twenty odd-looking figures mounted on ragwort stems. We made no sound as we watched. The little creatures were no bigger than my hand, and they clung tightly to their weedy steeds with scrawny fingers. Some rode astride, while others were seated 'side-saddle.' Their gauzy garments streamed out in black tatters across the yellow sunset as they directed their odd steeds up and away. Then they were gone, lost to view against the dim backdrop of the forest canopy."

Galiene sighed. "You ought to be a poet, Arran," she said earnestly. "No, I do not mock. You have a way with words. I have always asserted thus."

Again she fell to conversing with the purser. *Windweapon*'s support structure creaked as it shifted subtly in the currents, like the sound of dry branches abrading together, or crows muttering their avian curses. Arran spoke again to the sun-crystal and the color of its internal rays transmuted from apricot to sullen cerise.

"Crystals," said Jewel to regain his attention. "I presumed weathermasters had no power over them. They are, after all, extracts of the Land, not of Air, Water, or Fire."

" 'Tis true we have no mastery over most crystals," he said.

"Over *any* crystals," she insisted pedantically. "Salt, quartz, amethyst, basalt, coal—all are ultimately derived from the ground."

"There exists one kind of crystal," said Arran, "called Ice Seven, that was first created by the master-smith Alfardēne Maelstronnar, long ago."

"That renowned forefather of your house? He who fashioned the sword Fallowblade?"

"The very one. He bore great fragments of ice deep into the heart of Wychwood Storth. Then he rallied all his talent and learning, and put forth his power of the *brí,* calling upon the phenomenally high pressures that can be exerted by air and water. After being subjected to these extreme forces, the miniscule particles of the ice were crammed so closely together that even enormous heat could not prise them apart. Crystals of Ice Seven will not melt, even at temperatures that cause water to boil."

"I am astounded," said Jewel, candidly, "to think there are such toys as ice-crystals one can hold in one's palm without their melting. But what use are they?"

"Of great use and value, because we have mastery over them."

"Is the sun-crystal really ice?"

"No. It is a naturally occurring but rare type of matrix that absorbs heat energy."

"I own a crystal," Jewel said impulsively, drawing the white gem from concealment beneath her bodice. She had worn it once in a while ever since the urisk had so mysteriously returned it.

It glittered like a perfect tear wept by the moon in ages past.

Arran took the jewel in his fingers and examined it. The limit of the neck-chain caused him to lean close, and the damsel felt his breath, sweet as vanilla essence, caressing the side of her face. The sensation, so unanticipated and sensual, caused her to shiver. Apparently the young man failed to notice, for he did not draw back. "Ah yes, the Star from the Iron Tree. 'Tis beautiful," he murmured at length—so near to her that Jewel could feel his warmth against her skin as he spoke. " 'Tis not Ice Seven, but some marvelous mineral treasure from underground."

Beneath her blue-butterfly eyes, Jewel's cheeks were delicately brushed with a carnation tinge. "By my troth! That sun-rock's heat is excessive!" she protested, turning away and replacing the gem in its hiding place.

"Lo!" called Galiene, extending her arm. "I see the line of the Border Hills!"

After setting down for a brief stop in the Border Hills, where they took refreshment and a short stroll to ease their limbs after the cramped conditions of the basket, the company set off once more on their aerial voyage. There was little sensation of forward movement. The air seemed motionless, due to the fact that they were traveling with the wind, equaling its speed. The only sounds were the intermittent creak of the basketwork or the struts of the cradle, a desultory flapping as a gust punched the envelope, the miniature *ching* of a bell, and the occasional muffled sough of heat rising from the crystal, so soft it was almost subliminal.

On occasion, the craft abruptly lost altitude upon encountering a sudden change in air pressure, or unexpectedly shot upward as it crossed into a thermal updraught. These disturbances, however, were minor.

Arran, working a vent-line to release puffs of air from the balloon's crown, apologized to his passengers and crew. "I shall direct my efforts toward avoiding these sources of turbulence. It becomes more difficult, however, as we approach the region of high-speed winds."

"You need not bother to strive for perfection," said his sister Galiene, with a laugh. To Jewel, she said aside, "Flights with *some* pilots are like sledding down the side of a boulder-heap. They hardly bother to make adjustments."

The ground drifted closer.

"βȳřñ, ¥ē £ÿř-§tåɳɛ," said Arran in a low voice, making a rapid, subtle gesture. The crystal blazed up as before, exuding silent, shimmering blasts of energy. The perimeters of the landscape opened out as the aircraft regained altitude. A brief, whimsical gust pummeled the envelope. With another murmured command, the young weathermage directed the rogue current away.

High above the bellying curve of the envelope, fast-moving jet streams were driving the upper-atmosphere clouds toward the east. *Windweapon,* maintained at an altitude that ensured it was affected only by currents closer to the ground, continued its journey southeast.

As the aerostat neared the storm-whipped lands, capricious cross-winds buffeted it more and more frequently. The bells on the sides of the basket rattled their silver tongues in chorus. *Windweapon* passed over forests that raged and seethed like boiling spinach. In the villages, one or two tiny pocket-sized buildings lay open to the sky, their roofs torn off. Beside a river, trees lay on their sides where the winds had hauled them down. Their roots appeared to be reaching out, trying to grasp the clouds.

"We have reached the outskirts of this troublesome southern wind-system," Galiene told Jewel.

Appearing somewhat apprehensive, the purser was grimly hanging on to the rigid cane uprights that held the crystal-cradle in position. His eyes were squeezed shut, two puckered creases in his pallid visage. Jewel pitied the man. He was no weathermaster—besides which, he was as vulnerable as any mortal creature, leaving aside herself. For her part, she expected that if the winds tore open the envelope and they all fell out of the sky, she might merely bounce, or roll unhurt upon the grass. None of her companions would fare so well.

Yet she harbored no doubt that Arran was adept enough at piloting to ensure their safe passage, even through the roughest weather. She watched him as he worked to cheat and deflect the ever-strengthening gusts. It was the first time she had witnessed a weathermaster fully engaged in his profession. Facing south, toward Cathair Rua, he seemed to be hearing sounds she could not catch, seeing sights invisible to her. He uttered the arcane words of weathermastering, the calming phrases, the commands to subside, to weaken, to lie down and rest; and as he did so, he raised his arms like a conductor of a musical band and sketched the ancient, potent signs upon nothingness.

Tranquillity expanded from a center, and the center was him. Like concentric ripples traveling over water, it spread outward. First, *Windweapon* ceased to jump and rock. It floated smoothly and levelly, as if sliding on silk. Next, the surrounding clouds quit their panicky flight, slowing almost to a halt. Then the more distant sky-billows and the vapors at higher levels followed suit.

The chastened winds had fled away to the southeast, where the dark, impenetrable acres of the Tangle bordered Slievmordhu. There, far off, furious masses of steam, as white as a madman's spittle and as livid as strangulation, fumed and ripped themselves inside out, as evidence of the winds' torment. Yet they did no further harm to the lands of men.

Down below, the treetops were no longer being tossed and wrenched and whipped viciously about. Only a light shiver scampered through their leaves, as if unseen entities passed swiftly amongst the topmost boughs. By now the local winds had quieted to mere eddies, but they were still fretful and capricious.

Winter days were short. In the western sky, the sun was already a scarlet stain, its face grazed by horizontal streaks of cupreous cloud and scored by the rusty razors of dying smoke plumes. By now, the city was in view: a jumble of roofs and towers and belfries. This conglomerate of architecture was gradually increasing in size.

During her childhood in the Great Marsh of Slievmordhu, Jewel had twice visited the Summer Fair with her family, and once the Spring Fair. The last trip had been seven years previously, but she still retained clear memories of the terrain around Cathair Rua. Leaning over the side, she could make out the road leading to the marsh, and the line of frozen bulrushes marking the hidden channel of the Rushy Water on the other side of the Fair Field. She peered toward the southwest, but of course the marsh was much too far away to be spied. A thick fog was rising from the Water.

"If we land over there to the west," Jewel said to Arran, waving one hand, "there's a chance we'll escape the eyes of the city watchmen." He nodded acknowledgment.

Nearby cloud enveloped the balloon, and the skyscape began to fade from view. Soon, all that could be seen beyond the basket's rim was a dense, gray wall of insubstantiality. Arran seemed unperturbed, but Jewel began to imagine sudden collisions with unseen towers. Such accidents would be fatal to her friends.

She asked Galiene, "What is happening? How will Arran be able to navigate?"

"Be not afraid," replied Galiene. "Our people can penetrate fog in ways that do not require eyesight. Sensing air pressure, we can calculate our height above land-level with fair accuracy."

Now that the jolting had ceased and *Windweapon* was flying on an even plane, the purser had obviously returned to good spirits. He was a seasoned voyager, and known to be careful about protecting his hide, so Jewel decided to take her cue from him. If he was unconcerned about the lack of visibility, that was enough to encourage her. She thrust aside her apprehension.

The fog closed in, wrapping itself around the aircraft as firmly and imperviously as a wet cloak of fine weave. Arran Maelstronnar reached up and tugged on a vent-cord. High in the crown of the aerostat a small, temporary rift appeared. As there had been scant sensation of the climb into the sky, so there was barely a hint of descent, save for the rarest impression of lightness. No landmarks or horizons were visible to be used as measures of altitude. Thus, it was with surprise that Jewel saw, through the thinning fog, an expanse of grassy ground rushing up toward the gondola. Its pace slowed, and with barely a jolt the aircraft kissed the land, touching down. The buoyant envelope continued to tug restlessly, dragging the jangling basket along the bumpy terrain for several yards. The gondola, nonetheless, remained upright and did not overturn.

Soon *Windweapon* came to rest.

"This is where we must part," Arran said to his sister and Jewel. "If all goes to plan we shall meet again at sunrise tomorrow." He and Gauvain Cilsundror lifted the two damsels over the side of the basket and set them down. The girls would have been mightily hampered by their voluminous gowns and cloaks, had they attempted the feat unaided.

"Fear not for our safety," Galiene said cheerfully to her brother, while crewman Engres Aventaur handed out their bags. "If any man offers us ill, I shall summon such a gust as will sweep him out of his boots and into the nearest tree."

Arran looked skeptical, but, leaning from the gondola, he kissed his sister's brow and bade them both farewell.

As Jewel and her companion shouldered their bags and walked away, the fog began to lift. With it went the balloon. Like layers of gossamer curtains being parted, the vapors melted to translucency, then disappeared.

In front of the two girls loomed Cathair Rua, the Red City. The lofty machicolations and crenelations of the outer walls, and the conglomerate of rooftops and gables, towers and turrets, spires and belfries they enclosed were grilled red and orange by the radiation of the scarred sun. Above all, suspended like an apple of rosy wax, floated a sphere of silk, from beneath which dangled a tiny basket, like a child's plaything.

"This way!" said Jewel, beckoning to Galiene before gathering up her skirts. "This way to the Fair Field!"

Of Bards and Birds

As it sailed over the roofs of Cathair Rua, Windweapon *attracted much attention* from the populace. On the Fair Field, in the streets, on balconies, in courtyards, from windows, folk threw back their heads and flung up their pointing fingers, exclaiming, "The weathermasters are here!" Exuberantly they whipped off their caps and scarves and neckerchiefs, waving them to welcome the voyagers from High Darioneth. They guessed, accurately, that the visitors had soothed the violence of the maddened airs that had been plaguing them for the past two days. "Thanks be to ye, mighty lords!" they shouted gratefully. "All hail! All hail to the weathermasters!"

From an arched window in a lofty tower of the city Sanctorum, the druid Imperius stared stonily at the approaching aircraft. The envelope seemed to glow with a soft incandescence of its own, like a white lamp, opaline against the deep purple of the eastern sky. Without a word he turned and began to descend the spiral stair.

In over the walls of Uabhar's palace floated the sky-balloon, as though sliding effortlessly down an oiled ramp. It swam through a gap in the trees of the ornamental gardens. With the dexterity born of intense training, Arran Maelstronnar used his native *brí* to manipulate the local air streams and pressure zones, causing the vessel to drop gently and neatly into the center of a close-mown area of lawn in the palace grounds. This green rectangle was maintained and kept clear purely for the use of visiting weathermages.

Liveried stewards had been waiting at the perimeter of the balloon-lawn since first the aircraft had been identified through the long spyglasses of the watchmen on the parapets. As the basket touched the ground, they ran forward to secure the trailing ropes cast over the sides by the crew of journeymen.

With ceremony, Arran and the purser were conducted through the grounds, toward the palace. As they progressed, servants and courtiers alike watched them with awe, saluting respectfully. After the weathermasters had passed by, the women who had watched them fanned their faces with their aprons, or their peacock fans—depending on their station—and whispered to one another. So handsome was Arran that most of the ladies at the palace had long since been smitten with love for him. Each time they set eyes on him they loved him afresh. Never had they beheld a more comely youth; oft they secretly named him the noblest of bearing, the most courteous of speech, the handsomest amongst men.

The visitors were ushered into a splendid chamber overlooking the grounds. Soaring stained-glass windows depicted one of the former kings of Sliev-mordhu kneeling at the feet of Ádh, Lord Luck, who rested his benevolent hand on the man's bowed head. The glinting star bound to the brow of the Fate was a real topaz set into the leadwork. Beyond these intricate panes the gigantic dome of the sky-balloon could be seen, slowly collapsing inward as the crewmen deflated it.

Many ornaments decorated the magnificently furnished chamber, all to a common theme. On a sideboard stood the pentacular lucky star of Ádh, made of diamonds and set on a pinnacle. An oak cabinet upheld a cluster of horse-shoes cast in bronze, and a bunch of four-leafed clover fashioned from jade. Pairs of porcelain rabbits' feet dangled from a writing stand.

But by far the most numerous objets d'art were marble figurines of the Fates: the well-favored Lord Ádh exhibiting his charming smile; robust Míchinniúint, Lord Doom, shouldering his double-headed axe while tolling his bell with the other hand; a statuette of the seductress Mi-Ádh, armed with slings and arrows, carrying her black cat. At the feet of the latter an epigraph announced: "In the misfortunes of others we find solace." The scowling crone Cinniúint, with a drop-spindle and a pair of shears, stood in the center of a dish of flowers—these blossoms apparently another attempt to win favor with the obnoxious Lady Destiny, whose engraved motto was:

A man must ever strive to be
The master of his destiny.

The druids interpreted this couplet as meaning that whosoever donated the most generous funds to the Sanctorum could be assured of triumphing over his fate. Atop massive plinths, much-amplified statues of the Fates looked out from the four corners of the chamber. Each figure loomed twice the height of a man.

Uabhar's red-robed seneschal effusively welcomed the Storm Lord's son, and servants plied the young man with refreshments while the purser engaged in parley with the royal treasurer. Tax-levies funded weatherworking, but instead of coin, the weathermasters often preferred to receive their fee in the form of goods delivered to High Darioneth by way of road-wains. The exact measure of the fee depended on the destructive potential of the deflected weather system, and the amount of difficulty involved in mastering it. In the tradition of the marketplace, the purser's task was to inveigle the largest possible sum, while that of the treasurer was to allow a minimum of largesse to escape the royal coffers. The negotiations always took place with strict regard for protocol and the veneers of courtesy, according to diplomatic precepts.

"I congratulate you, sir, on your newly conferred magehood," said the seneschal to Arran. "Indeed, the Four Kingdoms must rejoice, that the Maelstronnar's son is now licensed to govern the winds of Tir."

The young man inclined his head as acknowledgment of the compliment.

"My liege wishes to offer his felicitations in person," continued the seneschal. "He regrets that duty has called him to matters of urgency so that he was unable to greet you upon your arrival, but he has left word that you are to be seated by his right hand at the dinner table this evening."

"I am honored," said Arran formulaically. Privately, he wished himself out of the palace and instead staying at some hostelry in the Red City, but it would appear discourteous to refuse to spend a single night with his hosts. He glanced with distaste at the garish curios arranged all around, glittering harshly, studded with gems in such a cacophony of jarring colors they threatened to induce nausea.

He had visited this chamber many times before, accompanying his father or any of the other weathermages with whom he had studied. The décor had hardly altered since his first visit in boyhood; it remained much as it had been during the reign of King Maolmórdha Ó Maoldúin. After the king's demise his son Uabhar had not bothered to change it in any way. Only a fine layer of dust now sifted over the bric-a-brac, where in earlier days every surface had shone speck-free.

Out of the window, the crown of the deflated sky-balloon finally sank from view. Arran's contemplation switched back to Jewel and his sister. He burned to know what they were doing at that instant. . . .

⁂

Darkness had gathered across the land by the time Jewel and Galiene reached the Fair Field. Clouds lidded the sky. Cathair Rua was wrapped in twilight, the expanse of ground beneath the city's walls illuminated only by innumerable campfires. A brisk breeze was coursing through the grounds, catapulting sparks from the flames, shaking tents, puffing dust and detritus into the air. The wind slapped at the woolen skirts of the two friends as they walked together amongst the campfires. On all sides the stall-holders were packing away their wares. A rough-looking man was leading away a mangy dancing-bear on a chain. The air smacked of smoky spice and roasted meats.

These familiar sights and smells evoked images of childhood for Jewel. She found herself in a ferment of agitation. Reflections danced in her wide-open eyes. "Look, over there is the head of the Rushy Water," she said, tugging at Galiene's sleeve. "You can see the willows lining the bank. My grandfather always set up his stall near the water, with the others of my people. We must direct our steps that way. Come!"

Galiene needed no urging, being infected by the enthusiasm of her companion, although she laughed and said, "Do not hasten so! 'Twill make us careless, and we will likely encounter some mishap in this gloaming!"

A moment after she uttered this gentle rebuke Jewel, in her hurry, stepped on a loose stone and stumbled against a stall-holder's covered wain. A commotion arose from within the parked vehicle, as of multitudinous metallic implements crashing down on top of one another. From the shadows nearby, a man's guttural voice snarled, "Hey, you! What are you about? You've knocked down every knife in my stock!" A face, broad and thick-lipped, was suddenly lapped into sight by lantern-glow.

"My apologies, sir," Jewel said hastily. She and Galiene exchanged guilty glances, then scooped up their skirts and fled into the windy darkness, the stall-holder's curses winging after them like vindictive bats.

Nonetheless, this accident did nothing to dampen Jewel's exhilaration. "We're almost there," she called to Galiene. "I'm sure we shall find him!"

"In that case, go with caution now, and not so precipitately," advised the Maelstronnar's daughter in murmurous tones. "Confine yourself to our plan, or be discovered by every marshman and marshwoman at the fair."

Acknowledging the wisdom of these words, Jewel slowed to a walk. Approaching close beside Galiene, she said in her ear, "There. You see those booths whose canopies are strung with goat-hides and braces of smoked fish? Those are the booths of the marshfolk." By now she was unable to stand still, jiggling with impatience even as they abated their pace further.

Observing a narrow alley between two carts piled high with barrels, Galiene said, "Now you must wait here in this dim aisle, while I go alone to find your grandfather. Remind me—how shall I know him?"

"By his grizzled hair and beard," said Jewel, "and the scar cutting across his left eyebrow, where a fish-hook raked him long ago. He is of middle stature, and his marshman's garb forever exudes the odor of fish and vinegar."

Galiene wrinkled her nose.

"Show him this," said Jewel, pressing the amulet of bone into her friend's palm. "By this token, he shall know I am nigh."

Her companion nodded and went silently forth. Unobtrusively, she flitted past the outskirts of the marshfolk's campsite, scanning all the faces that flickered into view. In this enclave, the stalls were already shuttered and secure. Sheltered from the breeze in the lee of their booths, the marshfolk sat around a large fire, drinking from tankards, conversing, waiting for their supper to cook.

The damsel could spy no man whose description corresponded to that of Earnán. She passed to and fro, advancing from varying angles in order to be certain she had not overlooked him. At last, conscious that repeated passage must invite attention, she gave up and began to return to the shadowy place where Jewel waited. No sooner had Galiene taken ten paces, however, than she came face-to-face with the man she sought. There could be no doubt of it; there was the broad and weathered face, the grizzled beard, the berry-round nose, and the weal distinctly interrupting the hoary eyebrow. Furthermore, to her gratification, he was alone. As he stood back to allow her to pass, she said quickly and softly, "Is your name Earnán Mosswell?"

Startled, he threw her a quizzical look, but said, "Aye."

Relief and gladness enveloped Galiene. "Your granddaughter Jewel is nigh," she said, discreetly displaying the amulet in her open hand. Turning her back toward the camp of the marshfolk, she used her body to shield her actions from their line of sight. The old marshman dithered, as if her news were too much to comprehend. At length, he said huskily, "Who are you?"

"I am a journeywoman weathermaster, a daughter of the Storm Lord himself." Pulling aside her flapping cloak, Galiene showed him the insignia embroidered on her shoulder. "Accompany me. I will lead you to her straightway."

The humble eel-fisher was quite taken aback, greatly awed by the presence of such an eminent personage and baffled by her announcement. Dazedly, he followed the damsel through the dim-lit maze of campsites, tents, booths, stalls, barrows, and animal pens. The breeze whipped their hair across their faces and pulled at their garments. Disturbed air currents, the aftermath of the windstorms, rattled chattels and makeshift edifices. Somewhere, two sheep called out in quavering tones.

When Jewel stepped out of the murk Earnán halted as if he had walked straight into a stone wall. He did not speak, only looked upon this well-dressed young friend of the weathermasters with the expression of a man who, for the first time in his life, beholds some wildly improbable eldritch phenomenon. Disbelief jostled with wonder, confusion, and eventually a dawning gladness.

Jewel, balanced between joy and uncertainty at his reaction, said, *"Seanathair!"* and moved forward. Next moment tears were pouring from the eyes of Earnán, and she ran into his embrace.

Galiene walked a few paces away, allowing them time for reacquaintance without intrusion. She was smiling to herself, pleased to have glimpsed Jewel's happiness at the reunion, delighted to have facilitated it. Presently, from the corner of her eye she saw Jewel reach into her bag and produce one of the gifts she had brought for her step-grandfather. Then a glimmer from overhead attracted Galiene's attention, and she looked up to see the clouds breaking apart. Moonlight shone down, silvering the looming walls and roofs of the Red City, and the towers of the palace.

Within those towers the royal dinner table was ranked with regiments of gold-plated cutlery, whose handles were all stamped with the burning-brand emblem of Slievmordhu. Arran, seated beside the young as-yet-uncrowned king—Uabhar was the senior by a year, having lived for twenty-two Winters—scrutinized the length of the white cloth, arrayed with ostentatious tableware.

At work on the seafood course, the royal carver was panegyrizing the mystique of his art by calling out the names of the cuts as he performed them: "Chine the bream; gobbet the trout!" he declared. "Unmail the crayfish, and as for the crab, tame and mime him, for the crab be a slut to carve and a froward creature! Give honor to the cod's head and shoulders, especially the palate, the sound, and the tongue. Spoon out the jelly parts with goodly temperance, for they be the most succulent!"

In case the carving display was not of sufficient interest to the assembled diners, an expert sand-artist was dribbling his colored sugar powders and tinted marble dust onto plateaux, designing exquisite pictures, which he then covered with transparent panes of glass. On and around his finished creations he placed dough and sugar statuettes, miniature topiaries, urns and fountains, in simulation of a formal garden.

The guests looked on without much curiosity. They included the purser of the weathermasters, the royal seneschal and other officials of the king's household, Uabhar's wife, the Lady Saibh, the Ambassador for High Darioneth in Cathair Rua, and the king's two brothers, as well as three druids from the Sanctorum.

Uabhar was renowned as a clever young man, but Arran had no love for him.

His own estimation of the king-in-waiting was augmented by the opinions of several other weathermasters who were acquainted with the son of Maolmórdha. Uabhar, they opined, was sly and manipulative, self-serving and callos to the extreme. His persistent self-righteous declarations of his own integrity belied—and to Arran's mind *confirmed*—his deceitful nature. He was fond of wearing fur, and kept a private farm on which ermines, minks, and other fur-bearing creatures were confined in cages and eventually slaughtered in agonizing internal ways, so that their pelts would remain unmarked. This, in combination with Uabhar's manner toward his family and his abuse of servants, disgusted the son of the Storm Lord. He could not help but dislike his host intensely, and therefore treated him with the utmost civility, to conceal his distaste. Diplomacy was an obligatory requirement of any weathermage. The unwritten statutes of High Darioneth demanded political harmony with the Four Kingdoms, unless the maintenance of that concord should bring peril upon the weathermasters.

Arran toyed with the food in his dish.

Across the chamber the king's mother reclined upon a couch, dining separately. She was clad all in shades of red: scarlet damask, crimson velvet, carmine silk. At her throat, ears, and fingers burned rubies, garnets, and carnelians. Her fingernails had been painted with cerise enamel. Even her meticulously coiffed hair blushed like fever. There was no relief from the redness save for her papery skin and her eyes, teak-brown, yellow-rimmed. On her feet she wore slippers of sanguine satin, and beside those dainty shoes sat an absurdly short-legged dog on a chain, its collar barnacled with carbuncles, its coat auburn, its selectively bred physique destined to be forever plagued with pains of the backbone. The chain was of reddish gold. The dowager queen was occupied with eating from dishes of the same material, and the food she placed between her poppy-painted lips consisted of strawberries, cherries, plums, and raspberries. From a goblet of rubicund glass she sipped wine the color of blood.

When the carver ceased his chant the old queen's minstrel, Luchóg, struck up on his lyre:

"Tra la la la, oh, merrily we go, yea, merrily we go along.
Tra la la la, we're merry as can be, so merrily we sing our song."

Prince Páid, brother to Uabhar and third in line for the throne, peered over the rim of his drinking vessel. "Luchóg, you are demented," he observed, before upending the goblet and draining it. No one else commented. As the seafood dishes were presented, the lead-panes rattled in the fitful breeze, and Arran glanced up at the window.

At the Fair Field, in the doubtful shelter of the carts Earnán and Jewel were deep in animated conversation, endeavoring, within the space of an hour, to describe all that had happened to them during the past few years. Galiene stood on watch, warning them if anyone approached, so that they might lower their voices to escape attention.

"There is one last question I wish to ask, dear *seanathair*," Jewel said earnestly. "It concerns my mother. How came she beneath that curse of madness, which proved her undoing?"

At Jewel's last parting from her father, Jarred, there had been no time for him to reveal the entire story of her background.

Then the marshman told her all he knew: how, some eighty years before, the beauteous Álainna Machnamh had been abducted by Janus Jaravhor, the Sorcerer of Strang; how the three sons of the House of A'Connacht had sought to rescue her and two had perished in the attempt; how Tierney A'Connacht, the youngest son, delivered Álainna Machnamh from her captor with the aid of Fallowblade, the golden sword, and the two were later wed; how in revenge for this thwarting of his ambition, Janus Jaravhor had set his malediction of madness upon them, and upon all their descendants.

"But," concluded Earnán, "when your father, the heir of Jaravhor, wed your mother, the heir of A'Connacht, the curse was destroyed by the sorcerer's own arts, which conferred immunity on his own lineage."

Jewel remained silent for some while.

"This tale is told among the weathermasters," she said at length. "Yet never before this moment have I fully understood my own connection to it. I am astonished. How curious, that my own history should be *doubly* entangled with that of the great sword Fallowblade. Now I detest that execrable sorcerer more than ever. If I could, I would tear out the part of me that springs from him." She laid her head upon Earnán's shoulder, and for a while he stroked her hair consolingly, as he used to do when she was a little child, while they desultorily discussed the story of the curse and its repercussions. "I wish someone would violate the foul Dome of Strang," Jewel said vehemently, "and seize the hoard the sorcerer hid so cunningly there. It would serve him right, if his precious monument were to be sacked."

"Be at peace," murmured the eel-fisher. "Do not be troubling yourself with notions of revenge. The man is dead. You are alive. Let that be retribution enough."

Jewel brooded awhile. "I have kept safe my father's gift all this time," she said eventually, lifting her head, "although I know full well it has no power as an amulet." Reaching her hand beneath a fold of her raiment, she drew out a hand-ful of spangles on a chain. Somehow, the jewel snagged radiance from the gloom, and multiplied it, and shot it forth in glistering rays.

"Cry mercy, but 'tis a rare and beauteous thing, *a muirnín*!" said Earnán, looking upon it wonderingly. "Valuable, too, no doubt."

A distant commotion started up. By the racket, it sounded as if a saucepan-stall had collapsed, blown over by the wind.

"You should take it," said Jewel, impulsively proffering the stone. "You might sell it, and live well off the proceeds."

The marshman shook his head. "Put it away, *a cailín*. Such a treasure is not for me. I am content enough with my life." He did not qualify *"except that I am lonely,"* but she could see it in his eyes. "Hide away your bauble," he urged again, "lest it attract thieves."

Jewel knew him well enough to take him at his word. It would be useless to press him. Besides, it suddenly occurred to her that the sale of such a rare prize might attract unwelcome attention to the vendor, bringing danger upon Earnán.

As she tucked away the clinquant inside her clothing, a flicker of movement caught her eye. A man in tradesman's garb was slouching down the narrow way between the carts. She was uncertain whether he'd had the opportunity to glimpse the gem. He greeted her grandfather as he went by.

"How now, water-man!"

"Wassail, sand-man," answered Earnán.

The stranger continued on his way.

"I wonder if he saw my father's gift," said Jewel anxiously.

"He did not mention it," replied her grandfather. "In any case, he is quite well known to me. He is a stall-holder, an Ashqalêthan by the name of Feroz Sohrab."

"Is he trustworthy?" Jewel tried to conceal her alarm.

"If high humor and good fellowship are a measure of trustworthiness, then yes, he is so. Ever since our erstwhile camp-neighbors ceased their seasonal visits some four years ago, Feroz and his comrade have made a habit of setting up their stalls next to ours at fair-time. The two of them are exceeding good-natured and jovial, always joking and singing. They have formed friendships with us. And they keep company with Cathal Weaponmonger, who grinds our knives cheaply because of the connection."

"I am relieved to hear of his good reputation," said the girl, glancing down the aisle in the direction the man had vanished. "Why did our camp-neighbors depart?"

"The knowledge is not at me, *a muirnín,*" answered her grandfather. "They simply ceased to appear, with no explanation or farewell. The campsite was empty, so the desert-men filled it."

Uneasily banishing the intruder from her thoughts, Jewel delved inside her bag and produced the other gifts she had brought for Earnán. Together they exclaimed over the gifts and exchanged memories, while Galiene hopped from one foot to the other, her agitation increasing.

At length she rejoined the pair, saying, "Our isolation cannot last. Someone is sure to come this way soon. Make haste! We must depart forthwith!"

"Someone has already come this way," said Jewel. "Did you not see him?"

"I did not!" exclaimed Galiene in astonishment.

"A man walked right by us."

"Well, I saw nothing," said Galiene. "Wait! Mayhap I missed seeing him when I was looking across the field toward some rowdy hubbub that broke out over yonder."

"There you have it," said Earnán. "But think no more on't. 'Tis in the past, now," he added soothingly to Jewel. "Let naught be marring this moment. For I am so glad to see you, *a muirnín,* that my poor heart overflows."

"Mine also!" affirmed Jewel. "Our meeting is both happy and sad together. And now we must say farewell."

They took their leave of one another, with many a fond embrace, before going their separate ways once again. Earnán returned to the campsite of the marshfolk, while Jewel and Galiene went into the city, to spend the night at a reputable inn.

A shadow trailed them, but they were unaware of it.

As they passed through the streets the two damsels could see the lighted windows high in the palace walls, and they played a game of guessing which embrasure might overlook Arran, dining therein.

On the other side of the window the meal, accompanied by the strains of a ballad, was drawing to a close.

"Madam, send that yowler away." Uabhar's words were directed to his mother. Turning his face away from her, he shot a conspiratorial look toward his guests, smiled wearily and shook his head, as if to insinuate that the queen's folly was exorbitant, but as a good son he must endure it.

"Begone, Luchóg," the dowager queen bade her minstrel. Luchóg broke off in the middle of a verse, quickly bowed, and made himself scarce.

"We enjoy the services of a far superior strummer," the king-designate informed his guests, widening his mouth in a benevolent smile. "My lady wife cherishes music, and since our only wish is to please her, we have obtained the best in the land." To the liveried page who stood behind his shoulder, Uabhar said, "Tell the ditty-man to enter forthwith."

The lad ran through a doorway, and returned in the company of a grave fellow clad in the crimson, vermilion, and carmine of the king's household.

"Ho, Master Bard," Uabhar said as the fellow bowed, "you are to entertain us with song." He turned to the young woman at his side. "What's your favorite, my dear?"

Saibh lifted her eyes. Her face was pretty, fine-boned and well shaped, if perhaps rather wan. Her subdued demeanour and pallid countenance might have been due to the fact that she had borne her first child not four weeks earlier, after a difficult lying-in. Frequently she turned her head in the direction of the palace's nursery, where a wet-nurse and a bevy of matrons had charge of the infant prince. "I am unsure, my lord," she said quietly. "Would you prefer to choose?"

Laughing, her husband proclaimed to the gathering, "See what a dutiful wife she is! A paragon! Every day of wedded bliss reminds us of the wisdom of our choice, and our sole aim is to pander to her every whim. Madam, it is for you to choose, not I."

"You are gracious, sir," she said. "May we hear 'The Swan Bride'?"

"A song unknown to me." Uabhar turned to the minstrel. "Your queen has issued her command. Now, play!" He settled back in his chair, folding his arms across his chest.

After performing a second genuflection, the minstrel took up his lute and sang:

> "They linger long, those mellow summer days
>   When o'er the country roads a golden haze
>   Of dust hangs thick, unfanned by breath or breeze,
>   And shadows lengthen, late, between the trees.

> "The muffling dust drifts deep, and dulls the sound
>   Of clopping hooves. A rider, homeward bound
>   Most leisurely along the roadway passes,
>   Between the hedgerows and the powdered grasses.

> "Scarcely a sound disturbs the evening air.
>   Hushed are the footfalls of his weary mare.
>   Gray moths and bats flit, as he draweth near
>   The leafy, wooded banks of Langorse Mere.

> "Then to his ears a lilting laughter chances.
>   The bold young horseman lifts his head and glances,

Beholding that which fills his thought with awe—
Nine graceful damsels dancing on the shore.

"But oh! Such damsels! Ne'er the like was seen
By this brave youth—unless within a dream.
Like flowers their rare beauty, like fine silk
Their hair. He doubts if they're of mortal ilk.

"In silence he dismounts and stealeth nigh,
The dancers all the better to espy,
Then softly gasps, amazed, for he hath found
A gleaming cloak of feathers on the ground.

"This mantle gathers he with eager arms,
Just as the swan-girls rouse, crying alarms
At lurking mortal presence by the lake.
And snatching up their feather-cloaks they take
Their flight into the sunset-painted sky—
All save for one, who can no longer fly."

"Enough!" interrupted Uabhar, clapping his hands so suddenly that his
young wife flinched. "Let the sweet pastries be served and we shall be regaled
with the rest of the jingle anon."

Saibh made as if to speak, but relapsed into silence, then bent down to caress
the ears of a spaniel that sat by her feet. As servants bustled around, the druid
Clementer, who neighbored Arran, leaned toward him and said softly, "She was
a reluctant bride, you know."

"Who?" said Arran, momentarily taken by surprise. "The swan-girl of the
ballad?"

The druid shook his balding head, and in a flash the weathermaster understood.

He nodded. "I comprehend."

"In confidence," continued Clementer, "I tell you this. She was in love with a
youth who had been her companion from childhood, but Uabhar saw her and
desired her for his queen."

"And had she no say in her betrothal?"

"Who shall gainsay a royal decree?" Clementer murmured sadly. "Such
deeds entail harsh penalties."

"Indeed," acknowledged Arran. He pitied the young bride. Her fragile loveliness reminded him, in some way, of Jewel.

In the Fair Field the night-wind threw itself against the covered wain of Cathal Weaponmonger and chivvied uselessly at the iron bolts securing it. Within, the cutlery clattered as fallen blades slid and clashed together. Saffron lantern light painted the faces of two men, their heads close together, conversing in low tones. One of them was the fellow who had hailed Earnán, calling him "water-man." He looked as lean and tough as cured cow-hide, and his shoulders sagged in a habitual stoop. The other was older, middle-aged. Beneath a flared nose his short, black beard covered a heavy jaw and pock-marked slab cheeks. His eyes drooped downward at the outer corners, as though his face were beginning to melt. His thick hair was cropped half an inch from the scalp.

"He will be interested," the bearded man was saying, in a guttural voice. "You have done well, Sohrab."

"Gaspar's ruse worked well, and the timing was perfect. At the exact moment, their watcher looked away, I passed."

Weaponmonger chuckled. "Some saucepan-seller will have a fiend of a job repairing his broken barrow!"

"Our years of watching have at last paid off," murmured the other, grinning like a crab.

"Not so fast. We have nothing in our grasp as yet," returned Cathal Weaponmonger. "But if aught comes of this, you both shall be well rewarded." The lantern-flame reflected twice in the facets of his eyes, and the wordless wind moaned beneath his wagon as if being tortured by the chassis-mechanisms. "Come," he said abruptly. "There is to be a cock-fight under the walls tonight, and I want to be sure and place my bets."

High in the upper levels of the palace, at the royal dinner table, Secundus Clementer was saying to the company at large, "'Tis the task of my assistant, Agnellus, to oversee the keeping of the carrier pigeons at the Sanctorum. He is keen on pigeons, you know. He used to live on an outflung farm owned by the druids, where novices are trained. He looked after the carrier pigeons there, and indeed the birds became a hobby. It was his habit to buy and sell unusually colored ones, breed them, and race them. Agnellus invented a bird-feeder that worked this way: whenever the pigeons pecked a lever, a grain rolled down a chute into their feed-tray. Thus, if a pigeon pecked six times, for example, it received six grains."

Stifled by boredom, Arran made a polite gesture he hoped would be interpreted as interest. Part of his mind was in the palace, another part extended out into the elements. He could sense, in the distance, the last remnants of the violent winds losing their power, writhing ever weaker, like water-eels cast onto dry land, asphyxiating. A third portion of his thought dwelled in the field beyond the city walls.

"Being an enterprising chap," Clementer droned on, "he wished to experiment with avian behavior. He next invented a device that dispensed food when the pigeons pecked first one lever, then another, in sequence. The birds learned quickly, and as time went on Agnellus's feeding devices grew more and more complicated, but the pigeons managed to master most of them eventually."

"Pigeons are pretty birds," Saibh contributed politely.

"Indeed they are, madam," agreed Clementer, bestowing on the queen-in-waiting a seated bow and a warm smile. "When Agnellus was called to serve the Fates at the Sanctorum here in the city," he said, "a new pigeon-keeper took over at the farm. He was erratic in restocking the feeders, and inept at repairing their mechanisms, so that they were forever jamming. Sometimes the pigeons had to peck many times to receive their reward; at other times they must peck only once or not at all. The grains rolled down the chute at random. Whether they would appear or not was entirely unpredictable. The pigeons had no idea what they must do in order to be regularly supplied with food."

"Poor creatures!" exclaimed Saibh.

Her husband grunted, his mouth filled with sweetmeats.

"Then a fascinating thing happened," said the druid.

Privately, Arran hoped he was right.

"The birds began bobbing their heads, pivoting on the spot, dancing, pecking at various things, and, on the whole, acting very strangely."

A flicker of interest illumined Arran's ennui. The Ambassador for High Darioneth, who had been listening attentively, said, "Whyfor?"

"Agnellus theorizes that they were trying to influence the feeding mechanism by their actions," expounded Clementer. "Sometimes the grain popped out for no reason at all, and they must have deduced that the set of actions they had performed in the previous instant caused the grain to appear. Thus, they repeated the actions. When this failed to produce results, they added more behaviors to their repertoires until they were hopping and ducking as if insane."

Several guests laughed.

"Queer rituals indeed," commented Arran.

"What's that you say? Rituals—but of course!" The druid's expression cleared as if he had just thrown back a curtain to reveal, unexpectedly, a wondrous sunrise, or else had at last comprehended the solution to some riddle. "Superstitious behavior!"

"A comic spectacle!" chuckled one of Uabhar's brothers.

"But tedious, you'll admit," Uabhar cut in, having swallowed his food. He laughed abundantly, as if he had made a great joke. "Bard, come hither! Your queen would hear you play again. You are not being paid to stand about, my good fellow!" From under the table there issued a yelp, as Uabhar kicked the spaniel that had wandered too close to his boot. "Finish that ditty you were playing before," the king said, with apparent geniality, to the musician.

Grave-faced, the minstrel obliged, his fingers lightly leaping on the lute-strings. His voice was true and resonant as he launched into the second portion of the ballad of the Swan Bride:

> " 'Give back my cloak!' she begs him piteously,
>   But though it grieves his pounding heart to see
>   Her weeping so, he keeps it from her reach
>   No matter how she pleads and doth beseech.
>
> "Instead, on bended knee he makes his vow.
>   'Oh, fairest swan-maid, this I promise now—
>   I'll honor thee and love thee all my life,
>   Protecting thee. Say thou shalt be my wife!'
>
> " 'Alas!' she moans. 'Alas, alackaday!
>   I only wish that I could fly away
>   To join my sisters, soaring on the wing!
>   I have no wish to wear a wedding ring.'
>
> "But when at length she sees he'll not relent
>   She says, 'You hold my cloak, so I'll consent
>   To be your servant, sir, if not your bride.'
>   And with those words he must be satisfied.
>
> "She serves him well, while morning, noon, and night
>   He woos this beauteous maid, this earthbound wight
>   Until at last, convinced by his addresses,
>   She yields unto his love and acquiesces.
>
> "Their marriage vows are sealèd with a kiss,
>   And then begin three years of wedded bliss.
>   The young man's house with happiness she fills,
>   Until the day she finds her cloak of quills.

"With high delight she wraps it o'er her shoulder
And flies away before the hour is older.
For no amount of mortal love and praise
Can keep a swan-girl from her eldritch ways.

"Beside the casement wide, the young man sits.
Sore grief threatens to drive him from his wits.
As evening draws in and the cold wind sighs,
He cranes his neck to gaze up at the skies.

"He strains his ears to catch a plaintive cry
And tries to glimpse the wild swans passing by.
Sad, lonely, and bereft he weeps in pain
And hopes, fruitlessly, she'll return again,
While knowing, as he yearns, his hopes are hollow.
For where the wild swans go, no man can follow."

As the melody ended and the last notes faded, Saibh smiled wistfully.

"By the Fates, 'tis a wretched, dolorous song," observed Uabhar. As if astounded, he gazed around at his guests, apparently convinced they must agree. "Will you choose a merrier one next time, madam?"

"Surely," his wife replied, calm and demure.

"Alas, I perceive you are weary, my dear," Uabhar said in tones of concern. To all and sundry, he suddenly announced, "Your queen wishes to retire. Her wish is my command; therefore, good night to all."

Without further ceremony he rose to his feet, which was the signal for all those present to do likewise. Watching the king-designate conduct his wife from the dining-room—she evidently still weak from the travails of childbed and walking laboriously—Arran was relieved to have endured to the conclusion of the occasion. He looked forward to the morning, when Jewel and Galiene would rejoin him for the flight back to High Darioneth.

Before sunrise Arran and the purser were aboard the reinflated sky-balloon and away. Like a plum of palest marble, *Windweapon* arose from the palace grounds out of a sea of mist. Summoned by weathermastery from their usual purlieu at the head of the Rushy Water, the coiling vapors enveloped the city's southwest perimeter. The obscurity allowed two figures, exiting early from the city gates, to melt and vanish before they had walked thirty feet from the walls.

Jewel and Galiene glided unerringly through the fog, until they reached the meeting place. The balloon dipped into view out of the haze, they were helped aboard, and soon *Windweapon* was climbing above the weltering mists into a pellucid sky.

As soon as they reached cruising altitude the travelers began to converse, exchanging tidings of all that had eventuated in Slievmordhu. Eager and animated, Jewel told of her happy meeting with Earnán, after which Arran recounted his story of dining with the royal family.

He did not neglect to emphasis the irksomeness of the affair. "Our destined monarch threw out one of the minstrels and had another dragged in. Having done so, he proceeded to cut off this second chap in mid-song, calling for sweet pastries!"

The purser dabbed at his eyes with his handkerchief. "Sain me!" he said, gasping for breath. "I though it not so comical at the time, young master, but the way you relate those events makes them seem surprisingly amusing!"

"And then Secundus Clementer began to expound upon the feeding habits of pigeons," Arran said, warming to his task, encouraged by the mirth of passengers and crew.

"What joy!" exclaimed Galiene. "How I wish we had attended!"

"Pigeons," said Jewel, clasping her hands ardently. "My favorite topic."

They went on in this merry manner for some time, while the balloon bowled across the countryside and the ascending sun threw stripes of gold across the landscape far below. At length Arran said, "We are in danger of drifting off course unless I turn my attention to navigation."

Jewel peered over the side of the basket. "Where are we now?" she asked. "Are those the Border Hills?" Lowering her voice, she whispered to Arran, "Would it matter if we drifted off course a little? Let us veer somewhat to the east, so that we may fly right over the Dome of Strang. What grand entertainment that would be!"

"Jewel," he whispered in return, "you know full well these flights are not for the purpose of sightseeing. If the crew suspected I was deliberately misdirecting this craft they would deeply disapprove. It is not meet for a weathermaster to do thus." After a pause he added, "My father informed us about your family's connection to the Dome. I cannot help but suspect that the real reason you wish to behold the fortress is more serious than mere divertissement, and the notion makes me uneasy."

"Not at all!" Jewel exclaimed dismissively. "Prithee, oblige me just this once!" she begged. "'Twould not be going very much out of our way. I might never have a chance to see the Dome again. Prithee!"

He averted his face, that she might not perceive how much her pleading moved him. And move him it did, to be sure. Every mote of him yearned to please her, to make her face light up with that luminous smile, visions of which were branded as if with hot iron onto his awareness. His mind revolved in turmoil as duty strove against desire, reason against sentiment, a lifetime of disciplined learning against a moment of spontaneous folly.

Unaware of his inner battle, Jewel interpreted his silence as refusal, and beyond his view, her brow darkened. Then he surprised her by saying quietly, "Very well. I shall do as you ask."

It was hard for her to conceal her glee. "Gramercie," she murmured, smiling up at the handsome weathermaster. Through charcoal streaks of her ungovernable hair, her eyes glowed gentian-blue.

The fortress of Strang.

First glimpsed as a dark smudge in the distance, it expanded.

Arran Stormbringer announced coolly to his passengers, "We appear to have deviated somewhat from our course. If you look to starboard you will behold a famous landmark."

As the balloon approached the building, those on board could make out a single massive dome rising out of the center like the humped back of a giant tortoise. Greenish-bronze in color, it was crowned with a matching bell-roofed cupola. Arched windows pierced the white walls beneath. Topped with similar mamelons, innumerable turrets, towers, and lesser halls crowded closely around the main hemisphere. The overall impression was of a clutter of round pillars and rectangular stacks upon which an assortment of upturned bowls had been arranged, all wrought from the same glaucous alloy.

"By all the Fates!" breathed Journeyman Engres. "The edifice does justice to the legends!"

No one else said a word while *Windweapon* cruised past the fortress. They could see a few tents pitched around the boundaries, and a solitary guard moving across the encampment. The watchers were close enough to note that he did not look up. He did not guess that he was spied upon.

Jewel caught herself wondering about the ineffable personage who had caused this stronghold to be raised: her own forefather, Janus Jaravhor, Lord of Strang. Some histories or legends concerning this mage had found their way even to the remote fastnesses of High Darioneth, where they had been passed around the school-ground of Fortune-in-the-Fields. The anecdotes described a man so saturated with hubris he had held himself to be superior to the world, so devoid of moral integrity he had violated every principle of rectitude with no

evidence of remorse, so lacking in sentiment he had seemed more like some unseelie monster or remorseless machine than the child of a human mother. Gifted
with razor-sharp acuity, he had devoted his long life to the study of sorcerous
arts, becoming more powerful in this regard than any mortal man before or
since. Long had he existed, but ultimately, even his most cunning stratagems
could not defeat the internal clock of the vital organism, and he had died. Only
the sealed fortress remained, as his memorial.

When they had left the Dome far behind, the purser broke the silence. "That
was worth the extra time taken on our return journey." He eyed Arran dubi-
ously. "Strange. I have never known you to be thrown off course before, young
master."

Apparently busy directing air currents, Arran offered no response. Away
scudded the balloon, into the broadening day.

Their arrival at High Darioneth was safe and uneventful. Back at the mill,
Jewel recounted her experiences to the family, who were avid to hear of the
flight. Hilde was so thrilled with Jewel's description that she forgave her for not
obtaining an invitation to join the adventure.

The marsh-daughter had imagined that a glimpse of the Dome of Strang
would set her restless mind at ease. She had assumed it would assuage her curiosity and annul her longing to find out what lay within. In fact, the sighting of
the sorcerer's fortress had had the opposite effect. Though she tried to dismiss it
from her mind, her thoughts frequently, inadvertently, returned there.

He who had raised it, her ancestor, had been a hateful tyrant. In sudden
dread, Jewel searched within her own character for evidence of any base inherited traits. It was true that she thought wistfully of power; however, whereas Jaravhor had used force solely for his own personal benefit, she genuinely wished to
help not only herself but others as well. She had once wandered bereft and
lonely, and therefore was drawn in sympathy to others who were destitute. Understanding the heartache of the forsaken, she yearned to heal it. No—she was
utterly different from her detestable forefather, and refused to consider him further, banishing him from her mind. The Dome, on the other hand—it was such
a wondrous mystery; built by sorcery, craved by kings, brimming with marvels,
utterly closed and inscrutable to the entire world.

Almost the entire world.

She seethed with frustration, feeling that so much was within her grasp, yet
ungraspable. Everyday life at High Darioneth went on, and she must endeavor
to subsume her desires.

Unexpectedly, she met the urisk again. She was walking, unaccompanied, to the house of the cobbler when she spied it. The road she traveled narrowed, and ran downhill through a dark grove of overhanging walnut trees. Among the gloomy boles, the wight was seated on the moldering coping of an abandoned well.

Jewel came to a halt.

"Greetings to you, sir," she said hesitantly, always uncertain of this unpredictable creature.

It stared at her, and might have nodded.

After a time she said, "Why won't you let other people see you?"

The wight's lip curled. "I have no love for weathermasters and their hangers-on. In any case, are you not aware that urisks are solitaries?"

"I believed urisks craved human company, yet you will not come to live at the mill."

"Many of your beliefs are mistaken, apparently. Why do you want me to live with you? I attract no good luck, or so the marshfolk always said."

"I like you," she dared. "You bring back memories of my childhood. I know my mother liked you, too."

The wight made no reply.

"Why did you give the jewel back to me?" she asked presently.

"I never took it away in the first place. Merely, I examined it."

Jewel could think of nothing to say.

"I will not accept it," said the wight, standing up on its cloven hooves. "What use would an urisk have for such a bauble?"

"I am sorry if I have offended you."

"You have not offended me." Was it mere fancy or did the wight's lip curl in sardonic amusement, as if to be offended by a mortal damsel was beneath its contempt?

"Well, I am glad."

The urisk hovered ephemerally in the shadows.

"Farewell," it said abruptly.

Unaccountably, it came to Jewel that it was saying goodbye for the last time, and she panicked.

"Don't leave. . . ."

But it had already gone. Her instinct proved correct, for she never saw the shaggy little goat-legged figure again.

That Winter in Cathair Rua, Uabhar Ó Maoldúin was crowned King of Sliev-mordhu, after which a naming-day celebration was held for Kieran, his first-born son. The naming ceremony was a magnificent affair. The royal families and aristocrats of the four kingdoms attended the festivities, along with the Council of Ellenhall and numerous druids from the upper echelons of the sanctorum. In Cathair Rua, a holiday was proclaimed in honor of the new prince. The merrymaking continued until it mingled with the celebrations for the new year, and in Slievmordhu it was said that 3470 had commenced auspiciously.

At High Darioneth the frosts set in. Rime picked out the bare twigs and boughs of the orchards in winking diadems. The health of Branor BlackFrost, Ryence's father, deteriorated drastically. Neither the carlin's skills nor the methods of a druid brought in from King's Winterbourne could prevent his slide toward the gates of death. He lay in his bed, more feeble and gaunt with every passing day, and all despaired of his recovery.

Throughout the deepening and changing of the season, Jewel could not rid herself of the haunting image of the Dome and its fabled treasures. The month of Mars brought her seventeenth birthday, but no decrease in her underlying discontent.

Occasionally she and Ryence Darglistel spent time together. It was clear to all who knew Ryence that he was profoundly affected by his father's impending death. He behaved as if he were trying to distract himself from sorrow; as if he were making a frenzied attempt to immerse himself so thoroughly in lighthearted frolicsomeness that sadness could not reach him. The prospect of having to endure grief terrified Ryence more than any mortal peril. His mad escapades were frequently fun for Jewel. He courted her in an offhand way, while courting others at the same time; she never could tell if he were trying to make her jealous or if his feelings for her were so shallow after all; and although she felt sorry for him she could not trust him enough to allow herself to invest in him anything more virtuous than friendship, fascination, and dislike, in constantly varying proportions.

Briefly, she wondered what truelove meant. Her parents had loved each other, there was nothing so certain; but it was a mystery to Jewel how any average person could sustain such incomprehensible depths of devotion. It was different for her parents—they had obviously been born for each other. In her opinion they were above the rest, an extraordinary couple she held in an affection that was close to reverence. Normal people could hardly be expected to form such a profound romantic alliance. Of course, Jewel had adored her whole family, and would have done anything for them, and she felt great fondness for the Millers and all her friends, but the *other* kind of love was a mystery. She considered it fortunate that she had long since vowed to grief-proof herself by never giving her heart to anyone. Otherwise she might have been disappointed that she could not seem to find it within herself to form an attachment to any of the young bucks about High Darioneth. As long as the companionship of Ryence remained enjoyable, perhaps her lack of high-principled sentiment for him did not matter. In any case, her greatest esteem was reserved for the Maelstronnar and his son.

Come Averil, the tree-clothed slopes of the storths still shone brilliantly with snow-glare, but the first mild southerlies were beginning to penetrate to High Darioneth. Daphne blossoms soaked these breezes with perfume, brave daffodils speared up through the cold soil, and the wattle trees in the wild woodlands of the lower elevations were alight with the play of sunshine on their golden blooms. The Oswaldtwistle Traveling Players came to the high plateau, as was their custom in early Spring. They entered by the East Road, heralded by the warner's cry. The watchmen spied their wagons, after which tidings of their arrival traveled swiftly. By the time the Players entered High Darioneth, passing through the gap between the mountain walls, crowds of children and dogs were running to greet them.

The usual gypsy peddlers trailed in the wake of the theatrical group, their wooden-walled carts gaily painted and adorned with simple carvings. These traders sold luxury items brought from distant regions: soaps, attars, and talcum powders; nougats, spices, and peppercorns; waxed oranges, truffles and rich liqueurs, embroidered clothing, combs of tortoiseshell and ivory, painted tableware of fine ceramic. The peddlers were welcomed by those inhabitants of the high plateau who rarely, if ever, journeyed beyond the ring of storths. This was a time for choosing special items to store away in readiness for future gift-giving.

Greatlawn Common was a twenty-five-acre meadow of frost-hardy grasses lying near the foot of the precipice below Rowan Green. It being a Salt's Day holiday, the Players set up their wooden stage there, and performed their virtual magick. They enthralled their audiences with the gaudiness of their costumes, the audacity of their wit, the astonishing credibility of their scenes of high drama. After the show, people strolled amongst the carts of the peddlers, examining the wares on display.

Scintillatingly clear was the alpine air, the sky feathered with clouds. On the slopes above, snow-covered stands of shining gum, alpine ash, satinwood, and mountain pepper reared like trees from some enchanted dream, pristine white, sparkling with tiny prisms.

Intercepting Jewel as she walked toward the peddlers' wagons, Ryence Darglistel said, "Are you afraid of cemeteries?"

"I am not. Why should I be?"

"Some folk believe the shades of the dead rise up from their graves and wander in such places."

"That is ridiculous," she retorted.

"The cemetery of our plateau is fair to look upon," he said. "Have you seen it?"

"No."

His mouth twitched, as if he repressed a smile, and his eyes expressed a deeper meaning. "Come with me."

From Ellenhall atop the cliff the bell sounded, four descending notes. Against her own better judgment, Jewel followed Ryence to the cemetery.

It was a pleasant spot. Some graves were fenced by knee-high wrought-iron railings; others were bordered by low walls of rock. All were marked by headstones of assorted shapes and sizes, decorated with various carvings, engraved with names and poetry. Flowers grew on the graves: alpine orchids, and frost-hardy boronia. The smooth trunks of satinwood and myrtle beech rose like pillars between the headstones, stretching out their boughs like a living ceiling over the resting-places of the dead. Leaves swayed and dipped. Birds chirruped, between sudden gaps of wind-sighing quietude, and an erratic butterfly dashed madly between patches of sunlight.

"Do you like it?" asked Ryence. "Rarely do folk come here. 'Tis peaceful, is it not?"

Jewel made no reply, for she had discovered she stood between him and a sun-warmed wall of stone. He moved toward her; she stepped back and felt the planed stones jammed hard against her shoulder blades. The young weathermaster leaned his hand against the wall right beside her, his face no more than six inches from her own.

He kissed her, and she considered it pleasant. Then he kissed her again, more ardently, closing in and crushing her against the wall, and all at once she felt stifled, and uncertain whether this was still pleasure or not.

Turning away her face, she said, "What if someone should come by and see us?"

"Do not think about others," he murmured.

"But I would speak of matters—"

"No," he said. "Do not speak. You do not need to speak. If you do, we shall only argue. Think your thoughts and keep them to yourself. I want no conversation from you. Talk would spoil what we have."

"But—"

Placing his hand over her mouth, he smiled tenderly. "Can you not be satisfied that I anticipate your every whim, and you need utter no word?"

After whisking away his hand he quickly kissed her a third time, and his mouth tasted sweet. With delight she again savored their embrace, spontaneously enjoying the moment, not beset by any desire for forethought or questioning, until a hubbub of chirruping and chattering came to their ears. Their privacy invaded, they drew apart as a flock of girls went gliding in the direction of the gypsy fair like colorful birds, all conversing simultaneously, at the tops of their voices. Ryence left off his amatory pursuit and disappeared around a corner of the wall.

Jewel spied Hilde and Elfgifu amongst the passing crowd and joined them as they headed for the gypsy encampment. She was in high spirits as she toured the wagons with her friends, and soon dismissed the encounter with Darglistel from her thoughts. It had, after all, been only one of several that had occurred recently, amusing but trifling. Such dalliances were no more than harmless frivolity.

Having bought several items, she was about to put away her purse when she noticed a gypsy woman staring at her. The woman, perched on the front seat of a wagon, was leathery-skinned, with the furrows of care graven deeply into her face. Her hair, pale gold like wattle-blossom at twilight, was swathed in a dark red head-scarf.

Discomfited by the woman's fixed gaze, Jewel turned to leave, but as she did so the gypsy called out, "Blue-eyes! I sense there is something special about you. Come hither!"

In a quandary, the marshgirl stood still. She was astounded that anyone would call out to her in that manner, but deeply shocked that the woman seemed—against reason—to know secrets about her that she did not wish to be disclosed. If she ran away, would the woman shout betraying comments after her? How much did the gypsy know, and how could she know anything at all?

"What is she talking about?" Hilde hissed in Jewel's ear.

"Likely, she says the same thing to many folk," surmised Elfgifu. "It's a way of bringing people to her wagon so that she can sell more wares."

"I will tell your fortune, Blue-eyes!" the woman called.

In the end, curiosity won the marsh-daughter's inner battle.

"Wait for me," Jewel advised her companions. "I will tell you all about it when I return."

Slowly, she walked to the wagon. The pale-haired woman smilingly helped her up the step, invited her inside, and let down a curtain behind them, screening them from passers-by.

The wagon's interior was dim, and incense-scented. The gypsy seated herself on a rug and motioned for Jewel to follow suit.

"So," said the woman, "you want your fortune told, eh?" Her pale eyes never left Jewel's face. She studied the damsel intently, searchingly.

"How much does it cost?" asked her client, warily.

"Only one copper penny."

Jewel nodded. She thought it a reasonable price—quite cheap, in fact. That is, unless the woman was a fraud. Inwardly Jewel laughed at herself, not truly believing that any mortal creature had the ability to foretell events that had not yet come to pass. As she hesitated, the gypsy said, "I perceive you are invulnerable."

The girl's fingers clenched. She felt stunned. Her ears seemed numb, as if they had been dealt a ringing blow. As serenely as she could manage, she said, "I will give you a silver threepence if you promise to tell no one else anything about what you see in me, or in my future."

"Of course, my dear!" exclaimed the woman. "All that passes within my wagon is confidential."

Jewel swallowed, trying to pacify her thumping heart.

"Give me your hand," the gypsy said. She bent her head over Jewel's extended palm, examining it closely. "I see sickness," she said. "Someone in your life is ill."

In response to her questioning look, Jewel nodded somberly. "Yes. You are right." Branor Blackfrost lay on his deathbed. Blostma's baby had the croup. Mildthrythe Miller was troubled with arthritis.

"And what is this?" the woman continued, conning Jewel's palm once more. "I see a certain shape—is it half an egg, perhaps? Or a bubble sitting on a flat surface?"

Her client squirmed. The woman's accuracy was unnerving. "Are you mortal, ma'am?"

"I am." The gypsy uttered a low, throaty laugh. "However, I am gifted with powers no ordinary mortal possesses. And now I see 'tis no bubble, but the domed roof of a fortress or castle. Indeed, if I am not mistaken, 'tis the Dome of Strang itself!"

Dumbfounded by amazement and trepidation, Jewel could only nod again.

"How strange, that I should see such a place so clearly, written upon your hand," the gypsy said musingly, "for 'tis an abode steeped in legend. Queer things happened there in ages past, so they say. But for the present, wondrous riches lie within, expertly crafted objects of great beauty, and coffers of jewels."

"Guarded by sorcery, so I have heard," said Jewel, faintly, "and by the king's men."

"No longer do Royal Guardsmen keep vigil at the Dome," the gypsy replied. "Have you not heard? King Uabhar has declared it a waste of manpower, since death awaits all who try to unlock it. I see adventure written in these lines upon your hand, and love—"

But Jewel had pulled her hand away. "You say the Dome is no longer guarded?" she exclaimed, endeavoring to conceal her excitement.

"Why yes, child. Have those tidings not yet arrived in this mountain fastness? You appear perturbed—"

"No." Hastily, Jewel returned her hand to the woman's gentle grasp. "I am not perturbed. Why should I be?"

"Perhaps you pictured the treasures of the Dome, and long for them, as many folk do."

"Not I," said Jewel, surprising herself by realizing her denial was close to the truth. "I do not long for wealth. All the fortune I require is right here in my home: friendship, merriment, and good food upon the table." To herself she acknowledged, *It is a fact, I have no desire to acquire wealth in the way most folk envisage it—the accumulation of gold and jewels for their own sake. What I long for is the means to safeguard the life I now live and the people who have shown me kindness, and the wherewithal to rescue others from such persecution and misery as I have endured.*

"Your values are meritorious," said the woman. "I am of one mind with you, although I confess I long to uncover the rare vellum-bound volumes of lore secreted within the Dome, the volumes of healing secrets that might benefit all mortalkind."

She returned to the topic of future romance, but Jewel heard nothing of her words. The notion of the books of healing lore had seized Jewel's awareness, imbuing her with inspiration. When the fortune-telling session was over she paid the woman the silver threepenny coin and departed in a state of disquiet.

After Jewel had gone, a curtain partitioning the rear of the wagon stirred, and was thrust aside. A man stepped out. His beard was the color of sun-bleached straw, and his features bore some resemblance to the woman's. He appeared to be about forty Winters old, but may have been younger than his looks indicated. Spare and gaunt was his frame, testament to a hard life.

"She believed all," the woman said to him. "I am certain of it."

"Perhaps," answered the man.

"I played the part well, did I not?"

"Perhaps," the man repeated. His pastel eyes were unfocused, as though he saw through the woman, as if she were some wraith.

"She resembles her father," his half-sister said wistfully. "Are you certain she can come to no harm from this venture?"

"You said yourself, she is invulnerable."

"To everything save for the weapon that slew *him,*" murmured Fionnuala, "whatever it was. What now?"

"We watch, as ever. We wait and watch," averred Fionnbar Aonarán.

The Oswaldtwistle Traveling Players and the peddlers had set up their encampment along one border of Greatlawn Common; over in the center, a football game was beginning. Rivalen Hagelspildar played the bagpipes while the ball, a large water-filled leather bag, was carried out to a step-ladder set up in the middle of the meadow. Bliant Ymberbaillé climbed up with the ball, then threw it off the top of the ladder, and the battle commenced. It was a catch-as-catch-can roughhouse, played according to very few rules by two teams of unrestricted size. These teams were known as the Upp'ards and the Down'ards and their object was simply to get the ball through the goals at either end of Greatlawn Common, almost half a mile apart. Up and down the pitch the players surged, with the ball moving by means of a succession of fiercely contested shoving matches. The event would finish at sunset, when Avalloc Stormbringer would award the ball, as a trophy, to the team with the most goals.

Jewel searched for the Storm Lord and found him amongst the spectators who traveled up and down on the sidelines, watching the game and cheering for the players.

"Sir, may I speak with you a moment?" she asked.

He walked with her away from the rowdy scene, and they halted beneath the eaves of some leafless oaks. The weathermaster turned his attention to the girl, who, as succinctly as possible, told him the tale of the sorcerer's curse and her family's hereditary madness, as related to her by Earnán. "But all is well now," she concluded, "because the curse is nullified."

Avalloc nodded, studying the damsel closely from beneath his beetling brows. "I see. Yours is an interesting history, to say the least. But there is something else you wish to tell me," he stated.

After taking a deep breath, Jewel launched into her rehearsed speech. "Indeed there is, sir. I ask your approval for an expedition I propose to make. Recently it has been made known to me that the old fortress built by the Sorcerer of Strang, sealed up for several score of years, is no longer under guard. The fortress is said to contain, in addition to precious treasure, many books of healing and other lore. As the sorcerer's sole living descendant, I am the only one who can retrieve them. Should I do so, 'twould benefit not only our people here, but all of mortalkind. I wish to journey to the Dome of Strang as soon as possible."

The Storm Lord did not reply straightaway. Contemplatively, he rubbed his hooked nose.

Then, somewhat acerbically he said, "Dear me. How do you intend to travel, this time, hmm?"

"With a well-provisioned company on horseback. If nobody can be spared from High Darioneth, I shall ask the Millers for the loan of a steed, and go alone."

"My dear child, are you fully aware of the perils that exist in the lands between here and Orielthir?"

"In every respect, sir. All regions may harbor unseelie wights or Marauders, or both. Yet my companions would be armed with steel and weathermastery, and I myself am well protected, don't you agree?"

"No, Jewel," he said sharply, "I do not."

Her eyes blazed with indignation, but she governed her temper, saying querulously, "What can you mean?"

"I mean, you may be invulnerable to fire and water, to rope and edge and all similar scourges of mortalkind, but you are not immune to captivity. Is that not why, in the past, you have desisted from trying this very course?"

"Indeed, but that is a risk no longer. As I have *told* you, the king's soldiers have given up watching the Dome!" Reading the displeasure on Stormbringer's face, Jewel regretted her disrespectful tone.

"Take care, my dear," he warned, "or your reckless ways might bring you grief. I know full well that the Dome is no longer guarded. The news came to our ears at Ellenhall some while ago."

Hanging her head, Jewel said, "Forgive my presumption. But," she subjoined, tilting up her chin again, "I must go. And I hope for your approval."

"That I can never give," Avalloc replied. "I never shall dispatch my people on a foolhardy journey to an unworthy destination. Nothing but wickedness is associated with that place. What do you really know of the supposed secrets of the Dome, hmm? All this talk of treasure and books of lore is only hearsay. The place may well be empty."

"But the sorcerer would not have sealed it if there were nothing inside," she insisted.

"How might you know how the mind of an unscrupulous madman works?" chided Stormbringer. "Come to your senses, dear girl. Instead of longing for that which is out of reach, look around you. Breathe deeply, and cherish the day."

"I *will* go," she said angrily, "whether you approve or not."

His wrath was ferocious but contained, like fire deep within the core of a mountain. "I advise against it," he said abruptly. With that he strode away, returning to the football game.

When his back was turned, Jewel kicked at the oak-roots that gripped the icy ground. "You cannot forbid me," she muttered. "You have no right to govern me; you are not my *father*."

Certain of the efficacy of the protective wards set on her, Jewel made up her mind to follow her desire. That same Salt's Day evening she paid a visit to Herebeorht and Blostma Miller in their apartments, as they sat by the cradle of their infant son, endeavoring to rock him to sleep. The child's frequent coughs were loud and hollow, more like the booming of some marsh-bird than a human utterance. Blostma had set bowls of steaming water near the cradle, to humidify the air.

After Jewel had inquired as to the baby's progress, she told them of her plan, as she had outlined it to the Storm Lord. Entrusting the secret of her identity to the Maelstronnar family had emboldened her, making her more inclined to yield it to others in whom she invested confidence; therefore she laid out her entire history, candidly, before the astonished couple.

"And so," she concluded, "I must ask if you would mind lending me a pony—perhaps Cloverleaf, for he is old and not much use about the place these days."

The infant wailed. Blostma lifted him from the cradle and began walking up and down the room, holding him on her shoulder and crooning softly.

Herebeorht shifted uncomfortably on his stool. "Jewel," he said, without meeting her gaze, "you know there is very little that Blostma and I would not do for you. We love you dearly, and you have done us a service we can never fully repay. However, the Maelstronnar spoke to me and my father at the football game this afternoon. He advised us not to lend you any form of transportation, if you should happen to ask."

Jewel fumed, biting back comments about unfair and heavy-handed intervention.

"Also," said Herebeorht awkwardly, "he told us to inform you that if you go alone despite his advice, it will be your own choice and you must face the consequences. He said, *'Tell her she is not our prisoner here. If she leaves, I will not order pursuit, neither will we rescue her from folly.'*"

Rising to his feet, he gently took from his wife the bundle of blankets within which the ailing child was wrapped. Blostma sat down to rest, while in her place her husband began pacing up and down holding the babe in his arms, humming tunelessly.

The young mother wiped a strand of damp hair from her forehead. Her face was strained and haggard. It was apparent to Jewel that being wedded inflicted this enervating effect on people. In general she did not think highly of marriage, and once had fleetingly wished that Ryence Darglistel would ask for her vow, so that she might refuse him.

Yet, what kind of future did High Darioneth hold in store for her? Trying to guess what the years ahead might bring if she remained there, she visualized only the mill and the orchards, hard work and times of high merriment, perhaps, after all, marriage and children, housekeeping, the passing of decades that would blend into one another, and, in the end, all seem the same. The concept of such a fate sent a frisson of dismay snaking down her spine. She was seized by a sudden urgency to use the days of her life in some mightily consequential manner, instead of frittering them away wastefully in mundane endeavors.

Earnestly, Blostma said to Jewel, "You say it was one of the gypsies who told you the Dome is now unguarded. I wish you would not give custom to those folk. Myself, I have no love for them. If their old overworked nags fall down in the road between the wagon-shafts, too exhausted to go on, the gypsies think nothing of digging a hole and lighting a fire beneath the poor beasts to force them to rise. I have seen it."

Jewel exclaimed in revulsion. "I will not visit the gypsies again, you may be certain!" she said vehemently.

Then, as if to console her visitor for conjuring such images of cruelty, Blostma said gently, "It is well that you are not going away. We are all looking forward to the forthcoming festivals of Spring—Mai Day will be upon us soon, with bonfires and heggin-cake and Bringing in the May. Moreover, with the change in the season, I am certain this dreadful croup will leave our darling. We shall all have jolly times together."

The young woman's innocent earnestness was moving. Jewel loved the Miller family and was unreservedly thankful to them for succoring her. Her desire to please them warred with her compelling hunger to venture forth in search of her inheritance. Irretrievably, her contentment at High Darioneth had been lost in any case; she knew that this restlessness would never allow her a moment's peace, if she did not set forth on this venture. Contrition threatened to swamp Jewel's eyes with tears—the words of her friends could not change her mind, but she felt ashamed that she was about to deceive them.

She spent the following week making preparations for her journey, in secret so as to postpone worrying the Millers and avoid their trying to dissuade her. The secrecy added to her moral discomfort, but did not sway her from her purpose.

Next War's Day night she departed under cover of darkness, leaving behind a note of explanation, gratitude, apology, and farewell. She left High Darioneth as she had first arrived—through the hidden passage of the Southeast Door.

The Dome

*With her, Jewel took her old pack—which was well provisioned with necessities, in-*cluding a map—and a well-worn cloak of waterproof oilcloth, lined with marten-pelts, which could be used as a blanket. At the worst, she knew she could go without food and survive, sustained by air and sunlight, like plants—perhaps nourished by the light of moon and stars as well, and even, perhaps, by rock and soil, although she did not care to try eating them.

The mountain nights were bitingly cold, although she hardly noticed. The warm layers of her clothing were fashioned from fabrics of high quality; trousers of dimity, cross-gartered up to the knee, a woolen petticoat, and a kirtle of frieze—both hemmed at mid-calf rather than at the ankle, to allow greater freedom of movement. Despite the original high quality of the fabrics, age and wear had stained them. They were patched, and ragged as dandelion leaves at the edges. To travel alone dressed in finery invited robbery. To go clad as a beggar would be safer. A capuchon like a confection of overlapping textiles adorned her head, while her feet were shod with stout, laced boots that reached up over the ankle. On a chain beneath her garments the white jewel dangled at her collarbone.

Through the defile she flitted, past the Hot Pool and down steep, meandering trails that were almost invisible, but more familiar to her now because she had sometimes passed that way with her friends, on jaunts and picnics. The air was sharp with a hint of ozone. Far off, thunder growled. As the night thickened, she descended the mountainside, her footsteps guided by a flickering torch in her hand. Its topaz brilliance threw up gigantic shadows on every wall of gneiss, every slope of mossy granite, every outcrop of stacked slates, and illuminated the crowds of tall, straight eucalyptus trees that towered up until lost from view. Darkness hemmed the torch's solitary globe of radiance.

That such a yellow glare flowering in the night must attract attention Jewel understood well. However, she needed the light, for no celestial glimmer penetrated the heavy canopy of cloud on this thunder-brewing night, and the going was not easy. She must tread carefully on the rocky slopes with their thin green skin of dew-beaded mosses, stepping over fallen boughs, avoiding squelchy sphagnum bogs, endeavoring not to slip on the ever-wet rocks, the dripping vegetation, the moist carpets of bark and old leaves. The possibility that she might mis-step and turn her ankle caused her to keep alight the flame. Lameness would heal swiftly, but if she tumbled down some smooth-sided slot or ravine she might remain alone at its nadir for days or weeks before any passer-by heard her calls and came to her rescue. Here on the steep southeastern flanks passers-by were few. The only mortal folk likely to come this way were weathermasters and other inhabitants of High Darioneth. Jewel doubted whether even Marauders would scour these slopes. There was nothing for them here. They could hardly hope to assail High Darioneth successfully, even if they could get in without being seen.

Nonetheless, the scarcity of humankind did not mean a lack of immortalkind. The lone traveler was aware that the outer walls of the mountain ring teemed with eldritch wights. Bogies, trows, and hillmen lurked aboveground, especially during the hours of darkness. The huldre—wights who looked like beauteous damsels except for their long tails, which they endeavored to conceal—played their pipes and tended the water-cattle grazing on the mountain pastures. Underground, various mining wights knocked and rattled in the lodes, while in other caverns spinners whirred their wheels. The mountain tarns were home to lake maidens, or the unseelie fuathan, or waterhorses, or elf-bulls. And there were other things, too grisly to be cataloging in one's head in the middle of the night, alone in the mountains.

One of them coagulated from the shadows in Jewel's path.

The girl jumped backward, burning her arm painlessly with the brand as she steadied herself against an outcrop. In front of her stood a hag whose skin was as wrinkled as a collapsed pig's bladder. It hung from her bony frame like rags. One hand emerged from tattered clothing, gripping the corner of a shawl. That hand, a filthy gray-brown, might have looked almost human except that it seemed fashioned only of bone and sinew, and instead of nails it sprouted talons. The eyes in the wight's head glowed balefully, dull red as the radiation from ancient stars. Long wisps of pallid hair dangled from the crone's chin like a sparse goatee. The entity manifested a hideous grin, revealing that the teeth embedded in its gums were not human, but those of some predatory ruminant.

Closer, thunder rumbled again. The wight extended a skinny claw and beckoned.

Jewel knew she was confronting one of the gwyllion, unseelie organisms that made it their business to accost and misdirect wayfarers by night on alpine paths. She understood, also, that it was imperative to greet such wicked anatomies with politeness, lest they wreak harm.

"Good evening," said Jewel.

The foul creature was nodding and summoning, encouraging her to follow it—doubtless to some ghastly fate, even for one who was invulnerable.

"You are too kind," said Jewel courteously, "but regrettably I cannot accept your invitation, for I have my own path to tread."

The hag bleated. It was not so much a bleat as a noise between a snarl, a bleat, and a shriek. The wight's menacing attitude made clear it did not love to be thwarted.

Aware that the gwyllion were especially susceptible to the effect of cold iron, the girl drew her knife and held it near the resinous torch-flame, so that the blade glittered. Two malignant red eyes glowed more brightly for a moment, then suddenly dimmed as the eldritch hag cringed and shied away. Jewel swung the knife in wide arcs, advancing as she did so. With one last shrill bleat, the wight folded itself back into the night. Jewel heard the sound of small hooves clattering away down the mountainside.

Determinedly she pressed on, thinking to herself that if a single unseelie wight were all she would encounter, Lord Fortune was on her side. Then she laughed softly, for she believed in the Four Fates no more than she believed that the stars were the lamps of Ádh, suspended in the skies.

Always, there was the tinkling of water falling on stone, and the silent fluttering of small brown moths that were drawn to the luminance of the torch. Down amongst the fallen leaves and cushions of moss something small scuttled into view at the edge of Jewel's light-sphere. It was a mouse-like animal with a long, pointed snout and soft, gray-brown, velvety fur. The shrew pounced on a worm, which it devoured juicily. It was about to do the same to an unwary stag-horn beetle when abruptly it fled, squeaking in alarm. The girl assumed it was her own presence that had startled the insectivore, until she noticed the hounds.

Elegant, white dogs, they merely stood, without moving, without looking as if they had approached at all, but had just been called into existence. Their collars of silver were studded with sparkling stones, and glistened in the torchlight.

A voice called through the air:

> "Slender-fay, slender-fay!
> Mountain-traveler, mountain-traveler!
> Black-fairy, black-fairy!
> Lucky-treasure, lucky-treasure!
> Grey-hound, grey-hound!
> Seek-beyond, seek-beyond!"

Then the dogs rushed away and the fanfare of a hunting horn rang through the night. It was followed by a percussion of hoofbeats, and the crying out of numerous riders, and a baying of hounds, and to Jewel it seemed a vast company of uncanny huntsmen swept past, somewhere out in the darkness, unseen. Despite her invulnerability, Jewel felt her nerves creep like caterpillars through her flesh, and wished that day might dawn soon.

Of all the wights that were reputed to infest the high places, those she feared most were goblins. Her fear was unfounded, merely the result of old tales she had heard as a small child, for she knew perfectly well that goblins no longer roamed the mountain ring, or any mountains in the four kingdoms, for that matter. They had all been driven out long ago, and for that she was thankful. Only the memories of their wickedness choked the lightless places. Only echoes of their unspeakable deeds still hung, like shades of moldering spiderwebs, between the dizzying crevasses. Recollecting old stories of horror, Jewel started at the slightest sound, and frequently glanced back over her shoulder.

Still she trudged on, slithering down the dew-slick slopes, scanning for footholds, leaping from rock to rock, grabbing hold of saplings and shrubs to keep her balance, sliding across mats of miniature ferns and slick layers of decaying vegetation. Down, ever down, while behind the low-slung clouds the threatening thunder rolled away to the west, fading. Until at last the landscape began to glimmer, and her torch burned out, but she needed it no longer, for a wash of light came creeping, so blue and dim it might have been glowing from behind a great rampart of amethyst. The first light of the new day. She imagined she heard a cry, faint, so far away and faint that it might have been a trick of her weary mind. It sounded like the crowing of a rooster.

The hours belonging to nocturnal wights were over. As the dawn blossomed,

Jewel lay down beneath a bushy outcrop, rolled herself in her sheet of canvas, and slept.

⁂

Pinches of gray-white cloud, teased out to translucency, fled across an aubergine sky. Breaking through suddenly, sunlight stippled the tops of the surrounding trees with fallow gold. The morning had worn well away by the time Jewel awoke, and the sun was nearing its zenith. She rose to her feet and looked around.

When she had first come this way, five years earlier, she had been too dazed by recent tragedy and loss to take much note of her surroundings. That was why she had strayed into the mountains. Now, her mind unclouded by grief, she scanned the vista before her with eager delight.

To the west a jumble of jagged peaks blocked up the sky, their mighty shoulders mantled with ermine. Vast rivers of cloud streamed from the rifts and valleys, swept diagonally back by an easterly breeze. Southward, the land dropped away, jeweled with misty tarns, begemmed with massive boulders, and spangled with frost hollows where patches of snow yet glistened, pristine. The lower lands of the Canterbury Valley floated in a blue haze, beyond. Dramatic and perilous was the terrain to the east, where the backs of the storths plummeted in sudden precipitous bluffs and chasms. Long cataracts hung there, vertical rivers shattering to splinters as they hurtled down the jagged cliffs. Behind them, to the southeast and barely visible on the far horizon, strode a distant line of mountains: the outflung arm of the Riddlecombe Steeps.

Down through the rugged scenery went Jewel, and the thoughts that chivvied through her mind were many. She puzzled about the Storm Lord's tremendous hatred of Castle Strang. She experienced pangs of loss and guilt, missing the company of her adopted family at the mill. Pictures of the son of Branor Darglistel drifted in and out of her musings. More often, she visualized the countenance of Arran Maelstronnar, his serious gaze alighting upon her, as happened with some frequency. Suddenly she was seized by an impulse to turn back, regretting her departure. *Yet if I turn back,* she thought, *I will be forever haunted by the summons of the Dome. I will go there, eventually. It might as well be now.*

Looming boulders, as high as houses, jutted up from the slopes. Their surfaces were pitted, encrusted with mosses, laminated with a lacework of lichen. Behind them, jagged ranks of frost-white pinnacles pointed to the sky, the hoary heads of the mountains. The air was cold as glass, and tingling with the scent of eucalyptus. Laughing rivulets of ice-melt fell down among the rocks, and sometimes pooled to become flawless mirrors of leaf and stone and sky. Bird-calls echoed from invisible haunts, and with every step, Jewel sensed the presence of watchers. Yet she saw no living creature, save for some black-and-yellow grasshoppers, and a splendid currawong perched on a monolith, its inky feathers sheened with an eerie blue.

After climbing laboriously around a rocky spur she came, unexpectedly, upon a wightish market. The little stalls were set up around one of the few level aprons on the mountainside, walled with lichened granite, arched over with boughs of mountain ash, and dripping with leaves. Vendors and customers alike were clad in green coats and red caps. By their size—they stood about three feet tall—Jewel guessed they were faynes, rather than siofra. This species of seelie wight differed from the diminutive siofra in more than looks and costume—where the latter were prone to be somewhat scatterbrained and shallow, naïve even in their guile, the former were of a more profound nature. Their stalls were prettily decorated with leaves and seed-pods and their wares were probably genuine, unglamoured. A siofran fair, on the other hand, would have been stocked with weevils and slugs, cocoons and the saliva of birds, all disguised as sweetmeats and objects of value.

Still, one could never be certain, with wights.

So suddenly had she stumbled upon the scene, Jewel was unable to withdraw before the faynes noticed her. They began gabbling at her in their queer language, beckoning and smiling. They were not unlovely to look at, and their gestures were so courteous, so enthusiastic, that Jewel could not restrain an answering smile. It appeared they were mightily glad to have a newcomer amongst them, to whom they could peddle their wares. And they were pleased with their market, showing it off to the mortal visitor with obvious pride.

In response to their eager invitations Jewel moved amongst the stalls, looking to right and left, examining the goods on display. Partly she did this because she found the faynes appealing, although in a spine-tingling way. Partly she was obeying her own common sense, which told her it was unwise to displease wights if one had a choice in the matter, whether they were seelie or not. A train of creatures followed her at a respectful distance, chattering and gesticulating to one another.

There were wooden bowls and dishes for sale, and tin mugs, and jugs made of pottery. There were bunches of dried herbs and strange little cheeses manufactured from the milk of some unidentified mammal, tiny pots of honey, and small bolts of woven fabric, dyed with the muted greens and dull reds of vegetation. As she walked, the girl wondered what she must do next. It would be too disappointing for the faynes if she were to depart without having bought anything; besides, it might appear ill-mannered. She had, however, very little coin in her possession, and balked at the idea of bartering with wights; it was said that some were apt to subtract one's hair or voice as payment. Nothing caught her fancy, so in the end she decided it would not matter what she purchased, as long as it was not purportedly edible.

Stopping at a booth selling tinware, Jewel saw a row of tin mugs hanging on hooks. She pointed to one of them.

"How much is the mug?"

The stall-holder, a little man in a coat of grass-green with acorn buttons, doffed his cap and bowed politely. His reply, although unintelligible, was delivered in such a pretty manner that Jewel could not help but be charmed. He unhooked the mug, and showed it to her, turning it around in his small brown hands so that she might admire its asymmetry from every angle. Giving a nod, she accepted the vessel from him, and after rummaging in her pack, she brought out a coin. It happened to be a golden half-crown, worth two shillings and sixpence. Of course the tin vessel could not be worth that much, but the little wight had whipped the money from her palm before she could draw breath to speak, and already he was handing over the change. That the change comprised a heap of dead leaves came as no surprise to Jewel. The tin-seller's expression was earnest and sincere; he did not appear to be making a jest with his customer. Taking her cue from him, she did not laugh but stowed the mug and the dead leaves in her pack with a serious demeanor, curtseyed gravely, and bade the vendors "good morning" before departing. A chorus of high-pitched voices accompanied her, evidently bidding farewell.

There was no point arguing about the change. She could not speak their language, and risked offending them if she objected. Heaving a sigh, she estimated that the mug could not have been worth more than threepence ha'penny. What a waste of two shillings and tuppence ha'penny.

Osweald Miller used to tell the tale of a pixy fair. An old farmer was riding home from market when he came upon this fair, and a glorious sight it was. The pixies were clothed in high fashion; the booths were ostentatious, and the merchandise most magnificent. The man saw, hanging up on one of the booths, a golden drinking-cup filled to the brim with gold pieces. There was enough precious metal in the cup to keep him in comfort for the rest of his days, so, spurring on his horse, he galloped right through the middle of the fair. The wightish crowds scattered, some dropping their bundles in their haste as they scurried from the horse's hooves. The farmer paid them no heed. Leaning from his mount, he scooped the cup from its hook and sped home as fast as his steed would carry him.

Greatly delighted with his acquisition, he took it to bed with him that night, for safe-keeping. However, when he woke in the morning all that he had beside him was a large toadstool, and when he got out of bed he was scamble-footed. His lameness plagued him until the end of his days.

If a golden mug turns into a toadstool, Jewel said to herself as she picked her way downhill, *come next morning, no doubt my new tin mug will have vanished altogether.* Then she laughed. *But it was worth all, to see such an odd and enchanting little fayne-market.*

At nightfall she stopped beside some trees whose damp boles were shelved with crescents of fungus in vibrant reds, oranges, and purples. Before curling up to sleep she placed the mug on a flat rock, and scattered the leaves all around it, resigned to the idea that they would be gone by morning.

She was mistaken.

The sun's early light, a thin shaft that glanced between the rocks and trees, gleamed on a fine silver mug atop the rock. It was surrounded by leaves of real gold. Uttering a cry of astonishment, Jewel gathered these gifts into her hands, and gazed, admiring their luster and workmanship. After a while she raised her head and looked around, fancying she had heard a snatch of laughter, but the slopes appeared as empty as usual, and there was only the fungus on the tree-trunks, glowing fluorescent in the colors of the dawn.

Down through the foothills of the mountain ring she traveled, with the eldritch treasures in her pack. Expansive views opened out at either hand: sharp valleys filled to the brim with lakes of sky; unscalable summits above, dissolved in cloud; lower peaks swimming in oceans of boiling vapor, silvered by sunlight. The land poured away in grand folds, from the heights down to the gorges, and every morning, mist screened the landscape with fine, white silk.

Her environment was as spectacular as it was desolate.

Having reached the Canterbury Valley, Jewel struck out eastward across open, rolling countryside, making for the Mountain Road. This region was sprinkled with low vegetation and dotted with stunted trees, bent-backed, like harps. The wind that had warped them played eerie tunes. Pools and lakes of dark, still water were cradled in the hollows of the land. These were fed by a multitude of narrow streams, bordered with alders and willows. Bitter winds gave way to the milder draughts of late Spring as the traveler made her way into more southerly climes.

Now and then Jewel would turn around and look back, but as she had expected, there was no sign of pursuit. The Storm Lord had not swerved from his advice; she would not be tracked. Alone she had made her choice; alone she must face the ramifications of that decision. At those times when she gazed over her shoulder, she would see the majestic storths rearing against the skies, their heads crowned with cloud, ever more distant. Ethereal mists scarved from their shoulders. Their skirts, sweeping in long swathes to the lowlands, were dappled with moving patterns of light and shade. They seemed, now, so solid and dependable, a fortress of protection against the wide world.

A belt of black-green pines crossed her path ahead, and Jewel stepped forward with renewed determination. As she approached, it became evident that the pines lined a road, fulfilling her expectations. Having encountered the Mountain Road, she headed south along its rutted surface. The road, bordered with banks of early-flowering wood anemones and lesser celandine, passed through the village of Saxlingham Netherby. Here Jewel paused in her journey and, after asking directions, found her way to the local cemetery. Cracked headstones leaned, and rotting wooden stakes marked the final resting places of the poor. The turf was cropped short by tethered goats that were permitted to graze here, to keep weeds at bay.

A weeping woman was kneeling beside a freshly dug plot. Jewel asked her, "Where is the burial place of the man slain at Black Goat, whose body was borne here by weathermasters?"

Without saying a word, the woman raised her arm and pointed to a low mound nearby. Jewel did not wonder at the fact the woman knew instantly to whom she referred. In a small rural village, the interment of the corpse of a stranger slain by wights would have attracted attention.

The weathermasters had treated Eoin's remains with honor. A small headstone marked his couch of clay beneath its emerald coverlet. They had paid the local stonemason to engrave it with his name and the weathermasters' sign for Water, ¥, a blessing.

Tenderly, Jewel placed on the grave her ivory-and-gold bouquet of wild anemones and celandine.

> "May rain fall around you," she whispered, "giving life to all
>   things.
> May rain quench your thirst and rinse you clean,
> Every drop a gift, musical in the giving.
> May rain fall around you."

It was a benediction she had heard chanted among the weathermasters. "Gramercie, my dear protector," she added. "And goodbye."

After a while she departed. Left behind, the flowers glowed richly in a shaft of sunlight, like bullion on the silent grass.

Next day, Jewel crossed the toll-bridge over the Canterbury Water with no difficulty, and pressed on. Traffic was sparse. Few travelers were using the road, but Jewel moved swiftly, and by late afternoon she had caught up with five covered horse-drawn wagons driven by families of nomadic cobblers and traders.

The laden wains trundled slowly, in such lack of haste that the children were able to walk alongside if they wished. The wagoners were returning south, from King's Winterbourne, where they had been bartering their goods for sought-after products of Narngalis: mirrors and glass objects, milled soap and aromatic cedar-wood, fine linen cloth, and wool.

Jewel greeted them cordially. "I am no beggar," she said. "I only wish for companionship. May I join you?"

"Join us and welcome!" the nomads said affably, and, heartily glad, Jewel fell in beside one of the wains. It was driven by a man whose nose appeared to have been smeared sideways across his face. Beside him sat a woman who was comely indeed: smooth-skinned, round of chin and oval of face, with chestnut braids showing from beneath the folds of her head-scarf.

Jewel told them her given name, circumspectly omitting her surname, and they asked why she traveled alone.

"I ran away from home," she replied, knowing it to be true. "I seek my fortune in Slievmordhu." This they understood, and the woman clucked sympathetically.

"Ren away from home mesilf," bellowed the man, "whin I was a led."

Their society proved pleasant. There were two families of Slievmordhuan cobblers who also traded in saddles and other equine tack accessories, and three groups of Grïmnørslanders, led by the man with the smeared nose, who introduced himself as Fridleif Squüdfitcher. Squüdfitcher's children ran and played with the other youngsters, or rode with their parents when they grew tired. The wagons of the west-coasters were as well bedecked with wight-repelling bells and talismans as any vehicle driven by humankind on the roads of Tir. They smelled of hempseed oil, and were littered with the dry fibers of the hempen rope, sacks, coarse fabrics, sailcloth, and packing cloth that was their stock in trade. The garments of the wagon-folk were covered by cloaks known as sclavines, which had wide, elbow-length sleeves, buttons down the front from neck to hem, and an attached hood. Some of the men wore narrow-brimmed hats over their hoods. The headgear of the women consisted of a long scarf serving as both head-kerchief and wimple combined. One end was held to the skull by a wide, leather headband; then the fabric was wound around the head and under the chin before being tucked under the band again and allowed to fall to one side in graceful folds. Their hair, dressed over the ears in the "ram's horn" style, peeped out on both sides of the face. Boy-children went bare-headed or topped with little bell-shaped caps, while their sisters' tresses were confined beneath simple, triangular kerchiefs tied beneath the hair at the nape of the neck.

From her perch up on the leading wagon Squüdfitcher's wife, Heidrun, informed the newcomer in strange accents, "Our hebut is to go from Grumnorsland to Northrilm, then down to Cethair, then across to Eshquelith to trade for sulk, then beck home. The untire journey takes about tin months."

Jewel nodded acknowledgment, coughing in the sprays of dust kicked up by the shaggy hooves of the draft horses. The Grïmnørslander considered herself a good raconteur, and whiled away the hours on the road by recounting her husband's life story, shouting over the rattle of the iron-rimmed wagon-wheels, the jingling of harness bells, and the cries of the children as they called to one another.

"You'll thunk he ez an ugly fillow, eh?" Heidrun yelled, shaping her pretty mouth into a wry grin as she waved her hand in the direction of her husband. "He used to be a fine hendsome led before huz nose was broken in a tevern brawl, five or sux years ago. Thet brawl arose after a dice-game in which he lost iverything he owned, includung a good gray gildung. Lost it all to one of your countrymin. But iver sunce then, he's not touched the dice, nor a drop of drunk. He's taken up the life of a trader, his luck hez returned, and he holds no melice against Slievmordhuan folk."

"I am joyful to hear it," Jewel called back.

An even more unsightly chap poked his head out of the wagon. The lower half of his face, which had collapsed inward, bawled indistinctly, "Good morrow, wench." His lips flapped wetly, like the lobes of a snail.

"Thet's my brother, Heiolf Meckerilnitter," yelled Squüdfitcher's wife cheerily. "He hez no teeth, and uz forced to eat foul goo et ivery meal."

The wagoners were heavily armed. Always, two horsemen were posted on watch, one at the rear and one at the front of the procession. They were prepared, at the first hint of Marauders, to draw the wagons into a circle with the women and children in the middle, while the men made ready to defend them all.

That night Jewel stayed with the wagoners, camped in a field neighboring the fortified hamlet of Kiln Green. As she sat with her companions, around the cooking fires, Jewel learned that of recent times, many traders were hired by wealthy merchants to travel the roads in convoys. The merchants owned the vehicles, the horses, and the merchandise, while the hired men were paid a percentage of the profit. Mercenary traders were beholden to an oath-bound foreman, who supervised every deal to ensure his master was not cheated.

"On the other hend," said Heidrun Squüdfitcher, "we trader femilies own our wegons. We hev sold our meager plots of lend to buy thim, choosing a life on the road. Aye, ut uz dangerous, but 'tuz also more profuteble then the lives we lift behind, and more unteristung by far!"

Two pairs of children were playing a hand-clapping game with each other, chanting as they performed the rhythmic movements:

> "Wind a cradle for a moth,
>   Tight against the Winter's wrath.
>   Spin a thread to make a cloth
>   Lighter than a puff of froth.
>   Needle, needle, stitch a thing
>   Pretty as a beetle's wing.
>   Cradle, cradle, lift me up
>   Till the raindrops fill my cup."

"What a quaint song," Jewel commented. "I have never heard it before."

"They learned thet in Eshquelith," said their mother, "from the sulk merchants."

The youngsters repeated the rhyme over and over, until Jewel was quite tired of it.

In the morning, villagers came to look over the wares of the nomads, and some commerce ensued. Awed, a village child gazed at Heiolf Meckerilnitter as he smacked his elastic lips over a bowl of porridge.

The wagons continued on their way through the rich agricultural regions of southern Narngalis lying between the Canterbury Water and the Border Hills. These gently undulating hills lay in limestone country, and the wagoners passed three deep quarries from which blocks were being hewn. Fumes arose from the tops of nearby brick lime-kilns, tainting the air with the stench of burning lime and coal. Pale gashes on the upper hillsides indicated smaller quarries dug by dry-stone-wallers. Miles of walls partitioned the countryside, clambering up slopes and plunging into vales, tenaciously gripping the contours and transforming into arched bridges when there were streams to be crossed. Two or three solitary laborers could be seen at work maintaining the barriers. With their spines curved like sickles they bent doggedly to their lonely task, fitting the stones together in interlocking patterns that would yield only to years of hard weathering.

The rutted way was lined with avenues of pin oaks, their arms outreaching and beseeching. White, flat-topped flowers and wild herbs hovered amidst the wayside grasses, on stems so fine as to be virtually invisible. Summer had arrived, casting golden nettings of dandelions across far-flung pastures that stretched away to green ridges in the middle distance. Behind the ridges rose the blue-gray shoulders of the Border Hills, row on row of gentle peaks paling from indigo to pastel blue as they receded toward the horizon.

On the following day the road passed between low, wooded spurs, its verges burgeoning with brakes of hazel. Soon it clove through a leafless birch-wood, then wound its way among groves of ash. After diving into a marshy vale of coppiced willows it climbed again, bringing the travelers out into another insignificant hamlet, no more than a collection of half a dozen cottages and an inn.

In a covered yard stacked with piles of birch trimmings, hazel wands, and ashen staves, men were hard at work. Clad in long leather aprons, and with their shirtsleeves rolled up to their elbows, they were making besoms. One sat astride a shaving-horse, working the jaws of the besom-grip to squeeze the birch twigs together while he bound them tightly with willow withies. Another trimmed ash-wood handles with his draw-knife, before ramming them into the birch bundles. A third broom squire hammered wooden retaining pegs through the bundles to strengthen the brooms.

"Thus vullege uz known ez Birchbroom," announced Heidrun Squüdfitcher, who, with her children, was walking at Jewel's side. "Ivery year we pass through, we barter for bissoms from the broom squires. The bist metterials are grown hereabouts, and these squires make the finest brooms un the Four Kungdoms."

Shortly after leaving Birchbroom the road led the wagons into a curious wood. Many hundreds of ash saplings grew here, and all were contorted in a most unnatural fashion. Their slender trunks stood perfectly straight until, about three or four feet from the ground, they bent over abruptly, into the shape of a shepherd's crook. On looking more closely, Jewel perceived that iron templates were strapped to many of the saplings.

"What manner of woodland is this?" she asked, amazed.

"Ut uz a walkung stuck wood!" Heidrun replied promptly, laughing. "They feshion fine walkung stucks in Birchbroom, ez will ez bissoms."

When they emerged from the wood they could see the Border Hills more clearly. Closer now, the rounded heads of the hills rolled across their path, like the frozen troughs and crests of some stormy ocean.

"Strange thungs dwill un those hulls," said Fridleif Squüdfitcher, narrowing his eyes calculatingly as he stared south toward the higher country.

"True enough!" agreed one of the Slievmordhuan traders. "But once past them it's back in Slievmordhu we shall be!" His countrymen cheered, absence from one's home soil being a catalyst to patriotism.

Following the direction of Squüdfitcher's gaze, Jewel felt her heartbeat accelerate. There lay the border. On the other side in Orielthir the Dome of Castle Strang squatted, like some monstrous fungus, her inheritance locked within.

The remainder of their passage through the Border Hills into Slievmordhu was relatively uneventful and they reached, without mishap, the village of Keeling Muir, in the marches of the Orielthir region. It was a large settlement, notable for the manor house on the hill, a sprawling, fortified mansion of stone.

"Here we halt for a seven-night," proclaimed Fridleif Squüdfitcher, handing out almonds to a gaggle of hungry children.

It was the custom of the convoy to spend a few days at some of the more substantial villages along their route. The Slievmordhuans amongst them were skilled cobblers. Their boots, each pair made to measure, would last for ten years of normal daily wear. It took each bootmaker two days of steady work to make one pair, using the high-quality Slievmordhuan leather and precision tools they carried with them. Every year, there would be a need for new footwear in the villages, as children grew, or as old boots reached the last step of their ten-year journey.

Jewel was relieved to learn of the wagoners' sojourn. She had been wondering what excuse she might fabricate, when it came time for her to leave the road and head east across Orielthir. Although she despised duplicity, she could not tell them she sought Castle Strang; the admission would only lead to awkward questions.

"I do not wish to tarry here," she announced to her benefactors. "Fain would I journey on." They protested, but could not sway her. "Ardent am I," she said, "to discover what lies ahead. 'Twould be passing irksome to remain here, when the road and the future beckon me."

"Go then, uff you must," said Heidrun Squüdfitcher, displaying a rueful grimace. "Perchence we shell meet agin, on the road, young jupsy. I hope you find what you seek. May good fortune go wuth you."

"And with you," said Jewel.

She handed her hostess a small cloth package, tightly knotted, and took her leave, in haste, lest they should repeat their arguments against her decision. The faynes' leaves of gold were wrapped inside the bundle, ample payment for the wagoners' hospitality.

Yet, when the wagons had been left far behind and Jewel darted, alone, along a weedy track branching from the road, her thoughts flew back to the campfires, voices murmuring in conversation, laughter, the smell of hay and apples as the horses were fed, the tapping of the cobblers' hammers, the limpid eyes of the children looking up at her as they tugged at her skirts to claim her attention. She missed them already.

But the Dome.

The Dome lay ahead, so close now. She need only continue on her easterly course and she must discover it, at last.

The wind sifted like fine dry sands over the hills of Orielthir. It hunted clouds across the firmament, their shadows, like gray thieves, flitting across the land. Away to the east raced the aerial vapors, and a chevron of charcoal birds passed swiftly above, their discordant squawks grating against the sky.

Tousled by the wind, Jewel sped lightly across a wide, rolling meadow, down a narrow footpath that ran through a Summer-verdant oak wood, and over a bridge into a wood of rowans where rain-pools lay on their backs like silvered looking glasses, framed by the roots of the trees. Her spirits were buoyed by her proximity to her goal, and she scarcely felt the need for rest. On the other side of the rowan wood rose a green hill, beyond which a sweeping vale fell away down to a river. Two stately houses faced each other across the valley. Their windows and chimneys were many, and so elegant was their architecture that Jewel felt impelled to pause and gape. The nearer mansion was old, and appeared to have been abandoned for many years. Crooked arms of ivy molested the mullioned windows and throttled the graceful turrets. Starlings and swallows had crammed nests beneath the eaves. The other house was too far away for Jewel to make out any details. Birds spiraled around its upper roofs, but there was no other sign of activity and she concluded that it, too, must be vacant of human life.

These vast tracts of meadowland and forest were seemingly uninhabited. No mortal dared dwell in that region, not anymore. This was Orielthir, whose lands were beloved by the sky, kissed and held close by the heavens, land of wide meadows and mighty forests and swift-flowing waters, a landscape haunted by countless eldritch wights, and perhaps by the lingering echoes of ancient human-wrought spells. At nights Jewel slept uneasily. Sometimes she would waken to glimpse a slitted glint of eyes, to feel fingers pinching her flesh or tweaking at her hair, to hear laughter, footsteps, insane bursts of music, or agonized sobbing that broke off into abrupt and total silence.

As she traveled, the season ripened.

Through these rolling pasturelands little streams meandered, and broader rivers. Wild deer grazed, knee-deep in the gold-dust powderings of dandelions. Gusts of white butterflies arose, and leaves spiraled down, colored peppermint and rust. Great, outspread oaks stood in pools of their own shadows, while willows lowered their fine, dragonfly-threaded draperies along the edges of the watercourses. Distant valleys were gauzed in softest, palest gray-blue. The air was an elixir, a tonic, each draft dizzying with its vitality. Jewel waded across narrow streams but had to swim across those that were wider. Sometimes there were bridges in various states of repair.

Jewel reckoned it must have been at least ten nights since she had left the wagoners at Keeling Muir when she crossed the stepping-stones of a shallow, fast-flowing brook and climbed a slope topped by a fence of living pines. As tall as towers were they, and so ancient that their boughs seemed to reach into the past. Dense and black-green was their needle-foliage combing the wind, and sweet-scented with resin. This soughing palisade stretched for many miles in either direction, and Jewel knew she had come at last to the borders of the domain of Strang. Quietly, despite her foment of excitement, she slipped through.

On she went in the direction of Castle Strang, despite being unsure how to reach that fortress. No visible road or track opened before her, and although she scanned the acres of meadowlands and forests she could discern no sign of any edifice. She passed the rotted and tumbled remnants of a wooden fence, perhaps once a barrier around a stock-yard. The crumbling timbers were overhung by venerable chestnut trees, some missing fallen boughs. Their roots were deeply buried in a thick litter of leaves and rotting chestnuts. Farther on, she passed a sycamore coppice, beyond which the hillsides were delicately terraced with the faded engravings of old sheep-tracks. As the day wore away she came to a shadowy oak wood as antique as any feature of that landscape, its floor littered with layers of decomposing acorns and leaves.

The afternoon was waning. Billows of alabaster cloud reared like monuments in the sky. Streaking through gaps between them, the lengthening sunrays were mellowing from palest gold to opulent amber. Jewel climbed up the slope of a grassy ridge. At the summit, she halted and looked down. Her gorge rose, as if she had taken a blow to the solar plexus, and she felt almost nauseous with excitement.

There below her on the other side of the valley stood the massive bulwarks of Castle Strang. The marsh-daughter had been unsure how to reach it, but perhaps that sorcerously built compound had its own way of being found.

Jewel could not know it but the stronghold remained much as it had appeared to her forefather Tierney A'Connacht, when he had first set eyes on it, more than eighty years earlier. A bulky dome, greenish-bronze in color, loomed out of the core. At its apex crouched a domed cupola. Countless round turrets, square towers, and minor structures crammed against its lime-washed walls, all with their hemispherical caps, looking like a rank infestation of toadstools. Fired by the florid tints of sunset, the pallid walls and metallic roofs burned, flamingo-pink in the light, hyacinth-purple in the shadow, like some fantastic confection. There were no signs of anyone guarding the fortress. Would it slay her, as it was said to slay all those who approached? By what method would it do so? She tried to recall all she had heard of the deaths of trespassers at the Dome. As soon as they touched a lock or tried to scale a wall or pass some invisible perimeter they had been struck down, but whether by lightning or some other agency none could say. The tops of the walls were lethal. Entrances were lethal. Men had been let down from enormous kites, on swinging ladders, but had perished before reaching the ground. The thought struck her—she could not know for certain whether she alone was able to open the Dome; what if it had been a false assumption in the first place? Nonetheless, Jewel took courage; nothing could harm her, except mistletoe, and maybe old age. Yet even of mistletoe she was uncertain. Unknowingly she had touched sprigs of the plant, handled its twigs and leaves, once toward Midwinter, when she and Elfgifu and Hilde had been visiting a lowland village and gone gathering greenery for decorations. Holding it had wrought no injury upon Jewel. Later she had found out what it was she had plucked and carried, and marveled that she remained hale.

There were double gates in the outer wall.

It was tempting to approach those gates, but the time of darkness was nigh and it would be folly to endanger one's existence in the gloaming. Besides, it was possible that the castle's invisible barriers were incapable of keeping out eldritch wights. Dunters were wont to inhabit the deserted buildings of men, and other species might have been attracted by any remnants of enchantment lingering in the stones, such as the very sorcery that locked out mortalkind.

If wights bided here, they would be most active at night. Better to risk one's safety in the morning, Jewel decided. She retreated down the ridge and found a scattering of elms, providing shelter from the wind. After a frugal supper subtracted from her waggoners' rations, she folded herself in comforting wrappings and lay down to sleep.

In the brazen light of morning the fortress still existed, as did the entrance in the outer wall. The night had been still, without a puff or eddy, but the dawn brought with it a rising wind and a wall of cloud riding in from the west that boded rain.

Jewel paid scant attention to the weather. After scanning the landscape a second time to make certain that no guards were posted anywhere nigh, she approached the gates, moving slowly, as in a dream. No fear churned through her mind—only exhilaration and avid curiosity. The bleached bones of doomed men lay scattered along the base of the castle wall—their comrades must have been too terrified to retrieve their remains—but, intent on her quest, the damsel scarcely noticed. Fleetingly she recalled again the tale about Tierney A'Connacht and his brothers, of how they had spoken to the sorcerer's servants and been told to circumnavigate the fortress three times, bidding the gate to open. They, however, had not been descendants of Jaravhor's line.

The gates were securely fastened. Marvelously the key remained, massive and ornate, its bit resting in the core of the lock. The knopped shank and scalloped handle protruded, the iron dully refusing to reflect early glints of sunlight. Jewel extended her hand toward the thing. Yet, at the final instant she drew back. To summon courage, she clutched at the gem dangling at her throat. Inhaling deeply, closing her eyes, whispering an entreaty to natural providence, she grasped the key. The contours and ridges pressed cool and hard between her fingers. Without opening her eyes she twisted the instrument. Deep within the lock a tumbler rotated. Pins slid into motion. Emitting a *click,* the gate opened, and the intruder stepped within.

Euphoria fountained in her veins. Joyous incredulity buoyed her, and she was hard put not to crow with exuberance. She had survived, while breaching the fortress. Her heart pounded rapidly, keeping tempo with the silent ovation racketing through her mind.

The courtyard that opened in front of her was spacious, and utterly deserted.

Again, had she known, this was close to the way her forefather Tierney A'-Connacht had first beheld it. No grooms, stable-boys, or equerries busied themselves about the stables. No pages, drudges, or footmen crossed the area on their errands. No scullery-maids filled their pails at the well. Thistles and tough grasses infested the crevices between the flagstones, and the fibrous remains of some aged birds' nests were scattered about. Atop a squat belltower, a petrified clock, its dial marked with eleven intervals, overlooked the scene. Here and there, chalky glimmers indicated fragments of disarticulated skeletons, the remains of some who had tried to enter without leave—and without leaving.

A sense of enchantment permeated the Dome's close. Even the air seemed petrified, at first, until a cold gust swept down over the outer wall, and raised spirals of withered leaves in a lunatic dance. Undaunted, seething with excitement, awe, and expectation, Jewel crossed the leaf-strewn flagstones and ascended a broad, shallow stairway. Two wide and lofty doors of brass-studded oak stood at the top. An insignia of two crossed axes was nailed in the middle of each. At their feet, the stairs were stained with a great splash of old blood, now as black as char. The doors were shut, but once again a key remained in the lock, and the girl broached this portal without trouble. Still grasping the white gem, she passed between the doors and into a hall so vast it could have encompassed a thicket of trees. From here a grander staircase led to a second pair of majestic doors, also easily opened. Beyond them stretched a vast refectory, in whose center stood a long table surrounded by tall-backed, vacant chairs.

The table was bare.

More than merely void and vacant was this chamber; the few furnishings that remained appeared to have been plundered. Grooves and small craters in the wood of table and chairs indicated places where costly inlays and gems might once have nestled.

Every room through which the intruder passed seemed to extend the entire length and height of the interior of a hill, and each one, so far, had been empty of living creatures. There was, however, no evidence of the wealth Jewel had expected in a structure so magnificent in proportion and design. The inner doors, the locks all yielding to their keys as she turned them, were embellished with neither gold nor silver. The fluted pillars supporting the ceilings loomed as tall as forest giants, but their stonework was unadorned. From the center of every ceiling, where the principal arches met, there hung ragged skeins of iron links. Marvelous chandeliers might once have been suspended therefrom, before being ripped from their chains. The castle did not merely *lack* precious ornament—it had apparently been *deprived* of any. Pedestals stood, surmounted by an absence of statuary. The gilt had been painstakingly peeled from painted murals; curtain rods had been robbed of their draperies; the floors were bereft of coverings, the walls innocent of tapestries or weapons; mantels deserted. In one corner, as if forgotten, stood an old brass beam balance; in another, covered with dust, an ancient and worm-eaten rocking chair. Yet, as far as Jewel could see, not a diamond glittered; not a gem flashed. Where were the famed valuables concealed?

The old weathermaster tale of Fallowblade and the rescue of Álainna Machnamh kept haunting the intruder. She wondered which was the chamber in which A'Connacht had at last found his sweetheart, and she tried to picture the three of them together—sorcerer and young lovers, all of them her ancestors.

As she wandered along a wide corridor it came to Jewel that something was following her. Swiftly she swung around, but nothing could be seen. Only the deserted passageway stretched behind her; only her own footprints marked the fine particles of dust layered like sheerest gossamer across the floor, and translucent beams of sunlight leaned in from the windows, swimming with dust motes and desiccated moths' wings, as if mists and the ghosts of insects were captured in cylinders of clearest glass. No figure tracked her with muted footsteps; no shadow slipped furtively into darker shadows.

She recalled then, belatedly, the sound of the front gate swinging at her back as she crossed the courtyard, and furtive sounds like the scratchings of mice, or the settling of sediments, occurring behind her as she moved from chamber to chamber. Suffused by her initial excitement she had ignored these signs, dismissing them as phenomena invoked by the freshening wind, or by rodents scuttling frantically in the walls. In hindsight, however, inspired by spontaneous fear, she recalled them clearly.

The certainty overwhelmed her that some unknown entity pursued her, and was about to appear from around some corner. Hastily she darted into the nearest hiding place, a wall recess half-concealed by a pilaster. She swallowed her fright, which turned into a stone, jumping and banging against her ribs. Holding her breath, she waited for the presence to rush by, searching, with a soft rustling of robes and the rhythmic susurrus of deliberately muffled footfalls.

But nothing went past.

'Tis a mere invention of my wayward imagination, she told herself. *My shrieking mind is playing tricks on me.*

After a while she gathered the courage to move again.

The chambers of Strang brooded, eerie but not entirely silent, for the wind caused unknown objects to rattle and knock in adjacent chambers and in distant places. The galleries were vacant, the stairwells and corridors and concave ceilings haunted by unquiet echoes. Yet the sparse furniture—a chair here, a table there, a dilapidated cuckoo-clock on a wall—was as austerely pleasing to the eye as the architecture.

Nonetheless Jewel was unable to shake off the sense of clandestine pursuit, until, after heaving open a door wide and high enough to admit a house on wheels, she was confronted with a spectacle so stupefying it drove off her anxieties.

She had reached the cavity of the main dome.

This barrel-vaulted interior, as vast as the gnawed-out hub of a mountain, was crowded with mechanical contraptions so remarkable, so utterly astonishing, as to defy description. The most extraordinary aspect of these engines was their sheer scale, which was so grand they seemed no less than the toys of giants. Recalling her studies at the schoolhouse in High Darioneth, Jewel guessed the names of several. They included an aeoliphile of copper, an abacus, a trebuchet or siege engine—the firing arm mounted on trestles as lofty as ancient forests— a telescope so huge it might scratch the stars, a tellurion, for demonstrating how the rotation and revolution of the world precipitates day and night, and the changing of the seasons, and a lofty waterglass, or clepsydra, a device for measuring time by recording the controlled flow of water through a small aperture. No water flowed here, however. All this apparatus was constructed of base metals such as iron, copper, brass, and some greenish-bronze alloy, everything stained, corroded, and tarnished with age. There was no precious metal. Alchemists or astrologers might have considered this a slowly decaying storehouse of wealth, but Jewel held no such opinion.

If this mass of machinery were ever to be set in motion this hollow place would be filled with feverish activity; the revolution of massive arms, the rotation of wheels, the arcing of pendula, and the constant transference of energies from point to point, like nerve impulses flashing through a cerebral system. For any onlooker, it would be like standing within a living brain housed in the dome of an improbable skull.

Central to this mechanical conglomeration, serpent-thin cylinders of copper soared up from the floor to the apogee of the Dome. Jewel ventured in amongst the monumental machinery, daring to touch her fingertips to a surface, here and there. All were cold, unyielding, save for the copper pipes running up through the Dome's axis. From them seemed to emanate a dim thrumming.

Quickly, Jewel snatched her hand back. The sensation had been not unlike that of a pulse, but without the rhythm of a beating heart. It was as if, deep amidst all these long-dead, silent behemoths, something was still functioning. The thought made her feel queasy.

Even as she hastened back to the door, the air of this vault thickened with darkness. Some potent shadow had passed across the face of the sun. Conceivably, the rainclouds blowing in from the west had arrived, and were racing across the skies above Castle Strang.

Many other contrivances met the eye of the intruder, and for these, despite mental gropings, she could find no name. Some were a snarl of springs and cogs, others a chaos of tubing, wires, and levers. Jewel could only surmise that they were not so much the tools of science as machines of torment.

Gravely disquieted, she hurried from that place. She ran down several flights of stairs and through a postern that gave onto a small, inner courtyard. Overhead the sky lowered, heavy with cloud-rack. The wind had risen to a stiff breeze that eddied in corners and dashed handfuls of withered leaves into the air. Dressed stones littered the ground, amongst thin copper pipes and rusted tools such as a stonemason might employ, all overgrown with weeds and interlaced by tangles of withered grass. A squat, square tower occupied the yard's center. Oddly, it appeared to possess no door or access of any kind, except for some windows set high up in the masonry.

"This is some secure exchequer," whispered Jewel in sudden delight. "The greatest treasure must be here!"

Without wasting another moment, she picked up a discarded length of piping and began thumping and prying at the stonework near the base. It seemed the only method by which she might penetrate the tower—the windows were too high to reach, and too narrow to allow ingress, and besides, the masonry was faulty and easy to disintegrate. The stones had been carelessly laid, and the ill-mixed mortar between them was crumbling.

It was as if the builder had been in a hurry, and had neglected to do his job properly.

Using the pipe as a crowbar, Jewel levered a loose stone and jumped backward as it spilled out. Eagerly she dug and jabbed. The wind lashed her hair across her face, and flogged her clothing. More powdery mortar showered down; another stone became dislodged. Her work became easier as blocks fell away, weakening the courses above.

Pausing for a brief rest, Jewel perceived a shallow inscription crudely carved on a slab set into the wall. It read:

THOSE WHO SEEK LOVE SHALL FIND ONLY CALAMITY,
FOR LOVE IS NO MORE THAN A VANITY.

A fleeting sense of wistfulness passed through her. Could such a declaration be true? Was love nothing but a sham?

More likely this epigraph was the work of some cynic, some social outcast who felt cheated, who believed he was owed loyalty and affection despite being incapable of giving it. Someone such as the Sorcerer of Strang.

To all purposes Jewel herself was an outcast now, having turned her back on those who cared for her in order to pursue this foolish quest. And what did she have to show for it so far? Dry bricks, worm-eaten rafters, and a bitter caption: little else. After all her labors she felt extremely frustrated at having found nothing of import so far.

"Hmph!" she snorted disparagingly, before resuming her work with vigor. The fourth stone fell, creating a window level with Jewel's face.

The mask of Death stared back at her.

Aghast, Jewel dropped the pipe, recoiling from the thing she had uncovered. She stumbled over a broken hod and fell to the ground, her gaze never leaving the apparition.

The skull of a deceased human being was peering out through the window in the wall. The sockets from which it seemed to watch were hollows brimming with blindness. The teeth with which it grinned were pearls in rows. When this grotesque and pathetic visage failed to speak or move, Jewel picked herself up and cautiously moved forward to examine it.

All flesh had long ago withered away, but the hair remained, unrotted. It was beautiful hair—as flowing, glossy, and dark as a river reflecting moonlight. And that hair was encased in a headdress of filigree gold, encrusted with rubies and skilfully wrought. The garments clothing the bony shoulders were of similar costly magnificence, fashioned of sumptuous fabrics and stitched with flamboyant embroideries. *She*—for judging by the clothes these were the mortal remains of a woman—was standing in the wall. Her claw-like remnants of hands were upraised, as if she tore at the stones with her nails. Indeed, long scratches were scored in the mortar.

This woman had been walled in alive.

Sick with horror, Jewel fled.

Knowing no other means of egress from the rubbish-strewn close, she returned by the way she had come, in through the postern, and up the several flights of stairs within the main building. On reaching a landing, she collapsed to the floor to regain her breath, and remained there, resting her shoulders against a newel post and listening to the ambient noise of loose articles, near and far, being slammed about by air currents. It was akin to being deep inside a network of mines and hearing the *tap-tap* of pickaxes coming through the rock, from hidden depths and gangs.

She pondered on what she had witnessed. The hallmarks of death were clearly visible in places about the castle. Beside the outer pales and in the courtyard had lain the bones of those who had perished while trying to enter the fortress. By the smear of blood on the very threshold any visitor ought to have been prepared for such sights as the lady in the wall. Jewel shuddered. For certain, extreme cruelty had reigned here in days of yore. The notion filled her with such revulsion that she felt queasy, and for one mad moment she wished she could slit open her own flesh and flush the sorcerer's blood out of her veins.

A soft sound near at hand made Jewel gasp. She held still and listened, with all her capacity. Had there been footsteps again? Inexorably, the concept of an invisible follower led her to recall her mother's madness. Lilith had been audience to sounds nobody else had heard. She had vowed they were the footsteps of a pursuer. In the end, the delusion had been the agent of her destruction. No one in the marsh had ever spoken to Jewel about the cause of her grandfather's death, but she had gathered, from talk overheard, that Old Man Connick, too, had been subject to that particular form of insanity, and Earnán had confirmed her conjecture at their meeting in the Fairfield. Those hallucinations were hereditary, engendered by the curse of Jaravhor. For an instant, Jewel's eerie surroundings and the macabre atmosphere of the abandoned fortress confused her, and illogically, an alarming notion struck her: *What if the curse had not been invalidated after all?*

The idea was too shocking to contemplate.

A long pull from her water bottle and a few bites of bread helped her recover from the fright and rally her common sense. Of course she was free of the curse; that was evident. She was invulnerable. The sorcerer's malediction no longer plagued her family. Looking about, she noted a small, arched door set into an inner wall. It was one she had not yet opened, and like the other doors it was furnished with a key. After unlocking the portal she climbed a narrow stair that coiled around in a fashion that led her to suspect she was moving up inside the ceiling of the main dome. Such a stair could only lead to the small vaulted chamber that crowned the main dome, the hand-bell on the back of the tortoise, which she had spied from the sky-balloon.

After much climbing she reached the utmost door and passed through to behold an interior even more extraordinary than those she had already visited.

The chamber was circular, the ceiling high and shaped—inevitably—like an inverted basin. Around the walls pilasters of white jasper, embellished with illustrious carvings, stood at intervals between tall, arched alcoves. Central to this apartment was a flat-topped plinth, rectangular in dimensions, about two yards long and one yard wide. It had been chiseled from rock-crystal shot through with a pale suspension of mist and swarms of miniature bubbles, locked in stasis. Its edges were beveled, and each of its sides displayed a relief sculpture of twin axes, their handles crossed. Nothing rested on this base block, which looked somehow destitute, as if it were intended to uphold some object no longer present—a statue, perhaps, or a coffer filled with wealth. Either way, whatever had once rested there had been removed or stolen. Most disturbing of all, the chamber's interior was lit by a strange fire whose flames flickered sapphire and heliotrope, rinsing the pallor of the stonework with lambent color, like a wash of dilute gentian-violet. Outside, the wind moaned. Inside, the numinous fire flickered with barely a sound—only the faintest hiss.

Who could have kindled the flames? Was someone here? There was no other sign of any presence, no footprints in the dust; therefore the fire must be of sorcerous manufacture. How puissant indeed was the Master of Strang, to produce a magickal flame that could exist throughout the decades!

It was worth exploring, this eyrie.

On the far side of the chamber, an alcove facing the door sheltered a dais upon which squatted a chair of snowy marble. It was above this throne that the strange fire blazed from a sconce. Jewel crossed the floor to examine the source of illumination. The sconce cupped a small bowl of white marble, but it was no oil lamp. In place of a wick of twisted fibers, a thin pipe came out of the wall and threaded through a hole in the center of the bowl. The flame clung to its tip. The mysterious hissing was emanating from this source, and there was a faint odor of putrefied cabbage. It reminded the marsh-daughter of the weird lights that glowed among the gases rising from the wetlands. She suspected that this was some kind of gas-flame, perhaps with an inexhaustible supply of fuel flowing up through the pipe. If that were true, no agent would have been required to tend it over the years since the Dome had been abandoned and sealed. The flame might have been lit decades ago, and abandoned to burn all by itself throughout the years. It was no sorcerous thing after all, but the product of artifice.

The alcove to the left contained three miniature drinking horns, no bigger than thimbles, elaborately mounted in precious metals. Other shelves and wall-niches harbored a collection of small jugs and drinking vessels, a cluster of candles, a bouquet of waxen tapers, brittle and flaking. A tall, stoneware oil jar occupied a stand in one corner of the room; near its base jutted a spigot with a wooden handle.

A lectern was housed in the alcove to the right of the flame-sconce, lapped by lavender tongues of radiance, which conjured illusions at the corners of the eyes. The damsel observed that the lectern supported an open tome of large proportions, which was chained to its stand. The pages were covered with lines of script, and as she bent her head to decipher the words Jewel experienced another surge of excitement. It was possible this was some volume of arcane lore. If so, these parchment leaves might well hold the key to unimaginable powers.

At that instant, there came a slight noise from behind her. It was the sound of footsteps, plain as daylight; there was no doubting it. She had heard them as clearly as she heard her own involuntary cry of terror. Dreading her family's madness, she whirled about to face that which hunted after her.

Quest

Long-limbed, striking, and possessed of effortless grace, the young man stood in the doorway. A canvas rucksack was strapped to his shoulders, and on his finger gleamed a signet ring of heavy gold. His garments were plain, like those of any peasant, his dark umber hair was tied back in a horse-tail, and he watched Jewel from eyes the color of limes.

"Desist," he warned. "Do not read the words."

"By all that's marvelous," the damsel breathed, unable to credit her own eyesight, "how came you here?" On reconsidering, she added, "Stay back! You are nought but illusion."

"No illusion," said Arran Stormbringer. "I followed you here, all the way from High Darioneth. Did you truly believe I would let you brave the dangers of travel on your own?"

"I cannot depend on you," said Jewel, shaking her head. "This is a place of cruelty and deception. You are some simulacrum."

The young Maelstronnar heaved a sigh of exasperation. "Jewel," he said, "ask any question. Interrogate me in any way you desire, in order to quell your doubts and satisfy yourself that I am indeed Arran Stormbringer."

If he were an eldritch wight he could never have uttered those words, for wights could only speak the truth. This calmed Jewel's qualms somewhat, but she would not be content until she had bombarded him with queries, the answers to which only the Storm Lord's heir would know.

At length, she was persuaded.

"Well," she said, folding her arms resolutely, "this is a wonder, and no mistake. Your father said that if I chose to depart, High Darioneth would spare me no succor. I suppose he changed his mind."

"Not really. He did not command me to pursue you. He told me that even as he dispensed that message he guessed, in his heart, that I would follow you. Had I not done so, I daresay he would have relented and sent someone after you, to keep you from harm. I know him too well to suppose otherwise. Yet he was greatly displeased with you, and with me also, for turning my back on my duties of weathermastery to indulge you in your escapade."

"How did he guess you would come after me?"

"You hardly seem grateful for my company," observed Arran mildly, deflecting her course.

"Why did you follow me in secret?" she persisted, so impatient to voice her questions that she did not wait to listen to the replies. "Why not openly?"

"In the hope you would turn back of your own accord, when danger threatened and you found yourself without a bodyguard."

"And danger I did meet. But not once did I see you or suspect your endeavor."

"Yet, I was watching, the while. I was nearby when you drove off one of the unseelie mountain hags. I was close at hand when you encountered the eldritch pack of white dogs, visited a market-fair of the faynes, and knelt beside the grave of your kinsman at Saxlingham Netherby. I was not far away when you joined the wagoners, and I was your shadow as you passed through Orielthir."

"I am ashamed, knowing how easily you tracked me without my knowledge."

"Do not be. Only a weathermaster or a highly proficient woodsman could have succeeded. It was not easy."

"How did you slip inside the castle domains without meeting destruction?"

"As you advanced, you left all the gates and doors open, not bothering to close them in your haste or carelessness. I merely walked in your wake, touching nothing with my flesh, and remained unscathed."

"I must admire your skill at progressing without detection," said Jewel.

"I know which way the wind blows," said the young man, allowing himself a somewhat enigmatic smile. "I have at my disposal methods unavailable to the greater population. For example, today's breeze I invoked, that its effect might cover the sound of my footfalls through these blighted halls."

"Footfalls!" exclaimed Jewel. "Alas!" She broke into a laugh. "I opined they were maddening hallucinations! Of all the terrors I encountered on my travels, the sound of footsteps affrighted me most!"

"Then I am sorry for it," Arran said. "Come, let us leave this vile place. It is over-ripe with the stench of sorcery."

"No. Behold, here lies an ancient book of lore! I wish to read it, and ascertain whether its wisdom might be of use. Or, if there is no wisdom herein, perhaps it contains clues to some vast store of treasure, or eldritch artefacts!"

"An ancient book of lore or clues it may be, but it belonged to a baneful owner. Who can say what malign erudition it might expound? 'Tis best left alone. To examine such a document in such an unlikely library might well prove folly. Come away! Surely you have seen enough. I watched you prise open the wall of a tower wherein a woman had been buried alive. Those who wrought such a shameful deed were malicious, to say the least. Old tales tell of murder and abduction at the Dome. There can be no good here. Depart with me now!"

"Exhort me not!" protested Jewel. "I have come this far and I shall stay to do my will." She was determined to track down and acquire whatever valuable items she could find in the Dome of Strang—whether wealth, or knowledge, or books of healing, or objects possessing supernatural virtues. It was her way of striving for some measure of security in an unpredictable world; furthermore, plundering Jaravhor's fortress was a method of retaliating against the malicious villain who had cursed her family.

Turning his face away from Jewel, Arran Stormbringer remained silent for a moment. Then he said evenly, "Very well. I cannot prevent you."

By his tone, she knew he was angry. This troubled her, but his warnings could not dissuade her from her purpose. She renewed her study of the massive tome. Creamy were the leaves of parchment, and unstained by the mildews of age. Between wide margins there flowed lines of text, penned in black ink. The outsized initial letter on each page was illuminated, wreathed with curling traceries of leafy vines, painted green and red, highlighted with gold leaf. Between each paragraph ran an illustrated motif shaped like two long, slender firedrakes, confronting each other in attitudes of aggression.

Without turning the pages or touching the book—for that at least was a concession to Arran's cautions—Jewel began to read aloud.

"Flesh of my Flesh, Bone of my Bone, Blood of my Blood, I, Janus Jaravhor, bid you welcome! Through these Pages I speak unto you. When my Scion deserted the Ways of Weird I could only hope that his Issue or the Offspring of his Issue would find a Way back to this my Stronghold in

Orielthir. Those whose Veins are quick with my Blood may unlock my Wards and remain unscathed."

"You who have returned, you seek, no doubt, the legendary Treasures of Castle Strang."

"Unless some trickster has been at work, it seems these words have been authored by the Sorcerer of Strang himself!" Jewel exclaimed. Eagerly, she read on:

"Indubitably, you believe those Treasures to comprise Gold and Jewels. Such Wealth was once stored here indeed, well hidden and guarded by Enchantment. Yet it is spent, and a greater Wealth awaits.

"Throughout my Life I sought a Terrible Secret, one that has eluded Mankind throughout History. Near the End, I discovered that Secret—but too late. My Strength had failed, and I was fading swiftly."

At this point the prose gave way to rhyme:

> *"Some Men build Monuments to stab the Sky,*
> *By these to be remembered when they die.*
> *Some seek to raise and publicize their Name,*
> *That they might be immortalized by Fame.*
> *But Ballads age, and Fashions change, anon.*
> *Pray, who will read your Story when you're gone?*
> *Proud Monuments are felled by Wind and Rain.*
> *Change governs. Nought can ever stay the same.*
> *At Life's end all Ambition shall be thwarted,*
> *Hope shall abandoned be, Beauty distorted.*
> *We're Tenants, Borrowers with Names unlisted*
> *And, unrecalled, might never have existed.*
> *Men strive for worldly Power or vast Treasure,*
> *Revenge, Love, Wisdom, Glory, Joy, or Pleasure.*
> *Yet one Goal cheats the Nets they're vainly casting—*
> *The greatest of them all—Life Everlasting."*

"There is a line appended," breathed Jewel. She read:

"Nonetheless, I, your Lord and Forefather, in my Wisdom and Fore-sight, have left clues and messages informing you how you may win that very Prize, that my Lineage shall continue forever."

Her voice petered out. Brushing her hand across her brow, she murmured, "To win the prize of immortality! Can that be possible?"

"Read on!" said Arran Stormbringer, now intensely interested. No cataclysm had occurred as a result of their perusal of the tome and, infected by Jewel's excitement, he was inclined to provisionally dispense with caution. Looking over her shoulder, he began to scrutinize the flowing script while she deciphered it aloud.

"Through Diligence and Scholarship I have discovered the Secret of true Life Everlasting, combined with eternal Youth and good Health. This Gift may be found in the Water from certain Wells, the which are not situated nigh unto one another but are located in several far-flung Countries of Tir.

"You will discover how to find all the Immortal Draughts. Howsoever: First you must pass two Tests. For the first, you must speak a bitterbynding Oath upon my Relics, the Bones of my right Hand, vowing that you will follow my Will in this Matter. That Hand hath wrought the most puissant Sorcery ever known in Tir and now, alas, is embalmed within a Reliquary in this very Chamber, this exalted Shrine, this Tope. Placing your living Palm upon the Reliquary, you must say aloud these very words: 'I swear by the Bones of my Ancestor that if I find the Draught from the Well of Rain I will bring it to the Tope of Castle Strang, and light the flame to signify the deed is done.'

"That is the first Test. The second is to fulfill the vow. Should you prove worthy by obtaining the Draught from the Well of Rain, the Locations of all other Wells shall be revealed to you.

"The Flame that must be lighted is thus: you must pour oil into the narrow Gutter that circumscribes the lowest portion of the Platform central to this Chamber, then take up one of the waxen Tapers you see nearby, light it from the weird-fire, and hold the Flame to the oil.

"After you have proved successful and performed these Tasks you will discover how to find the other Draughts. If you do not do as I have instructed, you will win only the First. If you obey my Commands and honor your Word—which indeed you must!—you shall win more.

"Do not deceive yourself into believing that one Draught would be as good as many, for there is contained only enough of the miraculous Water in each Well to bestow the greatest Gift of all upon one solitary Mortal Creature.

"Let your Mind's Invention conjure the Loneliness endured by the one and only Immortal Human Being, solitary throughout countless Centuries, finding Companionship only to lose it again and again, each Time forever. And when the full Horror of this Nightmare has become plain to you, then you will understand the Wisdom in obtaining all Draughts for distribution amongst those you love best.

"Furthermore, and not least, if you swear upon the Remains of my right Hand and then break that bitterbound Vow, Ill-Fortune and Catastrophe shall dog you faithfully unto the End of your Days, whether they be few or infinite in Number, and neither Druid nor Carlin nor Eldritch Wight shall save you."

Having used up its allotted space on the page, the writing ceased. As Jewel was speaking, a sense of dread had been creeping over her. For the first time since she had entered the fortress, she felt truly afraid of what might have been disturbed, here in these long-abandoned vaults.

The flames in the white bowl hissed, as if serpents whispered secrets together. Their radiance flowed across the leaves of the book like the palest liquor of grapes, smiting gleams from the gold leaf on the illuminated letters. For several minutes neither Jewel nor Arran said a word, while they pondered the antique message, the sorcerer's legacy.

"Threats and promises," muttered Stormbringer, at last. "What to make of them, I wonder?"

"I daresay there will be more information on the next page," said Jewel. Without further ado she flipped the page over, before Arran could intervene. Somehow the spread-eagled leaves now appeared perilous, drowning in the hyacinthine glow of a flickering ocean.

The young man said firmly, "Since you are so eager to know, I will take my turn and read now." Jewel acquiesced, stepping back to give him her position in front of the lectern, and he resumed:

"Now Follows the History of my Discovery.

"Long ago I traveled extensively throughout the four kingdoms, and during my Travels I was privy to many a Story and Fable. Amongst them were Tales of immortal Beasts—a Hare, a white Deer, a Dove. It was told that

such Creatures had long ago been trapped and held in Captivity by Humankind. For Decades, yea, for Centuries, they remained caged and displayed in Menageries, where Audiences were diverted and amused by their unique and mystifying Undyingness, until in the end the unfortunate Creatures were set free by Those who pitied them, or by Enemies of their Captors.

"Yet, by the Time this Knowledge came to me, nought had been seen of these Beasts and Fowl for Five Hundred Years or more, so I concluded that either they had perished, or they had never existed except in the Fancies of Storytellers.

"Always I believed the Tales to be of no Substance until by chance I stumbled across ancient Tablets inscribed by Philosophers of great Knowledge. While perusing an Account of a captive Deer that was Immortal, I first guessed there might be Truth behind the Legend.

"I postulated that these Beasts and Fowl that had become no more than Rumors might still exist, and if so, then due to their extraordinary Longevity they might well have accumulated a vast Store of Knowledge. Having grown acute, and wary of Traps, they had avoided Capture and fled where Humankind could no longer find them. This, then, was the reason they could no longer be found.

"To further my Research I trapped and questioned some of the feebler and more innocuous eldritch Wights. Their inability to tell Untruths proved an estimable Asset and I achieved Success, for after some Persuasion, the Wights informed me they had indeed encountered Beasts that could not die. Alas, despite my close Interrogation the Wights were unable to tell me how those Creatures had attained the State of Deathlessness.

"For many Years I endeavored to find out the Source of Immortality. By the Time I won the Answer I was old, far older than any common Man may become, and too weak to leave the Dome in person, in order to obtain the Draughts. And I trusted no Other to the Business! What Servant could resist the Temptation to take the Prize himself?

"This is how the Answer was found: At length I snared yet another Wight of eldritch, and it told me, from its very Mouth, that more than a

Millennium ago it had seen an ordinary Hare drink from a certain Well and that Hare became immortal. 'Does the Well endure yet, and are there any others like it?' I asked, and the small, chittering Thing answered yea, the Well endured, and there existed more. And I made it describe them to me.

"Then I wondered why, when the Wells had existed for Centuries, only three Creatures had ever benefited from them. But the Wight divulged that the Cailleach Bheur had spread a Warning amongst the Beasts and Birds and even among the Amphibians and Insects and all manner of Organisms: 'Do not drink from the Star-Wells!' The sufferings of the three immortal Beasts became widely known to the Creatures of the Wild, and they shunned the Wells as if the Waters were lethally poisonous. No Human Being had ever discovered the Wells. For me, however, a Man of superior Intellect, perilously close to Death, Time was running out.

"After that, knowing I had not the Strength to leave my Domains, I remained and studied my Lore-Books, while hastily plotting how I might gain a Draught to cure all my Ills, restore my Youth, and prolong my Existence for Eternity. Now that I knew their Locations, many more Revelations I uncovered about the Wells. If you pass the Tests you will learn all.

"Alas, my Time is running out and when you read this I will be long gone. Weep for me, Kinsman, for all you have of me now is my Estate, my written Records of Wisdom, the Bones of my Hand, and my Benediction flowing in your Arteries."

Arran paused in his monologue. His face was flushed and his eyes had become infused with a yearning sparkle. " 'Tis all true, then!" he marveled. "I, too, have heard the legends of the three undying beasts. It is beyond belief, that the gift of Immortality might be almost within our grasp! To live forever—that is a prize mankind has sought since time immemorial!" He continued to read:

"Herewith, the History of the Wells of Life Everlasting:

"Long ago, at an earlier Dawn, a Star fell from the Sky. It burned as it fell, and broke into Portions that flew widely apart. Their Size, by the Instant they struck the Rocks of Tir, were reduced to less than that of a Sparrow's Egg. Yet the Speed at which they fell was so great that the Force of Impact was severe. Each of these Portions created a small Crater where it struck, a deep cup-shaped Hollow no bigger than, say, an Eagle's Nest. On Impact the Pieces of the Missile's Core—all that was left—melted in a

great Heat. The alien Material sprayed out, coating the Sides of each De-
pression with a Substance not of this World; a curious Metal born in the
outer Choirs of the Heavens. Wights call this metal Star's Heart, and it cov-
ers the Interiors of each Crater-Well, as Velvet lines the Husk of a Walnut.

"After the Metal cooled one of the Wells filled with Water from the
Clouds, and the Wights called it the Well of Rain. The Water in the Wells
comes from the Skies and Airs and Rocks of Tir, but the extraordinary
Power of the Stars takes more than a thousand Years to seep from the Metal
into the Water, undergo a Reaction, and accumulate sufficient Concentra-
tion to prolong a Man's Life forever. Because the process takes so long each
Well contains only enough Water for one single Draught—a mere Thim-
bleful. Yet that is sufficient to save the Life of one Mortal Creature.

"I tell you this, Kinsman, so that you may live forever and my Dynasty
endure for all Time. At least in this manner I might attain some Degree of
Immortality.

"Now, Kinsman, if you wish to obtain the Draught from the Well of
Rain, you must swear the Oath and turn to the next Page. Then you will
learn where to find the Prize."

Immediately Arran tried to turn the page. It would not budge, even when his strong fingers scrabbled at the edges, and prised at the corners. "Some sorcery has made this fast," he concluded somberly.

"It would seem we must swear this oath, if we are to unseal the book," Jewel said uncertainly. "Can you deduce any harm coming from such a course?"

"I think not," said her companion, after a meditative pause. "I can find no harm in it, no matter which way I judge the matter. For if the oath is sworn, and the oath-swearer departs and does nothing, and returns not to this chamber, the curse will never fall. It is only if the oath-swearer finds this Draught and returns here without it that the bones of the sorcerer will take revenge."

Jewel had memorized the oath, and repeated it first without placing her hand on the reliquary. "I can find no catch in it, either," she said. "Let us try this quest! For if we fail to find it, we shall be no worse off than before, yet if we succeed—oh!" Her shining eyes and exuberant gestures articulated the excitement that rendered her speechless.

Arran could only share her enthusiasm. The prospect of obtaining the miraculous prize forever sought by humankind filled his young heart with a formidable excitement. In particular, it came to him that by means of such potent waters Jewel's prosperity might be made secure for all time. For years he had loved her

from afar. His love for her was as profound as it was abiding. It saturated his being, pervaded every breath he drew, and companioned his every moment. For
her delicate, fine-boned beauty he loved her, and for her unselfconscious charm;
for her open-handedness and forthright ways, her vehemence, her courage and
audacity, and for qualities that he could not name. Indeed, he even loved her for
her occasional conceitedness, for he judged that if people were to be capable of
thinking favorably of others, they must first have a high opinion of themselves.
The marsh-daughter attracted him like no other. To be sure, there were sweeter-
natured, meeker girls amongst his acquaintances, but it was only she who, by
her very existence, could answer his unspoken questions and fill the empty
places of his spirit.

He recognized that she either was unaware of his passion or wished to appear oblivious of it, furthermore, he was uncertain whether she would recipro-
cate even if she knew, but none of this diminished his ardency in any respect. He
desired only her welfare, her happiness—her company, too, whenever she cared
to grant it. His affection was so enduring he could continue to cherish her, stead-
fastly, without asking acknowledgment, or anything at all, in return.

"I wonder whether making this pledge will unseal the page and reveal information on how to reach this well, or if it is all just some trick," he mused.

The damsel crossed to the alcove opposite the one which contained the
lectern and book. Here, upon a marble stand, stood a ceramic urn, painted and
adorned with the ubiquitous crossed axes.

"See, Arran!" she proclaimed. "Herein, I daresay, are contained the relics of
the sorcerer. I shall swear on his bones, even if it has no effect."

Said the Storm Lord's son, waking from his reverie, "We shall not know, unless we try." Their gazes interlocked.

Placing her hand on the domed lid of the urn, Jewel said loudly, "I swear by the
Bones of my Ancestor that if I find the Draught from the Well of Rain I will bring
it to the Tope of Castle Strang, and light the flame to signify the deed is done."

They both looked expectantly at the book.

Nothing happened.

Once again, Arran tried to lever the pages apart, to no avail.

"How vexing!" cried Jewel, stamping her foot. Louder than ever, she called
out the oath, as if by sheer force of volume her voice could break the spell. As
she did so she pressed down hard on the reliquary, with both hands.

Two clicks echoed through the Tope.

The reliquary sank about an inch into its stand, and a clasp on the side of the
book flew undone.

"The page is turning!" Arran exclaimed. She darted to his side.

Jewel, single-mindedly intent on the book and thoughtlessly jostling close against him so that a wave of sweet heat seared through his body, followed the newly revealed words as he uttered them.

"In southern Ashqalêth, atop the Comet's Pinnacle in Saadiah, there you shall find the Well of Rain. Eldritch Wights guard the Pinnacles from Climbers. Local lore tells of a riddle: 'Who is borne by a Moth's Cradle, he may reach the Summit.'

"Take from this Tope the Vessel of Ivory, to carry the Draught. My true Kinsman will possess the Wit to reach the Prize."

Arran turned another page, but there was no further prose—only blank parchment. Frenziedly he rifled through the entire book; however, there was no more to be read, and even as he turned back to the inscribed pages the writing appeared to be bleaching and fading.

Under his breath he mumbled a curse.

Jewel, on the contrary, was pleased. "Atop one of the pinnacles of Saadiah!" she exclaimed. "I have heard of them. Saadiah is in Ashqalêth, and the famous pinnacles are tall and sheer. Their crowns are indeed far beyond the reach of the common man! Yet how easy it shall be, in a sky-balloon, to attain such a lofty perch."

"The statutes of Ellenhall do not permit the use of a sky-balloon for purposes other than weatherworking," her companion said somberly.

He sank deep into thought. Jewel paced the length of the chamber, defiantly tossing her hair. "I will not let the lack of a sky-balloon be an obstacle to this quest," she said eventually. "I have no idea how the pinnacles are to be scaled, but as my grandfather always said, *'Let us cross that bridge when we come to it, and not before.'*" She ceased pacing and came to a halt beside the alcove that sheltered the three ornate drinking vessels. "Here is the vessel of ivory," she said, picking up a tiny, lidded horn no bigger than her thumb, and clasped with gold. "The book says we may take it. And besides, it is mine already, for am I not the heir to all of this?" After loosening the drawstring of Arran Stormbringer's pack, she stowed the container within. He made no objection, merely resting his contemplative gaze upon her. Had she not been preoccupied she might have recognized the strength of feeling in that gaze.

"We *shall* seek the Well of Rain!" Jewel cried out impulsively.

Following this bold proclamation they both ceased to breathe for several moments, half expecting some momentous recognition of the words that had been spoken, a burst of light, the boom of a gong, some amazing revelation. Yet there was nothing. The flames continued to hiss softly, like the sigh of escaping steam, but no other sound came to their ears, for Arran had let his summoned breeze die away. They became conscious, all at once, of the labyrinthine halls and empty corridors of Castle Strang spread out around them, as repressive as a net, enclosing them with their tomb-like stillness and with a silence heavy with premonition, conscious, too, of the downstairs courtyard and the wall in which the woman had been incarcerated, where she still waited to be released, and of the tens of thousands of stones that bricked the structure of Castle Strang, each of which might be hiding secrets even more shocking.

Simultaneously, they wished to depart forthwith.

"But what if this Well is dry?" said Jewel in a low voice, as they hurried from the Tope and down the stair that coiled like a subcutaneous worm around the skull of the Dome.

"Then we shall go home," replied Arran Stormbringer, "and I will answer to my father for vexing him by hieing off on this expedition and neglecting my duties."

Along the deserted corridors the pair made haste. They were alternately illuminated with flashes of sunlight and drowned in purple shadow as they passed the windows, scuffing their own recent footprints in the dust. Through cavernous chambers they went, each hall stripped bare of precious ornament yet with its splendor preserved in the soaring arches, pleated columns, and monumental carvings of ebony. In and out of the echoing refectory they sped, past the barren table flanked by its tall-backed chairs, through the double doors, down the grand staircase, along the length of the outer hall, and out the portals whose feet were splashed with the black stains of ancient blood. Without stopping they descended the shallow steps into the courtyard. Desiccated leaves crunched beneath their boots as they crossed the cold flagstones, shadowed by the belltower with its seized-up clock. The gates in the wall still hung open on their hinges, but after the couple made their exit Jewel slammed the portals firmly shut, before locking them with the ornate key.

Outside the fortress the fresh air seemed pure and invigorating, and the soft caress of Orielthir's natural breezes was like swimming in silk. Together, the youth and damsel ran down the slope without a backward glance. Toward the southwest they set their faces, as if in unspoken agreement, for to the southwest lay the region called Saadiah, on the far side of Ashqalêth.

They did not look back at the bleached bones of slaughtered men scattered along the base of the wall, or the brooding Dome rising out of the castle's center like the carapace of a giant tortoise with a bell upon its back; nor did they review the sparse grove of elms where Jewel had taken shelter the previous night.

If they had done so, they might have noticed a furtive flicker of movement amongst the rustling trees. A man lurked there, watching them. Beneath the dappled shade his thinning hair glimmered, for an instant, like polished brass.

A long path lay before Jewel and Arran; the highway called the Valley Road, running from Cathair Rua, past the hills of Bellaghmoon and across the Ashqalêthan border, where it changed its name, becoming the Desert Road. Such a journey would be too extensive and arduous to undertake without the purchase of horses and extra provisions. With this in mind, the travelers made their way to Cathair Rua.

They entered the city by way of the road that passed through the Fair Field to the eastern gate. At this season the field lay empty; no pushcarts trundled hither and thither; no clowns or jongleurs performed for pennies. The clutter of tents, booths, and stands had given way to a sparse scattering of abandoned rubbish: torn hempen bags, frayed bits of string, bent nails, stones, fragments of pottery, nubs of charcoal, a few gnawed bones. The neighing of horses, the spruiking of vendors, and the laughter of children were no more than memories. Only a random breeze went swooping and complaining over the expanse of littered, stamped-down soil.

It was late in the month of Jule. Midsummer's Day was long past, and even Swan Upping would be over by now, in the Great Marsh. The marshfolk would be looking ahead to Rushbearing in Aoust. Meanwhile, the days lay warm and heavy on Slievmordhu, screened with motes of sunlight borne on dust-specks. The skies were unblemished and vividly blue, as if thickly painted with cyanic lacquers.

Within the city's walls of rufous sandstone, business continued as usual. Slievmordhuan citizens trafficked with Ashqalêthans garbed ostentatiously in raiment of ocher and apricot, or haggled with tough, vehement seafarers from Grïmnørsland, or paid their respects to the grave knights of Narngalis, or tried to ingratiate themselves with minions of the druids of the sanctorum. Above the streets, the alleys, the taverns, squares, hovels, and mansions, the flags of the palace stirred limply in the tepid and lazy airs.

Evening was drawing in as Jewel and Arran passed through the crowded thoroughfares. "We should avoid the *Three Barrels,* a lodging-house favored by my kindred," said the young weathermaster, "and we must endeavor not to draw attention to ourselves. My face is known in some quarters hereabouts. If I were to be recognized, questions would be asked. Who is my fair companion? And where are we going? Lying is distasteful to us both; therefore discretion is the better option."

"Verily," agreed Jewel. Her head swiveled from right to left as she tried to view everything in the populous precincts at once. "Should it be discovered that we journey to fetch the waters of eternal life, the entire population of the four kingdoms must surely descend on our shoulders!"

"I shall refer to you as some relation of mine," said Arran. "My wife, or my sister."

"Your sister," said Jewel.

"My sister," he repeated, smiling wryly. "Does that please you?"

"Even so." She returned his smile with guileful innocence, but genuine affection.

It was suppertime. Savory scents drifted from the vicinity of a curbside tavern whose signboard advertised it as the *"Ace and Cup,"* and the travelers decided to spend the night therein.

"I have never before set foot in this place," said Arran. "With luck, no one here will know my face."

"I have some coin," said Jewel.

"Keep your money. I carry a full purse."

"It troubles me to accept charity."

"Is it charity, or selfishness, that I enjoy your company? We are traveling together, and I am not short of currency. If you wish, I can sleep in feather beds while you slumber in barns. If you prefer, I can drink wine and eat plum puddings by the fire while you pluck blackberries and drink from puddles. But I would rather it were otherwise."

"Very well, if it pleases you so much," said Jewel. "I will let you spend your money on me, but only as a favor to you. Remember—you now owe me a favor."

Well-furnished with trestles, stools, and benches, the *Ace and Cup* remained one of the better-appointed taverns of Cathair Rua. Mellow evening light lingered, streaming in through its mullioned casements, but already the oil lamps swinging from hooks in the low-beamed ceiling had been set aflame. Their butter-yellow radiance washed over drinkers seated around several tables, men casting dice at another, card-players gaming at another, and a group in a corner gambling at knucklebones. Near the bar, some off-duty guardsmen were betting on the progress of a couple of cockroaches scuttling up the wall.

In his peasant garb of leggings, wide-sleeved shirt, thigh-length tunic belted at the middle, homespun cap, and stout walking-boots, Arran blended well with the throng. Neither was Jewel obtrusive, save for the unique beauty of her countenance. Her kirtle and capuchon were as weather-beaten and discolored as the raiment of any long-distance pedestrian. Over one shoulder she carried the fur-lined cloak of waterproof oilcloth, rolled tightly and tied with string.

The common-room was crowded—"Usually a reliable sign of decent fare," Arran commented as they maneuvered their way through the press. Indeed, he augured rightly, for the meal served to them on wooden platters was ample and delicious. The patrons proved to be as merry as they were many, and it was not long before someone, encouraged by his friends, clambered up onto one of the benches and began to sing:

> "Hairy little knobblin', hobblin' goblins,
> Horrid little goblins at my door.
> Grab 'em by the shinbone, thinbone, skinbone,
> Tie 'em to a broomstick, and mop the floor!
>
> "Nasty little knobblin', hobblin' goblins,
> Ugly little heads like oak-tree roots.
> Pick 'em up and slay them, splay them, flay them,
> Tan their stringy hides to make my boots!
>
> "Stupid little knobblin', hobblin' goblins
> Make a jolly game when they get caught.
> Roll 'em up and tie them, dry them, fly them,
> Kick 'em in the air, let's have some sport!
>
> "Dirty little knobblin', hobblin' goblins,
> Trap 'em in their caves and make 'em squirm!
> Clean 'em out and brush them, flush them, rush them,
> Chuck 'em in the Inglefire and watch them burn!"

"Oh," said Jewel, grimacing at Arran over her platter of dumplings, "what an obnoxious song. I almost feel sorry for unseelie wights."

Someone shouted at the singer, who began a second rendition, quite different from the first, slower, more lilting, and pitched in a minor key. It was a love song:

"Lady, break the spell on me, I beseech thee, set me free!
  For I've borne this bitter curse such a long time.
  Lady, take my misery, turn it into ecstasy!
  It's been growing so much worse for a long time.
  Weep and sigh, pass me by, let me live, make me die,
  Lofty peak, deep abyss, just a kiss.

"In the past I might have done wicked deeds beneath the sun,
  Or by starlight, or by moon, or in darkness.
  Is this penance for my crime? Surely I have served my time!
  Love is cruel. Release me soon from this darkness.
  Weep and sigh, pass me by, let me live, make me die,
  Lofty peak, deep abyss, just a kiss.

"Prithee, drive away the pain and unlock this heavy chain,
  For your kiss is now the key to my freedom.
  Thy sweet kiss. Is it so strange that you have the pow'r to change
  This enchanted thing I be? Grant me freedom!
  Weep and sigh, pass me by, let me live, make me die,
  Lofty peak, deep abyss, just a kiss."

Arran used a crust of bread to wipe the last of the gravy from his platter. "Do you prefer that song, then?" he asked.

"'Tis an improvement." Jewel licked her fingertips. In an undertone, she added, "Although, I am not over-fond of trite love ditties."

"Scorpion knows a deal of good songs," called out a small fellow seated on the other side of the long trestle table, who had not caught the girl's murmured codicil. He grinned like a pumpkin lantern at Arran and Jewel, and they recognized him as the most encouraging among the singer's friends.

"What's that you say, Lizard?" The singer himself elbowed his way toward the table. A lean fellow, he looked as leathery as old saddles, and his shoulders sagged in a habitual stoop. His head was capped by a red fez with a tassel of blue silk.

"The pretty lady likes your singing," said Lizard.

"She shows good taste," observed Scorpion. "Speaking of which, I could do with a taste of ale. Me throat's drier than the Fyrflaume after all that yodelling. Hey, landlord, bring a round of your finest for the whole table!"

Lizard clapped Scorpion on the shoulder. "Never was a more generous man," he chuckled. "May Ádh continue to look kindly upon him!"

Jewel and Arran suddenly found themselves part of a convivial group whose core members—and those who spent most freely on drinks for their acquaintances—were Scorpion and Lizard. Theirs was pleasant company. They expounded numerous jokes and humorous anecdotes and Scorpion, in particular, was adept at mimicking a wide range of sounds, the cleverest and most accurate of which was the auditory effect made by boots progressing through squelchy mire. Both hailed from Ashqalêth, it was clear, by the way they dressed and spoke.

When asked for his name, Arran said, "They call me Salt."

And Jewel said, "I am named Lily."

"By my troth!" exclaimed Lizard, "With such eyes, lady, they should have named you 'Hyacinth'!"

"Pray pardon my comrade for his boldness," Scorpion interjected quickly, as a look of displeasure crossed Jewel's countenance. "He makes too free and forgets courtesy. Curb your tongue, Lizard, my friend! Speak politely to your betters!" He slapped his friend lightly across the back of the head.

In return, Lizard flicked Scorpion's fez off his head. The two Ashqalêthans jumped up and a mock boxing match ensued, both participants moving away from the tables as they battled. Every time he swung his fist at Lizard, who expertly evaded the assault, Scorpion imitated the sound of two cabbages smacking together. A space opened around them, and the onlookers cheered as the combatants performed such a pantomime of high jinks and slapstick that the entire tavern rocked with laughter. Eventually, Scorpion said, "Schrrrriiiiii-innnnng!" and drew a nonexistent sword, with which he "decapitated" Lizard. Picking up the invisible head, Scorpion pretended to bounce it around the floor while Lizard chased after him, yelling, "Give back my poll, you thief!"

Arran and Jewel shared the general hilarity. "A mirthful pair of rogues, there's no doubt," the young man said appreciatively.

"Salt?" she inquired teasingly.

"'Twas all that came to mind on the spur of the moment," he admitted.

"I hope I can remember to call you that, in their hearing. Do you know, I suspect I have seen Scorpion somewhere before, but I cannot recall where."

Later, Arran and Jewel bade their acquaintances good night and made to leave the common-room. The two Ashqalêthans were sitting companionably side by side, their feet resting on a vacant bench, their "quarrel" forgotten. The red fez with the blue silk tassel was back on Scorpion's head, somewhat the worse for wear.

"Good night, friends!" said Scorpion jovially. "May Ádh bring you pleasant dreams and may you waken refreshed. Whither are you bound, on the morrow?"

Jewel glanced at Arran, who parried, "South."

"South, eh? Going far?"

"Mayhap," said the young man guardedly. He had been careful not to drink enough ale to blunt his wits. "Why do you ask?"

"Only because if you are going far you might be looking to purchase worthy steeds. And if you are, I know the honest horse dealers hereabouts. You want a nag that won't break down two miles from the city?"

Despite himself, Arran was interested. He nodded.

"Meet me here tomorrow at dawn," said Scorpion, tapping the side of his nose and winking waggishly. "I shall take you to a dealer who will make you a better bargain than you can dream of!"

"Very well," Arran replied, but doubt pooled in his eyes. To Jewel he murmured, "If they believe me to be a poor judge of horse-flesh they are mistaken. I shall soon know if he and his dealer crony are in the business of duping out-of-towners."

"I, too," said Jewel with dignity, "am a good judge of horse-flesh."

Arran raised an eyebrow, but made no reply.

At first light Jewel and Arran made their rendezvous with Scorpion and his friend, as promised. They spent the morning examining and haggling, and before noon they had purchased two horses in good fettle.

"You know a great deal about horses, young sir, I can see that," said Scorpion cheerfully. "And because you are perceptive, I daresay you perceive also that I am an honest man who only wishes good fortune to other fellows."

"It is true," said Arran, "that these steeds are young and in fine health. The price we paid was less than I had expected. You have done us a good turn and for that we give you thanks. Regrettably, now we must bid you both farewell, for there are other matters to which we must attend before we set off."

"You will be going on a long journey, if you require mounts," said Scorpion.

"Not so long," said Arran.

"Down the Valley Road?"

"Maybe."

"Lizard and me are going that way ourselves," said the Ashqalêthan. "Around town 'tis said that during the last few seven-nights it has been a dangerous path. Marauders have been plaguing lonely wayfarers. We are well armed, and experienced at skirmishes, and we have mettlesome steeds of our own, housed in the tavern stables. We shall soon depart. Join us!"

Arran deliberated.

"Why not?" asked Lizard, spreading his fingers, palms upward, in a gesture of open welcome.

"For the present we must leave our newly purchased horses with your friend the dealer while we make further arrangements," the young man said after some thought. "Early tomorrow morning we will exit the city by the southern gate. If you and Lizard are waiting for us when we leave, we might fall in with you, for a time."

"So be it!" shouted Scorpion over his shoulder as he and Lizard loped away down a cobbled alley. "'Twill be a merry meeting and a merrier journey!" He was whistling lightheartedly as the two Ashqalêthans rounded a corner and disappeared from view.

At a second-hand clothing stall Jewel and Arran purchased extra garments, voluminous and breezy, suitable for travel in the desert. A local milliner provided them with broad-brimmed hats. Afterward they visited a sausage-seller, a bakery, a saddler, and a stock-feed merchant. As they made their way about the urban streets they discussed Scorpion's offer.

"I am undecided. I'm grateful for their help in obtaining good horses at a good price," stated Arran.

"And I am mindful," said Jewel, "that they are men of Ashqalêth, who might be of help in the extreme conditions of the desert, if they should travel that far with us. I have visited the southern dry-lands before, as a child, but I have no notion of how to survive there if some catastrophe should occur."

"But do you trust them, Jewel?"

"Not entirely. But then, I am distrustful by nature," she said candidly. "I have been deceived and undeceived by too many illusions."

"But these are not wights, wielding glamour. They are men."

"All the more reason to be wary," she said.

"Yet," said the young man, "they have indeed aided us. The horses are excellent, and the price was fair. Should there be any hint of treachery—well, I sleep lightly, and at need, I can waken to full alertness. Like all my people, I am trained in martial skills . . ."

". . . and you have the *brí* at your fingertips . . ."

". . . a power I should not wield except in a life-threatening situation. But, should they try to take us unawares and rob us, they will find they are no match for a weathermaster."

"And an invulnerable marsh-daughter," subjoined Jewel.

"Then, are we agreed? Shall we travel in their company?"

"Even so, Salt my dearest brother. We are agreed!"

High amongst the towers of the city, the dawn bell rang. Like doves of gold metal its round notes flew out over the sleeping roofs. Jewel and Arran led their

saddled horses from the stables of the *Ace and Cup,* and along the twisting, narrow paths of the city. Soft blue-gray was the pre-dawn light, the color of veins
showing beneath translucent skin. Yolk-yellow radiance glowed from a few
windows here and there, behind which a few folk were stirring, stumbling from
their beds and rubbing their eyes. The hooves of the horses clapped hollowly on
the flagstones of the pavement, like ironic applause. A rat scuttled frantically
along a gutter.

Their route took them past the high walls at the rear of the sanctorum compound. Through the insipid gloom, the red walls gleamed ash-gray. Marble cockatrices glared balefully from sandstone blocks and piers. The travelers could hear
the crunch of the sentries' boots as they patrolled along the wall-walks above.

Here in the wealthier quarters tall houses of gray granite stood to attention
on either side of the streets. A long drain, covered over with a grating, ran down
the center of every cobbled road. The leafy branches of orange and lemon trees
swayed and dipped over courtyard walls, and the music of falling waters played
within those private cloisters. In the gardens of the affluent, blackbirds began to
twitter a greeting to the morning sun.

Jewel and Arran led their horses past some of the more highly esteemed Guild-
Houses, such as the Jewelers, the Perfumers, the Tailors, the Silk Merchants, and
the Distillers. Above the slate roofs, red as lobster carapaces, the sky paled. After a
time the travelers drew near an Oratorium, a high, colonnaded, beehive-roofed
structure reached by flights of stone stairs, and walled only by spaced columns. At
this early hour no King's Druids' Scribes' Hand held forth from the hallowed
platform of the Oratorium. The edifice stood as desolate as the Fairfield.

"Thanks be, we are not to be plagued with superstitious rantings this fine
morning," muttered Arran as he and his companion passed by.

Through the middle-income districts they went, curiously eyeing the abun-
dance of tavern signboards brightly painted with images symbolizing names such
as the "Hat and Feather," the "Boot and Last," the "Leaping Gnome." Doors and
windows were festooned with devices to repel unseelie entities—iron horseshoes,
sprigs of rowan-wood or hypericum, bells, carved roosters, the usual assortment.

Nearer the South Gate, wooden hovels were squeezed together shoulder to
shoulder, as if space were an unaffordable luxury. Sludge trickled down open
drains in the beaten dirt streets, and the travelers held muslin scarves to their
noses.

"No sign of our friends, yet," said Arran in a muffled voice.

But no sooner had they bypassed the yawning sentries and made their exit
from the city walls than they spied two men waiting outside the gate: Scorpion
and Lizard. Their horses were loaded with packs, and the grins that stretched
across their jaws were as broad as bridges.

"Hail and well remet!" shouted Scorpion. At the sight of his beaming face beneath the red fez, Jewel and Arran could not help but smile and respond in kind. Having mounted their steeds, the four travelers rode off together into the waxing morning. Their shadows walked beside them, spindle-legged and attenuated, stretching torturously across the dust of the road.

At this time of year the winds along the Valley Road lay down to rest for a while, and the air was still. It was only the currents stirred by their travel that tweaked at the hems of Arran's striped surcoat and rippled in the long folds of Jewel's hooded desert-cloak, the garment the Ashqalêthans called a *burnous*. As the travelers trotted along the shallow vale between the low green hills to the west and the jagged heights simmering in a haze on the eastern horizon, Jewel's thoughts strayed to the marsh, lying on the other side of Bellaghmoon. She longed to make a detour and visit her people there, but common sense told her there would be no profit in doing so, and maybe some harm.

Scorpion and Lizard had plenty of money to spend, and Arran did not lack coin either. The four travelers were able to buy good food and shelter at the villages scattered along the Valley Road. Thus, it was rare for them to spend a night camped by the wayside. The journey became a jaunt, a merry progression through lands that appeared strange to Jewel, for she had been quite young when she passed that way with her parents, and had forgotten much about that family excursion to R'shael. For her, this was an adventure enjoyed without deprivation, riding alongside one reserved but agreeable companion and two overtly jocular ones. They proceeded swiftly, with few halts, yet it was eighteen days before they crossed the Ashqalêthan border, just north of the farthest outpost of a line of hills. Here the northwest extremities of the mountainous arm called the Broken Scarps began to diminish and deflate, fusing with the dusty, waterless inner plain of Ashqalêth. The lands hereabouts were riven and jagged, but the Desert Road clove them resolutely.

The riders passed through a narrow defile in the foothills. Steep, rocky walls loomed high at either hand, blocking out most of the sky so that only a narrow strip of brilliant blue could be seen. The hoofbeats of their horses echoed doubly from the rough-hewn escarpments and a cool, profound shadow enveloped them.

Arran scanned their surroundings warily. To Jewel, he said quietly, "This would be a strategic emplacement for an ambush."

Their two Ashqalêthan companions had given no cause for distrust, yet Jewel and Arran preferred to keep most of their discourse private. Even the desert-men, riding a little distance ahead, had fallen silent as if apprehension stole over them.

Half a mile farther on, the rocky walls dropped away on either side, revealing expanses of broken ground strewn with the humped forms of crouching boulders and dwarf shrubs. A tiny stream tumbled from the distant heights. "The last water source before the dusky wells of the R'shael crossroads," announced Scorpion, calling out over his shoulder. "Let us water the horses here, and fill our bottles."

"We have been fortunate," Jewel said, as they led their mounts to the stream. "We have encountered no Marauders. And few travelers either," she added.

"It is yet high Summer," replied Scorpion, who was now wearing a turban of striped calico in place of the fez. He wiped a sleeve across his dripping brow. "Most folk prefer to wait for milder seasons before they take to the roads of the south. Even brigands avoid the desert Summer, if they have a choice," he added, "for that is when the southerly airstream called the Fyrflaume blows from the Stone Deserts. Let us hope the mountain-dwelling highwaymen have got good pickings elsewhere of late, and will have no need to plague desert wayfarers. By Lord Fortune, 'tis hot!"

Indeed, the air was like the breath of a furnace. Unaccustomed to ambient heat, Jewel and Arran had both been rendered uncomfortable by its effects, but despite Jewel's intermittent pleading whispers, the weathermaster refused to summon a cooling breeze.

"You called a wind to mask your footsteps in the Dome," she muttered. "Why not a refreshing gust or two in the desert?"

"I contravened weathermaster code," Arran murmured in return. "I should not have done so, and I'll not do it again. Does the heat much trouble one who is invulnerable to fire?"

"Not overly, but I am not used to it."

"You will adapt."

While their steeds drank copiously downstream, the travelers splashed their hair and garments, and refilled their water skins. They seated themselves in the thin shade of some stunted mallee eucalypts to partake of their noonday repast, rye bread and cheese wrapped in dampened muslin.

"Back there," said Scorpion, indicating with a jerk of his thumb the road they had already traveled, "back there was the last place you'll find between here and Jhallavad where an ambush might be successful."

"Do you refer to the place where the road is cloven between rock walls?" Arran asked.

"The very same. Except at that place, which we call 'Bandit's Alley,' those who made this road ensured there was scant cover at the verges, nothing much to provide concealment for archers and other snipers."

" 'Tis the same along many of the greater highways in all kingdoms," said Arran. "In regions where brigands are most active, local villagers endeavor to ensure the roadsides are kept clear of trees and large rocks, for the distance of a shotten arrow."

After taking refreshment, Scorpion and Lizard fell into a doze. Jewel and Arran seized the opportunity to move several yards away into the temperate shadow of a standing boulder, that they might converse without being overheard, or disturbing their companions.

"I have spied very few wights," Jewel commented, still chewing a last mouthful. "Had we met some of the seelie sort, I would have liked to approach them, to speak with them."

"Why?"

"I would like to ask them—" Jewel broke off momentarily. She swallowed, then resumed more softly, "what it is like to be immortal. . . ."

They spoke no more for a time, relaxing in sociable silence, listening to the gurgle of the water, the reedy *churr* and loud *tuk-tuk-tuk* of White-Browed Babblers in the boughs overhead, the muted jingling of harness as the horses grazed on low-growing glasswort and acacia.

"How strange," mused Arran. "If it is true that there is a well made from a star, and it holds the secret of eternity, then we find ourselves upon the threshold of momentous times. For a mortal creature to cross the border into deathlessness . . ." He paused, temporarily lost for words, then continued, "Indeed, countless sages and philosophers and druids have sought this prize for untold centuries. Some might regard it as the ultimate goal of humankind." He brushed three crumbs from his linen surcoat and said deliberately, "We mortal beings are heroes."

"What can you mean?"

"We walk—nay, we run down the path of Time while blindfolded. At any instant a chasm might open before us. At any moment we might run straight into a wall. Yet we keep on—most of us do, at any rate. We love, while knowing that someday our love might be lost forever. We laugh as we stride along, even while recognizing that doom lies at the end of the road. We give, while comprehending that in the end 'twill all be taken away. We are nothing less than heroes."

"What strange words you speak!" commented Jewel.

"They are merely words from a song," Arran told her, and in low but melodious tones he commenced to sing:

"Some wights play jestful tricks. Some are inclined
  To work malicious harm on humankind.
  Some help goodwives at spinning wheel and hearth,
  Or aid the honest farmer in his garth.

"Yet, while they oddly disparate may be,
  One attribute they hold in common fee—
  Their days and nights roll on forevermore
  And never reach the threshold of Death's door.

"No darkling grave awaits beneath the grass,
  No dreadful fear of what might come to pass.
  Oh, blithe and empty-hearted must be he
  Who's cosseted by immortality!

"But mortal creatures walk along the road
  Of Time—nay, we make haste! Despite our load
  Piled high with weary trouble. And withal,
  We're blindfold, so at any step might fall.

"At any instant chasms might unclose
  To swallow us, beneath our very toes!
  At any instant, blindfold and alone,
  We might run headlong into walls of stone.

"And yet we keep on running. On we go,
  Most of us, this despite the fact we know
  'Twill all be swept away. We love, aware
  That some dark hour, love shall be lost fore'er.

"We laugh and joke, we seek to banish gloom,
  Knowing the while, we speed toward our doom.
  We give, knowing all gifts will turn to dust,
  And still we keep on running, in blind trust.

"Like luminescent falling stars—"

Abruptly, the young man ceased his singing.
"What's amiss?" inquired Jewel.

"Naught," he replied casually. "Merely, I cannot recall the last couple of verses. Now, we had better rouse our snoring friends and be on our way once more." He sprang to his feet and went to attend his horse, brushing flies from its eyes and retightening the buckles of the surcingle. Jewel watched him, suddenly aware of the way he moved—so utterly self-assured, so graceful and lithe. His long hair swung with every shift of balance, and the dark strands whipped across his back. The look of him stirred an ember within her being, but she quickly turned away and let the sensation subside.

Like some unrelenting foe, the sun hammered its fists on the shoulders of the travelers. They took to journeying at nights, when the temperature dropped sharply and a bitter frost spread across the desert. During the noonday hours they dozed beneath awnings of bleached canvas stretched on poles hammered into the ground. Here in the southern desert there was scant natural shade to provide relief to humankind. Across hundreds of leagues the landscape on either side of the road rolled on as level as a placid lake, unrelieved by any projection more significant than the occasional small boulder. Bald patches of terra-cotta dirt showed like bloodstains between clumps of spinifex and dwarf acacia, and strewings of rusty rocks.

Jewel recalled her visit to her grandmother's village, R'shael, when she was five Winters old. The memory tugged at her heartstrings, giving rise to a half-formed desire to turn off the main road and revisit the place. Yet it was too far out of their way, and besides, she had no family living there now and it was unlikely that any of the villagers would remember her.

Sunfall, its spectacular vistas of splendor dazzling like wildfire across the skies, brought relief from the heat. Refreshed by the mild desert evenings, Scorpion would often lift his voice in song as they rode.

The highway crossed the sandy wastelands, making for Jhallavad, the capital city of that southern kingdom. Upright milestones, waist-high to a man, faithfully punctuated the road's edges. The surface itself was paved, here and there, and packed hard along other stretches. Restless windblown sands had made surprisingly small incursions; conceivably the highway was protected by some ancient, lingering enchantment; otherwise it might have been choked and buried long ago.

After sunfall, shy nocturnal animals would go scurrying amongst clumps of wiry grass, and hopping over stones: tiny kultarrs with their huge, dark eyes and their long tails, pointy-nosed bandicoots, long-eared bilbies digging in the sand for larvae, seeds, and fungi. Other creatures of the night were just as elusive but not so mortal. No water-loving wights haunted these regions; most were subterranean dwellers, including coblynau, buccas, gathorns, bockles, and nuggles. Occasionally, one or two such manifestations would skitter across the sand in the moonlight, darting from the shelter of a tussock to some small, secret cave-mouth, conceivably an entrance to underground labyrinths.

From time to time the riders met wayfarers coming from the other direction, unprosperous folk who, to eke a living, were forced to keep plying their trade no matter how hot the season. To replenish their water supplies from the wells the travelers broke their journey at hamlets along their route. Always they were met with hostility at first, for the desert-dwellers never ceased to be on guard against Marauders. When they proved themselves peace-loving, the travelers were offered hospitality in exchange for tidings, songs, tales, and coin. Yet never did the villagers allow their wariness to subside.

On a couple of occasions Jewel noted odd behavior on the part of the Ashqalêthans. Twice, as Scorpion left their lodgings in the morning, she spied him slipping money and some token to the inn-keeper, whispering the while. Scorpion was not aware that she saw him, and Lizard was otherwise occupied, but Jewel relayed her observations to Arran and they both increased their vigilance.

The farther west they rode, the drier the landscape became. Low, scrubby, and sparse was the vegetation clinging to the barren, hard-packed gravel that covered the ground. Dust clung to the ample folds of Jewel's *burnous,* and to the baggy sleeves of Arran's shirt. Grit infiltrated the camel-hide sebbats on the travelers' feet, and the fluid scarves of muslin that covered their heads beneath their hats and turbans. Not even weeds could steal a foothold in the dehydrated gravel. The only grass was tough-leafed spinifex, surviving tenaciously, but Arran and Scorpion had brought sacks of lucerne and oats to feed the horses.

"Sand everywhere," said Jewel, shading her eyes against the sun's glare. "As far as the eyes can see! Sand!"

"It hardly ever rains here, " said Arran, "perhaps once in four years, or nine, or fifteen. But when it does rain, the desert blooms everywhere like a garden, the fairest garden ever seen."

"You are a fount of knowledge," she bantered, "but I already knew that."

As always, he took her teasing in good part. He was, by nature, somewhat restrained and not given to extrovert behavior, yet he was a young man of common sense, wise, just, and fair, dependable and steadfast. Her badinage delighted him, even though he seldom replied in kind.

"Methinks you and your sister have passed this way before, young master," Scorpion said good-naturedly to Arran.

"That we have," replied the weathermaster, who had several times flown over Ashqalêth in a sky-balloon.

"We cannot help but wonder where a brother and sister might be bound, across these withered lands," Scorpion went on.

Arran remained sitting astride his horse, but the line of his body subtly altered. Jewel observed the change, noting his watchfulness.

"For our part, we cannot help but wonder why a couple of fellows who do not appear to be merchants or peddlers are traveling through Ashqalêth," the young man countered.

"We are happy to broadcast our enterprise. Neither merchants nor peddlers are we, but water-diviners. Our tools of trade are naught but a forked hazel rod and, in Lizard's case, a pair of sturdy copper wires. We are returning to our homes in Jhallavad."

This revelation alleviated Jewel's uneasiness; in the city she and Arran would be able to take their leave of their companions and be free to seek the Well of Rain in far-off Saadiah.

Courteously, Arran said, "We shall be sorry to part company with you both."

"Likewise," affirmed Scorpion.

"One can understand why water-diviners are sought after in arid lands, but what work did you find in Slievmordhu?" Jewel asked. "'Tis a kingdom abounding with rivers."

"Underground springs are always of value to farmers," said Scorpion. "What's more, sometimes we'll stumble across metal-lodes while we're looking for water."

"And sometimes we'll find nothing at all!" chuckled Lizard. "'Tis an uncertain business, water-divining!"

"For folk such as we, that is," amended Scorpion. "Not for weathermasters and the like. But *their* fees are too high for the common peasant to afford, so when farmers hear of us, they hire us instead! And now," he added, "'tis only fair that you must satisfy our enquiry in return. Whither go you?"

"We hie to Grïmnørsland," said Arran without hesitation, glad to deflect the topic from that of weathermasters. "To a small hamlet just over the border."

"Oh? What might be the name of this hamlet?"

"Müdgaard."

"I know of it," said Scorpion, flashing his usual grin. "It lies on the border between Grïmnørsland and Ashqalêth, on the road to Füshgaard. But you might have traveled a shorter path to get there from Cathair Rua."

"Shorter perhaps, but passing too close to the Wight Hills."

"What business have you in Müdgaard?"

"Our own."

The Ashqalêthan chuckled. "Hey, Lizard, the young master keeps close counsel!" he said, winking breezily. "Well, so be it. A man should not pry too deeply into his friends' affairs."

It was a seven-night more before they reached Jhallavad. The first sign of the distant city was a faint smear of smoke against the long shimmer of the western horizon. The hour was late, and the sun was falling into a welter of glory. Suffused ribbons of wine-red, long ovals of strawberry and soaking sheets of gold provided a backdrop to the dirty stain of smoke.

"The chimneys of the glass-furnaces are many," said Scorpion, ever the informative guide. "The smoke they pump out blows away to the north, on the prevailing winds."

"We always get nice sunsets in the desert," put in Lizard.

"The prettiest ones always happen when there's a lot of smoke and dust in the air," Scorpion said authoritatively.

"Indeed this sunset is surpassing fair!" said Jewel. Turning to Arran, she murmured, "But why?"

"Do you truly desire further explanation?"

"I do!"

The weathermaster grinned, amused at Jewel's enthusiasm for knowledge. "The fine particles in dusty atmospheres scatter the blue and green light from the sun's rays," he said, "and only the yellow, orange, and red beams shine through. But sunset is most beautiful when there is airborne moisture, such as those lenticular clouds you can see just above the horizon, from which the colors are reflecting with a tint of roses."

Admiring the panorama, they rode on.

Closer to the royal city the landscape altered, becoming greener, and sparsely wooded. Like supernatural trees, thousands of metal-bladed windmills whirled atop their tall stanchions, pumping up water from the city's aquifers and artesian wells. The sun's elongated shafts of rosy light lingered on legions of grapevines and battalions of crops, watered by irrigation channels. Goats and dromedaries grazed in fields surrounding farmhouses that squatted on stilts so that cooling airs might circulate beneath the floors. Such dwellings reminded Jewel of the marsh. The city itself, behind its high walls, had been constructed in and upon a vast hill of sandstone jutting out of the desert floor, riddled with deeply mined cellars that remained cool both day and night. The hovels of the poor had thick walls of dried mud and camel dung, while the abodes of the wealthy were primarily built of greenish slate, milky limestone, and sandstone the color of parchment. The western facets of the buildings were tinged carnation in the dying radiance of evening.

"Jhallavad is not an unlovely sight, no?" said Scorpion proudly. "Yet, an even better sight awaits within, and that is the king's palace. The gargoyles and adornments of our sovereign's halls are sculpted from fluorspar, a stone that glows like phosphorescence when illuminated in a certain way. Pale green and yellow are the colors of desert fluor, and the topmost turret of the palace is carved and sculpted entirely of butter-colored jasper. In the king's courtyards stand statues made of jadeite and nephrite, green as rushes and white as pups' milkteeth!"

As the riders approached the city gates a procession of heavily laden dromedaries came slowly marching out. The travelers reined in their horses and stopped by the roadside to watch the convoy pass. Their shadows undulated, long and slender, on the hard-packed dirt of the road.

"Glass merchants, I daresay," said Scorpion, "bound for eastern lands."

When at last they rode into Ashqalêth's royal city, Jewel gazed avidly about. Lamps were being kindled behind windows, and in metal cradles that swung from the fronds of palm trees. R'shael, her father's village, was only a small hamlet, a dwarf in comparison with the giant that was the capital city. She welcomed the opportunity to study this large Ashqalêthan settlement, staring with interest at the silk bazaars, the wine shops, the desert horses in sage-green bridles and saddles dyed with dark vermilion, the townsfolk garbed in hues of saffron and ocher.

The men wore flat-topped, turban-like hats, baggy leggings, and embroidered, calf-length tunics loosely belted at the waist. Sheathed scimitars and daggers hung from these belts. Many men sported finger-rings or earrings of bright yellow brass. Weathered and lean were their faces and their cardamom-colored hair was tied in a club at the nape of the neck—the tradition for men and boys in Ashqalêth. The garments of the women were long, voluminous, and flowing. Their headgear consisted of scarves, turbans, and veils, sometimes kept in place by twisted headbands of colored silks. They, too, decorated themselves with ornaments of brass: anklets, necklaces, armbands, bells, and pins that emitted a muted jingling with every movement. Amulets depended from thongs or chains about the necks of men, women, and children.

Lizard and Scorpion helped their companions find a suitable inn, where they made themselves comfortable.

"We go now to our own lodgings," said Lizard, "but do not be downcast, for we shall not abandon our new friends!"

"As long as you bide here in Jhallavad," said Scorpion, "we shall not be far away. If you need help, we shall be pleased to provide it!" They waved in a jolly manner as they departed, trotting down the street.

Later that evening, Jewel took Arran aside and spoke to him.

"I cannot help but distrust those two," she said. "They seem over-eager for our company, and that business with Scorpion slyly slipping money to inn-keepers disturbs me."

"I am of the same mind," said Arran.

"Still it escapes me—where have I glimpsed Scorpion's face before? Perhaps it was at the Fair Field. . . ." Jewel's musings petered out. She glanced up at Ar-ran. "What can they be about?"

"I cannot guess, but what you say strikes a chord within me. It has not es-caped my notice that they seem devious. Possibly, they are concealing something from us. The sooner we part company with them, the better."

Jewel burst out laughing, and said merrily, "It occurs to me that they might have the same opinion about us!"

There was no reason to stay in Jhallavad for long. For only two nights and one day Jewel and Arran remained there, stocking up on provisions at stalls in-dicated to them by their self-appointed guides, who insisted on accompanying them almost everywhere.

"We'll show you where to find the honest merchants," Lizard said.

As before, the prices asked by the recommended merchants were fair, and the goods received were sound. Nonetheless, this did nothing to allay the suspicions of Jewel and Stormbringer.

"You have been of great help to us," said the young man courteously as he and Jewel took their leave of the Ashqalêthans early in the morning. "May rain-fall bless you and your families."

"Ho! Sounds like a benediction of the weathermasters!" rejoined Scorpion. He smiled knowledgeably, perhaps a trifle smugly.

"May Lords Fortune and Doom favor you," Lizard bellowed, "may gracious Lady Ill-Fortune never cross your path, and may sublime Lady Destiny serve you well!"

Scorpion stuck a finger in one ear as if cleaning it out. He remarked to his companion, "And may the Fates mark well the ache-head volume at which you publicly praise them, as no doubt you intended."

Relieved to be parted from the Ashqalêthans at last, Jewel and Arran swung up into their saddles and set off, following the highway's meanderings. After riding through the gates of Jhallavad they passed through irrigated groves of olives and figs. In glaucous puddles of shade, small children frolicked. The ris-ing desert sun was a flaming cartwheel, iron-rimmed. Its rays reflected from a multitude of irrigation channels, chipping sparks from the water. Nodding palm fronds were stamped out in fine detail against the sky. As the breeze swung around, the travelers glanced back over their shoulders to catch a last view of the city. Thousands of flower-petal windmills were revolving, their directional vanes rotating them all to face south. After this brief glimpse, Jewel and Arran hastened on.

A band of weary riders approached from the other direction, plodding along the road toward Jewel and her companion. Dourly, they nodded acknowledgment as they went past, before disappearing in the direction of Jhallavad.

"Probably Grïmnørslanders," said Arran.

The farther they journeyed from the city, the more fantastic the landscape became. All was brick-red, sage-green, or duck-egg blue: the gravelly ground and the rocks, the faded foliage, the blistering sky. Across the plain, wind-eroded rock formations thrust up here and there like carvings sculpted by lunatics. Vast sweeps of sand piled high against unseen obstacles, their slopes etched with elongated rows of wavy lines. The wind lifted soft powdery veils. It plucked at the soft contours of tall sand-mountains, ceaselessly shifting them, uncovering the half-buried ruins of cities, bones of alabaster, slim spirals of horn, or the broken knees of gigantic statues, before concealing them again, conceivably for millennia. In these parts the sifting dusts sometimes covered the route. Only the tall monoliths, placed at intervals along the roadside, marked its course.

In the distance tall translucent funnels arose into the air, drilled their way along the ground, and subsided.

"What are they?" asked Jewel, pointing out these frenzied phenomena. "What causes them? Are they dangerous?"

"They are dust devils, sometimes called sand augers," said Arran. "They are born when a bubble of sun-warmed air rises rapidly in the vicinity of some pre-existing vorticity, such as the wind whipping about a rock. The rotating column of air picks up dust, leaves, feathers, and other debris, thus becoming visible."

"But are they dangerous?" Jewel repeated.

"Dust devils are only the infants of the tornado family. Typically, they last a very short span before dissipating, and do no damage, but the rare, larger ones can be destructive."

Scanning their surroundings, Jewel said, "Can they be seen, even if they do not collect dust?"

"I can perceive them, though you may not. Weathermasters can see differences in air pressure, although it is not really 'seeing,' but I have no other description for it."

"Look!" Jewel stood up in her stirrups. "There is one fast approaching down the road behind us, as we speak!"

Glancing back, Arran said, "That is no dust devil. The sand is being kicked up by the hooves of galloping horses. We are being pursued."

"Whyfor? Should we try to elude them?"

"Unless we jettison our saddlebags they will undoubtedly overtake us. In any case, where could we run? No. We can only wait. There may be no harm in whatever follows us, after all." His tone, nonetheless, was not convincing.

The shapes of two horsemen became outlined in the center of the fast-moving dust cloud. When they caught up with the travelers they resolved themselves into the robed forms of Scorpion and Lizard.

"Curses upon them," said Arran under his breath. "Why the haste?" he said aloud as the Ashqalêthans trotted up, their small desert horses snorting and glistening with sweat.

Lizard waved his hand cheerily. "Good morrow, friends!"

"Wayfarers from Grïmnørsland came into town this morning," shouted Scorpion. "They brought news. It seems there is a chance of work for us in Trøndelheim; therefore we intend to proceed there forthwith. We deemed we might as well travel in pleasant company."

Jewel and Arran exchanged a quick glance, steeped with meaning.

"Greetings," Arran said, formally and without warmth.

The Ashqalêthans appeared oblivious of the stolidness of their reception. After allowing their horses a shallow drink from their waterbags, they fell in beside the weathermaster and the damsel and rode on, chattering like mynah-birds.

In the simmering heat of noon, whenever the Ashqalêthans took their customary midday nap beneath some rubicund rock formation or skeletal desert bush, Jewel and Arran would consult together in muted tones.

"All along the way I have pondered," said the young man one day. "We must get rid of them before we reach Saadiah, but I cannot work out how to do it."

The edges of consciousness were chipped by the irritating drone of a single fly and the incessant, creaky *tootsie cheer* of a pair of chirruping wedgebills.

Jewel scooped up a fallen strip of bark and fanned the heat from her face. "I, too, am nonplussed," said she. "They are rogues, I am certain. We cannot have them following us to Saadiah, asking questions. I wish I could recall where I have seen Scorpion before . . . but perchance I have mistaken him for another. . . ."

On the third night, she came up with a suggestion. "We must pass the turn-off to Saadiah, wait until they are asleep one night, then slip away and double back. Darkness offers some slight chance of escaping unobserved."

Since he could advance no superior idea, Arran agreed.

Six days out from Jhallavad, the opportunity arose to execute their plan. That day they had bypassed the intersection whose left fork was the by-way leading to Saadiah. It was but one of several such forks, each one marked by a rune-etched stone to point the way. Early evening stretched out across the glimmering desert like a panther's shadow, and a quarter moon was rising behind the western ranges. The travelers were camped in a dry gulch that became a riverbed on the infrequent occasions when torrential downpours deluged the desert. Pale-boled river-eucalypts thrust skyward from the creamy gravel, their roots delving deep. Blue and green parrots, no bigger than a girl's hand, were nesting in the trees' woody hollows. The Ashqalêthans snored on their couches of river-sand. Their young companions apparently rested with them.

There was a faint, high-pitched shrilling, as of insects. A delicate bat flitted overhead, and a shadow momentarily crossed the faces of the two sleeping men. Next instant, the damsel and the young man were gone.

Serene shafts of moonlight glazed the sere watercourse and stood silently between the trees.

Quietly Jewel and Arran led the horses away. When they estimated they were out of earshot they remounted and began to canter back toward Jhallavad. About half an hour had passed when Arran chanced to look behind. A cloud of dust was moving along the road, and he knew Scorpion and Lizard were coming after them.

"They are following us," the young man called out. "They must have guessed we are hiding a secret. If they catch up, they will ask us why we were running away."

"Then we must urge our steeds to go faster!" cried Jewel.

"On the contrary!" Instead of bidding his horse to break into a gallop, Arran reined in. Following his example, Jewel also brought her mount to a halt. She asked no questions, only rested her quizzical azure gaze upon the young man.

With his weathermaster's senses, Arran reached out into his surroundings. He perceived the interplay of pressure gradients, and variations in temperature. His nerves felt the stirrings of the air, their directions, their velocities.

Nimbly he sprang from his saddle and crouched beside a stone whose flat surface had trapped the fierce heat of the sun that day and was still searingly hot to the touch. It was lying next to a wind-chiseled boulder almost the height of a man. Arran wove a pattern with his hands, and Jewel heard him speak.

"βȳřñ, ¥ē βéøřht βřöῄd!"

Excitement coursed through the damsel, as it always did when she watched weathermasters employing the words of power, the strange and potent language of the *brí*.

She saw a kind of shimmer arise from the stone, perhaps a heat haze. Meanwhile, the young man was muttering other words, making different gestures, and the corners of his striped surcoat began to move, fluttering out and away from the boulder. His attention was fixed on the flat stone. Then she caught a faint glimpse of it, a low spiral of dust twirling on the ground like a dog chasing its tail.

The conditions were almost right, in any case. He was not so much forcing a change as relocating and strengthening an existing state. So the young weathermaster told himself, as once again he defied the laws of Ellenhall for the sake of Jewel and her quest.

He stepped back. As the heated air rose through layers of cooler gases, its strong buoyancy enhanced the convergence. The air pressure at ground level dropped. Warm air rushing to fill the vacancy spiraled in a corkscrew motion. The effect was similar to that produced by a dancer who increases the speed of his pirouette by pulling his arms closer to his body. A curved current of air whipped from around the side of the boulder, making the air rotate even faster.

A vortex evolved. As the air spun more rapidly, the pressure in the center of the whirlwind dropped lower. More hot air was drawn within the cone, the tiny tornado feeding on itself, sucking up dirt and debris until it became clearly visible to Jewel. The funnel of twisting air grew tall enough to touch the top of a nearby mallee eucalypt, shaking the foliage. Then, with the sound of canvas being torn, the dust devil ran sideways across the ground, centering itself in the middle of the highway.

The garments of Jewel and Arran were blowing, flapping wildly now. Stormbringer leaped onto his horse's back and after one last long measuring stare at the phenomenon he had called into being, he cried out to Jewel, pulled around his horse's head, and sent it galloping down the road toward Jhallavad. The damsel followed closely in his wake.

Three times Arran slowed his steed and wheeled about to face the distant whirlwind, dropping the reins and sketching hieroglyphs in the air. His companion heard him speak and understood he was influencing the dust devil's eccentric ramblings, continually bringing it back to the road and ensuring it remained stationed between themselves and those who followed after.

On they galloped. Eventually, when the horses tired, they slowed to a walk.

"What will happen?" the damsel asked, peering over her shoulder. Her pulse stampeded; her sinews burned like cables of flame. At their backs the spiral, now full-grown, could be seen towering against the stars as it danced erratically through the desert. In front of them, rising majestically like some theatrical curtain, the night sky was peppered with a fantastic ice-storm of constellations.

"Dust devils eventually burn themselves out when the air pressure within the cone rises to equal the pressure of the surroundings. That one might last for one hour or several. At the very least, it will cover our tracks, drive our pursuers back, and prevent them from following us."

"It is a marvel," breathed Jewel.

Her companion fell silent, brooding. He seemed displeased with himself—she did not understand why.

Many miles later they reached the turn-off. By morning they were well along the by-way to Saadiah.

Without halting to rest they traveled on until the sun had reached its zenith. The heat poured down like boiling honey. At length, mindful of the well-being of the horses, they left the road and made camp in the shadow of a mighty dune, as tawny as a basking lion. They made certain they could not be seen from the road, in case they were being followed; there were not many places to which travelers might be heading in this part of the desert, and once the dust devil had subsided, the Ashqalêthans might have been able to work out their destination. The afternoon brought the now-familiar hot wind from the baking regions of the south, the Fyrflaume from the Stone Deserts, that ensured Ashqalêth remained in its arid condition. Finely granulated sheets of sand were blowing horizontally from the dune's uppermost ridge. Nearby, some beetles were burrowing beneath the ground to keep cool. In that place the travelers slept, while the sun swam lazily overhead and heat hazes quivered against the horizon, and the horses stood with drooping heads, and some insane insect trilled a monotonous opera.

The afternoon was already waning when Jewel and Arran awoke and scrutinized the landscape for evidence of Lizard and Scorpion. There was no sign of the pair, nor any overtaking hoofprints in the sand, so after taking some refreshment they moved on. Climbing steeply, the by-way was leading them toward the long range of mountains in the west. In the evening the setting sun was impaled upon the peaks; each hour those peaks loomed a little higher above the plain. The desert lay to the leeward side of the range, but Saadiah lay on the windward, seaward slopes, and travelers must cross through the mountains to reach it. This was usually achieved by means of the Khashayar Tunnel.

This vast underground traverse was an empty watercourse, the horizontal channel of an old underground river that had once pierced the mountain range from one side to the other. These days the river was dry, due to some ancient shiftings of the ground that had diverted the flow. It was a great arched passageway, worn through rock and soil by the action of the current over aeons.

Naturally vaulted, it was high, wide, and airy, and haunted by whistling winds. Mining wights could be heard at work in the walls, sometimes undercurrented by the drone and whirr of eldritch spinning wheels. Three miles long was this subterranean highway, and a safe road for humankind to travel during daylight hours, as long as they kept moving. It was perilous to stand still, more perilous to be in there at night.

Three days after setting forth on the by-way, Jewel and Arran reached the mouth of the Khashayar Tunnel, on the very outskirts of Saadiah. They spent the night in the open air, concealed by rocky outcrops covered in sagebrush, before venturing under the mountain the next day at dawn.

As they rode deeper into the subterranean way, the sun's light began to fail. The sound of their horses' hooves was partly muffled by swathes of sand that had drifted in from the desert. Farther still, and visibility was only possible by means of dim reflections from rock facets: ahead loomed blind darkness. From far off, somewhere in the secret cores of the mountain, there sounded a *tap-tap-tapping* and a chinking of metallic percussions, as if a dozen clockwork dolls were involved in rhythmically hammering and chopping, each slightly out of tempo with the rest.

Arran murmured outlandish words. Before they entered the Tunnel he had removed from his saddlebags a slender staff of ash that he had carried with him from High Darioneth. Such objects were known to the weathermasters as light javelins. The tip, sharpened to a point, was encased in a slim cone of brass. Raising this spear high in his right hand, Arran spoke again, now gesturing with his left hand. Overhead, the atmosphere jostled and tingled. The tapered end of the javelin gave off a crackling noise, as of droplets swiftly freezing to ice-crystals. A sudden blast screamed as two air currents gusted in opposite directions, not head-on but back to back, grating against each other as they passed. The air tasted like iron, and smacked of burning. A swarm of tiny blue-white sparks shot forth from the javelin's end. Scaldingly brilliant, they clustered about the brass point in a sphere of incandescent cloud, shedding a moonbeam radiance all around.

"A corona discharge," Arran explained to Jewel, who was taken aback. "Sometimes these glowing orbs are called 'corposants,' but their true designation is 'Erasmus's fires,' named after a fabled hero, the legendary patron of sailors. We shall use them to light our way."

"Does weathermaster law permit such use?"

Small lightnings fizzed and crawled on the brass cone.

"Indeed. Erasmus's fire can be contained as a local phenomenon, and is therefore not disruptive to larger systems."

Dazzles whizzed and jumped eerily in and out of the luminous sphere at the top of the javelin. Jewel's hair stood on end, and she exclaimed with astonishment.

Through the Tunnel they passed, and out the other side, and their traverse was uneventful. As they rode they cast many a backward glance to see if their hunters had tracked them down, but they could spy nobody following in their wake, and allowed themselves to hope that they had thrown Lizard and Scorpion off their trail.

After two and a half days more, Jewel and Arran arrived in the heart of the Saadiah region. During that time they met only one other party of travelers: a large convoy journeying toward the east. A string of dromedaries was laden with wrapped bales. Heavily armed outriders guarded the procession; two horsemen saluted the travelers with a wave of the hand, but the rest merely stared distrustfully.

Taking its native name from the unusual rock formations at its center, Saadiah was a remote district between Jhallavad and the Grïmnørsland border. It was cradled in the bosky foothills of the coastal ranges. The perennial wind current known as the Fyrflaume came racing across the hot stone wastelands to the south, while the freezing ocean current called the Glassingtide pounded against the rocky shores to the west. The moisture-laden breezes that crossed the mountains from the ocean dumped their burdens in the foothills, becoming as parched as husks by the time they blew across the hinterlands. These phenomena combined to produce Saadiah's local climate.

To the incoming travelers Saadiah seemed an oasis, lush and verdant. They rode amongst hills clothed with forests and orchards. The wind in the foliage moved the boughs gently, slowly, softly, and the sound was the sound of a thousand voices whispering. Leaves were falling down, twisting, gliding, fluttering as they descended in shoals, like fish. The sky was a pane of lapis lazuli, smoky at the edges, and, above the mountain range that reared steeply in front of them the riders saw the rugged, jagged shapes of the peaks echoed in a second range, one that climbed the sky and was formed of clouds building up over the distant ocean. Dark purple and stormy loomed the nearer clouds. Those rising behind them were purest silver-white.

They rode beneath dipping boughs, while winged things fluttered by like dislocated flowers. Patches of cool shade dappled their heads and shoulders. Deep in the groves young women were picking great quantities of leaves, thrusting branches inside their sacks and stripping them bare with their hands.

Some barefoot children accompanying the women were playing a game with sticks and seed-pods. Jewel smiled at them as she rode past.

The entire region appeared prosperous; the cottages were well built and in good repair. Beside most of the farmhouses stood long buildings perforated by tiny windows. In the middle of each village loomed an imposing structure with large, pointed-arch windows. The principal township, Spire, boasted a modest sanctorum, a distillery, several large wineries, and a couple of establishments devoted to the drying and storage of fruits.

That evening, in the Wheel and Spindle, the travelers put it about that they had come to Spire to view the well-known rock formations.

"Has anyone ever managed to climb them?" Arran asked a serving-lad.

"Hardly likely! They are guarded by the korred." The lad shook his head as if astonished. "You foreigners! Doesn't everybody know that?"

When the servant bustled away, Jewel said, "Saadiah is not as famous as the inhabitants suppose."

"No place is," said Stormbringer.

A woman sitting nearby, resting her elbows on the table, said, "Many have tried to climb the pinnacles."

"Oh yes," said her neighbor, nodding eagerly. "Many hopefuls have come here with their hammers and spikes and ropes, for there is naught as attractive to some folk as a peak that has never been conquered. But the pinnacles defeated them all, that they did!" She chuckled. "Couldn't get so much as a toe-hold, they couldn't! The korred wouldn't let 'em."

"What is the korred?" Jewel asked.

"They," corrected the first woman, now speaking more softly and glancing over her shoulder, "are short and stumpy wights with shaggy hair, dark wrinkled faces, and little deep-set eyes that are as bright as carbuncles. Their voices are cracked and hollow, their hands have claws like a cat's, and their feet are horny like a goat's."

"They are expert smiths and coiners," added the second woman, leaning close to the visitors and speaking in confidential tones, as if the wights themselves might be eavesdropping in the shadows nearby. "'Tis said they have great treasures hidden in the pinnacles where they dwell, and which some folk believe they themselves built. The korred dance around the pinnacles by night, and woe to the belated passer-by who is forced to join in their roundel, for he usually dies of exhaustion. King's Day is their weekly holiday, and the first King's Day in Mai their annual festival, which they celebrate with dancing, singing, and music."

Eager to prove herself equally as knowledgeable as her neighbor, the first woman elaborated, "They are always furnished with a large leathern purse, which is said to be full of gold."

"But if any man succeeds in getting it from them," the neighbor chimed in, "he finds nothing in his hands but hair and a pair of scissors!"

"These guardian wights sound formidable," Arran commented.

"In trying to reach the top of the pinnacles," the first woman went on, "some folk became quite inventive and tried to fling themselves up by way of human catapults and such. Always ended in disaster," she concluded, with an air of nostalgia.

"But I reckon the weathermasters might have a chance, floating in one of their balloons," speculated the neighbor.

"Not a hope," her friend disagreed. "The korred wouldn't let them get near; that's what everyone says."

Their difference of opinion evolved into a long-winded debate, during which the women paid no further attention to Jewel and Arran.

Spire township was situated less than one league away from the pinnacles, to which the travelers paid a visit next morning.

The track led through luxuriant groves. As they followed it, vertical splinters of sapphire slashed through the tree-stems ahead, and abruptly the trees opened out onto a vista; a great harbor of air flooded with blue sky, in which the massive petrified boles of ancient forest giants were standing; a gigantic forest of decapitated trees. Yet they were not trees.

Jewel and Arran found themselves in a natural bowl that was immense, possibly a mile wide but only about twenty-five feet deep. Its walls were formed of clay, colored ocher, raw sienna, burnt umber, hard material in which few plants could find purchase. The sides appeared vertical at first, but closer inspection showed they were pleated with minor landslides, scored with crevices and channels of erosion. The gradient of the incline was gentler in some parts, and it would not be difficult to navigate a route down to the hollow's floor.

The pinnacles, disposed about two hundred to four hundred yards apart, were perpendicular, sheer-sided towers of stone, too smooth to climb, too adamantine to be chipped with an axe to create footholds, apparently devoid of crevices. Unlike the stunted rock formations of the desert, they were very lofty, tall, ancient cores from around which the surrounding material had eroded away, and whose heads seemed to pierce the clouds. The wind sang amongst them. No vegetation clung to their flanks.

Myrtle bushes and short grasses sprang between and around the pinnacles, and the eastern half of the circular dell was blanketed by velvety shadows. There was no sign of any of the guardian korred, but the place had an eldritch feel. It was deserted.

That is, it appeared at first to be deserted.

Having clambered down, Jewel and Arran wandered amongst the inscrutable steeples, gazing ever upward, considering how the summits might be reached. Five small children were darting between the bases of the towers. They were clad in knee-length culottes, and loose-fitting shirts of silk or muslin. Thin brass bangles jangled on their wrists and ankles, which were bare and sun-browned. A cooing sound went up like a sudden release of bubbles. It was their giggling. Jewel guessed they were pretending to be hunted by wicked ogres, represented by herself and her companion. She had often played such games herself, as a child.

Arran was of the same mind. Playfully he feinted a lunge at one of the tots, who broke into a gleeful laugh and scampered away, only to reappear again in the next instant, peeping from behind a column. The young man threw himself energetically into the game, leaping and running, darting and dodging. Jewel followed his every movement, admiring his vitality and masculine beauty. Lithe and lean, he moved with the poise of an athlete. Impulsively she threw aside her hat and joined in. A romp ensued. The travelers chased the little ones until the exertion and the waxing heat of the day tired them all out.

As Jewel and Arran cast themselves down on the soft grasses in the shade of a myrtle bush, their erstwhile playmates self-consciously approached, trying to hide behind one another, fascinated and attracted by the appearance of newcomers.

"Which one is the Comet's Tower?" Jewel inquired.

"That one," said the tallest child, pointing a stubby, grubby finger.

It was not far from the center of the dell, and the loftiest of all. Predictably. Clouds scudded across the skies above its peak, seeming so near as to scrape its very crown. Close to the top a great chunk was missing from the pinnacle's side, as if some giant mouth had bitten it almost right through. Only a thin shelf of rock remained, overhanging the gap like a protective canopy. The onlookers could see right through this cavity, to the racing clouds beyond.

Such a height seemed impossible to reach.

The children giggled again. The smaller ones hid their impish faces behind the apron of the eldest girl.

The young man reclined against the slope and closed his eyes. His hair, which had worked loose from its bindings during the frolic, spilled in a tangle across the turf. Jewel lay flat on her stomach and cradled her head in her arms. The day was warm. They were weary from their travels, and stymied in their purpose. Now that they had at last arrived at their destination there seemed no way to achieve their ultimate goal.

In an attempt to regain their attention, three of the little girls lined themselves up in a triangular formation. Playing a game of clapping their own hands and one another's hands in rhythm, they chanted,

> "My mother said I never should
> Play with the gypsies in the wood.
> If I did, she would say,
> 'Naughty girl to disobey!
> Your hair won't curl; your shoes won't shine;
> Naughty girl, you shan't be mine!'"

After a second rendition of the verse, Stormbringer opened his eyes, but the singers had already decided there was more entertaining employment elsewhere, and run away. Their laughter effervesced through the sultry atmosphere.

Shadows inched across the dell. The wind sang between the pinnacles, and oceaned through the luxuriant foliage of the trees lining the rim.

"Thank the powers they have gone," murmured Jewel. "I was afraid they might begin on some similar doggerel, one that the wagoners' children used to sing interminably. They go round and round in your head, those chants." After a pause she said, "Too late. The other song is back in my brain. Wind a cradle for a moth, tight against the Winter's wrath. Ugh!"

Arran remarked quietly, "Did you say 'a cradle for a moth'?"

Jewel sat bolt upright. "Indeed I did!" she exclaimed. "How strange are the workings of the inner mind! Unintentionally, I may have solved the sorcerer's riddle.

> "Wind a cradle for a moth,
> Tight against the Winter's wrath.
> Spin a thread to make a cloth
> Lighter than a puff of froth.
> Needle, needle, stitch a thing
> Pretty as a beetle's wing.
> Cradle, cradle, lift me up
> Till the raindrops fill my cup.

"It is a song of the silk-merchants!"

"Ignorant foreigners that we are!" said the young man in mock disgust. "How could we have missed the obvious? Those are groves of *mulberry* trees, the fodder of silkworms."

The Comet's Tower

That very Sevember morning, five riders were trotting along the main road through Saadiah. They were the same distance away from Spire as Jewel and Arran Stormbringer had been at the identical time on the previous day. Their flowing Ashqalêthan robes were suited to the desert climate, albeit ragged. Two of them were the men known to Jewel and Arran as Scorpion and Lizard. Yet had the damsel and the young man looked upon them now, they would scarcely have recognized their erstwhile companions of the road. Gone were the smiles, the twinkling glances, the crow's-feet crinkles of habitual merriment. Scorpion scowled heavily, while the features of Lizard hung slack and vacuous.

This sullen pair rode in the dust kicked up by the hooves of the two leaders, one of whom was a middle-aged man who was swigging from a flask as he rode. Beneath a flared nose his short, black beard covered a heavy jaw and scarred slab cheeks. His eyes drooped downward at the outer corners, as though his face were beginning to melt, and his hair was close-cropped. The one who rode with him, slightly ahead, was somewhat younger, a spare fellow, morose and hungry-looking. Wisps of his thinning hair adhered to the sweat of his brow. The fifth wayfarer was a woman. A scarf muffled her face and she rode at the rear.

They were passing amongst the green and water-rich margins of the region. Trees drew in close to the road at either hand, their foliage rustling and nodding. As the morning wore on, the riders passed a long, many-windowed magnanerie attached to a farmhouse, where women were hauling in sack-loads of mulberry leaves to feed the ravenous caterpillars.

The lean fellow then dropped back to join the riders at the tail of the band.

"When we arrive," he said, "you three must lie low. They would recognize your faces. Weaponmonger and I shall go in search of them."

"If we are not too late," murmured the woman.

With earnest intensity, the fellow turned to her. "Should we ride any faster, these nags would likely drop dead beneath us. Even desert hacks have their limits in the heat of Summer. Tardy indeed we should be, if we had to walk into town!"

"Tardy for what?" interjected the man known sometimes as Lizard. "We do not even know what they are looking for!"

"Something of value," replied the gaunt leader. His pale eyes rolled sideways like two withered peas. "Something they learned about in the fortress of the sorcerer."

"We could as easily ambush them and seize this treasure as they ride back along the by-road! They are two to our five."

"You know not what you say."

"I know not, because you tell us naught! You guess some secret, but you keep it to yourself."

"Hold your clacking tongue, Gaspar. I tire of your noise."

"What do you mean by 'lie low,' Aonarán?" asked the man who often gave his name as "Scorpion."

"I mean, find some hovel and remain there until I summon you."

"But—"

"Argue not with me, Sohrab! It is your fault they became suspicious and tried to elude you. No doubt you were careless when you gave the landlords your garbled, almost unintelligible instructions to pass on to us."

"But the ploy worked and you were able to keep track—"

"I said, argue not!" Aonarán emphasized his command by landing a savage, backhanded blow across the jaw of Sohrab. Scorpion flinched but did not cry out. A tendril of blood trickled from his cut lip. The man with the cropped hair laughed gutturally.

The lean fellow, Fionnbar Aonarán, rode ahead once more. The woman's pallid gaze followed him, then remained fixed on the man who had laughed.

By now, the day was past noon. At one of the arch-windowed filatures in Spire, Arran and Jewel finished haggling with a silk-merchant. Having reached an agreement, they paid their money and departed, carrying a long bolt of gossamer-light fabric and several skeins of silken cord. Their steps were buoyant as they made their way toward the seamstress's shop.

"Borne by a moth's cradle!" chanted Stormbringer exuberantly. He shook his head in wonderment, at the simplicity of the solution, revealed in the children's song. "Borne by a moth's cradle!"

Jewel laughed, sharing his delight. "A riddle typical of eldritch wights," she said.

Upon reaching the shop, they explained their proposed design to the woman in charge. The gold coins displayed in Arran's outstretched hand impressed upon her the requirement for speed, and she led them straightaway to her pattern-maker. In a remarkably short time the pattern had been designed and cut out of brown paper, whereupon the head seamstress led her customers up-stairs to a large chamber. A table of impressive proportions occupied the center of the room.

"Put away your work," she instructed several industrious women who had been scissoring swirls of woven materials and stitching at seams. "You will com-mence a fresh project, this very hour." She bade her assistants unroll the new bolt of silk and spread it out on the now-cleared table-top. "Leave it to me," she said to her clients, winking with a confidential air. "I will make sure the work is done swiftly and well." Even as the two customers left the room, the seam-stresses were already beginning to pin some wedge-like paper shapes onto the silk.

Jewel and Arran made their way to the main thoroughfare of the township, where, at the blacksmith's, the grocer's, the chandler's and the general provi-sioner's, they purchased a sturdy canvas sack, ropes, bags of nails, salt, dried hy-pericum leaves, dried rowanberries and stale breadcrumbs, and two hand-bells.

Late that afternoon, the five riders entered the township of Spire. They were as dusty and bedraggled as any travelers, and the poor quality of their garments in-dicated that they were far from wealthy. As in any remote population center, un-familiar faces attracted interest from the local people; nonetheless, the raiment of the visitors was so dilapidated it seemed evident they were merely a band of rag-tag paupers; therefore the interest was mild and short-lived. The newcomers seemed unlikely to increase Spire's prosperity by much. Three of them found lodgings at one of the meaner dwellings at the edge of town. The other two vis-ited the taverns, where they made themselves most sociable, exhibiting a keen interest in the inhabitants and their observations.

Meanwhile, behind closed doors in their lodging-house, Sohrab-Scorpion and Gaspar-Lizard had spread a large goat's hide across the floor and laid out upon it a row of hardware for review. The former was using a whetstone to sharpen a scimitar, while the latter was squinting down the length of a blow-pipe.

"There's no warping," he said, placing the pipe aside and beginning to check a handful of darts. As he worked, he grumbled resentfully, "Weaponmonger ordered me to sharpen his sword and oil the chain on his morningstar. Why should he not do it himself? That pox-riddled maniac treats me like dirt. He has no right to deem himself so high and mighty. He thinks nobody knows, but *we* know that in truth he's a walking dead man, with his poisonous little bottles of quicksilver and bismuth and arsenic powder, useless remedies against the hideous malady he claims he does not have."

"That one is an apothecarium in man-shape. He also carries phenol and spirit of salts."

"Whyfor? Spirit of salts is etching acid, is it not? He's hardly likely to be decorating knife-blades with anything other than blood and guts, out here in the wilderness."

"The phenol is for treating his lues," replied Sohrab-Scorpion, busy with the whetstone. "'Tis his own idea—he puts a droplet onto the chancres and buboes when they pop up, believing it burns out the poison."

"By the bones of Ádh, I hope that is as painful as it sounds." Gaspar shuddered. "If you tell me he uses spirit of salts in the same manner, then I shall deem him to be a man of metal instead of flesh!"

"What would you deem a man who carries spirit of salts so that he might slyly drop it in the ale of his drunken enemy, or dash it in the face of any man who challenges him?"

"Cruel and corrupt," muttered Gaspar, examining another dart.

"Don't bother any more with that," said Sohrab, throwing him a glance. "Get on with putting an edge on Weaponmonger's sword and tending to his morningstar. You know what he can be like, especially when he's at the drink."

"What can he be like?" a cool voice inquired. The woman, now without her scarf, was standing in the doorway. Her face was framed by wisps of hair, pale as bleached straw. Hollow were her cheeks, and starved was her frame beneath the draperies of her desert robe. Her eyes were sunken into their sockets, as if retreating in horror from sights they had once been forced to behold. There was about her demeanor an unyielding quality, a ruthlessness that might have been rooted in a gruelling and hard-fought history.

"I told you to lock that door," Sohrab muttered to Gaspar.

"How could I do so, when there's no key?" the other snapped.

"You were speaking of Cathal Weaponmonger," the woman said.

"We did not speak him ill, madam," said Sohrab. "We never would."

"That is well. I would not love you if you did, and neither would my brother."

A resentful silence ensued. Apparently intent on their work, Sohrab continued to scrape at the scimitar's blade, while Gaspar busied himself with a small oil can.

At length, Sohrab said respectfully, "Madam, do you wish for us to inspect your bow and darts?"

"Do not trouble yourself. I have already done so."

Next time they looked up she was no longer standing there. The door swung gently, its hinges creaking.

Presently Sohrab elbowed Gaspar in the ribs and winked craftily. The other responded with a nod and a knowing look, after which Sohrab turned his head aside to spit on the floor.

"Lover girl," he whispered.

Into the long Autumn afternoon and all through the night the seamstresses of Spire stitched industriously, until by the afternoon of the following day they had fashioned a large hemisphere of silk. In places about the reinforced hem of this artefact they attached several long cords. By the time Arran and Jewel returned, all was complete.

"Thickness for thickness," said the head seamstress, displaying the finished product, "silk is stronger than steel."

"And very beautiful as well," said Jewel, gathering a handful of the gauzy stuff into her hands and letting it slip like water through her fingers.

"And virtually weightless!" added Stormbringer.

"You won't find better craftsmanship in the Four Kingdoms," boasted the seamstress.

Assuming a critical air, the weathermaster regarded the handiwork. "It is good enough," he pronounced, unwilling to eulogize in case the woman used his good opinion as an excuse to raise her price. After he paid the agreed fee, he and Jewel hastened away.

Watching them leave, the seamstress shook her head, nonplussed, as if the strange ways of the world continually astounded her. " 'Twill be a strange kind of boat, to be needing a sail like that," she said to her assistant. "I doubt whether such a design will discharge the function. Still, gold is gold, and customers get what they ask for."

The children tagged along after Jewel and Arran as they made their way back to the bowl of the pinnacles. There they stood watching the pair inquisitively.

It was close to sunset, and the sky had taken on the brilliant sheen of blue satin. Cloud-formations swam across the western quarter like shoals of mackerel, tinged gray along their streamlined backs and peach-colored along their underbellies. A light breeze came soughing from the east.

At the foot of the Comet's Tower, Arran turned his jade-green eyes upon Jewel. As she met his gaze, each of them recognized the tension and sense of awe in the other.

"Do you have the vessel at hand?" he asked quietly.

The damsel brought forth the tiny horn of ivory, the size of an eggcup or large thimble. He reached out to take it, but she drew back, saying, "No, I wish to be the one to fly up there!"

"It is possible some peril awaits. Recall, the pinnacles are said to be wight-guarded."

"You forget the gift with which I am shielded!"

"It cannot shield you from eldritch imprisonment."

"There is hardly likely to be a dungeon at the top of the pinnacle," she scoffed. "I want to see the Well!"

"Jewel, I cannot risk any harm coming to you."

"I am determined to set eyes on this thing. It is part of my heritage."

Clearly troubled, the young man looked searchingly at her, but perceived only a wall of stubbornness.

"If you wish," he said at last, "but I shall go up there first. I shall cast down the lifter, so that you may come after me."

In her turn, she studied his solemn aspect and discovered an equivalent resolution.

"Even so," she said presently, by way of compromise. He gave a single nod of acknowledgment, and set about his task.

To begin with, he attached several well-filled bags to his belt. Next, holding out both hands, palms upward, he waved them from right to left in a long arc in front of his middle, then beckoned toward the northeast. "βĺẵw̃, Ĉẵiqũẵşš ¥ē Ŋŏŕťĥ Ėẫşt Ŵỹńďĕ ƒỹ̃ťiğ ťẁā ⁴Fŏŕčĕ." It was a vector command he chanted, each syllable redolent with raw power. Holding both hands still fully open, his fingers pointing to the right, he placed his right palm toward his chest and his left palm forward. Then he repeatedly passed his hands across in front of him, reversing hand positions on opposite sides of his body.

"βĺẵw̃, Ĉẵiqũẵşš ¥ē Ŋŏŕťĥ Ėẫşt Ŵỹńďĕ ƒỹ̃ťiğ ťẁā ⁴Fŏŕčĕ!"

"'Caiquass'—the wind from the northeast," Jewel said, recalling some of the information she had picked up at the Seat of the Weathermasters.

"Coming in at fifty-two degrees, force four—a moderate breeze," explained Arran. He had tied the ends of the silken cords together to form a kind of supporting framework or harness. This web he passed under his arms so that it crossed his back at the level of his shoulder blades. With one swift, strong motion, he lifted an edge of the gossamer bubble and held it aloft.

The watching children fell silent, save for the smallest, who whimpered.

On the eastern edge of the natural bowl, the leaves stirred. A sound crescendoed through the thickets of mulberry trees, as if some dream-like, murmurous concourse robed in chain mail and silk poured in haste through the groves. Jewel felt a peppery breath scorch her cheek.

The desert airs were visiting.

Across miles of scalding sand the wind had swiftly passed. Over that distance, beneath the white-hot eye of the sun, it had gathered to itself a feverish energy. Into the bowl it flowed, only to encounter the imperatives of the *brí,* wielded by the young weathermaster. Thus directed, it streamed up into the seemingly flimsy envelope he held high. The envelope swelled. He let the hot breeze snatch it from his grasp. It bulged like a sail, continuing to rise, until the cords snapped taut. Beneath the flowering chute, Arran wound the cords about his wrists, gripped a bunch in each hand, and called out another vector command. The audience of children gawped, round-eyed with astonishment, and Jewel laughed aloud with sheer joy as the young man's sandal-shod feet slowly left the ground. Gracefully, almost leisurely, he rose, drawn by the gossamer wing, suspended on its spidery webs. The wide sleeves of his shirt billowed.

Higher he flew, until his altitude was greater than that of the tallest pinnacle, and then, with perfect control, he drifted sideways like an airborne leaf, and touched down elegantly on top of the Comet's Tower. The watching youngsters whooped and stamped with glee, their brass bangles jingling.

Gradually, the dollop of foamy silk deflated and vanished from sight.

Arran reappeared and began to lower a rope. Tied to the end was a canvas bag wrapped with cords. The silken sail was folded within. There was still no sign of any guardian wights, and Jewel had begun to think that the conquering of the Comet's Tower was, after all, much easier than she had expected when all at once there came a noise of stone grating swiftly on stone, and small rocky mouths unclosed up and down the entire length of the column. Swarthy, wrinkled little faces peered out from each of these crevices, and the owners of those heads began shouting, gesticulating, and throwing stones. The children retreated out of range, and Jewel ducked behind a myrtle bush.

The wights remained in their tiny caverns and did not jump down to attack the onlookers, so they waited and observed warily while Arran tried to let down the bundle. The korred snatched at the rope, and snagged it with their cats' claws, and hooked it with sticks, in an endeavor to reel in the parcel tied to the end. Looking down, with his feet braced against the rock, Arran perceived that something must quickly be done to drive off the wights, or they would soon steal the parachute. A number of options flitted through his mind. He could summon a weather-force, perhaps a storm of hailstones . . . but evoking hail would take too long . . . unless he could detect it already close by, high in the atmosphere . . . or perhaps he could make the wind gust hard at the wights, to flatten their pointy ears and make them squeeze shut their deep-set eyes—a dusty, gravely, abrasive wind.

The argument against using the *brí* was what bothered him most. Ellenhall's code forbade meddling with the forces of nature for personal advantage, except at extreme need in defense of life. He had already contravened the law yet again, by summoning the wind to lift the parachute, and he would soon repeat that offense. By their own law, weathermasters must wield the *brí* only for the greater good. Breaking that law was a reprehensible act that no responsible weatherlord should even consider, and he was surprised, anew, to find himself entertaining the notion of augmenting his misdemeanors, even for an instant.

In the end, he resorted to his original plan. He gripped the rope in one hand, while with the other he tore open the bags at his belt and proceeded to sprinkle handfuls of the contents down the side of the pinnacle. Iron nails showered, along with salt-crystals, breadcrumbs, hypericum leaves, and rowanberries. All the while, the young man was whistling tunelessly, piercingly. On the ground below, Jewel was swinging the hand-bells with as much energy as she could muster, and chanting wight-repelling rhymes.

Squealing and squeaking, the korred on Arran's side of the pinnacle whisked back inside their little hollows and angrily slammed the sliding rock-doors. They were only minor wights, which was why such ordinary wards were relatively efficacious against them. From the other faces of the column, the creatures continued to shriek and hurl missiles inaccurately at the conqueror of their tower. Yet if any mortal men had been so bold as to scale the rocky towers using rope and spike and ladder, the korred would have dislodged every foothold with their tricks and overwhelmed the men by sheer numbers, no matter how many charms the climbers carried.

Jewel paced impatiently. Presently, the canvas bag dropped within range. She ran and caught it, letting her broad-brimmed straw hat fall from her head. Looking up, she saw Stormbringer seated on the edge of the pinnacle's overhang, dangling his long legs and waving down at her. Now and then he tossed down a handful of wight-repellent debris, and instantly any korred that had experimentally poked out its head shot out of sight. Some of the nails struck Jewel, but bounced off without causing harm.

In eager haste she untied the parcel and laid out the folds of fabric on the ground, then passed the web of cords beneath her arms and around her back as Arran had done. She lifted an edge of the silken panes, but, lacking Arran's stature, she was unable to haul many of the folds off the ground. Then the children came running, and they gripped the material and stood on their toes, holding it as high above their heads as they were able. The far-off voice of Arran fell like the leaves of Autumn upon their ears, and they felt the lion's breath of Caiquass once more as the heated current swept in and under the fabric, making it billow like some marshmallow confection.

The children released their grasp.

Cords pressed into the flesh beneath Jewel's shoulder blades and arms, and she was lifted up, lightly, delicately, as if she were a puff of mist. Her feet brushed the top of the myrtle bush. The linen draperies of her *burnous* glided around her as if they floated on water, and the ground sank away. She saw the walls of the Comet's Tower descend past her eyes. As she rose, a small door would snap open here and there, and a pair of carbuncle-red eyes would glare at her. A wrathful korred would begin to jabber in cracked tones, and furiously fling pebbles at the invulnerable passer-by, before a hard rain fell about its shaggy head and forced it to withdraw into sanctuary.

With voice and gesture, Arran was guiding the breeze driving the parachute, but he was hard-pressed to continue dropping the charms of tree and salt and iron while maintaining control of his summoned wind. It was necessary for him to use one hand to dole out the fragments, which meant he was unable to accurately complete the vector commands. The wind gusted erratically, blowing Jewel's chute off course, and the weathermaster was compelled to exert his powers to bring her back.

On reaching the top at last she leaned forward, hovering briefly over the pinnacle's flat roof. Arran lightly held her elbow to help her to balance; then she stepped easily onto the surface and he pulled on a cord to deflate the silken wing. The squeaking and jabbering noises from below ceased, and when Jewel looked down, she perceived that the wights had all disappeared into the rock.

The overhang was only about twelve feet in diameter. Serrated slopes on either side made it easy to climb down into the sheltered, bitten-out niche below. Here, weltered in shade, a small hollow bored into the stony floor. It was lined with silvery metal, clean, shining, and free of growths. Fragile ferns nodded over it, like green fish-skeletons diamonded with dew.

"Behold," said Stormbringer, "the Well of Rain!" Mingled delight and amazement were clearly printed on his features.

Jewel tucked up her desert robes and knelt by the brink.

The Well was no more than an arm's length in depth. At the very nadir glistened a scoop of clear water—enough to fill a thimble, no more. Kneeling, Jewel coaxed every drop into the tiny, gold-clasped horn and closed the lid. The liquid flowed with a convex surface, like quicksilver, leaving no trace behind. It was as if it *wanted* to be contained in the sorcerer's receptacle, and trickled in of its own volition. Now, the silvery basin was dry.

Jewel clasped in her hand a Draught of Immortality. "After all, we have found and collected this remedy," she said wonderingly.

"Let us not dally," said Arran purposefully. "The wights might try some other trick. 'Twere better for us to be gone sooner than later. You must descend without delay."

The chute was only strong enough to carry one person at a time. Arran would follow Jewel, as soon as he had raised the silk to the top.

"In sooth!" Tucking the ivory vessel in her pocket, Jewel stood up. For the first time she noticed the panorama sprawling at the foot of their aerial perch: the other pinnacles, like a city of towers and steeples, the cliff embracing the bowl, the tossing greenery of the mulberry groves, the tiled rooves of Spire jutting like baked cakes in the distance, and, farthest of all, the mountains, seeming to hover in the firmament, as if floating on cloud layers.

Even as Jewel admired the scene, Arran was summoning thermal currents. The silk petals flowered again. Secure in the corded harness, Jewel stepped off the pinnacle's edge and drifted down.

Her wafting hair radiated upon the airs, while her *burnous* and riding-trousers fluttered gently, despite being caked with dust. She felt the miniscule weight of the jewel as it swung on its chain at her throat. A few pairs of small red eyes stared sullenly at her from crannies in the tower, but the korred left her in peace.

An extraordinary sense of tranquillity and happiness enfolded her while she hung suspended between clouds and grass. She and Arran had achieved their goal. They would be able to bear the water of life to the Dome of Strang, and realize her full legacy.

The western sky was a sheet of luminous fabric, palely shimmering with peach, gold, and pink tones, softly streaked with gray. In the forefront, lines of leaden cloud were outlined sharply against the shimmer-satin, as if they had been stretched and ripped across the face of it. As before, Jewel landed lightly. This time she took off the rudimentary harness and laid out the fabric, in preparation for Stormbringer's summoned wind to whisk it to the top of the pinnacle a third time, so that he could descend safely.

A blond stranger in dirty robes was walking toward her, across the floor of the bowl. He must have climbed down the clay cliffs when her attention was elsewhere, while she was admiring the view or lost in her daydreams of inheritance. She and the children watched him. He moved quickly, and as he drew near, fear suddenly skewered through Jewel. There was no time to do more than take two steps backward, before he was upon her, gripping her wrists with a hand of tempered wire, pinning her with a glare from eyes of palest blue, like the last rinsings of milk on the sides of a glass.

"Give it me," he said. His voice was hoarse, his breath rancid.

"What can you mean?"

She struggled. From high above, Arran's outraged shout rang forth. Without more ado, the pallid-eyed man ran his free hand over Jewel's clothing. Upon discovering the hard object in her pocket, he withdrew the precious horn of ivory and scrutinized it.

"I know not for certain, but I can guess," he murmured, "and no other shall have it."

It all happened too fast. He flipped back the lid and drank the contents on the spot, then threw down the container, stamping on it, shattering it.

Uttering a scream of dismay and disbelief, Jewel twisted within his powerful grasp, but by then others had appeared from the same part of the cliffs: a hooded woman, followed by three men, two of whom the girl recognized as Scorpion and Lizard. Squealing like frightened starlings, the audience of children scattered. The woman moved behind Jewel, trapping her by the elbows with a rope of twisted silk, so that when the man stepped away the girl was still held captive. Scorpion ran with a crouching stance to collect the broken remnants of the gold-and-ivory horn, which he presumably considered were worth selling, for the metal.

"Was there not a drop left over?" the woman asked the first man.

Brusquely, he shook his head. A brief but ugly scowl puckered the woman's forehead. Then she turned her attention to Jewel. "I told you the girl has the look of him," she said out of the side of her mouth. Startled by the tender longing in the voice, Jewel glanced at her captor. She bridled in shock, as it came to her that the raddled face beneath the calico hood was the face of the traveling gypsy fortune-teller she had met at High Darioneth. No longer was the woman dressed like a gypsy. A baldric was strapped diagonally across her torso. A crossbow and a quiver of bolts protruded from behind her bony shoulder.

The pale-eyed man, however, paid no heed to the woman. "What was the nature of that potion?" he demanded of Jewel. "What are its properties?"

Quickly the damsel marshaled her wits. "Lave your face in it and be beauteous forever," she said. "Drink it and die."

The man squealed. His hands flew to his throat and he began to gasp.

"A lie," said the woman, cuffing Jewel across the side of her head. "A man as

cunning as Jaravhor would hardly have expended any effort in search of cosmetics. It is just as McGabhann avowed, Finn, though you never believed him when
he screeched at us that Jaravhor had located the Wells. The drink is perpetuity."

Abruptly regaining composure, the man sneered at Jewel. "You are some vile
malapert!" He threw back his blond head and yelled up to Arran, who stood
helpless on the pinnacle, "Bring my friend up there, Maelstronnar, or else we
will slay your hussy." With a faint *snap,* a thin switchblade sprang from beneath
the cuff of his left sleeve.

Already one of his associates, a thick-set fellow with a short, black beard, was
donning the web of silken cords.

"Do not go up there, Cathal," said the woman who was restraining Jewel.
"Finn, it is you who should go."

She directed the second remark to the pale-eyed man, who uttered a short,
barking laugh. "The day Weaponmonger obeys the orders of a woman, that day
the sun will turn to ice. Ain't that so, Knife?"

The crop-haired man grunted, adjusting the cords beneath his armpits.

"The weathermaster is dangerous," protested the woman.

"D'ye think I cannot handle the pup?" Weaponmonger responded. "How
impotent you must think me, Fionnuala." He swigged deeply from a leathern
flask. As he moved, the sounds of ceramic surfaces clinking against glass emanated from his pockets.

"No, it is not that way at all," she said quickly. "On the contrary—"

"I wish to see what these two weanlings have found that is so precious, that
they would pursue it here, all the way from Strang."

"Aye," said the pale-eyed man. "That's what he wants."

"Do as you please, Cathal," Fionnuala said tightly.

"At the outer range of audibility, Jewel caught the whispers between Scorpion and Lizard: *"Aonarán is too great a lack-guts to fly up there himself. He sends
the poxy drunkard. . . ."*

Atop the Comet's Tower, Arran raged helplessly. He was fully aware that these
miscreants could not slay Jewel, yet it was conceivable they could do her other
harm. He possessed no certain knowledge of the extent of her invulnerability,
no idea whether they might be able to torment her in some way. The fair-haired
man had addressed him by his name. How could he have known? Who was he?

"I swear," he said aloud, "you shall pay for using her so."

Berating himself for allowing peril to threaten Jewel, he mulled rapidly over
the possibilities for action and concluded he could do nothing else, for now, but

submit to the scoundrel's demands. Swiftly he clambered back up to the roof of the overhang.

The *brí* flared through his body as he executed the sequence of word and sign. The summoned updraught applied its pressure, and the bulky form of the crop-haired man was hoisted skyward. Instantly, the cave-mouths in the rocky pillar snapped open, and a storm of missiles came flying out. Stormbringer took his time lifting the new passenger; the man cursed and roared as the barrage of pebbles hammered into his dangling body and threatened to cause the chute to fold up. As soon as their victim drew level with the top of the tower, the wights darted into their abodes and banged the doors shut. Arran elevated the silken hemisphere a little too high above the pinnacle's crown, then let it collapse and drop. The man landed heavily, calling down ill-fortune on all and sundry. His sword-hilt dug into his ribs.

"Should you play any of your tricks, Maelstronnar," Aonarán shouted up from the ground, "the wench will pay the price."

"Jackanapes, you will regret your cockiness," Weaponmonger growled, awkwardly getting to his feet. After extricating himself from the cords, he cast them off, then wiped blood from his injured face.

Arran contained his fury.

"Now show me what it is you have found up here," demanded the crophaired man. "What treasure trove have you discovered, eh, mooncalf?" A whiff of spirits was borne on his breath as he spoke. "Is there some drink up here? Your wench was carrying a vial. Is there more of that stuff? 'Tis down beneath this shelf you were. In that case, I shall make an inspection. But you must descend ahead of me, pup. I trust you not."

Keeping an eye on Jewel and leashing his desire for action, Arran climbed down to the well, with Weaponmonger following close behind.

The unwelcome guest peered at the silvery basin. "What's this? A hole, but 'tis dry. Have you taken it all, eh, and left naught for us?"

With increasing difficulty, Arran restrained his wrath. Ideas and possibilities tumbled through his mind as he sought a way to win through this predicament. The man was looking about now, examining the small area on which they stood, kicking at lumps of soil and stone. A natural breeze played languidly about their ears.

"Nothing else is here," the knife-merchant said at length. "You *have* seized all the plunder, whatever it might have been. Unbury this strange metal from its grave and give it me! It might be of some value."

"Such a feat is impossible," said Arran. "The stuff is welded there by forces of nature—melted into the living rock."

"Well, perhaps you speak truth, weathermaster, and perhaps you do not. But if I cannot have it, nobody shall!" With that, the intruder drew from his pocket a small earthenware flask and tipped the contents into the Well of Rain.

An unpleasant, penetrating stench arose. Weaponmonger instantly recoiled, but Arran coughed as acrid fumes burned his eyes and the back of his throat. The Well's silvery lining began to smoke and sizzle.

"Etching acid," said Cathal Weaponmonger with a sneer. "That will spoil your eldritch sink for you, whelp of puddle-makers!"

Arran ignored the taunts. Staring past his gloating adversary he fixed his attention on Jewel, constrained by the strangers on the ground below. The blond man had extended his arm toward her. He was fingering the chain around Jewel's neck, discovering the white gem, which he would steal while she stood helpless. His hands would be touching her skin.

Stormbringer's thoughts snapped to a conclusion. He flung up his arms, roaring, "βỹřñ, ¥ē βéøřhŧ βröη̇d, ꝁiłőŧhềřмє!" It seemed he hurled something from his hand, and then, far below, Jewel felt a freezing draught whip past her, and from a myrtle bush right beside Lizard bright flames burst violently, crimson and gold, like a gigantic torch, accompanied by a blast of intense heat. Without pause the weathermaster swung his arm the other way, lending his bodyweight to a backhand blow on the side of Weaponmonger's face.

Down on the ground the sudden conflagration was causing confusion. Lizard ran off, yelping and shrieking that his trousers were on fire. At the same time, Scorpion threw down his blow-pipe and fled toward the shelter of the trees, covering his head with his hands as if he expected the sky to unleash burning rain. Aonarán dropped Jewel's neck-chain. He crouched, cowering and whimpering, while his sister dragged Jewel away from the blaze and shouted at him. Sparks milled chaotically, while smoke rushed upward like escaping ghosts.

Up on the Comet's Tower, Cathal Weaponmonger aimed a blow at Arran, who blocked it with his forearm. The larger man bellowed his ire and leaped forward to attack, but Arran dodged and spun on his heel, fists clenched, ready to deliver a blow to the ribs. Weaponmonger, however, had miscalculated and thrown himself off balance. The platform was small, and his considerable momentum took him to the brink. There he teetered an instant, flailing his arms.

Then he disappeared.

From the Tower's foot, Fionnuala saw him fall. As his body crashed to the ground, an agonized cry wrenched itself from her throat, so harsh it must have torn her flesh in passing. After releasing Jewel she ran to where the man lay, spread-eagled and motionless.

Having cast herself on the grass beside him, she raised his head in her hands and kissed him repeatedly, calling out his name. His blood drenched her face and her hands, streaked her gown, clotted wet and glistening like cherry syrup in her hair. No matter how loudly or repeatedly she called, she could not make him respond. At last, in despair, she lifted his head into her lap and cradled him, crooning and wailing, swaying and mourning. Her tears mingled with the final gush of his life's fluids.

Meanwhile, the conflagration burned itself out.

Jewel shucked the rope from her arms. She saw Arran come plunging down from the pinnacle, hanging on to the cords of the open tulip of silk. Aonarán had already run away, and was nowhere to be seen. Having reduced the bush to a scrawl of blackened twigs, the fire smoldered as incandescent embers.

While still six or seven feet in the air, the young weathermaster let go of the cords, dropped deftly to the ground, and hastened toward Jewel. He took her by the shoulders, holding her at arm's length and scrutinizing her closely.

In turn, she inspected him. He was quivering with pent-up rage, and twin fires seethed behind his eyes.

"Are you unhurt?" she asked him.

"Of course. And you?"

She nodded.

Protectively, he put his arm about her. She leaned into the embrace, feeling the stampede of his pulse, the outraged tension of his musculature.

"You are angry."

Curtly he shook his head, dismissing her implied enquiry. They turned their attention to the man's lifeless body and the woman who held his head in her lap, bending over him, keening. A curtain of her blond hair swung down across his features.

The valedictory brilliance of the setting sun ran a line along the horizon. Dusk stole forth. Fionnuala lifted her tear-ravaged face and glared accusingly at Stormbringer. Her stare was so intense, it was as if she was emblazoning his features on her memory. "It was you who killed him."

"You are the gypsy who spoke to me in High Darioneth," cried Jewel now, stepping between the two. "What are you doing here? Who are you? Who are these robbers who accompanied you? Why have you followed us, duped us, and sent your spies with us? What is your purpose?"

"I will tell you naught," Fionnuala replied chokingly. "Your man has slain Cathal, my only love. He was all that was left to me."

"There was no slaying. 'Twas an accident. 'Twas plain for all to see."

But the grieving woman refused to say anything more.

Then Arran went to her. For the moment, pity mastered his wrath and he said, "I will go to Spire. I will send men to come and bear him to the Sanctorum." To Jewel, he said, "Come," and together they departed from the melancholy shadow of the Comet's Tower.

As evening thickened the air, wightish sounds evolved among the pinnacles of Saadiah, small mutterings and giggling, shrill arguments, eerie violin music, sudden shrieks, and a low, mournful cry. Like pin-pricks, the lights from tiny lanterns began to spangle the edges of the hollow. Arran and Jewel climbed the clay cliffs and struck out for Spire, but as they passed through a small clearing amidst the groves, Jewel spied a slight, fitful movement in the leaves at the perimeter. "One watches us," she cautioned.

Arran, still dark-faced with unexpressed fury, made no reply, but after a moment he leaped to one side and dived into a shadowy bower of greenery. Furious rustlings and shakings ensued, after which he emerged, pushing Lizard ahead of him. With one hand he crab-gripped the shoulder of the Ashqalêthan near the base of the neck; with the other he twisted the fellow's arm behind his back. He hauled his prisoner into the clearing, where Jewel waited beside the stump of a deceased mulberry tree.

The captive was pleading for mercy. "Prithee, sir, do not pinch so hard!"

"Why are you spying on us? Who are your cohorts?"

"I pray you, sir, in the name of gracious Lord Fortune, do not hurt me!"

"Answer my questions and you will be spared."

"Yes! Yes! I will answer them all!"

"Then I shall release you for the moment. But if you try to flee, or cause harm, be assured, fireballs and thunderbolts shall smite you." Stormbringer dumped Lizard on the ground. "Cast down your weapons!"

Obligingly, and in haste, Lizard unbuckled his scimitar. He also drew a dagger from his sleeve, and untied from his belt a pouch full of blow-darts.

"Where's the blow-pipe?"

"I dropped it," babbled Lizard, "As I ran—"

"Is that everything?"

"Yes, yes, I swear it!"

"What is your true name?"

"Bahram Gaspar."

"And Scorpion?"

"Fehroz Sohrab. The other three are from Slievmordhu. The man who fell, his name was Cathal Weaponmonger, but we called him 'Knife,' and the others are Fionnbar and Fionnuala Aonarán."

"Feroz Sohrab!" exclaimed Jewel. "Now I recall where I have seen Scorpion before. He walked past me at the Fair Field in Cathair Rua, when I was with my grandfather—"She broke off, as if she wished to reveal no more.

"A fair beginning to your disclosures," Arran said to the man. "Now, reveal your full story and omit nothing! If you lie, the vengeance of my kindred shall seek you out and fall upon you like boiling oil."

The Ashqalêthan commenced to speak, and the tale that unfolded was this:

Fionnbar Aonarán and his sister Fionnuala had for years been searching for a certain child born in the Great Marsh of Slievmordhu. To this end, they hired Fehroz Sohrab and Bahram Gaspar to keep watch on a marshman by the name of Earnán Mosswell. Eight months ago, in Jenever, the patient seasons of vigil had been rewarded. In the Fairfield outside Cathair Rua, Sohrab spied Mosswell in secretive converse with a young damsel. Better than that, Sohrab managed to glimpse a marvelous gem the girl carried with her. Exulting, he bore his tidings to Weaponmonger. He in turn relayed them to Aonarán, who seemed to possess some kind of hold over the weapons-dealer.

"Me and Sohrab supposed it was the pretty stone they were after," said Gaspar. "We thought Aonarán would tell us to steal it and that would be the end of all the games. But he wanted something more."

In Cathair Rua they observed and followed the damsel. It became evident she kept the company of weathermasters. Come Spring, Fionnuala had journeyed to High Darioneth in the guise of a gypsy peddler. As soon as she set eyes on the girl, the woman knew she was indeed the one they sought.

"By what did she recognize her?" growled Arran. "What is it about Jewel that betrayed her?"

"How would I know?" moaned the miserable Ashqalêthan, spreading out his hands in a pathetic gesture of appeal. "The young lady's looks are striking . . . perhaps her eyes . . ."

"This is purely conjecture," said Jewel sharply. The shock of these revelations and the man's over-familiar reference to her looks stung her, provoking her to retaliate with haughtiness. "I will not be discussed by a creature lowlier than a clod. There will be no more opinions." She turned to Arran. "As a gypsy, that woman informed me the Dome was no longer guarded. I stepped right into her trap, or else she put some spell on me, for from that moment on, all I desired was to visit Strang. They must have guessed I would not be able to resist seeking out my heritage—oh." Realizing she was once more in danger of saying too much, she broke off, glancing quickly at Gaspar, who only shrank from her. His attention flicked anxiously back and forth between her and Arran. "You," she said brusquely, "tell on."

"Aonarán followed you and the young lord to the Dome."

"What?" Stormbringer's tone was incredulous. "He followed us? Me?"

"Conceivably you were too intent on your own hunt to note you were also the hunted," Jewel murmured, aside.

"What Aonarán saw at the Dome he would not tell," gabbled the man of the desert. "Leastways, he would not tell us, nor even Weaponmonger. He told his sister, though. Ever thick as thieves, those two," he added, unconscious of the cliché's irony. "We tracked you to Saadiah, Sohrab and me. You tried your weathermaster tricks to throw us off your scent, but Aonarán is no fool. He found you." Gaspar drew his knees to his chest and clasped his wiry arms around them, as if trying to contract himself into a smaller space. "He's as brutal as a coward, is Aonarán. Savage as a cur that has been mistreated and knows no response other than attack."

"In that case, why do you work for him?" demanded Arran.

"He pays well. He has money. Lots of gold. Where he gets it from nobody knows for certain, but the word is that he and Weaponmonger sell arms to gangs of Marauders. That Fionnuala, the sister, she is better, but not much better. She fancied Knife, but 'twas plain he had only contempt for her. I'd avow he only tolerated her because she was Aonarán's kin."

"Better?" Jewel said sardonically. "I hardly think so. She tricked me and trapped me."

"Ah, but I heard her one day speaking with Aonarán, telling him she wished for no harm to come to the blue-eyed girl, for the sake of the memory of someone she had once known. He assured her you would remain unscathed."

Perplexity creased Jewel's brow for an instant, before a notion flashed into being and she muttered beneath her breath, "I wonder whether that woman ever met my father. . . ."

"How did they know what it was we sought in this place?" Arran demanded of Gaspar.

"They told us they did *not* know, sir!" The desert-man cringed from the young man's ferocity. "They said they guessed only that you hunted for some hidden thing of great value, some wealth that once, maybe, belonged to the Sorcerer of Strang. It is now clear they'd had some hint from a fellow named Mac Gabhann."

"Get up!" Arran nudged the captive with his boot.

Gaspar scrambled to his feet. "Do not hurt me," he whined. "Don't bring the flames! Where we come from, little is known of your kindred. None of us guessed you were one of the truly powerful weathermasters who could smite with fire—"

"I'll see justice done," barked Arran. "You'll come with us to Spire, and there I'll turn you over to the shire reeve, along with a litany of your crimes. But first you'll tell more of what you know."

The breeze, now freed from the persuasion of the *brí,* continued blowing gently from the east. On its shoulders it carried scents and sounds. The voices of Stormbringer and Gaspar were borne down the air currents to the woman who had been stealing toward them through the trees, her haggard face pink-splotched with the legacy of weeping. Fionnuala halted at the edge of the clearing, screened from view by the thick foliage of a mulberry. She peered out from her vantage point.

Two graceful figures stood near the waist-high stump of a dead tree, whose boughs had been carted away by the local folk to be used as firewood. A third person was bent into a half-crouch.

The daughter of Jarred Jaravhor was clad in a flowing *burnous* that looked to be a second-hand Ashqalêthan garment. A broad-brimmed hat on a cord dangled down her back, revealing a shock of hair the color of deep sleep and forgetfulness, the locks wisp-ended and pointy. Earlier, Fionnuala had taken note of the girl's amazing eyes—like amethyst cups brimming with snow-melt. By her eyes and black tresses the girl seemed unfamiliar—but in all other ways she did indeed resemble her comely brown-haired father.

Next, the spy trained her gaze on the taller form of the weathermaster, he who had cruelly slain Cathal Weaponmonger. The youth, also, was clad in flowing desert robes dyed in stripes with the coppery browns, oranges, and buttercup-yellows of Ashqalêth.

He was handsome, this son of the mountain lords. A dark-brown mane cascaded across his shoulders and down his back. The last gleams of sunlight sprinkled his hair with a powder of glints. He spoke accusingly to the fool Bahram Gaspar, who was ducking and bowing like a scolded cur. The desert man was travel-worn and dirty. His straggling beard jiggled like some large and lanky spider that had affixed itself to his lower jaw.

Fionnuala's cool, measuring regard concealed the turmoil of grief and rage boiling inside her head. Her mind dwelled on a single purpose: Weaponmonger was dead, therefore retribution must be exacted.

She silently slid two quarrels from her quiver and subtracted a small jar from her pocket. Carefully, she dipped the head of the first arrow into a dark ointment and laid it on the grass beside the open jar, then repeated the procedure with the second arrow, this time placing the jar at her feet and retaining her grasp of the quarrel. After unslinging her crossbow from her shoulder, she slotted the bolt into the chase and pulled back the lever to cock the weapon. The wood creaked as tension was loaded. Air streams murmured in her flaxen hair, pouring around her the sound of the weathermaster demanding of Gaspar, "Where does Aonarán hide himself? Where can he be found? Tell me or suffer my wrath!"

Gaspar was opening his mouth to speak when Fionnuala lifted the wooden stock, to which the bow was fixed crosswise. Stepping from the shelter of the trees, she raised the weapon and trained the sight on Arran Stormbringer.

From the corner of his eye the weathermaster glimpsed the movement, and in the next fragment of time several events rapidly took place. His first impulse being to protect Jewel, he flung himself between her and the archer and dragged the girl to the ground. Locking her in a tight embrace, he rolled with her behind the tree stump. Simultaneously, the quarrel that had been intended to slay him shot humming past his head, almost grazing his flesh, so close that turbulence ruffled his hair and the droning whine temporarily blocked his hearing. Even as Stormbringer fell, he was already calling out a vector command.

Gaspar's attention was riveted to the sight of the couple rolling unexpectedly at his feet. He stared in astonishment, at a loss as to why they should suddenly throw themselves down. Standing side on to the assassin, he was not yet aware of the danger.

In that same moment Fionnuala breathed a violent curse. With a swiftness engendered by practice, she fixed a second bolt in place and wound the lever back. She had seen how it was. The weathermaster had believed the girl to be in danger, and had sought to shield her with his own body. It was clear that he valued her life above his own. Now neither of them was in range, but the lack-wit Gaspar yet stood gawping and goggling, like some burrowing rodent forcibly dragged into broad daylight. The Ashqalêthan had been about to betray her brother. If she could not slay the weathermaster, she would destroy the traitor instead. There would be leisure, later, to hunt down the wretched youth. For now, she must waste not a moment.

She released the lever a second time. The crossbow twanged and the bolt flew. Gaspar fell sideways like a skittle. From nowhere a strident, shrieking wind leaped at Fionnuala, whipping at her garments, breaking boughs, almost lifting her from her feet. The current's force was too strong for an ordinary mortal to contest, and she knew it was driven by the *brí*. The weathermaster was now alert to her presence, and she could not oppose that kind of power. The wind battered at her, tipped her off balance, and pushed her over. It chivvied her, like some giant housewife sweeping with a besom, bowling her over and over and spilling the bolts from her quiver. It was all Fionnuala could do to hang on to the stock of her crossbow as she tumbled heels over head between the trees, until at last she regained her feet and began to run, with the wind fastened to her back like an unseelie rider. As she darted away, she glanced over her shoulder. Arran Stormbringer had leaped up and was giving chase.

Next to the decapitated tree-bole Jewel rested on her knees by Bahram Gaspar, as Fionnuala had knelt at the side of Cathal Weaponmonger. The shaft of a crossbow bolt was protruding from beneath his left armpit, and gouts of scarlet ichor pumped as if from a spigot.

"I think this is no mortal blow," she told him compassionately. "You will live.

We shall make haste and bear you to a carlin." She gathered handfuls of her garments and held them to the wound, trying to staunch the flow.

"I'll not live," gasped the Ashqalêthan. His flesh was turning gray, his chest rising and falling as he gulped huge breaths, overwhelmed by panic.

Before he could gather strength to speak again, Arran reappeared. "I have scanned the vicinity," he announced grimly. "The witch has escaped, leaving only a jar containing some species of fetid slime. You," he said to Gaspar, "I will carry you into town, where we shall seek a carlin." Squatting on his heels, he reached for the wounded man, preparing to hoist him into his arms.

Weakly, Gaspar shook his head. Terror clenched his visage. "Poison," he mouthed, as an eerie blue stain spread quickly over his skin, springing from his left side. "There is no cure. I beg of you, slay me now. I have seen her venoms at work. If you've any mercy at all, pray take my life with all speed. Prithee! Prithee!" His voice rose to a shriek and he struggled to say more, then began to scream as spasms racked his body. Bile and blood spurted from his swelling mouth.

Sick with horror, Jewel stared at the figure contorting at her feet. "You must do as he asks!" she cried to Arran. "And if you will not, then give me your sword and I shall do it myself!"

Arran needed no urging. Already he had pulled his sword from its sheath. Standing with feet braced apart, he grasped the hilt with both hands and raised the weapon above his head. The stricken man, however, was writhing so violently that the young man was afraid he might smite awry, and instead augment the man's suffering.

"Hold him! Hold him still!" Arran shouted to Jewel. The girl plunged her hands into the hair of Gaspar. Fighting his paroxysms and her own deep revulsion, she pinned his scalp to the ground.

Planting his foot on the man's chest in a desperate effort to hold him steady, Stormbringer lightly touched the blade's tip to Gaspar's throat to line up his target, then raised the sword a second time and brought it down with all his strength. At the last moment Jewel looked away, unable to endure the sight, but Stormbringer denied himself that luxury so as to be certain the blow was mortal.

The sharp edge sliced clean through the neck of the tortured victim. Gaspar's screaming ceased. His body heaved in a mighty convulsion, then lay still. In the severed head, the corneas of his eyes were already filming over.

Stricken, Jewel stared at the inert form.

"May rain fall around you," she whispered at last, leaning down to close the man's eyes with a tender sweep of her hand.

Stormbringer's flesh had paled to the color of milk. "I have never before slain a man," he whispered, looking down at the corpse.

Jewel said, "*You* did not slay him."

After a while, Stormbringer seemed to shake himself from an evil dream. He wiped his bloody sword on the grass. "Two lie dead," he said in anger and disgust, "because of this felon Aonarán. Come, let us leave this ill-fated place."

As evening closed around them like a funereal hood, he led her away.

The wind swung around to the west, and began to blow harder through the darkness, bringing with it the smack of salt and kelp. Stars blossomed in the east, but from the west an impenetrable cloak of cloud was moving across the sky, gradually blocking out all celestial light.

In the township of Spire, Arran and Jewel collected their horses and packs. They replaced their blood-stained garments with clean clothes, then paid a visit to the house of the shire reeve. The Lord of Saadiah—a peace-loving man—employed the reeve, who headed a small band of sergeants and constables for the purpose of maintaining order in the region.

"I am Arran Maelstronnar, son of the Storm Lord," said Arran, displaying his signet ring with its engraved lightning emblem. The officer bowed respectfully. "Send your agents to the Comet's Tower," the young man continued, "and to the clearing near the pinnacles, for two men have been slain there. The bodies are in need of burial. Be not tardy. Heavy rainfall is on the way. 'Twill be easier for your constables if they complete their task before the deluge commences."

The reeve, however, was no genius amongst men. It took quite some time and much discussion before he comprehended Arran's request. "Who might have perpetrated these fell deeds?" he asked, not without a trace of doubt as he eyed the visitors.

"The death of one man was caused by mischance," said Arran. "My sister and I both bore witness to the event. The death of the other was the work of an assassin, save that it was I who dealt the mercy stroke. Since doing the deed, the murderess has fled. I intend to hunt down both the assassin and her accomplice, since they each have crimes to answer for."

He described the physical characteristics of Aonarán, Fionnuala, and Fehroz Sohrab, adding that the latter went by the name of "Scorpion," after which he asked, "Sir, do you know aught of these folk?"

"I have seen them," replied the reeve. "Strangers never pass unnoticed, hereabouts. But I know nothing of their doings, for they were very close—as close as you are, my friend."

"Our business is our own," said Arran curtly.

"Meaning no offense," said the reeve hastily, shooting a sidelong glance toward the lustrous gold of the weathermaster signet ring adorning the young man's hand.

"You suspect I claim a false identity," said Arran bluntly, "but be informed, sir, nobody could steal such a weighty emblem as this ring. My kindred would put forth all their effort to find the thief and retrieve it."

The reeve looked unconvinced. "Perhaps, my lord, the calling of a small spark, a token of the *brí*—" he murmured, gesturing vaguely.

"My people are not required to prove their abilities," Arran said frostily, and by the look in his eye the official was at last convinced that the young man spoke the truth.

"If you wish, my lord, I shall send men to make inquiries, to discover where these offenders are lodging," he offered. At that moment the door flew open, harried by the wind. The constable who had lifted the latch plunged into the room and slammed the portal shut.

"'Tis a hurly-burly out there, and no mistake," he panted. "A rainstorm's bound this way, or I'm a Grïmnørslander."

"What's afoot, Kaveh?" grunted the reeve.

"Well, sir, just now I seen two men riding like maniacs out of town," said Kaveh, brushing tousled hair from his eyes and rearranging his cloak, "with the wind tearing at them like a starving jackal. They seemed to have no regard for the inclement weather, sir, or for the time of night. Mighty strange, I thought to meself."

"What did they look like?"

"One was dark, sir, like normal folk. The other had a head of yellow hair, which was easy to see, on account of the wind snatching off his hood."

"That'll be my man," said Arran abruptly. "If he has left town, so must I. Was there a woman in their company?"

"No, sir," said the constable. "Not that I saw."

The reeve said, "Alas; by now they'll be beyond the borders of my jurisdiction, no doubt." His expression became solicitous. "'Tis an evil night out there, my good lord. Won't you take a sup and a sip before you depart?"

Arran glanced at Jewel. With her shoulders drooping under the burden of weariness and her uncombed hair still in tangles, she looked like a wilting rose. He suspected she could endure no further exertions without refreshment. "We are in a hurry, but yes, we will partake of food and drink."

Jewel murmured her thanks. It was not food and drink she required so much as tranquillity. In her mind's eye she still envisioned the frightened face of the dying Gaspar.

They dined in haste and departed from the house of the reeve soon thereafter. As they set off, the first drops of rain from the storm blowing in from the west began to touch the ground like plump fingertips, raising tiny puffs like powdered glass. Soon, the dust would turn to mire.

Pacing their steeds so as not to overtax them, they rode through the night. There was no stopping to rest—Arran wanted to stay as close as possible on the trail of Aonarán, while Jewel was still too dazed from witnessing two brutal deaths to challenge anyone's ambition.

It was raining hard, but the downpour began to ease off as they left the vicinity of Spire. The sky began to clear, and swathes of stars flung themselves across the heavens like bridal veils exquisitely stitched with white flaxen daisies.

As they jogged onward, Jewel roused from her shocked silence.

"I am grateful that you risked your life to shield me," she said. "However, you forgot, as you always do, that I am invulnerable. There was no need for it."

Arran made no reply, and she glanced across at him. He was staring straight ahead, glowering. A hard light flashed in his eyes.

"You have hardly spoken to me," she said reproachfully. "Are you angry?"

As before, he offered no response.

"Now tell me, prithee," she persevered, "why you are in a towering rage!"

"Do you not know?"

"The thief Aonarán stole the sorcerer's draught," rejoined Jewel, "and his sister murdered a foolish man before our very eyes." She shuddered. "I, too, am vexed, but one cannot lose what one has never possessed. We were never immortal. Now Aonarán owns that miraculous gift—much ill may it do him. As for the treacherous sister, well, I hope she steps on a Stray Sod and wanders forever, lost amongst the mulberry trees."

"It is well that you take matters philosophically," said Arran. "For my part, I cannot."

"Why not?"

Riding alongside her, he looked her full in the face. When she read his countenance, she flinched. In his expression there was such an intensity of fierce tenderness, she felt shaken.

"I desired the water from the Well of Rain for one reason alone," said Arran. "I wanted it for you. Only you."

A clamp was squeezing Jewel's throat. Unexpectedly, she was lost for words.

"For you," he said, now directing his gaze away from her and apparently staring at the road ahead, "I broke weathermaster law, by wielding the *brí* to summon the dust devil, and to invoke the wind that lifted the chute of silk. All for you, all so that you might, if you chose, be the first to become immortal."

So tight-knotted were her vocal cords that the girl could not emit so much as a squeak. A fine mist of perspiration glistened on her brow. The intensity of passion behind his averment was overwhelming.

"Would you wish for that?" he said softly, but with enough volume that his voice carried over the patter of the last raindrops and the dull drubbing of hooves. "Would you like to live forever?"

Forcing her dry tongue to form the utterance, the damsel said, "Even so."

"Truly? For it would be no uncomplicated quality to possess. Think on it."

"I need not think a minute on it. I would like to live forever. I want to know what will happen next, through all the years. Curiosity drives me. I cannot bear the notion of never finding out, of letting the future unfold without me there to observe it."

"And I cannot bear the notion of a world without you."

In silence they rode on. At length, the young man added, quietly, "I love you beyond all measure."

The rain abated, the clouds thinned, and the wind decreased to a light breeze.

For a long time, even since before she had left High Darioneth, Jewel had gradually been becoming aware of his ardency toward her. Nonetheless, unable to interpret her own sensibilities, she had no idea how to respond to his words and therefore she said nothing about his declaration.

Disturbing thoughts hunted one another through Jewel's mind, and, when she found herself utterly unable to formulate a reply, she experienced a period of confusion, then fell to frantic pondering.

It was clear that Arran truly loved her, but although she liked him very much and was grateful for his help and companionship, she could not return his intense affection. Long ago she had vowed to herself never to entrust her love to anyone again. Two scenarios from her past fixed themselves firmly in her mind's eye—the first, herself as a child, wandering alone among purple-blossoming buddleias near a ruined watchtower, calling her uncle's name.

The second, herself a few weeks later at the mill in High Darioneth, lying awake at nights weeping, longing to be cradled in the arms of her parents.

From that time onward, the vow to avoid forming strong attachments had remained with her, encapsulating her heart. She esteemed the Storm Lord, she cared about the welfare of her friends, she enjoyed the company of Arran and— sometimes—of Ryence, but with a stubbornness born of a desperate desire to avoid the repetition of her terrible suffering, she allowed herself to feel no deeper sentiment toward anyone.

Be that as it may, the love of such a man as the son of the Storm Lord was no trifle. His passion was flattering, but more than that, he was kind and generous, brave and enterprising, and she began to wonder whether she had taken his help for granted, had perhaps been too headstrong and selfish in her dealings with him. With her obstinate insistence on examining the sorcerous book in the Tope at the Dome, for example, she might have endangered them both.

Covertly Jewel stole a glance at her companion, but he was staring straight ahead as he rode beside her, and the expression on his handsome face was unreadable. Unexpectedly, an extreme pulse of empathy, or sorrow, or longing, or some other fierce emotion welled within her, and she clenched her jaw, quelling the sensation by force of will.

Arran's declaration of love was not mentioned further between them. Yet, for a day or two, they were both awkward and shy with each other, as never before.

They traveled fast. Two days later they reached the Khashayar Tunnel, and crossed through without incident, emerging once again in the desert. No longer did the hooves of the horses kick up spatters of mud—now they struck only plumes of dust from the rock-hard roadway. The wayside trees dwindled and were replaced by low shrubs, which in turn diminished and disappeared as they reentered the arid region.

"How is it that you did not detect the presence of Aonarán when he tracked us to Strang?" Jewel asked presently. "If you had evoked breezes from all quarters, they would have brought you the scent of him on their backs. I recall, you did that trick once, when first we met."

"That breeze-stratagem is seldom effective in unfamiliar territory, or in regions sprinkled with villages. We found you in the remote mountains where creatures of fur and feather dwell amongst tree and stone and water. There it would not have been difficult to scent the wood-smoke of a traveler's campfire on the winds, or man-sweat, or the smell of tanned leather riding tack."

"On your way to the Dome you might have looked for sudden flights of birds disturbed by the passage of a stranger."

"Birds are disturbed by wild beasts as easily as by humankind. Besides, I had no reason to suppose I was being trailed. Methinks you look to find fault with me."

"Forgive me. That was not my intention."

They journeyed through the afternoon and the night, scarcely pausing. By the time morning strewed its snapdragon petals across the desert, the riders and their steeds were close to exhaustion. They had encountered no sign of Aonarán and Sohrab, and the hoofprints in the dust of the road were too muddled and crowded to be of any use. There was no option but to pull off to the verge, where they could rest and sleep amid the frosted sands.

When they awoke all rime had been vaporized, and the sun was suspended overhead like a flaming warrior, ruthlessly hurling down bolts of radiant energy. After watering the horses the travelers crawled deeper into the shade of an acacia clump and dined frugally on their provisions.

Having broken their fast, they continued on until they reached the crossroads where the road to Saadiah met the Desert Road. There they paused once more, unable to guess whether Aonarán had turned northwest toward Grïmnørsland or headed southeast, striking out for Jhallavad. He might even have left the road, or doubled back.

"We can go no further in our pursuit," Jewel announced. "We must return to the Dome and keep our promise, or part of it, ere we resume our search for the thief. Recall, I vowed, 'I swear by the bones of my ancestor that if I find the Draught from the Well of Rain I will bring it to the Tope of Castle Strang, and light the flame to signify the deed is done.'"

"Aye, we found the Draught, but we cannot bring it back."

"Through no fault of our own. Despite losing what we found, we should return and kindle the flame."

"But we can never fulfill the vow!" Arran exclaimed. "'Twould be sleeveless to return to that place without the Draught. Why not simply abandon the quest, and never go back to the Dome?"

"For two reasons," replied the damsel. "Firstly, the sorcerer's ancient enchantments might be strong enough to learn that we found the Well of Rain and yet did not return to the Dome. It would appear as if we were forsworn. What if his legacy is powerful enough to find us out and strike us down as punishment for our faithlessness? Secondly, if we go back, maybe we shall get a chance to find out where the other waters of eternal life can be obtained. I hold high hopes that the location of all the other Wells might be revealed to us, whether or not the Draught from the Well of Rain is present in the Tope when the fire is ignited. All that claptrap about passing tests might have been intended to fool us. We ought to go back and light the fire, and wait to find out what unfolds."

The young man was not convinced. "There is inconsistency in your reasoning, Jewel," he said, "for if the sorcerer's lingering enchantments were formidable enough to afflict us for failing to return to the Dome, then they would most certainly be able to punish us for returning to the Dome without the prize. For my part, I deem that his influence, though lasting beyond his death, is not far-reaching. His ancient spells endure within the walls of Strang, and in the blood of his heirs, but I surmise they have no efficacy in the world beyond his domains. Jaravhor was only a man, not an eldritch wight. Be certain: if we fail to return to the Dome, no supernatural punishment will hunt after us, but if we go back without the Draught, we risk becoming targets of his posthumous mischief."

"Jaravhor would hardly pre-arrange for his spells to harm his own heir when by his own written declaration his chief objective was preserving his lineage," Jewel countered. "But perhaps you are right about his influence being merely local. Now that I reflect on our experiences at the Dome, I begin to doubt very much whether the old trickster was as mighty as he would have people believe. Other than Castle Strang's wall-shield, you and I spied no evidence of lingering enchantment, and like you I wonder whether the shield is no spell at all, but some cunning, man-made contrivance. The flame that illuminates the Tope is fueled by commonplace gas, and the pages of the sorcerer's book unsealed themselves only when I pressed hard enough on the reliquary to budge some lever beneath, operating a hidden mechanism. The more I ponder, the more it seems clear that Jaravhor's tricks are mostly achieved by means of springs and cogs and other mechanical systems, rather than true magick."

"Aye," said Arran. "The man died years ago. What influence a dead sorcerer still possesses, in the form of weird engines and clockworks constructed before his demise, will exist only in his domain. If we never enter the Dome again, the breaking of the vow cannot harm us."

"But this does not annul my second reason for returning," said Jewel. "I would fain try to learn the locations of the other Wells."

"Jewel, the sorcerer dealt in troublemaking. All his works were devised for ill purpose. Even this well-intentioned quest for immortality has ended in misfortune, because the man who has ultimately obtained the gift of deathlessness is plainly unworthy."

"Only if the Draught is in fact everything it is claimed to be," Jewel interposed.

"Indeed. If so, then the immortality of a villain such as Aonarán could result in disastrous consequences for humankind. We might have unintentionally wrought some great wrong by heeding the words of the sorcerer's book and pursuing this absurd dream. I say we should have no further commerce with Castle Strang."

"Oh, but the Dome is my heritage!"

"You are mistaken. Your heritage is not a pile of moldering stones once built by a wicked man, no matter what secrets might be imprisoned within. All the most precious gifts you have inherited from your forebears I see before me now."

Jewel felt blood-heat rush to her cheeks. To cover her unwonted confusion she said quickly, "If you will not accompany me to Strang I shall go alone."

"Do so, if that is your wish," said Arran, surprising her, "for none of the sorcerer's tricks can scathe you. I choose another path. There is a man somewhere in the world, an unvirtuous man, whose span of days has been infinitely lengthened because of certain deeds of mine. I am honor-bound to endeavor to avert at least some of the harm he might unleash upon us all. My duty is to capture and imprison Aonarán."

"But we do not know where he has gone! What is your plan?"

"I shall go to Cathair Rua. Weathermasters often sojourn there on business, which gives me a chance of meeting some of my kindred and hearing news from home. The city is Aonarán's base, is it not? 'Tis likely he's heading there now, even as we speak."

"And from Cathair Rua whither?"

"I know not. Perhaps back to the mountain ring. It depends on how much information I can glean about the man I seek, and who will aid me."

A frown of indecision creased Jewel's brow as she turned over Arran's words in her mind. He was right—there was no knowing what a man like Aonarán might do, given all the days and nights of eternity to work his will. That he had consumed the Draught was beyond a calamity. Simultaneously, it came to Jewel for the first time that an aeons-long experience of forever losing the people he knew, while he himself outlived them, would surely be truly execrable. Immortality could be considered either the greatest gift or the worst possible curse for any mortal-born creature. There was also the question of pain. There was no knowing whether the Draught conferred anesthesia, or whether it entailed the possibility of eternal torment.

To endure decades, centuries, millennia of loss as generation after generation passed away . . . had Arran thoroughly thought the matter through, when he decided to seize deathlessness and present it to Jewel? Perhaps he had, and in saying to her, "All for you, all so that you might, *if you chose,* be the first to become immortal," he had left the decision in her hands. His gift was to have been the *option* of eternal life, rather than the obligation.

It would have been a gift unparalleled.

On the spur of the moment Jewel had told Arran candidly that she would like to live on. Now that she had mulled over the ramifications, she reconsidered. Her doubts led her to wonder whether pursuing the remaining Draughts was truly a commendable course of action. She and Stormbringer had set off on their mission at Jaravhor's behest from beyond the grave, despite both knowing the sorcerer had been a false and sadistic man with malicious designs. Jaravhor's posthumous message had intimated that he wished for his descendants to live forever, because since he himself had failed to obtain immortality, the next best arrangement was to secure it for those who were of his blood. Nonetheless, some hidden purpose might have driven Jaravhor to leave the message in the Tope, and if so, in all likelihood it was an ill-purpose.

It made sense to try to collect the remaining Draughts so that the weather-masters could then decide how to dispose of them in the best possible way, but Jewel was torn between distrust of the sorcerer's intentions and a desire to prevent the precious waters from falling into the wrong hands. . . .

At length she reached a decision. "I will aid you," she announced.

Arran raised an eyebrow in a querying fashion.

"You argue the right of it," Jewel admitted. "I have been hearkening to your words and weighing their good sense. We cannot fulfill the vow, so must try to undo the harm that has come of our enterprise."

The young man's grin was so warm and so engaging that she could only return it with a smile of her own. No more was said, and with that, they turned east and began to retrace their steps.

The road was long, hot, and wearisome. Scant conversation took place between them, and the sense of excitement with which they had undertaken the outward journey was dissipating along with every trace of cloud vapor in the scalding sky.

It occurred to Jewel, late one evening, that the road no longer lay beneath the feet of their steeds, and in fact, she could not recall having seen a milestone for some long while. Drawing rein, she sat up straight and looked about. The undulations of the slumbering desert lay beneath the brilliant sweep of the night sky, shimmering like a reflection of the star-field, spangled with frozen dew.

"We are lost," she announced.

Sharply, Stormbringer reined in his horse beside her. "Even so," he said, scanning the silver-plated but pathless landscape. "Somehow we have wandered from the road." He scratched his head. "How that came to occur I cannot say."

"Strange indeed," affirmed Jewel.

The weathermaster took his bearings from the stars, and they set off again, only to find that there was no sign of the road where he had calculated it ought to lie. The horses were behaving in an extraordinary manner, swinging their heads this way and that, as if unseen presences were urging them in conflicting directions. This happened a second time, and then a third. Eventually they halted again, bemused.

"More than strange," said Jewel. "I would say *eldritch*."

Arran smiled. "Of course! You have the answer. We must turn our clothes!"

Laughing with relief and amusement at their own obtuseness, they shrugged off their cloaks, reversed them, and put them on inside-out. The moment they did so, a cacophony of chortling, guffawing, and tittering broke out on all sides, followed by a loud whirring noise that seemed to draw away, as if a crowd of small creatures was scattering into the desert on insect-like wings.

Beneath the feet of their horses the road had reappeared, its surface beaten flat, its borders marked at intervals with tall stones.

"I have been letting down my guard," said Arran. "I ought to be more vigilant."

"Do not blame yourself," his companion answered. "I am equally at fault! 'Twas only pixies, in any case."

He held his peace, but Jewel guessed he shared her thought: *Worse things than pixies might be ahead.*

Next evening they came upon a scene that reminded them, if they needed reminding, of the truly terrible dangers that might befall unwary or ill-prepared travelers on any road in the Four Kingdoms. Looking ahead they could see, strewn across and to either side of the road, a scattering of indefinable shapes, like discarded rubbish. On closer inspection these articles turned out to be smashed coffers, human corpses, torn garments, and various vandalized objects of little value. This was the appalling aftermath of a recent attack on a band of travelers. Having dismounted, Arran and Jewel began to search for survivors.

Many sets of hoof-impressions, not yet spiced with blowing sand, led away into the desert. A boiled-leather gauntlet, studded with iron, lay half curled on the ground, like some armored desert reptile. Arran picked it up. "An artefact typical of Marauders," he said soberly, inspecting the glove. "And there are no beasts of burden in sight. All horses and dromedaries have been stolen, which confirms—as if it needed confirmation—this assault was not the work of malignant wights."

They buried the bodies in the sand and repeated the water-chant at the gravesides. Then they cleared the detritus from the road as best they could, before mounting up and riding on. Ever and anon they glanced vigilantly around, across the wide plains to the purple-headed ranges of the south, the shimmering wastes unrolling toward remote horizons in every other direction. Nocturnal desert-dwellers glided like half-formed concepts across the lilting dunes, and their eyes were sudden glints, like sequins, and swooping owls made the stars blink.

In Jhallavad, city of the whirling windmills, they could discover no information about Aonarán, or his sister, or Scorpion. Pushing on, they drew near the turn-off to R'shael ten days later.

It was very late in the afternoon and, as so often, the desert's western sky was putting on a fine display. Jewel could not help but frequently turn around in the saddle to admire it. The diving sun was a brass daisy radiating shining petals, with veils of brilliant orchid and orange caught amongst them. Gently, it slipped beneath the horizon, leaving a hot golden trail. In the afterglow the lower edges of cloud-rows in the sky's western quarter burst into puffs of pink spun sugar, stretched and torn across the gilt foil of the sun-path. Slowly the glory began to fade from bright tangerine to rose, streaked with soft brush-strokes of blue-gray, still smudged with rushing streams of pale amber. The rest of the sky, almost the entire bowl, solidified to silver.

The evening breeze was stirring up veils of dust, so according to the custom of desert-dwellers, Jewel and Arran wrapped scarves around the nostrils of the horses and the lower halves of their own faces, to keep out the airborne grit. As they approached the fork in the road they saw a band of horsemen traveling toward them from the direction of the village. By the time they spotted this phenomenon, there was no doubt the horsemen must have likewise spied them. They could choose to break into a gallop, but there was no guarantee their horses could outrun the steeds ridden by the strangers.

"Perchance they are Marauders," said Jewel. Her tone betrayed no fear, despite that she was afraid. Despising cowardice, she steeled herself to face this new encounter. She was shielded by invulnerability, and Arran possessed the powers of a weathermaster. The odds, she told herself, were good.

"Perchance," Arran agreed levelly. "We might as well confront them with a brave face."

They slowed to a halt and sat in their saddles, awaiting the strangers. Jewel noted that Arran had dropped the reins and his hands were moving, almost imperceptibly. He whispered a word, below the range of hearing, and she knew he was preparing to defend them both.

The strangers' steeds were the wiry horses of the desert tribes, bridled with green leather, saddled with dark vermilion. As for the riders, they were men of middle age, clad chiefly in hues of saffron and ocher. Hooded cloaks covered embroidered tunics. Sheathed scimitars and daggers hung at their hips. Beneath their tunics, amulets depended from thongs about their necks. Knee-high, flamboyantly embossed boots were pulled up over their deerskin leggings. Some sported clinking ornaments of brass. Their faces, too, were partially concealed, wrapped with light cloths about the nose and mouth to keep the dust from their lungs, so that only their eyes could be seen. The little that showed of their visages was suntanned and spare, and the hair of each man, streaked with salt-gray, was folded in a club behind his head.

The leader was a coarse-browed man of powerful build. His shoulders were as bulky as a bullock's, his chest as deep as a hogshead. He sat his horse with balanced and easy grace, even though his left leg had been severed below the knee. A wooden stump was strapped to his saddle.

"Hola!" he called out. "Be you friend or foe?"

A man who rode close by him said, amused, "How can they be foes, Caracal? Behold, one is a young woman and the other but a youth not much older than your own son!"

"Approach no further!" Stormbringer's voice rang out. "Hold, and identify yourselves!"

"The youth is bold, I'll grant you that!" the one called Caracal guffawed appreciatively. The horsemen brought their mounts to a standstill. The leader shouted, "We are liegemen of the Duke of Bucks Horn Oak in Narngalis, returning from our annual visit to our native village. What of you?"

Guardedly, Arran gave answer: "Our home is High Darioneth. We are bound for Cathair Rua."

"Weathermasters, eh?" shouted Caracal, as a stir of interest rippled through his band of comrades. "Why not keep us company on the road?"

"We have had such an invitation before," Jewel muttered to Arran, who grimaced. He deliberated before passing judgment. At length he called out, "Advance."

The horsemen shifted their weight forward, and in response their horses resumed walking. As the strangers caught up, Jewel turned her head and stared intently at each one. Despite that they were masked with scarves, she fancied there was some familiar look about them. Her own scarf was loose, and as she looked around it had begun to fall away from her face. She tucked it in again, but in return for her stares it seemed the strangers could not take their eyes from her, and they gazed at her in wonder. Perceiving this, Arran scowled, steering his horse between Jewel and the men.

Noting Arran's attitude, Caracal said to him, "Be not angered, young sir, for if we gawp unmannerly, it is not as you suppose." Still seated in his saddle, he ducked his head respectfully to Jewel. "Lady, forgive me," he said. "I mean no insult. In your countenance I see the countenance of another, who was dear to me long ago. His name was Jarred Jovansson."

Jewel felt her eyes fly wide in shock, before she mastered her demeanor. Who was this man? How could he have known her father? If she identified herself as a scion of the Jaravhor line, would she be in peril?

Averting her gaze from the Ashqalêthan's scrutiny, she murmured hoarsely, "I know not of whom you speak. High Darioneth is my home."

It was as if a lamp had been shedding radiance upon the big man and suddenly the light had been snuffed out. Hope faded from his eyes. He ducked his head a second time.

"Forgive me," he repeated. Unaccountably, Jewel wanted to reach out and touch him, but she made no move.

His comrade, the one who had been amused at the notion of a young woman and a youth being a threat, said, "I am known as Quoll, and my friend here is Caracal. The others of our troupe are called Jerboa and Snake. Of course, you know that such names are but kennings of the desert-lands."

"Naturally," said Arran. "We have our own kennings. I am Salt, and my sister is called Lily."

"Lily?" Caracal's head snapped up, but upon meeting Quoll's meaningful squint, he choked back his comment before it was uttered.

It was plain to Arran that Caracal must have been acquainted with Jewel's father, but it was also clear that these men meant no harm, and were endeavoring to show courtesy. Arran sensed they could be trusted, and besides, they might be of help along the road, should any further perils threaten. At the same time, he was not ready to invite strangers further into his confidence.

"If we are all introduced and agreed, pray let us ride on," he said.

The horsemen readily complied, and fell in beside them.

To while the leagues away, all parties engaged in amiable conversation. The one called Quoll told how he and his friends had left R'shael many years ago, to seek their fortune in other kingdoms. He himself had secured a position as Conjuror and Entertainer with the noble Duke of Bucks Horn Oak, while Caracal and Jerboa had turned their hands to various trades that came their way, including horse-breaking, hay-making, grave-digging, and cart-loading. As time went on and the duke's retainers declined into frailty or senility, or left his service, Quoll had recommended his friends as candidates for the vacated positions; however, they did not take to the idea of settling down in one place for too long, and were apt to skip between various employments.

"I was not amongst them when they first set out from our village," said one who called himself Snake. He was somewhat younger than the rest, a cheerful youth. "I joined this band of good-for-nothings last time they visited R'shael, desiring to see if their stories of great deeds and high adventure were true. So far the greatest deed I have seen them perform is the lifting of heavy tankards."

Caracal cuffed him good-naturedly.

"That accounts for all save for our old comrades Sand Fox and Gecko," concluded Quoll. "In Narngalis, Sand Fox entered the service of King Warwick, becoming a member of the household troops at the palace in King's Winterbourne. He is now Captain of the Guard, while his brother Gecko is second-in-command."

"And save also for Jovansson," interjected Caracal. "He stayed at the Great Marsh of Slievmordhu, for he fell in love with a marsh-daughter, and they were wed."

"Just as some of us found wives amongst the women of Narngalis," said Quoll.

Jewel observed, "You are well employed, yet every year you return to your home village."

"Every year," explained Snake, "we grow homesick. We long to feel the dry winds of Ashqalêth again, and so we go back, albeit for a short visit."

"Tell me about your friend who went to live in the marsh," Jewel said, unable to restrain her curiosity any longer.

"Ah well, he wed a damsel with eyes like blue lightning frozen to stillness, and they had a child, a daughter."

"What more of him?"

"He was brave and honest, strong and generous. His laugh would lighten anyone's mood, and he could shoot down a fell-cat at a hundred paces."

"He was skilled with both crossbow and sling," put in Jerboa, "and he was apprenticed to a blacksmith in R'shael. Also, he learned much from his own father, who was a carpenter. He played music, Jarred did, on a lyre he had fashioned with his own hands, and he was a creditable poet, to boot."

"A man of many talents," said Snake sadly. "Alas, now gone."

"By your words one would judge that he was dearly loved," Jewel ventured.

"Dearly loved," Caracal repeated for emphasis, "and we loved his family also." Again he eyed Jewel with a puzzled air, but voiced no question.

Impetuously, and without regard to the suspicions of the Bucks Horn Oak liegemen, Jewel was driven to quiz them about their dear friend, and they gladly regaled her with tales of Jarred's adventures in their company.

The dust settled as the breeze died, and the travelers were able to put aside their masks, yet in the starlit darkness it was difficult to discern facial features. Come morning, Jewel clearly saw the men from R'shael for the first time, and recognized them as her father's old friends, yet, having become cautious from years of living with the fear of identification, she refrained from mentioning the fact.

Both she and Stormbringer felt at ease with these high-spirited wayfarers in a way they had never enjoyed with Scorpion and Lizard. Sharing tales, songs, and laughter, they put the leagues behind them. As they crossed the border into Slievmordhu and headed along the Valley Road they fell in with a couple of jovial traveling minstrels who, in return for a few copper coins, regaled the company with the first stanzas of an east-kingdom ballad titled "Ropes of Sand":

"At Samradh Mile—the story tells—young student scribes at
    escritoires
Sat dipping quills in ink-filled wells, and studying their repertoires
Of runes and letters, toiling hard through hours of tedium each day.
When work was done—so says the bard—the lads were wont to lark
    and play.

But, as they idled at their ease, there came a knocking from below
The hearthstone. Thinking it some tease, they laughed and yelled,
    'Who's there? Hallo?'
No voice replied, but *rat-tat-tat,* the beat drummed from beneath the
    stone.
The grinning boys scoffed, 'Who is that who tries to fright us to the
    bone?'
Once more the knocking sounded from some sub-floor cave. 'Pray,
    let me in!'
A loud voice cried. Then, with aplomb the students answered, 'Hush
    your din!
Your prank grows stale. Three times you've knocked. Your game
    palls. 'Tis no longer rare.
Show us your face! The slab's not locked. Now, fellow, enter if you
    dare!'

"The stone arose into the air, revealing a horrific sight—
Up from the hole that opened there clambered a monstrous, hairy
    wight.
The lads were petrified with fear, all save for one, who slipped away
Unnoticed, in the atmosphere of disbelief and stunned dismay.
'You asked me in!' the sprite declared. 'Your invitation left no doubt.
Well might you tremble, meek and scared! Now that I'm in, I won't
    go out.
I'll cause you mischief night and day; I'll trick and taunt and harass
    you.
You won't be rid of me. I'll stay! There's nothing that I cannot do.'

" 'They're braggarts' words!' a man's voice cried. 'Words bow to deeds,
    you boastful elf!'
The voice's owner strode inside the door, the schoolmaster himself.
He'd heard the tidings from the youth who stole away, and come to
    try
To save the school from this uncouth malignant troll, so foul and sly.
'You say there's nothing you can't do?' the schoolmaster did boldly say.
'Prove that your claim is fair and true; if not, then you must flee
    straightway.'
'The wager's on!' the goblin howled. 'And I shall win! I'll guarantee!
Set me three tasks,' he shrieked and growled. 'I will perform them.
    You shall see.' "

Jewel was intrigued by the verses and begged the minstrels to name the three tasks without further ado, but the balladeers said, "For a coin or two, Mistress Lily, we shall sing you the second part!"

Close beside Jewel, Arran leaned and whispered, "They have got enough coin from us already. I know the song, and will later sing it to you for nothing."

Increasingly as they left behind the desert regions and passed deeper into Slievmordhu they came amongst acres of undulating grasslands. To the north, the land rose to become the low green hills of Bellaghmoon, while in the east a line of peaks stood sentinel, towering out of a sea of bluish fume. Here, many leagues from the stone deserts south of Ashqalêth, protected by two mountain ranges from the scouring winds of the Fyrflaume and well watered by the run-off from the Great Eastern Ranges, the landscape waxed lush and mellow.

It was late in Otember. Half-lost in the long grass, brown hares loped across the pastures, their fur gilded, and their whiskers fired into stiff wires of electrum by the slanting rays of the equinoctial sun. In the hedgerows along the margins of the road blackberries and hawthorns were ripening, turning from hard green nubs, to red globes, and then to carbuncles of deep, glossy black. Birds fed on them: song thrushes, redwings, blackbirds, and bullfinches. Kestrels hovered over meadows of maturing seed-heads, in search of harvest mice performing acrobatic feats amongst the stalks. Wooded areas were sparse, and no trees grew closer to the road than the distance of a bowshot. Villages were also rare in these outlying regions, but those through which the travelers passed were engaged in goose fairs, sheep fairs, and hiring fairs.

Early one evening, the travelers crossed a rickety wooden bridge over a brook that meandered away through the violet-studded wayside. Farther from the road, the waterway was lined with birches and beeches. Their foliage had begun to take on the rich tints of treasure, but the extravaganza of Autumn colors had not yet evolved. The clinging beech-leaves were heart-shaped shavings of gold. As if unattached to any twig, they hovered over the shimmering stream, whose dim banks of moss seemed as soft and inviting as couches of emerald velvet.

During the course of conversation, one of the minstrels informed Jewel and Arran that they were riding past a spot known as "Gibbet Corner." "For," he explained, "a long time ago a chimney-sweep was hanged and gibbeted here. He had committed a murder, right near this place. The gibbet stood for many years after the corpse disintegrated, until at last the timber succumbed to weather, and it, too, crumbled away. But the name remains."

"And more than the name, some say," his fellow troubadour muttered uneasily, peering into the gathering gloom. "We have dawdled too long on our way this afternoon, and are now upon the very doorstep of night."

To the right of the travelers, beneath the broken boughs of a derelict apple-orchard, piles of fruit lay rotting. The last rays of the sun illuminated fluttering cut-outs of brightly printed fabric—red admirals, tortoiseshells, and painted ladies, butterflies attracted by the sickly-sweet putrefaction of the apples.

A breeze shook the branches, and the abandoned orchard came awake with movement: leaves spiraling down, insects bouncing on the gaudy hinges of their wings, men moving silently and swiftly within the camouflage of the trees. The garb of the brigands was motley, dyed with the hues of natural vegetation, and they advanced with the easy stealth learned from practice in the wilderness. Harsh-faced, misshapen fellows were they, and their belts and baldrics sported a vast array of weaponry.

The first to spy them was Stormbringer.

"'Ware Marauders," he warned in a low, clear voice. Then, glancing over to the beech-wood, he added, "On both flanks! Ride hard!"

His alarm was timely. Even as the travelers urged their steeds into a gallop, a deadly hail of crossbow bolts seared through their ranks. The half-dozen Marauders were shooting at them, but even their most practiced archers found it harder to hit fast-moving targets. The young weathermaster let drop the reins, balancing skillfully astride his hurtling mount as his hands began to form subtle signals. Next moment he was flung from his seat as his horse unexpectedly toppled. Other Marauders had been lying hidden amongst the wayside weeds, on both sides of the highway, and had raised a trip-rope. Its legs entangled, Arran's horse crashed to the ground, closely followed by the mounts of Quoll and Jerboa. Jewel, instantly perceiving the dilemma, nudged her steed, which leaped high into the air and sailed gracefully over the three beasts prone and struggling in the middle of the road. The minstrels were unseated by their terrified, rearing horses, but somehow, both Snake and Caracal managed to swerve, avoiding further injury. Jewel, instead of riding to safety, turned her horse's head and rode back toward the melee.

As he was thrown down, Arran had reflexively rolled into the fall, then somersaulted to a halt, springing to his feet unharmed save for several bruises. He was in time to witness the second band of Marauders closing in. The fifteen brigands did not hesitate, but plunged toward the beleaguered travelers, running at full speed. They bore no shields, but were armored with chain mail and plates of hardened leather. Quickly they surged across the space between Jewel and Arran like the sweep and clash of two ocean currents. There was no opportunity to practice weathermastery. Flourishing his sword, Arran rushed to meet the enemy.

The close combat grew fierce. Quoll and Jerboa, having managed to survive being jettisoned from their saddles, had regained their feet. They were fighting valiantly, despite that one side of Quoll's head was soaked with blood. Caracal and Snake had wheeled about and charged into the fray on horseback, crouched low along the backs of their steeds and wielding long knives in both hands. Dextrously they spun their blades of Narngalis steel, which glittered like the spokes of chariot wheels, and would have plowed carnage among the ambushers had they not temporarily abandoned the fight and dodged out of reach. After discomfiting as many as possible, Snake jumped to the ground, unsheathed his weapons, and rejoined the fray on foot. Caracal, still in the saddle, wheeled and charged.

A multitude of pictures stabbed through the mind of Stormbringer, depicting the possible fates of Jewel: imprisonment and mistreatment at the hands of grotesque half-men; torment; terror; she alone in some remote mountain fastness without a champion to aid her, her blue eyes tear-filled . . . His most urgent desire was to force his way to her side. Even as he slashed and parried, he could see, through the gathering darkness, that she was surrounded by brigands and in imminent danger of being pulled from her saddle. Undaunted, she was laying about on all sides with a wooden club, dealing headaches to all within reach.

Caracal reached Jewel first, and commenced to beat back her assailants. Arran joined him a moment later. Together they became her defenders, flanking her horse. Arran was swapping sword-thrusts with a masked and ferocious opponent when the two weapons locked. The bloody blades slipped against each other, sliding up until the hilts jammed and the young weathermaster found himself staring into the mad eyes of his foe. A sudden glint sparkled from Arran's finger, where his seal-ring reflected an unexpected prickle of light. The ruffian was distracted, his attention wavered, and with a mighty heave of his shoulders he threw off the young man.

The light had emanated from a brilliant burst of fire that had abruptly blazed forth upon a bank at the roadside. Piercing the gloaming, the fire's radiance rinsed the profiles of the fighters with liquid brass, and they broke apart, shouting exclamations of surprise. The battle came to a dead stop. Every combatant froze with uncertainty, careful not to drop his guard. Jewel's horse shied and snorted loudly in fear. There was a sifting in the gloaming, an unwebbing of dark gauzes.

A gigantic dog was standing in the road.

If it *was* indeed a dog, then it was the strangest Arran had ever beheld, the size of a foal, but emaciated, as if it had been protractedly starved. Its shaggy hide was draped over an angular frame. It had lengthy ears, large, long teeth, and an extensive plume of a tail. Sunk within the long-muzzled skull the eyes glowed, orbs of garnet incandescence.

No one spoke a word.

The black dog opened its mouth as if grinning at the men. Instead of renewing their assault the Marauders dodged away, calling out to their accomplices. Arran wiped dripping sweat from his eyes and leaned on his sword, panting. The bandits, wounded and unwounded, were loping silently into the trees.

After several moments the strange dog disappeared, seeming to vanish like a shadow, or to sink into the ground. No clue remained at the spot where it had stood.

"Let us hie from this place forthwith!" one of the minstrels shrieked in a high-pitched and trembling voice. "That was none other than the Black Dog of Gibbet Corner! There's no knowing what will happen to us if we linger here. Fly! Escape!"

The Bucks Horn Oak liegemen whistled for their horses. Well-trained, the beasts obeyed their masters' summons, and when they returned the horses of the other travelers were nervously following in their wake. No longer was there any sign of the ominous bonfire on the road-bank. Shades of evening darkness thronged in like black-wrapped executioners. The minstrels were by now gibbering with fear; therefore, as soon as they had captured their steeds the riders mounted up and hastened on.

"We are not far from the hamlet of Snug," said Quoll as they rode. "There we will take our rest." He was pressing a wad of fabric to one side of his bleeding head.

"And there we should seek a carlin!" exclaimed Jewel, noting his injury. She herself remained, of course, unscathed.

"Our hurts are not lethal," replied Quoll, deftly binding a strip of linen around his head while he sat his moving horse. "No carlin's aid is necessary. From bitter experience of the road we have learned to carry salves and bandages, and to practice some rudimentary healing arts. We are well equipped enough to tend to our own scratches." He tossed a jar of ointment to Stormbringer. "Here, young warrior—smear it on your cuts. 'Twill help restore you to soundness."

A wasted moon, pale and diseased, oozed out from behind the clouds. By its bloodless light they made their way, only too aware that the wighting hours were upon them.

"Ironically the unseelie Black Dog has proved a boon to us," muttered Snake, "for had it not frightened off the Marauders, we must surely have been defeated."

Quoll said quietly, "I can never become accustomed to seeing so many misbegotten things banded together. Some of those brigands were as hairy as beasts, while others were bald as babies. Several seemed patched with scale-armored skin, or sprouted great long toes."

Caracal nodded, saying, "One or two were of enormous stature, perhaps seven feet tall."

Arran had not spoken for some time, and seemed lost in thought. At length, as they went on, he observed, "I looked into the eyes of one of those half-men and witnessed no hatred, rage, passion, or desire, no empathy whatsoever—only ignorance and pitiless brutality. If they all be such creatures, how they can even exist as a community defies imagination, for there was no warmth, no fellow-feeling, merely cold clockworks of madness behind those eyes."

"Aye," one of the minstrels agreed wholeheartedly. "But thanks be to the Lord Ádh, they did not know what haunts Gibbet Corner betimes. As your comrade said, the sight of that wight drove them off and doubtless saved our skins."

"Ignorant of local haunts they may be," said Arran grimly, "but did you mark, they are armed better than many a nobleman's garrison, with weapons of Narngalis steel and Grïmnørsland chain mail? How such gutter-dwelling wretches got their hands on high-quality arms and armor I cannot begin to guess."

"Oh, that is easily answered, I dare say," said the informative Quoll, still dabbing at his cuts and scratches with a blood-soaked rag. "Not long ago there began to be rumors of a network of arms-smugglers based in Cathair Rua, trading weapons to the murdering scum."

"The Sanctorum will soon find out who is selling arms to the Marauders," one of the minstrels put in self-righteously, "and then the guilty ones will be made to pay."

"Be not so certain, my friend," said Snake. "Other rumors would have it that certain of the druids are in the pay of these arms-runners."

"Profanity!" gasped the minstrel. "I'll warrant that any man who repeated such calumny would be flogged, by order of the Druid Imperius!"

Snake turned a hard stare on the musician, who subsided. Dampened, he and his friend dropped back to the rear of the group, and when they were out of earshot Arran asked Snake, "Has there been any mention of names? Of who might be behind this scheme?"

The Bucks Horn Oak liegeman nodded. "It is said that one trader is known as Weaponmonger, and there is another who might be his master—some back-alley fellow who knows how to discreetly grease the palms of High Court judges and other powerful druids."

"Perhaps not so discreetly," said Jerboa, "if his secrets are now the subject of whispers."

"Truth has a way of revealing itself eventually," said Caracal sagely.

"But what chance has Truth," remarked Arran dryly, "against the Sanctorum?"

The liegemen blinked at him in surprise at his outspokenness, then laughed together.

"Well," said Caracal good-naturedly, "I mark you are of one opinion with us, young sir!"

As he spoke, Jewel steered her horse beside him and handed him a stick of wood with a bowl-shaped end. "Here's your leg back," she said, "and I thank you for the use of it, for it drubbed a few skulls that required sense knocked into them!"

The big man guffawed again. On noticing Arran's mystified look, he explained, "I tossed it to the damsel as I was riding to her aid, back there on the road. Across the heads of the Marauders I threw it, and she caught my leg with one hand, while keeping her seat and thrusting her boot in the face of some grasping cur. A masterful rider you are, Mistress Lily!"

The corners of Jewel's mouth turned up in a sweet smile, until Arran reprimanded her, "Be that as it may, you should never have returned to the site of battle when you might have escaped."

"I came back to help," she answered him loftily.

"A fine help you are, a girl brandishing a wooden leg." The heat of anger still burned within the young man. Visions of losing her to the attackers had unsettled him, so that he spoke to her with uncharacteristic roughness.

Still flustered by the Marauder onslaught and the apparition, but elated at her band's reprieve, Jewel took his words at face value. She did not think to peer behind his mask of asperity. Her companions of the road were safe—that was her first consideration. Why Arran should rant at her was a mystery that, being beyond comprehension, she shrugged off. Now was a time for forging ahead, a time to be blithe.

"Well," she said, "the villains ran away, did they not?"

Perceiving she teased him, he could not help but return a grudging smile. Soon thereafter, they reached the hamlet of Snug, where they rested for the night.

Riddle

Beyond Snug the highway bent left and began a gentle, meandering descent toward
the next village, where it skirted the outlying hills of Bellaghmoon before winding its way across the countryside to Cathair Rua. Meadows rolled on both sides
like oceans of tranquilly waving grasses, and beneath the hedgerows violets
were producing a bounty of heart-shaped flowers, mere flecks of deep mauve exuding a heady perfume. Flocks of goldfinches skipped amongst clumps of
teasel and crowthistle, pecking at the ripe seeds. Long necklaces of migrating
birds threaded their way across the skies—chiffchaffs and redstarts, swallows
and house martins. In patches of flame-colored woodland, robins were feeding
on the busy clouds of gnats seduced by the mellow sunshine, while squirrels
scampered across the fallen leaves seeking beech mast and hazelnuts.

Outside the gates of the capital of Slievmordhu, the Fairfield lay empty. The
stamped-down soil of the market arena had lain desolate for four weeks, ever
since the closing of the Autumn Fair. A querulous wind had picked up, and was
playing at skittles with some broken sticks, remnants of dismantled stalls.

"The equinox approaches," said Arran, watching the skirls and patterns of
debris raised by eddies across the ground. "This is a season of flux."

Soon after they entered the city, Jewel and Stormbringer parted from their
companions of the road. The minstrels were the first to remove themselves,
while the Bucks Horn Oak liegemen were slower to take their leave.

"Already it is late Otember," said Quoll, "and by my reckoning it is only two weeks until Lantern Eve. Our plan is to remain here for one or two nights, before pushing on toward Narngalis. We shall be staying at an inn called the *Ace and Cup.*"

"We know of it, but alas, that is not close to the *Three Barrels,* where we intend to take our rest," said Arran. "Many streets lie between your inn and our hostelry."

Jewel said, "Notwithstanding, I hope we shall chance to meet again before we leave the city."

"Even so!" agreed Caracal and Snake.

Jerboa said, "It is with regret that we must leave you, my young friends. Whither are you bound, when you conclude your business here?"

"Home to Narngalis," the weathermaster replied circumspectly. "We shall not tarry long, here. My wish is to seek out any of my own kindred who might chance to be in the city. Afterward we shall take to the road north, and be not far behind you. If you prove slow, we might catch you up!"

"We do not travel slowly," said Quoll, laughing. "Not when a happy homecoming awaits us at the end of the road!"

"I am sorry that we must part," Jewel said to the liegemen. "Your company has been blithe, and without you we must surely have come to harm on the highway."

"Would you care to join us at the *Ace and Cup* for one last drink before you depart?" Caracal asked, and to this Jewel and Arran readily agreed.

With many more expressions of cordiality they exchanged salutations and went their separate ways. Jewel and Arran were left on their own in the city. They led their horses through the streets, and the milling crowd of citizens parted to let them through, flowing to rejoin like murmurous waters at their backs. It was just past noon, but the sun was invisible behind the overcast. A savage wind began to barrel through the city, issuing from the west, where a mighty bank of slate-blue storm clouds was rolling in. Garments flapped, detritus whirled past, and hats were snatched off heads.

"Rain and hail are on the way," observed Arran unnecessarily. "The sooner we get ourselves snug indoors, the better."

"Where are you guiding us?"

"To the inn of which I spoke, the Three Barrels. It is a hostelry favored by my kindred, who often choose to patronize it when they visit this town a-marketing, or for other reasons aside from royal business. Methinks if we sojourn there we might pick up recent tidings of High Darioneth, and I hope I might chance upon someone trustworthy who could bear a message to my father, letting him know we are safe and hale. I have been long away from Rowan Green, forsaking my duties. I daresay he's ill-pleased with me."

The beeswaxed timbers supporting the inner walls of the Three Barrels ran with liquid lampshine. Nailed thereon, hundreds of horse brasses winked cheerily. The inn looked clean and bright. As it happened, no sooner had they finished attending to the comfort of their horses in the hostelry's stables and set foot in the common-room than Jewel and her companion came face-to-face with Bliant Ymberbaillé-Rainbearer, in the company of a gray-haired weathermage and a young journeyman from the Seat of the Weathermasters. At once they fell upon one another's shoulders with gladness, exchanging heartfelt greetings.

The three from High Darioneth were elegantly clad. Their dyed leather belts and baldrics were fastened with intricately wrought buckles, the silver-white of platinum alloyed with iridium or the bluish-white of platinum blended with osmium. None wore weathermaster garb, which indicated they were in the city for purposes other than the taming of the elements. A thin ring of platinum pierced the lobe of Bliant's right ear. His wide mouth was stretched in a grin; his expressive countenance denoted sheer delight. Indeed, joy was shining from the faces of all the reunited friends.

Stormbringer called for a private dining-room and it was not long before all five were seated around a table beside a fireplace, with foaming tankards set before them, and a serving-man's promise that the cook would immediately prepare a substantial meal for their enjoyment. Cold raindrops began to patter against the windows and gusts shook the shutters, but indoors all was cozy and warm.

Then was many a tale recounted.

First, Arran demanded news of family and friends. "Not a word of our own ventures will pass our lips," he insisted, "until you have informed us how they are faring."

"I assure you that all is as well as can be hoped," said the weathermage, a flinty, middle-aged man named Tristian Solorien. "Sadly, Branor Darglistel has passed out of life. A welcome release for him, I would judge." All bowed their heads gravely, and there was a moment's respectful silence, before Solorien resumed: "The Maelstronnar does not often speak of his absent son, but I tell you this; he is not displeased with you. He trusts his son's good judgment in all undertakings, although he is saddened by the lack of your company."

"Aye, your father misses you sorely," said Bliant, "as do we all." He proceeded to outline details about the doings of Arran's siblings, Galiene, Lysanor, and Dristan, and his aunt Astolat, and his cousins, including young Ryence Darglistel.

"Darglistel is breaking the hearts of damsels all across the plateau," said Solorien, somewhat dismissively. "He acts like a bee crazed by fermenting honey."

Jewel laughed with the others, but could not prevent a twinge of annoyance that her admirer showed no signs of missing her, and instead was paying court to all and sundry. She noticed Arran's eyes upon her but he immediately looked away as if he had been unaware of her glance, which led her to wonder, in that moment, whether the Storm Lord's son had been jealous of her friendship with Ryence all along.

"Is Ettare Sibilaurë in sound health?" Arran asked Solorien.

"That she is, and happy as ever."

"What about the Miller family?" Jewel inquired.

"Prosperous, as far as I know."

"Does Blostma's baby still get the croup? How is Mildthrythe's arthritis?"

Solorien gave a shrug. "If you want news of aches and infants, ask a carlin." He took another pull at his tankard of ale.

Jewel said, "Beyond these walls, wind and rain beleaguer the city. Have you come here to tame them?"

"We will not disturb ourselves on account of anything less than a force nine strong gale," said Bliant. "That which blows outside is merely a force seven."

"By your clothes and your accommodation alone I deduced as much," said Arran. "But why have you come to the city?"

"We have just returned from a visit to a far-flung town in the northeast of Slievmordhu, called Carrickmore," Bliant replied. "Reports of civil disturbance there had come to the notice of the Maelstronnar, and he dispatched us to investigate."

"What disturbance?"

The weathermasters explained that a group of druids in the remote Carrickmore Sanctorum appeared to be forming a breakaway sect, claiming that Míchinniúint, Lord Doom, was the rightful Chieftain of the Fates. The druids were declaring that folk who continued to believe Ádh was Chieftain ought to be penalized, and they were talking of organizing "enlightenment parties" to patrol the town demanding that people state their allegiance to Míchinniúint. Most of the townsfolk were afraid that if they betrayed their allegiance to Ádh, they would lose the good favor of Lord Luck. He might then punish them by withdrawing his protection and allowing them to be harmed by Mí-Ádh, Lady Misfortune, and the hag Cinniúint, Lady Destiny.

Wearily, Arran sighed. "Therefore," he said, "the common-folk are pinched, as it were, in a forked stick, afraid to speak lest they offend one Fate or another."

"The entire town is ruled by fear," Solorien stated sourly, brooding as he stared into his half-empty tankard.

"Strange are the ways of humankind," mused Bliant. "There exist rain and wind and fire, and interdependent systems of organisms, and the myriad other elements that sustain Life. Instead of esteeming these elements we personify abstractions, that we may avoid responsibility for our own destinies and lay the blame elsewhere."

"All here present are agreed on that point," pointed out Solorien.

"And even if there *were* beings with as much power as the so-called Fates are claimed to wield," extrapolated Jewel, always keen to air her opinion, "such omnipotents would scarcely require to be constantly worshiped and fawned upon as if they were mortal kings. The truly great need no affirmation of their greatness."

"The faith of the druids is no more than unquestioning submission to the preposterous," muttered Bliant.

"This group in Carrickmore, the 'Sandals of Doom,' is saying that people who do not believe the Fates exist should be slain," Solorien said.

"The 'Sandals of Doom'?"

"They attest that their task is to disseminate the words of Lord Doom and be trodden beneath his feet."

Two serving-lads brought in platters and bowls of food to set upon the board. After the servants had departed and Bliant checked to ensure the door was firmly shut, the company fell to dining. Stories continued to be told throughout the repast.

The attention of the journeyman Gahariet Heaharním-HighCloud had obviously been wandering during the discussion. After the meal was over he begged leave to go hence to the inn's common-room, where he wished to renew his friendship with some old acquaintances lately spied there.

"And one of these acquaintances would have a pretty face, no doubt," said Solorien loudly. "And that one would be the buttery maid, no doubt. Be off with you, then, Gahariet. Go where your thoughts have already strayed. You've been propped up next to me like an empty vessel this last half hour."

When Heaharním had made his exit, Arran courteously informed the weathermasters that he wished to consult with Jewel in a private corner of the room. He took her aside and they conversed in murmurs, while Solorien and Ymberbaillé kept up a noisier conversation at the table.

"Jewel, the time has come to disclose your identity to Bliant," Arran said. "I recognize the look in his eye—he detects there is much left unsaid between the members of this group, senses he is an outsider, guesses there are secrets afoot but is too discreet to make enquiries. I value his counsel. He is my closest friend. Methinks we shall need his help, and for this purpose he must be made aware of your history. Solorien, as one of the councillors of Ellenhall, is, of course, already privy to the truth. Bliant Ymberbaillé-Rainbearer, as the son of a councillor and as my life-long comrade, is a man to be trusted. Besides, the habit of taciturnity is ingrained with weathermasters, who have to keep the secrets of weatherworking from an early age. For friendship's sake and also because I hold his advice in high esteem, let me tell Bliant who you are."

Jewel hesitated, then nodded in agreement. "You are right. Let him know."

They returned to the table. After eliciting a vow of secrecy from Bliant, they spoke of Jewel's heritage and narrated their recent adventures, keeping their voices low all the while, for as Stormbringer said, "A private chamber this may be, but gossipmongers have scant respect for privacy when there's a chance of discovering secrets. It is wise to forever assume, in public houses, that some Jack In The Wall is wagging his ears nearby. Our business is confidential."

Their tale riveted the attention of the listeners—Bliant was astonished at the revelations—and the hours passed quickly. It was very late by the time they had concluded their account; Solorien's head was nodding with exhaustion.

"We ought also to keep the existence of these other Wells secret," said Arran. "Make no mention to anyone—save, of course, for my father. If word got about that draughts of everlasting life are hidden somewhere in the Four Kingdoms, can you imagine the hordes that would stampede in search of them, inventing false rumors, following spurious trails, double-crossing and quarreling, cutting down all opposition in their desperation to cheat death? And if tyrants such as King Uabhar should seize this prize of everlasting life, why, Tir would never be rid of their predations!"

"It should be for the wisest of the wise, the Council at Ellenhall, to decide the future of such precious potions," said Solorien.

All present declared their concordance.

"Immortality, eh?" said Bliant. "I, for one, could never desire such a so-called gift."

"Why not?" Jewel wanted to know.

Ymberbaillé had ever been an honest young man, and it was obvious he spoke from the heart. "To me, it would be no gift, but a burden."

"To whom would *you* give the gift?" Jewel asked of Bliant.

"To whosoever could demonstrate they were both worthy of it and able to endure it."

"For example?"

"The Storm Lord."

"I, too, wished to offer one of the cups of life to my father," said Arran regretfully. Without glancing at Jewel, he added, "Had I successfully obtained the Draught from the Well of Rain for another."

Meanwhile the older weathermage unclosed his jaw in a gaping yawn and said, "We have traveled far this day. For myself, I would fain rest my head upon a pillow." He bade the company good night. After he had departed, Bliant fell to earnest discussion with Jewel and Arran.

The evening grew older, and more drinks were called for. Talk turned to the subject of arms-smugglers, with Bliant saying, "It has been lately evident some racketeering has been going on. Marauders all across the countryside are more brazen and successful in their attacks, now that they possess superior weapons."

"We have good reason to suspect that the leader of the operation is Fionnbar Aonarán," said Arran, "the self-same rogue who stole the Draught and has now—may the world be shielded from hideous folly—become immortal."

"Or so we must believe," said Bliant, "if the words written in the sorcerous book can be trusted."

"Alas," said Arran, "that such a potent potion should have found its final abode in the veins of a villain such as he!"

"And now we cannot fulfill the pledge we made at the Dome," said Jewel disconsolately. "For we vowed to bring back the Draught."

Outside, wind and rain battered on the whitewashed walls of the hostelry until they shuddered.

"Be not so certain," said Bliant, leaning back in his chair and worrying at his incisors with a toothpick. "On the contrary, it still remains possible to discharge the oath. This Aonarán quaffed the water. Bring Aonarán to Strang, and you bring the Draught."

Enlightenment struck his listeners simultaneously. Arran pounded the table with his fist, causing the dishes to jump, and Jewel laughed jubilantly.

"I like the idea this very instant!" Arran crowed.

"I offer you my help," said Bliant. "If we can capture the leader, then there is a good chance of breaking up the arms trade at the same time."

"Your offer is most welcome," said Stormbringer, "yet for a task as formidable as we propose, it might not be enough."

"I'll warrant my two companions will volunteer, when they hear of it!"

"Indeed. Gahariet Heaharním will also have to be told of Jewel's ancestry."

Jewel shot a glance of dismay at the Storm Lord's son. "But," she said, "it seems the whole world is to learn who I am! The more people who know, the more precarious my existence becomes!"

"I vouch for Gahariet's ability to keep his lips sealed," said Arran. "It is for your security that the truth must be revealed. You are safer with weathermasters knowing than not."

The marsh-daughter sighed. "Very well," she said reluctantly. "I accept your advice, on condition that he, too, must be sworn to secrecy before we commence the tale. We must warn him that I would be in danger if word leaked out to Uabhar that Jaravhor's heir walks the Four Kingdoms of Tir."

"In sooth!"

"Hoorah, good Gahariet shall join us!" Bliant said with glee.

This prospect led Arran to expand on the notion. "And I know of some men in the city who might also be inclined to aid us!"

"Who might they be? And are they worthy of our confidence?" Jewel asked.

"Most are liegemen to the Duke of Bucks Horn Oak, in Narngalis. Having traveled in their company, I deem they are creditworthy."

"Bucks Horn Oak?" repeated Bliant. "An honorable house! I know that Solorien has been a friend of that noble family for many a long year. The duke is said to be a wise and generous master, much-loved by his household, for he allows his retainers to take leave every year in order to visit their kindred."

"These liegemen were in our company when Marauders assailed us on the road. They aided us. I'll guarantee they would enjoy taking part in the downfall of the arms-traders."

"But can they be trusted with other secrets?"

"What is your meaning?"

"The confidential matter of Jewel's ancestry, for one. Furthermore, Aonarán has become immortal, if the sorcerer's book is to be believed. Anyone who deals with the rogue will be sure to discover his extraordinary condition, eventually. If the men of whom you speak learn about the remaining Wells, what will they do? Will they seek to betray us, in order to seize the Draughts for themselves?"

"I doubt it," replied Arran, "but who can read the minds of others? We can only hope, and have faith in our own good judgment."

"I, for one, am convinced the liegemen are of integrity beyond reproach," stated Jewel.

Over the next few hours the three of them put their heads together and devised stratagems, while in the clay saucers the tallow candles slouched into dwarfish, deformed shapes as they burned low. At length the conspirators became too tired to think coherently and sought their couches, eager to succumb to sleep.

Jewel lay in her narrow bed in an upstairs chamber of the inn, sensing the sweet abandonment of drowsiness steal over her. A furtive sound of brushing in the corridor roused her, drawing her to creep from her bed and peek through a crack in the door. A domestic brownie in ragged clothes was sweeping the floors with a birch besom, executing its self-imposed household duties during the hours of darkness. Reassured by the presence of the benevolent wight, she returned to her couch. The sound of voices drifted up from the common room below. They were singing the song "Ropes of Sand," the same ditty she had heard from the minstrels on the road. Striving to stay awake, she hearkened especially

to the portion she had wanted to learn, the verses concerning the betting between the schoolmaster and the unseelie wight:

" 'The wager's on!' the goblin howled. 'And I shall win! I'll guarantee!
Set me three tasks,' he shrieked and growled. 'I will perform them.
    You shall see.'

"The teacher said, 'A blackthorn fence doth run from here to Coran's
    Edge.
Rain lately fell theron. Go hence and count the droplets on that
    hedge!'
The wight was gone and back again more swiftly than a fox can
    cough.
'I shook the hedge with might and main, and all but thirteen
    tumbled off!
Just thirteen raindrops—that's the sum,' he sneered. 'Perhaps you'll
    think to ask
A harder question when you come to formulate the second task!'

"His jibes could not intimidate the hardy dean, who would not yield,
But bravely said, 'Enumerate the ears of corn in Tithepig's field!'
Once more the sprite employed his tricks—vanished and back all in
    a blink.
'Three million and twenty-six!' he crowed, with a triumphant wink.

"The schoolmaster waxed still as death. A shadow passed across his
    brow.
The scholars paled. They held their breath and shuddered. What
    would happen now?
But, misinterpreting the hush that fell upon the harrowed throng,
The ogre bellowed in a rush, 'If you believe I've got it wrong
Count them yourself, you mutton-head!' There were no means, the
    tutor knew,
To check the answer. So he said, 'I trust you, sir. Now you must do
One final task. Thus we've agreed. The first and second, you have
    done.
If at the third you don't succeed, you will have lost; I will have won.
And if I win, you must depart, ne'er to return. You've sworn you
    will.'

The other snarled, 'You won't outsmart me. Nothing is beyond my skill.
Say on! Say on, you foolish knave. Delay no more! You make me peeved.
I'll put you in an early grave when this last task I have achieved.'"

The rest of the song was lost to Jewel. She had fallen asleep.

Next day, Bliant Ymberbaillé announced to his two companions that he would not be returning with them to High Darioneth, but would instead join Arran Stormbringer in a hunt for the leader of the racketeers. Enthused at the prospect of injuring the arms-trade, Solorien and Heaharním immediately tendered their services. Arran accepted with thanks, adding as an afterthought, "Tristian, I have written a letter to my father and I had hoped to entrust it to you, to take to High Darioneth."

"Your father would rather I brought *you* home, than a message, young Maelstronnar," said Solorien grudgingly. "Still, if we can do some good here, our time will not be ill-spent."

Arran made his way swiftly through the streets to the Ace and Cup, where he had no difficulty recruiting the Bucks Horn Oak liegemen. "Our need for you is desperate," he said. "As weathermasters, my comrades and I will be too easily recognized by potential informants. I do not intend to keep you long from your employment and families—only long enough to help capture Aonarán and put an end to the arms-trade. If you can help us obtain the knowledge we seek, we shall take care of the rest."

"You can count on us, my friend!" said Caracal. "We are always ready for fun!"

Once a plan had been decided upon, events moved swiftly. Word was put about, through the thieves' dens, the clandestine warrens of racketeers and thugs, the illicit hideaways, the lairs of felons, the blind alleys and hidden crypts of Cathair Rua: Some men with purses full of gold crowns—Ashqalêthans, so it was said—were willing to pay generously for weapons, which they were buying on behalf of undisclosed purchasers. The purchasers, it was hinted, were outlaws. Their agents would, however, only buy from the top man. So keen were they that they offered to pay good money to anyone who would set up a meeting with him.

Cynical observers held that these merchants were really seeking factual information concerning the whereabouts of Fionnbar Aonarán, and would give a fortune in gold for his capture. Simultaneously, a directive began circulating in the more nefarious quarters of the city: anyone who betrayed their cohorts would wake up to find their heartstrings tied about the city gates.

There may be honor amongst thieves, but a thief's purpose is to accumulate wealth for himself. There may be a desire amongst men to survive, but there is always one who believes he can outsmart those who would take vengeance after he has exposed them. It was not long before the lure of gold had attracted a surreptitious informer, at pains to conceal his identity from his questioners, Quoll and Jerboa.

"Some powerful folk are involved in Aonarán's dealings," the whistle-blower muttered from beneath his makeshift mask of dirty rags. "If 'twere known I'd turned false, they'd be after murdering me. I will tell you what you want to know, but I will not tell you my name or show my face."

"You will not be paid until we verify your report."

"That is unfair, my lords. I have risked my life to bring you the tip-off!"

"Your advice might be mistaken or outdated. Depend on it, should you be proved right, we shall reward you well. Tell me: If we capture Aonarán, would you testify against him, in front of a judge? Would you bear witness to his role in selling arms to Marauders?"

"That is a different matter. Not for any amount of gold, good sirs. Not for any amount."

From the information gathered, it quickly became apparent that Aonarán had indeed preceded Jewel and Stormbringer to Cathair Rua, and that he currently lurked in some hidden precinct. The confirmation of the fellow's whereabouts fevered Arran with excitement.

Calm by contrast, Jewel observed, "If we know where he is, he must surely know where we abide. This city is his hunting-ground. Certainly, his spies will be telling him all our doings. Aonarán will always be one jump ahead of us."

"Not necessarily," Arran said.

Conceivably, Fionnbar Aonarán had grown overconfident, or else his enemies and competitors in Cathair Rua were craftier than he guessed, or maybe some cunning tactic of his had gone awry. On Love's Day, 29th Otember, two days before Lantern Eve, in a dingy room in a tawdry quarter of the metropolis, four men sat engrossed in a card-game. That is to say, they seemed engrossed. They might have been waiting for some transaction to begin.

A voice from the other side of the street door growled, "Gentlemen here to see you, sir."

"How many?" the pale-haired player called out, without taking his eyes from his cards.

"Two."

"Let them in."

The door opened to admit two men, who walked past the door sentinels and came to a halt at the table. They carried large bundles slung across their shoulders. If they noted two burly fellows lurking in the corners of the room, or the slight figure of a woman sitting near the fireplace, they gave no sign.

"Show me your merchandise," said Aonarán, laying his cards face down on the table and turning to the newcomers.

The bundles rattled as they were thrown to the floor.

"These are examples of the finest," said one of the bundle-bearers. "Lifted from the very armory of the Duke of Great Cheverell. Cheap at twice the price."

"Open the bags."

The strangers made as if to lean forward in order to unwrap their wares, but instead they threw off their hoods and cloaks. Their swords chimed from their scabbards. At the same instant the door burst inward, and six men charged into the chamber. Aonarán and the other card-players leaped to their feet, but before they or their bodyguards had time to unsheathe their weapons the assailants were upon them, wrestling them to the floor and rapidly binding their arms with cords.

The struggle was brief.

When Aonarán and his henchmen had been subdued, Arran Stormbringer took a closer look into the gloom of the poorly lit room. A woman crouched beside the hearth. She was bony, and frail of build, and her hair was a streak of phosphorescence. Nearby lay a quiver, from which jutted the feathers of a bundle of crossbow bolts, although no bow was in evidence. Fionnuala had evidently managed to find her own transport from Saadiah to Cathair Rua.

"You poisonous beldame!" the young weathermaster mouthed with loathing. "You must come with us and be tried for your crimes, as we intend to try your brother, after he has performed one last service for us."

Scooping up the quiver, he tossed it into the fire. As he did so, Fionnuala Aonarán flipped open the lid of a small trapdoor. Her narrow body slipped through an aperture in the floor, large enough to admit only a child or a small adult.

The door slammed shut.

She had escaped, because it was clear that nobody present was of small enough girth to fit through the trapdoor and there was no knowing how to pursue her.

In the dingy room, surrounded by his foes, Fionnbar Aonarán said in grating tones, "You cannot hurt me."

Arran's gaze was bleak as he stared at the felon. Aonarán's appearance had not altered, for all that he had ingested the water of life. The young man had half-expected him to look different, younger, perhaps, or more vital, but he remained exactly as he had been—pale and meager, sullen and prematurely balding. "Yes," Arran said aloud. "You cannot die, Aonarán; we are aware of that. But even an immortal being may be imprisoned forever."

"Without a trial?" the fellow sneered. "I thought justice was a hallmark of the weathermasters."

"Oh, you shall have your trial. But not in the corrupt courts of this town."

"And do you have witnesses to my so-called misdeeds?"

"That is enough talk from you. It is time to go. Walk now, or be hauled by the ears."

Now that the information leading to Fionnbar Aonarán's capture had been uncovered, the help of the Bucks Horn Oak liegemen was no longer needed. The men were eager to depart from Cathair Rua, for Quoll and Jerboa would now be late returning to their duties.

"Mistress Lily," said Caracal, bestowing on Jewel a troubled gaze, "before we bid you farewell, pray allow us to tell you and the young master our true names. For I speak for all of us when I say you seem to be worthy folk, and we would be glad to number you amongst our most trusted acquaintants."

"You do us great honor," said Jewel. Once again, the yearning to reach out to him welled up in her, but she held back.

"My name is Yaadosh," said Caracal, "and Quoll here is my cousin. He is called Michaiah."

"I am Gamliel," said Jerboa.

Snake said, "And I am Barakiel."

Jewel and Arran greeted the revelations with grave attentiveness, bowing formally to each man in turn as he introduced himself.

"Now we must take our leave of you both," said Michaiah, "but I hope we might meet again."

"If ever you visit High Darioneth," said the weathermaster, "ask for Arran Maelstronnar, son of the Storm Lord."

"Then it seems our journey has been more felicitous than we guessed," said Michaiah, while the liegemen, in their turn, bent their heads in salutation. "Few have the good fortune to travel in such esteemed company."

"Farewell, Master Stormbringer," Yaadosh said, his voice husky with emotion. "Farewell, Mistress Lily."

Impetuously, Jewel grabbed his hand and squeezed it hard. "Sir, I have known you aforetime," she cried. "My name is Jewel."

Solemnly, and for an extended moment, Yaadosh stared at her. His countenance expressed great tenderness and sadness. "I knew it all along," he said simply. "Your father was our dear friend. When you were a child I cradled you in my arms."

Drawing a sudden breath, Jewel flung herself into his embrace, where he held her gently.

When at length they drew apart, Arran, who had been looking on with compassion, said quietly, "Jewel has chosen to gift you with knowledge of her identity, good sirs, but that is a gift which must never be shared. For if such knowledge should come to the ears of certain powerful personages, it is likely her future would fall in ruins."

"On my life," said Yaadosh vehemently, "I pledge to keep the secret."

His comrades vowed likewise.

"Yet I would fain lend my protection to you, daughter of Jarred Jovansson," said the big man. "Weathermasters are formidable allies, yet a strong arm can be invaluable when foes are numerous. Prithee, let me go with you, at least for part of your journey. My wife and son will hardly be concerned if my arrival is a few days overdue, for I am often tardy. My son is a stonemason's apprentice and I daresay he will be so busy earning good wages he will not notice my lateness, while my wife will doubtless be too much occupied gossiping with her sisters and friends. Besides, I welcome some additional respite from wielding forks and shovels. My return to Narngalis is not pressing."

His honest, pleading expression touched Jewel. "Three men from High Darioneth are to be our companions," she said, "but Aonarán has many cohorts who might seek his release, and there is some chance they might attack us on the road. An extra man to guard us would not go amiss. Would you care to recount anecdotes of my father, along the way?"

"That I would, if 'twould please you!"

"Then come with us, and welcome!" The damsel glanced toward Arran to gauge his reaction. He nodded, adding, "Be warned, however, that we travel toward peril."

"Do not leave me out!" exclaimed Barakiel, pushing his way forward. "I departed from R'shael looking for adventure, and I sense it will be found more readily in the company of weathermasters than with this pack of aging camels."

"They would be hardly likely to welcome a mosquito in their midst," said Quoll.

"I can ride and fight as well as any son of the desert," declared the young Ashqalêthan, "and I do not eat as much as some. I carry my own provisions and cost nothing to keep. What say you, Lord Stormbringer and Lady Jewel?"

His enthusiasm and high spirits won their hearts. "Throw in your lot with us, if you wish," said Arran. "You have heard me tell of the risks. If you remain undaunted, then you are the man for us. Yet, if you are intent on this enterprise then you must make a vow, a solemn vow, that you shall keep faith with us and never, without my leave, disclose any secrets you might learn."

"Willingly!" said Yaadosh and Barakiel together.

They swore an oath on the seal-ring of the weathermasters, and so it was that Yaadosh and Barakiel became members of Jewel and Arran's party, while the Bucks Horn Oak liegemen went their separate way at last.

The return journey to Orielthir took more than two days. During the ride Arran took it upon himself to explain the entire story of the Wells to Yaadosh and Barakiel. They listened with awe, afterward repeating their vows to keep silent on the matter.

At this time of year the hours of sunlight were fewer, and the meteorological fluctuations caused by the Autumn equinox brought frequent atmospheric disturbances. Sometimes, across the hills, there drifted the eerie howl of eldritch warners predicting thunder and lightning. Although he never spoke of it, Stormbringer felt these equinoctial storms brewing in his veins well before they became apparent to the others. He experienced the charge in his blood, sensing the weather's instability as if he could reach out in all directions and touch it with his hands. One nightfall when they made camp he staved off a shower of rain, illicitly, to keep Jewel dry, even while reprimanding himself for repeatedly bending weathermaster law. Only for her would he ever have done such a thing. Nothing else in the world but love could have swayed him to defy the doctrine of Ellenhall. In all else he was resolute, fixed. In her presence his resolution melted like ice in a flame, and his convictions crumbled.

Having purchased some more garments in Cathair Rua, Jewel and Stormbringer were more suitably attired for the cooler climes of Slievmordhu. She wore a women's riding habit, consisting of an embroidered, long-sleeved waistcoat tailored sleekly to the waist and, below the girdle, a kirtle underneath a front-opening gown. A fur-lined mantle warmed her shoulders. Arran was dressed in a doublet that reached three-quarters of the way down his thighs. It fitted tightly to his figure, as fashion decreed. To this, sections of sleeves were attached by lacings. His fine linen shirt, worn beneath the doublet, showed through the lacings at shoulder and elbow. His boots rose to a little higher than the knee, and his outermost garment was a long cloak.

Aonarán had been roped to the back of his horse, his hands bound together with leather thongs. The men took turns to guard him. They treated the leader of the racketeers in a civil manner, providing him with plenty of food, a warm cloak, and a comfortable place to sleep at nights. He, too, was well clad, with a bycocket hat clamped over his head and a coat—gathered at the back and worn over a shirt—that reached below his hips. The cuffs of his thick trousers were tucked into sturdy shoes, and his cloak was made of good stout duretty, lined with armazine. His thin shoulder-length hair, the color of watery cream, brushed against his otters' fur collar

At the commencement of the journey he kept himself morose and withdrawn, his face like a mask of parchment stretched across a skull. On the second day, he broke his silence.

"Why are you taking me to Strang?" he barked.

"Because it is the only available method of bringing the Draught you swallowed to the Dome," replied Bliant.

"And why would you need to be doing that?"

"Aonarán," said Arran, riding close beside the captive, "your greed and ruthlessness have been the cause of endless suffering and injustice. In order to line your pockets with gold you have traded arms to murderers, who have slaughtered countless innocent families. Do not demand answers of me or my colleagues. Do not demand anything of us. It is only mercifulness and honor that prevent me from hauling you up the highest mountain in Tir and hanging you on an iron hook from the topmost mountain pinnacle where the snows never melt, there to languish throughout eternity."

Aonarán collapsed again into sullen taciturnity, but after many hours began his monologue again.

"'Tis fortunate you are," he said tonelessly to all who rode within earshot, "you with your ladies and your fine clothes and no fear of want or hunger. Would that I had been born with wealth. I have seen much of sickness and death. My mother and father died of the consumption. My great-uncle suffered from various ailments for as long as I can remember. All my boyhood years I was cooped up with him, sick and whining as he was, and no other choice available to me."

Aonarán's guards sat their steeds in stolid silence, endeavoring to ignore the tirade of complaints.

"Vile and malicious, that he was, my great-uncle. He used me for his own ends, knowing I feared him because he had once dwelled at the Dome."

Arran threw him a sharp glance but made no comment.

"I believed he had learned cruel magicks, while in service to the sorcerous lord." Jerking his head aside, Aonarán spat on the ground. "But he had learned nothing. He tricked me, deliberately, so that I should cringe from him and do his bidding."

He sat up straighter and continued his deprecations. "In the same way the druids trick us, with their claims of long life and robust health if we pay them to intercede with the Fates. Gold I gave the Sanctorum, and more, and the pockets of the druids went deeper than ocean trenches. After a time I came to perceive in them the same traits exhibited by my great-uncle: lust for power, treachery, greed. I learned from the druids. I learned that if a man wishes to better himself, to save himself, he must do it on his own, for none shall succor him."

"And have you bettered yourself?" Bliant inquired.

Aonarán hunched his head down between his shoulders and divulged no more.

Through the fence of living pines at the borders of Strang these eight riders passed, across acres of meadowlands and through guarded forests where, down amongst the roots, hedgehogs were busy hunting slugs and snails to fatten themselves in readiness for winter. In the gloaming, nimble-footed wights called grigs could be seen flitting hither and thither, like shrunken people. Sometimes Arran and Jewel raced ahead of the group to allow themselves some private conversation. At one such time Jewel asked the weathermaster to sing the rest of the song "Ropes of Sand," for she was intrigued as to how it ended.

"At what point did you hear the last of the song?" he inquired.

"The schoolteacher was about to set one last task for the ogre. If he could not do it, the wight would be forced to depart."

"Oh yes!" Arran laughed.

"What is the third task?" Jewel asked. "Methinks I can guess, but prithee, sing on!"

Stormbringer obliged:

"‘Go down along the river slopes, take handfuls of the yellow sands
    And twist them into sturdy ropes,’ the teacher said, ‘with your bare
        hands.
    Bundle these ropes into a skein and straightway bring them here to
        show.
    But if you lose a single grain you’ve failed the test. You’ll have to go.’

"The wight was longer absent this time. Back he came, but not so
        quick.
    And, rope-less, spluttered with a hiss, ‘That fickle, wayward stuff
        won’t stick!
    The grains will not cohere, so let me use some joiner’s glue, or tar.’
    ‘No,’ said the dean. ‘Recall our bet; you claimed you’d prove how
        skilled you are.’

'Then, let me mix some honey in!' 'No!" cried the teacher. 'That's not
    fair!'
The wight was desperate to win. 'Then chaff!' he pleaded in despair.
'Not even chaff. You foolish hob, some common sense might profit
    you.
You should have known that such a job was quite impossible to do.
You've lost; I've won. It's wager's end.' The hapless wight set up a roar
And in a trice he did descend to caverns deep beneath the floor,
Or some place unbeknownst to man, beyond the borders of the
    world,
Or some grim forest darker than Death's banners in the night
    unfurled.

"He ne'er was seen again. They say one fact can prove the story true,
For right up to this very day the hearthstone's cracked, where he
    passed through."

Dropping her horse's reins, Jewel applauded. "An entertaining ditty!" she
said. "And based on fact, I daresay! Ha—ropes of sand! What a clever notion."

Sitting straight-backed and relaxed in the saddle, Arran turned his head and
smiled at her. In that moment her attention was drawn to the shape of him once
again: tall and lean, wide-shouldered, tapered at the waist, muscular, and clean-
limbed. There was something unsettling about such masculine vitality.

The party trotted by the decaying and tumbled timbers of the fence overhung
by doddering chestnut trees, now gold-foiled in their Autumn splendor; past the
sycamore coppice, across windblown hillsides terraced with fading sheep-tracks
and between the mossy trunks of the oak-wood.

At last the riders found themselves cantering up the rain-rinsed slope of a
grassy ridge. At the summit they drew rein to allow their mounts to catch their
breath. Below, on the other side of the valley, rose the gigantic dome, crowned
with its matching bell-roofed Tope and surrounded by its multitude of cup-
roofed turrets, towers, and lesser halls.

It was a Moon's Day in early Ninember.

On the afternoon that they rode down the extensive lawns to Castle Strang a
light rainshower was falling, while simultaneously the sun shone. Every leaf on
every tree glittered and twinkled in the breeze. The sky to the east and south
was of a blue as sweet as the taste of sugared violets, low-banded with smoke-
gray wisps of thin cloud. In the southwest, the equinoctial sun idled languidly.
Opposite the sun, a rainbow shimmered. The central band appeared wider than

the others, a flawless, translucent arc of luminous green. To the west and north, gray storm-clouds edged with shining pearl loomed like slowly exploding mountains riven by crevasses.

Under the chill shadow of the outer wall the riders dismounted before the double gates, close enough to discern the miniscule mosses that clung to the interfaces between the wall-stones, and the spotted beetles that crawled thereon.

"Touch neither lock nor latch nor any aperture. Lay no finger on wall nor fence nor any perimeter. Follow only in my footsteps," instructed Jewel, "else you will perish."

To the three weathermasters, Tristian, Bliant, and Gahariet, Arran said, "I pray you bide here with Yaadosh and Barakiel, to mind the horses. Wait atop the slope before the gates. It needs only two of us to escort the miscreant to our destination inside the castle—Jewel to clear the way, and myself to guard the prisoner."

"I'd avow he'll not take much guarding," observed Weathermage Solorien. His nod indicated Aonarán, who had dropped to his knees on the grass. Head bowed, the pale-haired man was sniveling and whimpering.

"Do not take me in there," he entreated.

Arran's lip curled in distaste, but he knelt beside the quaking man, saying to him, "There is nought to fear. I have entered there and returned alive. If you do exactly as we say, no harm will come to you; this I swear."

"You will abandon me in that infernal house."

"We will not. You have my word on it." As Stormbringer rose to his feet he added, "It is my desire to bring you to justice in the courts of Narngalis, not to leave you wandering free to cause more mischief. Now, stand up, straighten your spine, and come with us."

Jewel and Arran, leading the terrified Aonarán, entered as before and made their way through the labyrinth of chambers and stairs. High in the Tope of the Dome, nothing seemed to have changed. In fact, the place was imbued with a timeless quality so intense it was as if all things enclosed within had died; even the very firelight seemed but the echo of a living flame. The high-backed throne of vanilla marble stood empty beneath the still-burning torch in its sconce, from which strange flames flickered purple and mauve, telling secrets at the edge of audibility.

Arran kept watch on Aonarán while Jewel crossed the floor to the great book, which lay open on the lectern, unaltered but for the fact that the writing was clearly visible once more.

She read again:

The Flame that must be lighted is thus: you must pour oil into the narrow Gutter that circumscribes the lowest portion of the Platform central to

this Chamber, then take up one of the waxen Tapers you see nearby, light it
from the weird-fire, and hold the Flame to the oil.

As inquisitive as ever, Jewel reexamined the two remaining miniature drinking horns, before turning and addressing the chamber at large: "We have returned," she said aloud. "We have fulfilled the Vow."

Her words seemed somehow fragile, breaking against the adamantine walls and shattering into eggshell fragments. The visitors watched warily, waiting for some sign or disturbance. A piteous whimper jumped from the lips of Aonarán and scurried away across the floor like a centipede.

"Husssh," said the lavender flames.

The silence of the Tope grew thicker and heavier, pressing in until the occupants seemed to have difficulty breathing.

Yet there came no reply.

Oppressed to the point of panic by the stultifying closeness of the chamber, Jewel felt her pulse accelerate. She yearned to lash out, to counteract the gelatinous weight of passivity with a swift stroke of activity. She darted to the alcove with the jar containing the sorcerer's bones, and placing both her own hands upon it, cried recklessly, "I swear that I have found the Draught of Immortality, and I have brought it with me to this place!" Next, she snatched up one of the clay jugs standing in a wall-niche, thrust it beneath the spigot of the oil jar, and wrenched at the tap's wooden handle.

Nothing happened.

Jewel gave vent to her frustration. "Curse this place!"

Arran reached across and twisted the cork that stoppered the slender neck of the oil jar. Air entered the vessel making a sucking noise, and with a *glug* as of a drain unblocking, the spigot excreted a cloudy ooze.

"This stuff is rancid!" said Jewel, as a barley-sugar twist of oil poured from the tap, filling the jug.

"It is old," said Arran. "Whale oil, perhaps, judging by the stench. It appears the sorcerer's magicks did not extend to the preservation of organic matter."

Jewel tipped the jug into the gutter girding the barren plinth. A syrupy arc leaned from the spout; the oil surged forth until it flowed all the way around. Having seized a waxen taper from a shelf, the damsel held it in the magnolia-hued pyre of the sconce until it transformed into a dahlia of fire; then she dashed this spitting flower against the gutter. Flames lapped. The oil began to smoke, then caught alight. Fire ran rapidly around the stone channel in both directions, meeting at the other side. Now the entire circumference of the narrow trough was burning furiously. The pedestal was skirted on all sides by leaping flamelets crowned with plumes of smoke.

Cowering against a milky pilaster, Aonarán squirmed. "What have you set in motion?" he shrieked.

But neither Jewel nor Arran could find an answer.

The heat from the blaze was extreme, so intense, it drove the watchers back against the walls, and they were forced to shield their faces with their upraised arms. A thin, sharp sound whipped across the air.

"The heat is cracking the stone!" Jewel shouted.

Aonarán gasped uncontrollably, crouching in his corner.

Impatiently she snapped at him, "Be silent!"

"Have no fear," Stormbringer advised the cringing man. "Fire can be mastered, if it becomes necessary."

Through the up-rushing curtains of radiant energy, they could see that the pedestal was, in fact, altering. The fire was transforming it. No crevices could be perceived, but the galactic mist and bubble-swarms locked in the rock-crystal were melting away. The material was unclouding, clearing to translucency.

The last wisps of opacity gave way to lucidity, and as the flames dwindled the smooth sides of the plinth were revealed in complete transparency, save for the delicate outlines of the relief carving of twin axes with crossed handles. The block was revealed as no pedestal after all, but a hollow container. Its outer planes of glass or crystal were speckled with the scorch-marks of burnt oil, but there was no mistaking: it was a coffin.

Within this glacial tomb lay a corpse.

Wonderingly, Jewel and Arran approached and looked down upon the prone figure framed by the beveled edge of what now turned out to be the casket's lid.

"Well," said Stormbringer at length, "I must revoke my criticism of the sorcerer's magicks."

The disclosed corpse seemed perfectly preserved, exhibiting no signs of fleshly decay. It was the body of an elderly man, clad in heavy black robes. The attenuated strands of his hair and beard, as white as rimed twigs on a winter's morning, flowed from his brow and jaw. His face was indented with the furrows of age. Swollen bags of slack skin sagged beneath his closed lids; his cheeks were sunken pits. His nostrils were wide and his mouth, visible as a slash of livid blue beneath the ashen moustaches, turned down at the outer corners. A scrawny, long-fingered hand rested at his side, resembling an albino crab. Dirt encrusted the fingernails.

"Perhaps it is he," said Arran in amazement.

"Indubitably," agreed Jewel. "The sorcerer himself!"

Reason decreed that this fossilized carcass could be none other than the body of Janus Jaravhor. Stories about this man described his arrogance, amorality, and ruthlessness, his cunning and scholarship, his acquired power, his appalling crimes, his terrible intellect, and his eventual demise. So full of his own self-importance was he, he must have had himself mummified after his death, that future generations might behold his worldly remains and remember him with awe. Between fascination and horror, Jewel could not tear her gaze from the sight of the perfectly preserved remains. Stormbringer, however, continually glanced toward Aonarán, who had fallen still and silent, obviously petrified by terror.

The last of the oil in the gutter having been consumed, the flames vanished.

"What now?" muttered Jewel as she and her companion stared at the recumbent form.

And the sorcerer stirred.

A great sigh seemed to pass through the Tope. Jewel's startled cry smote the masonry, and she stumbled backward. Arran caught his breath. His hand flew to the pommel of his sword. There was no doubt; the white-fringed lids of the old man were fluttering like anemic moths. His lips, the color of bruised plums, parted slightly.

"By thunder!" breathed Stormbringer. "He lives!"

The young man's first impulse was to restore and preserve life. Without thinking twice, he stepped forward. Gripping the edge of the casket's cover, he gave one mighty heave of his shoulders, and flung it aside. The pane crashed weightily to the floor, a glinting cobweb of fractures radiating across its surface. A gust of stale air erupted from within, churning the hair and beard of the occupant. Shallowly, his chest rose and fell. His lids unclosed. Two etiolated bulbs stared out. The calcified lobster of his hand came suddenly alive, and clawed at the prism walls of his comfortless bed.

"Is it illusion?" whispered Jewel, aghast.

"I think not."

"Oh, pitiful spectre!" she cried compassionately. "I do believe it is trying to sit up. It needs help—"

Leaning into the casket, Arran passed his arm beneath the spine of the macabre creature, hoisted it into a sitting position, then lifted it bodily out of its tomb and deposited it on the throne of marble. The apparition sprawled weakly against the arm-rests, panting and wild-eyed.

Then, "Water!" he grunted, raising a feeble finger in a gesture of command.

Jewel rummaged at her belt. She unhooked a small water flask, squirted some of the liquid into an earthenware cup, and, somewhat squeamishly, held the vessel to the man's mouth. His lips wriggled like bluish worms, sipping and spluttering. He fumbled to grasp the cup. Instead of his right hand, the stump of a wrist came up.

Jewel recoiled in disgust.

"Is that the water of life?" the ancient creature rasped.

"No," she replied, averting her eyes from the severed limb, "but—"

"Give me the water of life!"

Shocked at the sight of this gruesome thing shrieking commands at her from its putrefying mouth, the damsel stood for a moment, speechless. Jaravhor had *died*—or so it had been believed. His death, however, like much of his life, had been a trickery. Somehow this artful scholar had wrought a means to sustain and prolong his longevity, in a state of timeless stasis—perhaps indefinitely— waiting until the right person found a way into his stronghold, read the words in the book, and brought back the draught he needed for survival. Jewel recoiled from the idea of such long-simmering subterfuge. As all the *other* reasons she despised this man came to the forefront of her mind, her anger began to build.

Stormbringer, clearly as outraged as she, briefly endeavored to ease the tension with a quip. He murmured aside, "For a dead man, his strength is surprising."

Undeniably, the revived sage seemed to be gaining vitality by the minute. Rheumy eyes focused on his surroundings. He fixed a disconcerting stare on his rescuers.

"I am Janus Jaravhor, Lord of Strang," he said. His voice, though hoarse, was compelling. "Now that I wake, the sands begin again to tumble. It is you who woke me. You would not have done so, had you not obtained the elixir. Give it to me, now, before my time runs out. Give, and in return I shall reveal the location of the other Wells."

Jewel inhaled deeply, to fortify her resolve and calm her agitation. This *thing,* her ancestor, had faked his own death with the intention of tricking his benefactors into keeping him alive forever! He planned to drink the water of life—but what then? Would the water-bearer be rewarded, as the book had promised? Or would the Lord of Strang cast aside the implement of his salvation and proceed to rule the world? No matter—such conjectures were irrelevant now.

"That we cannot do," the damsel said boldly. With a flourish, she indicated Aonarán, curled up in the corner. "We found the Draught, it is true. But that fellow has taken it by force and cunning, and he has drunk it down, every drop."

Jewel was aware that she and her companion had failed the test. She understood they had lost the chance to discover the location of the other Wells, but it would be pointless to attempt deception.

The enthroned sage turned to Arran. "Does she speak truth?" he croaked.

"She does."

In the sconce above the mage's head, the fire fluctuated sibilantly. Violet reflections shimmered, lacing themselves through the rain of his silver locks. In the sockets beneath his brows, shadows accumulated, punctured by the wrathful gleam of his eyes.

Now, there was an added wrongness to his slumped posture in the chair. A series of subtle shudders rippled through his frame. His left hand gripped the arm of the chair like a grappling iron knotted with veins, and in his temple a cable throbbed. He seemed to be suffering from a fit of apoplexy, brought on by Jewel's news. The ferocity of his spasms threatened to cast him upon the floor. Stormbringer moved to support him, but from between clenched teeth the sorcerer growled, "Stay back!" Bloody foam spattered from his lips.

Gradually the convulsions of rage subsided. Jaravhor appeared to be forcing himself to regain composure, probably so that he could take steps to remedy his unexpected and desperate situation. He turned his grizzled head and pinned the shrinking Aonarán with a penetrating stare. It was clear this ruin of a human being still retained some of his original power. "You," he pronounced venomously, and every angle of his withered body projected incomprehensible depths of hatred.

The fair-haired man gibbered. "Weathermaster, do not let it near me!" he entreated Arran. "It will drink my blood!"

"You," the sage repeated savagely, ignoring the outburst. "You have the look of another. One who was my servant. Curse you for your offense against me! Yet, I shall be avenged. Be assured of it; I shall be avenged, you ill-gotten cur!" Returning his attention to Stormbringer, he said, with as much insistence as his weak constitution could evidently muster, "What year is it? Are you the son of Jovan? No matter—kinsman, there is little time. Now that the Pendur Sleep is no longer on me, a limited span of my natural life remains. I must speak with you privately. Kick this whining dog out the door, out of hearing range, but do not allow him to escape. And tell your wench she is dismissed, for the nonce." His lip curled, as his phlegmy regard flicked indifferently over Jewel.

She and Arran exchanged glances. They said nothing, but each knew the other was thinking: *The Lord of Strang is mistaken as to which of us is his heir.*

"Aonarán shall leave," Arran said levelly, disguising his abhorrence, "but not the damsel."

"Have your way. But make haste!" Ignoring Jewel, Jaravhor heaved himself upright until he sat straighter on the stone chair, resting his elbows on arms, half-reclining. The effort provoked a bout of coughing.

"Go," said Stormbringer to Aonarán. "Wait for us outside this room." As the terrified fellow began to scuttle toward the door, the young man called out a warning; "'Ware—the traps of the Dome are many. Should you try to exit alone, some fell doom may befall you."

"I am immortal!" Aonarán shouted shrilly.

"Much good may it do you, while you bide within my domains!" sneered the sorcerer. A cruel and secretive smile played at the edges of his mouth. "Ah, kinsman," he said, turning his attention once more to Arran, "succor not the miscreant. Let him go. Let him roam in my holdings and be prey to my devices, as he deserves. He will shortly wish for mortality."

As soon as Aonarán had disappeared from the Tope, the old man beckoned to Stormbringer, signaling that he should approach. "You must hasten to bring me another Draught," he wheezed with urgency.

"Of all the Wells, which is the closest?" asked Arran.

"All? Why, kinsman, there were only ever three Wells. Three portions of the Star fell from the sky and reached the ground. The rest were burned up."

"Three?" Stormbringer was incredulous. "Your book misled us. . . ."

"The second Well," rattled the sorcerer, "which is located in a place of mists and vapors, filled up with condensation and the wights called it the Well of Dew. The creation of the third Well fissured the ground beneath its crater, so that a subterranean spring seeped upward, drop by drop, to fill the bowl of Star-Metal. Being somewhat briny due to the absorption of salts from subterranean rocks, this became known as the Well of Tears. I know not whether these remaining Wells have been sipped and drained again, by beasts, or if they still exist, or have been destroyed by the ravages of weather over the years. Howsoever—you must go with all speed." Breezes cawed and whistled in his lungs. After a pause to catch his breath, he continued, "On Ragnkull Island in Grïmnørsland lies the Well of Dew. If there is a secret to crossing the waters of Stryksjø, I know it not. It is for you, my kinsman, to discover an answer. You are a weathermaster—aye, I heard the scoundrel say so. That is a fine thing!"

Again he hesitated, striving to recover from the exertion of speech. The initial burst of vigor that had sustained him when he first left the casket now appeared to be ebbing. During the quietude of that hiatus, a dim scraping could be heard, as of baggage shifting slyly across tiles. It emanated from the direction of the portal. The door stood ajar. As before, Arran and Jewel traded glances. With a slight movement of his head the young man indicated the doorway; she responded with a brief nod. *Aonarán lurks nigh. He listens at the crack of the door.*

"Begone, eavesdropper!" Stormbringer cried loudly.

"What? Has the cur overheard my words?" the mage bellowed.

Arran sprang to his feet. "I shall conduct him out of earshot," he said, but the old man forestalled him with a groan. His apoplectic shout was an expenditure of labor that had proved costly. "Stay! There is no time—" His head drooped feebly to his chest and he moaned, "Alas! Alas I fear 'tis all in vain. . . ."

"Not in vain," said Stormbringer. By nature the young man was compassionate. Despite his utter amazement at beholding the resurrection of the infamous villain, and his antipathy toward him, he was, for a moment, involuntarily moved to pity. Presently he collected his wits. "Tell us where the third Well is hidden."

"No," growled Jaravhor. "I'll not speak answers aloud while that accursed scum may be listening. Why did you bring him here?" Abruptly his hand shot out and grabbed Arran's sleeve. "You must not leave my side, kinsman. I fear I am failing. Despite all—despite all my endeavors, the end is approaching." He had begun to weep. It was a grotesque effect, the spilling of infantile tears from the tainted eyes, the child-like sobbing issuing from the portrait of death. "That wretch who swallowed the Draught has thwarted me," he sighed. "It is your task to avenge his deed. You must live on forever, exacting retribution until time's end." The tip of his tongue licked at the briny droplets and spittle beading his lips. For a moment his eyes glazed over, and his thoughts seemed to stray. "Ah, see how the tears fall! Were I undying, I would never weep again, for the gift of immortality annuls that weakness."

"Say where the third Well is hidden," insisted Stormbringer.

On occasion, the young weathermaster felt that perhaps his father had not been entirely wise to invest such faith in his son's judgment. In his heart he was aware that he desired to give a Draught of Immortality to Jewel for selfish reasons. First, it was a way of demonstrating the vehemence of his love for her, so that she could have no doubt of it. Second, he could not endure the idea of losing her to death, and would do everything within his scope to allow her the choice of being forever safe from that fate.

"Hearken." The voice of the ancient mage was growing fainter. He was sinking swiftly. "There is a riddle," he breathed, "It is written on a paper—"

His lids closed, his shoulders drooped, and his head collapsed to his forearm.

"A formidable fellow," the weathermage said to Jewel, awed in spite of his repulsion. "It is a marvel he survived for half a century in his enchanted sleep. He is antiquated and unwell, yet he has persevered. His powers must have been mighty indeed, to preserve him, so many years, from perishing. Yet I suspect he judges aright—he has not much longer to live."

"He has fallen into a faint," observed Jewel, keeping her distance.

But even as she uttered those words, the sorcerer rallied. He unlidded the sallow globes of his eyes and directed his scrutiny at Stormbringer, who drew back.

"I fear it is too late, after all. My time is nigh. Ah, kinsman—is it doubt I read in your aspect? I speak the truth about these Wells. Why should I not? As I lose my hold on life, you become of utmost importance to me. My sole hope of immortality lies with you, my heir. Some part of me must remain in this world! I cannot abide that I should go, and there be no mark of my existence save for songs and legends and a pile of masonry! Perform a task for me," he demanded. "It is my final request. Take the accursed one down to the tower in the lower courtyard. Stand him inside the hollow walls, and brick him up. Slather the mortar thickly. Thus shall the immortal knave be damned to eternal punishment."

"In the walls?" repeated Jewel. Her countenance twisted with repugnance. "Is that what you inflict on those who cross you? Whom else have you forced into that tower, to be walled alive?"

"Countless nonentities. *She* abides there," the sorcerer replied coldly, "my bride, who believed she could defy Janus Jaravhor." His laugh was flaccid, the chirruping of a cricket. "Those who wrong the Lord of Strang are, without exception, condemned to penalty."

"Your own *wife*?"

And Jewel thought, in horror: *His wife must have been my own great-grandmother!* How could anyone guess what notions had ultimately passed through the minds of Jaravhor's pitiable captives as the stone-masons bricked them in, as the walls rose higher around them? They might have strained to catch a final glimpse of some object, perhaps a fleck of color, some bird, or flower, even some weed, milkwort or the purple petals of crowthistle, a thing to gaze upon and commit to memory, to hold like an icon in the mind's eye, long after everything familiar had vanished forever from sight and the world had shrunk to a cold and airless chimney.

She recalled the skeleton behind the stones in the courtyard tower, with its beautiful hair, glossy and dark as a river reflecting moonlight, and the pathetic claw-like remnants of hands upraised, as if she had been tearing at the stones with her nails even until the moment of death. To stand bound in chains, witnessing the workmen with their shirtsleeves rolled up their thick brown arms as they labored to build the wall, stone by stone, to hear the slap of wet mortar and see it ooze like swamp mud as the next block was laid atop, and in the background, mallets pounding against chisels, and chips of rock flying as rough masonry was hewn into regular shapes, all the while aware that the sweet breath of the breeze on your face was the last kiss you would ever know, and the cold iron of the fetters was the last touch you would ever experience, and the clay beneath your feet was the floor of your very grave; how unspeakable, that punishment! To stand and watch as the terminal stone was fitted into place, shutting out the last gleam; perchance utter one final cry for mercy in the lightless pinch, and the tears coursing down your cheeks, the last warmth you would ever feel; and the silence after the builders went away, and the cold of the terrible cell, the mortar hardening only inches from your face, while knowing the silence and the cold would be the last companions you would ever have—that would be a fate cruel beyond comprehension.

Another bout of coughing racked the restored mage, but he persisted. "Some believe they have escaped my vengeance; however, they are mistaken. My malediction hunts them to this day, to this very hour, beyond the courtyards, beyond the borders of Strang, beyond the walls of the world. It will continue to pursue them and their issue until the last of their line perishes in madness."

The torment and injustice dispensed by this arrogant personage was more than Jewel could endure. Her outrage reached boiling point.

"It is you who are mistaken," she shouted. "I am descended from Álainna Macnamh, whose bloodline you blighted. My mother married your grandson. Yes, it is *I* who am your heir, despicable tyrant. And at my birth, your curse was extinguished. You beg us to take revenge on your behalf? Pah! There will be vengeance indeed—fittingly enough, against you! You cursed my mother's family—now wither to dust, Jaravhor, and let justice be done."

The dying mage gaped at Jewel as if a brilliant ray had struck her. His raddled visage contorted, becoming a caricature of wrath and dismay. A groan like the deflating bellows of a pipe organ escaped his vocal cords, but the shock of her revelation proved too great for his overtaxed systems. Hitting his chest with the stump of his arm, as if he tried to clutch his own heart, he toppled forward for the final time. Arran reached out to prevent his fall, but the mage slipped through his arms, crumpled to the floor, and lay still.

As the folds of his black robes settled, a scrap of paper rolled from the unclenching digits of his left hand. Jewel picked it up and began to decipher the script inked thereon. Meanwhile, Stormbringer placed two fingers on the side of the old man's neck. "There is no pulse," he said presently. "He's truly gone." The young man's expression was strained and taut. "So ends Janus Jaravhor, Lord of Strang, scholar of the sorcerous arts."

"The world is well rid of such despots," declared Jewel, her ire simmering, mingled with revulsion. "Henceforth I renounce the vile name 'Jaravhor' and adopt my father's patronymic of Jovansson. But see—at the very end the old villain has gifted us, for this is the riddle of which he spoke. I am certain of it. 'Tis a clue to the whereabouts of the third Well." After examining the writing, she tucked away the paper inside her garments.

Arran scanned the Tope's interior: the two tiny drinking horns in their alcove, the oil jar, the throne, the book on the lectern, the melancholy fire. "Let us leave this house of horrors, and all that is in it," he muttered.

A disturbance at the portal attracted their attention.

In one lissom movement, Stormbringer crossed the room and thrust open the door. Aonarán sprawled there, his hands still bound behind his back. "Come!" Arran hauled him to his feet. "It is time to depart. We did not need your presence after all, and I regret having brought you, for I daresay you learned more than was good for any of us."

"I heard nothing."

"Wait!" called Jewel. She remained in the Tope, taking care, as she stepped around the unbreathing heap of black fabric and ancient flesh, not to brush against it.

Her outrage still burned. "Too many wrongs have you wrought," she said to the lifeless form. "Because of your curse, my parents perished. Arrogant fool, to believe men have wrought songs and legends about you, for no one has done anything of the sort! No one will remember. You will become nothing, less than a memory, less than a flake of ash borne away on the wind." Her eyes, blue as the metallic mail of dragonflies, brimmed with tears. "This, for the poor prisoner in the wall," she cried. Setting her hand upon the tall oil jar, she pushed it over. It splintered on the floor, emptying its nauseating contents. "And this for my parents!" Having picked up the jar containing the bones of the sorcerer's hand, she hurled it at the flaming sconce. As the jar smashed against it, the bracket tore away from the wall. The flames blinked out, although the hissing continued, like the sound of escaping gases. Across the darkened chamber Jewel sped, imbued with sudden urgency, and out the door. She and Stormbringer joined hands, and, with Aonarán in tow, they fled down the stairs. The pale-haired man was shrieking with fear. Through the vitrified interior of Castle Strang they hastened, speaking not a word until they emerged at last beyond the outer gate and ran out onto the clean, crisp grass, beneath a wide sky streaked with windswept clouds.

The sun was sinking, a crimson disc boating on golden surf. High overhead, flocks of noisy starlings were flying to their roosts. A sudden gust whipped at Jewel's hair. Behind her, the gates of Strang slammed and banged erratically.

"You have locked neither gate nor door," said Arran, breathlessly.

"Let the gates swing!" declared Jewel, panting as they hurried up the incline. "Anyone might enter as they please, for I care not what happens to this place."

"No, no! Shut the gates!" screamed Aonarán. "Don't leave the Dome open for the sorcerer's wraith to come after me, or for all and sundry to plunder!"

"I hope it *shall* be despoiled," Jewel shot back. "No treasure is hidden within. If there were, I'd not want it. May the sorcerer's enchantments fail, and may his precincts be invaded!"

On the slope above the Dome their five companions were waiting with the horses, their hair ruffled by the breeze, and their cloaks flapping. The men's faces lit up when they beheld Jewel and Stormbringer climbing toward them. "Did you get what you came for?" they shouted, stepping forward eagerly.

"Yes and no," answered Arran. "We shall tell more, as we ride. For now, let us put as much distance as possible between ourselves and this pit of nightmares before the onset of night. Onward, to High Darioneth!"

Aonarán stumbled. Yaadosh and Bliant seized him by the elbows and propeled him to his steed. They thrust him into the saddle and, as before, tied him there with ropes. Without further ado they all mounted, turned their horses toward the sinking sun, and rode away.

At their backs the Dome's swellings and ornate protuberances gleamed in the dying light, as if soaked with colored washes, flesh-pink glowing on the western flanks, the east shaded with wrathful purple.

As they traveled into the lengthening shadows, Stormbringer and Jewel told their companions all that had happened inside the Dome—all the while ensuring that Aonarán remained guarded at a safe distance, unable to learn any more than he had already overheard.

"I perceive what will happen now," said Bliant, after hearing the tale. "The spells that guarded this fortress remained strong only because Jaravhor was still living. He is truly dead at last, or so it seems. Now his devices shall be rendered impotent and his enchantments shall crumble."

"Not necessarily," Gahariet said. "He was a man, not an eldritch wight. His devices, if any exist, are probably mechanical and may well remain potent until time erodes their substance, or their energy source fails."

"That remains to be seen," said Tristian Solorien.

The sun dipped at last below the horizon and darkness stretched across the wide solitude of Orielthir. A first hint of frost was borne on the night air. Beneath the eaves of a dim and ancient oak wood they halted to make camp, light a fire, and partake of a meal. The flames blazed welcomingly, beating like wings of tangerine glass. Jewel appreciated their friendly glow, after the cold, vein-blue radiance of the flames in the Tope. She was gradually moving closer to its warmth when Aonarán seated himself beside her.

He smiled ingratiatingly. "Sweet lady, do not go being too hasty to be leaving the Dome behind," he said in low tones. "Why not return there and stay awhile? Revisit it. 'Tis your heritage. There is no danger there for you."

"No danger in the Dome, perhaps, but danger here by my side," scoffed Jewel.

"Dear damsel, I am but a lamb. See, my hands are tied! But even were they not, I should be remaining innocuous. Never have I worked harm, in all my life."

She edged away from him. "You took me captive. You stole the Draught from me. You threatened me with a switchblade."

"Ah, but you see, sweet lady, I was by way of being forced to do all those things. It was against my will. Cathal Weaponmonger, he was the motivator of those ill deeds, he and my half-kin Fionnuala, working together, using me as their puppet. All the rumors about me are lies. I have never dealt in weapons. An honest man am I, and here's proof: I know you are the scion of the sorcerer, and I could be reaping a large reward for telling King Uabhar of your existence. But I have not done so. The king would like to broach the famous Dome and lay hands on its treasures—although I was seeing no treasures when I was inside. You have been in there once before—perhaps you are knowing where the treasure is hid, eh? If the king was about getting hold of you, no doubt he'd be making a sorry prisoner of you, and forcing you to open the Dome so that he could pillage your rightful inheritance. Why not be giving a little of the gold and jewels to your friend Aonarán, who has never betrayed you? Alas, I have scant income to be living on. I might be a rich man if I had exposed your identity, yet I remain poor. You might so easily relieve my poverty and reward my faithfulness by getting a coffer or two of gold and jewels for me, just as a token, some acknowledgment of my fidelity, you know."

Suddenly becoming aware of this discourse, Stormbringer stepped between them. "Never trouble this lady, perfidious contriver!" he cried. "I hear your wheedling, Aonarán, your incipient threats, your attempts at blackmail. Should you or any of your cohorts ever try to name this lady to the king, I swear, the wrath of all High Darioneth shall fall upon you. You would regret it for eternity. Moreover, weathermasters have ways of protecting our own. It would distill to this: your word against ours. To which of us would the king be more likely to attend?"

"I meant no mischief, weatherlord!" Aonarán ducked his head in an obsequious bow, and scrambled away to the rim of the firelight.

Stormbringer sat down beside Jewel, crossing his arms on his knees. "I am not troubled by Aonarán," said Jewel. "He may harp as he pleases—I shall close my ears to him." She turned her cerulean eyes upon the weathermaster. "But the mage of Strang," she said, "*he* troubles me. How strange and callous he was: He never asked our names; he never appeared pleased to meet his so-called heir. He could dwell on no thing beyond himself. I shudder to think I am sprung from such a horror as he."

"He was your great-grandfather, only one-eighth part of your ancestry. That is not a very close relationship."

Jewel stretched out her hand and let her fingers enter the amber film of the fire. Spontaneously, Arran knocked her arm aside. "Jewel, *what are you at?*"

"It has come to me that I cannot feel pain. I never truly realized it before. Not ever having known pain, how could I know what the word described? Pain is a warning. When no warning is needed, there's no pain."

"Well," replied her companion," at least the old vulture's existence gave rise to one commendable outcome."

Her fingers closed about her sleeve, where Arran had touched her.

Next morning, as the last stars were fading and waterlily light was beginning to glow in the east, they scattered the ashes of their fire, broke camp, and rode on. Translucent morning mists were rising from the meadows and long valleys like smoke, screening the landscape with muted shades of softest grays and blues. Against these swathes of pearly vapor, belts of leafless trees stood out starkly, every branch and twig distinct, interlocking in a pattern like black lace. A few late flowers stippled the meadows, the daisy-like blooms of mayweed, blue splashes of germander speedwell, and clusters of white deadnettle, thrumming with bees.

They rode along a narrow path through the oak wood, which eventually emerged onto grassy slopes engraved with disused sheep-tracks. In the distance shimmered the foliage of a sycamore coppice, burnished with autumnal gold.

Stormbringer was riding past Aonarán when the pale-haired man addressed him. "Weatherlord, may it please you to tell me what is your plan for me?" His manner was deferential. When not surrounded by his own henchmen, he feared the weathermaster. He kept his head down and would not meet Arran's eye.

"It is not yet decided. Perhaps we shall take you to High Darioneth, that you may stand trial."

"What wrong have I done?"

Arran glanced sharply at his questioner. "You deal illegally in weapons, selling them to Marauders and other felons who are the enemies of peace-loving travelers and law-abiding folk."

"With all respect, what proofs have you, good sir?" Aonarán's tone remained obeisant. "You'll not be finding a single witness to testify against me. What's the charge? 'Twould be unlawful to detain me without a charge. And yourself, honorable gentleman, would surely not be about breaking the law!" He shrank into himself, as if expecting a blow. "Or perhaps I err in my judgment—my hands are bound, and you have already detained me without excuse."

"You stole the Draught. There are witnesses."

"Forgive me for differing, sir, that was no theft. The Draught belonged to no one. The statutes of salvage allow possession to the first person who seizes the prize."

"You were the one who swallowed it, but not the first to seize it! It was Jewel who collected the Draught. In any event, Aonarán, there may not be a single person in Slievmordhu to testify against you, but at the trial, the testament of weathermasters will oppose your false assertions."

"The testament of weathermasters? But sir, what exactly have you and your people seen me at? Have you seen me after trading in arms, as you allege? And if you have not, I am certain such noble folk will not commit perjury in order to have me convicted!" His words were jarring, at odds with his fawning conduct.

"You threatened Jewel with a knife. That, at least, counts against you."

Aonarán said, "I understood full well she was invulnerable, like her father. There was no real threat. A lawyer could use that as argument on my behalf. I am by way of knowing something of your laws, weatherlord. I could press charges against you, for illegal detainment and abduction, if you do not return me to Cathair Rua."

For a long while, Arran brooded in silence. Then he swung his steed away from Aonarán's and joined the other riders to discuss the matter.

They passed the ruins of a wooden fence. Chestnut trees, layered with tooth-edged leaves of antique bronze, leaned over the moldering timbers. Prickly green-husked fruit clustered thickly on their boughs and lay scattered about their roots, bursting open to reveal the glossy brown nuts within.

Aonarán's horse was being led at the end of a long rope so that the rider might remain out of earshot. The young weathermage said to his companions, "As all know, the most secure place in Tir is High Darioneth, and it is there I first thought to take Aonarán. Yet in my heart I do not want him nesting at the core of my home, like a maggot in an apple."

"Aonarán has been privy to dangerous secrets," said Bliant. "It is possible he might try to bribe his way to freedom by divulging them—by disclosing Jewel's identity, and maybe also the whereabouts of the second Well."

"We must choose those who guard him with care," said Solorien. "They must be tight-lipped, and loyal to the Maelstronnar. They must be of the utmost probity."

"Methinks we are all agreed on that," said Yaadosh. The others murmured their concurrence.

"What then should we do with this worm?" asked Bliant.

"Gentlemen, we must deliver the arms-smuggler into the hands of the authorities in Cathair Rua and press charges against him," said Barakiel. "At the very least, he will be incarcerated for long enough that you, Master Stormbringer, with the other weathermasters, may reach the Well of Dew before he is able to start, if that is his plan. Moreover, while he is confined, others will have opportunity to collect evidence to convict him. Yaadosh has many contacts in Cathair Rua."

"You have much to learn, my friend," Yaadosh replied, smilingly. "In R'shael, everyone is privy to everyone else's business. 'Tis a small village. Wrongdoers are quickly caught. Not so in the metropolis. You speak of 'the authorities in Cathair Rua,' but King Uabhar employs no city guard, no civil constabulary. If there are disturbances of the peace, his household guards or the druids' henchmen from the Sanctorum might decide to quell them, should they become a nuisance. Wealthy merchants employ mercenaries for security."

"There is no state-run law enforcement in Slievmordhu, unlike in Narngalis and Grïmnørsland," said Solorien.

"Nor in Ashqalêth, save in Saadiah," said Bliant. "The Lord of Saadiah employs a constabulary to maintain order in the town of Spire, in addition to his own household guards."

"Considering the arbitrary nature of Uabhar's laws," Solorien said, "I see the lack of regulation as beneficial. However, to answer your question, Barakiel, we trust no authority in Cathair Rua."

Arran said, "And it seems the arms-runner might escape justice after all, if we can find no evidence against him."

"But we shall find evidence," Bliant Ymberbaillé asserted with confidence.

"All witnesses to his arms-trading will have mysteriously disappeared, no doubt," said Arran. "And, I daresay, all clues to boot."

"Yet we cannot set him free!" Yaadosh exclaimed feelingly. "He is a dangerous and slippery piece of work. What's more, he probably heard the sorcerer speak of the location of this other Well, and I suspect he would take the first opportunity to try to obtain that Draught. Who knows what he might do with it—give it to that witch he keeps company with, or some other vile rogue."

"Aye, he knows far too much," said Solorien.

"How shall we proceed?" asked the journeyman Gahariet.

"We should take him," said Solorien, "to Calogrenant Lumenspar, the Ambassador for High Darioneth in Cathair Rua. He dwells in a fortified consulate, well guarded. It were well to lock up Aonarán there, at least for a while, so that we may have time to somehow render harmless the two pieces of information he could wield against us once he is set free—Jewel's identity and the location of the Well of Dew."

They all agreed it was the best plan and, accordingly, changed their course. They had been heading southwest across the trackless meadows, making for the

Valley Road where it meandered in amongst the Border Hills. Now they veered farther southwest.

As they traveled, the discussion continued. Arran said, "In order to render useless Aonarán's knowledge of that Well, I would fain obtain the Draught. In fact, I would fain obtain both Draughts of which the sorcerer spoke."

"For whom?"

"For whosoever deserves the honor of immortality. That is a question the Council of Ellenhall shall decide."

"One must be for the Maelstronnar," proclaimed the weathermage Tristian, without hesitation. The others nodded to indicate their assent.

"I am glad you suggested him," said Arran. "I would have done so myself, had I not been hesitant to put forward my own kinsman. Gladly would I see him lead High Darioneth forever, and never would I envy him such a challenging task."

"If anyone is to live forever, it should be he," agreed Jewel. "In the Four Kingdoms of Tir, no alderman is so well loved."

"Aye," said Bliant Ymberbaillé-Rainbearer, "Stormbringer, these many years your father has guided High Darioneth with wisdom and justice—which is not to say you would not do the same, were you elected to the position, but I know you well enough to suppose you would not be entirely happy with the duties of a chieftain. You would rather live a life of adventure and freedom."

A grin flashed across Arran's face. "You understand me too well."

" I am in accord," interjected Jewel. "But tell me—if we can find the third Draught, the drop from the Well of Tears, to whom would it be offered?"

Turning in his saddle, the young Maelstronnar conferred upon her a gaze of such tenderness she felt herself catch alight, like a beacon. "Well, Jewel," he said softly, "that remains to be seen."

Once again, quite unexpectedly, she found herself quite unable to reply or, indeed, to speak at all.

Far ahead, a dark line marched across the hills: the row of pines that marked the borders of Strang's domains. No definable track ran before the riders, but they continued across the acres of meadowlands and forests on a southwesterly heading. Through the great palisade of black conifers they passed and, having descended the hillside into a sheltered vale, they splashed across a fast-flowing brook.

As they trotted along, Arran asked Solorien, "What do you know of this Ragnkull Island in Grïmnørsland?"

"It broods in the midst of a perilous lake called Stryksjø," answered the elder weathermage, "whose waters are uncrossable by any vessel. The drowners and fuaths inhabiting the waters rip apart all boats. It is said a waterhorse dwells in the deeps there also."

"I suppose it would be foolish to hope for a bridge," said Arran.

" 'Twould indeed! No bridge can stride the distance from shore to island, because 'tis too great a span, and besides, the water-wights might well destroy bridge-pylons."

"Is there any chance Stryksjø might be crossed by sky-balloon?"

"I doubt it. The many tiny islets on the lake are infested with unseelie marksmen whose habit is to shoot at mortal beings and their vehicles, with flinty barbs of ælf-shot, and wicked bolts. Their flights of cunning arrows would surely pierce the envelope and cause an aerostat to fall into the waters."

"Has any man ever set foot on Ragnkull Island?"

"That I cannot say."

Gahariet said boldly, "Men shall shortly set foot on it. We shall depart on this new quest as soon as we have seen the rogue Aonarán safely behind bars."

Arran nodded to the journeyman. "Aye," he said. "You and Bliant, and others amongst my comrades who are swift and strong and seeking adventure."

"For my part," said Jewel, "I would fain have naught to do with the sorcerer and his projects ever again. I want nothing to do with aught that is connected with him, including the Draughts. The getting of the first Draught led to deplorable events. The rest would be better left alone."

Ever since they had left the Dome, Jewel had been unable to rid her mind's eye of the image of her great-grandmother bricked into the walls. She had been brooding about Jaravhor's fatal curse on her dear mother, and about his abduction of Álainna Machnamh, his slaying of the two A'Connacht brothers, and the widespread tales of his various felonies. It seemed that everything he touched turned to tears. All that Jaravhor had ever wrought led immutably to catastrophe.

Arran murmured, "Jewel, I believed you craved immortality."

"I did. But now I discover that the asking price is too high."

"If we do not seize it," said Arran, "then some day someone else will do so, and the waters of life might then be imbibed by someone as spiteful as Aonarán, or worse."

"Yet, if you subtract these Draughts the empty Wells shall remain, and in a thousand years' time they will have refilled with potent liquid. Some new scoundrel might drink."

"No. After I take the Draughts I shall destroy the Wells."

"I want naught to do with it," she repeated, "and my rede to you all is thus: do not pursue this quest. I augur that only trouble shall come of it."

The young weathermage replied, "Jewel, you cannot sway my judgment in this matter. Furthermore, I would fain be certain of your safety while I go in search of the Draught. I do not wish to be distracted from my purpose. High Darioneth is where you must bide."

"Gladly."

"Arran, we might make our journey in a sky-balloon," suggested Bliant. "Then we should be surpassingly speedy."

"Nay. No longer will I break the laws of High Darioneth. It is forbidden to use aerostats for purposes other than pursuing our calling. Moreover, the waters of this lake, Stryksjø, are grievously dangerous and cannot be traversed by aircraft. With a good horse under me, I shall be able to make excellent time to Grïmnørsland. If I cannot win this prize without exploiting the privileges of a weathermage, I am not my father's son."

"What of the well-known tale of your own forefather, Aglaval Stormbringer, who employed a sky-balloon when Álainna Machnamh vanished and Tierney A'Connacht asked him to seek her!"

"That occurred in another era, long ago. The circumstances were different." The young Maelstronnar shook his head. Struck by his calm and assured aspect, Bliant broke off, ceasing his lobbying. Arran's demeanor was that of a rocky cliff that would not be broken by any tempestuous assault of the ocean.

Taken aback, Solorien asked, "What laws have you breached, Arran?"

"I have taken the liberty of working weather when such deeds were not necessary to protect life and property. Such actions are dishonorable."

Said the older weathermage, "An arguable point. Notwithstanding, I judge that the notion of traveling to Grïmnørsland by balloon is meritorious. I am inclined to believe the Council would have no objection to a sky-balloon being used for the purpose we propose—to prevent immortal villains from arising in the Four Kingdoms. Take the sky-route. None will deem this action unworthy."

"If I am to deserve any esteem," said Stormbringer, "I cannot employ an aerostat."

The older weathermage said, "For the sake of proving your worth, would you jeopardize the chance to obtain this miraculous Draught?"

Arran offered no reply.

After a moment, Solorien nodded curtly. "Let this matter rest, for now, while we make our journey to the city. Once we are rid of this pallid, cringing wretch, we shall strike out for High Darioneth, and when we reach it, we shall ask the councillors of Ellenhall for their judgments."

Above the sweeping pastures and woodlands of Orielthir, swallows trekked their way across the skies. Brambles sprawled, thick with ripening blackberries, and leaves rained down to carpet the foundations of hanging oak woods. On the willowy shores of streams wild deer grazed, lost in banks of flowering water-cress. Far away, long ridges and valleys stretched themselves out, veiled in Autumn haze. Dawn frosts made the air ring as sharp and clear as silver bells. At sunrise magpies would warble their heartbreakingly strange and beautiful melodies, music reputedly taught to them by elfin wights; or perhaps the legend had it topsy-turvy, and the birds had lessoned the immortals.

On a night when the travelers slept beneath the stars and the red embers of their fire glowed like bloodied garnets in the ashes, Gahariet Heaharním-HighCloud, seated with his back against the bole of a great oak, was keeping watch for wights and other perils. Wards and charms against unseelie incarnations had been set in many places throughout the camp, hanging about the necks of the travelers, plaited into the manes and tails of the horses, wound about their packs. Aonarán slept at the outskirts of their group—none wished to lie near him. His ankles were shackled with iron, but his captors had covered him with blankets and made him as reposeful as possible. A west wind arose out of the hills and combed through the woods. The journeyman was nodding with weariness. Not long after midnight, the sound of his gentle snores, rendered almost inaudible by the sighing of the wind, indicated he had succumbed to sleep.

It was then that a whitish shape slipped from the shadows and folded itself over Aonarán's prone form. The fair-haired man woke in fright, but already a handful of cloth was clapped firmly across his mouth, muffling his noise.

"Keep silent." A woman's voice, anemic and dim.

His mind still cloyed by the turgid pastes of his dreams, Aonarán stared up at her without comprehension.

"Hold still and do not be calling out. I shall cut the ropes that bind you."

"Fionnuala!" His whisper was fierce.

"Aye, and five mercenaries awaiting me in the woods. Yet I find you now in the company of four weathermasters and a couple of warriors. My men would stand no chance in an open fight against them, so I have come to you in secret."

"You cannot be freeing me unless you bring some blade that can slice through iron."

On perceiving the metal shackles, Fionnuala swore an oath under her breath.

"You cannot free me yet," said he, "but there is something of greater urgency you must do. Listen carefully." The woman leaned closer to her half-brother. He went on, "There is a second Well, in Grïmnørsland. It is on an island called Ragnkull, on Stryksjø Lake. You must get to this well before the weathermasters. Go swiftly. No doubt they shall be flying there by one of their balloons, so you must ride with all speed. Take the Draught before they can reach it, then seek me out and free me. I will be in the city. On the way back to me, first go by my quarters. Get Weaponmonger's diamond dagger. It is hidden behind a loose brick next to the fireplace. That dagger now belongs to me. It will cut through any steel they put on me. Will you do exactly as I've said?"

"That I will, Finn."

"Then go, now, before you rouse the whole lot of them. Get the water of life, and bring it to me. To me, understand!"

The woman slipped away as noiselessly as she had arrived.

Drifting out of his doze, Gahariet fancied he saw a wan figure melting into the wood. No doubt it was some wight, although what species he was unable to discern. The sight, although brief, was enough to shock him into alertness, and he returned to vigilance. Behind the wind's crooning, he thought he heard hoof-beats receding into the distance, but he could not be certain.

Two hours later Yaadosh relieved him of the watch, but by then, Gahariet had swept these incidents from his thoughts.

In the afternoon of the following day the riders reached the end of a barely discernible track and turned left onto the Valley Road toward Cathair Rua. As they rode along, a band of horsemen came cantering around the bend in front of them. Their tabards, resplendent with crimson and vermilion, and emblazoned with the emblem of a flaming torch, indicated they were members of King Uabhar's elite company, the Knights of the Brand. On spying the weathermasters, their leader raised his hand in a signal, and the men reined in their steeds, blocking the road. Likewise, Arran's party drew to a halt.

Yaadosh leaned to murmur confidentially in the ear of Aonarán. "Any noise from you and I shall hang you by your toes from the tallest tree in Slievmordhu, and leave you to dangle until the winds blow your beard back inside your chin."

Sullen Aonarán bared his teeth in a yellow snarl, and cast down his eyes with a furious air. He seemed to have shrunk into himself, like an emptied husk. Yaadosh maneuvered his horse close to Aonarán's right flank, while Arran closed in on the left.

"Good morrow, gentlemen!" The captain of the king's knights saluted, somewhat languidly.

"Good morrow, Captain," returned Solorien. "If your men will move aside we shall make better progress. We are bound for the city."

The officer shouted an order and a clear corridor opened down the center of the cavalrymen's ranks as they guided their mounts to the roadside.

"May Ádh smile upon you, my lords," said the captain, as the weathermasters rode past.

"And you, Captain," Solorien politely replied.

Next day Stormbringer and his companions entered the city, bringing their prisoner.

Lake

Straight to the house of Calogrenant Lumenspar hastened Stormbringer's company.
The Ambassador for High Darioneth, an old friend of Tristian Solorien, un-
hesitatingly agreed to provide the arms-dealer with comfortable circumstances
in the cellar of his official premises, which were as well guarded as Solorien had
indicated. After staying one night at the residence of the Ambassador, they set
off for High Darioneth. Leaving Fionnbar Aonarán at the consulate was like
the easing of a heavy burden.

Their progress was steady but unhurried. "We have plenty of time," said
Tristian Solorien. "Lumenspar is prepared to keep Aonarán until we send an order for his release."

"Yet, I would not dally," replied Stormbringer. "The slick-tongued knave
has made me aware that until now we have been holding him illegally, according to our own laws."

"Not, however, according to the haphazard laws of Slievmordhu," Bliant reminded him.

"In sooth. Howbeit, although we travel through Slievmordhu we are men
of High Darioneth. It does not rest well with me, to contravene our principles."

Unbeknownst to the weathermasters, Fionnuala Aonarán and her hired men had reached the city before them. The woman ordered the mercenaries to track the weathermasters upon their arrival, in order to find out where her brother was being held, and afterward to rendezvous with her at the Crock and Dwarf. Having certified these arrangements, she made her way swiftly and discreetly to her brother's empty rooms in certain notorious quarters of the city. Being in possession of a key, she entered without trouble. There, hidden in a cavity behind a dislodged brick next to the fireplace, she discovered Weaponmonger's diamond dagger, just as Fionnbar had described. She found also a bag of gold coins, which she took.

On meeting with her hirelings she learned of Fionnbar's incarceration at the consulate.

"You have done well," she said to them. "Now there is another task. You must prepare to ride with me to Grïmnørsland, and ride more swiftly than you have ever done. It will be a race against time, a race against the weathermasters. We must win."

"What do we seek?" asked the men. "Gold? Jewels? The blood of men?"

"Ask not," she said sharply. "You have always been paid on time. You will get your reward. Is it not enough to know that?"

Five days after their departure from Cathair Rua, Arran, Jewel and their companions reached the Border Hills. Four days later, they passed through the village of Market Deeping. From Market Deeping it was a long, hard ride, turning off at Blacksmith's Corner and climbing the steep byway through the hills to High Darioneth.

As they ascended the thickly wooded highland road, the travelers looked through the forest galleries towards the blue-misted walls of the neighboring valleys. Precipitous were the slopes, and hung with the emerald lace of treeferns. So steeply did the land drop away from the road's edge that the midpoints of the tallest trees growing merely a few yards down from the lip of the path were at eye-level and one could look down on the very tops of the trees growing out of the cliff a few yards farther below.

Boles crowded close together, tall and slender, holding up the sky. They were draped with hanging strips of bark, as damsels might be clad in loose-fitting robes. Sometimes, between the silver-white waists of the trees, one could glimpse the dark blue line of a distant mountain ridge, backed by a ribbon of pure cloud. Untamed rivulets chuckled as they fell down through the rocks of the hillsides into tiny pools brimming with fern-reflections. In the gullies, streams and miniature waterfalls gurgled, and the slopes echoed with birdsong.

At High Darioneth a joyous welcome awaited the travelers.

They came in through the East Gate, heralded by the eldritch frightener that resided in the mountain walls. As they made their approach it set up its usual clamor. Thus alerted, the watchmen on the heights noted the travelers through spyglasses. Joyful horns sounded. The gates were hauled open and the riders entered gladly into the embrace of the ring of storths.

It was the last month of Autumn. Already the alpine temperatures had plummeted. The air was chill, as bitter as a presage of grief.

Family and friends greeted the incomers effusively. There was scant recrimination for Jewel's stealthy departure; instead, chiefly gladness upon her return. Why this should be the marsh-daughter could not fathom, until later it came to her that these discerning people recognized she had not intended to hurt anyone, and made allowances for the fact that she was young and impetuous. They understood the flighty, erratic tendencies of youth, and while they did not condone irresponsible or duplicitous behavior, as scrupulous keepers of their own annals they recognized Jewel's ardent desire to learn about her heritage. Furthermore, they respected her courage and independence in embarking on a quest sustained by no help from anyone, they were relieved that she had returned unharmed, and they perceived, accurately, that she had gained wisdom from her experiences.

After welcoming the travelers, Avalloc tersely expressed his disapprobation of Jewel's reckless conduct; that was all. The Millers showered her with endearments and hugs, and she surprised herself by weeping with pleasure at seeing them once more. Her old friend and irritant Ryence Darglistel looked as sleek and cocksure as ever, and as if to confirm the impression he boldly seized and kissed her, then released her and seemed to turn all his attention to Stormbringer, as if Jewel were no longer present. In his turn, Arran appeared to be too busy to afford Ryence any more than a curt nod. Jewel's vexation lasted an instant only. Subsequently, hearty greetings were exchanged and the new arrivals were quizzed about their adventures, but they were impervious to appeals and would divulge nothing. On first setting foot in Rowan Green, Arran had asked his father to call for a Council moot in Ellenhall. All and sundry were advised that no tidings would be made publicly known until after the moot had concluded.

That same evening a feast was held in Long Gables under Wychwood Storth, in celebration of their return, and the warmth of the reception was well matched against the cold of the season. Jewel's eyes shone like two drops of liquid sky as she gazed up and down the tables running the length of the Common Hall. Golden lamplight cast a warm glow on a multitude of familiar and well-loved faces, young and old, families from the Seat of the Weathermasters and from the plateau below. The great chamber hummed with the discourses of cheerful folk; firelight gilded their hair and the rich fabrics of their raiment, and beneath the tables, patient mop-haired dogs waited for scraps.

Avalloc Maelstronnar presided at the head of the board, as straight and tall as a mountain ash, his hair falling like frosted cobwebs across his shoulders. Somber and gracious was he, with his deep-carved countenance and aquiline nose. His eyes of jade watched from beneath hooded lids. Like the other weathermages he wore magnificent raiment of velvet and watered silk, dyed in many shades of gray, storm-cloud, ash, iron, and slate, and embroidered with the runes for Water, Fire, and Air.

Jewel recalled the first time she had dined at Long Gables. Five years ago such a large crowd of strangers had seemed overwhelming. She had been allotted a place on a wooden settle, between Elfgifu and Ettare, where she attempted to make herself unnoticeable. This time, by contrast, she conversed easily and laughed much, while sharing in the generous supper and listening to the news of High Darioneth. Yet, often, she caught herself glancing toward Arran Stormbringer, who was seated at his father's side. Her outlook had altered. High Darioneth now seemed such a cherished and safe place after her travels—it felt more like her home than the marsh, which had receded into dim memory. Furthermore, now that Arran had made his declaration, Ryence seemed the more frivolous and vacuous by comparison, and Jewel wondered how she had ever found him so interesting.

Yaadosh and Barakiel freely told stories about their homeland, and the former expounded upon his travels, but both were strictly circumspect concerning other, more recent matters. The big man refused to touch a drop of strong drink, declaring that several years earlier he had vowed to remain sober for the rest of his days, because drinking was apt to loosen his tongue and bring him trouble.

"I'll not say a word until after your moot," he declared. "I am honored to be a guest amongst weathermasters, and I'll not abuse your hospitality, my lords, by flouting your request for discretion!"

The youth Barakiel, his eyes wide as he stared at his surroundings, was of the same opinion. In this he was aided by being tongue-tied with wonder.

As was customary at any celebration in High Darioneth, the gathering was regaled with music and song. The first to rise to her feet was Gvenour Nithulambar, weathermage and member of the Council of Ellenhall. Her voice soared, strong and clear, as she sang an old lay known as "The Drouth of Thirty-two":

"Bright blazed the sun in cloudless skies above the thirsty land
As rivers shrank to streams, and streambeds dried to dusty sand,
And lakes receded from their shores, and channels ceased to flow,

And farmers ceased to till the soil for crops that would not grow
Unless the rains began to fall. But showers came there none,
And all that poured from glaring skies were harsh rays of the sun.
Leaves parched and withered on the boughs; starved worms could
    wind no silk;
In once-green pastures sere and brown, gaunt cows could give no
    milk.
All mortal creatures suffered sore beneath the yoke of pain
With ne'er a hope for better times, unless there should be rain.

"Where are the mists, the clouds, the storms? Oh, let the sweet rains
    fall!
Now may the tears of weeping skies flow down to drench us all!
Grieve now for Tir, you smiling sky, 'ere naught is left alive.
Enshroud your face in cloud, and mourn, else we shall not survive.

"Then westward passed the weathermages, westward to the sea,
To gather on the shores, where they unleashed the force of *brí*.
They stirred the pressure systems, making anti-cyclones form,
They summoned moisture-laden winds and brewed a thunderstorm.

"A mighty cold front swelled. Its lightnings flickered like some ghost.
A line of clouds, ranged north to south, wheeled in toward the
    coast—
A towering wall of roiling steam, that with a crashing roar
Rolled right across the darkling land—and rain began to pour."

All those present who knew the words—and that was most—joined in chorus to sing the last verse:

"Here is the music! Silver droplets striking silver strings!
Here is the song of dripping leaves that steady rainfall brings.
Here is the diamond on the twig, the soft, gray overcast,
The perfume of the drinking garden, calm and slaked at last."

Afterward Ryence Darglistel began to sing a different lyric but was told to hush, because his song was inappropriate, being a satire on a powerful institution—the Sanctorum—and ill-composed, to boot. Somewhat later he made a brief sojourn out of doors with a merry group of friends and sang it anyway, beneath the febrile stars.

Ryence's coterie laughed and jested, then returned to the warmth of the hall. After the dining and singing, there was dancing. The wooden floors of Long Gables rocked to the pounding of feet; the walls resounded to the music of pipes, fiddles, and drums.

Jewel found herself making pictures in her mind. What would it be like to dance with the son of the Maelstronnar? To let him hold her closely, until he burned her with his heat, so close that the rhythm of the dance must be transmitted to her senses through his sinews, as his body slid against hers?

She turned around, and he was standing right beside her, in a casual, coincidental way. Immediately the room disappeared and her very identity shriveled out of existence. She was but dimly aware she was still balancing on her feet, by some automatic prompt. All that remained in focus was him, this tall weatherlord in the splendor of youth, his vigor, his breathtaking, sudden nearness. Only the length of a dagger separated them. He was so close she might have reached out and let her hand rest upon his elbow, allowing her flesh to catch alight with intense excitement, the sparks beginning at the fingers, flying along her arms, drilling through her bones to burst within her brain, violently destroying all longings, all desires, save one.

She said, "Oh," and then could not look away. Her eyes traced the contours of his form, caressed and discovered him, his hair, his face.

Then a different voice said impatiently, "Let's dance," and someone seized her by the wrist so that she lost equilibrium and must step away to regain it. Impelled by momentum and the insistent pull of Ryence Darglistel, she was dragged into a circle of revelers. A thrilling harmony of musical notes soared up to the rooftree, and before she had fully regained her wits Jewel was dancing with others, and Arran was lost to view.

There was never an opportunity, that night, to find out what it was like to partner him.

She was aware of his love—he had declared it. She believed in it—how could she not? She perceived it every time he looked at her. He was not demonstrative, but his ardor was all the more evident for the reins with which he restrained it, the mask of steel behind which he imprisoned it, his detached demeanor and deliberate gestures that, far from parading a lack of interest, displayed the strength of his self-discipline, that he could so tightly curb the intensity of his passion.

For her part, she was astounded. Never had she known such fierce and unwavering tenderness. Such resolution was hard for her to comprehend. She was intrigued by his steadfastness, and pleased, and flattered by his attention, but also she feared it. Somehow it seemed too great, too monumental and enduring. She did not know what to make of such a grand and formidable sentiment, and so she did not speak of it, never openly acknowledged its existence. Another marvel: He accepted her silence. He pressed no suit, he asked nothing of her, yet he remained as constant as the volcanic fires in the deeps of Wychwood Storth, with a patience so enduring that at times it seemed to Jewel almost terrible.

At the meeting place of the borders of the Four Kingdoms, the sky was overcast. A lofty obelisk loomed to stab the low-hovering clouds. It stood alone, with no other man-made edifice apparent nearby. Relief sculptures jutted from each of its four smooth sides, near the peak. The top of each sculpture featured a crown of chiseled stone. Below the crown, on the northern facet, a sword had been carved. On the western facet, the emblem was a square-sailed longboat. The east flank displayed a flaming torch, while the south depicted a cart-wheel.

Six riders congregated at the base of this monument. Their cloaks were weather-stained, their horses flecked with foam, slippery with sweat. Fionnuala Aonarán and her mercenaries had momentarily paused in their journey. The woman was swigging from a water flask. She wiped the back of her hand across her mouth, stoppered the flask, and stowed it in her saddlebags.

"We have reached the border," she said. "Now onward! Onward into Grïm-nørsland!"

At the prod of her spurs, her horse leaped forward. The other riders followed, and soon they had left the monolith far behind.

The day after the feast at High Darioneth the moot was convened. By favorable chance, the senior weathermages were free of their usual multitude of tasks, and none traveled abroad, so it was unnecessary to wait for their return. On Sun's Day, 21st Ninember, the Council of Weathermasters gathered in Ellenhall.

It was a day of brilliant, glassy light; such radiance as is peculiar to mountainous regions where the air is pure and distilled. Lemon-bright beams came flooding in through the tall windows, whose shutters had been thrown back. They illuminated the elegant interior of the Moot Hall, the wood paneling, the clean-swept floor, the steeply pointed arches of the vaults that sprang from narrow bays along the walls, soaring to the timbered ceiling. Hanging lamps softened any lingering shadows. Furniture gleamed: a cabinet on a stand, painted with mythical characters on a patterned background, long tables of oak, chairs and settles, massive copper candelabra, the burnished firedogs in the great fireplace, where no flame burned. In one corner, beneath a window, a notary sat on a stool before a lectern. He was industriously making records in a book, dipping the nib of his goose-quill pen in and out of an inkwell, scratching at the paper, blotting his work with handfuls of fine, dry sand.

The assembly included representatives of the nine chief families. Jewel and Arran sat with their traveling companions and the Council members, along the tables. At the meeting's outset Arran recounted all that had happened since Averil, when he had departed from High Darioneth, tracking Jewel. He had gone no further than describing the breaching of the Dome of Strang and the subsequent reading of the sorcerer's book with its account of the Waters of Eternal Life when the murmurs and exclamations of amazement among the councillors caused him to suspend his narrative.

"Wait," said Baldulf Ymberbaillé-Rainbearer. "Can this be true? Can it be possible to prolong a life-span eternally?"

"Conceivably it is *not* true," said Arran. "It may be that this notion of Wells and Stars and marvelous waters is naught but a ruse on the part of Jaravhor, a final trick, so that he might go to his grave knowing he had the last laugh. On the other hand, he might have believed it to be true, yet been mistaken or deceived."

Avalloc spoke, and all those present fell silent, turning their attention upon him. "Long ago," the Storm Lord said, "I heard of the immortal beasts. Yet never, even in the oldest tales, have I heard of such prodigies as these Wells. Of all the marvels known to humankind, surely these would be amongst the most extraordinary." He shook his head in wonderment. "These are tidings of singular consequence. Great deeds are afoot, if the secret to eternal life has indeed been uncovered. What this might mean for the world I cannot say, as yet; but there is no doubt the world must be altered by it. It is possible that changes have begun already." Briefly he glanced toward the open window. "But continue with the story, my dear boy, for we are eager to hear all."

His son needed no further urging. He told of the discovery of the Well of Rain, Fionnbar Aonarán's quaffing of the Draught, the accidental death of Cathal Weaponmonger and the murder of Bahram Gaspar by the poisoned bolt of Fionnuala Aonarán, the return to Strang, the awakening of the sorcerer, and subsequent events culminating in Aonarán's imprisonment in Cathair Rua.

"How can the alleged qualities of these waters be proven, save by trying to slay Aonarán?" pondered Nyneve Longiníme.

Baldulf replied, "There is no other method."

"I don't deny, such a test is not unattractive to me," said Arran wryly. "But we cannot know the answer, for such an ill-trial is not our way."

"Is it likely the sorcerer was leading you on? Is it likely he was mistaken or deceived?"

"I think not."

"Then we must assume, for the moment, that it is true."

Through the ensuing silence the dim echoes of birdcalls could be heard, ringing in the distant valleys of the mountains, and the scratching of the notary's nib as he scrawled hurriedly.

"To conclude," said the young Maelstronnar, "I would ask that the Council deliberate on the following questions: Should we claim the last two remaining Draughts of Immortality? If so, should we leave the Wells intact, their virtues seeping slowly into the water until they create another dose for whosoever should stumble upon them in a thousand years' time? If we take the Draughts from the Well of Dew and the Well of Tears, to whom should we offer them?"

"There is also the matter of the two Aonaráns," said Tristian Solorien. "He is an arms-smuggler, she a slaughterer, yet it might prove difficult to muster witnesses to testify against the former, while the latter roams at large throughout the Four Kingdoms."

"Honored gentlefolk, may I put forward my opinion?" Jewel asked abruptly. Somewhat overawed at having been accorded the privilege of attending a conference of the weathermasters, she had held her peace since the moot commenced.

Avalloc Stormbringer inclined his head. "Say on, Jewel."

From the moment Jewel had made her decision to aid Arran in tracking down Aonarán instead of returning from Saadiah to the Dome, the conundrum of the sorcerer's legacy had never been far from her thoughts. Her hopes of obtaining security against the caprices of an unjust world had been dashed. There had been no treasure of gold and jewels in the fortress of Strang after all, no library of lore, and no evidence of any objects with supernatural properties. The clues leading to the three Wells had been the only items of value. Jewel had reflected on the virtues and drawbacks of immortality, wondered whether hunting the remaining Draughts was a wise course of action, and ruminated on Jaravhor's maleficent and devious nature.

Moreover, she was still haunted by visions of the skeleton in the walls of Castle Strang, and she could hardly dismiss the matter of Jaravhor's curse on her dear mother, not to mention the rest of his multifarious offenses. Evidently, all his deeds were tainted by the stench of ultimate decay. Jewel repeatedly returned to the conclusion that any thing coveted by her morally corrupt ancestor must necessarily be odious, and any action arising from his works must lead to ruin. She wanted to excise him from her future; him and everything associated with him. It occurred to her, however, that even if she turned her back on his legacy, some of it would continue to run through her veins; after all, she was virtually indestructible. Did this mean she could never be free of his malign influence?

No! she argued to herself. *People are forever presuming that some ancestor or other determines their character, and it never does them any good. Many peaceable young men are taught that because their grandsires were great warriors they are obliged to follow in their footsteps and go to war. Many other youths and damsels, when informed of their ancestors' grand achievements in music, or oration, or some such discipline, are made to feel constrained to emulate them. The children are generally destined for disappointment, for their talents often lie in other directions and in the end they can rarely measure up to the benchmarks of their forefathers, which so often are historically exaggerated, in any case.*

No, we are not merely replicas of our ancestors! Each of us is a new person entirely, a unique individual with our own qualities. I cast off Jaravhor and all his works. Let my friends eschew him also, for their own good.

"The quest for the Draught from the Well of Rain went amiss and ended in tragedy," she said aloud to the councillors of Ellenhall. "It seems to me that all matters pertaining to the Sorcerer of Strang smack of depravity. Let there be no further meddling in the affairs of Janus Jaravhor. Let his memory die, and his legacy fade into the bones of Orielthir."

"Do you advise we should refrain from seeking the waters of life?" asked the Storm Lord.

"Indeed, sir."

"Your views are noted," Avalloc said noncommittally. In the sunlit corner, the notary at his lectern scribbled industriously, the quill pen dancing a mad jig. With that, Jewel had to be content.

The councillors, after lengthy debate voted on the issue, eventually deciding, to Jewel's chagrin, to claim the Draughts and destroy the Wells.

"The vote has gone against you, dear child," said the Storm Lord.

"So it has, sir," she replied. "The Council has spoken. I cannot feign approval, but none are wiser than the weathermasters of Ellenhall. It might be demonstrated that my judgment was at fault, after all."

"Weathermasters are of humankind," Avalloc said, "therefore not infallible." He turned to the whole assembly and declared, "As for the question of who should receive the waters of life, my response is this: Let him offer himself to deathlessness who has studied the ramifications of such a choice in all possible ways, and who is fully aware of the consequences. If after such study any volunteers remain, then shall a lottery decide the final outcome. Any man or woman who opposes my view, let them speak now."

The Council members murmured their acceptance. Consideration was next directed to the subject of Fionnbar and Fionnuala Aonarán.

Nyneve Longiníme clasped her slim fingers on the table's polished surface. "About the poisoner there seems little we can do save watch and wait," she said. "Where she wanders in the Four Kingdoms is anybody's guess."

"And I daresay she has access to rich funds," said Rivalen Hagelspildar. "She is her brother's accomplice, is she not? A partner in the arms-trade?"

"Even so," Arran averred gravely. "Doubtless the two of them have made their fortune. Pockets full of gold may command regiments of mercenaries. I daresay she has many hired men at her beck and call."

"On the other hand," Baldulf Ymberbaillé pointed out, "this Fionnbar Aonarán is currently our prisoner."

"Father, according to our laws, how long can we hold him without pressing a charge?" asked Bliant.

"Our system of justice forbids us to imprison any person unless we charge them with some crime," said Baldulf.

"Might he be charged without evidence?"

"The mountain-bandits are not selective about their prey," interjected Gvenour Nithulambar, her dark eyes flashing. "By assisting them, Aonarán has been injuring every good citizen of Tir! Let him not be spared!"

"Aye, said Baldulf, "trafficking with Marauders is against the laws of all four kingdoms. Based on reliable hearsay we could accuse him of racketeering, but the charges must be dropped after fourteen days if no evidence is presented."

"Aonarán is being held in Slievmordhu, where the administration of justice is no more than a token," said Tristian. "Indeed, I deem their judiciary a farce. Were we not honorable men and women we might make as if we are abiding by the laws of that kingdom, the most widespread of which is *'he prevails who is most powerful.'*"

"Yet we are honorable men and women," said Avalloc Maelstronnar, "and must ensure that justice is done."

"Supposing we can find witnesses to testify against him, where would the trial be held?" asked Cacamwri Dommalleo. He rubbed his jaw, his usual habit when deep in thought. "The accused is a citizen of Slievmordhu who has committed crimes against the populace of the Four Kingdoms, and is likely to be charged under the laws of High Darioneth. An authentic trial could only take place in Grïmnørsland, Narngalis, or here—and how can we know which are the locations where the offense of trafficking was committed?"

"Let us jump that stile when we come to it," said Nyneve Longiníme.

"For now, the most pressing dilemmas are these," said the Maelstronnar.

"Shall we hold Aonarán or must we set him free? For if we set him free he can wreak worse transgressions in at least two ways. He might raid the Well of Dew, and he can make Jewel's identity public, thus exposing her to possible harm."

"The first is easily solved," said Arran. "I shall waste no further time. With your blessing, gentlemen and gentlewomen, as soon as this meeting is over I shall travel by sky-balloon to Grïmnørsland, that I may claim the Draught of the Well of Dew for High Darioneth."

The councillors surrounding the table indicated their unanimous consent to his proposal.

"What of the last Draught?" asked Rivalen Hagelspildar. "That which lies in the Well of Tears?"

"Aonarán has no inkling of its location," Arran said. "The clue to that is written on a scrap of paper in Jewel's possession."

"May we see it, Jewel?" asked Avalloc.

Promptly the damsel drew the yellowing fragment from a pocket in her gown, and handed it to the Storm Lord. He unfolded it, smoothing out the creases, and read aloud to the gathering:

> " 'My hair is white, my bones are old.
> Steadfast I rest, for ages cold
> And still. So silent, lacking breath,
> That men think I've been touched by death.
> But deep within my chilly breast
> My living heart can find no rest.
> What falls and never breaks, but would
> Be broken if it ever should
> Stop falling? What is darkness? And
> Can mortalkind make ropes of sand?' "

"The Riddle of the Well of Tears. A riddle indeed," said the Maelstronnar. "An enigma of considerable magnitude. Are you certain Aonarán has not heard or read it?"

"We are certain."

"Then, there is no hurry to decipher the meaning," declared Lynley Ymber-baillé, the wife of Baldulf. "Unless I am misinformed, no one else in the world knows aught of this riddle save we who have heard it on this day. Furthermore, there exists no other clue to the whereabouts of the last Well—is that so, Arran?"

"As far as I am aware, it is so," he confirmed.

Avalloc offered to return the paper to Jewel, but instead of accepting it she shook her head. "Pray keep it, sir, or destroy it if you wish."

"We shall keep it." The Storm Lord handed the leaf to Baldulf Rainbearer, who folded it within a vellum pamphlet.

Nyneve Longiníme leaned forward in her chair. As she spoke, she looked earnestly about, to ensure she met the gazes of all those present. "Jewel's identity as the heir of the Sorcerer of Strang can only cause harm to her if she is revealed to be the sole person who can unclose the Dome. You say, Arran"—she focused her attention on the young man—"you say that you and Jewel left the Dome unsealed, the gates flung wide and dangling loose upon their hinges. If the Dome is already unlocked, Jewel may no longer be in jeopardy!"

Arran pondered. "Perhaps you are right," he said at length. "Nevertheless, taking her safety for granted is a risk I would fain avoid."

"That may be so, Nyneve," said Cacamwri Dommalleo. "Time will tell. Again, we must watch and wait."

"There is too much talk of waiting, and not enough action!" said Bliant. "Let us consider sending a message to Cathair Rua, advising Uabhar that it has come to our knowledge the Dome is his for the taking. Thereby we might hasten the process."

"If we merely inform him that the Dome has been opened he will know at once that an heir of Jaravhor is at large," the carlin warned. "He might instantly send forth search parties to track down this heir. Purely out of interest, and to find out if the heir possesses any unusual talents he might employ for his own gain, he would want to find her."

The councillors inquired whether she had a solution.

"We must inform Uabhar that the heir, Jewel, is under the auspices of Ellenhall," she replied. "He will know, then, that the heir and her whereabouts have been identified, but that she is out of his reach. Naturally he will assume that he might interview her at some later date, if it pleases the Council to allow it."

"An excellent notion!" approved Arran. "What say you, Father?"

"I say, let it be done straightway, if Jewel is willing." Murmurs of assent accompanied the Maelstronnar's words, and Jewel nodded her agreement. Shortly thereafter, the topic was closed and the Storm Lord called for a recess.

Refreshments were taken, the notary refreshed his inkwell, and then the meeting recommenced.

"Speaking of Cathair Rua," said Baldulf Ymberbaillé-Rainbearer, "this very morning a message arrived from the palace. We, the councillors, have been invited to attend the naming ceremony of King Uabhar's second-born son. The ritual is to take place on New Year's Eve."

"New Year's?" Avalloc's frown indicated his displeasure. "Are we to be summoned from our own celebrations at the whims of Uabhar Ó Maoldúin, hmm?"

"It appears the Druid Imperius has augured this is an auspicious date, beneficial for the naming of the young prince."

"Primoris Virosus, eh? We might have guessed," said Avalloc. His laugh was short and ironic. "No doubt it affords him much pleasure to disrupt the annual festivities of weathermasters."

"It seems we have attended so many royal festivities of late," sighed Cacamwri Dommalleo. "Only recently we returned from King's Winterbourne, and not long before that, Trøndelheim."

"The royal families of Narngalis, Grïmnørsland, and Ashqalêth will be sending representatives to the occasion," said Baldulf, "but Uabhar has specifically requested the pleasure of our company."

"And our generous gifts!" dourly said Gvenour Nithulambar.

"Diplomatically speaking, we can hardly refuse, of course," said Cacamwri Dommalleo.

"Even so," agreed Avalloc. "However, it is not necessary for us all to attend. Only a few of us need accept the invitation. There is time for each of us to decide. Now, if we have solved the most pressing issues to the satisfaction of the majority, let me call for Solorien's report about the dissenting druids of Carrickmore."

With the discussion of this and other knotty puzzles, the moot wore on throughout the afternoon, finally concluding toward dusk.

At dawn the following day, Arran set off for Grïmnørsland to seek the Well of Dew. With him went Gahariet and Bliant, and Rivalen Hagelspildar, who was familiar with the topography of the western kingdom. The members of the aircrew were warmly dressed, their heads covered by thickly padded hoods.

The final words of Avalloc Maelstronnar to his son at their parting were these: "Yours is a singular quest, Arran. Go subtly. Go with care. You are embarking on a momentous undertaking, and I would entrust it to none but you."

It was early morning. The mountain atmosphere chimed with cold, like a clear crystal cup. A layer of wispy cloud floated on the plain below the Seat of the Weathermasters. Dollops of white vapor, as billowy as the breath of icegiants, seethed about the lower summits of the storths, and steamed from valleys. Far above, high-altitude winds could be heard screaming amongst the snow-brilliant crags, but down on Rowan Green the atmospheric currents were playing at being breezes, for a time. The apex of the sky was vibrantly blue, softening to a talcum haze at the horizon.

On the launching apron, prentices unrolled the huge envelope of the sky-balloon *Wanderpath,* spilling a froth of fabric both strong and light, made from the silk spun for ten or eleven years by a million million spiders. They laid the basket of rattan and willow on its side, and into the mounted cradle they placed the covered sun-crystal.

Before he left, Arran drew Jewel aside and spoke with her. He said, "I will bring back the Draught for you."

"For me? What of the judgment of the Council on this matter?"

Calmly he replied, "If I bring it back, I will give it to you."

"Methinks I do not want it," she said, but she faltered.

"Once you did. Cast your mind back." After a moment Arran continued, "Next, forecast. The atmosphere churns. Weather erodes. Rock is gnawed away, bitten to gravel, minced to dust. Wind picks up the dust and sifts it over cities. Grain by grain, year by year, layers build up. In a thousand years, those cities will lie sleeping beneath depths of silt and clay, sand and marl. All monuments wrought by humankind will be altered or destroyed. The deeds that consume us, the people and places we consider so important, will be forgotten. What legacy remains with us, from a millennium ago? What names and deeds do we remember?" His voice dropped to a whisper, as if an invisible grip constricted his throat. "In a thousand years, who will recall your name?"

Stillness coalesced about Jewel. She appeared to be the axis of a pool of quiescence. Yet the core of that axis imprisoned a savage turbulence of thought.

"I told myself it did not matter," she said at length. "It is possible I was mistaken."

"You must survive," he said.

"And you?"

"And I." He leaned close to her. "What would you desire for me?"

In that moment his gaze riveted her, as if she were some feeble fly speared on a pin. There was some virtue of his eyes. She had noted it before—indeed, each time she looked at him—but on this occasion he was so near that she could feel the caress of his breath on her skin, and the potency of this quality overwhelmed her senses. His eyes were two orbs of cool flame, imbued with power; they were long leaves of jade, limpid, yet simmering with vitality.

She whispered, "You, too, must survive."

"It is time to go!" called Bliant, leaning from the wicker basket.

"Farewell," said Arran.

"Come back, with the Draught or without it, but come back," said Jewel.
He had kissed her lightly, on her forehead.
She remembered that kiss. Oh, how she remembered it.

Wanderpath stood upright, tugging on its moorings. Trembling bells jingled, hooked securely to the basket. Controlled energy was pouring upward from the pinnacle of the sun-crystal, into the skirt that bordered the mouth of the envelope. A gigantic, lustrous soap bubble hovered, its crown higher than the Tower of the Winds that loomed above the roof of Ellenhall. Arran stood in the gondola, his hand lightly grasping one of the rigid cane supports that attached the car to the frame of the cradle. The bubble ripened, until it seemed ready to burst. Eventually Arran signaled to the prentices, and they unleashed the mooring cables.

The balloon climbed swiftly and powerfully. It dwindled, becoming a tear in the blue eye of the sky.

Jewel watched it.

"Stare upward for too long," said Ryence Darglistel, "and you'll end up with a pain in the neck." He laughed and strolled past, then returned and beckoned, murmuring, "Come. Let me teach you how to summon fire."

"No."

"Ah, now don't be sulky, just because you're not going to ride the winds!"

She walked away from him. He seemed now trite and shallow, a buffoon.

That same morning a second aerostat, *Snowship,* departed from High Darioneth, bound for Cathair Rua. The weathermasters on board bore with them letters for the palace: notice of acceptance of the invitation to the royal naming ceremony, and another, more urgent announcement.

Late in the day Arran's sky-balloon scudded across the lakes and mountains of Grïmnørsland, three hundred feet above the ground. Sky blended with water; reflected images seemed indistinguishable from reality. Landmarks passed swiftly beneath the wicker car, which was wind-driven at Arran's governance. *Wanderpath* traveled at wind-speed, matching the rate of clouds at the same level, and airborne thistledown and, when they passed a village, smoke from hearth-fires. Ahead lay a deep bank of cloud. As the aircraft approached it, the shades and shapes of the countryside below gradually lost differentiation. Details blurred. A haze filmed the land, while overhead the vapors of the cloud layer wrapped themselves around the balloon. Within the cloud all was soft, damp, and muffled. As the aerostat rose above the cumulus, resplendent spears of sunlight rained down, dazzling the eyes of the crew. Billowing cloud-towers, mist-crags, and vapor-crevasses hurled the sun's glare into the profundities of the firmament.

"βɫẫẅ," Arran murmured, his hands performing the flight-commander's choreography. "βɫẫẅ, ¥μɾøš§, ¥ē §ðüþëẫ§ɫ Ẅỹṅɗê.'

After traveling for almost an hour, *Wanderpath* dived down through the clouds, and the envelope was surrounded by splintery powderings of suspended crystals that glimmered and glittered, before amalgamating with the cool, moist fog in a viscid environment that magnified any noises. Abruptly the frayed colors of the landscape emerged from invisibility. Dropping out through the bottom of the cloud ceiling, the aerostat emerged into the softer light of the atmosphere below.

Arran looked up past the load ring supporting the crystal, through the rigging wires and the panels of the balloon's heat-scoop. His appraising gaze swept the interior of a gigantic dome, its vaults symmetrically spaced in regular sections like the sliced rind of some waxy fruit. At the crown, like some spidery chandelier, a web of shroud lines and centralizing lines was attached to the parachute that covered the top opening. The aerostat was flying well, and appeared to be in good order as it approached the region of Stryksjø. As the last petals of carnation sunlight alchemized at day's end, the glimmering lakes of remote Grïmnørsland flared rose and pale gold, in reflection of the sunset. At the same time, sullen clouds were swiftly drawing in to suffocate this celestial splendor.

Rivalen Hagelspildar stood beside Arran. From their aerial vantage he pointed out various landmarks.

"See, the four great peaks that rise among the southernmost heights of the Nordstüren: Steinfjell, Hoyfjell, Sterkfjell, and Isfjell," he said. "And behold—the valleys between have been carved by three rivers, the Widflod, the Fiskflod, and the Østflod, leaping to join with each other and flow toward Ensomfjord on the west coast. Ah! Over there—that gleam of silver between the dark silhouettes of the junipers—I'll warrant 'tis the waters of Stryksjø."

"We should set our course across the lake!" suggested Gahariet. "Then we might spy the island!"

"Nay," Arran responded quickly. "If the tales are true, the arrows of wights might pierce the envelope, not to mention the basket, and our very flesh. I would not take the risk."

"The barbs of wights could hardly reach great heights," observed Bliant. "What is the greatest distance ever shot by a longbow?"

"Nigh on a land-mile," Rivalen informed him. "However, that was almost a legendary shot, achieved by a powerful man with a powerful bow."

"A land-mile!" exclaimed Gahariet. "Why then, we would have to climb to an altitude of more than fifty-two thousand feet to escape harm!"

"In which case we would merely freeze to death," put in Arran.

"I consider it implausible that minor wights such as are likely to inhabit remote islets would possess great strength," argued Bliant. "Besides, any marksman shooting his barbs straight up into the air is competing against the pull of gravity. Gravity alone would limit the range."

"True," said Arran, "yet how can we be certain some supernatural force does not propel their bolts? Very little is known about these isle-haunting species."

"Spidersilk is durable enough to resist arrowheads."

"For all we know it is only strong enough to resist barbs wrought by mortalkind and flung from a bow powered by a man. Who can say what malign forces propel eldritch darts? To risk damage to a balloon—that is too great a chance to take. Furthermore, despite the spidersilk lining on the floor of the car, as passengers we ourselves are not invulnerable."

"I am in accordance with you, Arran," said Rivalen. "Let us spy out the lie of this Ragnkull Island, for sure—but let us refrain from flying directly over the water, and instead float above the shores. We can survey the lake just as efficiently from that angle."

Stormbringer guided the balloon around the perimeter of the lake, holding it at a level of one thousand feet and staying well back from the shoreline. Meanwhile, Rivalen and Bliant consulted the map they had brought with them from the archives of Ellenhall. Many years ago the chart had been drafted by one of the cartographers who worked with the weathermasters, and on it were marked the islands in the lake. The detail was exact; the isles were clearly labeled with the names given them by local Grïmnørslanders.

"We have found our destination," Rivalen said softly. "See that patch of gray-green at forty-five degrees from the sun's path?"

The basket tilted to one side as they all peered over the edge. The island was triangular in shape. A small cove indented one end, while the other end tapered to a point.

"In sooth!" said Arran. He added, "'Tis formed like a love-heart."

Behind him, Bliant exchanged glances with Gahariet. They rolled their eyes.

Without turning around, Arran said, "Despite your knowing grimaces, my friends, I am not some love-smitten fool who sees hearts in every silhouette and hears harps playing on the wind. Be assured, you shall pay for your smugness, when next I wrestle you."

"Ha!" Bliant shouted happily, "'Tis you who will suffer when I have thrown you down!"

"Enough of your high jinks, lads!" Rivalen said, although his eyes were twinkling. "Next you'll be turning the basket upside down!"

The young Maelstronnar tugged on a vent-cord, opening a slit of a window in the canopy's crown. Smoothly, as if coasting down a snowy slope on runners, the aircraft began to descend. Mindful of warnings about unseelie manifestations haunting the shores, he guided *Wanderpath* toward a forest glade on a hillside about a furlong from the banks of the lake. As they skimmed over the pointed hats of the juniper trees toward their destination they watched vigilantly for signs of eldritch activity, but observed none. Immediately after landing, Bliant and Gahariet vaulted over the sides of the gondola and ran off into the gloaming to scout the locality at closer range. When the youths returned, reporting that the area appeared clear of peril, the balloonists allowed the envelope to deflate, then meticulously rolled and folded away the compacted spidersilk. They stored it, along with the sun-crystal, inside the charm-protected wicker basket. There all would be safe from eldritch assault.

"Here we must make camp and wait out the night," said Rivalen.

"Aye," said Arran, "but I suspect I shall not find rest. It irks me sorely, to wait. I burn to go directly to the lakeshore. We are so close, now."

"Close," said Bliant, "but divided from our ultimate goal by stretches of wood and water infested with nightmares."

"You are mistaken," said Rivalen dryly. "They are overrun with creatures we *wish* were merely nightmares."

"And who is to say this clearing is any less perilous than the rest of this region?" put in Gahariet. He stared warily about at the tall junipers palisading the landing site. Their dense, blue-gray foliage was beginning to merge with the thickening twilight.

"There is no certainty," said Arran. "We can only keep watch, taste the airs, and trust in our own proficiency."

After pitching a pair of tents they gathered armfuls of kindling for a campfire and employed flint and tinder to light it. The flames shredded against the darkness like torn cloth-of-gold while the weathermasters sat close to the warmth and partook of some food. They spoke infrequently, and in low voices. It was late when three of them lay down to sleep in the relative shelter of the canvas tents, leaving the fourth to take first shift at the Watch.

No moonlight penetrated the vapors curdling in the upper atmosphere. The murk was filled with surreptitious rustlings and sudden silences. Toward midnight a shrieking wind hurled itself against the trees as if a pack of giant, unseen horsemen barreled through the forest. The cacophony awoke the weathermasters, who sprang into the open. Their tents flapped wildly, shaking off frozen sequins that glittered through the air, straining at their moorings as if they would uproot themselves and flee in terror. Behind the roaring and thrashing of the junipers the men caught the spine-harrowing scrape of weird violins, wailing afar off.

As suddenly as it had blown up, the supernatural wind ceased.

There came no further incident that night.

Earlier that afternoon while Arran and his companions were landing their balloon near Stryksjø, Fionnbar Aonarán was striding up and down the length of a well-appointed, strongly guarded chamber at the house of Calogrenant Lumenspar. It was Aonarán's habit to pace. During his isolated incarceration he had leisure to ponder, as he had not pondered before. Never in his life had he experienced so much idle time, so many vacant moments to fill with speculation. It was becoming apparent to him, during his hours of brooding, that one thing was of paramount importance: the slaying of the young weathermage, Arran Maelstronnar. Aonarán hated Arran with a bitter, irrational loathing. It was his desire to inherit a world in which the son of the Storm Lord did not exist.

He reached the far wall, turned, and retraced his steps yet again.

Not far away, at the Royal Palace of Slievmordhu, the dowager queen existed in her parlor. Her sagging form was clad all in shades of yellow: tawny damask, creamy velvet, sulphurous silk. Glinting gold, topazes, and citrines adorned her person. Her fingernails were painted with gilt, or else crescents of gold leaf had been pasted on them. Curled and pinned was her hair, and powdered with gold dust. There was no relief from the sallowness; even her flesh appeared jaundiced, her skin like aged parchment; her eyes were two egg yolks. Wearing slippers of daffodil satin she reclined on her divan, surrounded by brazen birdcages, in which sixteen canaries were imprisoned. They hopped jerkily from perch to perch, and occasionally trilled piercingly. Seven handmaidens wafted about in xanthic robes. From a goblet encrusted with sparkling heliodors the widow of King Maolmórdha sipped wine the color of lemons. Her lips were puckered as though she did indeed taste the sour juice of lemons; but it was only the buttoning-up of old age.

"You look a hag, in yellow," King Uabhar said to his mother as he walked past.

A trumpet sounded from the parapets. It was the signal that a messenger of some importance had arrived at the palace gates. The king strode from his mother's parlor, slamming the door behind him.

The dowager queen trembled as she picked a yellow grape from a dish. She pinched the globule between tremulous talons, but did not eat.

A delicate hand pushed the door ajar.

"May I speak with you, madam?" a soft voice inquired.

"Is it you? Make haste and say what you need to say," the old queen replied peevishly. "I expect Adiuvo to attend me directly, and I desire no delay."

The young queen, Saibh, entered timorously. "Madam, I am troubled," she said, twisting her hands into the folds of her richly embroidered gown. "I ask for your support. In my position, there is no one else in whom I might confide."

"What are you saying? Is there some problem?"

"No, no. That is to say, there is a problem, in a way. I mean—" Desperately Saibh looked around for some source of inspiration and confidence, but found none. The shrilling of the canaries drilled thin holes in the air.

"You are not intending to complain to me about Uabhar, I hope," said the dowager queen.

"Oh!" The younger woman started. A blush of shame and confusion heated her pretty features. "Not at all. Never!"

"I have always deemed you were not fit to be his wife."

Aghast, Saibh stared at her for one moment, before hastening away.

The old queen popped the grape into her mouth and bit down on it.

Canaries shrieked. Handmaidens fluttered.

The next visitor was Secundus Adiuvo Constanto Clementer, his arrival announced by the queen's private secretary. The druid was clad chiefly in white, and his barren head shone like a polished ball of rosewood. A few wisps of hair fringed the lower edges of his scalp. He bowed before the mother of the king.

"You are come at last, Adiuvo," she said. "I have been waiting."

"At your service, Your Majesty."

"Tell me your opinion of my appearance."

"You look well in yellow, Your Majesty," he answered smoothly.

"Adiuvo, I live on summer squash and lemons, butter, egg yolks and honey, cheeses and mustard pickles, the flesh of yellow plums, the skin of yellow apples, and saffron cakes. How should I be well?"

"It sounds a reasonable diet to me, madam."

"No, no, no, Adiuvo, not this time around. I have been yellow on too many occasions. I wish to change, yet what color is left to me? I have tried all the colors. Sometimes I find myself on the verge of feeling I might like to try more than one color at a time. I am sick and tired of eating this way. I feel ill. I long for a variety of foods, a range of choices. But, Adiuvo, I am afraid to risk it."

Gently, he said, "Why?"

The dowager queen's face crumpled, as though she might cry. "I admit—I am frightened."

"Frightened of what?"

"Of breaking them."

"Breaking what?"

"The rules."

"They are your rules," the druid said perceptively. "You can change them."

" 'Tis not that easy."

Secundus Clementer clasped his hands behind his back and paced the floor. After nine steps a notion apparently struck him. He paused, took a deep breath, and raised his index finger instructively.

"Madam, what makes you happy?"

She said, "My three beautiful sons. They bring the only gladness in my life."

"In that case," he said, "think on them. It may be that in your source of happiness lies your answer."

"Very well. I shall consider this. Now go away, Adiuvo. I feel my palpitations coming on. Leave me!"

Having performed another bow, the druid obeyed.

Queen Saibh ignored the patter of satin slippers that betrayed the fact that her ladies-in-waiting were faithfully following her along the palace corridors. She made her way to the nursery, and entered swiftly. Her little son toddled toward her, and she stooped to gather him in her arms. Closely she held him, burying her face in his soft curls, murmuring, "My joy, my darling child, my sweet one."

Meanwhile in the East Wing Salon, Saibh's husband dismissed the messenger from High Darioneth and ordered his page to summon the Druid Imperius. His Majesty was restless. As the druid Clementer had done a few moments earlier, he strode up and down, but his demeanor was impatient rather than reflective. Draughts caused by his pacing stirred the extravagant tapestries adorning the walls and curtaining the doorways. The borders of his heavy velvet cloak brushed against one of the oaken tables, setting aquiver silver-gilt goblets and chalices, the wine-jug, the gold-mounted dishes of polished tiger's eye and agate.

A blaze thundered in the fireplace. Late afternoon light angled in spearshafts from the diamond panes of a tall casement, triple-arched, garlanded with carven imageries of fruits and flowers. It showed the King of Slievmordhu to be a man of middle height with solidly thewed, sloping shoulders. The once clear-cut bone-structure of his square face was beginning to be blurred by superfluous flesh. His mass of dark brown hair, carefully tended and gleaming, was combed back and bound at the back of the neck with a ribbon of crimson satin.

His household staff fidgeted uneasily. Their master was in a ferment. It was likely to mean trouble for them. They were relieved when Uabhar dismissed them from the chamber.

As usual, the Druid Imperius was clothed in robes of virginal baudekyn, appliquéd with expensive samite. Small of stature, wizened and stooped, he did not seem to have the bearing of an influential man. His fleams of eyes, however, betrayed the shrewd and calculating machinery housed in his skull. No sooner had the Master of the Sanctorum entered than Uabhar, without much preamble, began to speak.

"We have received word from High Darioneth. It seems the weathermasters have under their protection some girl who is a scion of the Sorcerer of Strang."

The eyes of Primoris Asper Virosus flamed like twin pyres. He was chilly of spirit; rarely were his emotions excited. This was one of those uncommon moments.

"A scion of Strang? Why then, we must demand that they hand her over at once!"

"You are too hasty," said Uabhar. "The Storm Lord has written that this chit has already, without our knowledge, opened the Dome and entered it. He professes she took no treasure out of the fortress, and left the gates standing wide open."

"By the axe of Míchinniúint!" swore Virosus. "How dare the puddle-makers steal into the Dome behind our backs!"

"The Storm Lord testifies this girl undertook the venture without his support."

"A likely tale. They have undermined us!"

"Primoris, surely you must be aware that Maelstronnar considers himself too honorable to propagate an outright lie. We must take him at his word. All the same, we shall send troops to the Dome this very hour."

"I am surprised you have not already ordered their dispatch."

Uabhar distended his mouth in a smile that some might privately have considered ingratiating or otherwise insincere. "Hardly would I have done so without consulting the Tongue of the Fates."

The druid acknowledged the comment with a rudimentary nod. "As for the sorcerer's get," he declared, "she is, it would appear, of no value to us."

"Nevertheless," rejoined his sovereign, "we shall have an appointment with her."

"Oh yes," agreed the druid. "Most certainly." A clapping and creaking of fast-beating wings drew his attention to the casement. Like a sudden flurry of ruffled petticoats, a flock of pigeons was flying past the palace on their way to the lofts at the Sanctorum.

A blizzard of shadows on golden radiance crossed the book that lay open before Secundus Adiuvo Constanto Clementer. Seated in the Sanctorum's scriptorium, the druid glanced up from his writing as the bevy of birds rattled by the window. Replacing his quill-pen in the ink-well, he leaned on his white-sleeved elbow and sighed.

A look of concern puckered his assistant's round face. He was anxious about his mentor's welfare, worried that he might have taken too much work upon himself. In addition to attending to his druids' duties and composing a treatise on ideology, Clementer was writing a book about the famous Iron Tree and the jewel that had once been trapped therein.

"What is it, master?" he inquired, approaching the Secundus. "Pardon my boldness, sir, but it seems to me you have been somewhat troubled, these past weeks, or maybe months."

"You are not mistaken, Almus." Clementer continued to gaze through the panes. He watched as the pigeons circled the lofts three times before swooping to alight. "I persevere with *A Treatise on the Iron Tree*; however, I find myself unable to focus. Last week," he expounded, "word came to me that Marquis Feighcullen won an enormous sum at the gaming tables of the Earl of Drum Criach. As you know, Almus, Drum Criach is an honorable gentleman who is benevolent toward his vassals and generous to the poor. Feighcullen, on the other hand, is a miser who is forever beating his servants, and would not so much as give the time of day to his own grandmother. Yet luck was on the side of the worse man. Where is the rightness in that?"

"Too lofty for the comprehension of mortalkind are the motives of the Fates," Almus Agnellus murmured formulaically.

"Another question perplexes me also," said Clementer, without turning around. "As you know, I like to pursue many branches of inquiry simultaneously. My recent study of longevity and happiness among the populace appears to be producing evidence that, contrary to what we have been taught, it is the manner in which people live and the way they view their circumstances that largely influences their life spans and their fortunes."

"Master," mumbled Agnellus, more agitated by the moment, "I am sure you are right, but when all is said and done it is the Four Fates who decide such matters."

"Do not be anxious," said Clementer, looking about and bestowing a preoc-cupied smile on his assistant. "I am not foolish enough to bring trouble upon us by confiding my doubts to others."

Secundus and his assistant subsided into a quiet, companionable reverie. Voices drifted faintly on the breeze from some distant cell of the Sanctorum, two Druids' Scribes' Hands deep in earnest debate. "But we need something *new*," insisted the first. "Too often have we prated about white stags and white horses. People are beginning to question the *authenticity* of our prophecies."

"What about a white unicorn?" the second voice suggested. "The white uni-corn shall—ehrm—shall bleed into the silver dish."

"No, no!" the first shouted irritably. "Not the silver dish again!"

"The silver chalice?"

"An improvement." After a pause, "And not blood. We *always* mention blood. It's becoming tedious."

"The white unicorn shall *spit* into the silver chalice? Cough hair-balls?"

"If you cannot talk sense don't talk at all," the first voice snapped.

"But what is the matter with—"

"The white unicorn shall *drink* from the silver chalice," the first interrupted, "and . . . and . . ."

"And the sword of the sun shall fall into darkness in the tomb beneath the mountain!" the second voice announced enthusiastically.

"For Ádh's sake! Can you not conjecture anything original? Swords, suns, darkness, tombs, mountains—the same old symbols, over and over again."

"All right, what about—ehrm—spoons and stars? Cradles and valleys?"

"Not bad. The silver—no, rather the *crimson* star shall shine upon the cradle in the valley—"

The second voice interrupted, as if struck with sudden inspiration, "And we always say *virgins*. What if we say instead *whores*? That would make the assem-blage wake up and listen. . . ."

The wind changed and the voices faded, blown away.

Persisting in his study of the sunset beyond the walls of the scriptorium, Clementer said, "And yesterday I was told that the wife of Neilus O'Breacáin passed from this life, and she having been so ill for such a long while. And Neilus with six little children to feed, and him with not a coin of his savings left, on ac-count of having given all his money to the Sanctorum to get intercession so that the Fates might permit his wife to live. Where is the rightness in that, Almus?"

His assistant admitted defeat. "There seems no rightness in it, master," he mumbled, hanging his head despondently.

"And these disturbances they are having at Carrickmore," said Clementer, "these druids giving themselves the title the 'Sandals of Doom.' They delude others, but what's worse, they delude themselves. Surely it is clear to any man of sound judgment that by claiming that Lord Doom allots them special preference, they are seeking to elevate their status, to gain more power over others, to try to undermine the Sanctorum."

"The Primoris certainly sees it that way," said Agnellus. "As you know, sir, he has proclaimed this splinter group disloyal to the Fates and therefore subject to their wrath. He declares the Fates decree that they must be punished."

"Well I, for one, question the judgment of the Fates," said Clementer.

"Master!" The moon of Agnellus's face broadened in alarm. "Speak softly, prithee, lest you are overheard!"

"Thank you for your concern, brother." The Secundus turned away from the window. He appeared to become truly aware of his assistant's presence for the first time, and smiled sadly. "I trust you," he said, "even while knowing my trust must be a terrible burden to you. Forgive me."

"There is nothing to forgive. I am honored by your confidence."

Clementer sat for a few moments with his head in his hands, then resumed his monologue. "A belief system imprisoned within the man-made trappings of hierarchies, punishments, rituals, and so forth, which are created solely for the purpose of giving certain people power over others—that is what I call a political institution. 'Tis wrong to manipulate people's beliefs as a way of making them do one's will."

"Sir, I caution you!" Agnellus darted a glance over his shoulder. "If anyone should hear—"

"I am discreet, Almus, but that is exactly my point! Am I not to be permitted to speak my own mind? Are my very thoughts to be censored?"

A lone feather drifted in at the window.

"The pigeons," said Clementer, capturing the airborne plume and twirling it between thumb and forefinger.

"Your pardon, sir, I do not follow you."

"The pigeons. *Your* pigeons, Almus, the birds you care for. Remember the bird-feeder?"

"Sir, shall I fetch you a cool drink?"

"No. If you are nervous that I am losing my wits, rest assured, my head is clearer than it has ever been. Listen; you built that first bird-feeder so that whenever the pigeons pecked a lever, a grain of corn rolled down a chute into their feed-tray. Thus, if a pigeon pecked seven times, for example, it received seven grains."

"Yes, sir. And then I experimented, building a device that dispensed food when the pigeons pecked first one lever, then another, in sequence. They learned quickly. Very clever, my pigeons!"

"Naturally you recall what happened when the lazy pigeon-keeper took over your job and, in his idleness, allowed the feeders to jam and become erratic, dispensing grains at random?"

"I do, for I saw the results myself when next I visited the farm. My pigeons had no idea how they should behave in order to be fed. They were nodding their heads, spinning about, hopping from one foot to the other, pecking hither and thither, and acting like muddle-heads. They were trying to direct the feeding mechanism. If the grain popped out they thought it must have done so because of some action they had, by chance, performed just prior to the appearance of the food, so they repeated the action. When this failed to produce consistent results, and when grains appeared seemingly in response to some different form of behavior, they added more performances to their repertoires until they were waddling and pecking and cooing as if mad."

"They were performing *rituals*," said Clementer. "Rituals to influence a machine that distributed bounty at random, and with-held largesse for no reason whatsoever. Rituals to make the irrational appear rational, to make the uncertain seem to have a purpose. Rituals invented by the birds in sheer desperation, believing they could influence their own haphazard destiny."

Agnellus cleared his throat. "Ah—we are talking about pigeons, sir, are we not?"

"Oh yes, Almus, of course. Pigeons. Birds who have become superstitious as a way of comprehending the incomprehensible." Clementer let the feather fall from his fingers. "Brother, I am shattered," he whispered. "My life's work has been without meaning."

Agnellus was at a loss for words.

"I am considering leaving the Sanctorum," said the Secundus. "Perhaps I ought to go out into the wide world, to make a proper search for meaning."

His assistant fell to his knees, as if his limbs would no longer support him. His face was now as pale as the moon it resembled, and his hands trembled. "If you leave," he said, "prithee do not tell them why. For the sake of your life, compose some pretense; otherwise they will call you a traitor to the Sanctorum, and you know—you *know* the punishments for that!"

"I know," said Clementer, calmly. "I know."

He turned back to the window again and stared out at the turrets of the royal residence. Bathed by the red light of sunfall, pennants and banners were fluttering merrily from all the masts. Hothouse-forced daffodils blossomed in window-boxes on the queen's balconies.

Arran had foretold accurately; he scarcely slept during the sunless hours. His fervent desire to offer Jewel the ultimate gift—the chance of immortality—inflamed him, gnawed at him, goaded him to restless agitation. Any consideration for the rights of others to this supreme prize had long since been burned to vapor by the blaze of his ardor. Daylight, when at last it filtered through the clammy fogs of dawn, illuminated his face; still comely, although drained of color, save for two purplish crescents underscoring his eyes. Over a quick bite of breakfast, he and his companions negotiated a plan.

"We must work in pairs," he said, "as a precaution."

They all agreed.

Bliant said, "Arran, you and I shall explore these surroundings, seeking a way to reach this island. I suggest that you, Rivalen, might look after the campsite and *Wanderpath,* with Gahariet's help."

"No," said the older weathermage. "There is no reason for anyone to remain here watching the balloon. No mortal men dwell in these parts and our aircraft is effectively protected from eldritch meddlers. You yourself know; a myriad wight-deterrents are built into it! The walls of the cars are interwoven with thin iron wires and rowan twigs, studded with amber and bedecked with bells. As for the envelopes—spidersilk has the strength of steel, many times over! As added reassurance, the Druid Imperius has interceded with Ádh, begging for his goodwill to follow all our voyages—for what *that* is worth."

"Worth? Not a fig, of course," said Bliant, his mouth full of hazelnut cake. "If our aerostats withstand the exigencies of weather and travel, it is not because the druids have subtracted our coins and spoken to the air; 'tis because our vessels are sturdily constructed and skilfully piloted."

"Perhaps, at first, we ought to post a guard over *Wanderpath,*" said Gahariet. "After all, if it is tampered with, we shall find ourselves faced with a long walk home."

Rivalen said, "Nay—the Maelstronnar has promised that an air-crew will be sent to find us, if we do not return by the 24th of Tenember, or if they have reason to believe we are in need of rescue."

"In that case, we have all the time in the world," said Bliant with a grin. "Surely it cannot take us three weeks to plunder this wonderful Well! What say you, Arran?"

"I agree with Gahariet," said Arran. "However, if you wish, Rivalen, I shall stay here while you reconnoiter."

"Ach! You are killing yourself with courtesy, lad!" said Rivalen. "You've been chafing at the bit ever since we arrived. Go forth with Bliant and survey the situation!"

Arran needed no further excuse.

"Come, Ymberbaillé!" he said, and they were away.

Downhill through steep groves of juniper and ash they plunged, between stands of leafless linden, bird cherry and hazel, and amongst thickets of aromatic pine, until some five minutes later they emerged from the cover of the trees.

From the top of a grassy incline dotted with goat willows, they looked down. Still, deep, and profound were the waters of Stryksjø, guarded by battalions of dark pines and goat willows reflected in its steel-blue surface. This natural cistern was so enigmatically fathomless, so unruffled and heavy, it must surely possess power beyond imagining. In the mists that floated over its waters, islands seemed to hover rootless, like mirages. Age-old forests clothing the slopes marched down to drink, in places, at the water's edge. The valley of the lake cradled a great silence, an immense tranquillity, pierced and threaded only by desultory birdcalls. As the young weathermasters gazed upon the placid water they felt the pace of their hearts slow. Haste, curiosity, and perplexity seemed to drain from them, as snow-melt drained down the slopes to the lake. And all that was left was stillness, peace, and serenity, folded within the muscular arms of the wooded hills.

Beyond the opposite shore, the vista opened onto sweeping gorges and soaring mountain ranges. The first rays of the rising sun transformed the overcast to a facade of muted pearl. Billows and strands of altocumulus embraced the faces of the mountains, caressed their shoulders, and lingered in their valleys. In Grïmnørsland the clouds and the mountains were in love with each other.

"There!" said Arran. He jabbed the map he held in his hand, before pointing across the lake. Bliant narrowed his eyes as he traced Arran's gesture. The source of their interest was a gray-green hump, irregularly shaped, near the lake's center. It floated between two skies: the real one above, and the slightly rippled mirror-image below.

"Ragnkull," murmured Bliant.

"Now that we've got our bearings," said Arran, "let us make further reconnaissance."

Warily they began to make their way around the mossy brink, among the bare-branched goat willows.

All seemed peaceful, yet there was a sense of watchfulness everywhere. The morning had dawned somber, but the clouds were clearing, and now weak sunlight dripped down through them, making pools of light and shade on the hillsides and the water. The air began to move, disturbed by a tremulous breeze. Nothing remained still. Everything was shifting constantly. The foliage on the trees swaying, boughs nodding and dipping, detached leaves falling like a sparse rain, clouds blowing across the sky, the water's surface wrinkling and quivering: all was as restless as the ocean, yet anchored by deep roots and plunging stone footings to timelessness and stillness and enduring patience.

Later that morning, as the sun climbed to burn away the last of the mists, Arran and Bliant finished conducting their surveillance and returned to the campsite.

"What have you discovered?" asked Gahariet.

"Very little," replied Arran. "We scouted along the southern shores but found naught save trees, sedges, and rocks."

"When we take our turn we shall scour the northern shores," said Rivalen.

"What do you know of this region, Rivalen?" Bliant questioned.

"Alas, not a thing. I have never visited here before."

"Ah, well, it matters not," Bliant declared optimistically. "We may take our time to explore. There is no great need for haste."

"So you keep saying, Master Ymberbaillé," said Rivalen. "Howbeit, my bones are older than yours, and sleeping on the ground is not to their liking. Fain would I return to my feather bed, before too many decades elapse!"

After the four explorers had taken some refreshment together, Rivalen and Gahariet went off to reconnoiter while the others remained to watch over the aerostat.

The two scouts pushed their way through a thicket of speckled alders choked with brakes of stunted hazel and clusters of snow daisies. They had not long been at it when Gahariet gave a shout. "Look, Master Hagelspildar! There is something ahead, showing through the trees!" After hastening toward the half-glimpsed shapes they found themselves at the foot of a broken stone column. Behind this pillar stood another, in worse repair. In his eagerness to find out more, Gahariet stumbled over some partially buried stairs, and fell, striking his knee on a crumbling outcrop of stone. Mumbling curses beneath his breath, he rolled on the ground, clasping his hands around the injured limb and nursing it to his chest.

"What's amiss?" Rivalen's throaty shout preceded his doughty form, which came crashing through the hazel bushes.

"'Tis naught," Gahariet said, between gritted teeth. "Give me a moment only, and I will be on my feet again."

The older weathermaster looked around. "Methinks these are the ruins of some ancient Oratorium," he said. "The pedestals of these columns stand on a circular platform. Between them lie blasted heaps of mortar and tile—the remains of a roof that has fallen in long ago. It was never in my knowledge that there was once an Oratorium in these parts."

He began to poke about among the lichen-blistered ruins. Gahariet rubbed his knee vigorously and decided to try putting some weight on the injured leg, but as he made to stand up he caught sight of a lick of color amidst the drifts of crushed masonry. Ignoring his discomfort, he brushed away some of the detritus and found, beneath, part of a floor inlaid with mosaic tiles. The mosaic formed a design, and as he cleaned away more of the debris he was able to discern an image that had once decorated the surface of the Oratorium's platform.

"What have you found?" Rivalen spoke from behind Gahariet's shoulder.

"Only some ceramic embellishment," answered the journeyman. "Somewhat of the type with which druids are wont to titivate their establishments, in order to impress the populace."

Both men regarded the tiled pictures for a few moments. Then, "Up you get," said Rivalen, helping Gahariet to his feet. "We must move on. There is a lot more to be investigated."

At the clearing amongst the junipers, for want of anything better to do Arran and Bliant had removed some gear from their packs for inspection and maintenance. Bliant was polishing a leather brigandine, studded with rivets where iron plates were fastened to the inside. Arran was checking the links of a hauberk.

"Do you believe such armor as this will be of much use against the arrows of Stryksjø's wights?" Bliant asked.

His companion shrugged his shoulders. "Narngalis chain mail is good protection against man-made barbs. Whether it can withstand the eldritch darts of Stryksjø's hunters remains to be seen."

He put away the mail shirt and was about to begin sharpening his knife when a figure that looked like a very small boy came walking out of the trees.

The two young men held themselves utterly still.

This newcomer was clad in baggy brown leggings, and a short green tunic belted at the middle. His leather slippers were extraordinarily elongated in shape, and tapered at the toes. His hat was brimless, fitting closely around the skull and rising to a point at the crown. In his hands he was holding a wooden tankard. He stopped right in front of the weathermasters and lifted a quaint little face to them. "Please, sirs," he piped, "gie me a drop o' ale for me poor old mither what's feeling poorly."

Simultaneously, the young men glanced at each other.

Bliant raised an eyebrow. "The lad's a mighty long way from home," he said under his breath. "There is not a village or hut or any shelter of humankind within a hundred miles of this place."

Arran stood up and fetched a half-empty four-gallon firkin from the storage area beside one of the tents. "We shall fill the cup for your mother," he said to their odd visitor. "Hold it out." The boy did so, whereupon Arran turned the tap and let the brown ale flow into the tankard.

It poured and poured.

A minute later, Bliant said suspiciously, "Isn't it full yet?" He peered into the vessel. The level of the foaming liquid reached only halfway up the sides. Startled, he exclaimed, "Blow me away!" Arran was as nonplussed as his friend. After another minute the firkin ran empty. Torn between reluctance to surrender a fine brew and the rules of courtesy, Bliant said, "Isn't a couple of gallons enough for your mother, lad?"

The little fellow merely stood there, still holding out his tankard. "Ye said ye'd fill it," he said, directing a reproachful gaze toward Arran.

"Indeed, I did say that. I shall fetch more."

As Arran went to retrieve a second cask, Bliant grabbed him by the sleeve and whispered in his ear, "That is the last one! We brought only two."

"No matter," hissed Arran. "A promise must be kept."

The other rolled his eyes and muttered something about "shameful tricks" and "supernatural greediness," but made no further objection.

The young Maelstronnar broached the second firkin and the boy, or boy-simulacrum, thrust his tankard beneath the tap. A single drop fell in, and at once the vessel was full to the brim.

A wide grin spread across the visitor's exotic features, "I'm mighty obliged to ye, sir," he said. After bowing politely without spilling so much as a fleck of froth, he trotted away.

"How wondrous strange," murmured Arran, staring after the retreating figure.

"Just make sure the tap's properly turned off," said his friend. "With only one firkin left we don't want any spillage."

"Did you see that?" cried Arran.

Bliant looked about, but the visitor had disappeared among the junipers. "See what?"

"Just before he reached the trees, he seemed to—to *shrink*."

"I should have thought he was small enough to begin with. The top of his cap was barely level with my knee."

"He dwindled to the size of my thumb. What's more, methinks he sprouted a rattish *tail*."

"Must have been using glamour on us," observed Bliant, "as if it were not enough to make fools of us by presenting a bottomless tankard." As he helped Arran lug the cask back to the storage area, he added glumly, "We'd best drink the rest of the ale tonight. Who can tell how many more of those little beggars are out there."

Evening turned the lake to sheets of solid pewter, the hills to slate, the clouds to ash outlined with shimmer, and the sky to nacre. Twilight was gathering by the time Rivalen and Gahariet returned to the campsite, where Arran and Bliant impatiently awaited them.

"We found a ruin, built long ago by the druids," said Rivalen, "but nothing else of consequence."

"'Tis a pity," said Arran. Exasperatedly he tossed a small branch into the campfire. "I had hoped for some small clue, at least, to aid us."

The four adventurers conversed in low voices while Bliant fed twigs to the flames, which threw themselves into the air like gouts of golden syrup and sent up sparks.

At length, Arran said, "I am tired of sitting here. So far we have discovered no way to reach the island, and despite what you say, Bliant, we do not have all the time in the world. We will soon be hunting for food if our rations run low, and besides, we are expected at the naming ceremony in Rua at New Year's."

"What's more," Bliant added knowledgeably, "you are fretting for the sight of a pair of blue eyes—oof!"

The breath was forced from his lungs with a *whoosh,* as he landed on his back. Next moment Arran threw himself at his friend in a headlong tackle, but Bliant rolled aside at the last instant. He was endeavoring to scramble out of reach when Arran pounced a second time, and they rolled over and over down the slope, locked in a bout of wrestling, yelling delightedly, grappling like pups suddenly released from captivity, overflowing with pent-up high spirits.

"You'll be drawing the attention of every nocturnal wight for miles around," Rivalen warned, and subdued by that sobering admonition, the two young men abandoned their mock fight.

Arran stood up and brushed dead leaves from his clothing. "If any night-loving lurkers dwell in the lake or on the isles, I should like to know what they look like," he announced. "I am going down to the water's edge."

"I shall accompany you," said Rivalen. His tone carried such authority that neither Bliant nor Gahariet offered argument.

The two weathermages shouldered their way through the trees and bushes until they reached the lake's reedy brink. There they stood side by side in silence, gazing out across the gleaming waters, where evening mists coagulated, coiling like translucent serpents. A loud and melancholy avian braying caused them to look up. A pair of birds was rowing across the darkening cloud ceiling.

"Strange," mused Rivalen. "Methinks I have not before seen or heard any sign of ducks hereabouts."

"All the ducks have migrated south for the winter, Master Hagelspildar. Those are brown bitterns."

No sooner had Arran spoken than a needle erupted from an islet and zoomed straight into the air. A puff of feathers exploded. One of the bitterns tumbled out of the sky, passing a second lethal bolt on the way down. An instant later its mate plummeted, scattering plumes. The stricken fowls fell into the lake, whereupon there was a flurry in the water, a splashing, a reaching arm the color of slime, then nothing but widening ripples.

"By all that's wicked!" said Rivalen. "It appears the tales are true. Unseelie marksmen do inhabit the islands—and the waters are perilous. Come away, Arran. Let us go back to the bright fireside!"

As they turned their backs on Stryksjø they could not help but note, at the corners of vision, the dusk forming itself into shapes that glided through the trees along the shore.

"Methinks we have attracted some of the Gray Neighbors," said Rivalen. They quickened their pace, half-running up the slope until they burst into the flame-illumined clearing.

"Trows are nigh," Arran said, as he and Rivalen dashed into the circle of light. "Be wary."

Gahariet and Bliant leaped to their feet and drew their knives, peering warily into the gloom.

For a time, nothing happened. Even the faint breeze of evening had stilled. The weathermasters could hear no sound save for the faint grunts and claps of waterfowl at some distant marsh. They sensed, nonetheless, the presence of creatures, and caught glimpses of movement outside the sphere of firelight.

The night grew older.

The weathermasters wrapped themselves in their furs and leathers against the bitter cold, but remained outside the tents, so that they could keep watch. None could sleep; the tension, the sense of being surrounded by unseen entities, was too compelling. Eventually, young Gahariet dozed. Around midnight, when the fire was dying down, a small stooped figure, clad in gray draperies, limped into the outer glow of the firelight. Its crumpled face was pitted with two sad, baggy eyes, its long nose drooped at the end, and its hands and feet seemed incongruously large for such a small, skinny body.

"Hae ye got ony sulver?" This was the eternal plea of trows, who loved silver above all things.

Gahariet awoke with a snort. His eyes widened in astonishment.

"No," said Rivalen.

The trow lingered, but said nothing more.

Then a trow-wife appeared a few feet away from the first wight, half obscured by darkness, half described by the dim radiance of the flames. Her large head was swathed in a gray shawl, and in her bony arms she was carrying a ragged bundle.

"Hae ye got ony clean water to bathe the bairn?"

"There's an entire lake full of water a stone's throw from here," Bliant muttered under his breath.

Disregarding his friend's comment, Arran poured some of the crew's drinking water into a pail and set it down in front of the dwarfish being. Aided by a second trow-wife, she unwrapped the bundle and began to wash the grotesque trow infant, much to Bliant's disgust and Gahariet's fascination.

While the weathermasters watched, Arran became aware of a soft rustling and shuffling amongst the shadows at his back. He spun around and swooped. Two child-sized figures scattered from his assault, their gray garments flapping.

"Be off with you!" Arran said, shooing them away.

Rivalen glared at the would-be thieves, who were scurrying off with an awkward, irregular gait. "So, you thought you'd distract us and then go nosing amongst our possessions! Trying to steal silver eh? We told you—we have none!"

"They did not disturb the aircraft," Bliant observed, with relief. "The charms kept them at bay. As long as the balloon remains safe, we have a means of escaping should any emergencies arise."

Apparently heedless of the commotion, the two trow-wives dried and rewrapped the bairn. Murmuring to each other in their own language, the wights were making as if to depart when Arran called out to them: "How can we cross the water?"

Eldritch wights lacked the ability to tell lies, as everyone knew, and trows were no exception.

"Tae our knowin', that ye cannae do," solemnly said the first trow-wife, she who had asked for the clean water. "Boats cannae cross Stryksjø. Drowners and fuathan rive boats. Waterhorses devour boatmen."

"Would it be possible to build a bridge?" asked Arran, as he had asked once before, in another place.

"Fuathan break bridges."

"Is there any chance we might cross Stryksjø by sky-balloon?"

"Ælf-archers are cunning. They are not shooting awry. Balloons shall fall."

The trow-wives continued to withdraw into the gloom, but Arran said desperately, "Tell us about the Well of Dew. Is it out there?"

The wights shrieked, and would have fled except that Arran thwarted them. He stared straight at them, without blinking, ignoring their moans. His unfaltering scrutiny seemed to hold them immobilized. "Tell us," he insisted.

"On Ragnkull Island in Stryksjø lies the Well of Dew," they cried shrilly. They would say nothing else. Ultimately Arran gave in and released them, whereupon they vanished into the night.

The impression of unseen crowds dissipated, and the weathermasters intuited that once again they were alone in the juniper glade. They relaxed a little, but did not let down their guard.

"I shall take first watch," said Rivalen. "The rest of you, bed down in the warmth of the tents and seize what sleep you can. There are precious few hours until the morning."

"Arran, how did you prevent the henkies from escaping when you wished to question them?" Gahariet wanted to know, as Rivalen stoked the fire and the young men rearranged their sleeping-furs and leathers.

" 'Tis an old trick I learned from my father. As long as one keeps one's eye on them they are unable to disappear. By that means I had hoped to learn something of use to us, but I have failed."

Diminutive points of light glowed forth from amongst the foliage of the junipers at the glade's borders. It was as if the boughs had been festooned with strings of miniature lamps; gentle pink, pastel green, and mellow gold, so soft and mild their shining seemed to be filtered through gauze.

"What's that?" Gahariet blurted.

After a pause, Rivalen said pensively, "Methinks 'tis nothing ill. I daresay they are merely the lights of the hurtless siofra. Be unworried. Sleep, now. I shall waken you all if anything seems amiss."

"I shall sleep under the stars tonight," said Arran. He rolled himself up in furs and a sheet of canvas, and stretched out on the ground.

The temperature dropped. A high-altitude wind was blowing the clouds away. In the clear skies, stars evolved. Those that shone from far off were dim, gauzy scarves of mist; the closer stars sparkled brilliantly, hard, crystalline points, purest dazzling white.

Crossing his arms behind his head, Arran lay back and gazed at the splendor of the constellations, without seeing it. Once, he had placed duty to Ellenhall above all else, but love had altered him. These days, fealty to that code stood second in line. Jewel was never absent from his thoughts. Always, in some guarded corner of his mind, he treasured a picture of her. Sometimes, when he was free to wander in the labyrinths of his own reasoning, he would allow himself to gaze at this mental image. He would dwell on her laugh, her gestures, the blue flash of her eyes, some chance remark she had made in passing, the way her hair lay against her cheek like a fan of softest swan's down. He would visualize the graceful way she walked, the lissom willow-wand of her waist, the svelte contours of her form, and after torturing himself with bittersweet fancies he would become sick with longing, and endeavor to thrust her from his awareness in order that he might find peace.

Gradually, slumber overtook Arran, Bliant, and Gahariet. Later, Rivalen passed the duty of the Watch to Bliant, who, at the end of his shift, was replaced by Gahariet.

Near morning before dawn, when darkness still lay across the countryside, the sleepers were roused by the voice of the journeyman calling urgently, "Awake! Awake!"

Immediately the weathermasters cast aside their covers and sprang from the tents, snapping to alertness. Gahariet hurled handfuls of kindling on the fire, causing it to flare.

A black horse was trotting around the outskirts of the clearing.

It moved so lightly through the soundless rain of starlight that it seemed not subject to the attraction of the ground, but suspended from above on invisible wires. Graceful and fluid were its steps, elegant its shape, exquisite the sheen of its hide. It was like a beast made of molten obsidian, the volcanic glass, with its shiny, curved surfaces.

Courteously, timorously, the lovely creature approached the men, extending its long head inquiringly, as if to sniff at them. Rivalen snatched a burning stick from the fire and the horse jumped back.

"Not so hasty, Master Hagelspildar," murmured Bliant, placing a restraining hand on Rivalen's elbow. "Conceivably this is a real horse. Perhaps it has escaped from its owners and is now lost, seeking human company. See how fine and well-bred it is."

"Do not be taken in," warned Rivalen. "There are things in the wilderness that are masters of deception. It is hardly likely one would find a tame horse out here in the remote regions of Grïmnørsland."

"And yet," Bliant said wistfully, "fain would I ride such a steed."

The horse pricked up its ears and trotted closer to Bliant. It stood shyly, at a safe distance from Rivalen and the fire; then, extending one foreleg like a dancer, it bowed prettily.

"See!" Bliant cried delightedly. "It offers itself to be ridden. How skillfully it has been trained!" He stepped toward the creature, but Arran pulled him back.

"Don't go near it," he advised. "Look away, Bliant. You ought to know better! It is drawing you under its spell. Take heed also, Gahariet; do not look at the horse." Firmly he grasped the arms of his friends, and refused to let them go.

Rivalen advanced on the creature, waving the firebrand in one hand, his long knife in the other. "Avaunt!" he shouted. "Avaunt, you wicked wight, or we shall smite you with cold iron!"

Coquettishly, the winsome steed pranced a little.

"Bo shrove!" Rivalen called out the ancient words of warding, and drew back his knife-wielding arm.

Suddenly the horse flattened its ears to its skull and drew back its lips. Its maw, instead of housing the square teeth of a herbivore, was filled with the long, cruel spikes of fangs. The manifestation snorted wrathfully and galloped away. Through the still freeze of the night, the men heard the sound of the splash as it entered the lake-water.

The fire ate itself away to a smolder.

"That was a wicked beguiler, and no mistake," said Rivalen, sheathing his knife.

There was no more sleep to be had before dawn.

The weathermasters sat cross-legged, or leaned against their packs. Scant conversation took place between them. It was a habit instilled by training that at times when there was little else to do but wait and watch, they would put forth their *brí*-working faculties to diagnose the current state of the weather. Invisible rivers became apparent to them; currents of chilled air flowing down the surrounding slopes into valleys and dingles and frost-hollows. As their awareness extended outward through the plenum they detected temperature, wind speeds and directions, and cloud cover. They traced systems of high or low pressure, and sensed electrical forces building up and discharging. They quantified humidity, and inhaled the scents of forest and soil.

The eight winds blew through their consciousness.

Arran, who could reach farthest, perceived gravity waves high in the troposphere, moving across deep convective clouds. They were creating lee waves above the mountains. Higher still, and he was cognizant of powerful jet streams flowing at great speeds through the lower stratosphere. Extending his perception in the opposite direction, he became aware of volcanic activity deep beneath the crust of the world, and of juvenile water being pumped up from far down in the mantle, to be expelled at the surface for the first time since its conception.

In the forest clearing where the weathermasters bivouacked, the temperature had plummeted. Vapor from the air had condensed, forming ice-crystals that coated the surfaces of each grass-blade. Some of the leaves and branches around the glade were now adorned with bunches of spiky white needles of hoar frost. Upon encountering the drop in temperature, the fogs that had stealthily arisen from Stryksjø began to congeal also, forming rough crystals, white and opaque, and depositing them as rime on every needle of every juniper tree. Black-boled, black-boughed stood the junipers, but their hair turned gray-white, as if they had aged many years over a few hours.

Far away, over the western ocean, a stationary depression with an associated cold front was building up. The weathermasters sensed it, as their *brí*-faculties coursed through the regional troposphere.

Yet, for all their skills, how could they guess that many leagues away Fionnuala and four of her mercenaries were sleeping, while the fifth kept watch? How could they suspect that with each passing day the archer with the poisoned arrows was closing in on them?

Later that morning the sun climbed high above the southern peaks of the Nordstüren, the lofty ranges fencing northern Grïmnørsland from Narngalis. Its dilute rays melted the frosts and hunted the mists of the lake country so that they must flee to hide in hanging valleys. Bright daylight flecked the diamond-clear water of Stryksjø with glinting silver fish-scales, and enriched the colors of the landscape: the brilliant greens of the mosses, the black-browns of the rocks, the albescence of the snows on the highest crags.

The most recent explorations of the weathermasters had proved fruitless, and they returned to the campsite in low spirits.

"Two nights have we bided here, and we are no closer to reaching the isle," Arran said. "Impatience gnaws at me."

"Hunger gnaws at *me,*" said Gahariet. "The sun is at its zenith. It must be time for the midday meal."

"Dine if you wish," said the young Maelstronnar. "For my part, I shall go to look at these ruins of which you and Rivalen spoke."

"In that case I will come with you," said Bliant, prudently filling a pouch with dried fruits, to bring as rations.

Without much difficulty the two young men forced a path through the hazel brakes and located the site of the abandoned Oratorium. Once they had arrived, Bliant sat on the remains of the stairs and munched desiccated medlars, while Arran investigated. In due course he came upon the mosaic floor discovered by Gahariet, and knelt to study the designs.

The pictures, although chipped and mutilated by weathering, were still legible. They appeared to depict an old druidic favourite, "The Marvels of the Fates," a tableau in which Lord Ádh was always shown walking on treetops or oceans or clouds, Míchinniúint, Lord Doom, flew unaided through the air, Cinniúint, Lady Destiny, passed unscathed through fire carrying her spindle, and an empty space was left for Mí-Ádh, Lady Misfortune, because she had become invisible.

"What have you learned?" Bliant's voice was distorted by a mouthful of food.

"Nothing," said Arran, in despair. "Nothing at all."

Having so far discovered nothing to further the quest, he sank into silent despondency.

Weathermastery

Deep in the wilds of Grïmnørsland, Fionnuala Aonarán and her five mercenaries were galloping through a beech forest. They had been traveling for more than a fortnight—since 6th Ninembre, when they set out from Cathair Rua. Their journey had been fast and hard.

Through dark forests they had passed, and over rolling water-meadows, across bridges that spanned rivers of ice, and around the rocky shores of tarns layered beneath mists. In this rugged land the streams flowed fast and noisy; the winds were edged with broken glass. Blowing clouds and snowy peaks pondered on their reflections in profound lakes whose steep shores were clothed with tiers of black alder, elm, birch, and maple. Long cascades of snow-melt, chained in rainbows, tumbled down sheer precipices.

The landscape's beauty eluded the travelers. Its harshness did not.

The wilderness of this western kingdom teemed with eldritch wights. It being a region of many waters, it was the haunt of numerous waterhorses, fuathan, lake-maidens, and watercattle. The placid surfaces of the lakes hid the secret abodes of aughiskis, phookas, cabyllushteys, and kelpies; the lairs of blood-thirsty fuathan that were nameless, the dwelling-places of the gentle, seelie asrai and the gwragged annwn, the crodh-mara and the gwartheg-y-llyn. The forests harbored an assortment of seelie and unseelie entities, including bogies and bogles, hobyahs and red-caps, warners and the melancholy trows. Murderous duergars roamed there, and hobgoblins and Jacks-in-Irons. Compared with these deadly incarnations, the wolverines and brown bears seemed relatively undaunting.

Encounters with dangerous wights hampered the progress of Fionnuala and her henchmen. More than once they were forced to flee for their lives, or to make wide detours around perilous places. Ruthlessly, the riders pushed their horses to the limits. Three of their mounts perished from exhaustion and ill-treatment. They stole replacements from remote settlements, and when the stolen horses collapsed beneath them they thieved some more.

These sparse villages were tiny. Steeply pitched roofs topped houses that huddled together for warmth. Built of locally quarried stone, they looked to be growing out of the hillsides. Their chimneys stood up like rows of trees, with smoke for foliage. Behind the houses the mountains towered, their shoulders patched with snow. Villages were useful to Fionnuala's band. They supplied horses; they also supplied food, which the men seized at knifepoint. Fionnuala had no time to waste on the courtesies of hospitality.

"Speed is of the essence," she would say. Ever she looked to the skies, searching for the white mote of thistledown that signified a weathermasters' balloon. "Curse them and their aircraft," she would rail. "We must beat them. We must be pressing on, without rest, or they will overtake us. Perhaps they have already done so. Perhaps they have passed us in the sky, and I have not spied them."

"What's the prize we seek?" the men wanted to know.

"You are not paid to ask questions. You shall see when we get there."

Settlements were few, and therefore food supplies were limited. Sometimes at dusk, they hunted, in order to avoid becoming weak from lack of nourishment. Wielding her crossbow, Fionnuala shot hares and squirrels. Once, she brought down a young reindeer.

"'Tis not inconceivable the weathermaster reached High Darioneth by the 20th," Fionnuala calculated, muttering to herself. "If he departed by air on the same day, he would have arrived at the lake by now. Nonetheless, if that is true 'tis possible he has not managed to obtain the prize yet. There might well be difficulties. He believes he has limitless time to surmount any challenges. He has no notion that I am on the trail. He has no reason to hasten. It might yet be myself who is the winner."

She scanned the skies once more, then jabbed her heels into her horse's flanks, shouted to the men, and galloped away.

At the site of the ruined Oratorium Bliant Ymberbaillé finished chewing and began idly throwing the medlar-pits at the decaying stub of a column.

His third pitch missed the mark and the missile landed amid a patch of alpine spear-grass. Instantly a shrill shrieking broke out, mingled with indignant jabbering. The grass-stems shivered. The shiver traveled, passing away through the hazels and snow daisies, and the hubbub faded.

"Methinks our presence here at Stryksjø has attracted plenty of onlookers," surmised Bliant. " 'Twould be wise of us to speak softly, if we speak of important matters. Our every word is likely to be overheard."

There was no response to be had from Arran.

"Let's go, my friend," Bliant said, hurling the last of the fruit-stones into the hazel brakes. "This place hides no secrets, and sleeveless pursuit grows tedious."

Arran left off his close examination of the old mosaics and rose to his feet. "As you wish," he said absently.

Together they beat a path back to the campsite, Bliant whistling as he walked, the other thoughtful and silent.

"What's on your mind?" Bliant asked, eventually noting his friend's unwonted taciturnity.

"An extraordinary notion has occurred to me. I am formulating a stratagem, which I shall reveal to all when we reach camp."

Bliant allowed his friend to deliberate and did not question him further.

Back at the campsite the four weathermasters seated themselves around the fire, crosslegged on their canvas groundsheets.

"Master Ymberbaillé tells us you have been inspired," Rivalen said to the young Maelstronnar.

"In sooth, I have. It came to me as I gazed upon the tiles in the Oratorium. In how many ways is it possible to cross water? One might go by boat or bridge or by air, but there is a fourth method."

His companions regarded him quizzically.

"One might walk across," said Arran.

After a pause, Rivalen said, "Surely you jest."

"One might walk across without sinking, if water were solid," said Arran. "And what is solid water, but ice?"

"By all the storms of Winter!" Gahariet said incredulously. "You don't mean to freeze the entire lake, do you?"

Bliant burst out laughing. "But that is marvelous!" he cried. "The best invention I've heard of since Darglistel engineered a secret entrance into the larder at Long Gables!" Then he subjoined, " 'Tis a shame it will not work, of course."

"Why should it not?" argued Arran. "We are four in number, and between us we can command formidable power. Hereabouts, the temperatures are already low. We could muster enough clouds to form heavy overcast during the day, thus keeping the area around Stryksjø shielded from incoming solar radiation, then drive away the clouds at night to allow maximum outgoing infrared radiation. If we can do that, there is a fair chance we might freeze the lake—or at least, solidify enough of it to form an ice-bridge between the near shore and Ragnkull Island."

"Even if such a feat were possible, 'twould take many days of prolonged effort to lower the temperature enough to crystallize such a huge volume of water," Rivalen pointed out.

"I have an idea!" said Gahariet excitedly. " 'Twould take but a single day to glaciate the lake if we were to devise some mechanism to rapidly bring down the sub-freezing air from the stratosphere!"

"That would have no success," Bliant contested. "The air would be warmed by adiabatic compression, so the required effect would be lost."

"To counteract adiabatic compression we might invoke extremely low surface pressure."

"Which would cause a super-storm of devastating magnitude and intensity, destroying every living thing throughout the length and breadth of Grïmnørsland!"

"Well then, you win," Gahariet conceded. "I had not considered the wider repercussions. Master Hagelspildar, is this notion of freezing a lake feasible at all?"

Animated discussion ensued. For an hour they debated, until, ultimately, it was mutually agreed that this wild proposition was in fact practicable. Furthermore, it appeared to be the only method that would enable them to reach the isle of the Well of Dew.

"Naturally, such an exploit will throw the normal weather into disorder," said Arran. "What say you, Rivalen? Would the Council condemn us?"

"It is never any slight matter to disturb the Great Equilibrium," the older mage said somberly, "yet since we weathermasters are willing to meddle with the atmosphere to save the orchards of Narngalis from ravaging winds, it seems even *more* appropriate to wield the *brí* to save the Four Kingdoms from the consequences of misuse of this Draught, in my opinion, and I am certain the other councillors would agree with me. I believe our course will be approved by Ellenhall in this singular case."

"Then our scheme has the support of both a senior councillor *and* the son of the Storm Lord," said Bliant, beaming triumphantly.

"And according to law," Rivalen continued, "in a situation such as this when a decision is required on the spot, and waiting for an exchange of messages with Rowan Green would cause unnecessary delay and keep us longer from our duties, the senior weathermage becomes the spokesperson for the Council."

Having settled this matter, they returned to the problem of how to go about freezing Lake Stryksjø.

Rivalen addressed Arran. "To speed up your suggested method," he said, "we might ensure that some snow falls during the days, perhaps by summoning part of the deep northerly airflow."

"An admirable plan," responded Arran. "Alternatively, instead of snow it might be easier to invoke enormous hailstorms, which would not cause such severe disruption of the broad-scale atmospheric flow."

"Prolific hailstorms would probably be permissible under our laws, but we would have to ensure the hailstones were not large enough to cause extensive damage to Grïmnørsland's forests."

Another hour passed in conference, while they assessed ways of harnessing and guiding various natural forces, and bending them to their will.

It was 24th Ninember, in the closing days of Autumn. Daylight hours were few, and the weathermasters spent the remainder of the afternoon studying the exact situation of local weather systems, making forecasts, and working out which systems to draw on, in what sequence, and to what measure.

"Such a prodigious exploit has never been attempted in the history of High Darioneth," muttered Bliant, not without pride and eager expectation.

"Another benefit," said Arran. "Locked beneath ice, any unseelie water-wights shall be unable to assault us."

"What of the archers that dwell on the islets?" Gahariet said.

"I have no remedy for that ill. That there will be risks associated with this undertaking, there is no doubt. The ice might be too thin in places to uphold the weight of a man, or malign island marksmen might pincushion an intruder with arrows, or our *brí*-powers might not endure for long enough to prevent a sudden thaw—many aspects of the plan may indeed go awry. One of us must go alone to find the Well of Dew while the rest remain ashore working and renewing the weathermastery. There will be peril for he who crosses the lake, and peril also for those who bide on land."

"I shall cross the lake," said Bliant.

"Nay, let it be me!" contended Gahariet.

"There is no man amongst us who would not play the hero," said Rivalen, "but who is best qualified? Can anyone deny that the *brí* is more potent in the son of the Maelstronnar than in any of us? If he is willing, which I doubt not, it should be he."

"I am willing," said Arran, and the way he said it caused his companions to stare wonderingly at him, for he had spoken those words as if swearing an oath of terrible significance. "I am willing," he repeated. "I shall assay for the Draught."

"They will make songs about this mighty deed," said Gahariet, grinning and clapping Arran on the back.

Come twilight, the four men of High Darioneth had completed their preparations and were ready to embark on their unprecedented venture. As the sun
began to deliquesce behind the trees in the west, and long shadows extended
their arms, a dim sound of singing came wafting from the lake. It sounded like
the voices of women, blending in disturbing harmonies.

"We'd better carry with us extra charms against wights," Rivalen said.

Down to the lakeshores they went, the keen air whistling like flutes in their
lungs as they passed through the groves of juniper and ash, the stands of bare-
branched linden, bird cherry, and hazel, and the thickets of sweet-smelling pine.

As they went, the singing grew louder, a chorus as melodious as it was uncanny. Abruptly, it ceased.

Above the slope of turf punctuated by a sparse scattering of goat willows, the
men paused and looked out across the lake. The sky seemed vast, sweeping
wider and deeper than usual. Across it, the last smudges of sunset, orchid and
lavender, darkened to indigo. Flocculent clouds corrugated the aerial meadows,
but high-altitude winds were thinning them, teasing them out into strands,
pulling them away.

A soft voice, lyrical and feminine, startled them. In the shallows at the foot of
the slope, nine damsels were reclining. Some were combing their hair; others laving themselves with the chilly lake water. The gloaming played tricks on the eye,
but it seemed to the men that these incarnations were nubile and comely. Their
copious tresses, green as watercress, flowed unbound to their lotus-stem waists.
Aside from this luxuriant hair, some fragments of verdant lace and ribbons and a
few necklaces and bracelets strung with snail-shells, the damsels were devoid of
covering. Pale gleamed their shapely limbs, as if sunlight had never touched them.

One of them turned her bewitching face toward the men and sang erotically:

"Come down to the water my luscious, my love,
   Come down to the water, my lonely.
   The kiss of cool water refreshes and calms.
   We'll banish your cares when you're twined in our arms.
   The kiss of cool lips shall entice and excite—
   'Tis thrilling to know a libidinous sprite!
   We'll clasp and enfold you. Your heart-pump is beating,
   The in-and-out rhythm of breathing repeating!
   Sweet courtesan 'Water' caresses and fills you.
   She enters your body; she soothes you and stills you.
   Come down to the water, my lusty, my lance.
   Come down to the water, my lively!"

"Avert your gaze! Stopper your ears!" Rivalen shouted to his companions. "They are drowners!" He rummaged feverishly in a bag, pulled out a box of salt, and scrabbled at the clasp of the lid. His fingers felt thick and heavy; they could get no purchase on the clasp.

The enchanting damsels clustered closer to the lake's edge. Each time they moved, the swathes of their green hair parted and closed like curtains, now revealing seductive curves, now hiding them.

Provocatively, they smiled at the men. Stretching out their arms in invitation, together they sang lewdly:

> "Twin buds of white lilies you'll cup in your hands;
> We'll bind you and wind you with silken hair-strands.
> And while you find bliss betwixt ivory limbs
> We'll dive down to seek where the eel-serpent swims.
> You'll dream of reclining on soft velvet couches,
> And fireworks of pleasure that slide in silk pouches.
> With each sure caress you shall rise like a fire;
> Lascivious nymphs saturate men's desire.
> We know how to tease you, immerse you, and drench you.
> We know how to please you; we know how to quench you.
> Come down to the water, my lawless, my lark.
> Come down to the water, my lovely!"

Arran, with his fingers plugging his ears, shook his head to clear his mind of the drowners' beguilements. From a corner of his eye he spied Gahariet, halfway down the slope, hurrying toward the brink of the lake. With a running tackle, Arran brought him down, pinned him to the sward, and struggled to keep him there. To prevent himself from hearing the singing he bellowed a chant, the first that occurred to him:

> "Hypericum, salt and bread,
> Iron cold and berries red,
> Self-bored stone and daisy bright,
> Save me from unseelie wight.

> "Red verbena, amber, bell,
> Turned-out raiment, ash as well,
> Rooster with your cock-a-doo,
> Banish wights and darkness, too."

"Get off! Let me go!" the journeyman shouted furiously, twisting and writhing. Rivalen had opened the box, while Bliant had wrenched the lid off another. They were flinging great handfuls of salt and iron filings at the damsels, while chanting wight-warding rhymes, ringing hand-bells, and uttering piercing whistles to override the song of the drowners.

The damsels recoiled from this onslaught, throwing up the waxen tapers of their arms in self-protection. Without faltering, Rivalen and Bliant continued their barrage of words, minerals, and noise. Weathermasters were not easy prey for unseelie wights. They strode right to the edge of the water, but no farther. Only a fool or an ignoramus would wade in and cross the threshold of the drowners' domain. At length, perceiving that the men were stubborn, the wights drew off into deeper waters. Even as they swam lazily away, their voices could be heard from across the lake; now, however, their intent was sinister, derogatory, mocking, and obscene:

> "Lords, when ev'ry part of your body is filled,
>   We'll rock you like babes till the spasms have stilled,
>   Till your cries, like women's in childbed, have passed,
>   Till your passionate climax has faded at last
>   And you're floating quiescent down in the long weeds
>   Where worms dwell in slime and the stickleback breeds.
>   In time you will swell like a mother with child,
>   While water soaks in and your flesh is defiled
>   By death and decay. As a mother does best,
>   You'll suckle the fishes that nibble your breast.
>   Come down to the water, my leery, my luce!
>   Come down to the water, my lowly."

Five hundred yards from the shore, barely perceptible in the gloaming, they dived. Their disappearance left scarcely a ripple.

High in the indigo heavens, white flowers blossomed.

Arran abandoned his capture of Gahariet, who scrambled to his feet. The young journeyman stared wretchedly at the lake, but made no comment; nor did his companions reprove him. It had been a lesson well learned. Gahariet did not cease shuddering until more than an hour had passed.

The single undulation caused by the departure of the lake-wights had spent itself. On the placid waters of Stryksjø reflections glimmered, flawless, unmarred by the slightest disturbance. Sky above, sky below. The firmament appeared to extend deep beneath the water's surface. Millions upon millions of stars hung suspended beneath the lake like glinting shoals of minnows. The lake merely meditated, wrapped in its own profound calm, pondering its peaceful eternity.

Across on the other side of the lake far-off peaks now faded to soft shapes, hazed, as if glimpsed through a silken screen tinted pale blue. Tall streaks of pines on distant ridges let down their perpendicular reflections into the water. Like the lake they were serene and self-contained. Straight-spined, they lifted their slender snouts to the skies as if baying like wolves.

Reflections of sharp crags dipped in marshmallow tried to plumb the water's depths, but could not reach. Only the images of the stars plunged to the true foundations of Stryksjø.

Warily, Rivalen scanned their surroundings. "All seems tranquil enough," he said in confidential tones. "I daresay we can hope for some peace now, so that we may complete our task without interruption."

A layer of mist crept surreptitiously across the water. All was mist, cloud, vapor, water, stone, and wood, illusion, light and darkness. The islands merely existed, aloof, untouchable.

"Ah, Ragnkull," murmured Arran, staring out at the gray-green hummock near the lake's center, "we shall conquer you yet!"

Then the four companions set to, and began their weatherworking.

On that same King's Day, 24th Ninember, Fionnuala Aonarán and her mercenaries were riding through a close and shadowy wood. They were following some narrow trail made, perhaps, by bears or wolves, a trail that meandered in the right direction, for the moment. This band looked the worse for wear. Hard riding, fighting, and cold nights bedded in the frost had cracked their skin, tied cruel knots in their hair, and ingrained their nails and flesh with grime. The whites of their eyes were the only splashes of brightness about them, pallid daubs of albescence in faces charcoaled by wind and cold. Guided by map, compass, and sextant, impelled by obsession, they had reached a point that was fewer than sixty miles—as the wild goose flies—from Lake Stryksjø.

Slowly but certainly, they were nearing their goal.

Down by the quiet banks of Stryksjø the men from High Darioneth were working in shifts. It was necessary for them to continuously exert influence on the weather, lest the normal structures should reassert themselves. The world's troposphere swirled, constantly moving toward equilibrium, yet never able to achieve it. Mighty forces and immutable cycles created complicated systems.

By means of the virtual thermometers, hygrometers, and barometers inside their skulls, the weathermasters were sensing invisible forces, even as they spoke the vector commands to guide them. That night, while Arran and Bliant slumbered, Rivalen and Gahariet summoned winds to drive away the clouds, leaving the skies clear and bristling with stars. Chill as the land and lake already were, the last few sluggish shreds of energy were departing, rising into the diamond air. The weathermasters reached far and deep into the northerly airflow and altered its passage, preparing for the next morning's work.

As sunrise drew nigh they reversed their summons. Small cumulus clouds scampered in and clustered together like flocks of sheep. Arran and Bliant awoke and took over from their exhausted companions. As if they were weather-shepherds, they called more moisture-laden winds, drawing together larger clouds until a thick billow of vapor lidded the lake and surrounds, locking out the sun's radiation. They could not afford to be too localized with their cooling. It was necessary for the cloud cover to extend several leagues beyond the lake, because if the land close around were to stay at normal temperatures, then horizontal energy exchange processes would work toward overcoming the imbalance. Once the clouds were in place, Arran and Bliant located the cold northerly airflow. Next, they began to invoke hail.

Supercooled water droplets were circulating within the updraughts of the cumulonimbus clouds. They were passing through regions of dissimilar temperatures and humidity, melting or freezing as they met warmer or colder air, collecting a build-up of alternating layers of clear and opaque ice.

"Let the stones grow no bigger than a fat wheat grain," Arran murmured to his friend. He returned to chanting a litany of vector commands and performing the directive gestures.

Soon afterward, Bliant became aware that the hailstones had reached the required size. He and Arran allowed the updraughts within the clouds to become weaker, until eventually they could no longer support the tiny balls of ice. There was a rattling and a pattering, and the weathermasters felt the sting of miniature ice-hammers striking their faces.

A hailstorm had commenced.

The storm of ice continued throughout the greater part of the day. By the following day the ground was so cold that the hail did not melt as it lay. Instead, it formed shallow drifts and clung to the boughs of trees.

Each night, Rivalen and Gahariet cleared the skies. Every day, Arran and Bliant invoked clouds and hail. Never before had the denizens of Grïmnørsland experienced such weird weather. The efforts of the weathermasters caused interruptions to the usual patterns of ridges and troughs in the airflow around the world, through a great depth of the atmosphere. As days passed, the lake grew colder. Plates of ice began to form on the surface. Hailstones ceased to liquefy when they touched the water. The ice layers deepened and strengthened.

It cost the weathermasters dearly to continue consistently with their effort. Working the *brí* was never easy, and their reserves of strength were running low. Despite their care, side-effects evolved at the outer rims of their influence. Uncanny balls of lightning made unexpected appearances, and other strange phenomena broke out over Grïmnørsland.

The weather hampered Fionnuala and her band. Now they must struggle through drifts of hailstones, and daily endure flails of ice.

"They are up to something, the puddle-makers," one of the mercenaries said. "Perhaps they know we are after their treasure. They are trying to drive us back."

"That is not their way," said Fionnuala. "They would not use their precious powers to counter the likes of us."

She added to herself, *Besides—'tis likely they have already been and gone.* The prospect, however, did not daunt her. Sheer stubbornness had ensured her survival during her childhood in the gutters of Cathair Rua, and it stood her in good stead on this venture.

Such unnatural weather caused eldritch wights to stir. Unusual numbers of them issued from their secret places and ventured abroad. The hair-raising harmonies and discords of their singing, their weeping and sobbing, their low chuckling and sudden shrieks of laughter punctuated the clear but blusterous nights. Attracted to the source of the *brí,* they drifted toward the shores of Stryksjø. Sometimes Arran and his companions glimpsed curious figures moving through the trees, or felt the pressure of eyes like augers drilling into the backs of their necks.

In High Darioneth the queer winds and disturbances and distant lightnings were sensed by the weathermasters. They knew that some major man-made event was taking place, and that only powerful weathermages could cause such upheaval. Many folk anxiously wondered what was to be done. Were Arran and his party in distress? Should they dispatch a search party straightaway?

"They ought to have taken a cage-full of carrier pigeons with them," said Nyneve Longiníme. "At least they would have been able to send us an *'all's well'* note now and then."

"They are four grown men!" argued Cacamwri Dommalleo. "How should we treat them so—as if they are merely small boys that cannot be let for an instant from their mother's sight without sending home notes!"

The councillors of Ellenhall gathered together. They agreed that Rivalen and

Arran must surely know what they were about, and decided to wait on further events.

By the evening of 30th Ninember the lake-ice was almost strong enough to bear the weight of a man.

The same twilight that enfolded its gray gauzes around the weathermasters on the shores of Stryksjø was also gathering about Fionnuala and her band of mercenaries, who were making their way through a juniper forest. The day's riding had been hard. Trails had petered out or doubled back, steep ridges had risen like walls before the riders, sink-holes had opened at their feet, hail-drifts had partially swallowed them, twigs and thorns had torn their garments and flesh, and they were cold to the very marrow of their bones. As the swallow flew, they were now fewer than six miles from Stryksjø.

The afternoon's cloud-cover had cleared, but the sun had long since vanished and it was getting too dark for the riders to go on. Like a thatched roof, the foliage of the junipers blocked out the weak light of the stars. When at last it became impossible to see where they were going they tethered the horses, made camp, partook of a rudimentary supper, and set one of their number to watch. Except when absolutely necessary, they did not speak to one another.

"Prepare to encounter the weathermasters tomorrow morning," said Fionnuala before she lay down by the fire to take her rest. "We shall depart at first light."

Privately, she believed she would arrive at Stryksjø too late. Although she had regularly scanned the skies throughout her journey, she had seen no balloon; this, however, she considered hardly surprising, because a clear view of the heavens could never be obtained from down amongst the trees.

She did not divulge her misgivings to the men. Should they believe they had battled the travails of the journey for naught, they must surely rise in rebellion against her. If the weathermasters were to be found at the lake and taken by surprise, then they would either slay the mercenaries or be slain themselves. Were they not there, she would wait a day or so in case they appeared, and if they failed to do so, she would slip away alone and ride home. The compass was in her possession. The men had no such instrument. Without her guidance they would have little chance of finding their way out of the wilderness of Grïmnørsland. In all likelihood they would perish, and it would not be necessary to pay them for a mission that had proved fruitless.

Her crossbow dug into her ribs. Although it was awkward and bulky she kept it always close to her body, beneath her clothing, so that it would not become frozen. She hugged it to herself like a lover, fiercely protecting this instrument of war. Unlike the human men who had left her desolate through abandonment or death, the crossbow had never failed her.

Closing her eyes, she sank at once into a slumber so deep it was akin to death.

Before sunrise a thick flocculence of cumulonimbus wadded the sky like mattresses. Gradually, it altered in color from slate-gray through pale ash to luminous platinum. The sun had arisen behind the overcast, ushering in a wan day. Everywhere, unmelted hail lay heaped like an overabundance of pearls. At the lakeshore the goat willows stood as stiff and crystallized as trees of glass. Weary were gray-haired Rivalen and young Gahariet as they waited there, yet they continued to make the gestures and say the words of gramarye. Out of the half-shadows came Arran and Bliant, their boots crunching on fallen hail.

"Good morrow," said Rivalen, timing his greeting between his utterance of vector commands.

"βłã̈w̃, Ãʃéliȫté§§ ¥ē Ėȧşt W̃ÿ̃ńd̃é! The ice on Stryksjø has become strong enough to walk on," said Gahariet.

"Yester-eve Bliant and I reckoned that this dawn would see our purpose fulfilled," said Arran. "I have come prepared."

"Go now, Arran," said Rivalen. "It is time. We can hold the ice for you, but you must make haste. The longer we hold it the weaker we become, and the greater will be the impact on the world's weather."

The young Maelstronnar had dressed in protective clothing. In his breast pocket he carried a tiny vial he had brought with him from High Darioneth, for the purpose of collecting the Draught from the Well of Dew. He checked that his sword slid easily in its sheath, and his knife was sharp.

"Farewell, friends," he said, but he hesitated. In response to his salute his comrades could do no more than nod, because they were occupied with keeping up the weathermastery. Arran's gaze took in the three of them standing in a row, side by side at the lake's edge, tall and graceful, in command of stupendous forces, frost caught in their hair and ice riming their beards. He felt a surge of pride and love for them, then stepped onto the ice.

His balance was faultless—he had the poise of a dancer. Besides, the tumbled hailstones lent some grip to the soles of his boots. Lightly he sped, reaching ahead with his weathermage's senses to predict any thin places in the ice.

It was as if he ran through some dim-lit, preternatural realm. All was ivory and alabaster, and soft tones of cobweb-gray. The lake surface was chiefly flat, buckled in places where the ice had burst upward. It was skittering with diminutive marbles, opaque hailstones that had frozen so quickly that bubbles of air had been trapped inside, each one no bigger than a pinpoint.

Islands shouldered their way up out of the frozen sea. From the nearest, arrows erupted. Eldritch archers were shooting at Arran, but he was covered with chain mail and thick leather, and his friends standing on the distant shore sent gusts of wind that threw the archers off balance so that, unaccustomed to slipperiness, they slid backward over the frozen layers. Rivalen, Bliant, and Gahariet also delivered swirls of hail to confuse the deadly wights. Arran ducked, dodged, and wove, moving rapidly.

Ragnkull Island stood up out of the ice like an elfin castle, pinnacled and turreted, jagged with stony battlements, pitted with natural crevices and clefts for windows. Its tall rock formations and peaked trees were frozen, coated in a lacework of frost. With shadows of glacial blue and highlights of silver it glittered, casting somber reflections of hyacinthine and swift argent on the gleaming lake.

Arran stepped onto the island. Instantly a rabble of small wights assaulted him; he drove them back with cold iron, flourishing his sword in one hand, his knife in the other. As a child, he had mastered a unique trick of activating an electrical charge on metal blades. Sparks flew from his weapons; he guessed the wights had never encountered such a device before. Some of his attackers he managed to injure. Black ichor gushed from their wounds, and they fled.

Frantically the young man searched for some sign of the Well, ever aware of urgency. He knew that if his companions should falter, if they succumbed to weariness and failed, then the ice would melt and he would be doomed.

Yet what did the Well of Dew look like? Was it merely a hole in the ground? Many depressions, large and small, pitted the surface of Ragnkull Island. Most were choked with hailstones. How could he know which of them was special?

He searched with ever-growing desperation, while dodging knee-high assailants and ducking for shelter from arrows. He was crouching behind the rough-barked bole of an ice-bedecked pine when a small voice piped up close to his ear.

"Look for a dingle."

Arran leaped sideways, dropped to the ground, and rolled, an instinctive reaction for one who had been trained in self-defense.

"Ooh, man, now I'm dizzy," moaned the voice, still right next to him.

Arran lay quite motionless in a bank of hailstones. He breathed shallowly. Softly he said, "Where are you?"

"I'm in your packet, man."

A head, impossibly small, like that of a child's doll, poked out of the breast pocket where Arran kept the vial. Its eyes were beady, and exhibited a pained expression. "Man, you might've broke all me bones," it said reproachfully.

"You are the boy with the tankard!"

"Ye've done us a good turn, man. I came with ye to gie ye a helping hand. Ye're lookin' for the Well o' Tears. I know where."

"Tell me!"

"We be nigh to a dingle. 'Tis small, no more than seven man-paces across, and not much deeper than the height of a man. 'Tis treeless within, but surrounded by trees that grow right up to the brink."

Arran peered over the top of the ridge of hailstones. Perceiving no immediate peril, he rose into a partial crouch and cast about, searching for anything that resembled the creature's description.

"Walk straight ahead now," the small voice said. "Now turn. No, not that way, t'ither!"

As Arran pushed his way through a wall of foliage, great heaps of ice came sliding from the boughs onto his shoulders. The tiny wight ducked back into the pocket for shelter. Abruptly the ground gave way beneath Arran's boots and he fell, sliding in a mass of melded hailstones. After sliding a short distance he came to a halt. The world had closed in. He was confined within a shadowy bowl, covered with a web of twilight. The wight popped its head out again and squeaked, "Here be the dingle!"

Ancient alders leaned out over the dell, their branches interlocking to weave a dense roof of living twigs and boughs, a shield against hail. Thick mosses carpeted the floor, which sloped downward toward the far end. As the floor descended, the walls of the hollow climbed steeper and higher until at last they closed in overhead, forming a sunken, low-ceilinged cavern on one side of the dingle.

"Go inside," the wight's voice advised. Arran had no doubt the creature could be trusted. Like all wights, it was incapable of lying. It had declared it had accompanied him in order to help him; therefore he knew it was not leading him into some trap.

Within the cavern the inclined floor continued for about fifteen yards until it met a stony wall, the back wall of the cavern, a dead end. About ten yards in from the entrance, the ground had been punctured, as if some fist-sized object had rapidly entered it on a diagonal trajectory. The hole that had been scooped out was not very deep; it was probable that rocks lying close to the surface had stopped the traveling object. This depression was lined with that silvery metal with which Arran was now familiar. It glimmered faintly in the gloom. Neither moss nor fern grew on that coating. No slime sullied the distillate therein, and no water-plants existed in that well. The water was clear, but there was no more than a thimbleful. That it remained in a liquid state and had not succumbed to the freezing conditions was no surprise to the weathermage; this was no ordinary liquor, after all.

At last he had reached the long-sought goal, this brew-vat of heart's desire and poison.

Kneeling beside the Well of Dew, Arran wept three tears.

"Here's your water-barrel," said the tiny wight. With both hands it proffered the vial, which it had discovered in Arran's pocket.

The young man withdrew the cork, leaned down, and carefully collected all the water. It was similar to the fluid in the Well of Rain and unlike natural water, in that somehow it allowed itself to be taken in a single mass, without leaving wasted dregs, or droplets clinging to the sides. When the silvery receptacle was dry and the vial securely plugged, the thought came to Arran that he had been holding his breath, and he let out a great sigh.

The pocket-wight chuckled merrily.

"Time to go hame," it said.

"If I put this vial in my pocket with you, will you guard it for me?"

"I'll guard it for ye, man. But I must be getting back to me mither now."

"We shall head straight back to the shore, I promise you, after I have completed one task more."

Arran had intended to destroy the Well of Dew with a dose of etching acid, in the same way Weaponmonger had ruined the Well of Rain, but even as he reached for the acid flask he recalled that in the excitement of preparation he had neglected to bring it from the campsite. For an instant he cursed his forgetfulness; then an idea occurred to him.

He broke a small chunk of material from the cavern's roof and held it close to his face for examination, noting the mineral and ore content. After letting the specimen drop from his fingers he crawled from the low-roofed cavern into the relative brightness of the shady dell. The exertion of the last six days had taxed him sorely. The channeling of enormous outputs of the *brí* in order to freeze the lake had drained and weakened him. There remained, however, one final challenge.

With or without the acid, he must destroy the Well of Dew.

Climbing out of the dell, shoving his way through the tight-knit branches of the alders, and brushing off the continual showers of hail that cascaded over him, Arran forced his way into the open. The dangers that surrounded him had not decreased; if anything, his presence had attracted further peril. A couple of small black darts whizzed past his ears. He ducked. His hands spun a shape in the air, while he uttered a swift phrase. A miniature whirlwind jumped up and blasted the unseelie marksmen that had slyly approached. They were bowled away across the ice, turning somersaults and shrieking as they tumbled.

The young weathermage continued to gesticulate and speak, but he had progressed from performing a simple wind-summons to executing a far more complicated and potent formula. Above Ragnkull Island the clouds darkened. As if exploding slowly from their foundations, they commenced piling on top of one another. Inside their gigantic bellies phenomenal amounts of energy were beginning to churn. The building of a thundercloud demanded the participation of violent updraughts, engendered by the heating of air close to the surface. Ramming together infinitesimal particles of water to form ice would release quantities of energy. The young weathermaster must drive the warming of the island's microclimate using the power of the *brí* alone—there were no fronts at hand to aid him. Simultaneously, he must fine-tune the conditions by ensuring the atmosphere's uniform moisture content. Fire, water, and air—all three moved at his command; yet it was against their nature to be tamed. Tremendous forces would lash out instantly, should he not remain vigilant.

Within the rising tower of cumulonimbus, ice-crystals and water droplets were circulating at high speeds, being smashed apart and thrown together with a brutality that unmade their neutrality. Sundered from one another, the positively charged particles accumulated near the crown of the thunder-head while those that were negatively charged gathered at the base.

From inside Arran's pocket, a voice screeched, "I mislike this! Let's go, man!" The wight's head appeared. Its hat had fallen off and its hair radiated in a frizz, like the bristles of a bottle-brush, framing the small, alarmed face.

"Fear not," said Arran. The thundercloud demanded all his attention; he was unable to bestow any more reassurance. He had directed the built-up charges in the base of the cloud, shifting them sideways until they hovered above a specific point. That point was the top of a tall alder rooted directly above the Well of Dew. The opposite electrical charges were straining to reach one another—negative at the base of the cloud, positive in the ground. Only a layer of air insulated them from each other.

The young man turned away from the alders concealing the dell. He ran across the island, then leaped off the gelid land, back onto the slippery surface of the frozen water. No eldritch archers harassed him. Indeed, suddenly there was no sign of any living thing on Stryksjø.

"Ooh, man, there's a terrible power a-breeding!" wailed the little thing in Arran's pocket. " 'Twill explode any moment now! Run, man!"

On the banks of the lake Arran's companions waited, obscured by the brumous murk. When Arran had reached a point midway between Ragnkull Island and the shore, he halted.

"Don't stop!" yelped the tiny wight. Only the tasseled tip of its skinny tail was visible, sticking out from the top of Arran's pocket.

A second time, Arran turned. This time he faced the island. He raised his right hand.

Deep in the ground the positive charge was waiting, beckoning, reaching a crescendo. A jagged leader-charge came zigzagging out of the thundercloud and smote the tip of the alder. An explosion of blue-white light lit up the entire region, so intensely brilliant that it seemed to Arran his eyes had vaporized in their very sockets. Instantly, that electric touch was answered.

Stryksjø blazed.

A second flare had followed, even more dazzling than the first. Cloven by searing energies, the air roared. A wall of compression lifted Arran off his feet and hurled him backward. Thunderclaps crashed so loudly that they splintered the lake ice with their percussions. Ragnkull Island vomited its heart, and a blazing tree crashed down, split in two pieces.

Then all became dark and silent.

In that moment a massive electrical current had surged up from the ground. It had blasted the well to fragments and zapped along the seam of ore in the cavern's roof, ascending through the roots of the alder. Soaring to a temperature of more than forty thousand degrees, it had sizzled up the tree, splitting it apart. The smell of ozone and smoke filled the air and the tree fell apart in two long, burning shards as the current discharged into the thundercloud.

Temporarily blind and deaf, and wracked with the agony of putting forth such phenomenal quantities of the *brí* in such a quick burst, Arran was unable to regain his feet. He gasped and retched. Every nerve in his body was a white-hot wire screaming its pain. He writhed helplessly on the hail-dusted ice, unaware of the bloody events that were unfolding back on the shore.

While Arran's companions were awaiting and aiding him at the lakeside, Fionnuala and her band of mercenaries had drawn near their campsite. The weathermasters had left *Wanderpath*'s envelope folded up in its basket, unguarded, while they performed the weathermastery necessary to keep the lake locked in a freeze.

Fionnuala was an expert hunter and markswoman. Her eyes, although insipid in color, pierced her surroundings keenly. Despite the deep gloom of the cloudy morning, she spied the pale folds of the envelope shimmering through the trees. In such a remote and unpopulated region the weathermasters had not bothered to conceal the aerostat; they had merely ringed it with charms of wight-protection.

The woman held up her hand in a signal for her followers to be alert.

"Dismount," she said in low tones. "I see something there. It might be their camp. Tie up the horses. We shall take the weathermasters by surprise."

As matters turned out, it was Fionnuala who was surprised. She and her henchmen moved stealthily amongst the junipers and surrounded the campsite, only to discover it was deserted.

"Go and reconnoiter," she ordered the men. They slipped away, their stain-blotched clothing blending with bark and leaves and beads of ice. It was hardly necessary for them to move noiselessly. Gusty winds were whipping the branches of the junipers, and random hail-squalls came beating down. The creak of wood, the sigh of blowing leaves, and the patter of hail obliterated any sounds the intruders might have engendered.

After double-checking the surroundings to ensure she was alone, Fionnuala strode into the clearing. She kicked over the wicker basket and began to vigorously tug at the contents. "Here's their cursed vehicle," she muttered, hauling out the spidersilk envelope, hand over hand. The silky masses billowed about her. She stood in an ocean of glimmering bubbles and shredded them to pieces. A diamond dagger was one of the rare blades that would cut spidersilk.

Later, her scouts returned.

"Three men stand at the edge of a frozen lake," they reported. "They are intent on watching something far across the water—so intent they did not note our presence."

"Take them unawares and slay them," she said. The ruined envelope lay gleaming like a pool of molten pewter on the ground.

Arran staggered to his feet. His hearing and sight were beginning to return, but he saw the world as if through a smoked glass pane and heard sounds as if from a distance, beyond a high-pitched whine and ringing of ceaseless shrill bells. Severe storms were raging all around him. Thunder trundled its iron-rimmed wheels around the horizon; the white calligraphy of lightning wrote itself upon roiling clouds, dancing on its own reflections in the lake of ice; winds careened here and there like invisible madmen, uprooting trees; hail threshed the landscape.

He staggered back toward the shore, dodging eldritch arrows. One struck him, but harmlessly lodged in the hard leather padding on his shoulder. He had no strength to pluck it out. Noting that the icy surface of the lake was starting to crack and melt, he peered through the storm, endeavoring to see what his friends were at. They no longer stood on the shore. Where they had been, gouts of red gore were splashed across the drifts of hail.

He slipped and toppled over, struggled upright, and walked on, keeping his head down so that he might watch where he stepped, in case the ice should betray him and he should fall through, to be lost beneath the haunted waters.

Next time he looked up, he saw, through swirls of windblown crystals, five men crossing the lake-ice toward him. Flashes of lightning sporadically illuminated their burly forms and grim faces. They were strangers, and they carried blood-stained swords.

Arran perceived at once how it would be. He was virtually alone on the ice, which was rapidly liquefying and breaking up now that the *brí* no longer constrained local temperatures. He guessed that these strangers had captured or slain his companions. If they had come here, to this remote place, they must know what he had been seeking. They would be certain that either he knew where it was or he had already found it.

Rapidly they drew near. Dazed and exhausted, Arran was barely able to balance on his feet. When they reached him he would be at their mercy, if any mercy moved their hearts. They would seize him, search his clothing, and discover the Draught. In all likelihood they would take it from him and slay him, as they had probably slaughtered his friends. His mind was tormented with anxiety on behalf of those he had left on shore. Yet he had been caught without warning. There was no time to work the *brí*: nor did he possess the vigor to do so, even if the chance had been given him.

The strangers drew apart, and from their midst stepped a woman, hitherto concealed behind them. She raised her crossbow and pointed it at Arran. He knew who she was: he knew her arrows were toxic.

They were almost upon him. He had no strength to flee, no strength to fight.

He said to the little wight in his pocket, "Attackers are coming. Can you help me?"

"I own only the power of glamour," moaned the wight, "and me mither's got a bottomless tankard. I can do naught to help you." It screwed shut its eyes, curled into a tight ball, and dived to the bottom of the pocket to hide.

"Then I am finished," said Arran. He sagged to his knees on the rotting, melting ice, bowed his head in defeat, and waited.

Hundreds of leagues to the east, beyond the walls of High Darioneth, four horsemen clad in the royal livery of Slievmordhu were climbing the East Road from Blacksmith's Corner. Far above their heads, the mountain heights echoed with the clamor of baying hounds, the rattling of heavy chains, and the slamming of gigantic doors. The eldritch frightener was issuing its warning. Watchmen looked out from the ramparts above the inner and outer portals of the East Gate. A horn sounded from a watchtower. Another answered from below, and a third responded from somewhere within the ring of storths.

The stridor of blowing horns reached a chamber in the house of the Maelstronnar, wherein he and several comrades had gathered. They paused in their conversation and hearkened to the coded signal, deciphering its meaning.

"'Tis messengers from Cathair Rua," said the Storm Lord, at length. The light of hope that had newly kindled in his eyes now dimmed, and he sighed.

"Alas; Uabhar's errand-boys are not the ones we long to see," said Lynley Ymberbaillé, the mother of Bliant.

"It has been nineteen days since *Wanderpath* departed in search of this Well," said Tristian Solorien. "Nineteen days! What can possibly be hindering them? Why do they not return?"

"I would not be overly concerned," said Avalloc, "were it not for the artificial storms."

"Ten days ago those storms raged at their height," said Lynley. "Since then, they have waned and dissipated. The weather begins to regain equilibrium. Still, no word comes out of Grïmnørsland."

"We wait no longer," said Avalloc. "This very day, *Snowship* shall be dispatched. We will send a rescue crew. Baldulf, will you see to it?"

"Without delay!"

"For my part, I must prepare to receive these messengers."

Under escort, the horsemen from Cathair Rua trotted up the main road from the plateau to Rowan Green. After receiving refreshment from the hands of a steward, the messenger and his three guards were ushered into Ellenhall for an audience with the Maelstronnar.

The emissary bowed. "Lord, I bring tidings from His Majesty, Uabhar Ó Maoldúin of Slievmordhu."

"Proceed," said Avalloc.

"Lord, I say this to you: King Uabhar has broken into the Dome of Strang in Orielthir."

"Indeed! These are tidings of great moment. Tell on!"

"His Majesty's servants, taking no harm from any curses that may once have been embedded into the outer architecture, made their way deep inside the Dome's interior. There being no windows piercing that inner core, they ignited torches, that they might have light to see by. At the precise moment the spark was struck from the tinder, or so it was later guessed, the innermost spaces of the Dome exploded. Men that later followed the advance party found tangles of fused piping amongst the human remains and rubble. The remnants of what must have been a library were found, too, for thousands of pages of books were strewn to the winds, later to wilt and wither in the rain. Investigators from the Sanctorum diagnosed that the Sorcerer of Strang had been tapping underground gases to fuel his lights and machineries. The pipes now being clogged by mortar-dust and broken brickwork, and the roof being burst asunder to let in the fresh air, there is no further danger of a blast.

"Since then, His Majesty's servants have scoured the bastion from pinnacle to foundations. They discovered no treasure or objects of gramarye, nothing whatsoever of any great value. All that has been brought to light are crumbling stones and rotting bones, worm-eaten wood, melted copper pipes, and rusted iron. This being the case, they have abandoned the site."

"By what right did they try to pillage it in the first place?" asked the Storm Lord.

"Why, by the right of the Crown of course!" The messenger was taken aback.

Diplomatically, Avalloc did not press the issue of the Dome's proprietorship. He quizzed the man further, and more information was divulged, after which the visitors retired to lodgings that had been prepared for them. They would depart from High Darioneth on the following day.

Immediately, Avalloc Stormbringer convened an informal meeting of the Council, to which he also summoned Jewel. Even as they hastened to Ellenhall, the councillors glanced across at the launching apron, upon which the balloon *Snowship* was being inflated. In their hearts they guessed where the aircraft would be bound, and when they gathered together Avalloc readily confirmed their conjectures.

"I am sending a flight to Grïmnørsland," he said. "*Wanderpath* has been too long away, and the contrived disturbances of the atmosphere are cause for concern."

"I am glad of this," said Cacamwri. "I believe I can speak on behalf of us all when I say, we have grown anxious, of late."

His colleagues voiced their concordance.

"I should like to accompany this flight," Jewel said to the Storm Lord. "Sir, will you give permission?"

During the extended wait for Arran's return the marsh-daughter had scarcely been able to sleep or eat. His long absence caused her an anguish so extreme that it was difficult to endure.

"Indeed I will not!" Avalloc's eyes flashed. "My dear Jewel, you try me too greatly. How can you ask, when you know full well that skilled hands are needed on missions that might prove dangerous, hmm? You have no skill at ballooning. You would only hamper the crew."

For an instant Jewel looked as if she might defy him, but she reined her temper.

"Pray forgive me."

The Storm Lord's expression softened. Gently he said, "Do not be downcast, dear child, for I have good news for you." Turning his attention to the assembly of councilors, he declared, "Word has come from Cathair Rua; Uabhar has penetrated and inspected the Dome. It appears the sorcerer's arcane inventions died with him, for no hurt came to those who invaded his domain, save for those who were killed in a subsequent explosion begot by their own torch-flames. Wealth was not found there, nor mysterious secrets—or so we are told. They are demolishing the compound. I daresay it has been a splinter in Uabhar's side for long enough.

"This means, of course, that our prisoner, Fionnbar Aonarán, has been rendered powerless to do Jewel mischief. It is no longer necessary for her identity to remain secret from the world. Until this time only a few folk in High Darioneth have known the truth. Now, anyone and everyone may become privy to the knowledge, and no harm done. If she is descended from Strang, what of it? She is heiress to nothing—only a worthless ruin. Aonarán knows the location of the Well of Dew, but when Rivalen and Arran return with the Draught, that information also will be of no value to him."

"These are excellent tidings!" said Nyneve Longiníme. "The scorpion loses its sting!"

A murmur of agreement rippled amongst the councillors.

"Tidings both good and ill," said Avalloc. "Notwithstanding the fact that Aonarán is undoubtedly guilty of supplying weapons to Marauders, his detention at the house of Lumenspar contravenes our own laws. As yet, despite our efforts we have gathered no definite evidence against him. His freedom is, therefore, long overdue."

"Surely you are not suggesting we should release him!" protested Tristian Solorien. "The fellow is a scoundrel, a miscreant without compunction! To set such a rogue on the loose would be ill enough in the usual way of things, but to liberate a man who is not only pitiless but probably immortal to boot—why, 'twould be a felony!"

"His perpetuity has not been proven for certain," Gvenour Nithulambar reminded the conclave.

"Deathless or not, the man is a criminal and ought to be fettered," growled Cacamwri Dommalleo. Someone shouted a question, another voiced a variant opinion, and vehement discussion broke out on all sides.

"Hearken!" Avalloc's peremptory tones thundered through the debate. All ceased their discourse and turned their attention to their leader.

"Gentlefolk, think you that I would recommend the liberty of this man without imposing conditions? Do you, hmm? If we free him, we shall set close watch on him day and night. This shall serve dual purposes—to ensure he does not work mischief, and perchance to lead us to his ring of accomplices and put a stop to his crimes."

"A sound plan, Maelstronnar," said Cacamwri.

"Whosoever is in accord with this course of action, raise your hand," intoned Baldulf Rainbearer. Readily the councillors demonstrated their consensus.

"And you, Jewel? Aonarán has been your bane. Would you have him released?" Avalloc's tone mellowed when he spoke to the damsel. She had been sitting quietly throughout the latter part of the meeting, obviously curbing her desire to contribute, remaining mute to show respect for the elected Council members.

Now she spoke boldly. "I am in accord, sir. The laws of Ellenhall must not be dealt with lightly. Let Fionnbar Aonarán be set free."

Avalloc nodded. "It shall be done."

"This very day, word shall be sent to Lumenspar," said Baldulf.

"Even so," Avalloc acknowledged, "but there is more. He who bears this news to our ambassador in Cathair Rua must also deliver a message to Uabhar. The king has invited Jewel to accompany us on our visit to his palace for his second son's naming ceremony, so that he might meet the heir of the sorcerer. On hearing of her existence, his interest was swiftly kindled. Jewel, you must make a second decision. Will you accept this invitation? Before you say yea or nay, know this: between the walls of Ellenhall it is recognized that Uabhar is false, a treacherous double-dealer. Outside this meeting-place we do not openly discuss such opinions. Uabhar is, however, canny and powerful. It is in our interests, at this time, to ensure a harmonious relationship between Cathair Rua and High Darioneth. With valid reason you might judge that presenting yourself at the court of Slievmordhu would not be without hazard. With valid reason you might consider that Uabhar has some secondary purpose in requesting this introduction. You might well suspect him of some hidden intention. If this is your doubt, be assured that we share it. Be assured also, dear child, that if you go with us, we promise to ensure your security."

"Sir, you have pre-empted all my arguments," said Jewel, bowing to the Storm Lord. A faint smile twitched at the corners of her mouth. "Thoroughly do you understand my mind! Thank you for your concern and assurances. I will go with you to Cathair Rua. I will wait upon the king. And I will do so in utmost confidence, being under the protection of High Darioneth."

After the meeting had concluded and Jewel returned to the mill, she imparted most of the news to her adopted family, who had come crowding around her as soon as she appeared. They were entranced to hear her tidings, especially when she revealed the secret of her identity.

"Your troubles are over, Jewel!" said Elfgifu delightedly. "This disclosure means that now you are free to revisit your friends and family in the marsh!"

"Yes, and how I long to see them. Yet my troubles are not yet over."

"Why not?"

Jewel turned her face up to the sky. "There is a balloon I wish to see, coming from the east, returning to the Seat of the Weathermasters."

The household ceased its animated chatter. Following Jewel's gaze, they tilted their heads. A balloon was flying above the ring of storths, rising into the cloud layer. It was leaving Rowan Green, however, and heading west.

"Aye," Osweald Miller said thoughtfully. "That is what we all wish to see."

High Darioneth kept vigil. The crew of the balloon that had flown to Grïm-nørsland would send back a carrier pigeon as soon as they arrived at Stryksjø. If there was a black band around the bird's leg, the news would be grave. A white band would mean good news; while yellow indicated no news at all.

The waiting was agony.

Next day a single pigeon winged in over the plateau, flying straight toward the lofts on Rowan Green. The loftmaster caught it and pulled the tag from its leg. The band was black.

Grief overwhelmed the weathermasters and denizens of the plateau. They knew not for certain what this sign could mean, and all wondered what had passed.

On the day after the pigeon's arrival, at sunfall, *Snowship* returned. All those who spied it wind-driven across the skies began lamenting, because it came home unaccompanied, and they could see there were no extra passengers on board—at least, none who were standing. The aerostat alighted on Rowan Green in the center of a throng of weathermasters who were standing by to meet it. Folk of the plateau hastened up the road to the launch apron, anxious to find out what had happened. By the time Jewel reached the apron, the word had spread; *Wanderpath* had been found, dismantled and shredded. Blood had been spilled at the lakeshore where the ground was churned to mud by a struggle.

One crew-member alone had been discovered.

The rescuers had brought Bliant with them, prone on the floor of *Snowship*'s gondola. He was seriously wounded, barely clinging to existence. There had been no sign of his companions on the banks of Stryksjø or in the surrounding forests. Bliant remembered seeing Rivalen fall, mortally hurt, and Gahariet fighting hard against impossible odds. Of subsequent events he had no recollection. He had fainted from loss of blood. The attackers, whoever they were, had left him for dead. Only the chill of the ice on which he lay had stemmed the flow, thus saving his life.

Incredulous, angry, and appalled, High Darioneth grieved for the crew of *Wanderpath*.

It was the 13th Tenember. At this season, High Darioneth would usually be preparing for the Midwinter celebrations. This year all festivities were canceled. Sorrow ruled both plateau and Seat.

Snowship flew a second time to Stryksjø. Deep within a rift in the ground, created when the storm winds uprooted a huge pine, they found the bodies of Rivalen and Gahariet lying where they had been dumped. Across the lake, Ragnkull Island had been torn apart, ravaged by a direct hit from a mighty lightning bolt. Of Arran there was no evidence. Perhaps the lake waters might have told his sad story, if they had possessed voices other than the whisperings and lappings of tiny wavelets.

The people of the plateau, the councillors of Ellenhall, and the entire population of the Seat of the Weathermasters went into mourning. They clad themselves in dismal colors and silently went about their business, red-eyed and wretched. As for the Storm Lord, he was beside himself with grief, and seldom spoke or remembered to partake of nourishment; he seemed to have aged ten years in the space of a day.

It came to Jewel that a void had opened in the world. More than a void: it was as if most of the world had been chopped away, and the little that remained was shriveled and juiceless. There was an absence, a negative space, a lack that could not be endured. She comprehended, eventually, that her longing for Arran was the consequence of love. Without her knowledge her resolve to steel her heart against deep sentiment had given way. She loved Arran, there was no denying it, and desired only to flee from High Darioneth so that that she might scour the Four Kingdoms, searching for him. It was not possible that he could be gone. Surely he must still exist somewhere. She would leave no corner unexplored, no leaf unturned, no shadow unilluminated. She would seek until she had found him, or until the final breath left her body.

Since the news of the loss of *Wanderpath,* she spent much time in the company of Mildthrythe Miller, to whom she revealed her plan.

"No, Jewel, you must not go to Grïmnørsland," said Mildthrythe. "The crew of *Snowship* has sought Arran twice, using the full extent of their powers, and all in vain. I have no doubt; were he living or dead in Grïmnørsland, they would have located him. Since skilled weathermasters have uncovered naught, what chance have you?"

"Against your advice I have gone away once before."

"Go then, if you wish. High Darioneth is no prison. But think twice before you act."

Jewel thought twice, then thrice. And as she deliberated, her disbelief turned to rage. The tentacles of wrath reached out to entangle her, wringing her heart and mind.

"There is no justice!" she ranted to Mildthrythe. "Why should he be taken from us? I hate whoever has done this deed. When we find the murderers we must make them suffer endless torment! Death is too good for the likes of them. It will be Aonarán's doing, somehow, I'll warrant. Let him be captured and forever locked away in the deepest dungeon."

"Aonarán was a prisoner when it happened," said Mildthrythe patiently. Her features were engraved with the furrows of profound sorrow.

"His recreant sister, then," Jewel shouted, through tears. "It will be *her* doing. Let us hunt her down and punish her! Cast her in a deep and sunless cavern, and there let her languish until her bones are dust!"

"Hush Jewel. Do not exert yourself."

"But it is my fault, do you not see? Arran journeyed to Stryksjø for my sake. If not for me he would be safe at home!"

"That is nonsense, and you know it. It was the will of Ellenhall that the Well should be sought, and Arran made his own decision to go. You were one who tried to dissuade him."

Jewel ceased her ranting. She met the gaze of the older woman. So grave were Mildthrythe's eyes, so brimming with desolate compassion, the damsel thought her heart swelled and burst. Throwing herself into Mildthrythe's arms, she pressed her face against her breast and sobbed wildly. Later, when Jewel had grown calmer, she realized that the teardrops scintillating on her hair and sleeves did not all belong to her.

Despite their mourning, the members of the Council of Ellenhall were determined to attend the naming ceremony of Uabhar's second son. To refuse would have been undiplomatic. Furthermore, as the Storm Lord had declared, "We are not being coerced into attending this ceremony. We promised to be present, and we keep our word." To the people of High Darioneth he said, "Do not publish news of the tragedy at Stryksjø as yet. I am loath to mar with ill tidings the name-day of the infant prince. Besides, all that is our own business, and the final outcome is not yet known—the fate of Arran, the fate of Bliant. I would not have these matters made the subject of speculation and gossip throughout the Four Kingdoms."

Taking Jewel with them, the weathermasters departed for Cathair Rua.

The streets of the city were gaily decorated with holly, and festooned with evergreen boughs. Most thoroughfares were crowded with folk celebrating the new year. Few revelers were abroad in the wealthier quarters hard by the palace, because Uabhar had decreed that no noisy or unseemly throngs should congregate near the royal precincts during the naming ceremony and New Year's festivities. The by-ways farther from the palace, however, were teeming with dancers, singers, musicians, vendors roasting hot chestnuts on charcoal braziers, pudding-sellers, bonfires, drinkers, wassailers, pranksters, people in disguise, and merrymakers of all descriptions.

The ceremonial naming of the infant prince, Ronin Ó Maoldúin, took place at the private Oratorium in the palace gardens. Afterward, in the evening, the feast was held at the Hall of Kings. No detail was omitted, no expense was spared, in ensuring the occasion was a sumptuous and intemperate affair. Yet, of all the marvels wrought in cuisine, music, and fashion, the one that most astonished the court was the late arrival of the dowager queen.

It was not that she was tardy—this was a common enough occurrence—but she appeared amongst them arrayed in three different hues.

The colors were red, gold, and black. Crimson was her gown, stitched all over with golden trefoils, and edged with sable. Her girdle and tiara were adorned with triangular jewels: rubies, topazes, and chips of jet. Looking pleased and triumphant, she smiled benignly upon the gathering as she dined on pyramidal redcurrant jellies, creamy triple-layered junkets and triangles of sweet liquorice. Three bracelets jingled on each wasted wrist, three rings encircled each finger, and three ladies-in-waiting hovered behind her chair.

The court of Slievmordhu was impressed, yet Jewel and the weathermasters sat stony-faced throughout the meal and the entertainments. Sorrow weighed heavily on them and they were unable to shake off their gloom. They hardly touched the rich fare or the sweet wines. It was urgent in their minds to complete the visit as soon as was politic, and return speedily to High Darioneth, where their people lamented, and where Bliant lay on the doorstep of death, closely tended by the carlin Luned Longiníme.

On being presented with the sorcerer's heir, Uabhar had stared hard at Jewel, but barely spared her a word. He seemed preoccupied with the ceremonies at hand, yet Avalloc was not deceived. He knew full well that the king had marked Jewel, noting her appearance in detail, as a portrait painter would examine his subject.

To his distaste, Avalloc Stormbringer found himself seated next to the Druid Imperius. Primoris Virosus commenced a brittle conversation, first unctuously inquiring about the welfare of Arran, as if he suspected something was amiss.

To divert the druid from the harrowing subject, Avalloc asked after the where-abouts of the amiable Secundus Adiuvo Constanto Clementer.

"Clementer has left the Sanctorum, in company with his assistant, Agnellus."

"Good gracious me. Then, has he renounced the druidry?"

"Not at all! I am surprised you even contemplate such a possibility! Natu-rally, Clementer remains faithful. He now devotes his time to research into the rarer meanings of life, by means of study and travel. 'Tis all done at his own ex-pense, however. The Sanctorum cannot afford to indulge the whims of these would-be philosophers. Having experienced the privations of a peripatetic life, he will eventually return to the Sanctorum, I expect."

Their conversation was interrupted by the twang of lute-strings. At Uabhar's command, his minstrels began to sing:

"There is virtue in allegiance to one's comrades,
And love's loyalty, all honest folk admire.
But of all the deeds that show if he is worthy,
A man's honor lies in duty to his sire.

"The obedience of sons decrees their value,
And throughout their lives it never must expire.
Those who strive against their patriarch are abject.
A man's honor lies in duty to his sire.

"All good sons, show gratitude for your begetting—
Never question, quarrel, argue, or inquire.
For your father's word is law. You must defend it!
A man's honor lies in duty to his sire."

Later during the course of the festivities, Uabhar quizzed Jewel closely—but with utmost courtesy—as to whether she possessed any special powers that might be to anyone's advantage, and whether she would like to sojourn for a while at the court of Slievmordhu, to keep his queen company. On both counts the marsh-daughter disappointed the monarch who, after failing to entrap her with cunning questions, became convinced of her uselessness, and left her to her own devices.

After all the pains she had taken to conceal her identity this seemed some-what of an anticlimax, yet, inevitably, relief washed through her.

While Jewel and the weathermasters endured the discourse of courtiers and druids in the candle-lit Hall of Kings, down in the dark streets outside the palace a shadow was lurking. Fionnbar Aonarán had been released from the custody of Lumenspar a fortnight earlier. He had gone back to his old haunts and discovered the diamond dagger was missing, but had not rallied his former cohorts, or recommenced his commerce in weapons, because he was aware that he was being watched by agents of the weathermasters.

In any event, seizing control of his erstwhile trade was not uppermost in his mind, for he owned plenty of wealth stashed away in secret hiding places. His single obsession was to slay the son of the Maelstronnar. Certain rumors spoke of the death of Arran and such of his companions as had accompanied him on some secret mission to the wilds of Grïmnørsland—no doubt, the quest for the Well of Dew. Hearsay, however, might prove incorrect.

Since his liberation Fionnbar had heard nothing from Fionnuala, despite having sought news of her by way of clandestine channels. No doubt she had gone hunting after the Draught, just as he had instructed—not necessarily in order to do him a favor, more likely to dedicate the Draught to her own benefit. Nonetheless, it had been worth giving her the directions to the Well of Dew, simply in order that she might prevent the weathermasters from laying their hands on the precious liquid. As far as he could guess from the unconfirmed reports, the weathermasters had failed to find it, but whether his sister had succeeded he knew not.

Other word was on the streets; the scion of Strang's sorcerer was coming to the city, to be presented to the king. Aonarán's choice was clear; he would loiter close to Jewel, so that if the young weathermage came nigh her, he might have the chance to smite him and, with luck, have time afterward to rifle his belongings in search of any valuables.

Aided by his knowledge of the by-ways and alleys of Cathair Rua, Aonarán was able to elude his watchers and skulk near the palace, with no clear plan other than to wait for some opportunity.

After all, what else was there to inspire, with endless years yawning before him?

Avalloc's desire to make a prompt departure from Cathair Rua was being thwarted. Uabhar had made it widely known that he would consider it an insult to his family if any of the guests took their leave from the protracted celebrations before moonrise on Moon's Day the 4th Jenever, at the earliest.

Late in the afternoon on that day, Jewel lingered in the company of the Storm Lord and his daughters, Galiene and Lysanor, on a west-facing balcony overlooking an upper courtyard and the top tiers of the palace gardens. They were blind to the flamboyant colors of the sunset, deaf to the fragrant music that wafted like expensive perfume from the palace's interior.

By now Galiene and Lysanor had become party to the secret of the wells— the secret that had stolen their brother from them. Moreover, the Maelstronnar family had known all along about Arran's love for Jewel, through they had never spoken of it. Since discovering that she returned his affections, Jewel had become aware of their knowledge and aware, too, that almost before she understood it herself they perceived she loved him. What's more, the family had welcomed the revelation.

"I was angry," mused Jewel, leaning on the marble balustrade. "Now my anger has melted, to be replaced by numbness."

"I have no appetite, no interest in anything," said Lysanor. "Sometimes I become aware I have been staring for hours at a wall, or some object, staring but unseeing."

Galiene said, "Sleep comes reluctantly to me at nights, yet during the days I wish only to sleep, that I might be free, for a while, of anguish. The pain that seeded in my heart has spread to take root throughout my person."

"It is the same for me," said Jewel. "'Tis a terrible, physical pain. When shall it go away?"

"It never really goes," said Galiene, "but it fades. I felt this way when our mother died. It was like standing on the brink of an abyss of horror, and watching the ground crumble beneath my feet. It was as if the world had altered fundamentally, had become disjointed in a way that was inexpressibly *wrong,* and could never be the same again."

"Yet we lived on," said Lysanor, "and after a year or two we discovered that the hurt had decreased to a background ache. Now, when I think of her— which is often—the wound stings but does not bleed."

"Come moonrise we will fly from here," muttered Avalloc. "Fain would I rest at my own hearthside."

"And fain would I be beside the healing-couch of Bliant," said Galiene.

"You might have stayed with him," said Avalloc.

"I might—but what could I do? I have not the skills of a carlin. I can do more good by being at your side, Father."

"Look!" Lysanor flung out her arm, indicating the entrance to the yard below. A man was running in. "Is that not one of our agents, Corbenic, son of Brennus?"

Her father scrutinized the courtyard. "Indeed it is! Corbenic is one who has been tracking Aonarán. He comes swiftly, as if bearing urgent tidings. Let us go down to meet him!"

The newcomer was sweating and panting, as if he had sprinted in a race. As soon as he set eyes on the Storm Lord he dropped to one knee, saying, "Sir, the most peculiar tidings have I!"

"Say on, Corbenic!"

"Just now I have seen a young man enter the city and walk slowly through the streets toward the palace. This man had the very look of Arran, if not his bearing."

Suddenly agitated, the Storm Lord gripped the agent by his shoulder. "What can you mean?" he demanded from bloodless lips.

"Sir, his face was the face of your son, but he stooped as he shambled, and when hailed he spoke no word nor showed any sign of recognition."

"I must see this man for myself! Where is he?"

"He will almost be here by now, if he has not halted or been hindered."

Avalloc called for any companions within hearing; then, with no further ado, he and Jewel and his daughters leaped downstairs. They sped from a postern, through the gardens, and out of the palace gates, sparing no explanation for the sentries.

Peering down a cobbled street that ran between tall buildings, they spied a weary wayfarer stumbling toward them. His back was bent as if he were exhausted. Grime covered him all over, and his clothes were ragged and stained black with old blood. He swayed as if he were about to lose balance. As soon as he set eyes on this apparition, Avalloc uttered a cry of pain and joy, for he recognized his own son, miraculously returned.

Even as the Storm Lord uttered this cry, a wiry form sprang out of the dense shadows between the buildings, pulled at the traveler, and threw him to the ground. A long sliver of a blade glittered. The assailant stabbed his victim in the back and neck, then took an instant to rifle his clothing, before making off with his fist clenched.

Although they ran as fast as they could, shouting aloud, Jewel and Avalloc and Corbenic were not able to reach the scene in time to prevent this atrocity. Galiene and Lysanor had been several paces behind; Lysanor stumbled on the cobbles and Galiene stopped to help her to her feet.

The attacker fled up the street.

"Seize him!" roared Avalloc, as Corbenic raced after the knife-wielder.

Within these precincts close by the palace few stragglers were abroad. Not many folk had witnessed the drama. Some clustered in gawking groups, keeping at a respectful distance from the weathermasters. Others discreetly departed the scene, in case they should be implicated in some way.

Jewel sank down on the cobbles beside the young man who lay sprawled on the street. The Maelstronnar and his daughters fell to their knees around the motionless figure. With horrified despair they gazed down and saw the handsome face of Arran, outlined against the eagle's wing of his hair. Frenziedly, in a desperate burst of strength fueled by terror, Jewel ripped strips of fabric from the hem of her petticoats, then rammed the makeshift bandages firmly against his neck and beneath his shoulder blade where the knife had struck. She pressed her fingertips to one of the arteries above his collarbone, as she had seen her great-grandmother do—as Arran himself had once done—but could detect no pulse.

"It is some trick," gasped Lysanor. "This is a sending, a simulacrum!" She drew back fearfully.

As Jewel swiftly bound the bandages in place, Galiene looked on wide-eyed, wringing her hands in distress. "Oh, but if it is *not,* then we have lost him a second time, for behold! He is slain."

Tenderly, Avalloc lifted the young man by the shoulders and laid him across his knees. Jewel stared at the comatose face turned up toward the pyre of the skies, which were streaming crimson and gold between the city's roofs. He looked vulnerable, as if he were sleeping. Dark lashes rested lightly against the pallor of the skin. Beneath the smears of dirt and dried blood, his extraordinary comeliness was apparent. Lean and taut was the line of his jaw; chiseled were his cheekbones. His features, as striking as those of a beautiful girl, were yet imbued with such masculinity that Jewel felt the force of it as a pang.

"It is truly he," the Storm Lord murmured hoarsely.

"Turn him on his side," said Jewel suddenly. "My great-grandmother taught me that if anyone falls unconscious you must lay him on his side, lest he choke on his own tongue."

Avalloc did as she had bidden.

Pushing back loose strands of her hair, Jewel laid her head close to the mouth of the young man, that she might hear whether he breathed or no. She was weeping as she did so. "Do not leave me," she whispered hopelessly. "Do not leave me, most cherished love." Copious tears flowed glistening down her cheeks, dropping lightly upon his lips. A fleck of darkness trickled from the corner of his mouth and blotted into the garments of the Maelstronnar.

Whereupon the young man moved.

Raven lashes fluttered. He licked his lips, and opened a pair of clear eyes as green as cut-glass goblets of absinthe.

"He lives!" The Storm Lord squeezed shut his own eyes, and bent his head, temporarily overcome.

By this time several weathermasters from their party had arrived, having heard rumor of Avalloc's call as he ran from the palace into the streets. Nyneve Longiníme held a flask to the mouth of the young man, and from it he sipped.

"In truth, is your name Arran?" quizzed Nyneve.

He smiled. "I am Arran Nithulambar Maelstronnar," he said; and with that, a great sigh went through those who surrounded him. There was no glamour deceiving the eyes of the beholders. Even so, some gramarye seemed to be at work, for Arran was making an exceptionally speedy recovery. He had already been helped to his feet, and was declaring he would walk to the palace. Crowds of onlookers were swelling in the thoroughfare. The weathermasters flocked around Arran as he made his way up the street, and some went ahead to clear the way, so that no member of the public might witness the son of the Maelstronnar, a weathermage, in that state of filth and degradation.

To the palace they all proceeded. The king had heard of the unlooked-for appearance of the Storm Lord's son, and Queen Saibh herself came to greet him.

"I am glad to welcome you, Arran Maelstronnar," said that dainty lady, "although I fear you have been in dire straits. Ask for anything you require for your good health. We shall not stint you, fair guest."

She conducted Arran to the best of apartments, where she left him in the company of his family and friends. All who were present noted that he could not take his eyes from Jewel, nor she from him. At first, his family would not leave him, and urged him to rest.

"I refuse to measure my length upon a couch like an ailing man!" he protested.

"But you were knifed!" exclaimed Lysanor.

"Naught but a scratch. I feel hale—better than I have ever felt before. But tell me, where are Rivalen, Bliant, and Gahariet, my companions from *Wanderpath*?"

"Bliant has returned, but his life is in peril," they told him. "The others were lost."

On hearing this news, Arran buried his face in his hands, and for a long while he was unable to speak. At length he bade them all leave him alone except for a single valet, so that he might bathe, and dress himself in clean garments.

He chose from an array of raiment sent to him with the compliments of the queen: an elaborately embroidered linen shirt next to his skin, linen leg-wrappings cross-gartered with leather thongs, a long tunic edged with knot-work, a sword-belt picked out in silver, high boots gilded with subtle designs, and a floor-length cloak lined with marten fur, fastened at the right shoulder by a disc brooch.

After Arran was refreshed, Jewel and the weathermasters sat with him in a private dining-room and he partook of food and drink with them. So handsome did he look that several of Queen Saibh's ladies-in-waiting made pretense of necessary journeys into that chamber, in order to glimpse him. Amongst the courtiers sighs of love murmured up and down the corridors of the palace like a flood of honeyed wine, and many of them glanced into looking glasses, primping and preening to ensure they looked their seductive best. Arran was oblivious of these reactions. His visage was etched with the grooves of sorrow for his ill-fated friends. He spoke very little, and ate less.

A paneled dado ran about the walls of the Oak Dining-Room. Coverings of patterned velvet interlaced with gold thread surmounted it. The ceiling was decorated with paintings by famous artists, set in gilded plaster frames. Tall windows overlooked the palace grounds. By night, the panes were lush with thick clusters of stars.

Something inside Jewel had broken, a hardness that for years had encapsulated her heart like the shell around a sweet almond kernel. It seemed to the damsel that this opulent chamber was empty save for the son of the Maelstronnar. To her own amazement, she opined she had never truly seen him before. He was a radiance that filled her vision, a flame that branded his image on her senses. It was with a sensation akin to shock that she looked upon him. Whenever his gaze alighted on her person she felt the thrill of a jolt, whereas merely to imagine his touch evoked an ecstasy of terrible delight. *It is true, what grandfather Earnán used to say,* she thought. *One never appreciates what one has, until it is lost. Arran was lost to me; now he is found. I would fain comfort him, for he feels the loss of his comrades keenly.*

During that meal extensive conversation took place between Arran and Jewel, none of it in words.

A messenger arrived bringing word that Aonarán had eluded capture. Streetwise and sly, he had escaped the net. For the satisfaction of his weathermaster guests, King Uabhar had issued a warrant for Aonarán's arrest, on charges of attempted murder.

"Arran, we are all marveling!" Galiene declared when the messenger had departed. "You survived a dagger in the back and neck, and now you eat and drink with us as if nothing had happened!"

"Tell how you survived and returned to us!" begged Lysanor.

Somberly but willingly, Arran related his story, describing the occurrences at Stryksjø that led up to the invocation of the lightning bolt to blast the Well of Dew, before elaborating on subsequent events.

"The destruction of the Well weakened me," he said. "For a while, I believe, I lost consciousness. When I had regained my wits and mustered sufficient strength, I began to make for land. I was stumbling along in somewhat of confusion when it came to me that I was splashing through water. Ice-melt was sloshing about my boots; the lake was melting rapidly. It could only mean that my companions had ceased to work their weathermastery. Visibility was poor, but I peered through the darkness to the shore, and saw that it was empty. At once I suspected foul play.

"It was then that I became aware of several armed strangers approaching across the ice. Alone and feeble as I was, I knew I stood no chance against them. I guessed that these men had overthrown my companions, and that they must surely be seeking the prize I was carrying. If I battled against them I would be defeated, and my life would be forfeit. They would plunder the Draught from my corpse and use it for their own ends.

"Worse was to come, for in the midst of these raiders there walked the woman Fionnuala Aonarán, and she aimed her crossbow at my heart, and I knew it would be loaded with a poisoned quarrel.

"For the space of a heartbeat or two I believed my doom was inescapable. Yet one path remained to me. In desperation I took the only choice left to me; I pulled the vial from my pocket and swallowed the Draught."

"You drank it?" Arran's family and friends echoed his words in astonishment.

"I was forced to do so, in order to stop it from falling into the wrong hands."

Simultaneously they showered questions upon him, but he lifted his hand in a gesture that requested silence, and courteously they held their peace.

"Indeed I drank it," he resumed. "However, this was no instant cure for my precarious plight. At the exact moment I gulped, she shot me through the chest. The dart's venom entered my bloodstream at the same time as the water of life. As both potions swirled through my veins, battling for my death or survival, I fell, half-insensible.

"Fionnuala's men—or perhaps they were Marauders; I could not tell, for their faces were muffled against the cold—lifted me in their arms. They dragged me to land, and laid me across the back of a horse. The entire party departed from Stryksjø and journeyed through Grïmnørsland. I had passed into delirium while the poison and the water waged their war in my flesh. For days, while I lay across the horse's crupper and was borne through the cold forests, I remained thus, unable to wield the *brí,* or even to reason. I was barely aware of my surroundings and what was happening to me. In hindsight I recall my captors reining in their mounts beneath evergreen trees, speaking of a balloon they had seen crossing the skies. They were keeping out of sight."

"What was their purpose?" asked Avalloc. "Where were they taking you, and why?"

"As the days passed, my mind grew clearer and I learned that they were heading back to Cathair Rua. I heard Fionnuala say she was waiting to see what would become of me. She said that if I lived she would lock me away forever. If I died, so be it. I believe she was in two minds about whether she wanted me to survive or not. Sometimes she wished I would die, because she was convinced I had slain Weaponmonger, a man for whom she cared. At other times she wanted me to live, because to be immortal in her cruel hands would be a worse punishment than death. She was wrathful—sorely wrathful—because I had consumed the Draught. That I had tasted it before her very eyes was insufferable to her, and she often revenged herself, treating me badly."

The Storm Lord made no comment. His silence was steel.

"Father has already despatched sleuths to track down Fionnuala and her cohorts," said Lysanor. "When Bliant told his story, we guessed the identity of the culprits. Somehow, in spite of precautions, Fionnbar Aonarán managed to pass details of the Well's whereabouts to his sister."

Arran kissed his sister's brow. "I look forward to seeing valiant Bliant again, and putting myself at his service until he is fully recovered."

"And he will be overjoyed to see you safe! But pray go on with your tale," murmured Lysanor.

"The henchmen of my tormentress begged her to ransom me if I lived," Arran continued, "but she would have none of it, and assured them they would be paid for their work in gold, as soon as we reached the city. As for the desperate war within my body, over time, the beneficial influence of the Draught was beginning to gain the advantage. As I lay head downward over the steed, I would sometimes spit bitter flecks from my lips. I reckoned they were drops of venom, expelled from my blood. Day by day my head cleared, my strength returned, and the blows rained upon me discomfited me less. We traveled for weeks, and during that time my captors gave me scant water to drink, and meager fare. Subject to such ill-usage, mortal man must surely have perished."

"In that case," Galiene said softly, clasping his hand in hers, "the efficacy of the Wells must be real. . . ." Her eyes were shining.

"The water defeated the poison, as you can see for yourselves. Instead of revealing my revived health, I feigned worsening illness until I was certain my powers had returned in full. Then, when their attention was focused elsewhere, I made my escape. By that time, the raiding party had almost reached Cathair Rua."

"Why were you so ill when you entered the city gates?"

"I had traveled for days. I was weary, even though the waters of life sustained me. Moreover, it was not until after I broke free that I was able to wrench the shaft of Fionnuala's cursed bolt from my ribs! Perhaps some last trace of pollution lingered in my system, causing my stupefaction. I had no thought, save to reach the palace, no idea what day of the year it was. I only knew that the season was Winter, and that soon you would all be gathering for the naming ceremony. At any rate, I was oblivious of my ambusher until he had cast me down."

"I fancied," said Jewel, "that he stole something from you."

Her eyes had turned a fascinating shade of blue, like highlights struck from an angled owl's feather.

"He stole nothing," said Arran. "I examined my pockets when I laid aside my ruined clothes. One thing of value I carried with me, and it remains still in my keeping."

"The empty vial?"

"Nay—a thing more strange; a tiny, harmless wight that aided me on my quest. It sleeps now, on the pillow of the curtained couch in my bedchamber. It is secretive of habit, and eschews large gatherings. I know not if it has a name, but it accompanied me all the way from Stryksjø. If ever a man was in need of friendship it was during that fell journey. As it seemed to me, that curious creature hiding itself in my pocket, half-crushed between me and the horse, was my sole ally. I suppose it would have bitten the hand of Aonarán, if that fellow tried to rob me. A nibble could not much harm a mortal man made immortal, yet it might have discomposed him!"

There was subdued laughter amongst the company, and much talk of their eagerness to see this wight if the creature should ever allow it; the hour, however, was late. Weariness came drifting down upon the lids of the assembly like the falling feathers of doves. They retired to their apartments for the night.

In the morning they bade farewell to their hosts and flew home to the mountain ring.

On their return Luned Longiníme informed them that Bliant's wounds were healing and his condition had improved. He was recovering. Throughout High Darioneth the sorrow of bereavement now mingled with the joy of friends reunited.

Jewel was invited to dine at the house of the Maelstronnar on the evening following their homecoming. It was an occasion of high jollity. After the meal Arran's sisters played music on harp and flute, and sang melodiously. Beside the hearth fire Avalloc sat, with his young son, Dristan, at his feet. Dristan's nurserymaid was amongst the merrymakers, and Avalloc's sister, Astolat Darglistel, with her five children, including Ryence.

Many people sang and made music. Ryence, who had imbibed large quantities of wine and mead, fell asleep on the hearth-rug. Tall jonquils of candles shed a mellow glow, and invoked restless shadows. Half enmeshed in those shadows, Arran danced with Jewel. Firmly in his arms he held her. For the moment it was sufficient just to be together; this was no time to be deliberating about a distant, uncertain future and what it might hold for such as they had become. Slowly they glided in unison, pressed so close together that at last he whispered, "I can feel your heart beating."

"I can feel yours."

They danced.

"You move so gracefully, like a swan," he murmured.

"You with your bird and animal comparisons!" she mocked gently.

" 'Tis because I love all things that live. Especially you."

They swayed.

"I have always loved you," said he.

She said, "I knew not what prize I had until it was taken from me."

The music played.

"I thought you were gone forever," she said. "I could not feel your pulse."

"You would make a sorry carlin, Jewel," he said. In his smile she glimpsed such profound and fettered passion she felt she toppled from some dizzying height. Excitement heightened her senses. "Feel it now." He captured her hand and pressed it to the side of his neck. Strong and firm was this muscular column, the skin smooth and warm. Beneath her fingers a tide throbbed, deep and swift; the tide of his life's blood.

He removed his hand, but she left hers in place, and presently her fingers found his hair, twisted themselves into the bewildering maze of twilight filaments, slid into the river of umber. Next thing she knew, the roughness of his jaw was pressed against her cheek; then blind torrents of sweetness came coursing as the contact between their mouths evolved into a kiss.

That night Arran and Jewel pledged themselves to each other.

XII

The Well

On Salt's Day, 28th Aoust 3471, five months after her eighteenth birthday, Jewel was wedded to Arran in the octagonal Tower of the Winds on Rowan Green. Her dress was of pure Saadian silk crêpe lasheen, with full, flared sleeves and a long train. It was trimmed with gold thread embroidery of intricate snowflakes around the neckline and sleeves, and laced at the back with gold ribbon. The boned and fitted bodice was of ivory velvet, and goldwork edged the over-skirt. A girdle of delicate filigree clasped the waist of the bride. Her headdress was a circlet of twisted yellow-gold and white-gold wires embellished with pearls and transparent crystals, holding in place a gold-bordered veil of ivory-colored silk chiffon. At her throat nestled a cluster of moonbeams, the gem her father had taken from the Iron Tree. Her eyes reflected the vivid blueness of flag-lilies studying their own images in clear waters.

What of Ettare Sibilaurë, who had been close to Arran? She was blithe to behold the couple's happiness, and delighted to be Jewel's bridesmaid along with Elfgifu and Hilde Miller. Bliant Ymberbaille, recovered from his wounds, played the part of best man. Avalloc Maelstronnar performed the ceremony, and afterward the Wedding Feast took place in Long Gables. The mighty Hall was crowded, for guests numbered in the hundreds. Representatives from the royal families of the Four Kingdoms had been invited: the wedding of the son of the Storm Lord was an affair of inter-realm importance.

Sustained by enormous entourages, there came Warwick Wyverstone, King of Narngalis, with Queen Emelyne; Halfrida, Queen of Grïmnørsland; King Uabhar's brothers Gearóid and Páid, and the sister of the King of Ashqalêth. The Druids Imperius of Narngalis and Grïmnørsland attended, accompanied by their assistants and an assortment of minions. The Sanctorums of Slievmordhu and Ashqalêth sent their Druids Secundus.

There were many other visitors, not so lofty. For Jewel the greatest joy was to be united with Arran. Second only to that was her delight at welcoming her friends and family from the Great Marsh of Slievmordhu, as wedding-guests. With open arms she greeted Earnán Mosswell, her grandfather—his hair and beard whitened by sixty Winters—and the marshfolk who arrived with him. Cuiva Rushford, the White Carlin of the Marsh, presented herself with her numerous clan: her father, the elderly Marsh Chieftain Maghnus; Muireadach, her brother; Keelin, her younger sister; her husband, Odhrán; her sons, Oisín and Ochlán; and her daughter, Ciara. They brought with them Rathnait Alderfen, and her husband the cooper, and Suibhne Tolpuddle with his sister Doireann. Neasán Willowfoil, the captain of the Marsh Watchmen, put in an appearance, along with Lieutenant Goosecroft.

Jewel seized the opportunity to relate her adventures to Earnán and Cuiva and to quiz them about the fateful connection between her father and the two Aonaráns.

"Who are these people, these Aonaráns?" she asked. "That dotard the sorcerer recognized Fionnbar as resembling one of his old servants; indeed, Fionnbar told us himself that his great-uncle served at Strang. But why did the woman, Fionnuala, seem to recognize me at our meetings? Why should she and her brother wish ill to our family? It is scarcely credible that they were ever associated with my father. I never heard him speak of them, and yet you tell me now that they were acquainted with him."

Apologizing for his sometimes-erratic memory, Earnán related everything he knew. "This is how it was told to me: The uncle of the Aonaráns was a servant of Janus Jaravhor. It was he who first discovered that your father was the sorcerer's scion. The man Fionnbar Aonarán supposed Jarred possessed special powers. He was wanting to make your father open the Dome for him, so that he might seize its fabled treasures. Your father, of course, refused to cooperate. It was Fionnbar's sister Fionnuala who was falling into an infatuation with Jarred. When he spurned her I daresay she was greatly angered, much as, long ago, Jaravhor of Strang was enraged by the rebuffs of Álainna Machnamh, your great-grandmother. So you see, because of their own greed, these two Aonaráns were fashioning for themselves a grudge against your father." Thus the eel-fisher revealed much that illuminated Jewel's past, and finally explained the history entwining Jarred and the Aonaráns.

Other eagerly looked-for guests included Yaadosh, Michaiah, Gamliel, Nasim, and Barakiel, Fridleif Squüdfitcher with his wife, Heidrun, and their children, and Heidrun's brother, Heiolf Meckerilnitter. By the time every introduction had been performed Jewel began to surmise she would require a notary's tome inscribed with genealogical lists in order to keep track of everyone.

The guests toasted the bride and groom:

> "Long may they live—happy may they be,
> Sained in contentment and from misfortune free!"

Of laughter and jollity there was sufficient and more, and as the newlyweds sat together upon their decorated chairs beneath the bridal canopy, they leaned together in private discourse, their hands continuously intertwining, their thoughts and breath mingling, their smiles inextinguishable.

"Of all the wedding gifts I have brought you," said Arran, "the one I most desired to bestow is not here."

"All that I crave is here before me now," she said.

"It is eternal life I wanted to give you."

"I am satisfied with your vow to be my husband."

"I am almost satisfied, but I cannot be completely so because I have failed you. I vowed to bring back for you the Draught from the Well of Dew, and I did not. In addition, I now desire the more urgently that you should be given the opportunity to join me in perpetual existence. Without you at my side, dearest love of my life, how shall I face infinity? Fortunately, there is a second chance. I will bring you the prize from the Well of Tears."

"There is no need for haste. Tarry a long while before you go questing."

"You might accompany me!"

Jewel pondered. During those terrible days when she and her uncle had fled from the tragedies of the marsh, when she wandered, burdened with grief, in the wilderness, she had privately determined that she would never again allow herself to suffer a plight so devastating. To avoid such misery she would strive to gain immunity from life's vagaries through the accumulation of wealth or knowledge or status, and moreover she would never entrust her heart to any living creature.

Now, everything had changed.

Events had radically altered her opinions; she had found security in her marriage to Arran and her home amongst the weathermasters at High Darioneth. She had cast to the eight winds the notion of eschewing love; love was too felicitous, too potent, to be avoided. Never had she guessed what joy true passion could bring. Loving Arran was an addiction that could not be cured, and she wished only to dwell with him indefinitely, in intimate affection and safety. Her former recklessness had been replaced by utter contentment.

"I have had enough of perilous adventure to last me for a goodly while," she said to her bridegroom. "I would prefer, for now, to stay at High Darioneth and rejoice in our new home, my new family, our friends, and other peaceful things."

"Then I might go without you."

"Prithee, do not!"

"Why not?"

"To be parted from you would sorely wound me!"

He looked straight into her eyes and said, "I swear I shall never wound you, except once, on this our wedding night."

She laughed and blushed, and then the musicians struck up a melody and it was time to dance.

It was a celebration of gigantic proportions, lasting for five days and nights. After the wedding Jewel dwelled with her husband in their own apartments, at the spacious and rambling house of the Maelstronnar. For more than two hundred years a domestic brownie had been attached to the household; like all the members of its species, it efficiently kept the premises spotless, working always during the night when mortalkind was sleeping. The new bride's duties were light. Married life began in gladness, and continued in bliss and harmony. Few concerns flawed the happiness of Arran and Jewel.

One such concern was the fact that neither Fionnbar Aonarán nor his sister Fionnuala could be found. The authorities in all Four Kingdoms had been informed that Fionnbar was in league with the Marauders, and he was wanted for questioning in every realm. King Warwick of Narngalis had issued a decree that the fellow should be arrested on sight, should he stray within the borders of the northern domain. Employed by the weathermasters of Rowan Green, sleuths went prying amongst the citizens of Cathair Rua. They learned much about the pale-eyed man and his half-sister, but not enough to discover where they were hiding themselves.

A second source of unrest for bride and groom was Arran's constant yearning to obtain the water from the Well of Tears. The reality that he was immortal while she was not drove him to distraction. She insisted that the matter need not plague him.

"There is no need to vex yourself. Let us linger in contentment. Besides, we do not know where the Well is located. We have only the riddle to guide us."

Arran spent numerous hours in the library of his father's house, trying to unravel the puzzle:

My hair is white, my bones are old.
Steadfast I rest, for ages cold
And still. So silent, lacking breath,
That men think I've been touched by death.
But deep within my chilly breast
My living heart can find no rest.
What falls and never breaks, but would
Be broken if it ever should
Stop falling? What is darkness? And
Can mortalkind make ropes of sand?

On an evening early in Autumn, he was thus occupied at home. Flames sizzled in the library fireplace. Brassware gleamed with licks of amber radiance. From floor to ceiling, the walls were lined with shelves of books. Fire-glow flashed and dithered up and down their gilded spines. Jewel sat on a cushion at Arran's feet, resting her head on his knee as he pored over tomes of vellum set out upon an escritoire. The fire was mirrored twice in her eyes, two miniature burning tiger-lilies.

Abruptly, Arran started up in a state of excitement.

"I may have solved the first part of the mystery!" he exclaimed. Without waiting for her response he spoke rapidly, "I believe the answer is 'A cascade of water in the core of a snowcapped mountain'! *'Deep within my chilly breast,'* " he quoted, " *'My living heart can find no rest. / What falls and never breaks, but would / Be broken if it ever should / Stop falling?'* The solution is, 'a waterfall'!"

"An insight indeed!" said Jewel, lifting her head to gaze up at him. "It makes sense, certainly. Yet, what of these *ropes of sand?*"

"That is more difficult to decipher," he said, thumbing through the book in front of him.

"The phrase puts me in mind of that song you sang to me," she said.

"I, too, have pondered on that song, in case any answer should be found between the lines. Recall, we found out how to reach the Well of Rain by listening to a children's ditty. Yet 'Ropes of Sand' gives no clue. In fact, the entire object of the song was to emphasize how impossible it is to weave ropes out of non-adhesive grains."

"Aye," she agreed ruefully. "Even an eldritch wight could not achieve it."

"An eldritch wight! That gives me another idea. I shall consult a book of weird lore."

"Since you are so determined to pursue these researches," said Jewel, "I shall admit defeat, and help you. Sometimes I wish we possessed the lore-volumes of Strang, which were destroyed in the explosion. Wondrous indeed they must have been, without doubt, antique and extensive anthologies! Does your father's library contain any books about the highlands of the Four Kingdoms? I now wish to read about a mountain that contains a waterfall."

"There must be many such mountains!"

"Nevertheless, I wish to aid you, and so I shall study!"

"Nay, you are merely bored, pursuing amusement."

"Not so! Or if I am, shall you not remedy my boredom in other ways?"

"In more ways than you can imagine!"

She climbed into his lap. The kiss they made together was long and sweetly languorous, but their indulgence was terminated unexpectedly when the door to the library burst open and Dristan came running in, laughing. His nurserymaid pursued him, entreating him vainly, "Come here, young man! It is well past your bed-time!"

Jewel jumped from her husband's knee and ambushed the errant child, scooping him in her arms. She planted a kiss on his brow and returned him to his protector, bidding him enjoy sweet dreams.

"Good night, Dristan!" Arran called out good-naturedly to his sibling.

Cheerfully the child returned the salute and permitted himself to be carried off by his nursemaid.

"Is there no privacy to be found in this house?" said Jewel, feigning indignation.

Arran replied dryly, "Not in the library."

Jewel wandered up and down the rows of books, peering inquisitively at the gilt-embossed titles upon their spines. While she examined the literary hoard, Arran returned to his musing, repeating the lines of the riddle.

Presently he said, "One line does not fit in with rest. *What is darkness?'* The phrase seems to be just stuck there with no link to the rest of the poem."

Returning to his side, Jewel said, "I understand your meaning. The initial six lines describe, as we believe, a mountain. After them follow three questions, the first hinting at a waterfall, the third setting forth the conundrum of rope-making. But there would seem to be no reason for the second question. It is as if the verse-maker has merely included it to keep the rhythm regular."

"Yet the rhymester might have possessed more cunning than we credit," said Arran. "Perhaps 'tis another clue in the riddle, to pinpoint the precise location of this mountain. *What is darkness?'* Of course, it is the lack of light. Any cavern at the root of a mountain must be lightless. How can this be a clue?"

"I daresay it is some anagram," suggested Jewel.

"Ah! Perhaps you're right! Let us work it out."

The escritoire's shelves held an assortment of inkbottles, quill pens, pen-sharpeners, blotting-sand, and blotting paper. Arran opened a drawer and withdrew a thick sheaf of paper. Together the couple scribbled away, forming various combinations of letters.

"Hearken to this," said Jewel, holding up a sheet covered with scrawled characters, mostly crossed out. *" 'Wards she knits.'* That might indicate an ancient site where some eldritch hag sits forever knitting metal wires into chain mail, or weaving indestructible hauberks from enchanted thread."

"That makes sense, but I have another for you," said Arran. *" 'Dark swan, he sits.'* It might mean large flocks of black swans inhabit this place."

" 'A hand strew kiss,' " said Jewel, kissing him quickly.

" 'A hand wrest kiss,' " he rejoined, reciprocating.

With much merriment they labored at their task. Every re-arrangement of the phrase's letters began to sound more foolish than the last.

" 'A shard west sink': A tall peak, in the shape of a jagged shard, looms against the setting sun!"

" 'A dart hews sinks': Pieces of rock shaped like arrowheads continually break off and fall from the heights. Over the decades, their impact hollows out a sink-like crater."

" 'A swan-herd skits': At a certain location, a village swan-herd regularly performs a short, usually comic theatrical performance."

By this time, both newlyweds were holding their sides and gasping with laughter. Tears streamed down Jewel's face.

" 'Dark sanest wish'!"

" 'Dark ashen wits'!"

" 'Sand hawk sister.' "

"Oh, *'sand'*!" exclaimed Jewel, sobering abruptly. "That is an excellent notion. We ought to include the word in all our conjectures. *'Sand saw the risk.'* "

" 'Sand was *the risk.' "*

" 'Sands at whisker.' " She tweaked the stubble on Arran's unshaven chin.

" 'Sand shaker wits.' " He entwined his fingers in her hair and gently shook her head.

" 'Sand wreaks this.' " She poked him in the ribs, where he was ticklish, and for a while they abandoned their paperwork.

Eventually they gave up on their puzzle solving. "There are too many possible permutations!" Jewel cried. "What's more, the phrase might not be an anagram at all!"

"What is even *more,*" said her husband, "there are distractions unnumbered between the walls of this library!"

"And the hour is late," said Jewel, pointing her finger toward a diamond-latticed window. "See, the moon has arisen." Beyond the embrasure a vast, illuminated disc hung in the void, almost filling the frame entirely. Thin purple smokes streamed across its face, which glimmered softly azure.

"A storm moon," commented Arran, "blue as your eyes."

Sudden solemnity overcame the couple. He wrapped his arms around her and she leaned against him, alive to his warmth. They stood together, gazing through the leaded panes to where the moon walked in her garden of sidereal blossoms. Her glow sifted over the watchers, like silvery dunes.

Arran bent his head close to his bride's ear and whispered, "Let us hie to our own apartments, where privacy *does* prevail."

The tiny wight that had accompanied Arran from Grïmnørsland, hidden in his pocket, had appeared unexpectedly out of the folds of his cloak when he arrived at his father's house.

"I have come to dwell with you," it had declared. When examined closely, it had shown itself to be about six inches high, with paw-like hands and a slender tail that ended in a tassel, like a cow's tail. It was in the habit of picking up this tail with one of its paws, and twirling it rapidly. Black as coal was its skin, as if the creature had been burned in a fire. A pair of eyes like shiny beads peered from a face that resembled a walnut, or a dried pea slightly squashed. Its garments comprised a collection of patches and rags, of the kind usually worn by wights of minor ilk.

After the wight's startling reappearance, when Arran had regained his composure he asked, "What about your ailing mother in the pine forests of Grïmnørsland? Does she not require you?"

"She's ailing no more. Besides, she's got me siblings to look after the bottomless tankard. They dwell with her, in the green mound. Besides, she's only feeling poorly when mortalkind with casks of beer come into the vicinity—which has happened only once or twice these past one hundred years. Trappers, woodcutters, fishers—they carry with them ale and stronger drink, and we test 'em, we do, to see if they keep their word. Besides, 'tis a good way to get some brew. None of 'em has ever kept his word, until you."

"Is that why you chose to come with me?"

"That and other reasons," the thing said loftily. "I'd a yen to travel."

"I have no objections to your making your home with me, if you are well intentioned toward mortalkind."

"That I am!"

Arran had been unable to work out whether this small impet-thing was male or female. It had appeared to be a boy, when the glamour was on it in the pine wood, but now that the illusion had passed, the creature's sex was indeterminate. "What's your name?" he had asked, unwilling to risk offending the entity and hoping for some clue.

"That I'm not a-telling you," the wight said smugly, twirling its tail.

The tail-twirling struck an echo in Arran's thoughts, causing him to recall a nursery tale. "Ah, you are one of *those* creatures, a spinner of straw into gold, a child stealer!"

"What?" squawked the impet.

"If you are one of that species, I shall drive you from my door!"

"I'm not!"

"What is your name?" the young weathermage demanded sternly. "Is it Tom-Tit-Tot? Is it Trwtyn-Tratyn? Terrytop? Habetrot?"

"No, no!" squealed the wight, scooting beneath the nearest piece of furniture. "Don't be calling me rude names!" Only the tip of its tail showed from beneath a three-legged stool. "Our mither tell'd us all," it said in muffled tones, " *'never say your name to mortalkind. Otherwise the big folk will get power over you.'* "

Once Arran had ascertained the thing was no sly child stealer, he made peace with it and allowed it to stay, even though it bluntly refused to divulge its true name. He dubbed it "Nimmy Nimmy Not," in token of the nursery tales, and it didn't object to the sobriquet. It took to living underneath various items of furniture, but was sometimes to be found in the kitchen or the cellars, in the shape of a small boy, drinking beer with the butler. The resident brownie ignored the newcomer.

Rarely, the impet volunteered data. Occasionally this data was unwelcome.

"The immortal animals did not breed," it said once.

"What do you mean?" they asked.

"The ones that got to be immortal by drinking the waters of life. They never had offspring."

"Go away," Arran said fiercely.

The wight's words weighed on Jewel, who aired the topic afterward, in consultation with the carlin of High Darioneth.

"I know 'tis not impossible for immortal beings to produce children," Jewel began. "Trows produce babies, and I daresay other wights do as well. But admittedly it is rare to hear stories of eldritch infants."

"As you say, 'tis unusual yet not impossible," said her advisor. "You yourself have told me the tale of how your uncle was repaid with good fortune for giving some wights a wrapping for their newborn child. Moreover, wights can be slain. It is only if they are not slain that they live forever. Those that die must be replaced, else all eldritch wights would vanish from the world. I would judge that immortal beings can reproduce well enough, but their fertility is low."

"I have a question to test your wisdom," said Jewel. "Three mortal creatures that were not of the human race drank of the waters of life: a hare, a deer, a bird.

Their case is different, because they were born mortal, not eldritch. They were the last of their line. Without death, shall there be birth?"

"If the immortal beasts produced no progeny," Luned said, "it was no doubt because others of their kind scented their strangeness, and would not mate with them."

"What of mortal men who have become immortal?"

"That we cannot know for certain."

Jewel and Arran had not embarked on a honeymoon after the wedding, for there was much work to be done. Tir's atmosphere had not yet regained its original stability in the aftermath of the freezing of Lake Stryksjø. Across the Four Kingdoms the weather had been capricious and violent, and the services of weathermages were greatly in demand.

Whenever weatherworking did not demand Arran's attention, he and Jewel would take advantage of the opportunity to depart on some jaunt, or attend various forms of organized amusement at locations throughout the kingdom. High Darioneth was situated in the heart of Narngalis, and the weathermasters were in close alliance with the palace at King's Winterbourne. Sundry, manifold, and diverting were the annual events that signposted the seasons of that northern realm. On 4th Sevember they and their friends were amongst the spectators at the lavishly antlered King's Winterbourne Horn Dance. By Lantern Eve, on 31st Otember, they had returned to High Darioneth for the equinoctial celebrations. Come Tenember, Midwinter's Eve and Midwinter's Day festivities rolled around again—too swiftly, it seemed. Yet the season brought welcome news, for Jewel discovered she was with child, and the couple's happiness knew no bounds. The old year fled, on slippers of snow diamonded with frost. The young year, 3472, tiptoed in, presenting Wassailing the Apple Trees on 6th Jenever, Averil Fool's Day on 1st Averil, and Mai Day on the first of that month. On 19th Juyn the King's Winterbourne Silver Arrow Contest was held. Hard on its heels came Midsummer's Day.

Jewel had been carrying the child for some seven months, but she refused to allow her gravidity to be an obstacle to traveling. Everywhere they visited, they asked knowledgeable folk whose discretion could be trusted—carlins, some druids, a few wanderers—if they knew the whereabouts of a mountain with a waterfall at its very heart.

The two Aonaráns were still in hiding, whether in some lonely charcoal burner's hut or deep in the labyrinthine alleys of some city nobody could tell. Their disappearance was of concern to Avalloc, Arran, Jewel, and their friends; nevertheless, seek as they might, the weathermasters and their agents could find no trace of the pale-haired siblings, or if clues turned up, the trail was always cold. Therefore they asked judiciously when trying to discover the mountain that housed the Well of Tears, for they had no wish to give their enemies any clue as to the trail they followed.

Arran's immortality was not made public knowledge. Amongst the weathermasters only the councillors of Ellenhall were aware of it; similarly, only a few knew about Jewel's invulnerability. These two matters were meticulously defended secrets, and if King Uabhar guessed the sorcerer's scion owned any singular qualities other than her rare beauty, he gave no evidence of his suspicions. The weathermasters had assured him that Jewel possessed no extraordinary powers, and now that she had become a weathermage's wife she enjoyed their utmost protection.

Arran requested that his weathermaster colleagues be vigilant, during their travels, in gleaning tidings of the elusive mountain. The conundrum was this: many thousands of mountains, mighty and minor, crowded the great ranges of Tir. What lay at their roots was usually a mystery; not only were they too numerous to have all been explored, but frequently their interiors were inaccessible. Arran hoped that local knowledge or traditional tales might provide some guiding information.

From time to time sky-balloon crews would bring news of a place that fitted the description. If Arran's missions took him near the location of the candidate he would make a detour and try to find a way of entering under the mountain. So far he had achieved no success in locating the Well of Tears.

Despite its remote location, there was a sparse but constant cycle of visitors at High Darioneth. One was an acquaintance of Avalloc Maelstronnar: Almus Agnellus, erstwhile assistant to the Storm Lord's old friend the ex-druid Adiuvo Constanto Clementer. Agnellus had become a wandering scholar, traveling in the company of his loyal squire.

Toward the end of Ninember in the previous year, Secundus Clementer had taken a courageous and unprecedented step, formally renouncing his belief in the existence of the Fates and cutting all ties with the Sanctorum. At great risk of the severe penalties for such heresy, he publicly broadcast his views, "declaring the truth," so that other druids and philosophers might learn his theories.

The Druid Imperius had reacted swiftly and ruthlessly. In the dead of night, burly thugs had burst into Clementer's bedchamber as he lay sleeping. They seized the Secundus and dragged him away. His possessions, too, had been confiscated, including many scrolls of his essays and other writings.

Before his arrest Clementer had visited the Great Marsh of Slievmordhu for the purpose of gathering research for his book *A Treatise on the Iron Tree: A Narrative Concerning the Tree, the Precious Stone Trapped Therein, and the Consequences of the Stone's Removal.* He had interviewed both Earnán Kingfisher Mosswell and Cuiva Featherfern Stillwater. Afterward he had investigated further, to fill in the missing segments of the tale—even going to the lengths of questioning such personages as a street beggar, an innkeeper in Cathair Rua, and one of King Uabhar's footmen—before writing down his discoveries in narrative form.

Clementer was fond of discussing his evolving doctrines and illuminations with close associates, but his field research was a different matter. He had never shown the text of *On the Iron Tree* to anyone, preferring—like many authors— to keep it to himself until the final word had been written. The book had grown into a formidable tome, which, since his detainment, was lost or destroyed.

Of what had happened to Clementer after this forcible abduction Agnellus could discover nothing. He became gripped by terror, lest in the stew of back- biting, social climbing, and undermining that was the political milieu of the Sanctorum, his master's offenses should somehow come to be laid at his own door. Moreover, the usually placid druid was incensed by the treatment meted out to his venerable mentor. The injustice and violence of these events hardened his resolve; he refused to allow the Secondus's thought-provoking ideas to be quashed, and determined that if Clementer could no longer keep them alive, he, Agnellus, would preserve, augment, and disseminate them on his behalf.

Agnellus and one of the novices who supported him had fled in secret. Now they passed their days traveling the Four Kingdoms, discussing Clementer's philosophical revelations with people from all walks of life, collecting knowl- edge, studying, sometimes even conversing with eldritch wights. Because of the edicts of the Sanctorum, which demanded death or life-imprisonment as the punishment for perfidy, they were forced to travel in disguise, never remaining for long in one place. Agnellus's once-plump frame had become gaunt, and his appearance wild and weather-beaten due to his earnest pursuit of knowledge in remote locations.

Avalloc and Agnellus spent long afternoons in discussion.

"I have no hesitation in confessing to you, my friend," the scholar said to the Storm Lord during one of their lengthy discourses, "that I feel demoralized. My career with the Sanctorum seems to have been without purpose. Adiuvo used to share all his speculations with me, and his reasoning cannot be faulted. Conse- quently it now appears to me that the way of the druids is merely superstition, a spurious method of comprehending the incomprehensible. In an effort to find some species of meaning, Adiuvo devoted much of his time to scientific re- search. At last he discovered the truth. The Fates are an invention of mortalkind, conjured to fulfill two functions: the myth is a wondrous source of income for the druids, and it gives false hope to the populace."

"There are some, my dear fellow," replied Avalloc, "who would hold that even false hope is better than none. Besides, who is to say that real hope might not ultimately be within reach, against all odds, perhaps in some previously inconceivable form?"

Yet Agnellus would not be convinced, and with his squire at his side, determinedly continued on his peregrinations, seeking wider knowledge.

While the days winged past at incredible speeds, the nameless tassel-tailed wight rarely appeared at the apartments of Jewel and Arran. Evidently it dwelled contentedly down in the furniture, now and then allowing itself to be spied reclining on the arm of a chair while biting an enormous apple, or sunning itself on a windowsill.

It seldom showed itself, even when Jewel and Arran spent hours in the Maelstronnar's library looking through the books in their endeavors to map the locations of hollow mountains, whose deepest interiors resounded to the music of falling waters.

Time passed, and none could solve the riddle. The members of the Council puzzled over it, discussed it, and consulted books and scrolls in the libraries of High Darioneth and the archives of the Sanctorums. Always they were careful to avoid broadcasting the riddle in their search for the answer, in case the sorcerer's rhyme should come to the attention of Aonarán, or any other adventurer who might seek to possess the final marvelous Draught.

Time and again, as they passed pleasant evenings in the Maelstronnar's library, Jewel and Arran mulled over the phrase *"What is darkness?"*

" 'She skirts a wand,' " hazarded Jewel one night, returning to the anagram theory.

" 'Sands swear kith,' " guessed Arran.

" 'We risk sand hats.' "

" 'Sand hews its ark.' "

"Surely it is impossible for this to be any anagram. . . ."

On an evening early in Aoust, the tiny wight popped out of Arran's pocket, twirled its tail, and said, "Indeed, 'tis an anagram."

"Ach, Nimmy Not!" snapped Jewel. "You made me jump, you mischief!"

The creature shaped its wide mouth into a grin like a canoe.

"Hello, Thing," said Arran. "Can you unravel it?"

"I can do anagrams in me noddle!"

"What's the solution?"

"Ah," the wight said sagely, "you cannot demand solutions from me, man. You have no power over me because you do not know my name."

"Well, what *is* your name?"

"'Tis . . ." The impet hesitated, then seemed to pull itself together. Crossly it declared, "You must not just *aks* me like that! Me mither tell'd us not to say our names to mortalkind!" Brightening, it added, "Then again, if you *guess* me name I'd be *obliged* to help you with the anagram." After bouncing down the length of Arran's arm it skittered across the floor and took up one of its favorite perches on the window seat.

"We all know how the name of your cousin the straw-spinner came to be guessed," said Arran. "It is the matter of legend."

"Yes, yes," scoffed the wight. "I have never claimed *that* as a cousin. *That* was foolish."

"I am not familiar with the story," said Jewel.

"Good." The wight clambered up some shelves laden with books.

Arran said, "Shall I tell it to you?"

"Pray do," said Jewel, seating herself beside him on the library settle.

"There once was a woman," said Arran, "who was so proud of her daughter's skills that she boasted to all and sundry, 'My daughter spins so well, she could spin straw into gold.'

"The boast came to the attention of a nobleman—a viscount, no less—who was seeking a bride for his son. 'Go and see this damsel,' he told the youth. 'If she pleases you, and if the rumors of her extraordinary abilities are true, you shall take her to wife.'

"The son, being obedient, did as his father had instructed. It was a fine Summer's day when he and his squire rode by the cottage where the damsel dwelled with her mother. The window shutters had been flung wide, and from within the house came the sound of melodious singing. The son of the viscount looked through the window and what he saw entranced him. The loveliest girl he had ever seen was sitting at her wheel, singing as she worked. Instantly he fell in love with her, as usually happens in these old tales."

"Love at the first encounter is not merely a fable," said Jewel.

Arran smiled, and kissed her on the mouth before resuming: "He knocked at the door, was granted entrance to the house, and spoke with the two occupants. When the woman learned that her daughter had the chance of marrying an aristocrat she was overjoyed. 'However,' said the young man, 'my father has imposed a condition. She must be able to spin gold from straw.' The damsel drew breath to deny the rumor, but the mother was too quick for her. 'Oh she can do that, of course!' she cried, eager for the grand wedding.

"The young man was greatly relieved. Although," Arran digressed, "he must have been dull-witted if he believed anyone who could turn straw into gold would be spending her days at a spinning wheel in a lowly cottage!"

"Perhaps he was made dull-witted by love," Jewel suggested.

"I believe he was thick-headed to begin with," Arran asserted. "Anyway, the daughter liked the son of the viscount well enough, for he was a well-favored fellow, so she asked if she would have to prove the claim before they were wed. At this juncture, I daresay the young chap commenced to see a glimmer of reason. If this lovely girl could not prove the claim he could not wed her, so he told them this: After the wedding, the daughter would be allowed to spend twelve months in idleness. At the end of this honeymoon period she would have to spin half a bale of straw into gold every day for a month. In his heart the son hoped his father would not insist on the test when he beheld the girl's comely face and heard her sweetly singing.

"'All right, she'll marry you,' said the mother. She was thinking: *As for the straw, when it comes to the time for spinning it there will be plenty of ways of getting out of it. Besides—most likely the whole idea will be forgotten by then.*

"The outcome was that the daughter married the son of the viscount, and the couple lived happily together in their stately mansion for eleven and a half months. At that time the old viscount started talking about the gold-spinning test, and the bride began to dread what might happen. He was a spiteful old gentleman, this peer of the realm, and he told her that if she did not pass the test she would have all her hair shorn off, and her two index fingers severed, and she would be cast out into the world to live or die, because the pact she had made would be broken."

"A most amiable father-in-law," Jewel commented.

"And a most gormless bridegroom, for he had not the courage to gainsay his father's cruel edict," said Arran sternly. "So the bride begins to weep and moan and wring her white hands, and she wanders about the house all sorrowful and distraught. She ends up in the kitchen, late at night when all the servants have gone to bed. And as she's sitting by the hearth, sobbing, she hears a knocking. It's coming from low down on the door that leads outside to the kitchen gardens. After drying her eyes with her handkerchief she opens the door; but nobody is there, and she's mystified, peering out into the lonely night.

"Then a strange voice like the complaining of a rusty hinge says, 'What are yew a-cryin' for?'

"The girl looks down and there on the doorstep is a small creature like a dried-out old man, all dusky and shrunken, but with a long, thin tail that's spinning around slowly. She backs away warily.

"'What's it to you?' she says.

"'Niver yew mind,' the thing replies, 'but tell me what you're a-cryin' for.'"

Amusement twitched at the corners of Jewel's mouth as she listened to Arran mimicking the queer accents of the wight.

He continued: " 'I won't be any better off if I do,' says the girl, starting to sob once more.

" 'Yew doon't know that for sure,' says the thing, and its tail spins a little faster.

"The girl reconsiders. 'Well,' she says, 'I suppose it won't do me any harm, even if it won't do me any good.' So she tells the thing all her woes: how she's going to be placed in a room on her own every day for a month, with a spinning wheel and half a bale of straw to transform into bullion, and if she does not pass the test, she will be mutilated and driven away.

" 'This is what I'll dew,' says the little dusky thing. 'I'll come to yar winder iv'ry mornin' an' take the straw an' bring it back spun iv'ry evening.'

"For the first time a glint of hope kindles in the damsel's spirits. Yet she would not allow herself to be joyful, for she understood the ways of the world.

" 'What pay do you want?' she inquired suspiciously.

"The thing looked out of the corners of its eyes and said, 'I'll give you three chances every night to guess my name, an' if you hain't guessed it afore the month's up yew shall be mine.' "

"A generous bargain," interrupted Arran's wight, who was perched on a bookshelf, leaning against a vellum-bound tome. "My cous—er, I mean, *that* was not only offering to save her from ruin; it was also giving her a chance to avoid payment!"

"In my opinion the thing was merely trying to prolong the girl's dread," said Arran. "With the unusual name it bore, how could it expect to fail?"

"There you go, seeing the worst in everybody," grumbled the wight. It sprang across to a curtain, shinned down, and disappeared again behind the window seat.

"The girl accepted the bargain," Arran told his wife. "After all, what option had she?"

"And she might have imagined she had a chance of guessing the name."

"Indeed. Then, when she told the thing she agreed, it twirled its tail madly and vanished into the night."

"Members of those species are most expert at sudden vanishings," said Jewel loudly, "or so I've heard. What happened next?"

"Early in the morning, before the sun came up, the spiteful old viscount had the damsel locked into a room on her own," said Arran, "along with some food and drink, half a bale of straw, and a spinning wheel. She was told not to come out until she had spun the straw into gold, or the punishment would be immediate."

"What of the gormless husband?"

"Perhaps he was threatened with disinheritance if he tried to help his bride.

Perhaps he was hatching some far-fetched plan. I suspect it was guilt at his own weakness that made facing her unbearable. At any rate, he must have stayed away from his wife, for the story does not mention him at this point. It tells how the damsel sat weeping by the wheel, certain that no help would come, until she heard a knocking at the window. She got up and opened it, and there she saw the little old thing, sitting on the ledge.

" 'Where's the straw?' it said.

" 'Here,' she said, handing it over.

"All day she stayed in the room, chewing on her fingernails and worrying. Not a bite of food did she eat, in her anxiety. Then the sun went down, and as before there came a knocking on the window. She ran to open it, and there was the thing, with a glittering skein of pure gold thread draped over its arm.

" 'Here it is,' said the thing, giving it to her. 'Now, what's my name?' it asked.

"She hazarded a guess, blurting out the first name that entered her head. 'Is it Bill?'

" 'No, that ain't,' said the thing. And it twirled its tail.

" 'Is it Ned?' said she.

" 'No, that ain't,' said the thing. And it twirled its tail.

" 'Well, is it Jim?' she said.

" 'No, that ain't,' said the thing, and it twirled its tail harder, before vanishing into the night.

"When the door was unlocked, the old viscount almost had an apoplexy in his astonishment, for there stood the damsel with the skein of gold ready in her hands. After grabbing the skein and admiring the way it shone before his eyes he recovered soon enough, saying, 'I see we shan't have to cut off your hair and fingers tonight, my dear. Off you go, but come back to work here in the morning and you'll have your straw and vittles.' Without another word he hobbled away to his treasury. She went to her bedchamber, where she slept alone. Her husband, apparently, had gone away on a long hunting trip, and was resting each night at the viscount's country lodge.

"Every day the straw and food were brought, and every day the little dusky thing would appear in the mornings and the evenings. The damsel would spend the entire day trying to decide on the best names to tell it when it arrived at night. But she never hit on the right one, and as it got toward the end of the month the thing's facial twitches became quite malicious, and it twirled its tail faster and faster each time she made a guess.

"The last day but one eventually dawned. When the thing came that night with the skein of gold, it said, 'What, hain't yew got my name yet?'

" 'Is it Nicodemus?' said she.

" 'Noo, t'ain't,' the thing said.

" 'Is it Hvergelmir?' "

" 'Noo, t'ain't,' the thing said. "

" 'Well,' she cried in desperation, 'is it Bozorgmehr?' "

" 'Noo, t'ain't that norther,' the thing said. Then it looked at her with eyes like coals of fire, saying, 'Woman, there's only tomorrer night, an' then yar'll be mine!' " "

"And then it vanished into the night?" Jewel inquired.

"Verily; whereupon, the damsel was overwhelmed with fear and alarm. She began to consider that wandering bald and fingerless in the wilderness might have been a better fate than the one she now faced."

A noise like a snort exploded behind the window seat.

"Just then," said Arran, "she heard the sound of footsteps coming along the passageway and knew someone was coming to unlock the door. She composed herself as best she could. The door opened and in came the viscount—this time, accompanied by his gormless son. When he saw the skein of gold in the hands of his wife the young husband looked delirious with joy.

" 'My sweet!' he said to her as his father appropriated the gleaming web. 'You have almost passed the test. Since you have come this far, I don't see any reason why you will not be able to have the gold ready tomorrow night as well! Our ordeal is as good as over!'

" '*Our* ordeal?' she repeated. Her irony was, however, lost on the infatuated and noticeably fatuous young man.

" 'Since all is going so well,' he enthused, 'let us dine together this night!'

" 'I am surpassingly tired,' she began frostily; but on catching the warning eye of the cruel old viscount she revised her intention. 'Nonetheless I would be delighted.'

"That night supper was laid out for the couple in the best dining hall. Despite that the food and drink were excellent, the bride could scarcely bring herself to touch a morsel. Whenever she looked at her husband, who was as good-looking as he was spineless, it came to her that his personal attentions would be more pleasant than those of the little old thing with the twirling tail. The son of the viscount prattled on, oblivious. They had hardly progressed to the second course when he ceased eating and talking, and began to laugh.

" 'What is it?' she asked.

" 'The funniest thing happened when I was out hunting,' he said. 'We found ourselves in a section of the forest we had never seen before. It seemed a very old part, for the trees were huge, and bedecked all over with long strands of moss. Amongst their great roots was an old chalk pit with a kind of humming sound coming out of its depths. Interested to discover what it might be, I dismounted, stole quietly up to the edge of the pit, and looked down. Well, it was rather dark down there, what with the overhanging trees and all; nevertheless, I could see the funniest little dusky thing you ever set eyes on, and what was it doing but sitting at a little spinning wheel! It was spinning wonderfully fast, while twirling its tail at the same time, and as it spun it sang:

> ' "Nimmy nimmy not,
> My name's Tom Tit Tot." '

"When his bride heard this she felt as if she could have jumped out of her skin with happiness, but she forced herself to appear calm, and said nothing.

"Next morning the little thing looked more malicious than ever when it came to take away the straw. When the sun had gone down, she heard the usual knocking on the windowpanes. She opened the window and the thing hopped right over on to the interior sill. It was grinning from pointed ear to pointed ear, and oh! its tail was twirling around so fast!

" 'What's my name?' it said as it gave her the golden skein.

" 'Is it Farrokhzad?'

" 'Noo, t'ain't,' the thing said, and it came further into the room."

Vastly entertained, Jewel broke in, "What a cool-nerved wench, to sport so impudently with the creature!"

"Why not, when she knew the answer, and it had taunted her for so long?" Arran replied with a smile. "So then the woman guessed again. 'Well, is it Zedbedee?' said she.

" 'Noo, t'ain't,' said the thing, and then it laughed and twirled its tail until the appendage was almost invisible. 'Take time, woman,' it said. 'Next guess and you're mine!' And it stretched out its shriveled hands toward her.

"She retreated a step or two, feigning terror as she stared at the creature. Then suddenly she laughed aloud, pointed her finger straight at it, and said:

> " 'Nimmy nimmy not,
> Your name's Tom Tit Tot.'

"When it heard her words, the creature shrieked like a hundred whistles. The table lamp fell over, and an enormous shadow seemed to flare from behind the creature's scrawny shoulders. There was a chaotic flapping, like pumping sails of leather, and with a *whoosh* the thing flew out the window into the dark.

"She never saw it again."

Arran's impet had emerged from its sanctuary. It now jumped up and down on the window seat. "That could not fly!" it chirruped shrilly. "That never had wings! Storytellers invented a false ending."

"Why are you so agitated?" Jewel asked, concealing her mirth at the little creature's antics.

"That was foolish enough to chant its name when that believed that could not be overheard!" said the wight scornfully. "Foolish enough to spin, while broadcasting that's name in a vapid example of doggerel. This is how that was thwarted!"

"Exactly!" agreed Arran.

"But I won't blather out my name, I won't make rhymes in private or public!" pontificated the impet. "I mind what my mither said. I remember the exact time she said it to me. It were a morning early in Spring, and the frost still unmelted on the ground, and she said to me, *'Fridayweed, don't you dare tell your name to any of the big folk. Hearken to me now—don't you do that!'*"

"So that's your name!" cried Jewel. "Fridayweed!"

The wight looked aghast. "Now, how would you be knowing that?" it screeched. "How did you guess my name?"

"You mentioned it just now," said Arran.

"Did I? Did I?" the wight shrieked, over-balanced, and fell over backward, disappearing into the corner shadows of the window seat.

Much later it reappeared, looking sheepish.

"What about that anagram?" it suggested.

"Fridayweed," said Arran, "come here and seat yourself upon the escritoire, and tell us all you know about the Well of Tears."

The impet obliged.

"I'll tell you about that well," it said. "'Tis at Whitaker's Sands. That is the name of the place where the mountain squats. It is the answer to the anagram."

Instantly Jewel began rifling through a pile of half-unrolled parchment maps. Arran held his breath, keyed up with expectation.

Its vocabulary and grammatical skills having become vastly more sophisticated since it had taken to frequenting the library and sleeping amongst the dictionaries, the impet fluently expounded: "At Whitaker's Sands in this very kingdom, there is a waterfall in the core of a haunted mountain called Whitaker's Peak. It can only be reached by way of a declension called the Deep Stair, accessed by a doorway that gives on to the high places near the summit. Four thousand, nine hundred, and thirty-one steps lead down to a cliff beside that waterfall. It is said by the wights inhabiting Whitaker's Peak that no mortal being can descend the cliff, except on ropes of sand. Near the foot of the cascade, but in a small, separate area, the ground is scooped out in the shape of a bowl. This is the Well of Tears. Long ago a Star, or part of a Star, fell through a fissure in the mountainside and plowed a downward shaft. In later centuries the shaft was hacked into the shape of a stairway by mining wights, the Fridean, Blue-caps, Knockers, and the like."

Between excitement and incredulity Arran said, "And can you take me to this doorway? Do you know how to find it?"

"That I can. That I do."

Jewel's forefinger stabbed a map. "We have found the place!" she yelled in triumph.

Arran jumped to his feet, his eyes blazing like embers imprisoned within emeralds. "I shall inform my father and depart this very hour!"

While Fridayweed jumped up and down twirling its tail, Jewel and Arran joined hands and swung around the library in a whirling dance, until Jewel, pausing for breath, said suddenly, "Wait."

"What is the matter?"

Jewel made no reply. Her face folded in on itself, and she pressed her hands to her distended sides. Arran's arms encircled his wife; all his attention was focused on her.

At length she drew a deep breath and murmured, "I suspect our child is on the way."

Her husband drew her to a settle and assisted her to rest there, while he knelt at her side. They stared at each other, and the look that passed between them was charged with all the incredulity, delight, and amazement of two lovers on the brink of parenthood for the first time.

"Well then," said Arran softly, "all else fades to shadows, when viewed by the light of this wonderful event!"

The child was born on 28th Aoust. They named her Astăriel, meaning *The Storm*. Black as thunder was her hair. In her flower of a face, her newborn eyes were two misty petals, the tint of sorrow.

Jewel and Arran were so lost in the joy of meeting their child, so delirious with awe at the miracle of her existence, and so obsessed with this small scrap of humankind that nothing else mattered to them. The Storm Lord and his councillors permitted the couple a period of uninterrupted peace to acquaint themselves with their infant and learn how best to nurture her. Astăriel's Naming Day was celebrated on 18th Sevembre, two weeks after the King's Winterbourne Horn Dance and the same week as the Autumn Fair in Cathair Rua. It was then, when the baby was three weeks old, that Avalloc called his son to a meeting.

"Ever since you and Jewel found the location of the Well of Tears the councillors have been anxious," said the Maelstronnar. "The Draught must be secured. If you will not go to the Well, someone else must make the journey. Already the sun has risen many times since the wight revealed the riddle's answer."

Emerging from his universe of flower-petal eyes, tiny hands waving like sea-anemones, and piercing wails that scored his brain and heart like nails, Arran looked upon his father with clear eyes and knew he had the implicit authority of the entire Council backing him. It was as if the young man suddenly awoke from a dream. All at once the pressing importance of the quest returned to the son of the Maelstronnar. The sheer urgency of his situation rushed at him as overwhelmingly as a tidal wave. Rapidly he began to calculate and plan, endeavoring to anticipate all contingencies.

"Yet there is little purpose in the quest unless we can answer the other portion of the riddle," he said. "What of these *'ropes of sand'*?"

"My dear boy, I surmised you would have consulted your wight on that matter. The creature appears to be knowledgeable enough, doesn't he? Hmm?"

"Indeed, Father, I shall quiz Fridayweed. And I shall immediately make preparations for the journey," Arran said. He was astounded at his own laxity. How could it be that three weeks had passed and he had scarcely spared a thought for the Well of Tears?

Avalloc's eyes crinkled at the outer corners. "You have been under the spell of fatherhood," he said, as if reading his son's thoughts. "A strong enchantment, I know. While you were immersed in your new role, the Council was not idle. Preparations were begun as soon as the riddle was solved. The quest for the Well of Tears will perhaps become a legend of our generation, and I am as eager for it to commence as any man. Now that *Wanderpath* has been destroyed, you must take *Northmoth*. All is in readiness."

Arran bowed to his chieftain and sire. "Then I shall depart directly."

When he informed Jewel of his decision she reacted with alarm. "I beg you, do not go yet." It was a warm evening and she was sitting in their bedchamber, upon a chair of carven applewood. With her hand resting on the edge of the crib, she was patiently rocking the infant to sleep.

"Why not? I am eager to bring you your gift!"

"A gift maybe not meant for me. The Council has passed no judgment on the fate of the third Draught."

"It is meant for you," he insisted.

Fridayweed slid down the side of the nearby firescreen, somehow elegant in spite of managing to find no purchase on the polished wood.

"Wait," Jewel repeated stubbornly. "The draining of the first two Wells brought grief and disaster. It may be that the third entails a similar doom. Stay with us a while longer! After all, this Well has lain undisturbed for centuries."

"Ever, while my companions and I camped on the shores of Stryksjø, we assured each other we had time aplenty to complete our task. Such assumptions proved our undoing. Hearken, love, to the reasons why I should set forth immediately. First, if Fridayweed knows the location, I daresay that information is common knowledge amongst all wights, and therefore available to Aonarán."

"Not all," said Fridayweed, sucking thoughtfully on the end of its paintbrush tail. "Some."

"Enough to thwart our plans," said Arran. He returned his attention to his wife. "Secondly, there is always a chance that those folk we have questioned on this topic might wonder why we seek a hollow mountain with water falling through its heart. Should they delve deeply enough into this issue they might learn the truth and go looking for the Well themselves. If those villainous Aonaráns hear of our enquiries I daresay they will suspect the existence of a third source of immortality."

"If, if, if!" said Jewel discontentedly. "Nothing of what you say is certain." She rocked the cradle harder than she intended, and the child stirred. "Hush! Hush!" soothed Jewel, stroking the wisps of dark hair. "I am sorry, little one."

"Another *if*: drink the waters of life while you suckle our darling, and perchance the gift will be doubled!"

"Possibly," began Jewel, "but—"

"That would be unnecessary, man," the wight interjected. "Your child is already immortal. It has inherited that from its father." The creature smugly twirled its tail, while Jewel and Arran stared at each other, dumbfounded.

She slumbered innocently in her tissue-curtained cradle, the child who was the issue of their love, that small gem who had suddenly become the reason for life, the focus of all happiness. She it was who held her parents hostage to fortune, she who needed no naming when spoken of—to them, there existed only one *her* and *she*. That she had received Jewel's legacy of invulnerability they had already guessed. Not that they would let anything come near that might hurt the cherished one, but it seemed she did not cry as often as other infants, and had not been prey to inexplicable outbreaks of rashes, cradle-cap, or gripes as her peers had. Yet their affection for their child was so overwhelming that they could not help but visualize possible dangers in order that such situations might be avoided, and ask themselves whether there was anything that could ever take her away from them.

But now, after the impet's unexpected announcement, the agony that constantly grazed the raw ends of their nerves, and honed the edge of their protective love for her, the mere shadow of the notion that any lethal harm might ever befall her—that suffering need no longer be endured.

Eldritch wights spoke only truth. Astăriel was immortal. It was all that needed to be known. She was safe—safer than her parents alone could ever have made her, despite their best efforts. No longer did fortune hold such terrible sway; no longer were they utterly vulnerable, as if spread-eagled against a target while Fate hurled darts.

Ever since their daughter's birth their sensibilities in general had amplified, simmering close to the surface. Their desire to shield and guard her was so vehement, so savage, that amidst their joy, they felt their hearts were being burned out hollow. Now it was as if cold water had sluiced over that burning, and in the place of the ravaged, tortured heart was a cool, clear shining, like elemental ice, a certainty that the most precious thing in the universe would forever remain inviolate.

Overwhelmed by that realization, the banks that restrained the heightened emotions of new parenthood broke asunder, and a torrent poured forth. Arran plucked the infant from her bed and together they enfolded her in a cradle of their loving arms, intertwined, leaning their heads over the sleeping baby, their hair cascading across the small, wrapped figure. Sobs wracked their bodies, and they cried with relief and happiness beyond describing.

Presently, Jewel raised her chin. Her face was wet, her eyes swollen. She smiled through the liquid moonlight of her tears. As ever with these two, he had only to smile in return and all was communicated, with no need for words.

Gently they laid their daughter down again, and drew a light coverlet over her. Then Jewel touched her fingertip to her husband's cheek.

"By my troth!" she said in astonishment. "You weep, yet there are no tears!"

He nodded. "'Tis strange indeed," he said. "Yet 'tis a fact that ever since I downed the Draught of Everlasting Life, I can no longer shed tears."

Jewel's brow puckered, as if she scoured her mind for a memory. "I recall some such thing said by the sorcerer, in the Dome." She leaned over the baby who, as flawless as a porcelain doll, slumbered peacefully in the cradle. "And now it comes to me that when *she* wails *she* is tearless also. A curious phenomenon."

"But of little account," said Arran. "Of what use are tears? A saline film, sufficient to cleanse and moisten, rinses my eyes. I need no more than that; apparently, neither does *she*. The absence of tears is a small price to pay. Indeed, I consider it a bounty."

Fridayweed, who had been sucking on the end of its tail, spat it out. "In sooth, squeezing water from one's eyes seems a wasteful activity," it said knowledgeably.

Arran rounded on the wight. "But why did you not enlighten us earlier, with this wonderful news about our child's immortality?"

The creature shrugged. "You never asked."

"Methinks that is one of your favorite phrases," Jewel commented, sighing with exasperation.

She and Arran glared at the impet. It came to them that Fridayweed was a valuable source of information and an asset to their household. Like the house-brownie it had lived for countless years, but unlike the domestic wight it had accumulated great store of knowledge, which it was sometimes willing to share. Only they must in future be careful to ask precisely formulated questions. In typical eldritch fashion it answered very literally, sometimes evasively, and frequently not at all if no answer was demanded.

A sudden concern struck Jewel. "Since our child is born immortal, will she remain forever in infancy? Will she ever reach adulthood?" she demanded.

"Of course she will grow up," said the wight. "She will reach her prime, then never age a whit more."

"You are a veritable goldmine of news," Arran stated.

Fridayweed grinned like a longbow and scampered behind a linen chest.

"Come back, you vagabond!" Arran chaffed. "You must tell us more. The riddle mentions 'ropes of sand.' How might we obtain such items?"

The wight's long nose appeared from behind the linen chest. "I know not."

"Is it possible to make ropes out of sand?" the young man asked, holding his irritation in check and choosing his words painstakingly.

"I know not." The wight emerged fully.

"You are no longer mortal," Jewel reminded her husband.

The recollection smote Arran like a fist. After a lifetime of taking mortality for granted, it was curiously easy to forget his altered condition.

"Of course! I would need no climber's lines or cables. I could merely leap from the cliff-top—"

"You wield no gramarye, man," said Fridayweed, "and therefore you could not fly in the face of it. To state the obvious, you cannot fly at all. It is the wights that dwell under the mountain who imposed the circumstances governing access to the Well. Gramarye will prevent your descending the cliff, because *once you were mortal*."

"Then, if mortalkind and once-were-mortalkind cannot descend the final precipice except on implausible strings," said Arran, "what if a wight were to climb down the cliff?"

"I daresay they do it, the Fridean, Blue-caps, Coblynau, Knockers, Buccas, Gathorns, Bockles, and Nuggies," said Fridayweed, conscientiously naming every subterranean wight that dwelt beneath Whitaker's Peak and neglecting to foresee where the topic was leading.

Arran said, "You might climb down on my behalf, and fetch the water."

Emitting a squeal of horror, the wight scurried beneath the bed. Its voice wafted indistinctly out of obscurity: "No."

The child stirred and whimpered.

"Hush! Now you've disturbed *her*," said Jewel, resuming her rocking of the cradle.

"Why not?" Arran demanded, lying flat on the floor and peering under the bed.

"I don't want to."

"I beg of you!"

"No. Never, man! Never."

"So be it," said Arran resignedly, getting to his feet and smacking the dust off his knees. "I shall have to find some other way. Ropes or no ropes, without further ado I shall prepare to visit this ironically named Well."

"But *she* is immortal, safe forever," said Jewel to her husband, "and I am invulnerable. So you see, there is no necessity for you to hasten away. You need not yet go to the Well of Tears. Delay!"

As Arran fixed his gaze upon his wife, an ache swelled beneath his ribs. Her beauty approached something mythical as she stood next to the gauze-draped crib. Her white gown, folded about her like a seagull's wing, was blowing in the night breeze from the window. Her hair fell down around her shoulders in a tempest of glossy darkness; her eyes bloomed with that unfathomable shade of cornflowers-in-essence-of sky.

"You are cruel," he cried, with unexpected passion, yet not so loudly as to startle the sleeping infant. "What if I am too late to claim the Draught? You say you are invulnerable, but that is not completely true. Death can still claim you. Would you condemn our daughter and me to everlasting years without you?"

"No!" Two sapphire spoonfuls glittered with tears. "It is only that I am frightened. I fear that something dreadful may befall you."

"What can happen? Death has no power over me."

"Something. I know not. I cannot name it."

After further discussion Jewel begrudgingly acceded to his wishes, yet a silence lingered between them. Morosely Arran strode to the window and stood with his feet braced apart, surveying the starlit roofs of the houses on Rowan Green.

"Since you are not to be dissuaded," Jewel said at length, "I might as well be of help to you. A notion has come to me." She was handling the fine textile that curtained the cradle. Embroidered with intricate stitchery and bordered with snowflakes of lace, the silken tissue had been a wedding present. "Once, when we visited the palace at Cathair Rua," she mused, "I saw there a tablecloth of extraordinary material, woven for the king, and I asked what it could be. The method by which this fabric was made is somewhat astonishing, for it was fashioned from spun glass. Molten glass was drawn out into threads as fine as gossamer, filaments that lost the brittleness of glass and became pliable enough for close-weaving. Spun-glass cloth is made on special looms in Ashqalêth, and is very expensive, for much labor is involved. The fabric is more ornamental than sturdy, for it has a limited life-span. With wear, the fibers disintegrate and fall apart. Holes begin to appear in places where elbows have leaned, or table corners have jutted. Yet it can be washed and dried and folded and stored, just like bolts of linen or wool. It engraved my mind with its strangeness, for I could not help but compare that soft, wax-smooth stuff with a glass windowpane or goblet—the one so soft and resilient, the other so hard and brittle. That cloth was made of glass. And," she added, "of what is glass made, but sand?"

Arran's features lit up with delight and surprise. "By thunder, there you have it!" he exclaimed, and leaving the window he drew her into his embrace, kissing her vigorously. "You have the solution! Glass is indeed manufactured from sand that has been melted and fused at considerable temperatures. And glass can be formed into fibers! We shall outfox the wights after all, and make ropes of sand!"

It was, however, a task more easily described than accomplished.

Next day Arran took *Northmoth* and a crew, and flew to the glassworks of Ashqalêth. During the ensuing days the weathermasters employed skilled glass-makers to produce fibers that were then twisted together to make ropes, but when tested for strength every rope tore apart under stress, and was not able to uphold more than the slightest of weights.

Despite this failure the glass-makers were proud to display their skills for the esteemed weatherlords, and the workshop foreman eagerly plied them with information.

"To make glass, we take a mixture of sand, soda, and lime, then heat it to a very high temperature, until it melts. As it begins to cool, it can be manipulated to form any shape, as of course you are aware, my lords. The colors of glass can be varied. For example, to make green bottle glass we simply use eleven parts of lime, sixty-three parts of sand, and twenty-six parts of soda ash. The latter is obtained from the burning of the saltwort plant, or found crystallized with other salts beneath the ground. For red glass we add red lead and copper oxide; for blue we use cobalt oxide—"

"Gramercie," said Arran gravely, raising his palm in a courteous signal. "Enough. Prithee do not reveal all of your trade secrets!"

The loquacious foreman bowed deeply in acknowledgment, and altered his topic. "Ashqalêthan glass is famed throughout the Four Kingdoms. Its clarity, strength, and beauty are prized everywhere, for windowpanes, mirrors, jewelry, and a multitude of vessels. But for ropes to be made from glass—that is another matter entirely, and I fear 'tis completely impracticable."

The weathermaster departed from the manufactories of Ashqalêth without any glass ropes.

Despite this setback Arran decided to depart for Whitaker's Sands, taking

with him a supply of rock-climbing equipment and the wight Fridayweed, opti-
mistic that the creature might change its mind when they arrived, and prove
helpful yet again. If it would not oblige, then he would attempt to conquer the
cliff using his own resources. On Salt's Day 2nd Otember 3472, he and his crew—
Bliant Ymberbaillé, Ettare Sibilaurë, and Gauvain Cilsundror—set forth from
High Darioneth in the airship *Northmoth*, bound for the Black Crags, the mountainous region on the northeast marches of the kingdom. The purpose of their
mission had been concealed from all except the councillors of Ellenhall. Others at
Rowan Green, and any from the plateau who knew of their departure, made the
assumption that they journeyed on a routine mission of weathermastery.

From west to east they crossed Narngalis, passing over the headwaters of the
Canterbury Water. In amongst the mountains flew *Northmoth,* until the weathermages found themselves gliding above rough terrain: steep valleys mantled with
forests, and gaunt peaks as barren as bones, or cloaked in virgin snows. The still
airs of Autumn had produced an inversion—an atmospheric condition in which
the air temperature rose with increasing altitude, pressing down the surface air
and inhibiting the dispersion of pollutants. In the timbered valleys charcoal burners and lime burners had been busy—the smoke from their fires hung in thick
swathes close to the ground, the upper layers reaching no higher than the treetops.

Whitaker's Peak loomed ever nearer. The impet poked its head out of Arran's
tunic pocket, yelling and gesticulating as it navigated. "Over there! A little to the
right! No, more to the left! Make for that crag shaped like the head of a goat!"
Until at last the creature screeched, "There, you see it? That gray rock that juts
like an otter leaping. The doorway is on the other side!"

As the balloon cruised toward its destination the crew drew out their spyglasses and pointed them at the ground, scanning their surroundings.

"It might be mere fancy, but I believe that for an instant I spied figures moving like swimmers beneath the murk of the inversion," said Ettare.

"Where?" Arran was quick to respond.

"In the valley below, and on the slopes near the place said to be the doorway
to the Deep Stair."

"Lime burners or shepherds, perhaps. At all events, since we are on important
business I shall reverse the inversion, and wrap our aircraft in obscurity."

The son of the Maelstronnar commenced to shape the signs and murmur the
vector commands, directing complex atmospheric events. As the balloon swept
farther into the mountain range, the air stirred. The inversion broke up, and the
trapped fumes began to rise, along with various river-mists that had been imprisoned with them. Slowly, the smokes drifted between the aerostat and the sun.

Northmoth now flew through a world in which the light of day was tinted amber. It was like moving through an antique painting on whose surface the lacquer

had yellowed with age, a quaint and charming effect. The dimness and the somber orange overcast painted a picture that was intriguing to Arran, until it occurred to him that those smudged clouds were in fact the ghosts of burned trees in the sky, passing overhead on the currents, flowing to the gray havens of ash, a pall of cremated timber passing eerily across the firmament before his eyes. Above the angular barrenness of the mountain crags, the sun was like a red eye staring through a keyhole at a dying world. Carboniferous air stung eyes and throats.

"I suspect we are too late with our strategy of concealment," said Bliant, still squinting through the bronze cylinder of his spyglass. "I myself have spied no strangers—Ettare has the sharpest eyes of all—but anyone moving down there must surely have witnessed our aircraft. It is to be hoped they were merely woodsmen, charcoal burners and the like."

"What if they were Marauders?" said Ettare. "Marauders are clever mountaineers, and have been known to pass through this region."

"If they were Marauders, then I suspect Aonarán has been up to his tricks," said Arran. "I have learned not to underestimate him and his relatives. They have trafficked with Marauders aforetime."

"This is all conjecture," said Bliant.

"True," replied Ettare, "but for added security, what say we land elsewhere, thus leading potential adversaries astray, and drawing them to some location far from this doorway into the mountain?"

"What's your opinion, Arran?" Gauvain asked.

"Fridayweed," said Arran to the creature in his pocket, "once you told me how many steps there are upon this Stair. Remind me of that number."

"Four thousand, nine hundred, and thirty-one," answered an indistinct voice.

The young man estimated the time required to travel down the length of the Stair and back, adding a swift reckoning of a suitable interval in which to scale the cliff in both directions, and the probable duration of the search for the Well at the foot of the precipice.

He said, "In my judgment there is no need for such games of leading interlopers astray. The travelers seen by Ettare are yet many furlongs from the place Fridayweed indicated. If that place is their planned destination we will still have leisure to land, find the doorway, descend the Stair, take the water, return to the aircraft, and take off before they arrive.

"In any case, the doorway might not be their planned destination," he added.

"Yet, even if it is not," said Ettare, "they must have glimpsed *Northmoth* in the sky. As Bliant stated, sky-balloons attract attention. There is a possibility that inquisitiveness alone will lead them in our direction. They might follow the balloon in order to find out what we are up to, with a desire to discover where we set down. Ordinary folk are forever interested in the deeds of weathermasters."

"Even if they see us descend behind the crags, they might well be deceived in our landing place. Amongst the heights a man's judgment of distance may play tricks; furthermore, steep slopes and deep valleys make formidable barriers."

"I am in accord with Arran," said Bliant. "We ought to land forthwith."

"Aye," said Gauvain.

"If I am out-voted, then so be it," Ettare acquiesced.

The terrain was so rough that it was difficult to find landing places for the balloon. *Northmoth* was forced to circle the doorway's location several times while the crew searched for a flat, level apron. Eventually a suitable spot was found, but even then, the aircraft could not be landed properly. Bliant had to use his most precise weatherworking skills to keep the balloon hovering, the floor of the basket floating about three feet above the ground. If it touched down completely, the gondola would be tipped over by the angle of the declivity.

The balloon, lightly anchored by ropes tied to sandbags, bobbed gently in the mists.

A slope of flint and shale led to a dim fissure beneath an overhang that was the doorway. Arran cast aside his cloak, so that it might not hamper him, and made ready to venture in, with Fridayweed curled up silently in the pocket of his tunic. He raised the light javelin he carried in his hand. "βȳřñ, ¥ē βéøřht βřöńd!" he commanded, and Erasmus's fire blossomed like a posy of sparks at the brazen point of the staff.

As soon as Arran entered, the ground dropped away from where he stood and the Deep Stair emptied itself down into the black depths, each tread standing about twelve inches high, each one narrowly hewn. Blank, solid walls hemmed unforgivingly on either side.

Lightly, sure-footedly, he stepped down.

While Arran plunged into the mountain's core his crew kept watch near the doorway, standing guard over the sky-balloon. Out on the foggy slopes they were debating the relative merits of concealing the balloon with vapors.

"In mists," Gauvain pointed out, "we are an easier target for stealthy attackers."

"In addition, while we use this method we cannot summon breezes to bring us scents, because breezes would blow away the vapors," said Ettare.

Bliant, who had taken over command in Arran's absence, deliberated for a while.

"We shall dissipate the mists," he decided, at length. His hands and lips began to move.

Presently, winds began converging toward the mountain from different directions, rising up the slopes. This, combined with the plumes of smoke in the atmosphere, caused a charge to begin developing in the air.

In lightless shafts buried deep beneath the feet of his friends, Arran moved steadily downward. The upper surfaces of the treads were constricted in area, and the ceiling pressed close. This was a precarious Stair, neither hewn by human agency nor fashioned in order to be easily traversed by human limbs. It twisted sometimes back on itself, or turned a sharp corner, or looped into tight spirals, or suddenly went up for a few steps instead of down. Faint hammerings knocked at the outer limits of audibility; in far-flung ventricles and arteries of the underground, mining wights were busy at their mysterious industries.

The Stair entered the mountain from the west and plunged at a precarious angle of forty-five degrees or more. As he descended, Arran could hear a murmur, the music of running water, faint, echoing from afar. Deeper he progressed, and the sounds grew ever louder. His heart beat more strongly; the rising noise of the flood must surely mean he was nearing his destination. Fridayweed's advice had proved well founded. Here was the mountain whose heart was hollow, yet filled with the movement of living waters.

The work of descent was demanding, but excitement empowered the young man. Down and down he sprang, from tread to tread, heedless of effort and hardship. The radiance of the light javelin, borne like a rare and alien jewel into this sunless sink, flickered over inscrutable walls and merciless panels of stone, bleeding into coughing bights of blindness.

The Stair ended on a cliff-top gallery overlooking an abyss.

Arran uttered a short word of command, and his corposant lamp briefly flared brighter.

Along the gallery, a hundred paces in front of him, the gleaming waters of a subterranean stream gurgled down out of a hole in the rock wall, as they had done for aeons. The stream flowed through a water-worn channel that crossed the gently sloping shelf in a series of shallow flumes, finally tumbling over the cliff's edge and spinning into space, hurtling perhaps a hundred feet to a floor far below, where it pooled briefly, before diving into a gap and vanishing.

To his left, the abyss.

It was as if some gigantic cleaver had split the stone platform on which he stood cleanly in two, and one half had fallen away to vanish into the foundations of the mountain while the other remained standing, upholding the base of the Stair. Down there, somewhere in the darkness at the foot of the waterfall, the Well of Tears waited.

"Fridayweed," Arran said quietly.

"Man, what?" The voice in his pocket sounded gruff.

"Will you not fetch something for me from below?" Arran said coaxingly.

"No."

"See for yourself. The cliff is not so formidable."

The impet popped its wizened head out and stared. "'Tis," it said, and the head snapped out of sight, followed by a flaccid paintbrush.

Privately, Arran had hoped that Fridayweed would descend the precipice if he pleaded with the wight. The creature, however, had made it clear it would not allow itself to be cajoled. Arran had gone so far as to issue a command weighted by his knowledge of the wight's true name, but even that powerful charm had not availed him.

"You know my name, but I am not your slave," squeaked the unruly impet.

Muttering imprecations under his breath, the weathermaster admitted defeat and resorted to his alternative plan.

Back and forth along the ledge he prowled, searching for a way down. In order to free his hands he wedged the light javelin firmly into its baldric-loop behind his left shoulder. Soon he had managed to climb, slipping and sliding, across the rocky balcony to the top of the waterfall. In the eroded channel limpid water flowed, chuckling and sparkling, over beds of coarse sand. Hempen ropes and iron hooks were amongst the equipment he had brought with him. He unslung them from his back, and set to work, preparing to lower himself down the cliff-face beside the waterfall.

Arran was no novice at rock-climbing, and knew what he was about, yet he encountered a peculiar phenomenon: none of his ropes would remain tied in a knot. Nor would the rock accept the iron spikes and hooks he tried to hammer into the crevices. After laboring futilely for almost an hour he gave up in disgust, and flung the tack aside.

Close to despair, he sat on the cliff-top, his arms wrapped about his knees. By the light of Erasmus's fire he could make out the floor below, barely discernible in the gloom.

From its refuge, Fridayweed spoke in muffled tones: "Your ropes won't hold a knot. No rope of hemp or flax or even wool shall hold a knot here in the heart of the mountain."

"How kind of you to inform me."

The wight huffed indignantly.

"Forgive me," Arran said, relenting. "You have helped me get this far, and for that I am grateful. Yet I may as well be back in High Darioneth as sitting here in the dark, on the brink of a precipice. The Well is out of my reach in either case." He fell silent, ruminating. Presently he asked, "Why is this region known as Whitaker's Sands?"

"Whitaker was a hermit who sued to scrape out a meager existence hereabouts, many lives of men before your birth."

"And the sands?"

"Beds of sand line the waterways that flow beneath this range, coarse river-sand weathered from granite and other rocks. There are great craters and sand pits down here. All the sand pits lie underground, for the alpine winds have long since scoured small grains from the outer slopes."

An idea struck the young man. "Fridayweed, you are a very fount of knowledge. Do the sands possess any particular qualities?"

"I know not."

Arran sighed. "Then I shall endeavor to find out."

The weathermage made his way to the banks of the stream and thrust his hand into the fast-moving water. As he cast about in the streambed, gathering up a handful of sediment, his exertions caused the light javelin to come loose from its brace. It tumbled into the shallows and the flames went out.

Like the tongue of a whip, but quicker, utter blindness licked out the orbs of his eyes. Blackness seeped in through his ears, his nostrils, his mouth, his wide and emptied oculars, a drowning, viscid blackness that was more palpable, more *alive,* than the mere absence of light.

Meanwhile, out on the mountainside above, Arran's friends waited restlessly. The air was turbulent and they sensed the rapid build-up of static electricity. Above their heads the silver apple of the balloon's envelope danced lazily in the hazy air, round and taut.

"It glistens like a beacon," said Ettare, uneasily. "We are too conspicuous."

She narrowed her eyes against the high-altitude glare. Her pulse jumped in her throat. As before, she was unsure whether it had been some trick of the light or the shadows; but she thought she had seen a figure, made small by distance, slipping from one hiding place to another.

"I reckon," she said to her companions, keeping her tone as even as possible, "that some watcher has indeed spied our vehicle, and they are furtively closing in."

"I see no one," said Bliant, scrutinizing the valleys through his spyglass. "Yet I daresay you are right."

"If they are Marauders," said the damsel, "they will be skilled at moving amongst high places and crossing steep slopes; those brigands are hardy and experienced mountaineers, experts with rope and hook."

"We can only hope," said Gauvain, shifting from one foot to another in his restlessness, "that Arran will be swift in completing his task."

When his lamp expired, Arran found himself in desperate straits. If sight had been killed, sound had not. As soon as the illumination disappeared, all around, throughout the vast cavern, a whispering started up. The young man crouched helplessly, feeling for the javelin in the dark, putting forth all his senses of weathermastery in an effort to overcome the disadvantage of blindness. Even as he groped through the swill of chill water the omnipresent whispering was joined by a low humming noise that grew in volume, becoming a penetrating drone that thrummed beneath the soles of his feet. Abruptly, at the very rim of vision, a dim light flashed on and off. Or was it a trick of fancy, played by sight-deprived eyes? But no—another faint incandescence popped into existence. And the first returned, remaining steady. Then the second was joined by a third to the right, and a fourth to the left, and more jumping out in all directions, until Arran blinked, and blinked again, and his eyes adapted to the weak glows, and he *saw*.

What he saw was this: The walls of the great, airy cavern were pocked by niches and small chambers, and it was from these that the wan radiances emanated. Within each of these cells, illumined by a subtle, shimmering radiance, grotesque crones were working at spinning wheels; and it was the whirling wheels that generated the humming.

A cracked old voice started to sing. Others augmented it. Their song was lilting but weird; its bizarre cadences and peculiar combinations of keys and dissonances and harmonies made the listener shudder, as if cold water had been poured down his spine.

They had not sung more than a few bars when Arran chanced to put his hand on the light javelin. Quickly he withdrew it from the water.

With a spoken command and a flutter of his fingers he rekindled his brighter light, which seemed suddenly dazzling. The singing ceased. All the preternatural lamps went out, and he was no longer able to discern the spinners in the shadowy walls.

It made him shiver anew, to realize they had been surrounding him all the time, ever since he set foot on the ledge. Odd-looking creatures they were, yet unlike the eldritch spinner-impet in the straw-to-gold story that he had recounted to Jewel. Perhaps they were less malicious. These spinning wights of Whitaker's Peak looked like quaint old goodwives working at their craft, pulling out their thread with skinny fingers and moistening the fibers with elongated lower lips that seemed specifically formed for the purpose.

As he was pondering on the spinners, a deep voice close to him boomed sepulchrally, "Get thee hence, weathermage. This is no place for thee. Begone from our doorstep."

Arran almost dropped the javelin a second time. Careful scrutiny of his surroundings failed to reveal the source of the voice. He could see no one else on the cliff-top.

"The underground-dwellers want me to leave their haunts," he said softly to Fridayweed, who crouched silently in his pocket

As he uttered those words he was reminded again of the song "Ropes of Sand," which had been hovering on the verges of his mind for many days. In that ballad the situation had been reversed: it had been the human beings who had yearned for the wight to depart.

And a bargain had been struck.

Arran stood quite still, holding up the javelin with Erasmus's fire sparkling at its tip.

"Begone," intoned the bass voice, cold as stone. It emanated from directly beneath Arran's feet. Hurriedly, he jumped backward.

"My departure is conditional," he cried recklessly.

The gurgling of the waters seemed to recede, as if the stream and the waterfall sullenly quieted to listen.

"I have heard of spinners," said Arran boldly, "who can perform extraordinary feats in their craft. It is difficult for a man to believe these tales. Give me proof."

"What proof, weathermage?"

"If the wheel-wives can perform a certain task and create a specific instrument I need to carry out my undertaking here, then when my work is done I shall depart as you request."

"If not?"

"I shall bide here as long as I wish. And I am deathless."

"What task?"

"They must spin sand into rope."

A rumble, like the iron-rimmed wheels of many wagons, rolled around the walls of the cavern.

"It cannot be done."

This was not the response Arran sought. He had no desire to languish forever in the guts of Whitaker's Peak. The cave-wight, or troll, or whatever it might be was calling his bluff, perhaps. Then again, it was incapable of lying.

As the young man's thoughts wrestled to and fro, he recalled a snippet of information the garrulous foreman had told him during the tour of the glassworks in Ashqalêth. Excitement surged in him, heady as a draught of potent wine.

He said, "I take it the wheel-wives can spin only filaments, such as lint, hair, and straw."

No reply.

"I shall depart," said Arran, "if they can spin strands of glass into rope."

"It can be done."

"Then the bargain is struck!"

Again the metallic thunder circled the cavern walls, the echoes phasing wide and narrow as wave-frequencies crisscrossed back and forth.

A muttering in his pocket reawakened Arran to the lurking presence of Fridayweed. "From where will you be getting glass?" the impet hissed.

"Wait and see."

The young man extinguished his lamp of coronal energy and thrust the javelin firmly into his belt. His heart was pounding wildly. In the dark, as he began to perform the gestures and whisper the vector commands that would evoke the necessary environment, the words of the glassworks foreman in Jhallavad ran through his mind.

"Glass ropes, such as you request, have no load-bearing capacity," the foreman had said, "yet in other shapes glass possesses huge strength and many other useful qualities besides. Even before glass-making was discovered, warriors valued glass for its sharpness, and used it to make knives, arrows, and spearheads—"

"Wait!" Arran had interjected, holding up his hand again. "Do you mean to say that glass existed before glass-making was invented?"

"Indeed, my lord," the foreman had answered, pulling his forelock politely. "Obsidian is formed when the fierce heat of volcanoes fuses sand."

"Of course," Arran had murmured, in the tones of an enlightened man. "I had forgotten."

"And sometimes when a fragment of a star falls from the sky," continued the erudite foreman, "its heat is so tremendous that it melts rock as it strikes the ground. Gobs of molten rock are hurled into the air by the force of the impact. When they cool they form smooth glassy tektites, shaped like sand-timers."

"From what you say," Arran had said, "I deduce that for glass to be formed naturally all that is required is sand containing the right combination of minerals, and a heat source of extreme intensity."

"Even so, my lord. Even so."

Under Whitaker's Peak Arran stood utterly still, as if locked into a timeless stasis. Reaching out his weathermaster's faculties, he explored the tons of rock suspended above his head, probing for variations in magnetic forces, pockets of air, trickles and gushes of water. It was the most difficult enterprise he had ever attempted. His ramifying senses could make nothing of the bones of the world, the strata and sub-strata formed from rocks of varying types and density and geological eras, some riddled with fossils, others veined with ores.

Yet, after much effort, he discovered something his *brí*-consciousness could decipher: behind the wall of the cavern a waterworn fissure, almost vertical, reaching right up to the very surface of the mountain. Had there been no lively water running down this channel, he would not have been able to recognize it. This perpendicular outlet was perfect for his plan, if only something else existed in the ground below his feet.

Downward he drove his superhuman perception. Heat grumbled and simmered in the depths. From the core of the world, tentacles of molten rock exuded. Not far away, in a hot subterranean dungeon, water was constantly accumulating. The natural chamber was filled with steam. As more water continuously seeped in, the pressure built up, until the cavern trembled like a gigantic cooking-pot with the lid tightly screwed on. All that separated the vertical fissure from the cauldron below was a thick plug made of small pebbles and sediment.

The hands of the young weathermage glided, outlining the contours of invisible shapes. Convoluted vowels streamed from his lips and ricocheted off the stones. To his knowledge, such an exploit as he embarked upon had never before been attempted from beneath a mountain. In fact, it might prove impossible. It was necessary for him to be very precise.

"Ooh, man, there's a terrible power a-breeding!" wailed the little thing in Arran's pocket. "'Twill explode any moment now! Run, man!"

Arran experienced an odd sensation of reversal, as if he had lived through this same moment in earlier times.

"Why do you wait until I'm with you, before you destroy everything in sight?" wailed the wight.

Arran ignored the outbursts and continued his work. He must focus on the task in hand, or fail. He was gambling on many variables, including whether the sands of Whitaker's Peak contained the right combination of minerals. Certainly, the exposed crags on the mountaintop far above were perfect for his purpose.

Somewhere below the floor on which he stood, something gave way. A blockage cleared. Silt and gravel emptied out from a natural tube, like sand from a timer. Instinctively Arran flung himself behind the shelter of a boulder as a screaming jet of overheated, moist air shot past, invisible on the other side of the rocky partition, and up through the escape vent that led to the outer slopes of Whitaker's Peak.

Thunderstorms are more likely to form over mountains than over flat land, especially when strong winds are converging toward the mountain from different directions. The atmosphere above the peak was already highly charged; into this projected the powerful jet of conductive steam, and the swirling gases of the heavens could no longer prevent their snapping, fretting, snarling currents from biting the ground.

The bolt, exceeding one hundred million volts, seared down the air and struck the pinnacle of the tallest crag on Whitaker's Peak. It drove down through highly transmissive seams of ore, into pits of dry quartz sand. As the lightning strike diffused through the mineral particles at a temperature of fifty thousand degrees it vaporized those in its direct path while melting and fusing those on the periphery, forming brittle, glassy tubes that preserved the shape of the current. Unfused grains were blasted aside by shock waves. The thin partition between the vent and the cavern burst asunder down its length, vomiting lethal missiles, skin-flaying detonations of sand and blobs of boiling vitreous. The return stroke—to the slow human eye, undifferentiated from the first— created yet more fulgurites.

No mortal man could have stood so close to that strike and survived. For the briefest of instants the current's path was as hot as the sun, generating pressures one hundred times that of the world's atmosphere.

The cavern now glowed with a lurid light that shone from holes in the sand. Before the fulgurite tubes had time to cool and solidify, Arran dredged them from their incandescent pits with his bare, immortal hands; his hooks and hammer would instantly have burned at the touch of the newly birthed compound. Still semi-liquid, the root-like structures warped as he handled them. Strings of glowing syrup sizzled when drops of moisture from the wet river-sand vaporized against them. Arran stood in the center of a surging steam-cloud, a spider-web of smoky gray cables strung between his fingers. The material clung stickily to his charmed skin as he drew out the mass like viscid honey, to create threads.

"Take it!" he yelled above the roaring and hissing of the steam. "Take it now and spin it while it is yet pliable!" He was unable to draw the threads skillfully enough to produce hair-fine filaments that would remain flexible when they cooled, and was forced to gamble again: this time, on whether the spinners would willingly work with molten glass.

Violent steam-billows obscured his surroundings. As he let fall the vitreous cords he became aware they were being dragged away. "You must comb it out, tease it into fibers," he cried, "before it can be spun."

His hair was pasted to his head, his skin dripping with sweat and condensation.

"After spinning you must ply the threads, and twist them to make strong cordage—strong enough to bear my weight!" he shouted into the murk.

"Do you presume to instruct craftsfolk at their own trade, weathermaster?" resonated the uncomfortably close Voice of the Cavern. Little could Arran perceive through the dimness, but as the vapors condensed on the rocky walls and the steam's sibilance faded, he heard the humming of rapidly turning wheels, and a cackling of ancient, cracked laughter. Arran guessed that if he tried to spy on the spinners they would disappear as soon as he generated his light-source. Motionless he stood, in an agony of suspense, wondering what would eventuate, until at length something heavy was thrown against his legs.

"Done," boomed funereal and somewhat aristocratic tones.

At the tip of Arran's light javelin, Erasmus's fire sprang open like a sunburst.

Beside the weathermage's feet the fulgurites were gone. In their place was a plentiful coil of glistening, smoky-gray rope.

He picked it up.

"Have you vanished, Fridayweed?" he asked, struggling to hold his jubilation in check.

"Mmph."

"I have them—ropes of sand!"

Without wasting another moment Arran tossed the flaming javelin over the cliff's brink. It seemed to descend gently, as if falling through water, until it came to rest on the dry stones and sand below. There it burned like a welcoming lamp in some distant tavern window. The young man tied one end of the strange rope to a sturdy boulder and paid out the other end over the edge of the precipice. After tugging experimentally to ensure the cable would bear his weight, he belayed it by passing it under one thigh and over the opposite shoulder, then rappelled down the precipice toward the light.

Upon reaching the cliff's foot he snatched up the light javelin and barked a command to Fridayweed: "Lead me!"

The wight directed the weathermage to the right of the waterfall's pool and across the stone-strewn floor. "I have never visited this place before," it grumbled. "I only know of it from hearsay! Me mither says the Well is conspicuous, and cannot be mistaken."

As he walked, Arran systematically inspected the ground in all directions.

Presently he gasped, as if startled. "If that is so," he said, "then we have found it."

In the world above, the day was waning. Through their weathermasters' senses the crew of the *Northmoth* had been fully aware of Arran's summoning of the lightning. Even so, they were astounded at the force of the strike, which had dislodged several large boulders from the higher buttresses of the summit. The questionable climbers on the slopes had turned back, retreating toward the lowlands. Conceivably they had been woodsmen curious to learn what weathermasters were doing on the heights, simple folk who, when confronted with the evidence of a weathermage's power, had thought better of interfering and re-turned to their huts. Peril had evaporated, unlike the mists of evening, which were beginning to coagulate in the lower dales.

Now Arran's companions waited.

Docile breezes shifted the airborne particles, and it was not long before the crew stood beneath clear skies, gazing out over the northern ranges. Glistening in the lucent airs, mountain peaks thrust like islands from oceans of translucent cloud-wisps. The weathermasters wondered what was happening deep beneath their feet.

So Arran Maelstronnar, weathermage of High Darioneth and scion of the Storm Lord, came at last to the Well of Tears.

As twice before, he came to kneel at the brink of an embedded stone chalice, lined with alien metals from beyond the stars. As before, he came to steal the strange water imbued with uncanny qualities, the Draught that could throw un-seen shields around beings of flesh and blood, screening them forever from the ravages of time, the inconceivable bane of non-existence, the finality of death. As before he knelt, but in this instance, the third, he fell to his knees as if an axe had smitten him a mighty blow across the shoulder. His palms struck the ground in front of him, and he leaned forward on his hands, staring wordlessly, while the intervals that linked time's chain clicked past one by one until the chain grew long and heavy.

Lying on its side in the sand, the light javelin flamed silently.

Arran stared, and not a word did he utter; nor did he breathe but shallowly. For the Well was as empty as daylight, dry as the moon.

XIII

Bane

The Well of Tears had long ago been cracked and choked and ruined by some ancient upheaval beneath the world's crust, some natural avalanche, perhaps, or tectonic shift, or a disturbance caused by those underground wights, the Fridean, in their delvings. Whatever the cause, the Well had been burst asunder, perforated and drained, until all that remained were fragments of dark silver stuff, rubble, and vacancies.

Later, as he continued to kneel at the brink, Arran discovered his hands were full of chips and slivers that sifted between his fingers. His nails were splintered. He remembered he had been digging, scrabbling, scratching wildly in the disintegrated rocks; seeking, seeking; finding no drop, no moisture, no seepage or osmosis, nothing but aridity and crumbling, parched gravel—sand that seemed even drier than bones in a desert.

Waterlessness.

It was then, sitting back on his heels and raising his face to the distant ceiling, that he sent forth a cry. Terrible was this cry, so filled with devastation that it was the utterance of profoundest horror, of desolation and loss too bitter to be endured. That single wordless plaint spoke of years, centuries, millennia of sorrow unassuaged. Ripped from his throat, it was a sound that belonged in the pits of madness.

Through hollows and shafts of the mountain it reverberated, bouncing from wall to wall, meeting and remeeting itself, doubling and redoubling in a clamor that fled away down the corridors into the deepest wounds of the mountain, into the darkest and most forbidden cavities where, since the dawn of days, sunlight had never reached.

At the sound, even the eldritch miners temporarily paused at their tasks, ceased their continual hammerings, and looked up. Even the Blue-caps with their tiny sapphire lanterns halted momentarily in their age-old labors, twitching their tufted ears. Even immortal entities could not remain unmoved.

It was with a haggard countenance and torn garments that Arran stumbled from the upper doorway of the Deep Stair to meet his comrades. The afternoon had aged. In the west, behind the mountains, the sun was a gigantic fireball. Its golden surface leaped and lapped with superheated fires, flaring with a myriad wings of translucent amber and boiling bronze. The seething furnace of the sky was falling below the horizon, but as its final rays struck the western faces of the ranges they teased out long, drowning shadows. One beam momentarily illuminated the man emerging from the door on the mountainside. Yet he spoke not, nor did he see the splendor of the day's passing as he hobbled, like some failing graybeard, across the slope, with his shoulders hunched, his head bowed, his eyes fixed and blind to such transient phenomena as beauty.

The last chance was gone. All hope was extinguished. His anguish metamorphosing to rage, Arran swore vengeance on those who had thwarted his hopes for Jewel's perpetual survival—Fionnbar and Fionnuala Aonarán. He would return to his wife at High Darioneth and gaze upon her, before he kissed her goodbye once more and went hunting.

A new sky-balloon had been delivered to Rowan Green from the spidersilk farms of Longville-in-the-Dale. After being inspected, tested, and proven to be airworthy, it was given the name *Mistmoor,* and officially launched. Delivered along with the gigantic envelope, borne in its covered wain and guarded by two dozen outriders, there came interesting intelligence: at a village in Narngalis an oracle had arisen, who declared himself a representative of the cult calling itself "The Sandals of Doom." This new leader had verified his approbation in the eyes of Lord Doom by, amongst other exploits, walking through fire and emerging unscathed. It seemed he was not short of marvels. He had, in addition, immersed himself in a barrel of water for fully an hour—some said a day, others a week—before reappearing alive and well, and had offered twenty golden guineas to the axe-man who could chop off his head. No man, churl or champion, had, as yet, succeeded in decapitating him. Many were the extraordinary feats said to be performed by this protégé of Míchinniúint. Consequently the diseased, the desperate, the needy and the indecisive had flocked to him, begging for succor and advice. Having gathered a following, he had commandeered the village hall as his headquarters and set up a hierarchy of sycophants to do his bidding. Their practice was to haul ordinary folk before the throne of the oracle, forcing them to kneel before him and praise his greatness as the chosen favorite of Lord Doom. Power and adulation, it seemed, were the primary goals of this mysterious miracle-worker. His influence was growing. Proportionately, the fears of the local populace were increasing, and it was widely rumored that King Warwick would not long tolerate such a tyrant within the borders of his kingdom.

"Where is the center of these odious activities?" Avalloc Maelstronnar asked the news-bearers.

"In the tiny hamlet of Marchington Hythe."

Avalloc's pronouncement to the Council on the matter was thus: "I daresay there is only one man who could be enacting such vulgar displays of invulnerability. Fionnbar Aonarán has reappeared."

Soon afterward, to the gladness of all, Arran and his crew returned to High Darioneth. Everyone was keen to hear of their adventures, which they recounted on the evening of their arrival, seated at the dining table of Avalloc's house in the company of family and councillors. The visage of Arran Maelstronnar was sorrowful indeed as he told of his discovery of the dry Well. He could not bear to look at his young bride while he made the disclosure. When at length he glanced at Jewel, he read in her eyes all the disbelief and despair that he himself had felt when he knelt at the broken brink and realized her last chance of immortality had been lost. She was to remain mortal, while her husband and child lived on through the ages. It was too much to bear.

The son of the Storm Lord was moody and preoccupied. The only ones whose presence could soften the hard lines of anger on his features were his wife and daughter. He was impatient to depart again as soon as possible, in order to track down his nemesis. Upon hearing the news of Aonarán's reemergence Arran waxed even more intolerant of delay, and declared he would remain at High Darioneth only long enough to collect a crew willing to accompany him on his mission of retribution.

It was a mission about which his father warned him: "Seek justice, not vengeance. Seek only to protect the world from the folly of this wretched mad-man."

"I have vowed to punish both brother and sister for their part in defrauding Jewel of her birthright. Our own sovereign has decreed that Aonarán should be arrested and charged with crimes against humankind, should he venture into Narngalis. He is guilty, no question, and ought to pay the price. Besides, I shall not be long away. It should be easy to discover this dissembler posing as a sooth-sayer, since he has made himself so famous. If I do not find them both within six weeks I shall set a bounty on their capture, and publish news of it throughout the Four Kingdoms."

"Aonarán will be surrounded by manifold guards and protectors," said the Storm Lord.

"Not enough to save him."

"My dear boy, it is out of character for you to put aside your duties in order to wreak harm. You are like a man driven by invisible unseelie creatures riding on his back."

Arran was indeed a changed man. He would not heed his father's advice. Next morning, accompanied by Bliant and Gauvain, eager companions, Arran set off for the village of Marchington Hythe.

On witnessing her husband's dire preoccupation and precipitate departure Jewel felt profoundly sorrowful, more for him than for herself, yet there was the child to care for, and little time to spend on melancholy musings. Besides, Jewel wished to raise her daughter in a milieu of happiness and contentment, not bit-terness and loss. Left behind once more, tied to home and hearth by the need to nurture her child, Jewel could not help but feel a twinge of resentment. She now learned the dilemma of motherhood, the tearing of one's desires in twain; on the one hand there were the great adventures of life, waiting to be experienced to the fullest; on the other, there was a selfish, demanding, and helpless creature to be sustained. Doubtless the child might have been entirely cared for by wet-nurses and nursemaids, yet every maternal instinct protested against it. No one else could attend to the needs of this being that was the center of the Uile—the universe—as satisfactorily as Jewel herself. Notwithstanding, Arran had em-ployed a nanny so that Jewel might rest if she needed to do so, and as it tran-spired, the new mother was grateful for the assistance.

There was little she could do to ameliorate her restlessness of spirit besides rejoicing every day in the smiles and fresh attainments of her daughter. Seeking ways to divert her thoughts from dismal pathways and make the time seem to elapse more swiftly during her husband's absence, Jewel took the child on a journey to the Great Marsh of Slievmordhu. It was Jewel's desire to proudly show the infant to her grandfather and the other marshfolk. Friends accompanied her; Elfgifu, Hilde, and Ettare. By coach-and-six they traveled, with several outriders providing the guard. The Storm Lord had insisted that mother and child should be carried in the equipage most comfortable for hard road travel.

With exuberant joy they were greeted by the people of the marsh, and as they were guided along the maze of causeways and bridges and elevated footpaths Jewel looked about in wonder, for it had been seven years since she had last seen her childhood home, and all seemed new and old at the same time. She watched herons stalking fish, and breathed the heavy perfume exuded by the waxy white flowers of water hawthorn. On forked spikes, the flowers raised their heads an inch or two above the surface of the marsh, and their pale green mats of foliage floated like rafts. Egrets dabbled amidst the round yellow flowers of "brass buttons," whose small oval leaves spread in dainty carpets across the water. Cormorants swam between blades of umbrella grass, each stem topped by circular heads of narrow leaves arranged like umbrella ribs. In places where no embroidery of vegetation floated, the water-surface was stippled and wavy, like distorted glass panes, and strewn with drifting petals.

Cuiva, White Carlin of the Marsh, welcomed the daughter of her dear friend Lilith. The passing years had only given Cuiva greater dignity; long ago the Winter Hag had taken her natural colors in payment for the extraordinary Wand of a carlin. With her silver rain of hair, her milk-white skin, and her colorless eyes, Cuiva seemed a creature of the permanent snows, an ethereal woman of striking looks who might melt away in the next warm breeze, or else burn you with her powerful touch. She was engaged in mixing medicines and cosmetics, decoctions of white willow bark to ease the pain of headache, toothache, and earache, pounding the dried rhizomes of iris to make orris root powder for use in toothpaste and for scented powders to dust the skin. Jewel remembered her great-grandmother performing those same tasks, and the memories induced tears of nostalgia.

Perceiving their guest's melancholy, Odhrán Rushford made Jewel laugh with his story about a strange phenomenon: a rain of tiny roseate frogs over the village of Carrickmore in Slievmordhu, far from the marsh. "Naturally the druids declared it was a sign from the Fates," he said, "but what the Fates might have meant by it is anyone's guess!"

"I can tell you what caused the rain of frogs," said Jewel. "It would have been nothing more than a trick of the weather, a small tornado lifting the creatures from their native lagoon and dropping them when its power petered out."

"Now Jewel, you are become so knowledgeable since dwelling with the weathermasters," said Cuiva, smiling.

Jewel spent many evenings in the company of her step-grandfather, resting with him by his hearth while the infant suckled. The appearance of the old eel-fisher had altered little over the years, despite that he had endured sixty-one Winters. His hair was sparser and grayer, and his shoulders sagged lower, but the broad face with its webs of wrinkles radiated the same common sense and quiet strength as always, and the scar once inflicted by a fish-hook was still visible through the wild patch of albino pasture that constituted his left eyebrow.

Jewel revered the old man's wisdom and hoped to glean from him the answers to many questions. She recounted the events that had taken place since she last spoke to him at her wedding, all about the Well of Tears, concluding by telling him of Arran's mission to punish Aonarán and his sister for their part in the whole business.

"As you explained to me, *a seanáthair,* out of their own greed, these two Aonaráns bred a grudge against my father. Yet *I* never did them harm."

"No, but do you think that would be mattering to such heartless monsters? The brother obsessed with preserving his own life, and the sister—O Unnatural woman!—a slave at her brother's heel, as ready to murder as to breathe? From what you have said, it appears she now bears a grudge against Arran also, believing it was his fault this Weaponmonger perished at the Comet's Tower."

"She cannot touch Arran."

"As you say, she cannot."

"Neither can she find any way to distress him by harming our child. As for myself, I am invulnerable."

"As you say," the eel-fisher murmured.

"I shall live long."

Earnán Mosswell gazed into the fire that danced on the hearth. The infant made noises like a kitten before settling into contentment again.

Jewel said, "*A seanáthair,* I am pleased to see you in good health as usual. The life of the marsh makes a man strong and hale. I believe you will go on forever."

He smiled. "I will tell you some of the ingredients of the recipe for long life. They include happiness, laughter, dance, song, honest labor, sound sleep, long walks, and fresh food in moderate quantities, eaten slowly at a convivial table, and enjoyed thoroughly. Those who are dwelling on pleasant thoughts are likely to be living longer. I have heard it said that married men live longer than those who are unwed, and that mothers live longer than childless women, but whether that is true or not, the knowledge is not at me. A cup of ale taken with the evening meal is a life-prolonger, so I believe."

"I shall bear in mind all you have said," Jewel told him earnestly. "By my efforts I shall live long, Draught or no Draught."

Jewel and her entourage remained at the marsh during the jollifications of Lantern Eve, but departed the following morning. As she took leave of her grandfather, he gave her a sprig of blossoming crowthistle, dried and pressed between two sheets of blotting paper.

"'Tis what we are calling a flower of souvenance," Earnán said. "This weed is disliked by most folk, for its spines are prickly, yet 'tis tough and resilient, and also beautiful, with its purple wings. Carry it with you to your mountain home as a reminder that what we see around us may at first glance appear common and even distasteful, but if we observe carefully we might be perceiving some worthy attribute, such as beauty.

"Besides," he added prosaically, "'tis a valuable food for goats."

Jewel's visit to her old haunts had triggered vivid memories of childhood. After arriving back at her family apartments in Avalloc's rambling house on Rowan Green, she went to the cedar-wood chest where she customarily stored linen, lace, and precious items. Taking out the fishmail shirt and the gem, she reexamined them, recalling events associated with these marvelous artefacts.

The jewel her father had seized from the Iron Tree sparkled as she held it high, a scattering of reflections and rays, snow-of-moonlight, intensely white. Gently she replaced it in its nest of silk. Then, the shirt. Years ago it had hung on the wall of her grandfather's cottage in the Great Marsh of Slievmordhu. Its workmanship was impeccable. Some process now lost from the lore of armorers had been employed to fashion the garment from the hide of a strong-armored deep-sea fish. The pearly scales interlocked densely yet flexibly, glistening with shades of turquoise, aquamarine, and metallic frost. Jewel wondered if the family legend was true—had the garment indeed been given to one of her forefathers by a mermaid who loved him? The fishmail shirt had been the only beautiful possession in the poor eel-fisher's cot. Now it had come to reside in luxurious surroundings, amongst the rich furnishings of a weathermaster's house. It should not be hidden in the chest, Jewel decided. It should be displayed in full view, as aforetime. With the approval of Avalloc, she had it hung on the wall of the dining hall. There it glittered like sunlight on ocean waves, not far from the great weapon above the fireplace: Fallowblade, the golden sword once called Lannóir, slayer of goblins and heirloom of the House of Stormbringer.

The Storm Lord himself had become a good friend to Jewel, and it was to him she frequently turned for advice. Often, taking Astăriel with them, they would go walking together through the orchards and wild places of the plateau.

The Maelstronnar's appearance had hardly changed since Jewel had first set eyes on him. His features were striking, the jade eyes hooded by deep lids, the aquiline nose, the noble face framed by a thick snowfall of hair. His bearing was proud, his strength still that of an ancient oak.

"Why are weathermasters so long-lived?" Jewel asked. "I have questioned others who dwell here, and I am told only, 'Longevity is in our blood.' Is there more to it? What promotes longevity?"

"Watching, my dear child," replied he. "Watching."

"Watching what?"

"There are three things a mortal creature can watch to calm the mind and revitalize the body. Leafy boughs blowing in the wind. Flames, when they are tame. Water—whether it be waves breaking on a shore, or deep ocean swell, or rain or flowing rivers or placid lakes—Water takes many forms and all are good to watch."

"I have seen leaves blowing in the wind," said Jewel, "yet it does not make me feel different at all."

"Have you watched them, hmm?"

"I have."

"Then tell me, what colors are upon them?"

"Why, green, of course! Except in Autumn."

"But what shades of green? And what other hues?"

"I do not understand your meaning."

"Note how the sun's light falls upon the foliage of that walnut tree. Where the light shines through from the back of the leaves it turns them golden-green. Where the leaves are in shadow they are dark green. And when the light strikes them on their glossy tops they shine purest silver, as dazzling as new-minted coins."

"Why, 'tis true!" cried Jewel in delight. For a moment she was content to dwell on her new discovery; then she said, "But if a person is blind, what then can they do? They cannot watch. . . ."

"But they can listen. There are two sounds that calm the mind and prolong the vitality of the body: birdsong and the music of water."

"Such as rain and rivers?"

"Just so."

"But what if someone is blind and deaf?"

"Then there is the fragrance of flowers, of citrus fruit and fresh-baked bread, of pine forests and new-mown hay. And there is the sensation of sunlight and breezes on the skin, the feeling of having one's hair combed, the touch of silk and satin and living fur, the rocking of a boat borne on the back of the sea."

"All these things will help?"

"Just so."

"But what if—"

Avalloc laughed. "My dear Jewel, let me guess. I'd warrant you are about to ask me about the sense of taste."

"I am. What is good to taste?"

"Your own tongue will tell you that, inquisitive child. Hunger and honey, cream and cheese, apples and bread and mushrooms, lettuce and beans and more hunger."

"Why hunger?"

"Hunger is the best condiment. It sharpens our sense of taste so that we may enjoy fare to the fullest."

"How else should folk proceed in order to live long?"

"Sleep, dance, work, play, sleep again."

Jewel was not entirely content with these answers. "But what are the most important things people must do to achieve longevity?"

"Give, love, laugh. Plentifully."

"And that will guarantee it?"

"No."

"Then what is the use of all you are saying?"

"Dear child, if you give love and kindness to all species of living creatures, if laughter comes easily to you, then no matter how long your span of days, you will have lived them to the fullest."

Despite this reassurance, Jewel had been made anxious by Arran's melancholy, and in typically perverse fashion could derive little satisfaction from Avalloc's words.

The Storm Lord's son, meanwhile, had arrived with the crew of *Mistmoor* at Marchington Hythe, where they had easily located Lord Doom's enthroned oracle. As had been conjectured, the soothsayer turned out to be none other than Fionnbar Aonarán. Arran and his comrades seized the Slievmordhuan in the name of King Warwick, and none of his henchmen or toadying supporters dared oppose the weathermasters.

"This caitiff needs no trial," Arran said roughly, as the pale-haired man was hustled from his throne room in chains. " 'Twould be a waste of resources to take him to the courthouse at King's Winterbourne. He is culpable, and must pay the penalty. Moreover, since he is incorrigible and will live forever, he must be prevented from ever wreaking further havoc on humankind. There is only one solution—eternal imprisonment."

Few would gainsay the son of the Maelstronnar in his intemperate fury. Bliant and Gauvain, to a lesser extent, shared his sentiments. Therefore they paid no heed to Aonarán's shrieks and protests but dumped him into the balloon's gondola and took him with them, ascending high into the sky, leaving his sycophants on the ground staring after them, bereft and agape, wondering if Lord Doom's chosen one had been so powerful, after all.

Mistmoor glided to the lofty range of peaks called the Northern Ramparts in Narngalis, one of the most remote regions of Tir. There, toward the east, Arran set down the sky-balloon high on a steep mountainside, and they toppled Aonarán from the basket.

Had the great-nephew of Ruairc MacGabhann faced his plight with dignity and courage, the hearts of the weathermasters might have been moved to pity. There was nothing dignified or courageous, however, about his shrill curses and threats, alternating with whining and complaining, his upbraiding and claims of having been framed.

"Do not leave me alone!" he wailed. "I am frightened of being immortal alone. Visions and nightmares plague me. In my fancy I am seeing generation after generation fading to dust; associations forged, only to be severed forever; the young growing old before my eyes, the world passing me by, perishable, while I endure immutable, in infinite loneliness!"

His captors ignored his clamor as they hauled him into the mouth of a disused adit, which had been part of a silver-mine in days of yore. Shored up by strong timbers, the adit ran straight into the mountainside for a league and a half, before joining with the rest of the abandoned mine-workings. It was known to be the last remaining entrance to the old diggings.

They removed Aonarán's gyves and left him in the adit, deep in the ground, warning him not to try following them to the outside world, for if he did so, they would blast him with strong winds and send him somersaulting back.

Terrible grief can breed terrible cruelty in humankind. Before he had been faced with the prospect of an endless future living without his beloved bride, Arran could never have brought himself to mete out such a harsh punishment. Anger and despair had warped his once-merciful nature. "This is your jail," he said coldly to the captive. "You need no food or drink to survive, now that you are immortal, and indeed why should His Majesty's Prisons be put to the trouble of feeding you for the rest of eternity? The only place suitable for incarcerating the likes of you is a dungeon that will last until the end of time. From here you can never escape, to work your ill on the world. Justice is served. Here in this sunless domain you must dwell forever, suffering loneliness and exile." Leaning closer to Aonarán, he muttered, "This is your punishment for stealing immortality from my bride, who was the rightful heiress."

With that he turned and walked away, accompanied by his comrades. But as he departed, the voice of Aonarán came shrieking down the lightless tunnel:

"How long is it until the end of time, brother? For when all else is gone I shall be your only kin!"

Arran spoke no word but strode faster, holding aloft his light javelin. When they reached the adit's exit he thrust the extinguished javelin through his belt, quickly spun around, and shouted a vector command, while performing elaborate gestures with his hands.

Even as the balloon had approached the landing place, he and his crew had been preparing for this moment. The atmosphere had already been primed. Air masses were rushing together, charges were building, the impet in Arran's pocket wailed and dived for cover, and next instant two consecutive bolts of lightning struck the entrance to the adit.

Walls and ceiling collapsed with a roar. Hefty timbers tumbled in, rocks crashed down, and clouds of dust billowed. When the vapors began to clear it could be seen that the door into the mountain existed no more. It was sealed with hundreds of tons of rock and soil and other debris.

"And they say that lightning never strikes twice," declared Bliant, brushing dirt off his hands.

"Claw your way out of *that,* you death-dealer," young Gauvain yelled at the settling material of the slope.

Pale-faced, Arran murmured, "A gruesome end to a gruesome career."

Soon afterward the aerostat lifted into the sky and carried the weathermasters away.

Mistmoor returned to High Darioneth on War's Day 16th Ninember with all crew on board, as hale as ever.

"Success we have achieved, yet it has been half-baked," Arran announced discontentedly, "for we have dealt with only one of the two offenders." He related the tale of how they had easily tracked down his hated foe, Fionnbar Aonarán, and incarcerated him in a cave deep below the northern mountains of Narngalis. "I seem to have become a dealer in lightning. With a well-placed strike I caused an avalanche of rocks to seal the sole exit, entombing the miscreant."

"A fate terrible beyond imagining," said Jewel when she heard this, and a look of horror crossed her features.

"Well deserved," her husband said bitterly.

The crew's encounter with Fionnbar had been almost immediate. Finding his half-sister, Fionnuala, however, had proved impossible and had wasted five of their six weeks of absence.

Later, when the heat of Arran's desire for vengeance had somewhat cooled and he was alone with Jewel, he said, "Somehow I cannot help feel the weight of my guilt at imprisoning the vile fellow. At the time I believed it to be a just and fitting penalty, but maybe I was too angry for rational thought. In hindsight I wonder if 'tis not over-severe. Yea, for Aonarán is, in some warped manner, my brother—the only other man in the Four Kingdoms who is no longer mortal. In inflicting this penance on him I am, in some strange way I cannot fathom, reflecting the harm upon myself. I am setting a precedent. If he can be treated this way, then so can I."

"Be at peace," said Jewel. "If your deed troubles you, then you must return to those mountains and dig him out. Set him free, or else devise some other way of dealing with him."

"Perhaps. I shall ponder the matter further."

The old year rolled away, and the new entered triumphantly through the portal of the seasons, welcomed by bonfires and festivities across the Four Kingdoms. Meanwhile, at private meetings in certain guarded rooms amidst the bountiful lands of Tir, subtle maneuverings were taking place. Changes were afoot.

At the palace of King Chohrab II in Ashqalêth yet another convoy arrived from Cathair Rua, bringing costly gifts from Uabhar Ó Maoldúin of Slievmordhu. Ever since his accession to the throne, Uabhar had been cultivating a cordial amity with Ashqalêth's sovereign. In addition to donations of presents, Uabhar would exalt his neighbor during occasions of state in Slievmordhu, and invite him to be present with his household at informal jollifications, where he was always offered the best of everything.

Chohrab II was much pleased by the flattery. He received this latest bounty with his customary sense of satisfaction, delighted that the sovereign of a neighboring realm should be so very particular in cultivating his goodwill. It seemed plain that Uabhar held him in high esteem. Ever watchful for enemies and rivals, Chohrab had perceived no threat from beyond his northeastern borders; it appeared that Slievmordhu's monarch wished only to strengthen the alliance of the two southernmost realms, not to undermine or overwhelm Chohrab's governance.

The King of Ashqalêth had daughters of an age to be wedded to any of the sons of Uabhar when they grew to manhood; therefore, he had at first reasoned that Uabhar might be hoping to inveigle a foothold in his kingdom by way of marriage ties. The King of Slievmordhu assured Chohrab II, however, that, to his regret, Queen Saibh—who sadly lacked foresight—had persuaded Uabhar to pledge his sons at an early age to young ladies from certain wealthy Slievmordhuan families "and Thorgild's daughter, I forget her name." That seemed to preclude any nefarious scheming for the throne of Ashqalêth. After some deliberation, Chohrab came to be of the opinion that Uabhar's friendship was genuine, and he could be trusted.

Besides, it was evident to the desert king that Uabhar trusted *him,* for he took him into his confidence. The two monarchs held many a discussion, guarded by their most loyal ministers, behind the closed doors of their private apartments. It had been Uabhar who had been honest enough with Chohrab to reveal to him the true stances of the monarchs of Narngalis and Grïmnørsland.

"I will not deny you the facts, my friend," he had said hesitantly, as if at pains to protect Chohrab's sensibilities. "Regrettably, Warwick and Thorgild have been heard to say they consider you to be obtuse, weak, and irresolute of character. It galls me more than I can endure, that such misrepresentations should be made of you."

Yet, when Chohrab in his indignation vowed to confront his detractors with their spurious remarks, demanding their withdrawal, along with recompense to demonstrate suitable penitence, Uabhar cautioned him.

"Patience, my dear friend. There are perhaps better ways to ensure that these scornful and deluded rulers open their eyes and see you in your true colors. I am sure you will be of one mind with me when I say that by rights they ought to be made to rue their insulting behavior. Patience, my virtual brother."

Uabhar spoke forthrightly when he revealed the opinion of those who walked other corridors of power. He failed to mention that he himself shared that disdainful view of Chohrab II, or that it was also judged in high places that the King of Slievmordhu was a cunning and clever man, intolerant of weakness in any form. Just why the monarchs of Slievmordhu and Ashqalêth should hold close conclave was a subject of speculation amongst courtiers and ministers across the lands, for a contriver like Uabhar would hardly heed the advice of Chohrab, nor would he joyfully endure the tedium of imparting his own counsel to one so unlikely to comprehend it.

In Narngalis, and more particularly in High Darioneth, tidings of reinforced political alliances between the southern and eastern realms were treated with watchful wariness. In a way, political events outside the mountain ring were like ocean waves battering themselves to pieces against stubborn cliffs. They seemed to have little influence on life on the plateau, or at the Seat of the Weathermasters. Nonetheless Avalloc and the councillors were fully aware that even a force as barely perceptible as the vibrations of the pounding seas can eventually erode the foundations of a precipice.

As the seasons took turns to splash the meadows, the woodlands, and the skies with their signature colors, and years glided by, Arran Maelstronnar sank into a gentle melancholy, brought on by his perceived failure to ensure Jewel's eternal life, his inability to locate Fionnuala, and his guilt at imprisoning Aonarán, who now could no longer be found. Belatedly taking Jewel's advice, the son of the Storm Lord had journeyed to the slopes where he had buried his foe alive. New entrances were excavated, but when the caverns were explored, no sign of the pale-haired man could be found. He was gone. There was no way out to the sunlit surface; he could only have descended to the nether regions and been lost in the labyrinth of tunnels far below fathoms of rock and soil. After their search the weathermasters resealed the openings they had created. Arran was adamant on one detail: if Aonarán were ever to emerge, Ellenhall must be informed of it.

What of Fionnbar's sister Fionnuala?

Hers was a curious and twisted tale.

So far, the weathermasters had been unable to discover her, even with the help of Fridayweed—"Man, I am not omnipotent! I am only a wee thing with a single glamour-guise." The Storm Lord's son vowed he would never rest until the markswoman had been captured, but for the time being, weathermastery missions demanded his urgent attention.

Aware that the lords of High Darioneth searched for her, Fionnuala assumed a series of false identities, a sequence of disguises. For years she roamed the by-ways of the Four Kingdoms of Tir, living off supplies bought with stored profits from the now-defunct illegal weapons-trade, an ignorant, ignominious, and tragic figure, puppetted by petty concerns. At night she could scarcely find repose, being tormented by dreams of voices taunting her in unintelligible languages. By day she was single-minded of purpose, yet ineffective, disorganized, and incompetent.

Relentlessly she sought a way to severely hurt Arran Maelstronnar. In her judgment the Storm Lord's son had caused the death of Cathal Weaponmonger, who, she believed delusively, would have one day asked her to be his wife. Before meeting Weaponmonger she had loved only one man: Jarred Jaravhor. Yet Jewel's father had rejected her, preferring Jewel's mother, and now, from all accounts, he was dead. Fionnuala Aonarán's hatred for Arran Maelstronnar was compounded when she learned he had imprisoned her half-brother in an inescapable tomb. Fionnbar had always been cruel to her. She had never truly cared for him; in fact, she feared and despised him; however, in her life of ephemerae, where people never stayed long and no place was home, his familiarity made him pivotal.

The knowledge that the Storm Lord's son was dwelling in wedded bliss was like salt excoriating her wounded psyche, inasmuch as her own existence had brought her nothing but misery. Jealousy fed her obsession. With Fionnbar gone and no other purpose driving her, Fionnuala acquired enough impetus to survive from day to day by blaming one man for all her woes.

But Arran was now indestructible.

Monomaniacally she pursued her goal: to find some method of exacting retribution.

"He loves the girl more than his own life," she would mutter to herself, "as I loved Jarred. As Cathal loved me." Her memory played tricks, for Weaponmonger had never held her in his affections, and her much-aggrandized "love" for Jarred had in fact been an empty fatuity.

The child Astăriel learned to walk and speak. She was taught her letters and numbers, she practiced the flute, and—when she was tall enough to sit a horse by herself and govern it—she rode through long grasses to the mill, in the company of her mother, to visit their friends. After that single ride Astăriel vowed never again to make a burden of herself to any beast, for she felt sorry that the innocent horse had been forced to carry her so far, when it might have been cantering free in the meadows amongst its own kind.

She groomed her pouring tresses, her total eclipse of black locks, with the brush and comb from a silver dressing-table set her Grandfather Avalloc had given her on her eighth birthday. A *brí*-child, she learned the basic principles of weathermastery from her father. She developed an ability to deflect and reflect the teasing mockeries of Ryence Darglistel, who played the role of honorary uncle (and who had declared his intention to remain a bachelor on the grounds that his marriage would deprive the flower of womanhood of their greatest source of joy). Timeless Summer days were spent roaming the countryside with friends of her own age. During long Winter's nights she explored the libraries of Rowan Green, or pestered Fridayweed with questions until it made itself scarce behind the wainscot.

At the age of nine, Astăriel went camping with her friends on Midsummer's Eve. It was an exciting treat for the children to pitch their tents beneath the stars, to tell stories around the campfire and try to remain awake until dawn. Her silver-backed brush and silver comb were the only instruments of coiffure that could untangle Astăriel's thick skeins of hair. She treasured them, and therefore took them with her on the outing.

It was after midnight by the time the children and the supervising adults finished celebrating the culmination of the sun's journey with songs, high jinks, and feasting. Exhausted, they had collapsed beside their fires, whereupon Astăriel began dressing her hair. Starlight laved the polished back of the brush, which was engraved with her initials: A.J.H.M., Astăriel Jewel Heronswood Maelstronnar. When she held up the device in front of her eyes, there appeared to be a hint of shape to the reflections on the gleaming surface and as she gazed, it seemed to her she could make out an image. It looked like a face but, curiously, not hers.

The reflection shifted.

Hastily, Astăriel turned around to glance over her shoulder. No one lurked behind her. Yet she felt as though someone had stood at her shoulder, moments before. At first stunned, then inwardly amused by her own unpredictable powers of invention, she turned back for a second look at the brush's mirror-like carapace.

The reflection remained.

She stared, spellbound, as it slowly began to fade.

Framed by hair blacker than wickedness, the face was male, wonderfully handsome, but radiating an air of extreme danger and maleficence. It was a countenance elemental, consummate, extreme, *patently* eldritch and not human. The flash of the eyes was violet lightning transformed to ice, and the lashes were outlined with black, as if the lids were penciled with kohl. Long strands of hair floated across that countenance in a sinuous dance, as if eddying in a river, or blown by a slow wind. A faint smile tugged at the corners of his mouth, and his glance seemed altogether knowing, ironic, intelligent, and arcane.

A moment later, the image was gone.

It had been as brief as the life of a flame in a snowstorm, that vision, but it stamped the damsel's memory with a vivid impression; those eyes, shards of dark amethyst, had been lit from within by sparks that might have signified viciousness or vengefulness, mockery or mischief, cruelty or callousness, amusement, antipathy, contempt, or cleverness, or all at once, fueled from the same source. And there was that *alien* quality . . . he was too eldritch, too impossibly beautiful to be any mortal man, there could be no doubt.

For Astăriel, it was as if she had been a pane of glass, smashed into a million splinters that flew apart, spinning and glittering. She could explain neither the phenomenon nor her reaction, could not define what had happened; therefore she made mention of the event to no one. Thus, it transpired she could not know that her mother had once seen the same image in a water-pool, while hoping that such a face could not exist.

Astăriel, perversely, found herself hoping that it *could*.

Jewel was particular about maintaining contact with old friends and relatives. Over the years she enjoyed many more visits to Great Marsh of Slievmordhu, often in the company of her husband and daughter.

If there was contentment and reassurance to be gained from renewing friendships in the marsh, sometimes there was also disquieting news. It was not until near the end of a visit in the Autumn of 3481 that Jewel's grandfather took her aside and spoke to her gravely, confidentially.

"Last Spring a stranger came prying about in the marsh," said Earnán. "A strange kettle of fish indeed. He was asking questions about Jarred. We told him nought. You understand how it is—we marshfolk protect our own. The stranger went away, but returned later that same year, still asking questions. At length, so that he would depart satisfied and trouble us no longer, Cuiva Rushford composed a false tale and recounted it to him.

"It now occurs to me," Earnán continued, "that the man who came prying must surely have been an agent of this Fionnuala Aonarán, she who has declared herself an enemy of your husband. She is aware that Arran cannot be slain. I daresay she had sent some mercenary to probe for ways to destroy the daughter of Jarred. You must guard yourself, dear one. Guard yourself painstakingly. Never underestimate the deceitfulness and cunning of your foes."

"I doubt if the she-fox would be able to push me over a mistletoed cliff," said Jewel. "I spend most of my days at High Darioneth. Mistletoe does not grow on the cold heights of the mountain ring. And when I visit here, I am surrounded by friends."

"Nevertheless, guard yourself," said Earnán.

"Arran will guard me, *a seanáthair*," said Jewel. "I have never known such love."

On learning of Fionnuala's search for a way to harm his wife, Arran was charged with anger so explosive, so consuming, he seemed like a thunderstorm clothed in the likeness of a man.

"You will be guarded," he said to her, "night and day, wherever you go."

She replied, "I am invulnerable! Almost."

Motherhood had mellowed her. She soothed him with words: "'Tis impossible for Fionnuala Aonarán ever to discover how my father died. The people of the marsh are the only ones who know the truth—and they will never tell."

"What if her aged relative, the servant of Strang, was privy to the secret and passed it on to her? Say what you will, I will remain forever vigilant on your behalf."

"Be so if you wish, dear love, but do not let this vex you and prey on your mind. 'Tis a strange fact: if we seek to avoid something we dwell on it all the time, and thus we have already succumbed to it, in a way."

Her peculiar methods of reasoning led her to wax philosophical, and she looked to her future with equanimity, though in her heart she said fatalistically to herself, *I am vulnerable only to one thing—mistletoe. Therefore, it is not unlikely that my bane will seek me out, in the end.*

Being herself a liar and a deceiver, Fionnuala Aonarán was readily able to recognize falsity in others. She knew full well the White Carlin of the Marsh had
tried to mislead her; therefore, Fionnuala employed her street-honed cunning
and her purses filled with blood-bought gold.

In Cathair Rua it was common knowledge that soldiers of King Maolmórdha had raided the Great Marsh of Slievmordhu in the Autumn of the year
3465. They had been hunting for a man who had, without scathe, taken the
white jewel from amongst the cruel thorns of the Iron Tree. He was, so said the
gossips, a marshman.

Fionnuala Aonarán knew exactly who he was, for it had been she who had
tricked Jarred into retrieving the jewel from its sixty-year-old resting place. He
was the scion of a mortal ancestor who had mastered several sorcerous arts and
made his descendants impossible to injure. After the soldiers had returned to
Cathair Rua the news had filtered through the usual channels to her ears: the
jewel-thief was dead.

But how had he died?

For Fionnuala, who was acquainted with the knowledge of Jarred's invulnerability, his death was a mystery. Her great-uncle, Ruairc McGabhann, had
never bothered to mention the sorcerer's bane in her hearing, nor had she ever
thought to ask before the old villain died. Seeking clues to the one weakness
that proved Jarred's undoing, she bribed and interviewed a soldier of the Household Cavalry, a member of the Royal Slievmordhu Dragoons. He had been
amongst those who entered the marsh and found Jarred's body on that fateful
Otember day.

Soon she learned exactly where Jarred's mortal remains had been discovered,
and in what condition.

A band of traveling players came to sojourn at the marsh. The watchmen were
initially loath to let them in, for they had not encountered this troupe before,
and knew not whether their performance would be entertaining, nor whether
they could be trusted. Yet they carried no weapons and seemed harmless
enough; besides, their prices were surprisingly low and one of their jugglers
showed off some amazing tricks for nothing. The players camped for a single
night near the *cruinniú,* where they enacted their comedic routine. On that evening, unnoticed by any marsh-dweller, one member of the troupe made a surreptitious journey.

The swift, sharp breeze racing along Lizardback Ridge chased the woman
walking up the slope from the marsh, tugging at her skirts, making the gray-

green grass-stems caress her stout boots and the hem of her woad-blue cloak. Her pale eyes darted from side to side, as if she looked for pursuers or watchers lurking in the shadows of early evening.

Yet no watchers were to be seen, only the grasses bending in waves to show the silvery undersides of their blades, and bright yellow splashes of late blooming rock-roses, and the dagged stars of maiden pinks and the purple wings of crowthistle.

When she reached the top, she paused.

At her feet lay the wide, undulating grasslands of southern Slievmordhu, tapestried with their leafy copses and belts of beech and ash, sprinkled in the near distance by the whitish blotches of grazing sheep and goats.

The woman displayed no interest in the view. On the cliff-face below, the three stunted ash trees, adorned with their swaying bunches of sage-green foliage, reached into chasms of wind. The woman knelt. She leaned forward. Perhaps she climbed down a short distance, then returned. Her sharp eyes darted, and she noted many things.

She did not stay long on the ridge-top. After she left, darkness gathered. The wind continued to hound the grasses and chivvy the nodding heads of crowthistle. And on the cliff-face something fluttered, snagged on the end of a dry mistletoe twig: a tiny scrap of fabric, woad-blue.

The Autumn Fair at Cathair Rua was to begin on 14th Sevember. Arran and Jewel had decided to attend it, in company with a group of weathermaster friends. There were purchases to be made on behalf of Rowan Green; besides, Jewel seized every opportunity to revisit Earnán and her friends of the marsh, who customarily set up their stalls at the Fair. Unwilling to take ten-year-old Astăriel away from her studies, they left her in the care of Avalloc, her governess, and her old nanny.

The four sky-balloons being engaged in far-off weathermastery missions, the company made their journey by carriage and on horseback. As they traveled along their way Jewel declared the Autumn colors of the equinoctial landscapes had never been more brilliant. Indeed this was probable, for during the past few weeks dry, sunny days and cool, dry nights had held sway throughout the southern regions of Tir, breaking down the green chlorophyll of the leaves and enhancing their production of red and purple anthocyanins.

The cortege from High Darioneth passed through a beech-wood in the morning. Early sunlight was shining through the leaves. Amongst the dark stems of the trees floated great drifts and bowers and spangled clouds of color, points and splashes of rich bronze and cinnibar, poignant green, fabulous gold, shimmering in sun and air, fair as some enchanted realm.

"I should fall on my knees and weep, at such a sight," said Jewel, gazing out of the carriage window, "a spectacle gorgeous beyond description, so glorious it breaks my heart. For with every moment it is all fading; another leaf falls, the sun rides to a different angle, and all this fleeting loveliness is ours to behold for only the briefest while. Yet I ache with love for this splendor."

"The trees will be bare in Winter," said Ettare, who was seated at her side, "but Spring will bring renewal, and next Autumn this spectacle will be repeated."

"Aye, but not the same. Never exactly the same. And there will come an Autumn when we are not here to see it, when this glory shall be denied us and we shall forever be parted from it. I should fall to my knees and weep."

"You are passionate, Jewel, to a fault."

"Perhaps you are right. For I love Autumn's beauty so dearly that it gives me what I can only describe as pain. Does that seem foolish, to you?"

Arran, riding behind the equipage, had chanced to overhear this exchange. He closed his eyes and turned his head aside, as if dodging a blow, or as if he suddenly felt a need to avoid seeing some particularly magnificent tracery of leaves against the sky.

Within the carriage a moment elapsed before Ettare replied to Jewel's question, and her tones seemed strained: "Be assured, it does not seem foolish at all."

The reddish sandstone and blood-slate roofs of the Red City gleamed warmly in the rich-tinted daylight of the season. Mists were rising from the street-gutters and wells, and from the head of the Rushy Water. Cathair Rua's conglomerate of rooftops and gables, towers and turrets, spires and belfries appeared to hover, free of footings, above the machicolations and crenellations of its battlemented walls. Atop the palace roofs, flocks of flags flapped against a sheer blue sky, each proudly bearing the fiery device of Slievmordhu: the Burning Brand. From that direction, staccato shouts and the regulated martial crunching of hundreds of boots on gravel indicated that a regiment of the Household Guards was performing a drill in the palace forecourt.

Set a little apart from the city, the Fair Field spread out beneath the high walls. The market that straggled across the field was a tangle of tents, booths, and stands. Man-powered pushcarts trundled back and forth, their wooden wheels groaning. Acrobats and jokesters bent their bodies into outlandish shapes in an effort to coax pennies from generous onlookers, rich or poor. Children hawked their parents' wares or played in the dust. An ancient dancing-bear in an iron collar, nose ring, and chain shambled hopelessly in the wake of his master. Fluid seeped from the bear's eyes, as if he were weeping. Weary nags pulling carts clip-clopped between the stalls, while dogs fought over scraps. A haze of dust, cooking-fire smoke, and mist veiled the scene, softening it and lending it a dream-like quality to contrast with the prosaic odors of fried onions and boiled cabbage.

Agents of the palace, the Sanctorum, and the higher echelons of the aristocracy were passing amongst the stalls, examining the goods and deciding which vendors would be commanded to present themselves at the palace or some majestic house, there to display their merchandise in privacy.

The entourage of Jewel and Arran moved through the small enclave, close to the city gates, which was always set aside for the vendors of high-quality or rare goods. They occupied a pleasant hour examining bolts of silk, damask, muslin, baldachin, velvet, linen, and fine woolen cloth, furs, crocodile skins, spices and ornaments, silver and bronze jewelry, glassware and perfumes, distilled liquors, ornate ceramic ware, musical instruments, and mechanical toys.

After leaving the guarded precinct of the upper-crust vendors, they strolled out into the main areas of the Fair Field. Here a wider variety of wares could be found: livestock and deadstock, sacks of nut-flour and corn-flour, preserved meats, eels and fish, dried vegetables, fruits, and herbs, waxed cheeses, barrels of beverages, candlesticks, cauldrons, lanterns, arrowheads, knives, saddles, harness, boots, bolts of cheap textiles, barrels of wine, candles, honey, glass beads, glassware, rope, chains, axes, bells, baskets, jugs, bowls, purses and belts, jars of oil, and sundry other articles. Jewel bought some penny-farthing griddle-cakes from a woman and her mother who toasted them on a griddle-iron over a fire. As traditional at seasonal fairs, entertainment was provided in the form of archery competitions, games of dice, jugglers, storytellers, musicians, fire-eaters, puppet-shows, and stilt-walkers.

They visited the marshfolk at their customary station on the southwest corner of the field, not far from the river-landings. Little had altered over the years since Jewel had first visited the fair as a child. There were the pyramidal piles of firkins stuffed with pickled eels, the goat-hides hung on display, the poles from which braces of smoked fish were suspended, the haberdashery.

Much conversation and purchasing having taken place, it was late in the afternoon by the time the travelers from the north decided to depart from the Fair Field and make for the house of Calogrenant Lumenspar, Ambassador for High Darioneth in Cathair Rua. There they would spend the night, before leaving for the mountain ring next morning.

Not far from the stalls of the marshfolk an itinerant jongleur had seated himself on a three-legged stool. He was playing a battered lute, accompanying him-

self while he sang. His instrument, although decrepit, was loud. The wistful
melody caught the attentions of the weathermasters and they paused to listen:

> "The fires of anger and passion, the daggers of envy and spite,
>   The acid of cruel sarcasm, or jealousy's viperous bite,
>   The arrows of humiliation, the glacial freezing of scorn,
>   The sweet warmth of gladness and rapture, the anguish of weepers
>   who mourn,
>   No sentiment, or thought can stir me; nay, nothing can touch me at all.
>   For mine is no longer the soaring, mine neither the heights nor the fall.
>   I walk on a plain that is barren; no mountain or vale marks my way.
>   No sunlight or darkness enfolds me—just limitless shadows of gray.
>   I long for the fires to burn me; I yearn for the ice and the knives,
>   I wish I could once more be roused by the passions that quicken our
>   lives,
>   Yet only when I am beside you can I feel some emotion again—
>   'Tis only your presence that moves me, restoring both pleasure and
>   pain."

With a flourish of his fingers the minstrel ceased his crooning. He rose to his
feet and bowed. "You fortunate lord and ladies have been regaled by the music
of one who once sang at the court of King Uabhar Ó Maoldúin himself. The
lyrics are mine alone, yet the melody is not, for, growing weary on my journey
homeward one evening, I fell asleep upon a lonely hill, and when I awoke I
heard a lilting pipe-tune of the Fridean coming from beneath the ground, which
I memorized."

"Which explains why the melody is passing pleasing to the ear, while the
words grate depressingly on the same organ," said Ryence Darglistel. "Why
sing sorrowful love songs on a jolly afternoon? Would you have us bawling into
our gravy by dinnertime?"

The musician bowed a second time. "Alas. Forgive me if I have displeased
you, lord."

But Ettare, who had been loitering at the edge of the group, put her hand on
Jewel's sleeve. "Did you hear it?"

"The song? Of course."

"Not the song. I scarcely paid heed to the ditty. There was another sound,
dimmer, as if coming from far off. Yet keener and more disturbing, by far."

"What sound?"

"The sound of weeping. . . ."

Now that Ettare had mentioned it, Jewel recalled, in hindsight, hearing a low accompaniment to the song of the minstrel, an eerie lamenting and sobbing.

An eldritch weeper was forecasting someone's death.

"Best not to mention it," Jewel advised her friend. "There is no knowing for whom the weepers cry. It might be anyone at all in this vast city."

Arran gave two silver threepences to the troubadour, who prostrated himself in gratitude, and the company moved on.

Through the busy streets of Cathair Rua they walked. As usual the doors and windows of every house, shop, and inn were decorated with assortments of devices to ward off unseelie manifestations—horseshoes, sprigs of rowan or hypericum, strings of small bells, cast-iron roosters, daisies and ivy leaves carved in relief on timbers of ash-wood, rare river-stones worn hollow by the natural action of water, and cheerful bundles of red ribbons.

Within the more privileged quarters the streets were bordered by tall houses built of gray granite, with a cobbled and grated drain down the center of every road. The fragrant boughs of citrus trees nodded over the walls of courtyards where fountains played tunefully. Well-dressed personages strolled the footpaths taking the evening air, or rode in their carriages on their way to formal dinners.

The uppermost tiers of the Sanctorum peered over the walls of the Royal Citadel. It was the only city edifice constructed of white sandstone; however, the chastity of its masonry had long been corrupted by red dirt. The walls were smeared, and from each sill, gutter, and drainpipe dripped a long black-red blemish, as if the buildings were bleeding. Staring serpents of marble twined about fluted columns. The crests on their heads and backs proclaimed them to be cockatrices. More of their ilk glared from the bell-shaped roofs atop the square towers and turrets and belfries. Splinters of broken glass jutted along the lofty tops of the walls, and sentinels patrolled the wall-walks.

After bypassing the Sanctorum the company entered the streets leading up to the house of Lumenspar. Their course took them across a public square at a crossroads. Here, enclosed by a striking edifice of blushing sandstone—a high, colonnaded, beehive-roofed structure reached by flights of stone stairs—a speaker was holding forth. Five young boys supported oil lamps on tall poles, which illuminated the speech-maker with their radiance. Dressed in the raiment of a King's Druids' Scribes' Hand, the orator stood high on the rubicund platform of the Oratorium. His voluminous, deeply hooded robes were made of fustian, dyed red with the roots of madder. A scarf of etiolated linen enfolded his neck and shoulders, and the insignia of the White Cockatrice was embroidered on his sleeve beneath the sigil of the Burning Brand. At the Hand's back two henchmen stood like rough-hewn statues. A little aside stood a nervous youth all in ruddled fustian, a small cockatrice sigil gleaming on his shoulder.

This attendant stepped forward and called to the crowd, "Be silent for Tertius Malandria!"

The weathermasters hastened past, making all efforts to remain as inconspicuous as possible so that they would not be expected to halt and listen to the Oration. As they rounded a corner at the far end of the street, they could hear, at their backs, the opening words of the Tertius's speech, "threading up the road," as Ryence described it, "like an intestinal worm."

"Hear now the Word of the King's Druids," he warbled, as if trying to enunciate around a gall in his throat, "and as the druids prophesy, so shall it be. For it shall come to pass that the white unicorn shall drink from the silver chalice, and the crimson star shall shine upon the cradle in the valley. . . ."

"Hasten!" Arran muttered under his breath. "Without doubt, bloodsuckers will be nearby. I have no wish to contribute to the swelling of their over-stuffed coffers."

None of his companions needed urging. All were well acquainted with the intercessionary collectors and their inevitable bodyguards, whose habit was to go amongst crowds that gathered in uneasy neediness whenever a representative of the druidhood expounded at an Oratorium. The collectors would ask for the names of the audience members, so that the druids might intercede with the Fates on their particular behalf. Citizens need only cross the Scribes' Hand's Assistant's Intercessionary Collector's palm with silver or gold coinage and later, at the Sanctorum, a druid would speak directly to the Fates, asking that the donor receive Good Fortune and avoid Ill Luck.

The weathermasters were not the only folk endeavoring to distance themselves from the Oratorium. They merged with the flow of a moving crowd. To be hurrying, almost running, up a street amidst a throng of people, all feigning nonchalance in case the druids should suspect deception by stratagem, struck several members of the group as hilarious. Jewel, Ettare, and Ryence had to stifle their laughter as they went. Arran hid his grin behind his hand. It was as if they were children again, trying to avoid the attention of their elders after some misdeed.

Bliant, who strode at the front of the group, called out, "The house of Lumenspar is close by!"

After all those years of living in safety their vigilance had decreased. When no danger seems to threaten, it is difficult to be constantly on one's guard; it is easy to slip into the tranquillity of peace when no war is apparent. To post bodyguards and watchers around Jewel at every moment would seem to be an overreaction. It was more pleasant to relax and enjoy life's adventures.

Therefore, as they hastened, laughing breathlessly, they did not notice—nobody in that scurrying crowd noticed—that, flanked by two shabby mercenaries, a stringy figure stepped from around a corner of a building. This archer raised a crossbow—already loaded and cocked—waited for a gap to appear in the crowd, took careful aim, and fired.

A sound like a *zing* ripped the air.

As Jewel fell, pierced by the quarrel of mistletoe, Fionnuala lowered her weapon, slipped it to a lurking hireling, and darted out of sight. Her agent disappeared in the opposite direction. Fionnuala passed swiftly away into the maze of Rua's back-alleys, toward the streets where she had been born, raised, and taught the meaning of "survival." She became just another face in the crowd, just another fair-goer, another rat in the slums.

Cries and gasps rippled through the crowd when they witnessed Jewel's fall. Many took to their heels and fled, fearing to be caught up in a random eruption of street warfare. Others fanned out, searching for the assassin. The swiftest amongst the weathermasters ran in search of a carlin, while the rest formed a protective shield around Jewel.

As his wife lay breathing her last, Arran eased the quarrel from beneath her breastbone and cast it aside. He drew her into the haven of his arms and rocked her softly, and kissed her forehead.

At first, dazed, Jewel did not know what had happened.

"I seem to have fallen," she said in surprise, "into a pit." She brought her hand close to her face. There was blood on it.

Gazing up at her husband, she said, "No, not a pit. I feel my spirit fading."

He could not speak. His throat felt choked.

"I think I am dying," she said.

A mist seemed to be blowing across her eyes, like vapor across a sky-pool, and by that he knew her sight was failing. Her last words to Arran were, "I will love you both, even when you can no longer see me."

Then she was gone.

Just like that she was gone, and Arran was inconsolable. Refusing to release her from his embrace, he bore her inert form to the house of Lumenspar. There he laid Jewel on a couch covered with cloth-of-gold, and would not leave her side.

He ranted, "She should have been immortal, with me. We should have dwelled side by side forever. Now my gift is wasted and I would cast it from me if I could."

At times when he seemed to have rallied his wits he cried, "The only means by which humankind can defeat death is to earn everlasting fame. Fame is achieved by means of songs sung by bards, and sagas made by poets, and they must be great ballads, in order to endure the trials of time. I shall make songs for her. I shall commission the best bards to compose unforgettable epics in her honor."

But he was unable to shed tears, because he was mortal made immortal.

Jewel's body was borne to High Darioneth in the sky-balloon *Northmoth*. During the following days, men and women, children, carlins, lords and ladies, and representatives from the four royal families of Tir journeyed to the mountain ring to pay their respects.

In Ellenhall Jewel's coffin rested on a seven-foot-high catafalque covered with Narngalish purple velvet, gold braid, and crimson felt. The casket itself was draped and entirely hidden beneath the fair banner of the weathermasters, with its four quadrants, each containing a symbol: Water, ¥; Fire, Ψ; Air, §; and, in the fourth quadrant, the longsword emblem of Narngalis. The coffin's lid was surmounted by a garland of gentians and alpine lupins, placed around a transparent crystal vessel of clear water. Half-hidden amongst the flowers was a card, inscribed with words in an elegant, flowing hand, and other words in a more childish script. Six carved and gilded pedestals had been placed around the catafalque. Each stood five feet tall, and supported a white candle three feet long and as thick as a man's upper arm.

The coffin was guarded by four senior councillors of Ellenhall, who in turn would yield their places to four prentices, and so everyone who dwelled on Rowan Green could, if they so wished, participate in this last gesture of farewell. A long queue of mourners waited at the doors of Ellenhall. People from the plateau had come to file past the coffin and pay their respects. Marshfolk had made the long journey, and members of all the royal families.

On the eve of the ceremonial funeral a quartet of young men stood vigil at the four corners of the catafalque: Bliant Ymberbaillé, Ryence Darglistel, Herebeorht Miller, and Oisín Rushford, Jewel's old playmate from the marsh. Bliant and Ryence wore their weathermaster raiment, while Herebeorht and Oisín were clad in their best clothes. They stood guard over her memory, in the great silence and the dim candle-light and the scent of the flowers brought to honor her.

When the morning of the funeral dawned, the bell in the tower atop Ellenhall tolled twenty-nine times, reflecting every year of Jewel's life. While the bell solemnly pealed, the mourners filed into Ellenhall. The great building could not hold them all: some must listen from beyond the doors as Avalloc Maelstronnar conducted the rites. He performed the ancient ceremony of the sprinkling of the waters, saying, "Life is a cosmic imperative, and Water is its key. The source of purification, sustenance, and cleanliness, Water signifies transparency and tranquillity. Water's natural beauty is emblematic of the grace and loveliness of life in harmony. Its primal, creative power symbolizes the restoration of life and the promise of the future. It is the wellspring of the spirit, of life, and of health; it confers prosperity on our communities, and safeguards the harvest. Every living creature is a conduit of unseen Water. Water is constantly flowing around and through all people in the world. Humankind, like all other species, is a river."

The Storm Lord then talked of Jewel's fearlessness, quick-wittedness, kindness, and grace. As he spoke, Arran battled with his emotions, while Astăriel listened intently, her head bowed.

"You may weep that she has gone," Avalloc said, "but better that you be joyful she has lived."

The Bard of High Darioneth had written an elegy for Jewel, which he chanted in his rich voice, unaccompanied by music. Cuiva Rushford of the marsh rendered a heartfelt eulogy, and all persons gathered there joined their voices in a song that Jewel had loved:

> "Life is to live. Pray, do not mourn the falling of each blossom day,
>   Nor sigh for memories, nor pine for some thing that has passed away;
>   Spare it a thought, a word, a dream, but never dwell on what has
>   gone.
>   Open your eyes and seize the day. The sun still shines as once it
>   shone.
>
> "No time to lose! 'Tis time to laugh, to look and leap, to love and live.
>   Fondly embrace this present hour and all the choices it can give.
>   Now ride against the wind! Now jump from dune to strand; now
>   challenge wave
> Of curling surf; now sing the stars, be overjoyed; be bold, be brave!
>
> "The world is kind, the world's benign, our cradle floating in the void,
>   Enwrapped with cloudy scarves, a gem, sapphire-in-silver unalloyed,
>   Pulsing to seasons of the moon. The land's alive with tidal breath.
>   Young seedlings sprout from withered moss, and new life springs
>   from every death."

Then the crystal bowl of water was removed and, to the accompaniment of two young trumpeters playing a military farewell, the coffin, still decorated with a spill of fresh flowers, was taken out of Ellenhall. Eight stalwart weathermasters lifted it and hoisted it to their shoulders. Slowly, with measured steps, they bore it from the stately building. Arran, Astăriel, Avalloc, and Earnán followed through the oaken doors, sorrow written cruelly on their faces. In their wake came Cuiva and Odhrán Rushford, and Avalloc's chil-

dren, Galiene, Lysanor, and Dristan, accompanied by his sister, Astolat
Darglistel-BlackFrost, with her son Ryence at her side, and her four younger
children in tow. Behind them came a long line of other family members and
friends.

As they passed through the doors, the mountain wind blew the cloaks of the
mourners, ruffled the foam of blue flowers on the coffin lid, and swept the hems
of the flag draping it. The crowd waited in silence, watching as the casket was
eased into a hearse drawn by six matching horses, the color of melancholy, the
leading pair under the charge of a mounted postilion. With extraordinary care
the pallbearers lowered their light burden from their shoulders, then took two
steps sideways. As the casket slid into place, the young men bowed.

Arran looked on, fighting for composure, his mouth a compressed seam of
grief. As the light of a lamp is dimmed by soot, so his handsome face was dulled
by sadness, his brows knitted, his lower eyelids sagging into bruised bags. Furrows incised themselves into his flesh where no line or mark had appeared before, two deep symmetrical grooves etched from each side of his nose, running
down to the outer corners of his drooping mouth.

The four sky-balloons of the weathermasters hovered in formation over the
scene, their baskets festooned with swags of raven silk. When the hearse pulled
away, the bell of Ellenhall rang out again, echoing over the plateau and the high
valleys, sounding one peal every sixty heartbeats. Then began the final journey. A
procession, led by Avalloc, Arran, Astăriel, and Earnán, walked behind the coffin.
As the cortege in full panoply passed through the crowd, people tossed flowers
and petals upon them. Pipers were playing a lament, accompanied by drummers
whose instruments were all draped in black, the sumptuous color of secrets and
mystery. Incongruously, yet somehow comfortingly, larks and currawongs were
warbling their wild melodies, heard whenever the pipes and drums fell silent.

Preceded by a trio of horsemen on ebony steeds, the procession made its way
up the steeply winding path that led from behind the stables. The road climbed
pine-clothed slopes, crossing bridges over high mountain gullies and rocky gorges
cloven by fast-flowing waters, finally reaching the higher places of Wychwood
Storth where, in a tiny, peaceful dale, lay the cemetery of the weathermasters.

Throughout the journey Arran kept his jaw firmly clenched, upholding the
honor of Rowan Green by keeping his emotions in check, yet all those who
knew him understood what it cost him to appear to march with detachment.
His eyes were terrible sinks of pain, and he stared fixedly into the distance as if
he wished to see nothing more, ever again. He seemed to be dazed.

In the cemetery stood a building of vaulted stone. It was a place that offered
peace and solitude, a reflectory, a venue in which to reflect, contemplate, medi-
tate. The lustrous water-pools surrounding the outer walls mirrored the moun-

tains and sky. Within, a great silver-lined bowl was kept clean and filled with pure water, cared for by the Keeper of the Reflectory, a gentle, kindly man.

Whereas it was for kings and queens to be buried beneath roofs and floors of barren stone, weathermasters were laid in fertile soil underneath the open skies, so that rain might dance with silver-shod feet on their graves, and flakes of sunlight fall softly thereon, and flowers grow. After a quiet, private ceremony in Lord Alfardēne's Reflectory, Jewel was laid to rest amongst the tombs of many weathermasters, including the famous lords Avolundar, Alfardēne, and Aglaval Stormbringer. The coffin of Narngalis oak was lowered on ropes and positioned in its resting place, marked by a black headstone that had been engraved with the words *"Jewel Heronswood Jovansson, 3453–3482, Beloved Wife of Arran Maelstronnar, Mother of Astăriel."*

Then Avalloc sprinkled water from a wooden bowl while Cuiva symbolically broke her ceremonial carlin's Wand in half, formally marking the close of the service.

As for Arran, his eyes were stones.

Officially, the mourning period lasted for a sevennight. The son of the Storm Lord averred he would remain in mourning forever.

Every day he climbed the steep path and visited the grave. Sometimes, as he knelt on the newly turned soil, he murmured the last two verses of a song he had once sung to Jewel, but had left unfinished:

> "Like luminescent falling stars, we shine
> With one brief flash, then fade into decline.
> Like mayflies, we dance for one fleeting day,
> Till dusk comes stealing. Then we pass away.

> "But humankind's ephemerality
> Makes heroes of us. Our mortality
> We bear, eschewing madness, though we see
> Death is the prize for heroes such as we."

Springtime of the year 3483 filled the gardens of the plateau and Rowan Green with the colors and scents of climbing roses, clematis, azaleas, rhododendrons, camellias, dogwoods, and magnolias. The uncultivated places blossomed, too. Satinwood bushes thrived in the damp forests, putting forth small white flowers on thick scaly stalks; the small, creamy flowers of mountain pepper showed themselves, ready to ripen later into shiny black fruit-globes. Wild alpine gardens were richly sprinkled with the whitish-green flowers of elderberry panax, the fragrant blossoms of coral boronia, the long pale-gold catkins of sallow wattle, and the reddish pea flowers of mountain mirbelia.

In that season of renewal, Cuiva Rushford returned again to High Darioneth. Avalloc had invited her to remain for a while, as a guest of his household. He held her wisdom in high esteem, and hoped she might share some of her carlin's knowledge with the lore-gatherers of Ellenhall, while simultaneously imparting comfort to Arran and Astăriel. Another guest at that time was the wandering scholar Almus Agnellus, with his squire.

Agnellus was a man who had never been short of words, but when he arrived at High Darioneth and witnessed the family of Maelstronnar in their grief he was struck dumb. Their devastation and desolation were severe, and from his treasure-hoard of philosophies he could find no words of sufficient comfort to offer them.

It was a bright alpine morning when he and Cuiva accompanied Arran to the cemetery of the weathermasters and stood once more at the graveside. Rain had been pouring down throughout the night, but the showers had dwindled to the east, and the morning dawned clear and radiant. Glittering clouds of ice-crystals hovered like gauze above the highest peaks, backed by an agapanthus sky.

Wild roses were growing on the grave, twining their slim stems over the headstone. The pink-gold-ivory blooms glistened with nectar. Tiny wildflowers blanketed the plot like fantastic embroideries: purple violets, sweet forget-me-not, orchids, woodruff, and everlastings.

Arran subsided to his knees amongst the flowers. Unable to accept his loss, he spent every moment of his life desperately trying to find ways to somehow transform his wife's mortality into immortality. At his behest, many a song had been made for her. As he knelt, heedless of the two who stood beside him, he spoke, as if to himself alone, or to someone who could not be seen.

"For most people, perpetuity can come only through fame. Some are famous because of their looks. Great beauties may be famed throughout history: artists paint them; poets laud them. *Your* beauty outshone them all. Some, such as kings and queens, are famous because of their ancestry. Monuments are built for them; scholars write their histories. *Your* lineage was unparalleled. Others are famed not for the beauty or the forefathers they were born to own, but for their intellect, their skill. All these qualities you possessed. Surely, you must live on."

But Cuiva knelt beside the grieving man, and to him she said: "Everyone is immortal. Recall the words of the Maelstronnar when he spoke of Water. Mortalkind is a river. We are, and will be, in the rain, the clouds, the ocean. More: the body to dust, dust to flowers, the pollen blown on the wind, to be inhaled, the nectar to be collected by birds, for nourishment.

"Behold," she said, indicating the trailing stems that festooned the headstone. The three figures at the grave had attended so quietly that small birds had felt secure enough to come down and sip at the flowers. Amongst pairs of stiff, pointed leaves, they were feasting on the sweetness already refilling the petal-cups after the rains. A tinkling twitter played up and down the air's lute-strings, the call of Blue Honeyeaters. Ultramarine was their chief coloring, with deeper edges to the wing feathers, pale blue throat and breast, brown eyes, and black legs.

From Arran's coat pocket, a blackcurrant eye peered out. The end of a limp paintbrush twitched.

A male honeyeater darted upward, beginning his aerial display to impress his mate. Having reached the apogee of his flight, he folded his wings and dived, uttering a shrill chatter. He swooped skillfully before reaching the ground, but not before a loose pinion, dislodged by his rapid movements, slipped free.

Arran rose to his feet. A beautiful blue feather drifted down. He reached up and caught it. Cradled in his palm, it shimmered with every shade of blue: jacaranda, lapis lazuli, sapphire, cornflower, antique ice, oceans, skies, sadness, tranquillity. As blue as Jewel's eyes.

"This I shall keep," Arran said, "in her memory."

In great astonishment the wandering scholar Agnellus had hearkened to the words of the carlin. Afterward he dwelled on her meaning. Not for the first time he wondered about the lore of the Winter Hag, and over the following weeks, during many an evening in discussion with Cuiva and Avalloc, another change gradually began to be wrought in him. Before he left High Darioneth he spoke earnestly to them, saying, "I have come to believe it is my duty not to expose false ideas and reveal truth, but to spread hope and comfort amongst humankind. I should like to further study the ways of the carlins."

"You are a man of honor, Master Agnellus," said Cuiva. "In sooth, I had never thought to endure the company of any man tainted by the dogma of the Sanctorum; yet you, sir, have turned my expectations upside down. You and your squire are welcome," she added, "to visit the marsh at any time. The door of the Rushford house is always open to you."

Gravely, Agnellus thanked her for her invitation, and the two sages parted on the best of terms.

Despite words of consolation from the carlin and the scholar, Arran's distraction did not decrease. He seemed unable to shake off his despondency. The counseling of his father and his peers could not assuage his grief. Even the company of his daughter—so like her mother in appearance—could not do more than temporarily alleviate his pain. It was in the Autumn of the same year that, driven by sorrow, he decided to retreat from the world. With his mind made up, he commenced to make ready for departure.

But what was the fate of Fionnuala Aonarán?

For ten years she had spent every waking moment trying to find a way to come close to Jewel undetected. After a decade of futile endeavor, attempting to gain access to the inaccessible, to break through the barriers of protection that surrounded the bride of the weathermage, she had succeeded. Having let fly the lethal bolt of mistletoe, she returned to the streets from whence she came, the gutters and alleys of Cathair Rua. Her goal had been achieved; now there was no longer any purpose. A substitute purpose might have been happiness, for she perceived it in other people and longed for it, but she understood she had been only a destroyer of happiness and could never hope for it.

Bitter, then, was her repentance.

One wintry morning her body was found suspended from the Iron Tree in Cathair Rua, she having hanged herself from its icy branches.

Yet that was not the end of her story. For although she had hanged herself, she had done the job inefficiently, and thus it happened the sister of Fionnbar Aonarán was not yet dead when a commander of the Knights of the Brand, leading a few men of his squadron, came riding through Fountain Square. This commander, in his late twenties, was named Conall Gearnach. He was a man of extreme passions, fervent devotion to honor, and a strong sense of justice.

At the center of the square stood a well with low walls of stone, and it was beside the well that the leafless plant grew, the extraordinary tree known as the Thorn of Iron, or the Iron Tree. Slender spikes thrust eagerly from every bough and twig, long and cruel as a northern Winter. So numerous were the thorns, jutting at all angles, that they formed a kind of basketwork of swords.

At the sight of the forlorn figure swaying from the boughs of this barbarous tree, Conall Gearnach gave a mighty shout, unsheathed his knife, and flung it with all his strength and skill. His aim was true; the blade sliced the rope and down fell Fionnuala, gasping and half-throttled, into the lowest barbs.

"Get her out," Gearnach ordered his knights, and so they did. Fionnuala had been but superficially wounded by the sharp spines, for she had fallen at the outer limits of the tree, but her face, arms, and hands were badly scratched, and congested, too, by semi-strangulation. She was awake, in pain, and unable to speak.

"You abject slattern!" the commander reprimanded. "How dare you presume to take your own life? I have seen men desperate to stave off death, who would surrender all their gold to live for just one more day. Life is a priceless treasure! And you—you would treat it as a worthless thing, while at the same time flouting the king's law. To leave a corpse abandoned in a public place is a crime punishable by imprisonment. Now you have a second chance. Recover your wits and get ye gone before I change my mind and have you clapped in irons. Go and do some good!"

After voicing his rough and somewhat arbitrary concern for the well-being of one of the citizens, Conall Gearnach rode off with his troops. A kindly woman who had poked her head out of her window in order to find out the cause of the noise now came creeping from her lodgings. She helped the unsuccessful suicide to her feet, then took her home and gave her shelter, caring for her until she was mended.

Fionnuala did not know what to make of these events. She had expected to die, and at first it was difficult to know what to do, how to think, when death was replaced by life. The woman who had taken her in told her, "You ought to look upon your rescue as a gift."

"How should I proceed?" Fionnuala asked in bewilderment.

"You must go to one of the carlins. They will know."

However, when Fionnuala was physically healed it was not to a carlin she took herself, but to the druids.

"For," she said to herself through the mists of her confusion, "they are most powerful."

To the druids she made confession in an incoherent, rambling manner, mentioning no names but asking for absolution for her terrible deeds, which haunted her, making her thoughts unbearable, her dreams intolerable.

The druids said, "You must give twenty pieces of gold to the Sanctorum so that the druidhood might intercede on your behalf. Then go away from here and kneel in the dust, and repeat this chant five hundred times:

> "'O Fates, wise and magnificent.
> O Fates, splendid and powerful.
> O Fates, be generous to your lowly servant.
> O Fates, prithee grant me peace.'"

So she did as the druids bidden her, but when the penance was finished she felt no closer to lightness of spirit, and was tempted again to try to end her own life. In a final attempt to find an answer she consulted a carlin, who said, "It is much easier to chop down an oak tree than to cultivate one from an acorn and nurse it to maturity. From what you have told me, you have chopped down many trees during your miserable life. You must become a gardener. Devote your days to the nurturing of living things, so that in selflessness you might make recompense for your heinous acts and learn what is truly valuable."

Fionnuala went away, and took a lease on a piece of land in Slievmordhu which had been abandoned, rendered barren by bad farming practices that had leached the soil of goodness. There she made a garden.

So tirelessly did she work, so unremittingly did she break the clods and spread the compost, and sow, and sprinkle water, and carefully pick the snails off the new sprouts, that the garden took shape and began to flourish. The more it expanded upward and outward the more ardently she tended it and brought fresh seeds to plant. She lived on the vegetables she grew therein, and the eggs of the hens that scratched and ate the insects, enriching the ground with their droppings. Lovely trees raised luxuriant heads. Beneath their eaves sprang flowers and hedges and worts and all manner of herbs. Word of the wonderful garden began to spread, and people came to look at it. The scarred crone let them pluck fresh herbs to treat their ailments, allowed them to wander freely amongst the flowerbeds and groves, never hindering them from sitting on the lawns or strolling by the rocky pools. She hardly ever spoke to them, nor they to her, and she would tell her name to no one, but visitors found comfort in the place she had brought to fruitfulness: this bower of greenery and beauty, and no one despoiled it. Fionnuala Aonarán toiled in the garden for years, until the night she died at a venerable age; thus, her life was not utterly destructive and wasted after all, and when she had passed away they buried her under a stone in her garden, naming her "The Crone of the Herbs."

But that was all in the future.

In High Darioneth, Arran was preparing to leave his family and friends and the Four Kingdoms of Tir when the scholar Agnellus suddenly reappeared in their midst. He was flustered and excited, making great haste; his face was flushed and his eyes bright. At first they thought he had been taken by a fit of madness, for he was burbling and gesticulating urgently. His words seemed to make no sense.

"Raise her from the grave!" he was shouting. "Raise her now! For I have learned strange news, and it might be that there is hope at last!"

When the scholar's meaning had sunk in, Arran gave the agitated man one terrible look. Quietly he said, "If this turns out to be some false news, if she is disturbed for no reason, if she is brought to light only for me to see her fair face in ruins, I will be haunted forever, and I will hold you responsible, Agnellus."

Such behavior and speech had awful impact, coming from the son of the Storm Lord. Agnellus was momentarily frightened, but he did not waver. "Take her from the ground!" he insisted. "Do it, for I have read the truth as it was written down by an eldritch wight, who cannot lie, and I say to you this must be done!"

Without another word Arran sped away up the mountainside to the cemetery of the weathermasters, and there were many who followed after.

The grave was breached. From amongst the thorny briars the coffin was raised. They carried it to the gracious reflectory that stood nearby, surrounded by its lustrous water-pools mirroring the mountains and sky, and placed it upon a catafalque of green-veined marble. Then Arran Maelstronnar commanded everyone to leave him alone with the casket while he opened it, and so harsh was he, and so dangerous, that all acquiesced, but Avalloc kept guard just outside the door, and Agnellus with him, and the child Astăriel was enfolded in the protection of others who held her dear.

There was not a sound outside or inside the reflectory. It seemed as if even the wind had ceased to blow. Those who waited heard the sound of the lid's clasps being snapped back. They heard the creak of the soil-clogged hinges as the cover was raised, and then a very long silence ensued.

At last, when no one could endure it any longer, Avalloc made to enter the building, but he stopped abruptly and reeled back, as if he had run into an invisible barrier, for from the interior came a keening, a song like weeping, wordless, high, and almost inhuman.

Then the Storm Lord threw back the door and entered, while the rest of them followed at his back.

This is what they saw within.

Atop the plinth of jade-streaked marble the coffin remained, the lid cast aside. Beside it sat Arran, and in his arms he cradled the pristine, flawless body of his wife. Her black hair was spilling like ink-drawn lines across the ash-gray folds of his doublet.

Jewel seemed to be merely sleeping. Death had not touched her, had not corrupted her flesh in any way. She remained as beautiful as falling water.

The song of Arran ceased, and he rocked his bride very gently. Almus Agnellus fell to his knees, as did all those who had entered behind them, but Avalloc Maelstronnar looked long upon his son, and the wife he held in his arms, and he said, "What can this mean?"

Agnellus spoke. "After I left here I had cause to consult my notes and books of lore, and as I was searching amongst my papers I came across a scroll which I could swear I had never seen before. On it were words written in an archaic tongue of eldritch, by means of a wondrous hand, a calligraphy of spiky flourishes and gothic ornamentation. Fortunately I am learned in that esoteric speech and was able to decipher the meaning. I learned this: that a woman who mothers an immortal child must inevitably be tinged by that immortality. If she is fatally wounded she shall not die, but shall instead fall into a deep and lasting sleep that resembles death." He drew breath and appended, "Jewel lives."

And it was true.

The voice of the Storm Lord, wontedly assured and commanding, trembled as he asked, "But how can she be awakened?"

"Alas," replied the scholar. "The scroll could not tell me that. Yet in the past I have studied widely, and methinks no answer can be found in the Four Kingdoms of Tir."

"Then is there no hope?"

"There is always hope," said the scholar, but he was weeping.

They bore her to the house of Maelstronnar. Agnellus and every trusted carlin and druid known to the weathermasters endeavored to find ways to waken her. Cuiva the White Carlin was summoned from the marsh. Potions were smeared on Jewel's lips; hartshorn was wafted beneath her nose; music was played; rhymes were chanted, all to no avail. But Arran attended the physicians closely, and would allow no one to meddle with his bride. He administered all unguents with his own hand and would permit no radical procedures to be attempted.

"She will not be violated," he avowed.

After all possible measures had been tried the enterprise was abandoned. Cuiva departed for the Great Marsh of Slievmordhu, carrying both good and bad news to Earnán.

An octagonal cupola perched atop the house of Maelstronnar. Its walls were not fashioned from timber or stone but from panes of thick, transparent glass. They were double-glazed, strong enough to withstand bitter cold, and strong winds. This high chamber commanded a panoramic view across Rowan Green to the mountains on the far side of the plateau. Before his eyesight began to fail Avalloc had used this cupola as an observatory and housed his telescope there. To this lovely eyrie the weathermasters carried the sleeping beauty.

There they laid her on a canopied couch, amongst soft cushions of damasked silks and crimson velvets. Here, vigilantly watched night and day, she rested in perfection. The eight walls of glass looked out upon spectacular alpine scenery, but if Jewel beheld any landscape at all, it must have been the landscape of a dream, for her eyes were closed, and it was as though the gossamer wings of the Blue Lycaenidae butterfly rested motionless thereon.

Below the cupola, hard against the outer walls of the house, wild roses began to sprout. Dristan Maelstronnar would cut them down, only to discover they had burgeoned again, more vigorously than ever, so in the end Avalloc advised him to let them be. The sinuous stalks scrambled up the walls and across the slate tiles until they reached the cupola, where they entwined themselves together, loosely framing the eight glass panes with their tiny thorns, their spearhead leaves, and their five-petaled rosettes. Jewel on her couch of silks seemed encaged in an open wickerwork, a bower of flowers and thorns. Yet on the empty grave down in the cemetery, the briars withered.

As he traveled the by-ways of Tir, Almus Agnellus continued to marvel at the strange manner in which he had learned of Jewel's continuing vitality. "It was the oddest thing," he was inclined to murmur, "but the scroll looked to have been freshly written, on clean papyrus, in a hand so bizarre it could only have been eldritch, and an ink so sharp and luminous I have not seen its like before. Or since," he would add, "for the scroll has now vanished from my archives, as mysteriously and conveniently as it appeared. It is as if some*one* or some*thing* deliberately furnished me with that knowledge at a time when it would be useful, so that Jewel might be rescued from the grave!" And he would shake his head in amazement.

Declaring he would seek forever, until he could find a way to bring back his lost bride, Arran departed from the Four Kingdoms after all. The fever of true devotion burned in his countenance, in his every movement and sigh, waking or sleeping. "The places to which I am bound," he said as he took his leave, "are not fit for a child. Nor will I take with me any mortal creature, and as for luggage, I would fain travel unhampered."

Amongst the briar roses he kissed the petal-pink lips of his icon wife and bade her goodbye. He left behind his daughter, his father, his family and friends, and all his inheritance, including the Storm Lord's golden sword, Fallowblade.

"Fare thee well, my darling," he murmured to Astăriel. "Ever shall I think of thee."

Neither father nor daughter possessed the ability to let fall tears, but upon their brows grief was graven deeply as they parted.

Accompanied only by the impet Fridayweed, who chose to go with him, Arran Maelstronnar disappeared from the known lands of Tir, and no one knew whether he would evermore be seen there. Over the northern mountains he went, and it is thought he wanders afar in the Unknown lands.

Arran now passes from this tale. If the rest of his story is ever to be told, it will be told elsewhere.

Autumn ornamented the Four Kingdoms of Tir with the colors of fire opals. At High Darioneth, clouds clung lovingly to the mountain peaks, mists lay dreaming in the valleys, and soft hazes veiled the horizon. The sun's rays were as rich and mellow as saffron wine. Cerulean shadows lazily stretched their lengths across the ground; it was as if the mountain ring steamed gently in a vat of amber dyes suffused with blue. Leaves indolently fluttered from their twigs like shavings of copper, rust, gold, and verdigris, scattering light as they floated down.

The harvests were bountiful that year.

As sacks of nuts were trundled to the storehouses, nutteries and silos by the wagonload, the harvesters sang in chorus to make their workload seem lighter. Some played instruments; at Rowan Green the thin melodies of pipes or flutes could sometimes be heard, plaintively spiraling up from the plateau.

Once a month, Astăriel tended the empty grave of her mother, which, now that the briars had vanished, she had whimsically fashioned into a wild garden. Late on a golden Autumn afternoon as she made her solitary journey up the winding road to the cemetery, she met the urisk. She had encountered it twice before, and even conversed with it. Having grown up in a house with a domestic brownie and an impet that lived in the furniture, she felt no awkwardness in the presence of eldritch wights. The creature's appearance did not discomfit the girl. To her it seemed not extraordinary in the least to be confronted with a creature that, from the waist up, looked like an ugly little man with pointed, tufty ears, a turned-up nose, and eyes set slantwise. Two stumpy horns protruded from the urisk's curly hair. It was dressed in its habitual shabby jacket and torn waistcoat, with dilapidated breeches covering its shaggy goats' legs. The cloven hooves pattered softly on bare slabs of rock, where the thin soil had washed away. In silence, keeping to the shade of the pines, the wight accompanied her.

At sunset, having weeded the plot and set it to rights, Astăriel found her way to a high place above the cemetery. Here grew liquidambar trees lush with fans of jeweled foliage, and a great mossy boulder crowned a rocky shoulder. The boulder was almost a hundred feet tall, but its sides were weathered and cracked, providing plenty of footholds. The child liked to climb it, because from the top an unbroken view of the entire surrounding area could be obtained.

Astăriel and the urisk seated themselves on this vantage point, looking out across the ranges toward the distant lands. She had positioned herself in a lingering pool of sunlight, while the wight immersed itself in the indigo shadows of a standing boulder. The day was not yet over, but already the moon hovered in the sky, a curved glimmer like the reflection of a white feather. The little girl let her weathermaster's awareness float out in concentric ripples. Around her the air was chilly, the temperature plummeting. The still airs would soon be in motion. A low-pressure trough over Narngalis was moving eastward as a cold front approached from the west. There would be scattered showers and thunderstorms that night, before the northerly wind freshened a little. The next few days would bring heavy falls and isolated thunderstorms easing to showers, after which the weather would continue cold and windy. Subsequently, snow would fall on the peaks, but the winds would ease.

As she sat atop the rock the child could read the invisible signs of the weather and feel the *brí* surge in her, responding to the tides of air, but she could not know all about the myriad human activities, personal dramas, and natural occurrences that were playing themselves out across the Four Kingdoms of Tir. An old vagrant called Cat Soup was sleeping, huddled in rags, beneath a tangled vine in the garden of a house at King's Winterbourne. At the royal palace of Narngalis, the pages were lighting the lamps. Far away in Grïmnørsland an evening breeze was causing the pine trees to sigh, while down amongst their roots several pairs of oddly shaped eyes peered and blinked, and the silken soughing of the resinous boughs was briefly embossed by a burst of high-pitched laughter. Beyond the forest two boy-princes, one with hair of gold, the other with hair of bronze, raced each other on horseback under the watchful eye of their guardian, a Knight of the Brand.

In Slievmordhu's Lake District a young apothecary with a half-smoked pipe growing cold in his hand sat slumped in a chair beside his hearth, sleeping soundly. Somewhere beneath a mountain, in the sunless cold, a rock fell from a cavern wall, dislodged by unusual vibrations along a mineral seam.

And amongst the ruined stones of the Dome in Orielthir the accursed weed crowthistle thrust a new green spear.

On the surface the world seemed serene enough, but beneath the impassive cliffs of stone and the silent expanses of lakes; behind the facades of political protocol and the veneers of civilization; within the domes of human skulls and the hearts of schemers there rampaged various activities and machinations that would soon—before Astăriel's twenty-first birthday—irrevocably change the four kingdoms of Tir. It was impossible for the daughter of Jewel and Arran to foresee, but that extraordinarily spine-tingling reflection briefly glimpsed in the polished back of the hairbrush, that disturbingly handsome face, was perhaps the most significant portent of her future.

The child could know nothing of these events. She had lately come from the glass-walled chamber where her mother lay like a finely modeled figurine amongst the flowers, and thoughts of the loss of both her parents had cast her into a doleful, yearning mood. A broken line of birds passed swiftly and noiselessly overhead, the last swallows migrating south before the season of the Winter Hag laid its chill grip upon soil, stone, and leaf. Yet Astăriel's father had set out in the opposite direction, and as she gazed northward, a terrible wistfulness seized her heart. She longed to take wing, to fly from her perch out across the misty landscape to the northern mountains and beyond.

"Your sorrowfulness is irksome," commented the urisk.

She replied, "If you do not like it, you need not stay."

"Be of good cheer."

"I will not."

They reverted to silence and sat beneath the pink-streaked sky, watching the sun melt in a glorious pyre behind the mountains. Soon it would give way to the solemn majesty of the stars.

"If you choose melancholy," said the urisk, "then, the more fool you."

She said, "It is easy for you to say those words, ignorant immortal creature. You cannot know what it is to forever lose someone you love."

The wight, a being that was unable to lie, who had existed for many lives of men and accumulated more knowledge in those lifetimes than could ever be measured, said pityingly, "It is you, not I, who is ignorant. You fail to understand. Loss may be reversed. Even death is not the story's end."

Here ends

The Crowthistle Chronicles, Book 2: The Well of Tears

The story commenced in

The Crowthistle Chronicles, Book 1: The Iron Tree

and continues in

The Crowthistle Chronicles, Book 3: Weatherwitch

and

The Crowthistle Chronicles, Book 4: Fallowblade

NOTES

A beautiful, interactive, 3D fantasy world.

A free CD accompanies this book, depicting scenes from Book 1: *The Iron Tree* and this book. It is planned that the next in the Crowthistle series, Book 3: *Weatherwitch,* will also be associated with a CD, letting you walk through the windows of imagination into the kingdoms of Tir. The existing scenes will be extended, and others will be added.

In answer to readers' requests, Book 4: *Fallowblade* tells much more about the face glimpsed in the pool at the marsh, the same face also seen in the reflection on the silver hair-brush. And for readers of the Bitterbynde trilogy, as I have promised, there will indeed be a character who resembles Morragan.

ACKNOWLEDGMENTS

THE BROWN MAN OF THE MUIRS: Inspired by an event said to have occurred in 1641, and recorded in *Notes on the Folk-Lore of the Northern Counties of England and the Borders*, by William Henderson, London, 1866.

THE BRAG: Inspired by "The Picktree Brag," from *Notes on the Folk-Lore of the Northern Counties of England and the Borders,* by William Henderson, London, 1866.

THE BLUE-EYED DAMSEL: Inspired by "The Phantom of the Fell," from *Goblin Tales of Lancashire,* by James Bowker, London, 1883.

THE DOOM OF EOIN: Inspired by "Uter Bosence and the Piskie," from *Traditional and Hearthside Stories of West Cornwall,* by William Bottrell, Penzance, 1870. ". . . like a black buck-goat, with horns a yard long, flaming eyes, and a long, twirling tail" is directly quoted from this source.

THE TRAVELING TREE: Inspired by "The Travelling Tree," in *Forgotten Folk-Tales of the English Counties,* by Ruth L. Tongue, Routledge and Kegan Paul, London, 1970. "'I don't know about you,' said the tree, 'but I'm getting soaked through. I'm off home to a nice fire.' And it went" is paraphrased from this source.

THE BROWNIE AND THE MIDWIFE: Inspired by a) "The Brownie of Dalswinton," in *The Fairy Mythology,* by Thomas Keightley, new edition, London, 1850, p. 357, and b) "The Brownie and the Midwife," in *Minstrelsy of the Scottish Border,* by Sir Walter Scott, Volume 1, Oliver & Boyd, Edinburgh, 1932, p. 149. "'Do not ride by the Auld Pool! We might meet the brownie!' [And he replied:] 'Have no *fear,* Goodwife. . . . You've met *all* the . . . brownies you're likely to meet!' With that, he plunged the horse into the water and [bore me] safely to the other shore" is quoted directly from the text of "The Brownie of Dalswinton."

THE TROWS AND BLOSTMA: Inspired by and partially quoted from "Sandy

Harg's Wife," in *Remains of Galloway and Nithsdale Song,* by R. H. Cromek London, 1810, p. 305.

THE BROWNIE DRIVEN FROM THE MILL: Inspired by "Brownie-Clod," in *Popular Superstitions of the Highlanders of Scotland,* by Grant Stewart, Archibald Constable, London, 1823, pp. 142–143. "[Robin] has got a cowl and coat, and never more will work a jot!" is quoted directly from this source.

THE SHIOFRA BATHE IN THE CIRCULAR BASINS: Inspired by *Northumberland,* examples of printed folklore concerning Northumberland. Mrs. and Thomas Balfour, *Country Folk-Lore IV,* N.W. London, 1903.

THE SHIOFRA IN THE STOREROOMS: Inspired by and partially quoted from "Fairy Thefts," in *The Fairy Mythology, Illustrative of the Romance and Tradition of Various Countries,* by Thomas Keightley, new edition, Bohn Library, London, 1850, pp. 305–306.

THE SHIOFRA IN THE KILN-HOUSE: Inspired by and partially quoted from "Rothley Mill," in *Northumberland*, examples of printed folklore concerning Northumberland. Mrs. and Thomas Balfour, *County Folk-Lore IV,* N.W. London, 1903, p. 16. "Burnt and scalded! Burnt and scalded! The sell of the mill has done it!" is quoted directly from this source.

THE BROKEN SHOVEL: Inspired by "The Broken Ped," an ancient legend retold in several versions. The version I discovered can be found in *A Dictionary of British Folk-tales in the English Language,* by K. M. Briggs, Routledge and Kegan Paul, London, 1970.

THE HAUNTED MILL BENEATH THE LAKE: Inspired by a tale in *Folklore and Legends, Scotland*. W. W. Gibbings, London, 1889.

TORNADOES CAN PROVIDE TRANSPORTATION: This has been documented. In western China, on May 29, 1986, a tornado sucked up twelve schoolchildren. It deposited them on a sand dunes twelve miles away, without harming them at all.

THE ROYAL CARVER'S CHANT: Inspired and partially quoted from John Lydgate's poem "The Hors the Shepe and the Goos" (1498) and Wynkyn de Worde's "Boke of Kervynge" (1508, 1513), from *Early English Meals and Manners,* ed. F. J. Furnivall. London: N. Trubner, 1868, reprinted in *The Rituals of Dinner,* by Margaret Visser, Penguin, 1992.

THE TWO STRANGE HOUNDS: Inspired by a note about the *cu-sith,* the fairy hound, in Carmina Gadelica, 4 vols., A. Carmichael, Edinburgh, 1928. From this source is quoted the chant:

"Slender-fay, slender-fay!
Mountain-traveler, mountain-traveler!

Black-fairy, black-fairy!
Lucky-treasure, lucky-treasure!
Grey-hound, grey-hound!
Seek-beyond, seek-beyond!"

THE FAYNES' MARKET: Inspired by "Fairy Merchandise," in *Folk-Tales of England*, ed. K. M. Briggs and R. L. Tongue, University of Chicago Press, 1965. Heard in summer 1906 from haymakers at Galmington, near Taunton, Somerset, England.

THE PIXY FAIR: Inspired by a tale of the same name in *Somerset Folklore*, by Ruth Tongue, *County Folk-Lore VIII*, Folk-Lore Society, 1965.

MISTLETOE AS BANE: The concept of being invulnerable to all things except mistletoe springs from an ancient Norse legend.

THE BOGGART: Inspired by "The Boggart" in *The World Guide to Gnomes, Fairies, Elves and Other Little People*, by Thomas Keightley, Avenel Books, 1978, originally published in 1880 by G. Bell, London, as *The Fairy Mythology*.

THE KORRED: The description of the korred is derived and partially quoted from Thomas Keightley's description in *The World Guide to Gnomes, Fairies, Elves and Other Little People*, Avenel Books, 1978, originally published in 1880 by G. Bell, London, as *The Fairy Mythology*. The korred are a race of small, troll-like supernatural beings whose folklore originated in Brittany.

"MY MOTHER SAID I NEVER SHOULD . . .": This is an old schoolyard chant I learned years ago. It really does belong with a hand-clapping game.

THE BLACK DOG OF GIBBET CORNER: Inspired by "The Black Dog of Tring," in *The Ghost World*, by T. F. Thistleton Dyer, London, 1893, p. 107: "[the strange dog] disappeared, seeming to vanish like a shadow, or to sink into the ground" was quoted from this source.

THE BOY ASKING FOR ALE: Inspired by the story "The Laird o' Co," recorded in *Personnel of Fairyland*, by K. M. Briggs, Alden Press, Oxford, 1953.

THE EIGHT WINDS: The weathermaster names for the eight winds are based on personifications originally invented by the ancient Greeks:

The north wind: Boreas
The northeast wind: Kaikias
The east wind: Apheliotes
The southeast wind: Euros
The south wind: Notos
The southwest wind: Lips

The west wind: Zephyros
The northwest wind: Skiron

Source: *The Wonders of Weather,* by Bob Crowder, Australian Bureau of Meteorology.

THE WEDDING TOAST:

> Long may they live—happy may they be,
> Sained in contentment and from misfortune free!

During the annual celebration of May Day, this rhyme (with the word "sained" replaced by "blessed") is traditionally repeated outside the homes of the "May Queen" and her courtiers in Knutsford, Cheshire, England.

SPINNING STRAW INTO GOLD: Inspired by and partially quoted from the well-known story *Tom Tit Tot: An Essay on Savage Philosophy,* by Edward Clodd, Duckworth, London, 1898.

FRIDAYWEED: My lost copy of *A Dictionary of Names* indicates that "Friday-weed" is a spelling corruption of the Old English "Frideweard." It is a name too enchanting to overlook.

WEATHERMASTERY: I am sincerely grateful to the knowledgeable and imaginative meteorologist John, who helpfully donated his advice when I was doing the background research on weathermastery. My advisor cannot be named because his profession is concerned with serious science; in his own words, "Clearly this is outside our normal line. Despite what some people might say about us, we try to steer away from fantasy as far as possible." I can only hope that any meteorologists, geologists, or fulgurite experts reading this book will not be too scandalized by the spurious nature of the weathermastery phenomena described. This is, after all, a work of fiction!

AVALLOC'S EULOGY TO WATER was partly inspired by episodes in the excellent six-part CPTV documentary *Water: The Drop of Life.*

BRIAR ROSES GROWING AROUND THE CUPOLA: Readers of fairy tales will recognize this motif from the wonderful story "The Sleeping Beauty," which inspired it.

MY SINCERE THANKS to the Irish people for having such a wonderful language. The words of Irish Gaelic sound so musical, and look so beautiful when written down, that I could not resist borrowing some, although I am the first to admit that my knowledge of Irish grammar is nonexistent.